Great Short Works
of
Mark Twain

Great Short Works of Mark Twain

Edited by JASON S. ROBERTS

BARNES & NOBLE
BOOKS
NEW YORK

This edition published by Barnes & Noble, Inc.

1993 Barnes & Noble Books

ISBN 1-56619-121-1

Book design by Charles Ziga, Ziga Design

Printed and bound in the United States of America

M 9 8 7 6 5 4 3 2 1

Contents

The American Puritan

After reading Hemingway and Faulkner and speculating upon the breach of the American novel with its English tradition, we go back to the two decisive, indigenous Americans who opened the new vein—Mark Twain and Edgar Allan Poe. Everything really American, really non-Engilsh comes out of that pair of spiritual derelicts, those two scarecrow figures with their half-lynched minds. Both of them, but particularly Twain, represent the obverse side of Puritanism. We have never had this obverse in England, for the political power of Puritanism lasted for only a generation and has since always bowed if it has not succumbed to civilised orthodoxy. If an Englishmen hated Puritanism, there was the rest of the elaborate English tradition to support him; but American Puritanism was totalitarian and if an American opposed it, he found himself alone in a wilderness with nothing but bottomless cynicism and humorous bitterness for his consolation. There has never been in English literature a cynicism to compare with the American; at any rate we have never had that, in some ways vital, but always sardonic or wretched, cynicism with its broken chopper edge and its ugly wound. We have also never had its by-product: the humorous philosophers; Franklin's Poor Richard, the Josh Billingses, the Artemus Wards, the Pudd'nhead Wilsons and Will Rogerses with their close-fisted proverbs:

> 'Training is everything. The peach was once a bitter almond: cauliflower is nothing but a cabbage with a college education.'

Or

> 'Consider well the proportion of things. It is better to be a young June bug than an old bird of Paradise.'

I say we have never had this kind of thing, but there is one exception to prove the rule and to prove it very well, for he also is an uprooted and, so to speak, colonial writer. Kipling with his 'A woman is always a woman, but a good cigar is a smoke' is our first American writer with a cynicism, a cigar-stained humour and a jungle book of beliefs which, I think, would be a characteristic of our literature if we become seriously totalitarian in the future. For English totalitarianism would create the boredom and bitterness of the spiritual wilderness, as surely as Puritanism did in America.

When Mark Twain turned upon the religion of his childhood because it was intolerable, he was unaware that it would destroy him by turning him into a money-grubber of the most disastrously Puritan kind. Fortunately the resources of the imagination are endless even when a fanatical philosophy wrecks human life, genius and happiness. Out of the mess which Twain made of his life, amid the awful pile of tripe which he wrote, there does rise one book which has the serenity of a thing of genius. *Huckleberry Finn* takes the breath away. Knowing his life, knowing the hell from which the book has ascended, one dreads as one turns from page to page the seemingly inevitable flop. How can so tortured and so angry a comedian refrain from blackguarding God, Man and Nature for the narrow boredom of his early life, and thus ruin the gurgling comedy and grinning horror of the story? But an imaginative writer appears to get one lucky break in his career; for a moment the conflicts are assimilated, the engine ceases to work against itself. The gears do not crash and *Huckleberry Finn* hums on without a jar. America gets its first and indisputable masterpiece. The boyhood of Huck Finn is the boyhood of a new culture and a new world.

The curious thing about *Huckleberry Finn* is that, although it is one of the funniest books in all literature and really astonishing in the variety of its farce and character, we are even more moved than we are amused by it. Why are we moved? Do we feel the sentiment of sympathy only? Are we sighing with some envy and self-pity? 'Alas, Huck Finn is just what I would have been in my boyhood if I had had half a chance.' Are we sorry for the vagrant, or are we moved by his rebellion? These minor feelings may play their part; but they are only sighs on the surface of the main stream of our emotion. Twain has brought to his subject far more than this personal longing; he has become the channel of the generic American emotion which floods all really American literature—nostalgia. In that brilliant, hit-or-miss book, *Studies in Classical American Literature,* which is either dead right or dead wrong, D. H. Lawrence called this feeling the longing of the rebel for a master. It may be simply the longing for a spiritual home, but it is as strong in Mark Twain as it is implicit in Hemingway. One finds this nostalgia in Anglo-Irish literature which is also colonial and, in a less lasting way, once again in the work of Kipling. The peculiar power of American nostalgia is that it is not only harking back to something lost in the past, but suggests also the tragedy of a lost future. As Huck Finn and old Jim drift down the Mississippi from one horrifying little town to the next and hear the voices of men quietly swearing at one another across the water about 'a chaw of tobacco'; as they pass the time of day with the scroungers, rogues, murderers, the lonely women, the frothing revivalists, the maundering boatmen and fantastic drunks, we see the human wastage that is left behind in the wake of a great effort of the human will, the hopes frustrated, the idealism which has been whittled down to eccentricity and mere animal cunning. These people are the price paid for building a new country. The human spectacle is there. It is not, once you have faced it—which Dickens did not do in *Martin Chuzzlewit,* obsessed as he was by the negative pathos of the immigrant—it is not a disheartening spectacle; for the value of a native humour like Twain's is that it records a profound reality in human nature: the ability of man to adjust himself to any circumstance and somehow to survive and make a life.

Movement is one of the great consolers of human woe; movement, a process of continual migration is the history of America. It is this factor which gives Twain's wonderful descriptions of the journey down the Mississippi its haunting overtone and which, naturally enough, awakens a sensibility in him which is shown nowhere else in his writings and which is indeed vulgarly repressed in them:

. . . then we set down on the sandy bottom where the water was about knee-deep and watched the daylight come. Not a sound anywhere—perfectly still—just like the whole world was asleep, only sometimes the bull-frogs a-clattering may be. The first thing to see, looking away over the water, was a kind of dull line—that was on the woods on t'other side—you couldn't make nothing else out; then a paleness, spreading around; then the river softened up, away off, and wasn't black any more but grey; you could see little dark spots drifting along, ever so far away—trading scows . . . and such things; and long black streaks—rafts; sometimes you could hear a sweep screaking; or jumbled-up voices, it was so still, and sounds come so far; and by-and-by you could see a streak on the water which you know by the look of the streak that there's a snag in the swift current which breaks on it and that streak looks that way; and you see the mist curl up off the water, and the east reddens up, and the river, and you make out a log cabin in the edge of the woods, away on the bank t' other side of the river, being a woodyard likely, and piled by them cheats so you can throw a dog through it anywheres . . .

And afterwards we would watch the lonesomeness of the river, and kind of lazy along and by-and-by, lazy off to sleep. Wake up, by-and-by, and look to see what done it, and may be see a steamboat, coughing along upstream, so far off towards the other side you couldn't tell nothing about her only whether she was sternwheel or side wheel; then for about an hour there wouldn't be nothing to hear nor nothing to see—just solid lonesomeness. Once there was a thick fog, and the rafts and things that went by was beating tin pans so the steam boats wouldn't run over them. A scow or a raft went by so close we could hear them talking and cussing and laughing—heard them plain; but we couldn't see no sign of them; it made you feel crawly, it was like spirits carrying on that way in the air. Jim said he believed it was spirits; but I says, 'No, spirits wouldn't say "dern this dem fog".'

(Note the word 'way' in this passage; it is a key nostalgic word in the American vocabulary, vaguely vernacular and burdened with the associations of the half-articualte. It is a favourite Hemingway word, of course: 'I feel *that way*'—not the how or what he feels of the educated man.)

The theme of *Huckleberry Finn* is the rebellion against civilisation and especially against its traditions:

> I reckon I got to light out for the Territory ahead of the rest, because Aunt Sally she's going to adopt me and sivilize me and I can't stand it. I been there before.

Huck isn't interested in 'Moses and the Bulrushers' because Huck 'don't take no stock of dead people'. He garbles European history when he is discussing Kings with Jim, the Negro. Whether Huck is the kind of boy who will grow up to build a new civilisation is doubtful; Tom Sawyer obviously will because he is imaginative. Huck never imagines anything excepts fears. Huck is 'low down plain ornery', always in trouble because of the way he was brought up with 'Pap'. He is a natural anarchist and bum. He can live without civilisation, depending on shrewd affections and loyalty to friends. He is the first of those typical American portraits of the underdog, which have culminated in the poor white literature and in Charlie Chaplin—an underdog who gets along on horse sense, so to speak. Romanticism, ideas, ideals are repugnant to Huck; he 'reckons' he 'guesses', but he doesn't think. In this he is the opposite of his hero, Tom Sawyer. Tom had been telling 'stretchers' about Arabs, elephants and Aladdin's lamp. Huck goes at once 'into a brood'.

> I thought all this over for two or three days, and then I reckoned I would see if there was anything in it. I got an old tin lamp and an irony ring and went out into the woods and rubbed it till I sweat like an Injun, calculating to build a palace and sell it; but it wasn't no use, none of the genies came. So then I judged that all that stuff was only just one of Tom Sawyer's lies. I reckoned he believed in the A-rabs and elephants, but as for me I think different. It has all the marks of a Sunday school.

That is, of American Puritan civilisation, the only civilisation he knew.

'Ornery', broody, superstitious, with a taste for horrors, ingenious, courageous without knowing it, natural, sound-hearted, philosophical in a homely way—those are the attributes of the gorgeous, garrulous Huck and they give a cruelly extravagant narrative its humanity. He obliges you to accept the boy as the devastating norm. Without him the violence of the book would be stark reporting of low life. For if *Huckleberry Finn* is a great comic book it is also a book of terror and brutality. Think of the scenes: Pap and d.t.'s chasing Huck round the cabin with a knife; Huck sitting up all night with a gun preparing to shoot the old man; Huck's early familiarity with corpses; the pig-killing scene; the sight of the frame house (evidently some sort of brothel) floating down the Mississippi with a murdered man in it; the fantastic events at the Southern house where two families shoot each other down in vendetta; the drunken Boggs who comes into town to pick a quarrel and is eventually coolly shot dead before the eyes of his screaming young daughter by the man he has insulted. The 'Duke' and the 'King', those cynical rascals whose adventures liven up the second half of the story, are sharpers, twisters and crooks of the lowest kind. Yet a child is relating all this with a child's detachment and with a touch of morbidity. Marvellous as the tale is, as a collection of picaresque episodes and as a description of the mess of frontier life, it is strong meat. Sometimes we wonder how Twain's public stomached such illusionless reporting. The farce and the important fact that in this one book Mark Twain never forced a point nor overwrote—in the Dickens way for example—are of course the transfiguring and beguiling qualities. His corpse and coffin humour is a dry wine which raises the animal spirits. Old Jim not only looked like a dead man after the 'King' had painted him blue, but like one 'who had been dead a considerable time'.

Judiciousness is carried to the comic limit. And then, Mark Twain is always getting the atmosphere, whether he picks up the exact words of loafers trying to borrow tobacco off one another or tells a tall story of an hysterical revival meeting.

Atmosphere is the decisive word. *Huckleberry Finn* reeks of its world. From a sensitive passage like:

> When I got there it was all still and Sunday-like, and hot and the hands was gone to the fields; and there was them kind faint dronings of bugs and flies that makes it seem so lonesome and like everybody's dead . . .

to descriptions of the silly, dying girl's ridiculous poetry, the sensibility draws a clear outline and is never blurred and turned into sentimentality. One is enormously moved by Huck's view of the world he sees. It is the world not of Eden, but of the 'old Adam', not the golden age of the past, but the earthly world of a reality which (we feel with regret) we have let slip through our fingers too carelessly. Huck is only a crude boy, but luckily he was drawn by a man whose own mind was arrested, with disastrous results in his other books, at the schoolboy stage; here it is perfect. And a thousand times better than the self-conscious adventures of Stevenson's *Treasure Island* and *Kidnapped*.

Is *Huckleberry Finn* one of the great works of picaresque literature? It is, granting the limits of a boy's mind in the hero and the author, a comic masterpiece; but this limitation is important. It is not a book which grows spiritually, if we compare it to *Quixote, Dead Souls* or even *Pickwick;* and it is lacking in that civilised quality which you are bound to lose when you throw over civilisation—the quality of pity. One is left with the cruelty of American humour, a cruelty which is softened by the shrewd moralisings of the humorous philosophers—the Josh Billingses, the Artemus Wards, and the Will Rogerses. And once Mark Twain passed this exquisite moment of his maturity, he went to bits in that morass of sentimentality, cynicism, melodrama and vulgarity which have damned him for the adult reader.

V.S. Pritchett

Those Extraordinary Twins

A man who is not born with the novel-writing gift has a troublesome time of it when he tries to build a novel. I know this from experience. He has no clear idea of his story; in fact he has no story. He merely has some people in his mind, and an incident or two, also a locality. He knows these people, he knows the selected locality, and he trusts that he can plunge those people into those incidents with interesting results. So he goes to work. To write a novel? No—that is a thought which comes later; in the beginning he is only proposing to tell a little tale; a very little tale; a six-page tale. But as it is a tale which he is not acquainted with, and can only find out what it is by listening as it goes along telling itself, it is more than apt to go on and on and on till it spreads itself into a book. I know about this, because it has happened to me so many times.

And I have noticed another thing: that as the short tale grows into the long tale, the original intention (or motif) is apt to get abolished and find itself superseded by a quite different one. It was so in the case of a magazine sketch which I once started to write—a funny and fantastic sketch about a prince and a pauper; it presently assumed a grave cast of its own accord, and in that new shape spread itself out into a book. Much the same thing happened with "Pudd'nhead Wilson." I had a sufficiently hard time with that tale, because it changed itself from a farce to a tragedy while I was going along with it,—a most embarrassing circumstance. But what was a great deal worse was, that it was not one story, but two stories tangled together; and they obstructed and interrupted each other at every turn and created no end of confusion and annoyance. I could not offer the book for publication, for I was afraid it would unseat the reader's reason. I did not know what was the matter with it, for I had not noticed, as yet, that it was two stories in one. It took me months to make that discovery. I carried the manuscript back and forth across the Atlantic two or three times, and read it and studied over it on shipboard; and at last I saw where the difficulty lay. I had no further trouble. I pulled one of the stories out by the roots, and left the other one—a kind of literary Caesarean operation.

Would the reader care to know something about the story which I pulled out? He has been told many a time how the born-and-trained novelist works. Won't he let me round and complete his knowledge by telling him how the jack-leg does it?

Originally the story was called "Those Extraordinary Twins." I meant to make it very short. I had seen a picture of a youthful Italian "freak"—or "freaks"—which was—or which were—on exhibition in our cities—a combination consisting of two heads and four arms joined to a single body and a single pair of legs—and I thought I would write an extravagantly fantastic little story with this freak of nature for hero—or heroes—a silly young miss for heroine, and two old ladies and two boys for the minor parts. I lavishly elaborated these people and their doings, of course. But the tale kept spreading along, and spreading along, and other people got to intruding themselves and taking up more and more room with their talk and their affairs. Among them came a stranger named Pudd'nhead Wilson, and a woman named Roxana; and presently the doings of these two pushed up into prominence a young fellow named Tom Driscoll, whose proper place was away in the obscure background. Before the book was half finished those three were taking things almost entirely into their own hands and working the whole tale as a private venture of their own—a tale which they had nothing at all to do with, by rights.

When the book was finished and I came to look around to see

what had become of the team I had originally started out with—Aunt Patsy Cooper, Aunt Betsy Hale, the two boys, and Rowena the light-weight heroine—they were nowhere to be seen; they had disappeared from the story some time or other. I hunted about and found them—found them stranded, idle, forgotten, and permanently useless. It was very awkward. It was awkward all around; but more particularly in the case of Rowena, because there was a lovematch on, between her and one of the twins that constituted the freak, and I had worked it up to a blistering heat and thrown in a quite dramatic love-quarrel, wherein Rowena scathingly denounced her betrothed for getting drunk, and scoffed at his explanation of how it had happened, and wouldn't listen to it, and had driven him from her in the usual "forever" way; and now here she sat crying and broken-hearted; for she had found that he had spoken only the truth; that it was not he, but the other half of the freak, that had drunk the liquor that made him drunk; that her half was a prohibitionist and had never drunk a drop in his life, and, although tight as a brick three days in the week, was wholly innocent of blame; and indeed, when sober, was constantly doing all he could to reform his brother, the other half, who never got any satisfaction out of drinking, anyway, because liquor never affected him. Yes, here she was, stranded with that deep injustice of hers torturing her poor torn heart.

I didn't know what to do with her. I was as sorry for her as anybody could be, but the campaign was over, the book was finished, she was side-tracked, and there was no possible way of crowding her in, anywhere. I could not leave her there, of course; it would not do. After spreading her out so, and making such a to-do over her affairs, it would be absolutely necessary to account to the reader for her. I thought and thought and studied and studied; but I arrived at nothing. I finally saw plainly that there was really no way but one—I must simply give her the grand bounce. It grieved me to do it, for after associating with her so much I had come to kind of like her after a fashion, notwithstanding she was such an ass and said such stupid, irritating things and was so nauseatingly sentimental. Still it had to be done. So, at the top of Chapter XVII, I put a "Calendar" remark concerning July the Fourth, and began the chapter with this statistic:

"Rowena went out in the back yard after supper to see the fireworks and fell down the well and got drowned."

It seemed abrupt, but I thought maybe the reader wouldn't notice it, because I changed the subject right away to something else. Anyway it loosened up Rowena from where she was stuck and got her out of the way, and that was the main thing. It seemed a prompt good way of weeding out people that had got stalled, and a plenty good enough way for those others; so I hunted up the two boys and said "they went out back one night to stone the cat and fell down the well and got drowned." Next I searched around and found old Aunt Patsy Cooper and Aunt Betsy Hale where they were aground, and said "they went outback one night to visit the sick and fell down the well and got drowned." I was going to drown some of the others, but I gave up the idea, partly because I believed that if I kept that up it would arouse attention, and perhaps sympathy with those people, and partly because it was not a large well and would not hold any more anyway.

Still the story was unsatisfactory. Here was a set of new characters who were become inordinately prominent and who persisted in remaining so to the end; and back yonder was an older set who made a large noise and a great to-do for a little while and then suddenly played out utterly and fell down the well. There was a radical defect somewhere, and I must search it out and cure it.

The defect turned out to be the one already spoken of—two stories in one, a farce and a tragedy. So I pulled out the farce and left the tragedy. This left the original team in, but only as mere names, not as characters. Their prominence was wholly gone; they were not even worth drowning; so I removed that detail. Also I took those twins apart and made two separate men of them. They had no occasion to have foreign names now, but it was too much trouble to remove them all through, so I left them christened as they were and made no explanation.

I

The conglomerate twins were brought on the stage in Chapter I of the original extravaganza. Aunt Patsy Cooper has received their letter applying for board and lodging, and Rowena, her daughter, insane with joy, is begging for a hearing of it:

"Well, set down then, and be quiet a minute and don't fly around so; it fairly makes me tired to see you. It starts off so: 'HONORED MADAM—'"

"I like that, ma, don't you? It shows they're high-bread."

"Yes, I noticed that when I first read it. 'My brother and I have seen your advertisement, by chance, in a copy of your local journal—'"

"It's so beautiful and smooth, ma—don't you think so?"

"Yes, seems so to me—'and beg leave to take the room you offer. We are twenty-four years of age, and twins—'"

"Twins! How sweet! I do hope they are handsome, and I just know they are! Don't you hope they are, ma?"

"Land, I ain't particular. 'We are Italians by birth—'"

"It's so romantic! Just think—there's never been one in this town, and everybody will want to see them, and they're all *ours!* Think of that!"

"—'but have lived long in the various countries of Europe, and several years in the United States.'"

"Oh, just think what wonders they've seen, ma! Won't it be good to hear them talk?"

"I reckon so; yes, I reckon so. 'Our names are Luigi and Angelo Capello—'"

"Beautiful, perfectly beautiful! Not like Jones and Robinson and those horrible names."

"'You desire but one guest, but dear madam, if you will allow us to pay for two we will not discommode you. We will sleep together in the same bed. We have always been used to this, and prefer it.' And then he goes on to say they will be down Thursday."

"And this is Tuesday—I don't know how I'm ever going to wait, ma! The time does drag along so, and I'm so dying to see them! Which of them do you reckon is the tallest, ma?"

"How do you s'pose I can tell, child? Mostly they are the same size—twins are."

"Well then, which do you reckon is the best looking?"

"Goodness knows—I don't."

"I think Angelo is; it's the prettiest name, anyway. Don't you think it's a sweet name, ma?"

"Yes, it's well enough. I'd like both of them better if I knew the way to pronounce them—the Eyetalian way, I mean. The Missouri way and the Eyetalian way is different, I judge."

"Maybe—yes. It's Luigi that writes the letter. What do you reckon is the reason Angelo didn't write it?"

"Why, how can I tell? What's the difference who writes it, so long as it's done?"

"Oh, I hope it wasn't because he is sick! You don't think he is sick, do you, ma?"

"Sick your granny; what's to make him sick?"

"Oh, there's never any telling. These foreigners with that kind of names are so delicate, and of course that kind of names are not suited to our climate—you wouldn't expect it."

[And so-on and so-on, no end. The time drags along; Thursday comes: the boat arrives in a pouring storm toward midnight.]

At last there was a knock at the door and the anxious family jumped to open it. Two negro men entered, each carrying a trunk, and proceeded upstairs toward the guest-room. Then followed a stupefying apparition—a double-headed human creature with four arms, one body, and a single pair of legs! It—or they, as you please—bowed with elaborate foreign formality, but the Coopers could not respond immediately; they were paralyzed. At this moment there came from the rear of the group a fervent ejaculation—"My lan'!"—followed by a crash of crockery, and the slave-wench Nancy stood petrified and staring, with a tray of wrecked tea-things at her feet. The incident broke the spell, and brought the family to consciousness. The beautiful heads of the new-comer bowed again, and one of them said with easy grace and dignity:

"I crave the honor, madam and miss, to introduce to you my brother, Count Luigi Capello," (the other head bowed) "and myself—Count Angelo; and at the same time offer sincere apologies for the lateness of our coming, which was unavoidable," and both heads bowed again.

The poor old lady was in a whirl of amazement and confusion, but she managed to stammer out:

"I'm sure I'm glad to make your acquaintance, sir—I mean, gentlemen. As for the delay, it is nothing, don't mention it. This is my daughter Rowena, sir—gentlemen. Please step into the parlor and sit down and have a bite and sup; you are dreadful wet and must be uncomfortable—both of you, I mean."

But to the old lady's relief they courteously excused themselves, saying it would be wrong to keep the family out of their beds longer; then each head bowed in turn and uttered a friendly good-night, and the singular figure moved away in the wake of Rowena's small brothers, who bore candles, and disappeared up the stairs.

The widow tottered into the parlor and sank into a chair with a gasp, and Rowena followed, tongue-tied and dazed. The two sat silent in the throbbing summer heat unconscious of the million-voiced music of the mosquitoes, unconscious of the roaring gale, the lashing and thrashing of the rain along the windows and the roof, the white glare of the lightning, the tumultuous booming and bellowing of the thunder; conscious of nothing but that prodigy, that uncanny apparition that had come and gone so suddenly—that weird strange thing that was so soft-spoken and so gentle of manner and yet had shaken them up like an earthquake with the shock of its gruesome aspect. At last a cold little shudder quivered along down the widow's meager frame and she said in a weak voice:

"Ugh, it was awful—just the mere look of that phillipene!"

Rowena did not answer. Her faculties were still caked, she had not yet found her voice. Presently the widow said, a little resentfully:

"Always been *used* to sleeping together—in fact, *prefer* it. And

I was thinking it was to accommodate me. I thought it was very good of them, whereas a person situated as that young man is—"

"Ma, you oughtn't to begin by getting up a prejudice against him. I'm sure he is good-hearted and means well. Both of his faces show it."

"I'm not so certain about that. The one on the left—I mean the one on *it's* left—hasn't near as good a face, in my opinion, as its brother."

"That's Luigi."

"Yes, Luigi; anyway it's the dark-skinned one; the one that was west of his brother when they stood in the door. Up to all kinds of mischief and disobedience when he was a boy, I'll be bound. I lay his mother had trouble to lay her hand on him when she wanted him. But the one on the right is as good as gold, I can see that."

"That's Angelo."

"Yes, Angelo, I reckon, though I can't tell t' other from which by their names, yet awhile. But it's the right-hand one—the blond one. He has such kind blue eyes, and curly copper hair and fresh complexion—"

"And such a noble face!—oh, it *is* a noble face, ma, just royal, you may say! And beautiful—deary me, how beautiful! But both are that; the dark one's as beautiful as a picture. There's no such wonderful faces and handsome heads in this town—none that even begin. And such hands—especially Angelo's—so shapely and—"

"Stuff, how could you tell which they belonged to?—they had gloves on."

"Why, didn't I see them take off their hats?"

"That don't signify. They might have taken off each other's hats. Nobody could tell. There was just a wormy squirming of arms in the air—seemed to be a couple of dozen of them, all writhing at once, and it just made me dizzy to see them go."

"Why, ma, I hadn't any difficulty. There's two arms on each shoulder—"

"There, now. One arm on each shoulder belongs to each of the creatures, don't it? For a person to have two arms on one shoulder wouldn't do him any good, would it? Of course not. Each has an arm on each shoulder. Now then, you tell me which of them belongs to which, if you can. *They* don't know, themselves—they just work whichever arm comes handy. Of course they do; especially if they are in a hurry and can't stop to think which belongs to which."

The mother seemed to have the rights of the argument, so the daughter abandoned the struggle. Presently the widow rose with a yawn and said:

"Poor thing, I hope it won't catch cold; it was powerful wet, just drenched, you may say. I hope it has left its boots outside, so they can be dried." Then she gave a little start, and looked perplexed. "Now I remember I heard one of them ask Joe to call him at half after seven—I think it was the one on the left—no, it was the one to the east of the other one—but I didn't hear the other one say anything. I wonder if he wants to be called too. Do you reckon it's too late to ask?"

"Why, ma, it's not necessary. Calling one is calling both. If one gets up, the other's *got* to."

"Sho, of course; I never thought of that. Well, come along, maybe we can get some sleep, but I don't know, I'm so shook up with what we've been through."

The stranger had made an impression on the boys, too. They had a word of talk as they were getting to bed. Henry, the gentle, the humane, said:

"I feel ever so sorry for it, don't you, Joe?"

But Joe was a boy of this world, active, enterprising, and had a theatrical side to him:

"Sorry? Why, how you talk! It can't stir a step without attracting attention. It's just grand!"

Henry said, reproachfully:

"Instead of pitying it, Joe, you talk as if—"

"Talk as if *what?* I know one thing mighty certain: if you can fix me so I can eat for two and only have to stub toes for one, I ain't going to fool away no such chance just for sentiment."

The twins were wet and tired, and they proceeded to undress without any preliminary remarks. The abundance of sleeve made the partnership-coat hard to get off, for it was like skinning a tarantula; but it came at last, after much tugging and perspiring. The mutual vest followed. Then the brothers stood up before the glass, and each took off his own cravat and collar. The collars were of the standing kind, and came high up under the ears, like the sides of a wheelbarrow, as required by the fashion of the day. The cravats were as broad as a bank bill, with fringed ends which stood far out to right and left like the wings of a dragon-fly, and this also was strictly in accordance with the fashion of the time. Each cravat, as to color, was in perfect taste, so far as its owner's complexion was concerned—a delicate pink, in the case of the blonde brother, a violent scarlet in the case of the brunette—but as a combination they broke all the laws of taste known to civilization. Nothing more fiendish and irreconcilable than those shrieking and blaspheming colors could have been contrived. The wet boots gave no end of trouble—to Luigi. When they were off at last, Angelo said, with bitterness:

"I wish you wouldn't wear such tight boots, they hurt my feet."

Luigi answered with indifference:

"My friend, when I am in command of our body, I choose my apparel according to my own convenience, as I have remarked more than several times already. When you are in command, I beg you will do as you please."

Angelo was hurt, and the tears came into his eyes. There was gentle reproach in his voice, but not anger, when he replied:

"Luigi, I often consult your wishes, but you never consult mine. When I am in command I treat you as a guest; I try to make you feel at home; when you are in command you treat me as an intruder, you make me feel unwelcome. It embarrasses me cruelly in company, for I can see that people notice it and comment on it."

"Oh, damn the people," responded the brother languidly, and with the air of one who is tired of the subject.

A slight shudder shook the frame of Angelo, but he said nothing and the conversation ceased. Each buttoned his own share of the night-shirt in silence; then Luigi, with Paine's "Age of Reason" in his hand, sat down in one chair and put his feet in another and lit his pipe, while Angelo took his "Whole Duty of

Man," and both began to read. Angelo presently began to cough; his coughing increased and became mixed with gaspings for breath, and he was finally obliged to make an appeal to his brother's humanity:

"Luigi, if you would only smoke a little milder tobacco, I am sure I could learn not to mind it in time, but this is so strong, and the pipe is so rank that—"

"Angelo, I wouldn't be such a baby! I have learned to smoke in a week, and the trouble is already over with me; if you would try, you could learn too, and then you would stop spoiling my comfort with your everlasting complaints."

"Ah, brother, that is a strong word—everlasting—and isn't quite fair. I only complain when I suffocate; you know I don't complain when we are in the open air."

"Well, anyway, you could learn to smoke yourself."

"But my *principles*, Luigi, you forget my principles. You would not have me do a thing which I regard as a sin?"

"Oh, bosh!"

The conversation ceased again, for Angelo was sick and discouraged and strangling; but after some time he closed his book and asked Luigi to sing "From Greenland's Icy Mountains" with him, but he would not, and when he tried to sing by himself Luigi did his best to drown his plaintive tenor with a rude and rollicking song delivered in a thundering bass.

After the singing there was silence, and neither brother was happy. Before blowing the light out Luigi swallowed half a tumbler of whisky, and Angelo, whose sensitive organization could not endure intoxicants of any kind, took a pill to keep it from giving him the headache.

II

The family sat in the breakfast-room waiting for the twins to come down. The widow was quiet, the daughter was alive with happy excitement. She said:

"Ah, they're a boon, ma, just a boon! don't you think so?"

"Laws, I hope so, I don't know."

"Why, ma, yes you do. They're so fine and handsome, and

high-bred and polite, so every way superior to our gawks here in this village; why, they'll make life different from what it was—so humdrum and commonplace, you know—oh, you may be sure they're full of accomplishments, and knowledge of the world, and all that, that will be an immense advantage to society here. Don't you think so, ma?"

"Mercy on me, how should I know, and I've hardly set eyes on them yet." After a pause she added, "They made considerable noise after they went up."

"Noise? Why, ma, they were singing! And it was beautiful, too."

"Oh, it was well enough, but too mixed-up, seemed to me."

"Now, ma, honor bright, did you ever hear 'Greenland's Icy Mountains' sung sweeter—now did you?"

"If it had been sung by itself, it would have been uncommon sweet, I don't deny it; but what they wanted to mix it up with 'Old Bob Ridley' for, I can't make out. Why, they don't go together, at all. They are not of the same nature. 'Bob Ridley' is a common rackety slam-bang secular song, one of the rippingest and rantingest and noisiest there is. I am no judge of music, and I don't claim it, but in my opinion nobody can make those two songs go together right."

"Why, ma, I thought—"

"It don't make any difference what you thought, it can't be done. They tried it, and to my mind it was a failure. I never heard such a crazy uproar; seemed to me, sometimes, the roof would come off; and as for the cats—well, I've lived a many a year, and seen cats aggravated in more ways than one, but I've never seen cats take on the way they took on last night."

"Well, I don't think that that goes for anything, ma, because it is the nature of cats that any sound that is unusual—"

"Unusual! You may well call it so. Now if they are going to sing duets every night, I do hope they will both sing the same tune at the same time, for in my opinion a duet that is made up of two different tunes is a mistake; especially when the tunes ain't any kin to one another, that way."

"But, ma, I think it must be a foreign custom; and it must be right too, and the best way, because they have had every opportunity to know what is right, and it don't stand to reason that with their education they would do anything but what the highest musical authorities have sanctioned. You can't help but admit that, ma."

The argument was formidably strong; the old lady could not find any way around it; so, after thinking it over a while she gave in with a sigh of discontent, and admitted that the daughter's position was probably correct. Being vanquished, she had no mind to continue the topic at that disadvantage, and was about to seek a change when a change came of itself. A footstep was heard on the stairs, and she said:

"There—he's coming!"

"*They,* ma—you ought to say *they*—it's nearer right."

The new lodger, rather shoutingly dressed but looking superbly handsome, stepped with courtly carriage into the trim little breakfast-room and put out all his cordial arms at once, like one of those pocket-knives with a multiplicity of blades, and shook hands with the whole family simultaneously. He was so easy and pleasant and hearty that all embarrassment presently thawed away and disappeared, and a cheery feeling of friendliness and comradeship took its place. He—or preferably they—were asked to occupy the seat of honor at the foot of the table. They consented with thanks, and carved the beefsteak with one set of their hands while they distributed it at the same time with the other set.

"Will you have coffee, gentlemen, or tea?"

"Coffee for Luigi, if you please, madam, tea for me."

"Cream and sugar?"

"For me, yes, madam; Luigi takes his coffee black. Our natures differ a good deal from each other, and our tastes also."

The first time the negro girl Nancy appeared in the door and saw the two heads turned in opposite directions and both talking at once, then saw the commingling arms feed potatoes into one mouth and coffee into the other at the same time, she had to pause and pull herself out of a faintness that came over her; but after that she held her grip and was able to wait on the table with fair courage.

Conversation fell naturally into the customary grooves. It was a little jerky, at first, because none of the family could get smoothly through a sentence without a wobble in it here and a break there, caused by some new surprise in the way of attitude or gesture on the part of the twins. The weather suffered the most. The weather was all finished up and disposed of, as a subject, before the simple Missourians had gotten sufficiently wonted to the spectacle of one body feeding two heads to feel composed and reconciled in the presence of so bizarre a miracle. And even after everybody's mind became tranquilized there was still one slight distraction left: the hand that picked up a biscuit carried it to the wrong head, as often as any other way, and the wrong mouth devoured it. This was a puzzling thing, and marred the talk a little. It bothered the widow to such a degree that she presently dropped out of the conversation without knowing it, and fell to watching and guessing and talking to herself:

"Now that hand is going to take that coffee to—no, it's gone to the other mouth; I can't understand it; and now, here is the dark complected hand with a potato on its fork, I'll see what goes with it—there, the light complected head's got it, as sure as I live!" Finally Rowena said:

"Ma, what is the matter with you? Are you dreaming about something?"

The old lady came to herself and blushed; then she explained with the first random thing that came into her mind: "I saw Mr. Angelo take up Mr. Luigi's coffee, and I thought maybe he—sha'n't I give *you* a cup, Mr. Angelo?"

"Oh no, madam, I am very much obliged, but I never drink coffee, much as I would like to. You did see me take up Luigi's cup, it is true, but if you noticed, I didn't carry it to my mouth, but to his."

"Y—es, I thought you did. Did you mean to?"

"How?"

The widow was a little embarrassed again. She said:

"I don't know but what I'm foolish, and you mustn't mind; but you see, he got the coffee I was expecting to see you drink, and you got a potato that I thought he was going to get. So I thought it might be a mistake all around, and everybody getting what wasn't intended for him."

Both twins laughed and Luigi said:

"Dear madam, there wasn't any mistake. We are always helping each other that way. It is a great economy for us both; it saves time and labor. We have a system of signs which nobody can notice or understand but ourselves. If I am using both my hands and want some coffee, I make the sign and Angelo furnishes it to me; and you saw that when he needed a potato I delivered it."

"How convenient!"

"Yes, and often of the extremest value. Take the Mississippi boats, for instance. They are always over-crowded. There is table-room for only half of the passengers, therefore they have to set a second table for the second half. The stewards rush both parties, they give them no time to eat a satisfying meal, both divisions leave the table hungry. It isn't so with us. Angelo books himself for the one table, I book myself for the other. Neither of us eats anything at the other's table, but just simply works—works. Thus, you see there are four hands to feed Angelo, and the same four to feed me. Each of us eats two meals."

The old lady was dazed with admiration, and kept saying, "It is *per*fectly wonderful, perfectly wonderful!" and the boy Joe licked his chops enviously, but said nothing—at least aloud.

"Yes," continued Luigi, "our construction may have its disadvantages—in fact, *has*—but it also has its compensations of one sort and another. Take travel, for instance. Travel is enormously expensive, in all countries; we have been obliged to do a vast deal of it—come, Angelo, don't put any more sugar in your tea, I'm just over one indigestion and don't want another right away—been obliged to do a deal of it, as I was saying. Well, we always travel as one person, since we occupy but one seat; so we save half the fare."

"How romantic!" interjected Rowena, with effusion.

"Yes, my dear young lady, and how practical too, and economical. In Europe, beds in the hotels are not charged with the board, but separately—another saving, for we stood to our rights and paid for the one bed only. The landlords often insisted that as both of us occupied the bed we ought—"

"No, they didn't," said Angelo. "They did it only twice, and in both cases is was a double bed—a rare thing in Europe—and the double bed gave them some excuse. Be fair to the landlords; twice doesn't constitute 'often.'"

"Well, that depends—that depends. I knew a man who fell down a well twice. He said he didn't mind the first time, but he thought the second time was once too often. Have I misused that word, Mrs. Cooper?"

"To tell the truth, I was afraid you had, but it seems to look, now, like you hadn't." She stopped, and was evidently struggling with the difficult problem a moment, then she added in the tone of one who is convinced without being converted, "It seems so, but I can't somehow tell why."

Rowena thought Luigi's retort was wonderfully quick and bright, and she remarked to herself with satisfaction that there wasn't any young native of Dawson's Landing that could have risen to the occasion like that. Luigi detected the applause in her face, and expressed his pleasure and his thanks with his eyes; and so eloquently withal, that the girl was proud and pleased, and hung out the delicate sign of it on her cheeks.

Luigi went on, with animation:

"Both of us get a bath for one ticket, theater seat for one ticket, pew-rent is on the same basis, but at peep-shows we pay double."

"We have much to be thankful for," said Angelo, impressively, with a reverent light in his eye and a reminiscent tone in his voice, "we have been greatly blessed. As a rule, what one of us has lacked, the other, by the bounty of Providence, has been able to supply. My brother is hardy, I am not; he is very masculine, assertive, aggressive; I am much less so. I am subject to illness, he is never ill. I cannot abide medicines, and cannot take them, but he has no prejudice against them, and—"

"Why, goodness gracious," interrupted the widow, "when you are sick, does he take the medicine for you?"

"Always, madam."

"Why, I never heard such a thing in my life! I think it's beautiful of you."

"Oh, madam, it's nothing, don't mention it, it's really nothing at all."

"But I say it's beautiful, and I stick to it!" cried the widow, with a speaking moisture in her eye. "A well brother to take the medicine for his poor sick brother—I wish I had such a son," and she glanced reproachfully at her boys. "I declare I'll never rest till I've shook you by the hand," and she scrambled out of her chair in a fever of generous enthusiasm, and made for the twins, blind with her tears, and began to shake. The boy Joe corrected her:

"You're shaking the wrong one, ma."

This flurried her, but she made a swift change and went on shaking.

"Got the wrong one again, ma," said the boy.

"Oh, shut up, can't you!" said the widow, embarrassed and irritated. "Give me *all* your hands, I want to shake them all; for I know you are both just as good as you can be."

It was a victorious thought, a master-stroke of diplomacy, though that never occurred to her and she cared nothing for diplomacy. She shook the four hands in turn cordially, and went back to her place in a state of high and fine exaltation that made her look young and handsome.

"Indeed I owe everything to Luigi," said Angelo, affectionately. "But for him I could not have survived our boyhood days, when we were friendless and poor—ah, so poor! We lived from hand to mouth—lived on the coarse fare of unwilling charity, and for weeks and weeks together not a morsel of food passed my lips, for its character revolted me and I could not eat it. But for Luigi I should have died. He ate for us both."

"How noble!" sighed Rowena.

"Do you hear that?" said the widow, severely, to her boys. "Let it be an example to you—I mean you, Joe."

Joe gave his head a barely perceptible disparaging toss and said: "Et for both. It ain't anything—I'd a done it."

"Hush, if you haven't got any better manners than that. You don't see the point at all. It wasn't good food."

"I don't care—it was food, and I'd 'a et it if it was rotten."

"Shame! Such language! Can't you understand? They were starving—actually starving—and he ate for both, and—"

"Shucks! you gimme a chance and I'll—"

"There, now—close your head! and don't you open it again till you're asked."

[Angelo goes on and tells how his parents the Count and Countess had to fly from Florence for political reasons, and died poor in Berlin bereft of their great property by confiscation; and how he and Luigi had to travel with a freak-show during two years and suffer semi-starvation.]

"That hateful black-bread! but I seldom ate anything during that time; that was poor Luigi's affair—"

"I'll never *Mister* him again!" cried the widow, with strong emotion, "he's Luigi to me, from this out!"

"Thank you a thousand times, madam, a thousand times! though in truth I don't deserve it."

"Ah, Luigi is always the fortunate one when honors are showering," said Angelo, plaintively, "now what have I done, Mrs. Cooper, that you leave me out? Come, you must strain a point in my favor."

"Call you Angelo? Why, certainly I will; what are you thinking of! In the case of twins, why—"

"But, ma, you're breaking up the story—do let him go on."

"You keep still, Rowena Cooper, and he can go on all the better, I reckon. One interruption don't hurt, it's two that makes the trouble."

"But you've added one, now, and that is three."

"Rowena! I will not allow you to talk back at me when you have got nothing rational to say."

III

[After breakfast the whole village crowded in, and there was a grand reception in honor of the twins; and at the close of it the gifted "freak" captured everybody's admiration by sitting down at the piano and knocking out a classic four-handed piece in great style. Then the Judge took it—or them—driving in his buggy and showed off his village.]

All along the streets the people crowded the windows and stared at the amazing twins. Troops of small boys flocked after the buggy, excited and yelling. At first the dogs showed no interest. They thought they merely saw three men in a buggy—a matter of no consequence; but when they found out the facts of the case, they altered their opinion pretty radically, and joined the boys, expressing their minds as they came. Other dogs got interested; indeed, all the dogs. It was a spirited sight to see them come leaping fences, tearing around corners, swarming out of every by street and alley. The noise they made was something beyond belief—or praise. They did not seem to be moved by malice but only by prejudice, the common human prejudice against lack of conformity. If the twins turned their heads, they broke and fled in every direction, but stopped at a safe distance and faced about; and then formed and came on again as soon as the strangers showed them their back. Negroes and farmers' wives took to the woods when the buggy came upon them suddenly, and altogether the drive was pleasant and animated, and a refreshment all around.

[It was a long and lively drive. Angelo was a Methodist, Luigi was a Freethinker. The Judge was very proud of his Freethinkers' Society, which was flourishing along in a most prosperous way and already had two members—himself and the obscure and neglected Pudd'nhead Wilson. It was to meet that evening, and he invited Luigi to join; a thing which Luigi was glad to do, partly because it would please himself, and partly because it would gravel Angelo.]

They had now arrived at the widow's gate, and the excursion was ended. The twins politely expressed their obligations for the pleasant outing which had been afforded them; to which the

Judge bowed his thanks, and then said he would now go and arrange for the Freethinkers' meeting, and would call for Count Luigi in the evening.

"For you also, dear sir," he added hastily, turning to Angelo and bowing. "In addressing myself particularly to your brother, I was not meaning to leave you out. It was an unintentional rudeness, I assure you, and due wholly to accident—accident and preoccupation. I beg you to forgive me."

His quick eye had seen the sensitive blood mount into Angelo's face, betraying the wound that had been inflicted. The sting of the slight had gone deep, but the apology was so prompt, and so evidently sincere, that the hurt was almost immediately healed, and a forgiving smile testified to the kindly Judge that all was well again.

Concealed behind Angelo's modest and unassuming exterior, and unsuspected by any but his intimates, was a lofty pride, a pride of almost abnormal proportions, indeed, and this rendered him ever the prey of slights; and although thy were almost always imaginary ones, they hurt none the less on that account. By ill fortune Judge Driscoll had happened to touch his sorest point, *i. e.*, his conviction that his brother's presence was welcomer everywhere than his own; that he was often invited, out of mere courtesy, where only his brother was wanted, and that in a majority of cases he would not be included in an invitation if he could be left out without offense. A sensitive nature like this is necessarily subject to moods; moods which traverse the whole gamut of feeling; moods which know all the climes of emotion, from the sunny heights of joy to the black abysses of despair. At times, in his seasons of deepest depressions, Angelo almost wished that he and his brother might become segregated from each other and be separate individuals, like other men. But of course as soon as his mind cleared and these diseased imaginings passed away, he shuddered at the repulsive thought, and earnestly prayed that it might visit him no more. To be separate, and as other men are! How awkward it would seen; how unendurable. What would he do with his hands, his arms? How would his legs feel? How odd, and strange, and grotesque every action, attitude, movement, gesture would be. To sleep by himself, eat by himself, walk by himself—how lonely, how unspeakably lonely! No, no, any fate but that. In every way and from every point, the idea was revolting.

This was of course natural; to have felt otherwise would have been unnatural. He had known no life but a combined one; he had been familiar with it from his birth; he was not able to conceive of any other as being agreeable, or even bearable. To him, in the privacy of his secret thoughts, all other men were monsters, deformities: and during three-fourths of his life their aspect had filled him with what promised to be an unconquerable aversion. But at eighteen his eye began to take note of female beauty; and little by little, undefined longings grew up in his heart, under whose softening influences the old stubborn aversion gradually diminished, and finally disappeared. Men were still monstrosities to him, still deformities, and in his sober moments he had no desire to be like them, but their strange and unsocial and uncanny construction was no longer offensive to him.

This had been a hard day for him, physically and mentally. He had been called in the morning before he had quite slept off the effects of the liquor which Luigi had drunk; and so, for the first half hour had had the seedy feeling, and languor, the brooding depression, the cobwebby mouth and druggy taste that come of dissipation and are so ill a preparation for bodily or intellectual activities; the long violent strain of the reception had followed; and this had been followed, in turn, by the dreary sight-seeing, the Judge's wearying explanations and laudations of the sights, and the stupefying clamor of the dogs. As a congruous conclusion, a fitting end, his feelings had been hurt, a slight had been put upon him. He would have been glad to forego dinner and betake himself to rest and sleep, but he held his peace and said no word, for he knew his brother, Luigi, was fresh, unweary, full of life, spirit, energy; he would have scoffed at the idea of wasting valuable time on a bed or a sofa, and would have refused permission.

IV

Rowena was dining out, Joe and Harry were belated at play, there were but three chairs and four persons that noon at the home dinner-table—the twins, the widow, and her chum, Aunt Betsy Hale. The widow soon perceived that Angelo's spirits were as low as Luigi's were high, and also that he had a jaded look. Her motherly solicitude was aroused, and she tried to get him interested in the talk and win him to a happier frame of mind, but the cloud of sadness remained on his countenance. Luigi lent his help, too. He used a form and a phrase which he was always accustomed to employ in these circumstances. He gave his brother an affectionate slap on the shoulder and said, encouragingly:

"Cheer up, the worst is yet to come!"

But this did no good. It never did. If anything, it made the matter worse, as a rule, because it irritated Angelo. This made it a favorite with Luigi. By and by the widow said:

"Angelo, you are tired, you've overdone yourself; you go right to bed after dinner, and get a good nap and a rest, then you'll be all right."

"Indeed, I would give anything if I could do that, madam."

"And what's to hender, I'd like to know? Land, the room's yours to do what you please with! The idea that you can't do what you like with your own!"

"But, you see, there's one prime essential—an essential of the very first importance—which isn't my own."

"What is that?"

"My body."

The old ladies looked puzzled, and Aunt Betsy Hale said:

"Why bless your heart, how is that?"

"It's my brother's."

"Your brother's! I don't quite understand. I supposed it belonged to both of you."

"So it does. But not to both at the same time."

"That is mighty curious; I don't see how it can be. I shouldn't think it could be managed that way."

"Oh, it's a good enough arrangement, and goes very well; in

fact, it wouldn't do to have it otherwise. I find that the teetotalers and the antiteetotalers hire the use of the same hall for their meetings. Both parties don't use it at the same time, do they?"

"You bet they don't!" said both old ladies in a breath.

"And, moreover," said Aunt Betsy, "the Freethinkers and the Baptist Bible class use the same room over the Market house, but you can take my word for it they don't mush up together and use it at the same time."

"Very well," said Angelo, "you understand it now. And it stands to reason that the arrangement couldn't be improved. I'll prove it to you. If our legs tried to obey two wills, how could we ever get anywhere? I would start one way, Luigi would start another, at the same moment—the result would be a standstill, wouldn't it?"

"As sure as you are born! Now ain't that wonderful! A body would never have thought of it."

"We should always be arguing and fussing and disputing over the merest trifles. We should lose worlds of time, for we couldn't go down stairs or up, couldn't go to bed, couldn't rise, couldn't wash, couldn't dress, couldn't stand up, couldn't sit down, couldn't even cross our legs, without calling a meeting first and explaining the case and passing resolutions, and getting consent. It wouldn't ever do—now would it?"

"Do? Why, it would wear a person out in a week! Did you ever hear anything like it, Patsy Cooper?"

"Oh, you'll find there's more than one thing about them that ain't commonplace," said the widow, with the complacent air of a person with a property-right in a novelty that is under admiring scrutiny.

"Well, now, how ever do you manage it? I don't mind saying I'm suffering to know."

"He who made us," said Angelo reverently, "and with us this difficulty, also provided a way out of it. By a mysterious law of our being, each of us has utter and indisputable command of our body a week at a time, turn and turn about."

"Well, I never! Now ain't that beautiful!"

"Yes, it is beautiful and infinitely wise and just. The week ends every Saturday at midnight to the minute, to the second, to the last shade of a fraction of a second, infallibly, unerringly, and in that instant the one brother's power over the body vanishes and the other brother takes possession, asleep or awake."

"How marvelous are His ways, and past finding out!"

Luigi said: "So exactly to the instant does the change come, that during our stay in many of the great cities of the world, the public clocks were regulated by it; and as hundreds of thousands of private clocks and watches were set and corrected in accordance with the public clocks, we really furnished the standard time for the entire city."

"Don't tell me that He don't do miracles any more! Blowing down the walls of Jericho with rams' horns wa'n't as difficult, in my opinion."

"And that is not all," said Angelo. "A thing that is even more marvelous, perhaps, is the fact that the change takes not of longitude and fits itself to the meridian we are on. Luigi is in command this week. Now, if on Saturday night at a moment before midnight we could fly in an instant to a point fifteen degrees west of here, he would hold possession of the power another hour, for the change observes *local* time and no other."

Betsy Hale was deeply impressed, and said with solemnity:

"Patsy Cooper, for *de*tail it lays over the Passage of the Red Sea."

"Now, I shouldn't go as far as that," said Aunt Patsy, "but if you've a mind to say Sodom and Gomorrah, I am with you, Betsy Hale."

"I am agreeable, then, though I do think I was right, and I believe Parson Maltby would say the same. Well, now, there's another thing. Suppose one of you wants to borrow the legs a minute from the one that's got them, could he let him?"

"Yes, but we hardly ever do that. There were disagreeable results, several times, and so we very seldom ask or grant the privilege, nowadays, and we never even think of such a thing unless the case is extremely urgent. Besides, a week's possession at a time seems so little that we can't bear to spare a minute of it. People who have the use of their legs all the time never think of what a blessing it is, of course. It never occurs to them; it's just their natural ordinary condition, and so it does not excite them at all. But when I wake up, on Sunday morning, and it's my week and I feel the power all through me, oh, such a wave of exultation and thanksgiving goes surging over me, and I want to shout 'I can walk! I can walk!' Madam, do you ever, at your uprising want to shout 'I can walk! I can walk!'?"

"No, you poor unfortunate cretur', but I'll never get out of my bed again without *doing* it! Laws, to think I've had this unspeakable blessing all my long life and never had the grace to thank the good Lord that gave it to me!"

Tears stood in the eyes of both the old ladies and the widow said, softly:

"Betsy Hale, we have learned something, you and me."

The conversation now drifted wide, but by and by floated back once more to that admired detail, the rigid and beautiful impartiality with which the possession of power had been distributed between the twins. Aunt Betsy saw in it a far finer justice than human law exhibits in related cases. She said:

"In my opinion it ain't right now, and never has been right, the way a twin born a quarter of a minute sooner than the other one gets all the land and grandeurs and nobilities in the old countries and his brother has to go bare and be a nobody. Which of you was born first?"

Angelo's head was resting against Luigi's; weariness had overcome him, and for the past five minutes he had been peacefully sleeping. The old ladies had dropped their voices to a lulling drone, to help him steal the rest his brother wouldn't take him up stairs to get. Luigi listened a moment to Angelo's regular breathing, then said in a voice barely audible:

"We were both born at the same time, but I am six months older than he is."

"For the land's sake!"

"Sh! don't wake him up; he wouldn't like my telling this. It has always been kept secret till now."

"But how in the world can it be? If you were both born at the same time, how can one of you be older than the other?"

"It is very simple, and I assure you it is true. I was born with a full crop of hair, he was as bald as an egg for six months. I could walk six months before he could make a step. I finished teething six months ahead of him. I began to take solids six months before he left the breast. I began to talk six months before he could say a word. Last, and absolutely unassailable proof, *the sutures in my skull closed six months ahead of his.* Always just that six months difference to a day. Was that accident? Nobody is going to claim that, I'm sure. It was ordained—it was law—it had its meaning, and we know what that meaning was. Now what does this overwhelming body of evidence establish? It establishes just one thing, and that thing it establishes beyond any peradventure whatever. Friends, we would not have it known for the world, and I must beg you to keep it strictly to yourselves, but the truth is, *we are no more twins than you are.*"

The two old ladies were stunned, paralyzed—petrified, one may almost say—and could only sit and gaze vacantly at each other for some moments; then Aunt Betsy Hale said impressively:

"There's no getting around proof like that. I do believe it's the most amazing thing I ever heard of." She sat silent a moment or two and breathing hard with excitement, then she looked up and surveyed the strangers steadfastly a little while, and added: "Well, it does beat me, but I would have took you for twins anywhere."

"So would I, so would I," said Aunt Patsy with the emphasis of a certainty that is not impaired by any shade of doubt.

"*Any*body would—anybody in the world, I don't care who he is," said Aunt Betsy with decision.

"You won't tell," said Luigi, appealingly.

"Oh, dear, no!" answered both ladies promptly, "you can trust us, don't you be afraid."

"That is good of you, and kind. Never let on; treat us always as if we were twins."

"You can depend on us," said Aunt Betsy, "but it won't be easy, because now that I know you ain't you don't *seem* so."

Luigi muttered to himself with satisfaction: "That swindle has gone through without change of cars."

It was not very kind of him to load the poor things up with a secret like that, which would be always flying to their tongues' ends every time they heard any one speak of the strangers as twins, and would become harder and harder to hang on to with very recurrence of the temptation to tell it, while the torture of retaining it would increase with every new strain that was applied; but he never thought of that, and probably would not have worried much about it if he had.

A visitor was announced—some one to see the twins. They withdrew to the parlor, and the two old ladies began to discuss with interest the strange things which they had been listening to. When they had finished the matter to their satisfaction, and Aunt Betsy rose to go, she stopped to ask a question:

"How does things come on between Roweny and Tom Driscoll?"

"Well, about the same. He writes tolerable often, and she answers tolerable seldom."

"Where is he?"

"In St. Louis, I believe, though he's such a gadabout that a body can't be very certain of him, I reckon."

"Don't Roweny know?"

"Oh, yes, like enough. I haven't asked her lately."

"Do you know how him and the Judge are getting along now?"

"First-rate, I believe. Mrs. Pratt says so; and being right in the house, and sister to the one and aunt to t'other, of course she ought to know. She says the Judge is real fond of him when he's away; but frets when he's around and is vexed with his ways, and not sorry to have him go again. He has been gone three weeks this time—a pleasant thing for both of them, I reckon."

"Tom's ruther harum-scarum, but there ain't anything bad in him, I guess."

"Oh, no, he's just young, that's all. Still, twenty-three is old, in one way. A young man ought to be earning his living by that time. If Tom were doing that, or was even trying to do it, the Judge would be a heap better satisfied with him. Tom's always going to begin, but somehow he can't seem to find just the opening he likes."

"Well, now, it's partly the Judge's own fault. Promising the boy his property wasn't the way to set him to earning a fortune of his own. But what do you think—is Roweny beginning to lean any toward him, or ain't she?"

Aunt Patsy had a secret in her bosom; she wanted to keep it there, but nature was too strong for her. She drew Aunt Betsy aside, and said in her most confidential and mysterious manner:

"Don't you breathe a syllable to a soul—I'm going to tell you something. In my opinion Tom Driscoll's chances were considerable better yesterday than they are to-day."

"Patsy Cooper, what *do* you mean?"

"It's so, as sure as you're born, I wish you could 'a' been at breakfast and seen for yourself."

"You don't mean it!"

"Well, if I'm any judge, there's a leaning—there's a leaning, sure."

"My land! Which one of 'em is it?"

"I can't say for certain, but I think it's the youngest one—Anjy."

Then there were handshakings, and congratulations, and hopes, and so on, and the old ladies parted, perfectly happy—the one in knowing something which the rest of the town didn't, and the other in having been the sole person able to furnish that knowledge.

The visitor who had called to see the twins was the Rev. Mr. Hotchkiss, pastor of the Baptist church. At the reception Angelo had told him he had lately experienced a change in his religious views, and was now desirous of becoming a Baptist, and would immediately join Mr. Hotchkiss's church. There was no time to say more, and the brief talk ended at that point. The minister was much gratified, and had dropped in for a moment now, to invite the twins to attend his Bible class at eight that evening. Angelo accepted, and was expecting Luigi to decline, but he did not, because he knew that the Bible class and the Free-thinkers met in the same room, and he wanted to treat his brother to the embarrassment of being caught in free-thinking company.

V

[A long and vigorous quarrel follows, between the twins. And there is plenty to quarrel about, for Angelo was always seeking truth, and this obliged him to change and improve his religion with frequency, which wearied Luigi, and annoyed him too; for he had to be present at each new enlistment—which placed him in the false position of seeming to endorse and approve his brother's fickleness; moreover, he had to go to Angelo's prohibition meetings, and he hated them. On the other hand, when it was *his* week to command the legs he gave Angelo just cause of complaint, for he took him to circuses and horseraces and fandangoes, exposing him to all sorts of censure and criticism; and he drank, too; and whatever he drank went to Angelo's head instead of his own and made him act disgracefully. When the evening was come, the two attended the Freethinkers' meeting, where Angelo was sad and silent; then came the Bible-class and looked upon him coldly, finding him in such company. Then they went to Wilson's house and Chapter XI. of "Pudd'nhead Wilson" follows, which tells of the girl seen in Tom Driscoll's room; and closes with the kicking of Tom by Luigi at the anti-temperance mass meeting of the Sons of Liberty; with the addition of some account of Roxy's adventures as a chambermaid on a Mississippi boat. Her exchange of the children had been flippantly and farcically described in an earlier chapter.]

Next morning all the town was a-buzz with great news; Pudd'nhead Wilson had a law case! The public astonishment was so great and the public curiosity so intense, that when the justice of the peace opened his court, the place was packed with people, and even the windows were full. Everybody was flushed and perspiring; the summer heat was almost unendurable.

Tom Driscoll had brought a charge of assault and battery against the twins. Robert Allen was retained by Driscoll, David Wilson by the defense. Tom, his native cheerfulness unannihilated by his back-breaking and bone-bruising passage across the massed heads of the Sons of Liberty the previous night, laughed his little customary laugh, and said to Wilson:

"I've kept my promise, you see; I'm throwing my business your way. Sooner than I was expecting, too."

"It's very good of you—particularly if you mean to keep it up."

"Well, I can't tell about that yet. But we'll see. If I find you deserve it I'll take you under my protection and make your fame and fortune for you."

"I'll try to deserve it, Tom."

A jury was sworn in; then Mr. Allen said:

"We will detain your honor but a moment with this case. It is not one where any doubt of the fact of the assault can enter in. These gentlemen—the accused—kicked my client at the Market Hall last night; they kicked him with violence; with extraordinary violence; with even unprecedented violence, I may say; insomuch that he was lifted entirely off his feet and discharged into the midst of the audience. We can prove this by four hundred witnesses—we shall call but three. Mr. Harkness will take the stand."

Mr. Harkness, being sworn, testified that he was chairman upon the occasion mentioned; that he was close at hand and saw the defendants in this action kick the plaintiff into the air and saw him descend among the audience.

"Take the witness," said Allen.

"Mr. Harkness," said Wilson, "you say you saw these gentlemen, my clients, kick the plaintiff. Are you sure—and please remember that you are on oath—are you perfectly sure that you saw *both* of them kick him, or only one? Now be careful."

A bewildered look began to spread itself over the witness's face. He hesitated, stammered, but got out nothing. His eyes wandered to the twins and fixed themselves there with a vacant gaze.

"Please answer, Mr. Harkness, you are keeping the court waiting. It is a very simple question."

Counsel for the prosecution broke in with impatience:

"Your honor, the question is an irrelevant triviality. Necessarily, they both kicked him, for they have but the one pair of legs, and both are responsible for them."

Wilson said, sarcastically:

"Will your honor permit this new witness to be sworn? He seems to possess knowledge which can be of the utmost value just at this moment—knowledge which would at once dispose of what every one must see is a very difficult question in this case. Brother Allen, will you take the stand?"

"Go on with your case!" said Allen, petulantly. The audience laughed, and got a warning from the court.

"Now, Mr. Harkness," said Wilson, insinuatingly, "we shall have to insist upon an answer to that question."

"I—er—well, of course, I do not absolutely *know*, but in my opinion—"

"Never mind your opinion, sir—answer the question."

"I—why, I *can't* answer it."

"That will do, Mr. Harkness. Stand down."

The audience tittered, and the discomfited witness retired in a state of great embarrassment.

Mr. Wakeman took the stand and swore that he saw the twins kick the plaintiff off the platform. The defense took the witness.

"Mr. Wakeman, you have sworn that you saw these gentlemen kick the plaintiff. Do I understand you to swear that you saw them *both* do it?"

"Yes, sir,"—with decision.

"How do you know that both did it?"

"Because I *saw* them do it."

The audience laughed, and got another warning from the court.

"But by what means do you know that both, and not one, did it?"

"Well, in the first place, the insult was given to both of them equally, for they were called a pair of scissors. Of course they would both want to resent it, and so—"

"Wait! You are theorizing now. Stick to facts—counsel will attend to the arguments. Go on."

"Well, they both went over there—*that* I saw."

"Very good. Go on."

"And they both kicked him—I swear to it."

"Mr. Wakeman, was Count Luigi, here, willing to join the Sons of Liberty last night?"

"Yes, sir, he was. He did join, too, and drank a glass or two of whisky, like a man."

"Was his brother willing to join?"

"No, sir, he wasn't. He is a teetotaler, and was elected through a mistake."

"Was he given a glass of whisky?"

"Yes, sir, but of course that was another mistake, and not intentional. He wouldn't drink it. He set it down." A slight pause, then he added, casually and quite simply: "The plaintiff reached for it and hogged it."

There was a fine outburst of laughter, but as the justice was caught out himself, his reprimand was not very vigorous.

Mr. Allen jumped up and exclaimed: "I protest against these foolish irrelevancies. What have they to do with the case?"

Wilson said: "Calm yourself, brother, it was only an experiment. Now, Mr. Wakeman, if one of these gentlemen chooses to join an association and the other doesn't; and if one of them enjoys whisky and the other doesn't, but sets it aside and leaves it unprotected" (titter from the audience), "it seems to show that they have independent minds, and tastes, and preferences, and that one of them is able to approve of a thing at the very moment that the other is heartily disapproving of it. Doesn't it seem so to you?"

"Certainly it does. It's perfectly plain."

"Now, then, it might be—I only say it might be—that one of these brothers wanted to kick the plaintiff last night, and that the other didn't want that humiliating punishment inflicted upon him in that public way and before all those people. Isn't that possible?"

"Of course it is. It's more than possible. I don't believe the blond one would kick anybody. It was the other one that—"

"Silence!" shouted the plaintiff's counsel, and went on with an angry sentence with was lost in the wave of laughter that swept the house.

"That will do, Mr. Wakeman," said Wilson, "you may stand down."

The third witness was called. He had seen the twins kick the plaintiff. Mr. Wilson took the witness.

"Mr. Rogers, you say you saw these accused gentlemen kick the plaintiff?"

"Yes, sir."

"Both of them?"

"Yes, sir."

"Which of them kicked him first?"

"Why—they—they both kicked him at the same time."

"Are you perfectly sure of that?"

"Yes, sir."

"What makes you sure of it?"

"Why, I stood right behind them, and *saw* them do it."

"How many kicks were delivered?"

"Only one."

"If two men kick, the result should be two kicks, shouldn't it?"

"Why—why—yes, as a rule."

"Then what do you think went with the other kick?"

"I—well—the fact is, I wasn't thinking of two being necessary, this time."

"What do you think now?"

"Well, I—I'm sure I don't quite know what to think, but I reckon that one of them did half of the kick and the other one did the other half."

Somebody in the crowd sung out: "It's the first sane thing that any of them has said."

The audience applauded. The judge said: "Silence! or I will clear the court."

Mr. Allen looked pleased, but Wilson did not seem disturbed. He said:

"Mr. Rogers, you have favored us with what you think and what you reckon, but as thinking and reckoning are not evidence, I will now give you a chance to come out with something positive, one way or the other, and shall require you to produce it. I will ask the accused to stand up and repeat the phenomenal kick of last night." The twins stood up. "Now, Mr. Rogers, please stand behind them."

A Voice: "No, stand in front!" (Laughter. Silenced by the court.) Another Voice: "No, give Tommy another highst!" (Laughter. Sharply rebuked by the court.)

"Now, then, Mr. Rogers, two kicks shall be delivered, one after the other, and I give you my word that at least one of the two shall be delivered by one of the twins alone, without the slightest assistance from his brother. Watch sharply, for you have got to render a decision without any if's and and's in it." Rogers bent himself behind the twins with his palms just above his knees, in the modern attitude of the catcher at a base-ball match, and riveted his eyes on the pair of legs in front of him. "Are you ready, Mr. Rogers?"

"Ready, sir."

"Kick!"

The kick was launched.

"Have you got that one classified, Mr. Rogers?"

"Let me study a minute, sir."

"Take as much time as you please. Let me know when you are ready."

For as much as a minute Rogers pondered, with all eyes and a breathless interest fastened upon him. Then he gave the word: "Ready, sir."

"Kick!"

The kick that followed was an exact duplicate of the first one.

"Now, then, Mr. Rogers, one of those kicks was an individual kick, not a mutual one. You will now state positively which was the mutual one."

The witness said, with a crestfallen look:

"I've got to give it up. There ain't any man in the world that could tell t'other from which, sir."

"Do you still assert that last night's kick was a mutual kick?"

"Indeed, I don't, sir."

"That will do, Mr. Rogers. If my brother Allen desires to address the court, your honor, very well; but as far as I am concerned I am ready to let the case be at once delivered into the hands of this intelligent jury without comment."

Mr. Justice Robinson had been in office only two months, and in that short time had not had many cases to try, of course. He had no knowledge of laws and courts except what he had picked up since he came into office. He was a sore trouble to the lawyers, for his rulings were pretty eccentric sometimes, and he stood by them with Roman simplicity and fortitude; but the people were well satisfied with him, for they saw that his intentions were always right, that he was entirely impartial, and that he usually made up in good sense what he lacked in technique, so to speak. He now perceived that there was likely to be a miscarriage of justice here and he rose to the occasion.

"Wait a moment, gentlemen," he said, "it is plain that an assault has been committed—it is plain to anybody; but the way things are going, the guilty will certainly escape conviction. I cannot allow this. Now—"

"But, your honor!" said Wilson, interrupting him, earnestly but respectfully, "you are deciding the case yourself, whereas the jury—"

"Never mind the jury, Mr. Wilson; the jury will have a chance when there is a reasonable doubt for them to take hold of—which there isn't so far. There is no doubt whatever that an assault has been committed. The attempt to show that both of the accused committed it has failed. Are they both to escape justice on that account? Not in this court, if I can prevent it. It appears to have been a mistake to bring the charge against them as a corporation; each should have been charged in his capacity as an individual and—"

"But, your honor!" said Wilson, "in fairness to my clients I must insist that inasmuch as the prosecution did not separate the—"

"No wrong will be done your clients, sir—they will be protected; also the public and the offended laws. Mr. Allen, you will amend your pleadings, and put one of the accused on trial at a time."

Wilson broke in: "But, your honor! this is wholly unprecedented! To imperil an accused person by arbitrarily altering and widening the charge against him in order to compass his conviction when the charge as originally brought promises to fail to convict, is a thing unheard of before."

"Unheard of *where?*"

"In the courts of this or any other State."

The Judge said with dignity: "I am not acquainted with the customs of other courts, and am not concerned to know what they are. I am responsible for this court, and I cannot conscientiously allow my judgment to be warped and my judicial liberty hampered by trying to conform to the caprices of other courts, be they—"

"But, your honor, the oldest and highest courts in Europe—"

"This court is not run on the European plan, Mr. Wilson; it is not run on any plan but its own. It has a plan of its own; and that plan is, to find justice for both State and accused, no matter what happens to be practice and custom in Europe or anywhere else." (Great applause.) "Silence! It has not been the custom of this court to imitate other courts; it has not been the custom of this court to take shelter behind the decisions of other courts, and we will not begin now. We will do the best we can by the light that God has given us, and while this court continues to have His approval, it will remain indifferent to what other organizations may think of it." (Applause.) "Gentlemen, I *must* have order!—quiet yourselves! Mr. Allen, you will now proceed against the prisoners one at a time. Go on with the case."

Allen was not at his ease. However, after whispering a moment with his client and with one or two other people, he rose and said:

"Your honor, I find it to be reported and believed that the accused are able to act independently in many ways, but that this independence does not extend to their legs, authority over their legs being vested exclusively in the one brother during a specific term of days, and then passing to the other brother for a like term, and so on, by regular alternation. I could call witnesses who would prove that the accused had revealed to them the existence of this extraordinary fact, and had also made known which of them was in possession of the legs yesterday—and this would, of course, indicate where the guilt of the assault belongs—but as this would be mere hearsay evidence, these revelations not having been made under oath—"

"Never mind about that, Mr. Allen. It may not all be hearsay. We shall see. It may at least help to put us on the right track. Call the witnesses."

"Then I will call Mr. John Buckstone, who is now present, and I beg that Mrs. Patsy Cooper may be sent for. Take the stand, Mr. Buckstone."

Buckstone took the oath, and then testified that on the previous evening the Count Angelo Cappello had protested against going to the hall, and had called all present to witness that he was going by compulsion and would not go if he could help himself. Also, that the Count Luigi had replied sharply that he would *go,* just the same, and that he, Count Luigi, would see to that himself. Also, that upon Count Angelo's complaining about being kept on his legs so long, Count Luigi retorted with apparent surprise, '*Your* legs!—I like your impudence!'"

"*Now* we are getting at the kernel of the thing," observed the Judge, with grave and earnest satisfaction. "It looks as if the Count Luigi was in possession of the battery at the time of the assault."

Nothing further was elicited from Mr. Buckstone on direct examination. Mr. Wilson took the witness.

"Mr. Buckstone, about what time was it that that conversation took place?"

"Toward nine yesterday evening, sir."

"Did you then proceed directly to the hall?"

"Yes, sir."

"How long did it take you to go there?"

"Well, we walked; and as it was from the extreme edge of the town, and there was no hurry, I judge it took us about twenty minutes, maybe a trifle more."

"About what hour was the kick delivered?"

"About thirteen minutes and a half to ten."

"Admirable! You are a pattern witness, Mr. Buckstone. How did you happen to look at your watch at that particular moment?"

"I always do it when I see an assault. It's likely I shall be called as a witness, and it's a good point to have."

"It would be well if others were as thoughtful. Was anything said, between the conversation at my house and the assault, upon the detail which we are now examining into?"

"No, sir."

"If power over the mutual legs was in the possession of one brother at nine, and passed into the possession of the other one during the next thirty or forty minutes, do you think you could have detected the change?"

"By no means!"

"That is all, Mr. Buckstone."

Mrs. Patsy Cooper was called. The crowd made way for her, and she came smiling and bowing through the narrow human lane, with Betsy Hale, as escort and support, smiling and bowing in her wake, the audience breaking into welcoming cheers as the old favorites filed along. The Judge did not check this kindly demonstration of homage and affection, but let it run its course unrebuked.

The old ladies stopped and shook hands with the twins with effusion, then gave the Judge a friendly nod, and bustled into the seats provided for them. They immediately began to deliver a volley of eager questions at the friends around them: "What is this thing for?" "What is that thing for?" "Who is that young man that's writing at the desk? Why, I declare, it's Jack Bunce! I thought he was sick." "Which is the jury? Why, is *that* the jury? Billy Price and Job Turner, and Jack Lounsbury, and—well, I never!" "Now who would ever a' thought—"

But they were gently called to order at this point, and asked not to talk in court. Their tongues fell silent, but the radiant interest in their faces remained, and their gratitude for the blessing of a new sensation and a novel experience still beamed undimmed from their eyes. Aunt Patsy stood up and took the oath, and Mr. Allen explained the point in issue, and asked her to go on now, in her own way, and throw as much light upon it as she could. She toyed with her reticule a moment or two, as if considering where to begin, then she said:

"Well, the way of it is this. They are Luigi's legs a week at a time, and then they are Angelo's, and he can do whatever he wants to with them."

"You are making a mistake, Aunt Patsy Cooper," said the Judge. "You shouldn't state that as a *fact*, because you don't know it to *be* a fact."

"What's the reason I don't?" said Aunt Patsy, bridling a little.

"What is the reason that you do know it?"

"The best in the world—because they told me."

"That isn't a reason."

"Well, for the land's sake! Betsy Hale, do you hear that?"

"*Hear* it? I should think so," said Aunt Betsy, rising and facing the court. "Why, Judge, I was there and heard it myself. Luigi says to Angelo—no, it was Angelo said it to—"

"Come, come, Mrs. Hale, pray sit down, and—"

"Certainly, it's all right, I'm going to sit down presently, but not until I've—"

"But you *must* sit down!"

"*Must!* Well, upon my word if things ain't getting to a pretty pass when—"

The house broke into laughter, but was promptly brought to order, and meantime Mr. Allen persuaded the old lady to take her seat. Aunt Patsy continued:

"Yes, they told me that, and I know it's true. They're Luigi's legs this week, but—"

"Ah, *they* told you that, did they?" said the Justice, with interest.

"Well, no, I don't know that *they* told me, but that's neither here nor there. I know, without that, that at dinner, yesterday, Angelo was tired as a dog, and yet Luigi wouldn't lend him the legs to go up stairs and take a nap with."

"Did he ask for them?"

"Let me see—it seems to me somehow, that—that—Aunt Betsy, do you remember whether he—"

"Never mind about what Aunt Betsy remembers—she is not a witness; we only want to know what you remember yourself," said the Judge.

"Well, it does seem to me that you are most cantankerously particular about a little thing, Sim Robinson. Why, when I can't remember a thing myself, I always—"

"Ah, *please* go on!"

"Now how *can* she when you keep fussing at her all the time?" said Aunt Betsy. "Why, with a person pecking at *me* that way, I should get that fuzzled and fuddled that—"

She was on her feet again, but Allen coaxed her into her seat once more, while the court squelched the mirth of the house. Then the Judge said:

"Madam, do you know—do you absolutely *know,* independently of anything these gentlemen have told you—that the power over their legs passes from the one to the other regularly every week?"

"Regularly? Bless your heart, regularly ain't any name for the exactness of it! All the big cities in Europe used to set the clocks by it." (Laughter, *suppressed by the court.*)

"How do you *know?* That is the question. Please answer it plainly and squarely."

"Don't you talk to me like that, Sim Robinson—I won't have it. How do I know, indeed! How do *you* know what you know? Because somebody told you. You didn't invent it out of your own head, did you? Why, these twins are the truthfulest people in the world; and I don't think it becomes you to sit up there and throw slurs at them when they haven't been doing anything to you. And they are orphans besides—both of them. All—"

But Aunt Betsy was up again now, and both old ladies were talking at once and with all their might; but as the house was weltering in a storm of laughter, and the judge was hammering his desk with an iron paper weight, one could only see them talk, not hear them. At last, when quiet was restored, the court said:

"Let the ladies retire."

"But, your honor, I have the right, in the interest of my clients, to cross-exam—"

"You'll not need to exercise it, Mr. Wilson—the evidence is thrown out."

"Thrown out!" said Aunt Patsy, ruffled; "and what's it thrown out for, I'd like to know."

"And so would I, Patsy Cooper. It seems to me that if we can save these poor persecuted strangers, it is our bounden duty to stand up here and talk for them till—"

"There, there, there, *do* sit down!"

It cost some trouble and a good deal of coaxing, but they were got into their seats at last. The trial was soon ended now. The twins themselves became witnesses in their own defense. They established the fact, upon oath, that the leg-power passed from one to the other every Saturday night at twelve o'clock sharp. But on cross-examination their counsel would not allow them to tell whose week of power the current week was. The Judge insisted upon their answering, and proposed to compel them, but even the prosecution took fright and came to the rescue then, and helped stay the sturdy jurist's revolutionary hand. So the case had to go the jury with that important point hanging in the air. They were out an hour and brought in this verdict:

"We the jury do find: 1, that an assault was committed, as charged; 2, that is was committed by one of the persons accused, he having been seen to do it by several credible witnesses; 3, but that his identity is so merged in his brother's that we have not been able to tell which was him. We cannot convict both, for only one is guilty. We cannot acquit both, for only one is innocent. Our verdict is that justice has been defeated by the dispensation of God, and ask to be discharged from further duty."

This was read aloud in court and brought out a burst of hearty applause. The old ladies made a spring at the twins, to shake and congratulate, but were gently disengaged by Mr. Wilson and softly crowded back into their places.

The Judge rose in his little tribune, laid aside his silver-bowed spectacles, roached his gray hair up with his fingers, and said, with dignity and solemnity, and even with a certain pathos:

"In all my experience on the bench, I have not seen justice bow her head in shame in this court until this day. You little realize what far-reaching harm has just been wrought here under the fickle forms of law. Imitation is the bane of courts—I thank God that this one is free from the contamination of that vice—and in no long time you will see the fatal work of this hour seized upon by profilgate so-called guardians of justice in all the wide circumstance of this planet and perpetuated in their pernicious decisions. I wash my hands of this iniquity. I would have compelled these culprits to expose their guilt, but support failed me where I had most right to expect aid and encouragement. And I was confronted by a law made in the interest of crime, which protects the criminal from testifying against himself. Yet I had precedents of my own whereby I had set aside that law on two different occasions and thus succeeded in convicting criminals to whose crimes there were no witnesses but themselves. What have you accomplished this day? Do you realize it? You have set adrift, unadmonished, in this community, two men endowed with an awful and mysterious gift, a hidden and grisly power for evil—a power by which each in his turn may commit crime after crime of the most heinous character, and no man be able to tell which is the guilty or which the innocent party in any case of them all. Look to your homes—look to your property—look to your lives—for you have need!

"Prisoners at the bar, stand up. Through suppression of evidence, a jury of your—our—countrymen have been obliged to deliver a verdict concerning your case which stinks to heaven with the rankness of its injustice. By its terms you, the guilty one, go free with the innocent. Depart in peace, and come no more! The costs devolve upon the outraged plaintiff—another iniquity. The court stands dissolved."

Almost everybody crowded forward to overwhelm the twins and their counsel with congratulations; but presently the two old aunties dug the duplicates out and bore them away in triumph through the hurrahing crowd, while lots of new friends carried Pudd'nhead Wilson off tavern-wards to feast him and "wet down" his great and victorious entry into the legal arena. To Wilson, so long familiar with neglect and depreciation, this strange new incense of popularity and admiration was as a fragrance blown from the fields of paradise. A happy man was Wilson.

VI

A deputation came in the evening and conferred upon Wilson the welcome honor of a nomination for mayor; for the village has just been converted into a city by charter. Tom skulks out of challenging the twins. Judge Driscoll thereupon challenges Angelo (accused by Tom of doing the kicking); he declines, but Luigi accepts in his place against Angelo's timid protest.

It was late Saturday night—nearing eleven.

The Judge and his second found the rest of the war party at the further end of the vacant ground, near the haunted house. Pudd'nhead Wilson advanced to meet them, and said anxiously:

"I must say a word in behalf of my principal's proxy, Count Luigi, to whom you have kindly granted the privilege of fighting my principal's battle for him. It is growing late, and Count Luigi is in great trouble lest midnight shall strike before the finish."

"It is another testimony," said Howard, approvingly. "That young man is fine all through. He wishes to save his brother the sorrow of fighting on the Sabbath, and he is right; it is the right and manly feeling and does him credit. We will make all possible haste."

Wilson said:

"There is also another reason—a consideration, in fact, which deeply concerns Count Luigi himself. These twins have command of their mutual legs turn about. Count Luigi is in command now; but at midnight, possession will pass to my principal, Count Angelo, and—well, you can foresee what will happen. He will march straight off the field, and carry Luigi with him."

"Why! sure enough!" cried the Judge, "we have heard something about that extraordinary law of their being, already—nothing very definite, it is true, as regards dates and durations of power, but I see it is definite enough as regards to-night. Of course we must give Luigi every chance. Omit all the ceremonial possible, gentlemen, and place us in position."

The seconds at once tossed up a coin; Howard won the choice. He placed the Judge sixty feet from the haunted house and facing it; Wilson placed the twins within fifteen feet of the house and facing the Judge—necessarily. The pistol-case was opened and the long slim tubes taken out; when the moonlight glinted from them a shiver went through Angelo. The doctor was a fool, but a thoroughly well-meaning one, with a kind heart and a sincere disposition to oblige, but along with it an absence of tact which often hurt its effectiveness. He brought his box of lint and bandages, and asked Angelo to feel and see how soft and comfortable they were. Angelo's head fell over against Luigi's in a faint, and precious time was lost in bringing him to; which provoked Luigi into expressing his mind to the doctor with a good deal of vigor and frankness. After Angelo came to he was still so weak that Luigi was obliged to drink a stiff horn of brandy to brace him up.

The seconds now stepped at once to their posts, half way

between the combatants, one of them on each side of the line of fire. Wilson was to count, very deliberately, "One—two—three—fire!—stop!" and the duelists could bang away at any time they chose during that recitation, but not after the last word. Angelo grew very nervous when he saw Wilson's hand rising slowly into the air as a sign to make ready, and he leaned his head against Luigi's and said:

"Oh, please take me away from here, I can't stay, I know I can't!"

"What in the world are you doing? Straighten up! What's the matter with you?—*you're* in no danger—nobody's going to shoot at you. Straighten up, I tell you!"

Angelo obeyed, just in time to hear:

"One—!"

"Bang!" Just one report, and a little tuft of white hair floated slowly to the Judge's feet in the moonlight. The Judge did not swerve; he still stood erect and motionless, like a statue, with his pistol-arm hanging straight down at his side. He was reserving his fire.

"Two—!"

"Three—!"

"Fire—!"

Up came the pistol-arm instantly—Angelo dodged with the report. He said "Ouch!" and fainted again.

The doctor examined and bandaged the wound. It was of no consequence, he said—bullet through fleshy part of arm—no bones broken—the gentleman was still able to fight—let the duel proceed.

Next time Angelo jumped just as Luigi fired, which disordered his aim and caused him to cut a chip out of Howard's ear. The Judge took his time again, and when he fired Angelo jumped and got a knuckle skinned. The doctor inspected and dressed the wounds. Angelo now spoke out and said he was content with the satisfaction he had got, and if the Judge—but Luigi shut him roughly up, and asked him not to make an ass of himself; adding:

"And I want you to stop dodging. You take a great deal too prominent a part in the thing for a person who has got nothing to do with it. You should remember that you are here only by courtesy, and are without official recognition; officially you are not here at all; officially you do not even exist. To all intents and purposes you are absent from this place, and you ought for your own modesty's sake to reflect that it cannot become a person who is not present here to be taking this sort of public and indecent prominence in a matter in which he is not in the slightest degree concerned. Now, don't dodge again; the bullets are not for you, they are for me; if I want them dodged I will attend to it myself. I never saw a person act so."

Angelo saw the reasonableness of what his brother had said, and he did try to reform, but it was of no use; both pistols went off at the same instant, and he jumped once more; he got a sharp scrape along his cheek from the Judge's bullet, and so deflected Luigi's aim that his ball went wide and chipped a flake of skin from Pudd'nhead Wilson's chin. The doctor attended to the wounded.

By the terms, the duel was over. But Luigi was entirely out of patience, and begged for one more exchange of shots, insisting that he had had no fair chance, on account of his brother's indelicate behavior. Howard was opposed to granting so unusual a privilege, but the Judge took Luigi's part, and added that indeed he himself might fairly be considered entitled to another trial, because although the proxy on the other side was in no way to blame for his (the Judge's) humiliatingly resultless work, the gentleman with whom he was fighting this duel was to blame for it, since if he had played no advantages and had held his head still, his proxy would have been disposed of early. He added:

"Count Luigi's request for another exchange is another proof that he is a brave and chivalrous gentleman, and I beg that the courtesy he asks may be accorded him."

"I thank you most sincerely for this generosity, Judge Driscoll," said Luigi, with a polite bow, and moving to his place. Then he added—to Angelo, "Now hold your grip, hold your *grip,* I tell you, and I'll land him sure!"

The men stood erect, their pistol-arms at their sides, the two seconds stood at their official posts, the doctor stood five paces in Wilson's rear with his instruments and bandages in his hands.

The deep stillness, the peaceful moonlight, the motionless figures, made an impressive picture and the impending fatal possibilities augmented this impressiveness to solemnity. Wilson's hand began to rise—slowly—slowly—higher—still higher—in another moment:

"*Boom!*"—the first stroke of midnight swung up out of the distance; Angelo was off like a deer!

"Oh, you unspeakable traitor!" wailed his brother, as they went soaring over the fence.

The others stood astonished and gazing; and so stood, watching that strange spectacle until distance dissolved it and swept it from their view. Then they rubbed their eyes like people waking out of a dream.

"Well, I've never seen anything like that before!" said the Judge. "Wilson, I am going to confess now, that I wasn't quite able to believe in that leg-business, and had a suspicion that it was a put-up convenience between those twins; and when Count Angelo fainted I thought I saw the whole scheme—thought it was pretext No. 1, and would be followed by others till twelve o'clock should arrive, and Luigi would get off with all the credit of seeming to want to fight and yet not have to fight, after all. But I was mistaken. His pluck proved it. He's a brave fellow and did want to fight."

"There isn't any doubt about that," said Howard, and added, in a grieved tone, "but what an unworthy sort of Christian that Angelo is—I hope and believe there are not many like him. It is not right to engage in a duel on the Sabbath—I could not approve of that myself; but to finish one that has been begun—that is a duty, let the day be what it may."

They strolled along, still wondering, still talking.

"It is a curious circumstance," remarked the surgeon, halting Wilson a moment to paste some more court plaster on his chin, which had gone to leaking blood again, "that in this duel neither of the parties who handled the pistols lost blood, while nearly all the persons present in the mere capacity of guests got hit. I have not heard of such a thing before. Don't you think it unusual?"

"Yes," said the Judge, "it has struck me as peculiar. Peculiar and unfortunate. I was annoyed at it, all the time. In the case of Angelo it made no great difference, because he was in a measure concerned, though not officially; but it troubled me to see the seconds compromised, and yet I knew no way to mend the matter."

"There was no way to mend it," said Howard, whose ear was being readjusted now by the doctor; "the code fixes our place, and it would not have been lawful to change it. If we could have stood at your side, or behind you, or in front of you, it—but it would not have been legitimate and the other parties would have had a just right to complain of our trying to protect ourselves from danger; infractions of the code are certainly not permissible in any case whatever."

Wilson offered no remarks. It seemed to him that there was very little place here for so much solemnity, but he judged that if a duel where nobody was in danger or got crippled but the seconds and the outsiders had nothing ridiculous about it for these gentlemen, his pointing out that feature would probably not help them to see it.

He invited them in to take a nightcap, and Howard and the Judge accepted, but the doctor said he would have to go and see how Angelo's principal wound was getting on.

[It was now Sunday, and in the afternoon Angelo was to be received into the Baptist communion by immersion—a doubtful prospect, the doctor feared.]

VII

When the doctor arrived at Aunt Patsy Cooper's house, he found the lights going and everybody up and dressed and in a great state of solicitude and excitement. The twins were stretched on a sofa in the sitting-room, Aunt Patsy was fussing at Angelo's arm, Nancy was flying around under her commands, the two young boys were trying to keep out of the way and always getting in it, in order to see and wonder, Rowena stood apart, helpless with apprehension and emotion, and Luigi was growling in unappeasable fury over Angelo's shameful flight.

As has been reported before, the doctor was a fool—a kind-hearted and well-meaning one, but with no tact; and as he was by long odds the most learned physician in the town, and was quite well aware of it, and could talk his learning with ease and precision, and liked to show off when he had an audience, he was sometimes tempted into revealing more of a case than was good for the patient.

He examined Angelo's wound, and was really minded to say nothing for once; but Aunt Patsy was so anxious and so pressing that he allowed his caution to be overcome, and proceeded to empty himself as follows, with scientific relish:

"Without going too much into detail, madam—for you would probably not understand it, anyway—I concede that great care is going to be necessary here; otherwise exudation of the œsophagus is nearly sure to ensue, and this will be followed by ossification and extradition of the maxillaris superioris, which must decompose the granular surfaces of the great infusorial ganglionic system, thus obstructing the action of the posterior varioloid arteries, and precipitating compound strangulated sorosis of the valvular tissues, and ending unavoidably in the dispersion and combustion of the marsupial fluxes and the consequent embrocation of the bicuspid populo redax referendum rotulorum."

A miserable silence followed. Aunt Patsy's heart sank, the pallor of despair invaded her face, she was not able to speak; poor Rowena wrung her hands in privacy and silence, and said to herself in the bitterness of her young grief, "There is no hope—it is plain there is no hope;" the good-hearted negro wench, Nancy, paled to chocolate, then to orange, then to amber, and thought to herself with yearning sympathy and sorrow, "Po' thing, he ain' gwyne to las' throo de half o' dat;" small Henry choked up, and turned his head away to hide his rising tears, and his brother Joe said to himself, with a sense of loss, "The baptizing's busted, that's sure." Luigi was the only person who had any heart to speak. He said, a little bit sharply, to the doctor:

"Well, well, there's nothing to be gained by wasting precious time; give him a barrel of pills—I'll take them for him."

"You?" asked the doctor.

"Yes. Did you suppose he was going to take them himself?"

"Why, of course."

"Well, it's a mistake. He never took a dose of medicine in his life. He can't."

"Well, upon my word, it's the most extraordinary thing I ever heard of!"

"Oh," said Aunt Patsy, as pleased as a mother whose child is being admired and wondered at, "you'll find that there's more about them that's wonderful than their just being made in the image of God like the rest of His creatures, now you can depend on that, *I* tell you," and she wagged her complacent head like one who could reveal marvelous things if she chose.

The boy Joe began:

"Why, ma, they *ain't* made in the im "

"You shut up, and wait till you're asked, Joe. I'll let you know when I want help. Are you looking for something, doctor?"

The doctor asked for a few sheets of paper and a pen, and said he would write a prescription; which he did. It was one of Galen's; in fact, it was Galen's favorite, and had been slaying people for sixteen thousand years. Galen used it for everything, applied it to everything, said it would remove everything, from warts all the way through to lungs—and it generally did. Galen was still the only medical authority recognized in Missouri; his practice was the only practice known to the Missouri doctors, and his prescriptions were the only ammunition they carried when they went out for game. By and by Dr. Claypool laid down his pen and read the result of his labors aloud, carefully and deliberately, for this battery must be constructed on the premises by the family, and mistakes could occur; for he wrote a doctor's hand—the hand which from the beginning of time has been so disastrous to the apothecary and so profitable to the undertaker:

"Take of afarabocca, henbane, corpobalsamum, each two drams and a half: of cloves, opium, myrrh, cyperus, each two drams; of opobalsamum, Indian leaf, cinnamon, zedoary, ginger, coftus, coral, cassia, euphorbium, gum tragacanth, frankincense, styrax calamita, celtic, nard, spignel, hartwort, mustard, saxifrage, dill, anise, each one dram; of xylaloes, rheum ponticum, alipta, moschata, castor, spikenard, galangals, opoponax, anacardium, mastich, brimstone, peony, eringo, pulp of dates, red and white hermodactyls, roses, thyme, acorns, pennyroyal, gentian, the bark of the root of mandrake, germander, valerian, bishop's weed, bayberries, long and white pepper, xylobalsamum, carnabadium, macedonian, parsley-seeds, lovage, the seeds of rue, and sinon, of each a dram and a half; of pure gold, pure silver, pearls not perforated, the blatta byzantina, the bone of the stag's heart, of each the quantity of fourteen grains of wheat; of sapphire, emerald and jasper stones, each one dram; of hazel-nut, two drams; of pellitory of Spain, shavings of ivory, calamus odoratus, each the quantity of twenty-nine grains of wheat; of honey or sugar a sufficient quantity. Boil down and skim off."

"There," he said, "that will fix the patient; give his brother a dipperful every three-quarters of an hour—"

—"while he survives," muttered Luigi—

—"and see that the room is kept wholesomely hot, and the doors and windows closed tight. Keep Count Angelo nicely covered up with six or seven blankets, and when he is thirsty—which will be frequently—moisten a rag in the vapor of the tea-kettle and let his brother suck it. When he is hungry—which will also be frequently—he must not be humored oftener than every seven or eight hours; then toast part of a cracker until it begins to brown, and give it to his brother."

"That is all very well, as far as Angelo is concerned," said Luigi, "but what am I to eat?"

"I do not see that there is anything the matter with you," the doctor answered, "you may, of course, eat what you please."

"And also drink what I please, I suppose?"

"Oh, certainly—at present. When the violent and continuous perspiring has reduced your strength, I shall have to reduce your diet, of course, and also bleed you, but there is no occasion for that yet awhile." He turned to Aunt Patsy and said: "He must be put to bed, and sat up with, and tended with the greatest care, and not allowed to stir for several days and nights."

"For one, I'm sacredly thankful for that," said Luigi, "it postpones the funeral—I'm not to be drowned to-day anyhow."

Angelo said quietly to the doctor:

"I will cheerfully submit to all your requirements, sir, up to two o'clock this afternoon, and will resume them after three, but cannot be confined to the house during that intermediate hour."

"Why, may I ask?"

"Because I have entered the Baptist communion, and by appointment am to be baptized in the river at that hour."

"Oh, insanity!—it cannot be allowed!"

Angelo answered with placid firmness:

"Nothing shall prevent it, if I am alive."

"Why, consider, my dear sir, in your condition it might prove fatal."

A tender and ecstatic smile beamed from Angelo's eyes, and he broke forth in a tone of joyous fervency:

"Ah, how blessed it would be to die for such a cause—it would be martyrdom!"

"But your brother—consider your brother; you would be risking his life, too."

"He risked mine an hour ago," responded Angelo, gloomily; "did he consider me?" A thought swept through his mind that made him shudder. "If I had not run, I might have been killed in a duel on the Sabbath day, and my soul would have been lost—lost."

"Oh, don't fret, it wasn't in any danger," said Luigi, irritably; "they wouldn't waste it for a little thing like that; there's a glass case all ready for it in the heavenly museum, and a pin to stick it up with."

Aunt Patsy was shocked, and said:

"Looy, Looy!—don't talk so, dear!"

Rowena's soft heart was pierced by Luigi's unfeeling words, and she murmured to herself, "Oh, if I but had the dear privilege of protecting and defending him with my weak voice!—but alas! this sweet boon is denied me by the cruel conventions of social intercourse."

"Get their bed ready," said Aunt Patsy to Nancy, "and shut up the windows and doors, and light their candles, and see that you drive all the mosquitoes out of their bar, and make up a good fire in their stove, and carry up some bags of hot ashes to lay to his feet—"

—"and a shovel of fire for his head, and a mustard plaster for his neck, and some gum shoes for his ears," Luigi interrupted, with temper; and added, to himself, "Damnation, I'm going to be roasted alive, I just know it!"

"Why, Looy! Do be quiet; I never saw such a fractious thing. A body would think you didn't care for your brother."

"I don't—to *that* extent, Aunt Patsy. I was glad the drowning was postponed a minute ago, but I'm not now. No, that is all gone by; I want to be drowned."

"You'll bring a judgment on yourself just as sure as you live, if you go on like that. Why, I never heard the beat of it. Now, there,—there! you've said enough. Not another word out of you,—I won't have it!"

"But, Aunt Patsy—"

"Luigi! Didn't you hear what I told you?"

"But, Aunt Patsy, I—why, I'm not going to set my heart and lungs afloat in that pail of sewage which this criminal here has been prescri—"

"Yes, you are, too. You are going to be good, and do everything I tell you, like a dear," and she tapped his cheek affectionately with her finger. "Rowena, take the prescription and go in the kitchen and hunt up the things and lay them out for me. I'll sit up with my patient the rest of the night, doctor; I can't trust Nancy, she couldn't make Luigi take the medicine. Of course, you'll drop in again during the day. Have you got any more directions?"

"No, I believe not, Aunt Patsy. If I don't get in earlier, I'll be along by early candlelight, anyway. Meantime, don't allow him to get out of his bed."

Angelo said, with calm determination:

"I shall be baptized at two o'clock. Nothing but death shall prevent me."

The doctor said nothing aloud, but to himself he said:

"Why, this chap's got a manly side, after all! Physically he's a coward, but morally he's a lion. I'll go and tell the others about this; it will raise him a good deal in their estimation—and the public will follow their lead, of course."

Privately, Aunt Patsy applauded too, and was proud of Angelo's courage in the moral field as she was of Luigi's in the field of honor.

The boy Henry was troubled, but the boy Joe said, inaudibly, and gratefully, "We're all hunky, after all; and no postponement on account of the weather."

VIII

By nine o'clock the town was humming with the news of the midnight duel, and there were but two opinions about it: one, that Luigi's pluck in the field was most praiseworthy and Angelo's flight most scandalous; the other, that Angelo's courage in flying the field for conscience's sake was as fine and creditable as was Luigi's in holding the field in the face of the bullets. The one opinion was held by half of the town, the other one was maintained by the other half. The division was clean and exact, and it made two parties, an Angelo party and a Luigi party. The twins had suddenly become popular idols along with Pudd'nhead Wilson, and haloed with a glory as intense as his. The children talked the duel all the way to Sunday-school, their elders talked it all the way to church, the choir discussed it behind their red curtain, it usurped the place of pious thought in the "nigger gallery."

By noon the doctor had added the news, and spread it, that Count Angelo, in spite of his wound and all warnings and supplications, was resolute in his determination to be baptized at the hour appointed. This swept the town like wildfire, and mightily reinforced the enthusiasm of the Angelo faction, who said, "If any doubted that it was moral courage that took him from the field, what have they to say now!"

Still the excitement grew. All the morning it was traveling countrywards, toward all points of the compass; so, whereas before only the farmers and their wives were intending to come and witness the remarkable baptism, a general holiday was now proclaimed and the children and negroes admitted to the privileges of the occasion. All the farms for ten miles around were vacated, all the converging roads emptied long processions of wagons, horses, and yeomanry into the town. The pack and cram of people vastly exceeded any that had ever been seen in that sleepy region before. The only thing that had ever even approached it, was the time long gone by, but never forgotten, nor even referred to without wonder and pride, when two circuses and a Fourth of July fell together. But the glory of that occasion was extinguished now for good. It was but a freshet to this deluge.

The great invasion massed itself on the river bank and waited hungrily for the immense event. Waited, and wondered if it would really happen, or if the twin who was not a "professor" would stand out and prevent it.

But they were not to be disappointed. Angelo was as good as his word. He came attended by an escort of honor composed of several hundred of the best citizens, all of the Angelo party; and when the immersion was finished they escorted him back home: and would even have carried him on their shoulders, but that people might think they were carrying Luigi.

Far into the night the citizens continued to discuss and wonder over the strangely-mated pair of incidents that had distinguished and exalted the past twenty-four hours above any other twenty-four in the history of their town for picturesqueness and splendid interest; and long before the lights were out and burghers asleep it had been decided on all hands that in capturing these twins Dawson's Landing had drawn a prize in the great lottery of municipal fortune.

At midnight Angelo was sleeping peacefully. His immersion

had not harmed him, it had merely made him wholesomely drowsy, and he had been dead asleep many hours now. It had made Luigi drowsy, too, but he had got only brief naps, on account of his having to take the medicine every three-quarters of an hour—and Aunt Betsy Hale was there to see that he did it. When he complained and resisted, she was quietly firm with him, and said in a low voice:

"No—no, that won't do; you mustn't talk, and you mustn't retch and gag that way, either—you'll wake up your poor brother."

"Well, what of it, Aunt Betsy, he—"

"'Sh-h! Don't make a noise, dear. You mustn't forget that your poor brother is sick and—"

"Sick, is he? Well, I wish I—"

"Sh-h-h! Will you be quiet, Luigi! Here, now, take the rest of it—don't keep me holding the dipper all night. I declare if you haven't left a good fourth of it in the bottom! Come—that's a good boy."

"Aunt Betsy, don't make me! I feel like I've swallowed a cemetery; I do, indeed. Do let me rest a little—just a little; I can't take any more of the devilish stuff now."

"Luigi! Using such language here, and him just baptized! Do you want the roof to fall on you?"

"I wish to goodness it would!"

"Why, you dreadful thing! I've a good notion to—let that blanket alone; do you want your brother to catch his death?"

"Aunt Betsy, I've *got* to have it off, I'm being roasted alive; nobody could stand it—you couldn't yourself."

"Now, then, you're sneezing again—I just expected it."

"Because I've caught a cold in my head. I always do, when I go in the water with my clothes on. And it takes me weeks to get over it, too. I think it was a shame to serve me so."

"Luigi, you are unreasonable; you know very well they couldn't baptize him dry. I should think you would be willing to undergo a little inconvenience for your brother's sake."

"Inconvenience! Now how you talk, Aunt Betsy. I came as near as anything to getting drowned—you saw that yourself; and do you call this inconvenience?—the room shut up as tight as a drum, and so hot the mosquitoes are trying to get out; and a cold in the head, and dying for sleep and no chance to get any on account of this infamous medicine that that assassin prescri—"

"There, you're sneezing again. I'm going down and mix some more of this truck for you, dear."

IX

During Monday, Tuesday, and Wednesday the twins grew steadily worse; but then the doctor was summoned South to attend his mother's funeral, and they got well in forty-eight hours. They appeared on the street on Friday, and were welcomed with enthusiasm by the new-born parties, the Luigi and Angelo factions. The Luigi faction carried its strength into the Democratic party, the Angelo faction entered into a combination with the Whigs. The Democrats nominated Luigi for alderman under the new city government, and the Whigs put up Angelo against him. The Democrats nominated Pudd'nhead Wilson for mayor, and he was left alone in this glory, for the Whigs had no man who was willing to enter the lists against such a formidable opponent. No politician had scored such a compliment as this before in the history of the Mississippi Valley.

The political campaign in Dawson's Landing opened in a pretty warm fashion, and waxed hotter every week. Luigi's whole heart was in it, and even Angelo developed a surprising amount of interest—which was natural, because he was not merely representing Whigism, a matter of no consequence to him, but he was representing something immensely finer and greater—to wit, Reform. In him was centred the hopes of the whole reform element of the town; he was the chosen and admired champion of every clique that had a pet reform of any sort or kind at heart. He was president of the great Teetotalers' Union, its chiefest prophet and mouthpiece.

But as the canvass went on, troubles began to spring up all around—troubles for the twins, and through them for all the parties and segments and fractions of parties. Whenever Luigi had possession of the legs, he carried Angelo to balls, rum shops, Sons of Liberty parades, horse races, campaign riots, and everywhere else that could damage him with his party and the church; and when it was Angelo's week he carried Luigi diligently to all manner of moral and religious gatherings, doing his best to regain the ground he had lost before. As a result of these double performances, there was a storm blowing all the time, an ever rising storm, too—a storm of frantic criticism of the twins, and rage over their extravagant, incomprehensible conduct.

Luigi had the final chance. The legs were his for the closing week of the canvass. He led his brother a fearful dance.

But he saved his best card for the very eve of the election. There was to be a grand turnout of the Teetotalers' Union that day, and Angelo was to march at the head of the procession and deliver a great oration afterward. Luigi drank a couple of glasses of whisky—which steadied his nerves and clarified his mind, but made Angelo drunk. Everybody who saw the march, saw that the Champion of the Teetotalers was half seas over, and noted also that his brother, who made no hypocritical pretensions to extra temperance virtues, was dignified and sober. This eloquent fact could not be unfruitful at the end of a hot political canvass. At the mass meeting Angelo tried to make his great temperance oration, but was so discommoded by hiccoughs and thickness of tongue that he had to give it up; then drowsiness overtook him and his head drooped against Luigi's and he went to sleep. Luigi apologized for him, and was going on to improve his opportunity with an appeal for a moderation of what he called "the prevailing teetotal madness," but persons in the audience began to howl and throw things at him, and then the meeting rose in wrath and chased him home.

This episode was a crusher for Angelo in another way. It destroyed his chances with Rowena. Those chances had been growing, right along, for two months. Rowena had partly confessed that she loved him, but wanted time to consider. Now the tender dream was ended, and she told him so the moment he was sober enough to understand. She said she would never marry a man who drank.

"But I don't drink," he pleaded.

"That is nothing to the point," she said, coldly, "you get drunk, and that is worse."

[There was a long and sufficiently idiotic discussion here, which ended as reported in a previous note.]

X

Dawson's Landing had a week of repose, after the election, and it needed it, for the frantic and variegated nightmare which had tormented it all through the preceding week had left it limp, haggard, and exhausted at the end. It got the week of repose because Angelo had the legs, and was in too subdued a condition to want to go out and mingle with an irritated community that had come to distrust and detest him because there was such a lack of harmony between his morals, which were confessedly excellent, and his methods of illustrating them, which were distinctly damnable.

The new city officers were sworn in on the following Monday—at least all but Luigi. There was a complication in his case. His election was conceded, but he could not sit in the board of aldermen without his brother, and his brother could not sit there because he was not a member. There seemed to be no way out of the difficulty but to carry the matter into the courts, so this was resolved upon. The case was set for the Monday fortnight. In due course the time arrived. In the meantime the city government had been at a standstill, because without Luigi there was a tie in the board of aldermen, whereas with him the liquor interest—the richest in the political field—would have one majority. But the court decided that Angelo could not sit in the board with him, either in public or executive sessions, and at the same time forbade the board to deny admission to Luigi, a fairly and legally chosen alderman. The case was carried up and up from court to court, yet still the same old original decision was confirmed every time. As a result, the city government not only stood still, with its hands tied, but everything it was created to protect and care for went a steady gait toward rack and ruin. There was no way to levy a tax, so the minor officials had to resign or starve; therefore they resigned. There being no city money, the enormous legal expenses on both sides had to be defrayed by private subscription. But at last the people came to their senses, and said:

"Pudd'nhead was right at the start—we ought to have hired the official half of that human phillipene to resign; but it's too late now; some of us haven't got anything left to hire him with."

"Yes, we have," said another citizen, "we've got this"—and he produced a halter.

Many shouted: "That's the ticket." But others said: "No—Count Angelo is innocent; we mustn't hang him."

"Who said anything about hanging him? We are only going to hang the other one."

"Then that is all right—there is no objection to that."

So they hanged Luigi. And so ends the history of "Those Extraordinary Twins."

The $30,000 Bequest

I

Lakeside was a pleasant little town of five or six thousand inhabitants, and a rather pretty one, too, as towns go in the Far West. It had church accommodations for 35,000, which is the way of the Far West and the South, where everybody is religious, and where each of the Protestant sects is represented and has a plant of its own. Rank was unknown in Lakeside—unconfessed, anyway; everybody knew everybody and his dog, and a sociable friendliness was the prevailing atmosphere.

Saladin Foster was book-keeper in the principal store, and the only high-salaried man of his profession in Lakeside. He was thirty-five years old, now; he had served that store for fourteen years; he had begun in his marriage-week at four hundred dollars a year, and had climbed steadily up, a hundred dollars a year, for four years; from that time forth his wage had remained eight hundred—a handsome figure indeed, and everybody conceded that he was worth it.

His wife, Electra, was a capable helpmeet, although—like himself—a dreamer of dreams and a private dabbler in romance. The first thing she did, after her marriage—child as she was, aged only nineteen—was to buy an acre of ground on the edge of the town, and pay down the cash for it—twenty-five dollars, all her fortune. Saladin had less, by fifteen. She instituted a vegetable garden there, got it farmed on shares by the nearest neighbor, and made it pay her a hundred per cent. a year. Out of

Saladin's first year's wage she put thirty dollars in the savings-bank, sixty out of his second, a hundred out of his third, a hundred and fifty out of his fourth. His wage went to eight hundred a year, then, and meantime two children had arrived and increased the expenses, but she banked two hundred a year from the salary, nevertheless, thenceforth. When she had been married seven years she built and furnished a pretty and comfortable two-thousand-dollar house in the midst of her garden-acre, paid half of the money down and moved her family in. Seven years later she was out of debt and had several hundred dollars out earning its living.

Earning it by the rise in landed estate; for she had long ago bought another acre or two and sold the most of it at a profit to pleasant people who were willing to build, and would be good neighbors and furnish a general comradeship for herself and her growing family. She had an independent income from safe investments of about a hundred dollars a year; her children were growing in years and grace; and she was a pleased and happy woman. Happy in her husband, happy in her children, and the husband and the children were happy in her. It is at this point that this history begins.

The youngest girl, Clytemnestra—called Clytie for short—was eleven; her sister, Gwendolen—called Gwen for short—was thirteen; nice girls, and comely. The names betray the latent romance-tinge in the parental blood, the parents' names indicate that the tinge was an inheritance. It was an affectionate family, hence all four of its members had pet names. Saladin's was a curious and unsexing one—Sally; and so was Electra's—Aleck. All day long Sally was a good and diligent book-keeper and salesman; all day long Aleck was a good and faithful mother and housewife, and thoughtful and calculating business-woman; but in the cosey living-room at night they put the plodding world away, and lived in another and a fairer, reading romances to each other, dreaming dreams, comrading with kings and princes and stately lords and ladies in the flash and stir and splendor of noble palaces and grim and ancient castles.

II

Now came great news! Stunning news—joyous news, in fact. It came from a neighboring State, where the family's only surviving relative lived. It was Sally's relative—a sort of vague and indefinite uncle or second or third cousin by the name of Tilbury Foster, seventy and a bachelor, reputed well-off and correspondingly sour and crusty. Sally had tried to make up to him once, by letter, in a by-gone time, and had not made that mistake again. Tilbury now wrote to Sally, saying he should shortly die, and should leave him thirty thousand dollars, cash; not for love, but because money had given him most of his troubles and exasperations, and he wished to place it where there was good hope that it would continue its malignant work. The bequest would be found in his will, and would be paid over. *Provided,* that Sally should be able to prove to the executors that he had *taken no notice of the gift by spoken word or by letter, had made no inquiries concerning the moribund's progress towards the everlasting tropics, and had not attended the funeral.*

As soon as Aleck had partially recovered from the tremendous emotions created by the letter, she sent to the relative's habitat and subscribed for the local paper.

Man and wife entered into a solemn compact, now, to never mention the great news to any one while the relative lived, lest some ignorant person carry the fact to the death-bed and distort it and make it appear that they were disobediently thankful for the bequest, and just the same as confessing it and publishing it, right in the face of the prohibition.

For the rest of the day Sally made havoc and confusion with his books, and Aleck would not keep her mind on her affairs, nor even take up a flower-pot or book or a stick of wood without forgetting what she had intended to do with it. For both were dreaming.

"Thir-ty thousand dollars!"

All day long the music of those inspiring words sang through those people's heads.

From his marriage-day forth, Aleck's grip had been upon the

purse, and Sally had seldom known what it was to be privileged to squander a dime on non-necessities.

"Thir-ty thousand dollars!" the song went on and on. A vast sum, an unthinkable sum!

All day long Aleck was absorbed in planning how to invest it, Sally in planning how to spend it.

There was no romance-reading that night. The children took themselves away early, for the parents were silent, distraught, and strangely unentertaining. The good-night kisses might as well have been impressed upon vacancy, for all the response they got; the parents were not aware of the kisses, and the children had been gone an hour before their absence was noticed. Two pencils had been busy during that hour—note-making; in the way of plans. It was Sally who broke the stillness at last. He said, with exultation—

"Ah, it'll be grand, Aleck! Out of the first thousand we'll have a horse and a buggy for summer, and a cutter and a skin lap-robe for winter."

Aleck responded with decision and composure—

"Out of the *capital?* Nothing of the kind. Not if it was a million!"

Sally was deeply disappointed; the glow went out of his face.

"Oh, Aleck!" he said, reproachfully. "We've always worked so hard and been so scrimped; and now that we are rich, it does seem—"

He did not finish, for he saw her eye soften; his supplication had touched her. She said, with gentle persuasiveness—

"We must not spend the capital, dear, it would not be wise. Out of the income from it—"

"That will answer, that will answer, Aleck! How dear and good you are! There will be a noble income, and if we can spend that—"

"Not *all* of it, dear, not all of it, but you can spend a part of it. That is, a reasonable part. But the whole of the capital—every penny of it—must be put right to work, and kept at it. You see the reasonableness of that, don't you?"

"Why, ye-s. Yes, of course. But we'll have to wait so long. Six months before the first interest falls due."

"Yes—maybe longer."

"Longer, Aleck? Why? Don't they pay half-yearly?"

"*That* kind of an investment—yes; but I sha'n't invest in that way."

"What way then?"

"For big returns."

"Big. That's good. Go on, Aleck. What is it?"

"Coal. The new mines. Cannel. I mean to put in ten thousand. Ground floor. When we organize, we'll get three shares for one."

"By George, but it sounds good, Aleck! Then the shares will be worth—how much? And when?"

"About a year. They'll pay ten per cent. half-yearly, and be worth thirty thousand. I know all about it; the advertisement is in the Cincinnati paper here."

"Land, thirty thousand for ten—in a year! Let's jam in the whole capital and pull out ninety! I'll write and subscribe right now—to-morrow it may be too late."

He was flying to the writing-desk, but Aleck stopped him and put him back in his chair. She said:

"Don't lose your head so. We mustn't subscribe till we've got the money; don't you know that?"

Sally's excitement went down a degree or two, but he was not wholly appeased.

"Why, Aleck, we'll *have* it, you know—and so soon, too. He's probably out of his troubles before this, it's a hundred to nothing he's selecting his brimstone-shovel this very minute. Now, I think—"

Aleck shuddered, and said:

"How *can* you, Sally! Don't talk in that way, it is perfectly scandalous."

"Oh well, make it a halo, if you like, *I* don't care for his outfit, I was only just talking. Can't you let a person talk?"

"But why should you *want* to talk in that dreadful way? How would you like to have people talk so about *you*, and you not cold yet?"

"Not likely to be, for *one* while, I reckon, if my last act was giving away money for the sake of doing somebody a harm with it. But never mind about Tilbury, Aleck, let's talk about something worldly. It does seem to me that that mine is the place for the whole thirty. What's the objection?"

"All the eggs in one basket—that's the objection."

"All right, if you way so. What about the other twenty? What do you mean to do with that?"

"There is no hurry; I am going to look around before I do anything with it."

"All right, if your mind's made up," sighed Sally. He was deep in thought awhile, then he said:

"There'll be twenty thousand profit coming from the ten a year from now. We can spend that, can't we, Aleck?"

Aleck shook her head.

"No, dear," she said, "it won't sell high till we've had the first semi-annual dividend. You can spend part of that."

"Shucks, only *that*—and a whole year to wait! Confound it, I—"

"Oh, do be patient! It might even be declared in three months—it's quite within the possibilities."

"Oh, jolly! oh, thanks!" and Sally jumped up and kissed his wife in gratitude. "It'll be three thousand—three whole thousand! how much of it can we spend, Aleck? Make it liberal—do, dear, that's a good fellow."

Aleck was pleased; so pleased that she yielded to the pressure and conceded a sum which her judgment told her was a foolish extravagance—a thousand dollars. Sally kissed her half a dozen times and even in that way could not express all his joy and thankfulness. This new access of gratitude and affection carried Aleck quite beyond the bounds of prudence, and before she could restrain herself she had made her darling another grant—a couple of thousand out of the fifty or sixty which she meant to clear within a year out of the twenty which still remained of the bequest. The happy tears sprang to Sally's eyes, and he said:

"Oh, I want to hug you!" And he did it. Then he got his notes and sat down and began to check off, for first purchase, the luxuries which he should earliest wish to secure. "Horse—buggy—cutter—lap-robe—patent-leathers—dog—plug hat—church-pew— stem-winder—new teeth—*say,* Aleck!"

"Well?"

"Ciphering away, aren't you? That's right. Have you got the twenty thousand invested yet?"

"No, there's no hurry about that; I must look around first, and think."

"But you are ciphering; what's it about?"

"Why, I have to find work for the thirty thousand that comes out of the coal, haven't I?"

"Scott, what a head! I never thought of that. How are you getting along? Where have you arrived?"

"Not very far—two years or three. I've turned it over twice; once in oil and once in wheat."

"Why, Aleck, it's splendid! How does it aggregate?"

"I think—well, to be on the safe side, about a hundred and eighty thousand clear, though it will probably be more."

"My! isn't it wonderful? By gracious! luck has come our way at last, after all the hard sledding. Aleck!"

"Well?"

"I'm going to cash-in a whole three hundred on the missionaries—what real right have we to care for expenses!"

"You couldn't do a nobler thing, dear; and it's just like your generous nature, you unselfish boy."

The praise made Sally poignantly happy, but he was fair and just enough to say it was rightfully due to Aleck rather than to himself, since but for her he should never have had the money.

Then they went up to bed, and in their delirium of bliss they forgot and left the candle burning in the parlor. They did not remember until they were undressed; then Sally was for letting it burn; he said they could afford it, if it was a thousand. But Aleck went down and put it out.

A good job, too; for on her way back she hit on a scheme that would turn the hundred and eighty thousand into half a million before it had had time to get cold.

III

The little newspaper which Aleck had subscribed for was a Thursday sheet; it would make the trip of five hundred miles from Tilbury's village and arrive on Saturday. Tilbury's letter had started on Friday, more than a day too late for the benefactor to die and get into that week's issue, but in plenty of time to make connection for the next output. Thus the Fosters had to wait almost a complete week to find out whether anything of a satisfactory nature had happened to him or not. It was a long, long week, and the strain was a heavy one. The pair could hardly have borne it if their minds had not had the relief of wholesome diversion. We have seen that they had that. The woman was piling up fortunes right along, the man was spending them—spending all his wife would give him a chance at, at any rate.

At last the Saturday came, and the *Weekly Sagamore* arrived. Mrs. Eversly Bennett was present. She was the Presbyterian parson's wife, and was working the Fosters for a charity. Talk now died a sudden death—on the Foster side. Mrs. Bennett presently discovered that her hosts were not hearing a word she was saying; so she got up, wondering and indignant, and went away. The moment she was out of the house, Aleck eagerly tore the wrapper from the paper, and her eyes and Sally's swept the columns for the death notices. Disappointment! Tilbury was not anywhere mentioned. Aleck was a Christian from the cradle, and duty and the force of habit required her to go through the motions. She pulled herself together and said, with a pious two-per-cent. trade joyousness:

"Let us be humbly thankful that he has been spared; and—"

"Damn his treacherous hide, I wish—"

"Sally! For shame!"

"I don't care!" retorted the angry man. "It's the way *you* feel, and if you weren't so immorally pious you'd be honest and say so."

Aleck said, with wounded dignity:

"I do not see how you can say such unkind and unjust things. There is no such thing as immoral piety."

Sally felt a pang, but tried to conceal it under a shuffling attempt to save his case by changing the form of it—as if changing the form while retaining the juice could deceive the expert he was trying to placate. He said:

"I didn't mean so bad as that, Aleck; I didn't really mean immoral piety, I only meant—meant—well, conventional piety, you know; er—shop piety; the—the—why, *you* know what I mean, Aleck—the—well, where you put up the plated article and play it for solid, you know, without intending anything improper but just out of trade habit, ancient policy, petrified custom, loyalty to—to—hang it, I can't find the right words, but *you* know what I mean, Aleck, and that there isn't any harm in it. I'll try again. You see, it's this way. If a person—"

"You have said quite enough," said Aleck, coldly; let the subject be dropped."

"*I'm* willing," fervently responded Sally, wiping the sweat from his forehead and looking the thankfulness he had no words for. Then, musingly, he apologized to himself. "I certainly held threes—I *know* it—but I drew and didn't fill. That's where I'm so often weak in the game. If I had stood pat—but I didn't. I never do. I don't know enough."

Confessedly defeated, he was properly tame now and subdued. Aleck forgave him with her eyes.

The grand interest, the supreme interest, came instantly to the front again; nothing could keep it in the background many minutes on a stretch. The couple took up the puzzle of the absence of Tilbury's death notice. They discussed it every which way, more or less hopefully, but they had to finish where they began, and concede that the only really sane explanation of the absence of the notice must be—and without doubt was—that Tilbury was not dead. There was something sad about it, something even a little unfair, maybe, but there it was, and had to be put up with. They were agreed as to that. To Sally it seemed a strangely inscrutable dispensation; more inscrutable than usual, he thought; one of the most unnecessarily inscrutable he could call to mind, in fact—and said so, with some feeling; but if he was hoping to draw Aleck he failed; she reserved her opinion, if she had one; she had not the habit of taking injudicious risks in any market, worldly or other.

The pair must wait for next week's paper—Tilbury had evidently postponed. That was their thought and their decision. So they put the subject away, and went about their affairs again with as good heart as they could.

Now, if they had but known it, they had been wronging Tilbury all the time. Tilbury had kept faith, kept it to the letter; he was dead, he had died to schedule. He was dead more than four days now and used to it; entirely dead, perfectly dead, as dead as any other new person in the cemetery; dead in abundant time to get into that week's *Sagamore,* too, and only shut out by an accident; an accident which could not happen to a metropolitan journal, but which happens easily to a poor little village rag like the *Sagamore.* On this occasion, just as the editorial page was being locked up, a gratis quart of strawberry water-ice arrived from Hostetter's Ladies' and Gents' Ice-Cream Parlors, and the stickful of rather chilly regret over Tilbury's translation got crowded out to make room for the editor's frantic gratitude.

On its way to the standing-galley Tilbury's notice got pied. Otherwise it would have gone into some future edition, for *Weekly Sagamores* do not waste "live" matter, and in their galleys "live" matter is immortal, unless a pi accident intervenes. But a thing that gets pied is dead, and for such there is no resurrection; its chance of seeing print is gone, forever and ever. And so, let Tilbury like it or not, let him rave in his grave to his fill, no matter—no mention of his death would ever see the light in the *Weekly Sagamore.*

IV

Five weeks drifted tediously along. The *Sagamore* arrived regularly on the Saturdays, but never once contained a mention of Tilbury Foster. Sally's patience broke down at this point, and he said, resentfully:

"Damn his livers, he's immortal!"

Aleck gave him a very severe rebuke, and added, with icy solemnity:

"How would you feel if you were suddenly cut off just after such an awful remark had escaped out of you?"

Without sufficient reflection Sally responded:

"I'd feel I was lucky I hadn't got caught with it *in* me."

Pride had forced him to say something, and as he could not think of any rational thing to say he flung that out. Then he stole a base—as he called it—that is, slipped from the presence, to keep from getting brayed in his wife's discussion-mortar.

Six months came and went. The *Sagamore* was still silent about Tilbury. Meantime, Sally had several times thrown out a feeler—that is, a hint that he would like to know. Aleck had ignored the hints. Sally now resolved to brace up and risk a frontal attack. So he squarely proposed to disguise himself and go to Tilbury's village and surreptitiously find out as to the prospects. Aleck put her foot on the dangerous project with energy and decision. She said:

"What can you be thinking of? You do keep my hands full! You have to be watched all the time, like a little child, to keep you from walking into the fire. You'll stay right where you are!"

"Why, Aleck, I could do it and not be found out—I'm certain of it."

"Sally Foster, don't you know you would have to inquire around?"

"Of course, but what of it? Nobody would suspect who I was."

"Oh, listen to the man! Some day you've got to prove to the executors that you never inquired. What then?"

He had forgotten that detail. He didn't reply; there wasn't anything to say. Aleck added:

"Now then, drop that notion out of your mind, and don't ever meddle with it again. Tilbury set that trap for you. Don't you know it's a trap? He is on the watch, and fully expecting you to blunder into it. Well, he is going to be disappointed—at least while I am on deck. Sally!"

"Well?"

"As long as you live, if it's a hundred years, don't you ever make an inquiry. Promise!"

"All right," with a sigh and reluctantly.

Then Aleck softened and said;

"Don't be impatient. We are prospering; we can wait; there is no hurry. Our small dead-certain income increases all the time; and as to futures, I have not made a mistake yet—they are piling up by the thousands and the tens of thousands. There is not another family in the State with such prospects as ours. Already we are beginning to roll in eventual wealth. You know that, don't you?"

"Yes, Aleck, it's certainly so."

"Then be grateful for what God is doing for us, and stop worrying. You do not believe we could have achieved these prodigious results without His special help and guidance, do you?"

Hesitatingly, "N-no, I suppose not." Then, with feeling and admiration, "And yet, when it comes to judiciousness in watering a stock or putting up a hand to skin Wall Street I don't give in that *you* need any outside amateur help, if I do I wish I—"

"Oh, *do* shut up! I know you do not mean any harm or any irreverence, poor boy, but you can't seem to open your mouth without letting out things to make a person shudder. You keep me in constant dread. For you and for all of us. Once I had no fear of the thunder, but now when I hear it I—"

Her voice broke, and she began to cry, and could not finish. The sight of this smote Sally to the heart and he took her in his arms and petted her and comforted her and promised better conduct, and upbraided himself and remorsefully pleaded for forgiveness. And he was in earnest, and sorry for what he had done and ready for any sacrifice that could make up for it.

And so, in privacy, he thought long and deeply over the matter, resolving to do what should seem best. It was easy to *promise* reform; indeed he had already promised it. But would that do any real good, any permanent good? No, it would be but temporary—he knew his weakness, and confessed it to himself with sorrow—he could not keep the promise. Something surer and better must be devised; and he devised it. At cost of precious money which he had long been saving up, shilling by shilling, he put a lightning-rod on the house.

At a subsequent time he relapsed.

What miracles habit can do! and how quickly and how easily habits are acquired—both trifling habits and habits which profoundly change us. If by accident we wake at two in the morning a couple of nights in succession, we have need to be uneasy, for another repetition can turn the accident into a habit; and a month's dallying with whiskey—but we all know these commonplace facts.

The castle-building habit, the day-dreaming habit—how it grows! what a luxury it becomes; how we fly to its enchantments at every idle moment, how we revel in them, steep our souls in them, intoxicate ourselves with their beguiling fantasies—oh yes, and how soon and how easily our dream-life and our material life become so intermingled and so fused together that we can't quite tell which is which, any more.

By-and-by Aleck subscribed for a Chicago daily and for the *Wall Street Pointer.* With an eye single to finance she studied these as diligently all the week as she studied her Bible Sundays. Sally was lost in admiration, to note with what swift and sure strides her genius and judgment developed and expanded in the forecasting and handling of the securities of both the material and spiritual markets. He was proud of her nerve and daring in exploiting worldly stocks, and just as proud of her conservative caution in working her spiritual deals. He noted that she never lost her head in either case; that with a splendid courage she often went short on worldly futures, but heedfully drew the line there—she was always long on the others. Her policy was quite sane and simple, as she explained it to him: what she put into earthly futures was for speculation, what she put into spiritual futures was for investment; she was willing to go into the one on a margin, and take chances, but in the case of the other, "margin her no margins"—she wanted to cash-in a hundred cents per dollar's-worth, and have the stock transferred on the books.

It took but a very few months to educate Aleck's imagination and Sally's. Each day's training added something to the spread and effectiveness of the two machines. As a consequence, Aleck made imaginary money much faster than at first she had dreamed of making it, and Sally's competency in spending the overflow of it kept pace with the strain put upon it, right along. In the beginning, Aleck had given the coal speculation a twelvemonth in which to materialize, and had been loath to grant that this term might possibly be shortened by nine months. But that was the feeble work, the nursery work, of a financial fancy that had had no teaching, no experience, no practice. These aids soon came, then that nine months vanished, and the imaginary ten-thousand-dollar investment came marching home with three hundred per cent. profit on its back!

It was a great day for the pair of Fosters. They were speechless for joy. Also speechless for another reason: after much watching of the market, Aleck had lately, with fear and trembling, made her first flyer on a "margin," using the remaining twenty thousand of the bequest in this risk. In her mind's eye she had seen it climb, point by point—always with a chance that the market would break—until at last her anxieties were too great for further endurance—she being new to the margin-business and unhardened, as yet—and she gave her imaginary broker an imaginary order by imaginary telegraph to sell. She said forty thousand dollars profit was enough. The sale was made on the very day that the coal-venture had returned with its rich freight. As I have said, the couple were speechless. They sat dazed and blissful that night, trying to realize the immense fact, the overwhelming fact, that they were actually worth a hundred thousand dollars in clean, imaginary cash. Yet so it was.

It was the last time that ever Aleck was afraid of a margin; at least afraid enough to let it break her sleep and pale her cheek to the extent that this first experience in that line had done.

Indeed it was a memorable night. Gradually the realization that they were rich sank securely home into the souls of the pair, then they began to place the money. If we could have looked out through the eyes of these dreamers, we should have seen their tidy little wooden house disappear, and a two-story brick with a cast-iron fence in front of it take its place; we should have seen a three-globed gas-chandelier grow down from the parlor ceiling; we should have seen the homely rag carpet turn to noble

Brussels, a dollar and a half a yard; we should have seen the plebeian fireplace vanish away and a recherché, big base-burner with isinglass windows take position and spread awe around. And we should have seen other things, too; among them the buggy, the lap-robe, the stove-pipe hat, and so on.

From that time forth, although the daughters and the neighbors saw only the same old wooden house there, it was a two-story brick to Aleck and Sally; and not a night went by that Aleck did not worry about the imaginary gas-bills, and get for all comfort Sally's reckless retort, "What of it? we can afford it."

Before the couple went to bed, that first night that they were rich, they had decided that they must celebrate. They must give a party—that was the idea. But how to explain it—to the daughters and the neighbors? They could not expose the fact that they were rich. Sally was willing, even anxious, to do it; but Aleck kept her head and would not allow it. She said that although the money was as good as in, it would be as well to wait until it was actually in. On that policy she took her stand, and would not budge. The great secret must be kept, she said—kept from the daughters and everybody else.

The pair were puzzled. They must celebrate, they were determined to celebrate, but since the secret must be kept, what could they celebrate? No birthdays were due for three months. Tilbury wasn't available, evidently he was going to live forever; what the nation *could* they celebrate? That was Sally's way of putting it; and he was getting impatient, too, and harassed. But at last he hit it—just by sheer inspiration, as it seemed to him—and all their troubles were gone in a moment they would celebrate the Discovery of America. A splendid idea!

Aleck was almost too proud of Sally for words—she said *she* never would have thought of it. But Sally, although he was bursting with delight in the compliment and with wonder at himself, tried not to let on, and said it wasn't really anything, anybody could have done it. Whereat Aleck, with a prideful toss of her happy head, said:

"Oh, certainly! Anybody could—oh, anybody! Hosannah Dilkins, for instance! Or maybe Adelbert Peanut—oh, *dear*—yes! Well, I'd like to see them try it, that's all. Dear-me-suz, if they could think of the discovery of a forty-acre island it's more than *I* believe they could; and as for a whole continent, why, Sally Foster, you know perfectly well it would strain the livers and lights out of them and *then* they couldn't!"

The dear woman, she knew he had talent; and if affection made her over-estimate the size of it a little, surely it was a sweet and gentle crime, and forgiveable for its source's sake.

V

The celebration went off well. The friends were all present, both the young and the old. Among the young were Flossie and Gracie Peanut and their brother Adelbert, who was a rising young journeyman tinner, also Hosannah Dilkins, Jr., journeyman plasterer, just out of his apprenticeship. For many months Adelbert and Hosannah had been showing interest in Gwendolen and Clytemnestra Foster, and the parents of the girls had noticed this with private satisfaction. But they suddenly realized now that that feeling had passed. They recognized that the changed financial conditions had raised up a social bar between their daughters and the young mechanics. The daughters could now look higher—and must. Yes, must. They need marry nothing below the grade of lawyer or merchant; poppa and momma would take care of this; there must be no mésalliances.

However, these thinkings and projects of theirs were private, and did not show on the surface, and therefore threw no shadow upon the celebration. What showed upon the surface was a serene and lofty contentment and a dignity of carriage and gravity of deportment which compelled the admiration and likewise the wonder of the company. All noticed it, all commented upon it, but none was able to divine the secret of it. It was a marvel and a mystery. Three several persons remarked, without suspecting what clever shots they were making:

"It's as if they'd come into property."

That was just it, indeed.

Most mothers would have taken hold of the matrimonial matter in the old regulation way; they would have given the girls a talking to, of a solemn sort and untactful—a lecture calculated to defeat its own purpose, by producing tears and secret rebellion; and the said mothers would have further damaged the business by requesting the young mechanics to discontinue their attentions. But this mother was different. She was practical. She said nothing to any of the young people concerned, nor to any one else except Sally. He listened to her and understood; understood and admired. He said:

"I get the idea. Instead of finding fault with the samples on view, thus hurting feelings and obstructing trade without occasion, you merely offer a higher class of goods for the money, and leave nature to take her course. It's wisdom, Aleck, solid wisdom, and sound as a nut. Who's your fish? Have you nominated him yet?"

No, she hadn't. They must look the market over—which they did. To start with, they considered and discussed Bradish, rising young lawyer, and Fulton, rising young dentist. Sally must invite them to dinner. But not right away; there was no hurry, Aleck said. Keep an eye on the pair, and wait; nothing would be lost by going slowly in so important a matter.

It turned out that this was wisdom, too; for inside of three weeks Aleck made a wonderful strike which swelled her imaginary hundred thousand to four hundred thousand of the same quality. She and Sally were in the clouds that evening. For the first time they introduced champagne at dinner. Not real champagne, but plenty real enough for the amount of imagination expended on it. It was Sally that did it, and Aleck weakly submitted. At bottom both were troubled and ashamed, for he was a high-up Son of Temperance, and at funerals wore an apron which no dog could look upon and retain his reason and his opinion; and she was a W.C.T.U., with all that that implies of boiler-iron virtue and unendurable holiness. But there it was; the pride of riches was beginning its disintegrating work. They had lived to prove, once more, a sad truth which had been proven many times before in the word: that whereas principle is a great and noble protection against showy and degrading vanities and vices, poverty is worth six of it. More than four hundred thousand dollars to the good! They took up the matrimonial matter again. Neither the dentist nor the lawyer was mentioned; there was no occasion, they were out of the running. Disqualified. They discussed the son of the pork-packer and the son of the village banker. But finally, as in the previous case, they concluded to wait and think, and go cautiously and sure.

Luck came their way again. Aleck, ever watchful, saw a great and risky chance, and took a daring flyer. A time of trembling, of doubt, of awful uneasiness followed, for non-success meant absolute ruin and nothing short of it. Then came the result, and Aleck, faint with joy, could hardly control her voice when she said:

"The suspense is over, Sally—and we are worth a cold million!"

Sally wept for gratitude, and said:

"Oh, Electra, jewel of women, darling of my heart, we are free at last, we roll in wealth, we need never scrimp again. It's a case for Veuve Cliquot!" and he got out a pint of spruce-beer and made sacrifice, he saying "Damn the expense," and she rebuking him gently with reproachful but humid and happy eyes.

They shelved the port-packer's son and the banker's son, and sat down to consider the Governor's son and the son of the Congressman.

VI

It were a weariness to follow in detail the leaps and bounds the Foster fictitious finances took from this time forth. It was marvellous, it was dizzying, it was dazzling. Everything Aleck touched turned to fairy gold, and heaped itself glittering towards the firmament. Millions upon millions poured in, and still the mighty stream flowed thundering along, still its vast volume increased. Five millions—ten millions—twenty—thirty—was there never to be an end?

Two years swept by in a splendid delirium, the intoxicated Fosters scarcely noticing the flight of time. They were now worth three hundred million dollars; they were in every board of directors of every prodigious combine in the country; and still, as time drifted along, the millions went on piling up, five at a time, ten at a time, as fast as they could tally them off, almost. The three hundred doubled itself—then doubled again—and yet again—and yet once more.

Twenty-four hundred millions!

The business was getting a little confused. It was necessary to take an account of stock, and straighten it out. The Fosters knew it, they felt it, they realized that it was imperative; but they also knew that to do it properly and perfectly the task must be carried to a finish without a break when once it was begun. A ten-hours' job; and where could *they* find ten leisure hours in a bunch? Sally was selling pins and sugar and calico all day and every day; Aleck was cooking and washing dishes and sweeping and making beds all day and every day, with none to help, for the daughters were being saved up for high society. The Fosters knew there was one way to get the ten hours, and only one. Both were ashamed to name it; each waited for the other to do it. Finally Sally said:

"Somebody's got to give in. It's up to me. Consider that I've named it—never mind pronouncing it out loud."

Aleck colored, but was grateful. Without further remark, they fell. Fell, and—broke the Sabbath. For that was their only free ten-hour stretch. It was but another step in the downward path. Others would follow. Vast wealth has temptations which fatally and surely undermine the moral structure of persons not habituated to its possession.

They pulled down the shades and broke the Sabbath. With hard and patient labor they overhauled their holdings and listed them. And a long-drawn procession of formidable names it was! Starting with the Railway Systems, Steamer Lines, Standard Oil, Ocean Cables, Diluted Telegraph, and all the rest, and winding up with Klondike, De Beers, Tammany Graft, and Shady Privileges in the Post-office Department.

Twenty-four hundred millions, and all safely planted in Good Things, gilt-edged and interest-bearing. Income, $120,000,000 a year. Aleck fetched a long purr of soft delight, and said:

"Is it enough?"

"It is, Aleck."

"What shall we do?"

"Stand pat."

"Retire from business?"

"That's it."

"I am agreed. The good work is finished; we will take a long rest and enjoy the money."

"Good! Aleck!"

"Yes, dear?"

"How much of the income can we spend?"

"The whole of it."

It seemed to her husband that a ton of chains fell from his limbs. He did not say a word; he was happy beyond the power of speech.

After that, they broke the Sabbaths right along, as fast as they turned up. It is the first wrong steps that count. Every Sunday they put in the whole day, after morning service, on inventions—inventions of ways to spend the money. They got to continuing this delicious dissipation until past midnight; and at every séance Aleck lavished millions upon great charities and religious enterprises, and Sally lavished like sums upon matters to which (at first) he gave definite names. Only at first. Later the names gradually lost sharpness of outline, and eventually faded into "sundries," thus becoming entirely—but safely—undescriptive. For Sally was crumbling. The placing of these millions added seriously and most uncomfortably to the family expenses—in tallow candles. For awhile Aleck was worried. Then, after a little, she ceased to worry, for the occasion of it was gone. She was pained, she was grieved, she was ashamed; but she said nothing, and so became an accessory. Sally was taking candles; he was robbing the store. It is ever thus. Vast wealth, to the person unaccustomed to it, is a bane; it eats into the flesh and bone of his morals. When the Fosters were poor, they could have been trusted with untold candles. But now they—but let us not dwell upon it. From candles to apples is but a step: Sally got to taking apples; then soap; then maple-sugar; then canned-goods; then crockery. How easy it is to go from bad to worse, when once we have started upon a downward course!

Meantime, other effects had been milestoning the course of the Fosters' splendid financial march. The fictitious brick-dwelling had given place to an imaginary granite one with a check-board mansard roof; in time this one disappeared and gave place to a still grander home—and so on and so on. Mansion after mansion, made of air, rose, higher, broader, finer, and each in its turn vanished away; until now, in these latter great days, our dreamers were in fancy housed, in a distant region, in a sumptuous vast palace which looked out from a leafy summit upon a noble prospect of vale and river and receding hills steeped in tinted mists—and all private, all the property of the dreamers; a palace swarming with liveried servants, and populous with guests of fame and power, hailing from all the world's capitals, foreign and domestic.

This palace was far, far away towards the rising sun, immeasurably remote, astronomically remote, in Newport, Rhode Island, Holy Land of High Society, ineffable Domain of the American Aristocracy. As a rule, they spent a part of every Sabbath—after morning service—in this sumptuous home, the rest of it they spent in Europe, or in dawdling around in their private yacht. Six days of sordid and plodding Fact-life at home on the ragged edge of Lakeside and straitened means, the seventh in Fairyland—such had become their programme and their habit.

In their sternly restricted Fact-life they remained as of old—plodding, diligent, careful, practical, economical. They stuck loyally to the little Presbyterian Church, and labored faithfully in its interests and stood by its high and tough doctrines with all their mental and spiritual energies. But in their Dream-life they obeyed the invitations of their fancies, whatever they might be, and howsoever the fancies might change. Aleck's fancies were not very capricious, and not frequent, but Sally's scattered a good deal. Aleck, in her Dream-life, went over to the Episcopal camp, on account of its large official titles; next she became High-church on account of the candles and shows; and next she naturally changed to Rome, where there were cardinals and more candles. But these excursions were as nothing to Sally's. His Dream-life was a glowing and continuous and persistent excitement, and he kept every part of it fresh and sparkling by frequent changes, the religious part along with the rest. He worked his religions hard, and changed them with his shirt.

The liberal spendings of the Fosters upon their fancies began early in their prosperities, and grew in prodigality step by step with their advancing fortunes. In time they became truly enormous. Aleck built a university or two per Sunday; also a hospital or two; also a Rowton hotel or so; also a batch of churches; now and then a cathedral; and once, with untimely and ill-chosen playfulness, Sally said, "It was a cold day when she didn't ship a cargo of missionaries to persuade unreflecting Chinamen to trade off twenty-four carat Confucianism for counterfeit Christianity."

This rude and unfeeling language hurt Aleck to the heart, and she went from the presence crying. That spectacle went to his own heart, and in his pain and shame he would have given worlds to have those unkind words back. She had uttered no syllable of reproach—and that cut him. Not one suggestion that he look at his own record—and she could have made, oh, so many, and such blistering ones! Her generous silence brought a swift revenge, for it turned his thoughts upon himself, it summoned before him a spectral procession, a moving vision of his life as he had been leading it these past few years of limitless prosperity, and as he sat there reviewing it his cheeks burned and his soul was steeped in humiliation. Look at her life—how fair it was, and tending ever upward; and look at his own—how frivolous, how charged with mean vanities, how selfish, how empty, how ignoble! And its trend—never upward, but downward, ever downward!

He instituted comparisons between her record and his own. He had found fault with her—so he mused—*he!* And what could he say for himself? When she built her first church what was he doing? Gathering other blasé multimillionaires into a Poker Club; defiling his own palace with it; losing hundreds of thousands to it at every sitting, and sillily vain of the admiring notoriety it made for him. When she was building her first university, what was he doing? Polluting himself with a gay and dissipated secret life in the company of other fast bloods, multimillionaires in money and paupers in character. When she was building her first foundling asylum, what was he doing? Alas! When she was projecting her noble Society for the Purifying of the Sex, what was he doing? Ah, what, indeed! When she and the W. C. T. U. and the Woman with the Hatchet, moving with resistless march, were sweeping the fatal bottle from the land, what was he doing? Getting drunk three times a day. When she, builder of a hundred cathedrals, was being gratefully welcomed and blest in papal Rome and decorated with the Golden Rose which she had so honorably earned, what was he doing? Breaking the bank at Monte Carlo.

He stopped. He could go no farther; he could not bear the rest. He rose up, with a great resolution upon his lips: this secret life should be revealed, and confessed; no longer would he live it clandestinely; he would go and tell her All.

And that is what he did. He told her All; and wept upon her bosom; wept, and moaned, and begged for her forgiveness. It was a profound shock, and she staggered under the blow, but he was her own, the core of her heart, the blessing of her eyes, her all in all, she could deny him nothing, and she forgave him. She felt that he could never again be quite to her what he had been before; she knew that he could only repent, and not reform; yet all morally defaced and decayed as he was, was he not her own, her very own, the idol of her deathless worship? She said she was his serf, his slave, and she opened her yearning heart and took him in.

VII

One Sunday afternoon some time after this they were sailing the summer seas in their dream-yacht, and reclining in lazy luxury under the awning of the after-deck. There was silence, for each was busy with his own thoughts. These seasons of silence had insensibly been growing more and more frequent of late; the old nearness and cordiality were waning. Sally's terrible revelation had done its work; Aleck had tried hard to drive the memory of it out of her mind, but it would not go, and the shame and bitterness of it were poisoning her gracious dream-life. She could see now (on Sundays) that her husband was becoming a bloated and repulsive Thing. She could not close her eyes to this, and in these days she no longer looked at him, Sundays, when she could help it.

But she—was she herself without blemish? Alas, she knew she was not. She was keeping a secret from him, she was acting dishonorably towards him, and many a pang it was costing her. *She was breaking the compact, and concealing it from him.* Under strong temptation she had gone into business again; she had risked their whole fortune in a purchase of all the railway systems and coal and steel companies in the country on a margin, and she was now trembling, every Sabbath hour, lest through some chance word of hers he find it out. In her misery and remorse for this treachery she could not keep her heart from going out to him in pity; she was filled with compunctions to see him lying there, drunk and content, and never suspecting. Never suspecting—trusting her with a perfect and pathetic trust, and she holding over him by a thread a possible calamity of so devastating a—

"*Say*—Aleck?"

The interrupting words brought her suddenly to herself. She was grateful to have that persecuting subject from her thoughts, and she answered, with much of the old-time tenderness in her tone:

"Yes, dear."

"Do you know, Aleck, I think we are making a mistake—that is, you are. I mean about the marriage business." He sat up, fat and froggy and benevolent, like a bronze Buddha, and grew earnest. "Consider—it's more than five years. You've continued the same policy from the start: with every rise, always holding on for five points higher. Always when I think we are going to have some weddings, you see a bigger thing ahead, and I undergo another disappointment. *I* think you are too hard to please. Some day we'll get left. First, we turned down the dentist and the lawyer. That was all right—it was sound. Next, we turned down the banker's son and the pork-butcher's heir—right again, and sound. Next, we turned down the Congressman's son and the Governor's—right as a trivet, I confess it. Next, the Senator's son and the son of the Vice-President of the United States—

perfectly right, there's no permanency about those little distinctions. Then you went for the aristocracy; and I thought we had struck oil at last—yes. We would make a plunge at the Four Hundred, and pull in some ancient lineage, venerable, holy, ineffable, mellow with the antiquity of a hundred and fifty years, disinfected of the ancestral odors of salt cod and pelts all of a century ago, and unsmirched by a day's work since; and then! why, then the marriages, of course. But no, along comes a pair of real aristocrats from Europe, and straightway you throw over the half-breeds. It was awfully discouraging, Aleck! Since then, what a procession! You turned down the baronets for a pair of barons; you turned down the barons for a pair of viscounts; the viscounts for a pair of earls; the earls for a pair of marquises; the marquises for a brace of dukes. *Now,* Aleck, cash-in!—you've played the limit. You've got a job lot of four dukes under the hammer; of four nationalities; all sound in wind and limb and pedigree, all bankrupt and in debt up to the ears. They come high, but we can afford it. Come, Aleck, don't delay any longer, don't keep up the suspense: take the whole lay-out, and leave the girls to choose!"

Aleck had been smiling blandly and contentedly all through this arraignment of her marriage-policy; a pleasant light, as of triumph with perhaps a nice surprise peeping out through it, rose in her eyes, and she said, as calmly as she could:

"Sally, what would you say to—*royalty?*"

Prodigious! Poor man, it knocked him silly, and he fell over the garboard-strake and barked his shin on the cat-heads. He was dizzy for a moment, then he gathered himself up and limped over and sat down by his wife and beamed his old-time admiration and affection upon her in floods, out of his bleary eyes.

"By George!" he said, fervently, "Aleck, you *are* great—the greatest woman in the whole earth! I can't ever learn the whole size of you. I can't ever learn the immeasurable deeps of you. Here I've been considering myself qualified to criticise your game. *I!* Why, if I had stopped to think, I'd have known you had a lone hand up your sleeve. Now, dear heart, I'm all red-hot impatience—tell me about it!"

The flattered and happy woman put her lips to his ear and whispered a princely name. It made him catch his breath, it lit his face with exultation.

"Land!" he said, "it's a stunning catch! He's got a gambling-hell, and a graveyard, and a bishop, and a cathedral—all his very own. And all gilt-edged five-hundred-per-cent. stock, every detail of it; the tidiest little property in Europe. And that graveyard—it's the selectest in the world: none but suicides admitted; *yes*, sir, and the free-list suspended, too, *all* the time. There isn't much land in the principality, but there's enough: eight hundred acres in the graveyard and forty-two outside. It's a *sovereignty*—that's the main thing; *land's* nothing. There's plenty land, Sahara's drugged with it."

Aleck glowed; she was profoundly happy. She said:

"Think of it, Sally—it is a family that has never married outside the Royal and Imperial Houses of Europe: our grandchildren will sit upon thrones!"

"True as you live, Aleck—and bear sceptres, too; and handle them as naturally and nonchalantly as I handle a yardstick. It's a grand catch, Aleck. He's coralled, is he? Can't get away? You didn't take him on a margin?"

"No. Trust me for that. He's not a liability, he's an asset. So is the other one."

"Who is it, Aleck?"

"His Royal Highness Sigismund-Siegfried-Lauenfeld-Dinkelspiel-Schwartzenberg Blutwurst, Hereditary Grand Duke of Katzenyammer."

"No! You can't mean it!"

"It's as true as I'm sitting here, I give you my word," she answered.

His cup was full, and he hugged her to his heart with rapture, saying:

"How wonderful it all seems, and how beautiful! It's one of the oldest and noblest of the three hundred and sixty-four ancient German principalities, and one of the few that was allowed to retain its royal estate when Bismarck got done trimming them. I know that farm, I've been there. It's got a rope-walk and a candle-factory and an army. Standing army. Infantry and cavalry. Three soldiers and a horse. Aleck, it's been a long wait, and full of heartbreak and hope deferred, but God knows I am happy now. Happy, and grateful to you, my own, who have done it all. When is it to be?"

"Next Sunday."

"Good. And we'll want to do these weddings up in the very regalest style that's going. It's properly due to the royal quality of the parties of the first part. Now as I understand it, there is only one kind of marriage that is sacred to royalty, exclusive to royalty: it's the morganatic."

"What do they call it that for, Sally?"

"I don't know; but anyway it's royal, and royal only."

"Then we will insist upon it. More—I will compel it. It is morganatic marriage or none."

"That settles it!" said Sally, rubbing his hands with delight. "And it will be the very first in America. Aleck, it will make Newport sick."

Then they fell silent, and drifted away upon their dream-wings to the far regions of the earth to invite all the crowned heads and their families and provide gratis transportation for them.

VIII

During three days the couple walked upon air, with their heads in the clouds. They were but vaguely conscious of their surroundings; they saw all things dimly, as through a veil; they were steeped in dreams, often they did not hear when they were spoken to; they often did not understand when they heard; they answered confusedly or at random; Sally sold molasses by weight, sugar by the yard, and furnished soap when asked for candles, and Aleck put the cat in the wash and fed milk to the soiled linen. Everybody was stunned and amazed, and went about muttering, "What *can* be the matter with the Fosters?"

Three days. Then came events! Things had taken a happy turn, and for forty-eight hours Aleck's imaginary corner had been booming. Up—up—still up! Cost-point was passed. Still up—and up—and up! Five points above cost—then ten—fifteen—twenty! Twenty points cold profit on the vast venture, now, and Aleck's imaginary brokers were shouting frantically by imaginary long-distance, "Sell! sell! for Heaven's sake *sell!*"

She broke the splendid news to Sally, and he, too, said, "Sell! sell—oh, don't make a blunder, now, you own the earth!—sell, sell!" But she set her iron will and lashed it amidships, and said she would hold on for five points more if she died for it.

It was a fatal resolve. The very next day came the historic crash, the record crash, the devastating crash, when the bottom fell out of Wall Street, and the whole body of gilt-edged stocks dropped ninety-five points in five hours, and the multimillionaire was seen begging his bread in the Bowery. Aleck sternly held her grip and "put up" as long as she could, but at last there came a call which she was powerless to meet, and her imaginary brokers sold her out. Then, and not till then, the man in her was vanquished, and the woman in her resumed sway. She put her arms about her husband's neck and wept, saying:

"I am to blame, do not forgive me, I cannot bear it. We are paupers! Paupers, and I am so miserable. The weddings will never come off; all that is past; we could not even buy the dentist, now."

A bitter reproach was on Sally's tongue: "I *begged* you to sell, but you—" He did not say it; he had not the heart to add a hurt to that broken and repentant spirit. A nobler thought came to him and he said:

"Bear up, my Aleck, all is not lost! You really never invested a penny of my uncle's bequest, but only its unmaterialized future; what we have lost was only the increment harvested from that future by your incomparable financial judgment and sagacity. Cheer up, banish these griefs; we still have the thirty thousand untouched; and with the experience which you have acquired, think what you will be able to do with it in a couple of years! The marriages are not off, they are only postponed."

These were blessed words. Aleck saw how true they were, and their influence was electric; her tears ceased to flow, and her great spirit rose to its full stature again. With flashing eye and grateful heart, and with hand uplifted in pledge and prophecy, she said:

"Now and here I proclaim—"

But she was interrupted by a visitor. It was the editor and proprietor of the *Sagamore*. He had happened into Lakeside to pay a duty-call upon an obscure grandmother of his who was nearing the end of her pilgrimage, and with the idea of combining business with grief he had looked up the Fosters, who had been so absorbed in other things for the past four years that they had neglected to pay up their subscription. Six dollars due. No visitor could have been more welcome. He would know all about Uncle Tilbury and what his chances might be getting to be, cemeterywards. They could, of course, ask no questions, for that would squelch the bequest, but they could nibble around on the edge of the subject and hope for results. The scheme did not work. The obtuse editor did not know he was being nibbled at; but at last, chance accomplished what art had failed in. In illustration of something under discussion which required the help of metaphor, the editor said:

"Land, it's as tough as Tilbury Foster!—as *we* say."

It was sudden, and it made the Fosters jump. The editor noticed it, and said, apologetically:

"No harm intended, I assure you. It's just a saying; just a joke, you know—nothing in it. Relation of yours?"

Sally crowded his burning eagerness down, and answered with all the indifference he could assume:

"I—well, not that I know of, but we've heard of him." The editor was thankful, and resumed his composure. Sally added: "Is he—is he—well?"

"Is he *well?* Why, bless you he's in Sheol these five years!"

The Fosters were trembling with grief, though it felt like joy. Sally said, non-committally—and tentatively:

"Ah, well, such is life, and none can escape—not even the rich are spared."

The editor laughed.

"If you are including Tilbury," said he, "it don't apply. *He* hadn't a cent; the town had to bury him."

The Fosters sat petrified for two minutes; petrified and cold. Then, white-faced and weak-voiced, Sally asked:

"Is it true? Do you *know* it to be true?"

"Well, I should say! I was one of the executors. He hadn't anything to leave but a wheelbarrow, and he left that to me. It hadn't any wheel, and wasn't any good. Still, it was something, and so, to square up, I scribbled off a sort of a little obituarial send-off for him, but it got crowded out."

The Fosters were not listening—their cup was full, it could contain no more. They saw with bowed heads, dead to all things but the ache at their hearts.

An hour later. Still they sat there, bowed, motionless, silent, the visitor long ago gone, they unaware.

Then they stirred, and lifted their heads wearily, and gazed at each other wistfully, dreamily, dazed; then presently began to twaddle to each other in a wandering and childish way. At intervals they lapsed into silences, leaving a sentence unfinished, seemingly either unaware of it or losing their way. Sometimes, when they woke out of these silences they had a dim and transient consciousness that something had happened to their minds; then with a dumb and yearning solicitude they would softly caress each other's hands in mutual compassion and support, as if they would say: "I am near you, I will not forsake you, we will bear it together; somewhere there is release and forgetfulness, somewhere there is a grave and peace; be patient, it will not be long."

They lived yet two years, in mental night, always brooding, steeped in vague regrets and melancholy dreams, never speaking; then release came to both on the same day.

Towards the end the darkness lifted from Sally's ruined mind for a moment, and he said:

"Vast wealth, acquired by sudden and unwholesome means, is a snare. It did us no good, transient were its feverish pleasures; yet for its sake we threw away our sweet and simple and happy life—let others take warning by us."

He lay silent awhile, with closed eyes; then as the chill of death crept upward towards his heart, and consciousness was fading from his brain, he muttered:

"Money had brought him misery, and he took his revenge upon us, who had done him no harm. He had his desire: with base and cunning calculation he left us but thirty thousand, knowing we would try to increase it, and ruin our life and break our hearts. Without added expense he could have left us far above desire of increase, far above the temptation to speculate, and a kinder soul would have done it; but in him was no generous spirit, no pity, no—"

Some Learned Fables for Good Old Boys and Girls

IN THREE PARTS

PART FIRST HOW THE ANIMALS OF THE WOOD SENT OUT A SCIENTIFIC EXPEDITION

Once the creatures of the forest held a great convention and appointed a commission consisting of the most illustrious scientists among them to go forth, clear beyond the forest and out into the unknown and unexplored world, to verify the truth of the matters already taught in their schools and colleges and also to make discoveries. It was the most imposing enterprise of the kind the nation had ever embarked in. True, the government had once sent Dr. Bull Frog, with a picked crew, to hunt for a northwesterly passage through the swamp to the right-hand corner of the wood, and had since sent out many expeditions to hunt for Dr. Bull Frog; but they never could find him, and so government finally gave him up and ennobled his mother to show its gratitude for the services her son had rendered to science. And once government sent Sir Grass Hopper to hunt for the sources of the rill that emptied into the swamp; and afterward sent out many expeditions to hunt for Sir Grass, and at last they were successful—they found his body, but if he had discovered the sources meantime, he did not let on. So government acted handsomely by deceased, and many envied his funeral.

But these expeditions were trifles compared with the present one; for this one comprised among its servants the very greatest among the learned; and besides it was to go to the utterly unvisited regions believed to lie beyond the mighty forest—as we have remarked before. How the members were banqueted, and glorified, and talked about! Everywhere that one of them showed himself, straightway there was a crowd to gape and stare at him.

Finally they set off, and it was a sight to see the long procession of dry-land Tortoises heavily laden with savants, scientific instruments, Glow-Worms and Fire-Flies for signal service, provisions, Ants and Tumble-Bugs to fetch and carry and delve, Spiders to carry the surveying chain and do other engineering duty, and so forth and so on; and after the Tortoises came another long train of ironclads—stately and spacious Mud Turtles for marine transportation service; and from every Tortoise and every Turtle flaunted a flaming gladiolus or other splendid banner; at the head of the column a great band of Bumble-Bees, Mosquitoes, Katy-Dids, and Crickets discoursed martial music; and the entire train was under the escort and protection of twelve picked regiments of the Army Worm.

At the end of three weeks the expedition emerged from the forest and looked upon the great Unknown World. Their eyes were greeted with an impressive spectacle. A vast level plain stretched before them, watered by a sinuous stream; and beyond there towered up against the sky a long and lofty barrier of some kind, they did not know what. The Tumble-Bug said he believed it was simply land tilted up on its edge, because he knew he could see trees on it. But Professor Snail and the others said:

"You are hired to dig, sir—that is all. We need your muscle, not your brains. When we want your opinion on scientific matters, we will hasten to let you know. Your coolness is intolerable, too—loafing about here meddling with august matters of learning, when the other laborers are pitching camp. Go along and help handle the baggage."

The Tumble-Bug turned on his heel uncrushed, unabashed, observing to himself, "If it isn't land tilted up, let me die the death of the unrighteous."

Professor Bull Frog (nephew of the late explorer) said he

believed the ridge was the wall that inclosed the earth. He continued:

"Our fathers have left us much learning, but they had not traveled far, and so we may count this a noble new discovery. We are safe for renown now, even though our labors began and ended with this single achievement. I wonder what this wall is built of? Can it be fungus? Fungus is an honorable good thing to build a wall of."

Professor Snail adjusted his field-glass and examined the rampart critically. Finally he said:

"The fact that it is not diaphanous convinces me that it is a dense vapor formed by the calorification of ascending moisture dephlogisticated by refraction. A few endiometrical experiments would confirm this, but it is not necessary. The thing is obvious."

So he shut up his glass and went into his shell to make a note of the discovery of the world's end, and the nature of it.

"Profound mind!" said Professor Angle-Worm to Professor Field-Mouse; "profound mind! nothing can long remain a mystery to that august brain."

Night drew on apace, the sentinel crickets were posted, the Glow-Worm and Fire-Fly lamps were lighted, and the camp sank to silence and sleep. After breakfast in the morning, the expedition moved on. About noon a great avenue was reached, which had in it two endless parallel bars of some kind of hard black substance, raised the height of the tallest Bull Frog above the general level. The scientists climbed up on these and examined and tested them in various ways. They walked along them for a great distance, but found no end and no break in them. They could arrive at no decision. There was nothing in the records of science that mentioned anything of this kind. But at last the bald and venerable geographer, Professor Mud Turtle, a person who, born poor, and of a drudging low family, had, by his own native force raised himself to the headship of the geographers of his generation, said:

"My friends, we have indeed made a discovery here. We have found in a palpable, compact, and imperishable state what the wisest of our fathers always regarded as a mere thing of the imagination. Humble yourselves, my friends, for we stand in a majestic presence. These are parallels of latitude!"

Every heart and every head was bowed, so awful, so sublime was the magnitude of the discovery. Many shed tears.

The camp was pitched and the rest of the day given up to writing voluminous accounts of the marvel, and correcting astronomical tables to fit it. Toward midnight a demoniacal shriek was heard, then a clattering and rumbling noise, and the next instant a vast terrific eye shot by, with a long tail attached, and disappeared in the gloom, still uttering triumphant shrieks.

The poor camp laborers were stricken to the heart with fright, and stampeded for the high grass in a body. But not the scientists. They had no superstitions. They calmly proceeded to exchange theories. The ancient geographer's opinion was asked. He went into his shell and deliberated long and profoundly. When he came out at last, they all knew by his worshiping countenance that he brought light. Said he:

"Give thanks for this stupendous thing which we have been permitted to witness. It is the Vernal Equinox!"

There were shoutings and great rejoicings.

"But," said the Angle-Worm, uncoiling after reflection, "this is dead summer-time."

"Very well," said the Turtle, "we are far from our region; the season differs with the difference of time between the two points."

"Ah, true. True enough. But it is night. How should the sun pass in the night?"

"In these distant regions he doubtless passes always in the night at this hour."

"Yes, doubtless that is true. But it being night, how is it that we could see him?"

"It is a great mystery. I grant that. But I am persuaded that the humidity of the atmosphere in these remote regions is such that particles of daylight adhere to the disk and it was by aid of these that we were enabled to see the sun in the dark."

This was deemed satisfactory, and due entry was made of the decision.

But about this moment those dreadful shriekings were heard

again; again the rumbling and thundering came speeding up out of the night; and once more a flaming great eye flashed by and lost itself in gloom and distance.

The camp laborers gave themselves up for lost. The savants were sorely perplexed. Here was a marvel hard to account for. They thought and they talked, they talked and they thought. Finally the learned and aged Lord Grand-Daddy-Longlegs, who had been sitting in deep study, with his slender limbs crossed and his stemmy arms folded, said:

"Deliver your opinions, brethren, and then I will tell my thought—for I think I have solved this problem."

"So be it, good your lordship," piped the weak treble of the wrinkled and withered Professor Woodlouse, "for we shall hear from your lordship's lips naught but wisdom." [Here the speaker threw in a mess of trite, threadbare, exasperating quotations from the ancient poets and philosophers, delivering them with unction in the sounding grandeurs of the original tongues, they being from the Mastodon, the Dodo, and other dead languages.] "Perhaps I ought not to presume to meddle with matters pertaining to astronomy at all, in such a presence as this, I who have made it the business of my life to delve only among the riches of the extinct languages and unearth the opulence of their ancient lore; but still, as unacquainted as I am with the noble science of astronomy, I beg with deference and humility to suggest that inasmuch as the last of these wonderful apparitions proceeded in exactly the opposite direction from that pursued by the first, which you decide to be the Vernal Equinox, and greatly resembled it in all particulars, is it not possible, nay certain, that this last is the *Autumnal* Equi—"

"O-o-o!" "O-o-o! go to bed! go to bed!" with annoyed derision from everybody. So the poor old Woodlouse retreated out of sight, consumed with shame.

Further discussion followed, and then the united voice of the commission begged Lord Longlegs to speak. He said:

"Fellow-scientists, it is my belief that we have witnessed a thing which has occurred in perfection but once before in the knowledge of created beings. It is a phenomenon of inconceivable importance and interest, view it as one may, but its interest to us is vastly heightened by an added knowledge of its nature which no scholar has heretofore possessed or even suspected. This great marvel which we have just witnessed, fellow-savants (it almost takes my breath away), is nothing less than the transit of Venus!"

Every scholar sprang to his feet pale with astonishment. Then ensued tears, hand shakings, frenzied embraces, and the most extravagant jubilations of every sort. But by and by, as emotion began to retire within bounds, and reflection to return to the front, the accomplished Chief Inspector Lizard observed:

"But how is this? Venus should traverse the sun's surface, not the earth's."

The arrow went home. It carried sorrow to the breast of every apostle of learning there, for none could deny that this was a formidable criticism. But tranquilly the venerable Duke crossed his limbs behind his ears and said:

"My friend has touched the marrow of our mighty discovery. Yes—all that have lived before us thought a transit of Venus consisted of a flight across the sun's face; they thought it, they maintained it, they honestly believed it, simple hearts, and were justified in it by the limitations of their knowledge; but to us has been granted the inestimable boon of proving that the transit occurs across the earth's face, *for we have* SEEN *it!*"

The assembled wisdom sat in speechless adoration of this imperial intellect. All doubts had instantly departed, like night before the lightning.

The Tumble-Bug had just intruded, unnoticed. He now came reeling forward among the scholars, familiarly slapping first one and then another on the shoulder, saying "Nice ('ic!) nice old boy!" and smiling a smile of elaborate content. Arrived at a good position for speaking, he put his left arm akimbo with his knuckles planted in his hip just under the edge of his cut-away coat, bent his right leg, placing his toe on the ground and resting his heel with easy grace against his left shin, puffed out his aldermanic stomach, opened his lips, leaned his right elbow on Inspector Lizard's shoulder, and—

But the shoulder was indignantly withdrawn and the hard-handed son of toil went to earth. He floundered a bit, but came up smiling, arranged his attitude with the same careful detail as before, only choosing Professor Dogtick's shoulder for a support, opened his lips and—

Went to earth again. He presently scrambled up once more, still smiling, made a loose effort to brush the dust off his coat and legs, but a smart pass of his hand missed entirely, and the force of the unchecked impulse slewed him suddenly around, twisted his legs together, and projected him, limber and sprawling, into the lap of the Lord Longlegs. Two or three scholars sprang forward, flung the low creature head over heels into a corner, and reinstated the patrician, smoothing his ruffled dignity with many soothing and regretful speeches. Professor Bull Frog roared out:

"No more of this, sirrah Tumble-Bug! Say your say and then get you about your business with speed! Quick—what is you errand? Come—move off a trifle; you smell like a stable; what have you been at?"

"Please ('ic!) please your worship I chanced to light upon a find. But no m (*e-uck!*) matter 'bout that. There's b ('ic!) been another find which—beg pardon, your honors, what was that th ('ic!) thing that ripped by here first?"

"It was the Vernal Equinox."

"Inf ('ic!) fernal equinox. 'At's all right. D ('ic!) Dunno *him*. What's other one?"

"The transit of Venus."

"G (ic!) Got me again. No matter. Las' one dropped something."

"Ah, indeed! Good luck! Good news! Quick—what is it?"

"M ('ic!) Mosey out 'n' see. It'll pay."

No more votes were taken for four-and-twenty hours. Then the following entry was made:

"The commission went in a body to view the find. It was found to consist of a hard, smooth, huge object with a rounded summit surmounted by a short upright projection resembling a section of a cabbage stalk divided transversely. This projection was not solid, but was a hollow cylinder plugged with a soft woody substance unknown to our region—that is, it had been so plugged, but unfortunately this obstruction had been heedlessly removed by Norway Rat, Chief of the Sappers and Miners, before our arrival. The vast object before us, so mysteriously conveyed from the glittering domains of space, was found to be hollow and nearly filled with a pungent liquid of a brownish hue, like rain water that has stood for some time. And such a spectacle as met our view! Norway Rat was perched upon the summit engaged in thrusting his tail into the cylindrical projection, drawing it out dripping, permitting the struggling multitude of laborers to suck the end of it, then straightway reinserting it and delivering the fluid to the mob as before. Evidently this liquor had strangely potent qualities; for all that partook of it were immediately exalted with great and pleasurable emotions, and went staggering about singing ribald songs, embracing, fighting, dancing, discharging irruptions of profanity, and defying all authority. Around us struggled a massed and uncontrolled mob—uncontrolled and likewise uncontrollable, for the whole army, down to the very sentinels, were mad like the rest, by reason of the drink. We were seized upon by these reckless creatures, and within the hour we, even we, were undistinguishable from the rest—the demoralization was complete and universal. In time the camp wore itself out with its orgies and sank into a stolid and pitiable stupor, in whose mysterious bonds rank was forgotten and strange bedfellows made, our eyes, at the resurrection, being blasted and our souls petrified with the incredible spectacle of that intolerable stinking scavenger, the Tumble-Bug, and the illustrious patrician my Lord Grand Daddy, Duke of Longlegs, lying soundly steeped in sleep, and clasped lovingly in each other's arms, the like whereof hath not been seen in all the ages that tradition compasseth, and doubtless none shall ever in this world find faith to master the belief of it save only we that have beheld the damnable and unholy vision. Thus inscrutable be the ways of God, whose will be done!

"This day, by order, did the engineer-in-chief, Herr Spider, rig the necessary tackle for the overturning of the vast reservoir, and so its calamitous contents were discharged in a torrent upon the thirsty earth, which drank it up, and now there is no more danger, we reserving but a few drops for experiment and scrutiny, and to exhibit to the king and subsequently preserve among the wonders of the museum. What this liquid is has been determined. It is without question that fierce and most destructive fluid called lightning. It was wrested, in its container, from its storehouse in the clouds, by the resistless might of the flying planet, and hurled at our feet as she sped by. An interesting discovery here results. Which is, that lightning, kept to itself, is quiescent; it is the assaulting contact of the thunderbolt that releases it from captivity, ignites its awful fires, and so produces an instantaneous combustion and explosion which spread disaster and desolation far and wide in the earth."

After another day devoted to rest and recovery, the expedition proceeded upon its way. Some days later it went into camp in a pleasant part of the plain, and the savants sallied forth to see what they might find. Their reward was at hand. Professor Bull Frog discovered a strange tree, and called his comrades. They inspected it with profound interest. It was very tall and straight, and wholly devoid of bark, limbs, or foliage. By triangulation Lord Longlegs determined its altitude; Herr Spider measured its circumference at the base and computed the circumference at its top by a mathematical demonstration based upon the warrant furnished by the uniform degree of its taper upward. It was considered a very extraordinary find; and since it was a tree of hitherto unknown species, Professor Woodlouse gave it a name of a learned sound, being none other than that of Professor Bull Frog translated into the ancient Mastodon language, for it had always been the custom with discoverers to perpetuate their names and honor themselves by this sort of connection with their discoveries.

Now Professor Field-Mouse having placed his sensitive ear to the tree, detected a rich, harmonious sound issuing from it. This surprising thing was tested and enjoyed by each scholar in turn, and great was the gladness and astonishment of all. Professor Woodlouse was requested to add to and extend the tree's name so as to make it suggest the musical quality it possessed—which he did, furnishing the addition *Anthem Singer,* done into the Mastodon tongue.

By this time Professor Snail was making some telescopic

inspections. He discovered a great number of these trees, extending in a single rank, with wide intervals between, as far as his instrument would carry, both southward and northward. He also presently discovered that all these trees were bound together, near their tops, by fourteen great ropes, one above another, which ropes were continuous, from tree to tree, as far as his vision could reach. This was surprising. Chief Engineer Spider ran aloft and soon reported that these ropes were simply a web hung there by some colossal member of his own species, for he could see its prey dangling here and there from the strands, in the shape of mighty shreds and rags that had a woven look about their texture and were no doubt the discarded skins of prodigious insects which had been caught and eaten. And then he ran along one of the ropes to make a closer inspection, but felt a smart sudden burn on the soles of his feet, accompanied by a paralyzing shock, wherefore he let go and swung himself to the earth by a thread of his own spinning, and advised all to hurry at once to camp, lest the monster should appear and get as much interested in the savants as they were in him and his works. So they departed with speed, making notes about the gigantic web as they went. And that evening the naturalist of the expedition built a beautiful model of the colossal spider, having no need to see it in order to do this, because he had picked up a fragment of its vertebrae by the tree, and so knew exactly what the creature looked like and what its habits and its preferences were by this simple evidence alone. He built it with a tail, teeth, fourteen legs, and a snout, and said it ate grass, cattle, pebbles, and dirt with equal enthusiasm. This animal was regarded as a very precious addition to science. It was hoped a dead one might be found to stuff. Professor Woodlouse thought that he and his brother scholars, by lying hid and being quiet, might maybe catch a live one. He was advised to try it. Which was all the attention that was paid to his suggestion. The conference ended with the naming the monster after the naturalist, since he, after God, had created it.

"And improved it, mayhap," muttered the Tumble-Bug, who was intruding again, according to his idle custom and his unappeasable curiosity.

PART SECOND HOW THE ANIMALS OF THE WOOD COMPLETED THEIR SCIENTIFIC LABORS

A week later the expedition camped in the midst of a collection of wonderful curiosities. These were a sort of vast caverns of stone that rose singly and in bunches out of the plain by the side of the river which they had first seen when they emerged from the forest. These caverns stood in long, straight rows on opposite sides of broad aisles that were bordered with single ranks of trees. The summit of each cavern sloped sharply both ways. Several horizontal rows of great square holes, obstructed by a thin, shiny, transparent substance, pierced the frontage of each cavern. Inside were caverns within caverns; and one might ascend and visit these minor compartments by means of curious winding ways consisting of continuous regular terraces raised one above another. There were many huge, shapeless objects in each compartment which were considered to have been living creatures at one time, though now the thin brown skin was shrunken and loose, and rattled when disturbed. Spiders were here in great number, and their cobwebs, stretched in all directions and wreathing the great skinny dead together, were a pleasant spectacle, since they inspired with life and wholesome cheer a scene which would otherwise have brought to the mind only a sense of forsakenness and desolation. Information was sought of these spiders, but in vain. They were of a different nationality from those with the expedition, and their language seemed but a musical, meaningless jargon. They were a timid, gentle race, but ignorant, and heathenish worshipers of unknown gods. The expedition detailed a great detachment of missionaries to teach them the true religion, and in a week's time a precious work had been wrought among those darkened creatures, not three families being by that time at peace with each other or having a settled belief in any system of religion whatever. This encouraged the expedition to establish a colony of missionaries there permanently, that the work of grace might go on.

But let us not outrun our narrative. After close examination of the fronts of the caverns, and much thinking and exchanging of theories, the scientists determined the nature of these singular formations. They said that each belonged mainly to the Old Red Sandstone period; that the cavern fronts rose in innumerable and wonderfully regular strata high in the air, each stratum about five frog-spans thick, and that in the present discovery lay an overpowering refutation of all received geology; for between every two layers of Old Red Sandstone reposed a thin layer of decomposed limestone; so instead of there having been but one Old Red Sandstone period there had certainly been not less than a hundred and seventy-five! And by the same token it was plain that there had also been a hundred and seventy-five floodings of the earth and depositings of limestone strata. The unavoidable deduction from which pair of facts was the overwhelming truth that the world, instead of being only two hundred thousand years old, was older by millions upon millions of years! And there was another curious thing: every stratum of Old Red Sandstone was pierced and divided at mathematically regular intervals by vertical strata of limestone. Up-shootings of igneous rock through fractures in water formations were common; but here was the first instance where water-formed rock had been so projected. It was a great and noble discovery, and its value to science was considered to be inestimable.

A critical examination of some of the lower strata demonstrated the presence of fossil ants and tumble-bugs (the latter accompanied by their peculiar goods), and with high gratification the fact was enrolled upon the scientific record; for this was proof that these vulgar laborers belonged to the first and lowest orders of created beings, though at the same time there was something repulsive in the reflection that the perfect and exquisite creature of the modern uppermost order owed its origin to such ignominious beings through the mysterious law of Development of Species.

The Tumble-Bug, overhearing this discussion, said he was willing that the parvenus of these new times should find what comfort they might in their wise-drawn theories, since as far as he was concerned he was content to be of the old first families and proud to point back to his place among the old original aristocracy of the land.

"Enjoy your mushroom dignity, stinking of the varnish of yesterday's veneering, since you like it," said he; "suffice it for the Tumble-Bugs that they come of a race that rolled their fragrant spheres down the solemn aisles of antiquity and left their imperishable words embalmed in the Old Red Sandstone to proclaim it to the wasting centuries as they file along the highway of Time!"

"Oh, take a walk!" said the chief of the expedition, with derision.

The summer passed, and winter approached. In and about many of the caverns were what seemed to be inscriptions. Most of the scientists said they were inscriptions, a few said they were not. The chief philologist, Professor Woodlouse, maintained that they were writings, done in a character utterly unknown to scholars, and in a language equally unknown. He had early ordered his artists and draftsmen to make facsimiles of all that were discovered; and had set himself about finding the key to the hidden tongue. In this work he had followed the method which had always been used by decipherers previously. That is to say, he placed a number of copies of inscriptions before him and studied them both collectively and in detail. To begin with, he placed the following copies together:

THE AMERICAN HOTEL	MEALS AT ALL HOURS
THE SHADES	NO SMOKING
BOATS FOR HIRE CHEAP	UNION PRAYER MEETING, 4 P.M.
BILLIARDS	THE WATERSIDE JOURNAL
THE A1 BARBER SHOP	TELEGRAPH OFFICE
KEEP OFF THE GRASS	TRY BRANDRETH'S PILLS
COTTAGES FOR RENT DURING THE WATERING SEASON	
FOR SALE CHEAP	FOR SALE CHEAP
FOR SALE CHEAP	FOR SALE CHEAP

At first it seemed to the professor that this was a sign-language, and that each word was represented by a distinct sign; further examination convinced him that it was a written language, and that every letter of its alphabet was represented by a character of its own; and finally he decided that it was a language which conveyed itself partly by letters, and partly by signs or hieroglyphics. This conclusion was forced upon him by the discovery of several specimens of the following nature:

He observed that certain inscriptions were met with in greater frequency than others. Such as "FOR SALE CHEAP"; "BILLIARDS"; "S. T.—1860—X"; "KENO"; "ALE ON DRAUG." Naturally, then, these must be religious maxims. But this idea was cast aside by and by, as the mystery of the strange alphabet began to clear itself. In time, the professor was enabled to translate several of the inscriptions with considerable plausibility, though not to the perfect satisfaction of all the scholars. Still, he made constant and encouraging progress.

Finally a cavern was discovered with these inscriptions upon it:

WATERSIDE MUSEUM
Open all hours—Admission 50 Cents
WONDERFUL COLLECTIONS OF
WAX-WORKS, ANCIENT FOSSILS, ETC.

Professor Woodlouse affirmed that the word "Museum" was equivalent to the phrase *"lumgath molo,"* or "Burial Place." Upon entering, the scientists were well astonished. But what they saw may be best conveyed in the language of their own official report:

"Erect, in a row, were a sort of rigid great figures which struck us instantly as belonging to the long extinct species of reptile called MAN, described in our ancient records. This was a peculiarly gratifying discovery, because of late times it has become fashionable to regard this creature as a myth and a superstition, a work of the inventive imaginations of our remote ancestors. But here, indeed, was Man, perfectly preserved, in a fossil state. And this was his burial place, as already ascertained by the inscription. And now it began to be suspected that the caverns we had been inspecting had been his ancient haunts in that old time that he roamed the earth—for upon the breast of each of these tall fossils was an inscription in the character heretofore noticed. One read, 'CAPTAIN KIDD THE PIRATE'; another, 'QUEEN

VICTORIA'; another, 'ABE LINCOLN'; another, 'GEORGE WASHINGTON,' etc.

"With feverish interest we called for our ancient scientific records to discover if perchance the description of Man there set down would tally with the fossils before us. Professor Woodlouse read it aloud in its quaint and musty phraseology, to wit:

"'In ye time of our fathers Man still walked ye earth, as by tradition we know. It was a creature of exceeding great size, being compassed about with a loose skin, sometimes of one color, sometimes of many, the which it was able to cast at will; which being done, the hind legs were discovered to be armed with short claws like to a mole's but broader, and ye forelegs with fingers of a curious slimness and a length much more prodigious than a frog's, armed also with broad talons for scratching in ye earth for its food. It had a sort of feathers upon its head such as hath a rat, but longer, and a beak suitable for seeking its food by ye smell thereof. When it was stirred with happiness, it leaked water from its eyes; and when it suffered or was sad, it manifested it with a horrible hellish cackling clamor that was exceeding dreadful to hear and made one long that it might rend itself and perish, and so end its troubles. Two Mans being together, they uttered noises at each other like this: "Haw-haw-haw—dam good, dam good," together with other sounds of more or less likeness to these, wherefore ye poets conceived that they talked, but poets be always ready to catch at any frantic folly, God he knows. Sometimes this creature goeth about with a long stick ye which it putteth to its face and bloweth fire and smoke through ye same with a sudden and most damnable bruit and noise that doth fright its prey to death, and so seizeth it in its talons and walked away to its habitat, consumed with a most fierce and devlish joy.'

"Now was the description set forth by our ancestors wonderfully indorsed and confirmed by the fossils before us, as shall be seen. The specimen marked 'Captain Kidd' was examined in detail. Upon its head and part of its face was a sort of fur like that upon the tail of a horse. With great labor its loose skin was removed, whereupon its body was discovered to be of a polished white texture, thoroughly petrified. The straw it had eaten, so many ages gone by, was still in its body, undigested—and even in its legs.

"Surrounding these fossils were objects that would mean nothing to the ignorant, but to the eye of science they were a revelation. They laid bare the secrets of dead ages. These musty Memorials told us when Man lived, and what were his habits. For here, side by side with Man, were the evidences that he had lived in the earliest ages of creation, the companion of the other low orders of life that belonged to that forgotten time. Here was the fossil nautilus that sailed the primeval seas; here was the skeleton of the mastodon, the ichthyosaurus, the cave-bear, the prodigious elk. Here, also, were the charred bones of some of these extinct animals and of the young of Man's own species, split lengthwise, showing that to his taste the marrow was a toothsome luxury. It was plain that Man had robbed those bones of their contents, since no toothmark of any beast was upon them—albeit the Tumble-Bug intruded the remark that 'no beast could mark a bone with its teeth, anyway.' Here were proofs that Man had vague, groveling notions of art; for this fact was conveyed by certain things marked with the untranslatable words, 'FLINT HATCHETS, KNIVES, ARROW-HEADS, AND BONE ORNAMENTS OF PRIMEVAL MAN.' Some of these seemed to be rude weapons chipped out of flint, and in a secret place was found some more in process of construction, with this untranslatable legend, on a thin, flimsy material, lying by:

" '*Jones, if you don't want to be discharged from the Museum, make the next primeaveal weppons more careful—you couldn't even fool one of these sleapy old syentiffic grannys from the Coledge with the last ones. And mind you the animles you carved on some of the Bone Ornaments is a blame sight too good for any primeaveal man that was ever fooled.—Varnum, Manager.*'

"Back of the burial place was a mass of ashes, showing that Man always had a feast at a funeral—else why the ashes in such a place; and showing, also, that he believed in God and the immortality of the soul—else why these solemn ceremonies?

"To sum up. We believe that Man had a written language. We *know* that he indeed existed at one time, and is not a myth; also, that he was the companion of the cave-bear, the mastodon, and other extinct species; that he cooked and ate them and likewise the young of his own kind; also, that he bore rude weapons, and knew nothing of art; that he imagined he had a soul, and pleased himself with the fancy that it was immortal. But let us not laugh; there may be creatures in existence to whom we and our vanities and profundities may seem as ludicrous."

PART THIRD

Near the margin of the great river the scientists presently found a huge, shapely stone, with this inscription:

"In 1847, in the spring, the river overflowed its banks and covered the whole township. The depth was from two to six feet. More than 900 head of cattle were lost, and many homes destroyed. The Mayor ordered this memorial to be erected to perpetuate the event. God spare us the repetition of it!"

With infinite trouble, Professor Woodlouse succeeded in making a translation of this inscription, which was sent home, and straightway an enormous excitement was created about it. It confirmed, in a remarkable way, certain treasured traditions of the ancients. The translation was slightly marred by one or two untranslatable words, but these did not impair the general clearness of the meaning. It is here presented:

"One thousand eight hundred and forty-seven years ago, the (fires?) descended and consumed the whole city. Only some nine hundred souls were saved, all others destroyed. The (king?) commanded this stone to be set up to . . . (untranslatable) . . . repetition of it."

This was the first successful and satisfactory translation that had been made of the mysterious character left behind him by extinct man, and it gave Professor Woodlouse such reputation that at once every seat of learning in his native land conferred a degree of the most illustrious grade upon him, and it was believed that if he had been a soldier and had turned his splendid talents to the extermination of a remote tribe of reptiles, the king would have ennobled him and made him rich. And this, too, was the origin of that school of scientists called Manologists, whose specialty is the deciphering of the ancient records of the extinct bird termed Man. [For it is now decided that Man was a bird and not a reptile.] But Professor Woodlouse began and remained chief of these, for it was granted that no translations were ever so free from error as his. Others made mistakes—he seemed incapable of it. Many a memorial of the lost race was afterward found, but none ever attained to the renown and veneration achieved by the "Mayoritish Stone"—it being so called from the word "Mayor" in it, which, being translated "King," "Mayoritish Stone" was but another way of saying "King Stone."

Another time the expedition made a great "find." It was a vast round flattish mass, ten frog-spans in diameter and five or six high. Professor Snail put on his spectacles and examined it all around, and then climbed up and inspected the top. He said:

"The result of my perlustration and perscontation of this isoperimetrical protuberance is a belief that it is one of those rare and wonderful creations left by the Mound Builders. The fact that this one is lamel-libranchiate in its formation, simply adds to its interest as being possibly of a different kind from any we read of in the records of science, but yet in no manner marring its authenticity. Let the megalophonous grasshopper sound a blast and summon hither the perfunctory and circumforaneous Tumble-Bug, to the end that excavations may be made and learning gather new treasures."

Not a Tumble-Bug could be found on duty, so the Mound was excavated by a working party of Ants. Nothing was discovered. This would have been a great disappointment, had not the venerable Longlegs explained the matter. He said:

"It is now plain to me that the mysterious and forgotten race of Mound Builders did not always erect these edifices as mausoleums, else in this case, as in all previous cases, their skeletons would be found here, along with the rude implements which the creatures used in life. Is not this manifest?"

"True! true!" from everybody.

"Then we have made a discovery of peculiar value here; a discovery which greatly extends our knowledge of this creature in place of diminishing it; a discovery which will add luster to the achievements of this expedition and win for us the commendations of scholars everywhere. For the absence of the customary relics here means nothing less than this: The Mound Builder, instead of being the ignorant, savage reptile we have been taught to consider him, was a creature of cultivation and high intelligence, capable of not only appreciating worthy achievements of the great and noble of his species, but of commemorating them! Fellow-scholars, this stately Mound is not a sepulcher, it is a monument!"

A profound impression was produced by this.

But it was interrupted by rude and derisive laughter—and the Tumble-Bug appeared.

"A monument!" quoth he. "A monument set up by a Mound Builder! Aye, so it is! So it is, indeed, to the shrewd keen eye of science; but to an ignorant poor devil who has never seen a college, it is not a Monument, strictly speaking, but is yet a most rich and noble property; and with your worship's good permission I will proceed to manufacture it into spheres of exceedings grace and—"

The Tumble-Bug was driven away with stripes, and the draftsmen of the expedition were set to making views of the Monument from different standpoints, while Professor Woodlouse, in a frenzy of scientific zeal, traveled all over it and all around it hoping to find an inscription. But if there had ever been one, it had decayed or been removed by some vandal as a relic.

The views having been completed, it was now considered safe to load the precious Monument itself upon the backs of four of the largest Tortoises and send it home to the king's museum, which was done; and when it arrived it was received with enormous *éclat* and escorted to its future abiding-place by thousands of enthusiastic citizens, King Bullfrog XVI. himself attending and condescending to sit enthroned upon it throughout the progress.

The growing rigor of the weather was now admonishing the scientists to close their labors for the present, so they made preparations to journey homeward. But even their last day among the Caverns bore fruit; for one of the scholars found in an out-of-the-way corner of the Museum or "Burial Place" a most strange and extraordinary thing. It was nothing less than a double Man-Bird lashed together breast to breast by a natural ligament, and labeled with the untranslatable words, *"Siamese Twins."* The official report concerning this thing closed thus:

"Wherefore it appears that there were in old times two distinct species of this majestic fowl, the one being single and the other double, Nature has a reason for all things. It is plain to the eye of science that the Double-Man originally inhabited a region where dangers abounded; hence he was paired together to the end that while one part slept the other might watch; and likewise that, danger being discovered, there might always be a double instead of a single power to oppose it. All honor to the mystery-dispelling eye of god-like Science!"

And near the Double Man-Bird was found what was plainly an ancient record of his, marked upon numberless sheets of a thin white substance and bound together. Almost the first glance that Professor Woodlouse threw into it revealed this following sentence, which he instantly translated and laid before the scientists, in a tremble, and it uplifted every soul there with exultation and astonishment:

"In truth it is believed by many that the lower animals reason and talk together."

When the great official report of the expedition appeared, the above sentence bore this comment:

"Then there are lower animals than Man! This remarkable passage can mean nothing else. Man himself is extinct, but they may still exist. What can they be? Where do they inhabit? One's enthusiasm bursts all bounds in the contemplation of the brilliant field of discovery and investigation here thrown open to science. We close our labors with the humble prayer that your Majesty will immediately appoint a commission and command it to rest not nor spare expense until the search for this hitherto unsuspected race of the creatures of God shall be crowned with success."

The expedition then journeyed homeward after its long absence and its faithful endeavors, and was received with a mighty ovation by the whole grateful country. There were vulgar, ignorant carpers, of course, as there always are and always will be; and naturally one of these was the obscene Tumble-Bug. He said that all he had learned by his travels was that science only needed a spoonful of supposition to build a mountain of demonstrated fact out of; and that for the future he meant to be content with the knowledge that nature had made free to all creatures and not go prying into the august secrets of the Deity.

The Notorious Jumping Frog of Calaveras County

In compliance with the request of a friend of mine, who wrote me from the East, I called on good-natured, garrulous old Simon Wheeler, and inquired after my friend's friend, Leonidas W. Smiley, as requested to do, and I hereunto append the result. I have a lurking suspicion that *Leonidas W.* Smiley is a myth; that my friend never knew such a personage; and that he only conjectured that if I asked old Wheeler about him, it would remind him of his infamous *Jim* Smiley, and he would go to work and bore me to death with some exasperating reminiscence of him as long and as tedious as it would be useless to me. If that was the design, it succeeded.

I found Simon Wheeler dozing comfortably by the barroom stove of the dilapidated tavern in the decayed mining camp of Angel's, and I noticed that he was fat and bald headed, and had an expression of winning gentleness and simplicity upon his tranquil countenance. He roused up, and gave me good day. I told him that a friend of mine had commissioned me to make some inquiries about a cherished companion of his boyhood named *Leonidas W.* Smiley—*Rev. Leonidas W.* Smiley, a young minister of the Gospel, who he had heard was at one time a resident of Angel's Camp. I added that if Mr. Wheeler could tell me anything about this Rev. Leonidas W. Smiley, I would feel under many obligations to him.

Simon Wheeler backed me into a corner and blockaded me

there with his chair, and then sat down and reeled off the monotonous narrative which follows this paragraph. He never smiled, he never frowned, he never changed his voice from the gentle-flowing key to which he tuned his initial sentence, he never betrayed the slightest suspicion of enthusiasm; but all through the interminable narrative there ran a vein of impressive earnestness and sincerity, which showed me plainly that, so far from his imagining that there was anything ridiculous or funny about his story, he regarded it as a really important matter, and admired its two heroes as men of transcendent genius in *finesse*. I let him go on in his own way, and never interrupted him once.

"Rev. Leonidas W. H'm, Reverend Le—well, there was a feller here once by the name of *Jim* Smiley, in the winter of '49—or maybe it was the spring of '50—I don't recollect exactly, somehow, though what makes me think it was one or the other is because I remember the big flume warn't finished when he first come to the camp; but anyway, he was the curiousest man about always betting on anything that turned up you ever see, if he could get anybody to bet on the other side; and if he couldn't he'd change sides. Any way that suited the other man would suit *him*—any way just so's he got a bet, *he* was satisfied. But still he was lucky, uncommon lucky; he most always come out winner. He was always ready and laying for a chance; there couldn't be no solit'ry thing mentioned but that feller'd offer to bet on it, and take any side you please, as I was just telling you. If there was a horse-race, you'd find him flush or you'd find him busted at the end of it; if there was a dog-fight, he'd bet on it; if there was a cat-fight, he'd bet on it; if there was a chicken-fight, he'd bet on it; why, if there was two birds setting on a fence, he would bet you which one would fly first; or if there was a camp-meeting, he would be there reg'lar to bet on Parson Walker, which he judged to be the best exhorter about here, and so he was too, and a good man. If he even see a straddle-bug start to go anywheres, he would bet you how long it would take him to get to—to wherever he was going to, and if you took him up, he would foller that straddle-bug to Mexico but what he would find out where he was bound for and how long he was on the road. Lots of the boys here has seen that Smiley, and can tell you about him. Why, it never made no difference to *him*—he'd bet on *any* thing—the dangdest feller. Parson Walker's wife laid very sick once, for a good while, and it seemed as if they warn't going to save her; but one morning he come in, and Smiley up and asked him how she was, and he said she was considerable better—thank the Lord for his inf'nite mercy—and coming on so smart that with the blessing of Prov'dence she'd get well yet; and Smiley, before he thought, says, 'Well, I'll resk two-and-a-half she don't anyway.'

"Thish-yer Smiley had a mare—the boys called her the fifteen-minute nag, but that was only in fun, you know, because of course she was faster than that—and he used to win money on that horse, for all she was so slow and always had the asthma, or the distemper, or the consumption, or something of that kind. They used to give her two or three hundred yards' start, and then pass her under way; but always at the fag end of the race she'd get excited and desperate like, and come cavorting and straddling up, and scattering her legs around limber, sometimes in the air, and sometimes out to one side among the fences, and kicking up m-o-r-e dust and raising m-o-r-e racket with her coughing and sneezing and blowing her nose—and always fetch up at the stand just about a neck ahead, as near as you could cipher it down.

"And he had a little small bull-pup, that to look at him you'd think he warn't worth a cent but to set around and look ornery and lay for a chance to steal something. But as soon as money was up on him he was a different dog; his under-jaw'd begin to stick out like the fo'castle of a steamboat, and his teeth would uncover and shine like the furnaces. And a dog might tackle him and bully-rag him, and bite him, and throw him over his shoulder two or three times, and Andrew Jackson—which was the name of the pup—Andrew Jackson would never let on but what *he* was satisfied, and hadn't expected nothing else—and the bets being doubled and doubled on the other side all the time, till the money was all up; and then all of a sudden he would grab that other dog jest by the j'int of his hind leg and freeze to it—not chaw, you understand, but only just grip and hang on till they throwed up the sponge, if it was a year. Smiley always come out winner on that pup, till he harnessed a dog once that didn't have no hind legs, because they'd been sawed off in a circular saw, and when the thing had gone along far enough, and the money was all up, and he come to make a snatch for his pet holt, he see in a minute how he'd been imposed on, and how the other dog had him in the door, so to speak, and he 'peared surprised, and then he looked sorter discouraged-like, and didn't try no more to win the fight, and so he got shucked out bad. He give Smiley a look, as much as to say his heart was broke, and it was *his* fault, for putting up a dog that hadn't no hind legs for him to take holt of, which was his main dependence in a fight, and then he limped off a piece and laid down and died. It was a good pup, was that Andrew Jackson, and would have made a name for hisself if he'd lived, for the stuff was in him and he had genius—I know it, because he hadn't no opportunities to speak of, and it don't stand to reason that a dog could make such a fight as he could under them circumstances if he hadn't no talent. It always makes me feel sorry when I think of that last fight of his'n, and the way it turned out.

"Well, thish-yer Smiley had rat-tarriers, and chicken cocks, and tomcats and all them kind of things, till you couldn't rest, and you couldn't fetch nothing for him to bet on but he'd match you. He ketched a frog one day, and took him home, and said he cal'lated to educate him; and so he never done nothing for three months but set in his back yard and learn that frog to jump. And you bet you he *did* learn him, too. He'd give him a little punch behind, and the next minute you'd see that frog whirling in the air like a doughnut—see him turn one summerset, or maybe a couple, if he got a good start, and come down flat-footed and all right, like a cat. He got him up so in the matter of ketching flies, and kep' him in practice so constant, that he'd nail a fly every time as fur as he could see him. Smiley said all a frog wanted was education, and he could do 'most anything—and I believe him. Why, I've seen him set Dan'l Webster down here on this floor—Dan'l Webster was the name of the frog—and sing out, 'Flies, Dan'l, flies!' and quicker'n you could wink he'd spring straight up and snake a fly off'n the counter there, and flop down on the floor ag'in as solid as a gob of mud, and fall to scratching the side of his head with his hind foot as indifferent as if he hadn't no idea he'd been doin' any more'n any frog might do. You never see a frog so modest and straightfor'ard as he was, for all he was so gifted. And when it come to fair and square jumping on a dead level, he could get over more ground at one straddle than any animal of his breed you ever see. Jumping on a dead level was his strong suit, you understand; and when it come to that, Smiley would ante up money on him as long as he had a red. Smiley was monstrous proud of his frog, and well he might be, for fellers that had traveled and been everywheres all said he laid over any frog that ever *they* see.

"Well, Smiley kep' the beast in a little lattice box, and he used to fetch him down-town sometimes and lay for a bet. One day a feller—a stranger in the camp, he was—come acrost him with his box, and says:

" 'What might it be that you've got in the box?'

"And Smiley says, sorter indifferent-like, 'It might be a parrot, or it might be a canary, maybe, but it ain't—it's only just a frog.'

"And the feller took it, and looked at it careful, and turned it round this way and that, and says, 'H'm—so 'tis. Well, what's *he* good for?'

" 'Well,' Smiley says, easy and careless, 'he's good enough for *one* thing, I should judge—he can outjump any frog in Calaveras County.'

"The feller took the box again, and took another long, particular look, and give it back to Smiley, and says, very deliberate, 'Well,' he says, 'I don't see no p'ints about that frog that's any better'n any other frog.'

" 'Maybe you don't,' Smiley says. 'Maybe you understand frogs and maybe you don't understand 'em; maybe you've had experience, and maybe you ain't only a amature, as it were. Anyways, I've got *my* opinion, and I'll resk forty dollars that he can outjump any frog in Calaveras County.'

"And the feller studied a minute, and then says, kinder sad-like, 'Well, I'm only a stranger here, and I ain't got no frog; but if I had a frog, I'd bet you.'

"And then Smiley says, 'That's all right—that's all right—if you'll hold my box a minute, I'll go and get you a frog.' And so the feller took the box, and put up his forty dollars along with Smiley's, and set down to wait.

"So he set there a good while thinking and thinking to himself, and then he got the frog out and prized his mouth open and took a teaspoon and filled him full of quail-shot—filled him pretty near up to his chin—and set him on the floor. Smiley he went to the swamp and slopped around in the mud for a long time, and finally he ketched a frog, and fetched him in, and give him to this feller, and says:

" 'Now, if you're ready, set him alongside of Dan'l, with his fore paws just even with Dan'l's, and I'll give the word.' Then he says, 'One—two—three—*git!*' and him and the feller touched up the frogs from behind, and the new frog hopped off lively, but Dan'l give a heave, and hysted up his shoulders—so—like a Frenchman, but it warn't no use—he couldn't budge; he was planted as solid as a church, and he couldn't no more stir than if he was anchored out. Smiley was a good deal surprised, and he was disgusted too, but he didn't have no idea what the matter was, of course.

"The feller took the money and started away; and when he was going out at the door, he sorter jerked his thumb over his shoulder—so—at Dan'l, and says again, very deliberate, 'Well,' he says, 'I don't see no p'ints about that frog that's any better'n any other frog.'

"Smiley he stood scratching his head and looking down at Dan'l a long time, and at last he says, 'I do wonder what in the nation that frog throw'd off for—I wonder if there ain't something the matter with him—he 'pears to look mighty baggy, somehow.' And he ketched Dan'l by the nap of the neck, and hefted him, and says, 'Why blame my cats if he don't weigh five pound!' and turned him upside down and he belched out a double handful of shot. And then he see how it was, and he was the maddest man—he set the frog down and took out after the feller, but he never ketched him. And—"

[Here Simon Wheeler heard his name called from the front yard, and got up to see what was wanted.] And turning to me as he moved away, he said: "Just set where you are, stranger, and rest easy—I ain't going to be gone a second."

But, by your leave, I did not think that a continuation of the history of the enterprising vagabond *Jim* Smiley would be likely to afford me much information concerning the Rev. *Leonidas W.* Smiley, and so I started away.

At the door I met the sociable Wheeler returning, and he buttonholed me and recommenced:

"Well, thish-yer Smiley had a yaller one-eyed cow that didn't have no tail, only just a short stump like a bannanner, and—"

However, lacking both time and inclination, I did not wait to hear about the afflicted cow, but took my leave.

The Diary of Adam and Eve

PART I—EXTRACTS FROM ADAM'S DIARY

Monday This new creature with the long hair is a good deal in the way. It is always hanging around and following me about. I don't like this; I am not used to company. I wish it would stay with the other animals . . . . Cloudy today, wind in the east; think we shall have rain . . . . *We?* Where did I get that word?—I remember now—the new creature uses it.

Tuesday Been examining the great waterfall. It is the finest thing on the estate, I think. The new creature calls it Niagara Falls—why, I am sure I do not know. Says it *looks* like Niagara Falls. That is not a reason, it is mere waywardness and imbecility. I get no chance to name anything myself. The new creature names everything that comes along, before I can get in a protest. And always that same pretext is offered—it *looks* like the thing. There is the dodo, for instance. Says the moment one looks at it one sees at a glance that it "looks like a dodo." It will have to keep that name, no doubt. It wearies me to fret about it, and it does no good, anyway. Dodo! It looks no more like a dodo than I do.

Wednesday Built me a shelter against the rain, but could not have it to myself in peace. The new creature intruded. When I tried to put it out it shed water out of the holes it looks with, and wiped it away with the back of its paws, and made a noise such as some of the other animals make when they are in distress. I wish it would not talk; it is always talking. That sounds like a cheap fling at the poor creature, a slur; but I do not mean it so. I have never heard the human voice before, and any new and strange sound intruding itself here upon the solemn hush of these dreaming solitudes offends my ear and seems a false note. And this new sound is so close to me; it is right at my shoulder, right at my ear, first on one side and then on the other, and I am used only to sounds that are more or less distant from me.

Friday The naming goes recklessly on, in spite of anything I can do. I had a very good name for the estate, and it was musical and pretty—Garden of Eden. Privately, I continue to call it that, but not any longer publicly. The new creatures says it is all woods and rocks and scenery, and therefore has no resemblance to a garden. Says it *looks* like a park, and does not look like anything *but* a park. Consequently, without consulting me, it has been new-named—NIAGARA FALLS PARK. This is sufficiently high-handed, it seems to me. And already there is a sign up:

KEEP OFF
THE GRASS

My life is not as happy as it was.

Saturday The new creature eats too much fruit. We are going to run short, most likely. "We" again—that is *its* word; mine, too, now, from hearing it so much. Good deal of fog this morning. I do not go out in the fog myself. The new creature does. It goes out in all weathers, and stumps right in with its muddy feet. And talks. It used to be so pleasant and quiet here.

Sunday Pulled through. This day is getting to be more and more trying. It was selected and set apart last November as a day of rest. I had already six of them per week before. This morning found the new creature trying to clod apples out of that forbidden tree.

Monday The new creature says its name is Eve. That is all right, I have no objections. Says it is to call it by, when I want it to come. I said it was superfluous, then. The word evidently raised me in its respect; and indeed it is a large, good word and will bear repetition. It says it is not an It, it is a She. This is probably doubtful; yet it is all one to me; what she is were nothing to me if she would but go by herself and not talk.

Tuesday She has littered the whole estate with execrable names and offensive signs:

THIS WAY TO THE WHIRLPOOL
THIS WAY TO GOAT ISLAND
CAVE OF THE WINDS THIS WAY

She says this park would make a tidy summer resort if there was any custom for it. Summer resort—another invention of hers—just words, without any meaning. What is a summer resort? But it is best not to ask her, she has such a rage for explaining.

Friday She has taken to beseeching me to stop going over the Falls. What harm does it do? Says it makes her shudder. I wonder why; I have always done it—always liked the plunge, and coolness. I supposed it was what the Falls were for. They have no other use that I can see, and they must have been made for something. She says they were only made for scenery—like the rhinoceros and the mastodon.

I went over the Falls in a barrel—not satisfactory to her. Went over in a tub—still not satisfactory. Swam the Whirlpool and the Rapids in a fig-leaf suit. It got much damaged. Hence, tedious complaints about my extravagance. I am too much hampered here. What I need is change of scene.

Saturday I escaped last Tuesday night, and traveled two days, and built me another shelter in a secluded place, and obliterated my tracks as well as I could, but she hunted me out by means of a beast which she has tamed and calls a wolf, and came making that pitiful noise again, and shedding that water out of the places she looks with. I was obliged to return with her, but will presently emigrate again when occasion offers. She engages herself in many foolish things; among others, to study out why the animals called lions and tigers live on grass and flowers, when, as she says, the sort of teeth they wear would indicate that they were intended to eat each other. This is foolish, because to do that would be to kill each other, and that would introduce what, as I understand it, is called "death"; and death, as I have been told, has not yet entered the Park. Which is a pity, on some accounts.

Sunday Pulled through.

Monday I believe I see what the week is for: it is to give time to rest up from the weariness of Sunday. It seems a good idea. . . . She has been climbing that tree again. Clodded her out of it. She said nobody was looking. Seems to consider that a sufficient justification for chancing any dangerous thing. Told her that. The word justification moved her admiration—and envy, too, I thought. It is a good word.

Tuesday She told me she was made out of a rib taken from my body. This is at least doubtful, if not more than that. I have not missed any rib. . . . She is in much trouble about the buzzard; says grass does not agree with it; is afraid she can't raise it; thinks it was intended to live on decayed flesh. The buzzard must get along the best it can with what it is provided. We cannot overturn the whole scheme to accommodate the buzzard.

Saturday She fell in the pond yesterday when she was looking at herself in it, which she is always doing. She nearly strangled, and said it was most uncomfortable. This made her sorry for the creatures which live in there, which she calls fish, for she continues to fasten names on to things that don't need them and don't come when they are called by them, which is a matter of no consequence to her, she is such a numskull, anyway; so she got a lot of them out and brought them in last night and put them in my bed to keep warm, but I have noticed them now and then all day and I don't see that they are any happier there than they were before, only quieter. When night comes I shall throw them outdoors. I will not sleep with them again, for I find them clammy and unpleasant to lie among when a person hasn't anything on.

Sunday Pulled through.

Tuesday She has taken up with a snake now. The other animals are glad, for she was always experimenting with them and bothering them; and I am glad because the snake talks, and this enables me to get a rest.

Friday She says the snake advises her to try the fruit of that tree, and says the result will be a great and fine and noble education. I told her there would be another result, too—it would introduce death into the world. That was a mistake—it had been better to keep the remark to myself; it only gave her an idea—she could save the sick buzzard, and furnish fresh meat to the despondent lions and tigers. I advised her to keep away from the tree. She said she wouldn't. I forsee trouble. Will emigrate.

Wednesday I have had a variegated time. I escaped last night, and rode a horse all night as fast as he could go, hoping to get clear out of the Park and hide in some other country before the trouble should begin; but it was not to be. About an hour after sun-up, as I was riding through a flowery plain where thousands of animals were grazing, slumbering, or playing with each other, according to their wont, all of a sudden they broke into a tempest of frightful noises, and in one moment the plain was a frantic commotion and every beast was destroying its neighbor. I knew what it meant—Eve had eaten that fruit, and death was come into the world. . . . The tigers ate my horse, paying no attention when I ordered them to desist, and they would have eaten me if I had stayed—which I didn't, but went away in much haste . . . . I found this place, outside the Park, and was fairly comfortable for a few days, but she has found me out. Found me out, and has named the place Tonawanda—says it *looks* like that. In fact I was not sorry she came, for there are but meager pickings here, and she brought some of those apples. I was obliged to eat them, I was so hungry. It was against my principles, but I find that principles have no real force except when one is well fed . . . . She came curtained in boughs and bunches of leaves, and when I asked her what she meant by such nonsense, and snatched them away and threw them down, she tittered and blushed. I had never seen a person titter and blush before, and to me it seemed unbecoming and idiotic. She said I would soon know how it was myself. This was correct. Hungry as I was, I laid down the apple half-eaten—certainly the best one I ever saw, considering the lateness of the season—and arrayed the discarded boughs and branches, and then spoke to her with some severity and ordered her to go and get some more and not make such a spectacle of herself. She did it, and after this we crept down to where the wild-beast battle had been, and collected some skins, and I made her patch together a couple of suits proper for public occasions. They are uncomfortable, it is true, but stylish, and that is the main point about clothes . . . . I find she is a good deal of a companion. I see I should be lonesome and depressed without her, now that I have lost my property. Another thing, she says it is ordered that we work for our living hereafter. She will be useful. I will superintend.

Ten Days Later She accuses *me* of being the cause of our disaster! She says, with apparent sincerity and truth, that the Serpent assured her that the forbidden fruit was not apples, it was chestnuts. I said I was innocent, then, for I had not eaten any chestnuts. She said the Serpent informed her that "chestnut" was a figurative term meaning an aged and moldy joke. I turned pale at that, for I have made many jokes to pass the weary time, and some of them could have been of that sort, though I had honestly supposed that they were new when I made them. She asked me if I had made one just at the time of the catastrophe. I was obliged to admit that I had made one to myself, though not aloud. It was this. I was thinking about the Falls, and I said to myself, "How wonderful it is to see that vast body of water tumble down there!" Then in an instant a bright thought flashed into my head, and I let it fly, saying, "It would be a deal more wonderful to see it tumble *up* there!"—and I was just about to kill myself with laughing at it when all nature broke loose in war and death and I had to flee for my life. "There," she said, with triumph, "that is just it; the Serpent mentioned that very jest, and called it the First Chestnut, and said it was coeval with the creation." Alas, I am indeed to blame. Would that I were not witty; oh, that I had never had that radiant thought!

Next Year We have named it Cain. She caught it while I was up country trapping on the North Shore of the Erie; caught it in the timber a couple of miles from our dug-out—or it might have been four, she isn't certain which. It resembles us in some ways, and may be a relation. That is what she thinks, but this is an error, in my judgment. The difference in size warrants the conclusion that it is a different and new kind of animal—a fish, perhaps, though when I put it in the water to see, it sank, and she plunged in and snatched it out before there was opportunity for the experiment to determine the matter. I still think it is a fish, but she is indifferent about what it is, and will not let me have it to try. I do not understand this. The coming of the creature seems to have changed her whole nature and made her unreasonable about experiments. She thinks more of it than she does of any of the other animals, but is not able to explain why. Her mind is disordered—everything shows it. Sometimes she carries the fish in her arms half the night when it complains and wants to get to the water. At such times the water comes out of the places in her face that she looks out of, and she pats the fish on the back and makes soft sounds with her mouth to soothe it, and betrays sorrow and solicitude in a hundred ways. I have never seen her do like this with any other fish, and it troubles me greatly. She used to carry the young tigers around so, and play with them, before we lost our property, but it was only play; she never took on about them like this when their dinner disagreed with them.

Sunday She doesn't work, Sundays, but lies around all tired out, and likes to have the fish wallow over her; and she makes fool noises to amuse it, and pretends to chew its paws, and that makes it laugh. I have not seen a fish before that could laugh. This makes me doubt. . . . I have come to like Sunday myself. Superintending all the week tires a body so. There ought to be more Sundays. In the old days they were tough, but now they come handy.

Wednesday It isn't a fish. I cannot quite make out what it is. It makes curious devilish noises when not satisfied, and says "goo-goo" when it is. It is not one of us, for it doesn't walk; it is not a bird, for it doesn't fly; it is not a frog, for it doesn't hop; it is not a snake, for it doesn't crawl, I feel sure it is not a fish, though I cannot get a chance to find out whether it can swim or not. It merely lies around, and mostly on its back, with its feet up. I have not seen any other animal do that before. I said I believed it was an enigma; but she only admired the word without understanding it. In my judgment it is either an enigma or some kind of a bug. If it dies, I will take it apart and see what its arrangements are. I never had a thing perplex me so.

Three Months Later The perplexity augments instead of diminishing. I sleep but little. It has ceased from lying around, and goes about on its four legs now. Yet it differs from the other four-legged animals, in that its front legs are unusually short, consequently this causes the main part of its person to stick up uncomfortably high in the air, and this is not attractive. It is built much as we are, but its method of traveling shows that it is not of our breed. The short front legs and long hind ones indicate that it is of the kangaroo family, but it is a marked variation of the species, since the true kangaroo hops, whereas this one never does. Still it is a curious and interesting variety, and has not been catalogued before. As I discovered it, I have felt justified in securing the credit of the discovery by attaching my name to it, and hence have called it *Kangaroorum Adamiensis*. . . . It must have been a young one when it came, for it has grown exceedingly since. It must be five times as big, now, as it was then, and when discontented it is able to make from twenty-two to thirty-eight times the noise it made at first. Coercion does not modify this, but has the contrary effect. For this reason I discontinued the system. She reconciles it by persuasion, and by giving it things which she had previously told me she wouldn't give it. As already observed, I was not at home when it first came, and she told me she found it in the woods. It seems odd that it should be the only one, yet it must be so, for I have worn myself out these many weeks trying to find another one to add to my collection, and for this one to play with; for surely then it would be quieter and we could tame it more easily. But I find none, nor any vestige of any; and strangest of all, no tracks. It has to live on the ground, it cannot help itself; therefore, how does it get about without leaving a track? I have set a dozen traps, but they do no good. I catch all small animals except that one; animals that merely go into the trap out of curiosity, I think, to see what the milk is there for. They never drink it.

Three Months Later The Kangaroo still continues to grow, which is very strange and perplexing. I never knew one to be so long getting its growth. It has fur on its head now; not like kangaroo fur, but exactly like our hair except that it is much finer and softer, and instead of being black is red. I am like to lose my mind over the capricious and harassing developments of this unclassifiable zoological freak. If I could catch another one—but that is hopeless; it is a new variety, and the only sample; this is plain. But I caught a true kangaroo and brought it in, thinking that this one, being lonesome, would rather have that for company than have no kin at all, or any animal it could feel a nearness to or get sympathy from in its forlorn condition here among strangers who do not know its ways or habits, or what to do to make it feel that it is among friends; but it was a mistake—it went into such fits at the sight of the kangaroo that I was convinced it had never seen one before. I pity the poor noisy little animal, but there is nothing I can do to make it happy. If I could tame it—but that is out of the question; the more I try the worse I seem to make it. It grieves me to the heart to see it in its little storms of sorrow and passion. I wanted to let it go, but she wouldn't hear of it. That seemed cruel and not like her; and yet she may be right. It might be lonelier than ever; for since I cannot find another one, how could *it?*

Five Months Later It is not a kangaroo. No, for it supports itself by holding to her finger, and thus goes a few steps on its hind legs, and then falls down. It is probably some kind of a bear; and yet it has no tail—as yet—and no fur, except on its head. It still keeps on growing—that is a curious circumstance, for bears get their growth earlier than this. Bears are dangerous—since our catastrophe—and I shall not be satisfied to have this one prowling about the place much longer without a muzzle on. I have offered to get her a kangaroo if she would let this one go, but it did no good—she is determined to run us into all sorts of foolish risks, I think. She was not like this before she lost her mind.

A Fortnight Later I examined its mouth. There is no danger yet: it has only one tooth. It has no tail yet. It makes more noise now than it ever did before—and mainly at night. I have moved out. But I shall go over, mornings, to breakfast, and see if it has more teeth. If it gets a mouthful of teeth it will be time for it to go, tail or no tail, for a bear does not need a tail in order to be dangerous.

Four Months Later I have been off hunting and fishing a month, up in the region that she calls Buffalo; I don't know why, unless it is because there are not any buffaloes there. Meantime the bear has learned to paddle around all by itself on its hind legs, and says "poppa" and "momma." It is certainly a new species. This resemblance to words may be purely accidental, of course, and may have no purpose or meaning; but even in that case it is still extraordinary, and is a thing which no other bear can do. This imitation of speech, taken together with general absence of fur and entire absence of tail, sufficiently indicates that this is a new kind of bear. The further study of it will be exceedingly interesting. Meantime I will go off on a far expedition among the forests of the north and make an exhaustive search. There must certainly be another one somewhere, and this one will be less dangerous when it has company of its own species. I will go straightway; but I will muzzle this one first.

Three Months Later It has been a weary, weary hunt, yet I have had no success. In the mean time, without stirring from the home estate, she has caught another one! I never saw such luck. I might have hunted these woods a hundred years, I never would have run across that thing.

Next Day I have been comparing the new one with the old one, and it is perfectly plain that they are the same breed. I was going to stuff one of them for my collection, but she is prejudiced against it for some reason or other; so I have relinquished the idea, though I think it is a mistake. It would be an irreparable loss to science if they should get away. The old one is tamer than it was and can laugh and talk like the parrot, having learned this, no doubt, from being with the parrot so much, and having the imitative faculty in a highly developed degree. I shall be astonished if it turns out to be a new kind parrot; and yet I ought not to be astonished, for it has already been everything else it could think of since those first days when it was a fish. The new one is as ugly now as the old one was at first; has the same sulphur-and-raw-meat complexion and the same singular head without any fur on it. She calls it Abel.

Ten Years Later They are *boys;* we found it out long ago. It was their coming in that small, immature shape that puzzled us; we were not used to it. There are some girls now. Abel is a good boy, but if Cain had stayed a bear it would have improved him. After all these years, I see that I was mistaken about Eve in the beginning; it is better to live outside the Garden with her than inside it without her. At first I thought she talked too much; but now I should be sorry to have that voice fall silent and pass out of my life. Blessed be the chestnut that brought us near together and taught me to know the goodness of her heart and the sweetness of her spirit!

PART II—EVE'S DIARY

(Translated from the original)

Saturday I am almost a whole day old, now. I arrived yesterday. That is as it seems to me. And it must be so, for if there was a day-before-yesterday I was not there when it happened, or I should remember it. It could be, of course, that it did happen, and that I was not noticing. Very well; I will be very watchful now, and if any day-before-yesterdays happen I will make a note of it. It will be best to start right and not let the record get confused, for some instinct tells me that these details are going to be important to the historian some day. For I feel like an experiment, I feel exactly like an experiment; it would be impossible for a person to feel more like an experiment than I do, and so I am coming to feel convinced that this is what I *am*—an experiment; just an experiment, and nothing more.

Then if I am an experiment, am I the whole of it? No, I think not; I think the rest of it is part of it. I am the main part of it, but I think the rest of it has its share in the matter. Is my position assured, or do I have to watch it and take care of it? The latter, perhaps. Some instinct tells me that eternal vigilance is the price of supremacy. [That is a good phrase, I think, for one so young.]

Everything looks better to-day than it did yesterday. In the rush of finishing up yesterday, the mountains were left in a ragged condition, and some of the plains were so cluttered with rubbish and remnants that the aspects were quite distressing. Noble and beautiful works of art should not be subjected to haste; and this majestic new world is indeed a most noble and beautiful work. And certainly marvelously near to being perfect, notwithstanding the shortness of the time. There are too many stars in some places and not enough in others, but that can be remedied presently, no doubt. The moon got loose last night, and slid down and fell out of the scheme—a very great loss; it breaks my heart to think of it. There isn't another thing among the ornaments and decorations that is comparable to it for beauty and finish. It should have been fastened better. If we can only get it back again—

But of course there is no telling where it went to. And besides, whoever gets it will hide it; I know it because I would do it myself. I believe I can be honest in all other matters, but I already begin to realize that the core and center of my nature is love of the beautiful, a passion for the beautiful, and that it would not be safe to trust me with a moon that belonged to another person and that person didn't know I had it. I could give up a moon that I found in the daytime, because I should be afraid some one was looking; but if I found it in the dark, I am sure I should find some kind of an excuse for not saying anything about it. For I do love moons, they are so pretty and so romantic. I wish we had five or six; I would never go to bed; I should never get tired lying on the moss-bank and looking up at them.

Stars are good, too. I wish I could get some to put in my hair. But I suppose I never can. You would be surprised to find how far off they are, for they do not look it. When they first showed, last night, I tried to knock some down with a pole, but it didn't reach, which astonished me; then I tried clods till I was all tired out, but I never got one. It was because I am left-handed and cannot throw good. Even when I aimed at the one I wasn't after I couldn't hit the other one, though I did make some close shots, for I saw the black blot of the clod sail right into the midst of the golden clusters forty or fifty times, just barely missing them, and if I could have held out a little longer maybe I could have got one.

So I cried a little, which was natural, I suppose, for one of my age, and after I was rested I got a basket and started for a place on the extreme rim of the circle, where the stars were close to the ground and I could get them with my hands, which would be better, anyway, because I could gather them tenderly then, and not break them. But it was farther than I thought, and at last I had to give it up; I was so tired I couldn't drag my feet another step; and besides, they were sore and hurt me very much.

I couldn't get back home; it was too far and turning cold; but I found some tigers and nestled in among them and was most adorably comfortable, and their breath was sweet and pleasant, because they live on strawberries. I had never seen a tiger before, but I knew them in a minute by the stripes. If I could have one of those skins, it would make a lovely gown.

To-day I am getting better ideas about distances. I was so eager to get hold of every pretty thing that I giddily grabbed for it, sometimes when it was too far off, and sometimes when it was but six inches away but seemed a foot—alas, with thorns between! I learned a lesson, also I made an axiom, all out of my own head—my very first one: *The scratched Experiment shuns the thorn.* I think it is a very good one for one so young.

I followed the other Experiment around, yesterday afternoon, at a distance, to see what it might be for, if I could. But I was not able to make out. I think it is a man. I had never seen a man, but it looked like one, and I feel sure that that is what it is. I realize that I feel more curiosity about it than about any of the other reptiles. If it is a reptile, and I suppose it is; for it has frowsy hair and blue eyes, and looks like a reptile. It has no hips; it tapers like a carrot; when it stands, it spreads itself apart like a derrick; so I think it is a reptile, though it may be architecture.

I was afraid of it at first, and started to run every time it turned around, for I thought it was going to chase me; but by and by I found it was only trying to get away, so after that I was not timid any more, but tracked it along, several hours, about twenty yards behind, which made it nervous and unhappy. At last it was a good deal worried, and climbed a tree. I waited a good while, then gave it up and went home.

To-day the same thing over. I've got it up the tree again.

Sunday It is up there yet. Resting, apparently. But that is a subterfuge; Sunday isn't the day of rest; Saturday is appointed for that. It looks to me like a creature that is more interested in resting than in anything else. It would tire me to rest so much. It tires me just to sit around and watch the tree. I do wonder what it is for; I never see it do anything.

They returned the moon last night, and I was *so* happy! I think it is very honest of them. It slid down and fell off again, but I was not distressed; there is no need to worry when one has that kind of neighbors; they will fetch it back. I wish I could do something to show my appreciation. I would like to send them some stars, for we have more than we can use. I mean I, not we, for I can see that the reptile cares nothing for such things.

It has low tastes, and is not kind. When I went there yesterday evening in the gloaming it had crept down and was trying to catch the little speckled fishes that play in the pool, and I had to clod it to make it go up the tree again and let them alone. I wonder if *that* is what it is for? Hasn't it any heart? Hasn't it any compassion for those little creatures? Can it be that it was designed and manufactured for such ungentle work? It has the look of it. One of the clods took it back of the ear, and it used language. It gave me a thrill, for it was the first time I had ever heard speech, except my own. I did not understand the words, but they seemed expressive.

When I found it could talk I felt a new interest in it, for I love to talk; I talk, all day, and in my sleep, too, and I am very interesting, but if I had another to talk to I could be twice as interesting, and would never stop, if desired.

If this reptile is a man, it isn't an *it,* is it? That wouldn't be grammatical, would it? I think it would be *he*. I think so. In that case one would parse it thus: nominative, *he;* dative, *him;* possessive, *his'n*. Well, I will consider it a man and call it he until it turns out to be something else. This will be handier than having so many uncertainties.

Next week Sunday All the week I tagged around after him and tried to get acquainted. I had to do the talking, because he was shy, but I didn't mind it. He seemed pleased to have me around, and I used the sociable "we" a good deal, because it seemed to flatter him to be included.

Wednesday We are getting along very well indeed, now, and getting better and better acquainted. He does not try to avoid me any more, which is a good sign, and shows that he likes to have me with him. That pleases me, and I study to be useful to him in every way I can, so as to increase his regard. During the last day or two I have taken all the work of naming things off his hands, and this has been a great relief to him, for he has not gift in that line, and is evidently very grateful. He can't think of a rational name to save him, but I do not let him see that I am aware of his defect. Whenever a new creature comes along I name it before he has time to expose himself by an awkward silence. In this way I have saved him many embarrassments. I have no defect like his. The minute I set eyes on an animal I know what it is. I don't have to reflect a moment; the right name comes out instantly, just as if it were an inspiration, as no doubt is, for I am sure it wasn't in me half a minute before. I seem to know just by the shape of the creature and the way it acts what animal it is.

When the dodo came along he thought it was a wildcat—I saw it in his eye. But I saved him. And I was careful not to do it in a way that could hurt his pride. I just spoke up in a quite natural way of pleased surprise, and not as if I was dreaming of conveying information, and said, "Well, I do declare, if there isn't the dodo!" I explained—without seeming to be explaining—how I knew it for a dodo, and although I thought maybe he was a little piqued that I knew the creature when he didn't, it was quite evident that he admired me. That was very agreeable, and I thought of it more than once with gratification before I slept. How little a thing can make us happy when we feel that we have earned it!

Thursday My first sorrow. Yesterday he avoided me and seemed to wish I would not talk to him. I could not believe it, and thought there was some mistake, for I loved to be with him, and loved to hear him talk, and so how could it be that he could feel unkind toward me when I had not done anything? But at last it seemed true, so I went away and sat lonely in the place where I first saw him the morning that we were made and I did not know what he was and was indifferent about him; but now it was a mournful place, and every little thing spoke of him, and my heart was very sore. I did not know why very clearly, for it was a new feeling; I had not experienced it before, and it was all a mystery, and I could not make it out.

But when night came I could not bear the lonesomeness, and went to the new shelter which he has built, to ask him what I had done that was wrong and how I could mend it and get back his kindness again; but he put me out in the rain, and it was my first sorrow.

Sunday It is pleasant again, now, and I am happy; but those were heavy days; I do not think of them when I can help it.

I tried to get him some of those apples, but I cannot learn to throw straight. I failed, but I think the good intention pleased him. They are forbidden, and he says I shall come to harm; but so I come to harm through pleasing him, why shall I care for that harm?

Monday This morning I told him my name, hoping it would interest him. But he did not care for it. It is strange. If he should tell me his name, I would care. I think it would be pleasanter in my ears than any other sound.

He talks very little. Perhaps it is because he is not bright, and is sensitive about it and wishes to conceal it. It is such a pity that he should feel so, for brightness is nothing; it is in the heart that the values lie. I wish I could make him understand that a loving good heart is riches, and riches enough, and that without it intellect is poverty.

Although he talks so little, he has quite a considerable vocabulary. This morning he used a surprisingly good word. He evidently recognized, himself, that it was a good one, for he worked it in twice afterward, casually. It was not good casual art, still it showed that he possesses a certain quality of perception. Without a doubt that seed can be made to grow, if cultivated.

Where did he get that word? I do not think I have ever used it.

No, he took no interest in my name. I tried to hide my disappointment, but I suppose I did not succeed. I went away and sat on the moss-bank with my feet in the water. It is where I go when I hunger for companionship, some one to look at, some one to talk to. It is not enough—that lovely white body painted there in the pool—but it is something, and something is better than utter loneliness. It talks when I talk; it is sad when I am sad; it comforts me with its sympathy; it says, "Do not be downhearted, you poor friendless girl; I will be your friend." It *is* a good friend to me, and my only one; it is my sister.

That first time that she forsook me! ah, I shall never forget that—never, never. My heart was lead in my body! I said, "She was all I had, and now she is gone!" In my despair I said, "Break, my heart; I cannot bear my life any more!" and hid my face in my hands, and there was no solace for me. And when I took them away, after a little, there she was again, white and shining and beautiful, and I sprang into her arms!

That was perfect happiness; I had known happiness before, but it was not like this, which was ecstasy. I never doubted her afterward. Sometimes she stayed away—maybe an hour, maybe almost the whole day, but I waited and did not doubt; I said, "She is busy, or she is gone a journey, but she will come." And it was so: she always did. At night she would not come if it was dark, for she was a timid little thing; but if there was a moon she would come. I am not afraid of the dark, but she is younger than I am; she was born after I was. Many and many are the visits I have paid her; she is my comfort and my refuge when my life is hard—and it is mainly that.

Tuesday All the morning I was at work improving the estate; and I purposely kept away from him in the hope that he would get lonely and come. But he did not.

At noon I stopped for the day and took my recreation by flitting all about with the bees and the butterflies and reveling in the flowers, those beautiful creatures that catch the smile of God out of the sky and preserve it! I gathered them, and made them into wreaths and garlands and clothed myself in them while I ate my luncheon—apples, of course; then I sat in the shade and wished and waited. But he did not come.

But no matter. Nothing would have come of it, for he does not care for flowers. He calls them rubbish, and cannot tell one from another, and thinks it is superior to feel like that. He does not care for me, he does not care for flowers, he does not care for the painted sky at eventide—is there anything he does care for, except building shacks to coop himself up in from the good clean rain, and thumping the melons, and sampling the grapes, and fingering the fruit on the trees, to see how those properties are coming along?

I laid a dry stick on the ground and tried to bore a hole in it with another one, in order to carry out a scheme that I had, and soon I got an awful fright. A thin, transparent bluish film rose out of the hole, and I dropped everything and ran! I thought it was a spirit, and I *was* so frightened! But I looked back, and it was not coming; so I leaned against a rock and rested and panted, and let my limbs go on trembling until they got steady again; then I crept warily back, alert, watching, and ready to fly if there was occasion; and when I was come near, I parted the branches of a rose-bush and peeped through—wishing the man was about, I was looking so cunning and pretty—but the sprite was gone. I went there, and there was a pinch of delicate pink dust in the hole. I put my finger in, to feel it, and said *ouch!* and took it out again. It was a cruel pain. I put my finger in my mouth; and by standing first on one foot and then the other, and grunting, I presently eased my misery; then I was full of interest, and began to examine.

I was curious to know what the pink dust was. Suddenly the name of it occurred to me, though I had never heard of it before. It was *fire!* I was as certain of it as a person could be of anything in the world. So without hesitation I named it that—fire.

I had created something that didn't exist before; I had added a new thing to the world's uncountable properties; I realized this, and was proud of my achievement, and was going to run and find him and tell him about it, thinking to raise myself in his esteem—but I reflected, and did not do it. No—he would not care for it. He would ask what it was good for, and what could I answer? for if it was not *good* for something, but only beautiful, merely beautiful—

So I sighed, and did not go. For it wasn't good for anything; it could not build a shack, it could not improve melons, it could not hurry a fruit crop; it was useless, it was a foolishness and a vanity; he would despise it and say cutting words. But to me it was not despicable; I said, "Oh, you fire, I love you, you dainty pink creature, for you are *beautiful*—and that is enough!" and was going to gather it to my breast. But refrained. Then I made another maxim out of my own head, though it was so nearly like the first one that I was afraid it was only a plagiarism: *"The burnt Experiment shuns the fire."*

I wrought again; and when I had made a good deal of fire-dust I emptied it into a handful of dry brown grass, intending to carry it home and keep it always and play with it; but the wind struck it and it sprayed up and spat out at me fiercely, and I dropped it and ran. When I looked back the blue spirit was towering up and stretching and rolling away like a cloud, and instantly I thought of the name of it—*smoke!*—though, upon my word, I had never heard of smoke before.

Soon, brilliant yellow and red flares shot up through the smoke, and I named them in an instant—*flames*—and I was right, too, though these were the very first flames that had ever been in the world. They climbed the trees, they flashed splendidly in and out of the vast and interesting volume of tumbling smoke, and I had to clap my hands and laugh and dance in my rapture, it was so new and strange and so wonderful and so beautiful!

He came running, and stopped and gazed, and said not a word for many minutes. Then he asked what it was. Ah, it was too bad that he should ask such a direct question. I had to answer it, of course, and I did. I said it was fire. If it annoyed him that I should know and he must ask, that was not my fault; I had no desire to annoy him. After a pause he asked:

"How did it come?"

Another direct question, and it also had to have a direct answer.

"I made it."

The fire was traveling farther and farther off. He went to the edge of the burned place and stood looking down, and said:

"What are these?"

"Fire-coals."

He picked up one to examine it, but changed his mind and put it down again. Then he went away. *Nothing* interests him.

But I was interested. There were ashes, gray and soft and delicate and pretty—I knew what they were at once. And the embers; I knew the embers, too. I found my apples, and raked them out, and was glad; for I am very young and my appetite is active. But I was disappointed; they were all burst open and spoiled. Spoiled apparently; but it was not so; they were better than raw ones. Fire is beautiful; some day it will be useful, I think.

Friday I saw him again, for a moment, last Monday at nightfall, but only for a moment. I was hoping he would praise me for trying to improve the estate, for I had meant well and had worked hard. But he was not pleased, and turned away and left me. He was also displeased on another account: I tried once more to persuade him to stop going over the Falls. That was because the fire had revealed to me a new passion—quite new, and distinctly different from love, grief, and those others which I had already discovered—*fear.* And it is horrible!—I wish I had never discovered it; it gives me dark moments, it spoils my happiness, it makes me shiver and tremble and shudder. But I could not persuade him, for he has not discovered fear yet, and so he could not understand me.

Extract from Adam's Diary

Perhaps I ought to remember that she is very young, a mere girl, and make allowances. She is all interest, eagerness, vivacity, the world is to her a charm, a wonder, a mystery, a joy; she can't speak for delight when she finds a new flower, she must pet it and caress it and smell it and talk to it, and pour out endearing names upon it. And she is color-mad: brown rocks, yellow sand, gray moss, green foliage, blue sky; the pearl of the dawn, the purple shadows on the mountains, the golden islands floating in crimson seas at sunset, the pallid moon sailing through the shredded cloud-rack, the star-jewels glittering in the wastes of space—none of them is of any practical value, so far as I can see, but because they have color and majesty, that is enough for her, and she loses her mind over them. If she could quiet down and keep still a couple of minutes at a time, it would be a reposeful spectacle. In that case I think I could enjoy looking at her; indeed I am sure I could, for I am coming to realize that she is a quite remarkable comely creature—lithe, slender, trim, rounded, shapely, nimble, graceful; and once when she was standing marble-white and sun-drenched on a boulder, with her young head tilted back and her hand shading her eyes, watching the flight of a bird in the sky, I recognized that she was beautiful.

Monday noon. If there is anything on the planet that she is not interested in it is not in my list. There are animals that I am indifferent to, but it is not so with her. She has no discrimination, she takes to all of them, she thinks they are all treasures, every new one is welcome.

When the mighty brontosaurus came striding into camp, she regarded it as an acquisition, I considered it a calamity; that is a good sample of the lack of harmony that prevails in our views of things. She wanted to domesticate it, I wanted to make it a present of the homestead and move out. She believed it could be tamed by kind treatment and would be a good pet; I said a pet twenty-one feet high and eight-four feet long would be no proper thing to have about the place, because, even with the best intentions and without meaning any harm, it could sit down on the house and mash it, for any one could see by the look of its eye that it was absent-minded.

Still, her heart was set upon having that monster, and she couldn't give it up. She thought we could start a dairy with it, and wanted me to help her milk it; but I wouldn't; it was too risky. The sex wasn't right, and we hadn't any ladder anyway. Then she wanted to ride it, and look at the scenery. Thirty or forty feet of its tail was lying on the ground, like a fallen tree, and she thought she could climb it, but she was mistaken; when she got to the steep place it was too slick and down she came, and would have hurt herself but for me.

Was she satisfied now? No. Nothing ever satisfies her but demonstration; untested theories are not in her line, and she won't have them. It is the right spirit, I concede it; it attracts me; I feel the influence of it; if I were with her more I think I should take it up myself. Well, she had one theory remaining about this colossus: she thought that if we could tame him and make him friendly we could stand him in the river and use him for a bridge. It turned out that he was already plenty tame enough—at least as far as she was concerned—so she tried her theory, but it failed: every time she got him properly placed in the river and went ashore to cross over on him, he came out and followed her around like a pet mountain. Like the other animals. They all do that.

Friday Tuesday—Wednesday—Thursday—and to-day: al

without seeing him. It is a long time to be alone; still, it is better to be alone than unwelcome.

I *had* to have company—I was made for it, I think—so I made friends with the animals. They are just charming, and they have the kindest disposition and the politest ways; they never look sour, they never let you feel that you are intruding, they smile at you and wag their tail, if they've got one, and they are always ready for a romp or an excursion or anything you want to propose. I think they are perfect gentlemen. All these days we have had such good times, and it hasn't been lonesome for me, ever. Lonesome! No, I should say not. Why, there's always a swarm of them around—sometimes as much as four or five acres—you can't count them; and when you stand on a rock in the midst and look out over the furry expanse it is so mottled and splashed and gay with color and frisking sheen and sun-flash, and so rippled with stripes, that you might think it was a lake, only you know it isn't; and there's storms of sociable birds, and hurricanes of whirring wings; and when the sun strikes all that feathery commotion, you have a blazing up of all the colors you can think of, enough to put your eyes out.

We have made long excursions, and I have seen a great deal of the world; almost all of it, I think; and so I am the first traveler, and the only one. When we are on the march, it is an imposing sight—there's nothing like it anywhere. For comfort I ride a tiger or a leopard, because it is soft and has a round back that fits me, and because they are such pretty animals; but for long distance or for scenery I ride the elephant. He hoists me up with his trunk, but I can get off myself; when we are ready to camp, he sits and I slide down the back way.

The birds and animals are all friendly to each other, and there are no disputes about anything. They all talk, and they all talk to me, but it must be a foreign language, for I cannot make out a word they say; yet they often understand me when I talk back, particularly the dog and the elephant. It makes me ashamed. It shows that they are brighter than I am, and are therefore my superiors. It annoys me, for I want to be the principal Experiment myself—and I intend to be, too.

I have learned a number of things, and am educated, now, but

I wasn't at first. I was ignorant at first. At first it used to vex me because, with all my watching, I was never smart enough to be around when the water was running uphill; but now I do not mind it. I have experimented and experimented until now I know it never does run uphill, except in the dark. I know it does in the dark, because the pool never goes dry, which it would, of course, if the water didn't come back in the night. It is best to prove things by actual experiment; then you *know;* whereas if you depend on guessing and supposing and conjecturing, you will never get educated.

Some things you *can't* find out; but you will never know you can't by guessing and supposing: no, you have to be patient and go on experimenting until you find out that you can't find out. And it is delightful to have it that way, it makes the world so interesting. If there wasn't anything to find out, it would be dull. Even trying to find out and not finding out is just as interesting as trying to find out and finding out, and I don't know but more so. The secret of the water was a treasure until I *got* it; then the excitement all went away, and I recognized a sense of loss.

By experiment I know that wood swims, and dry leaves, and feathers, and plenty of other things; therefore by all that cumulative evidence you know that a rock will swim; but you have to put up with simply knowing it, for there isn't any way to prove it—up to now. But I shall find a way—then *that* excitement will go. Such things make me sad; because by and by when I have found out everything there won't be any more excitements, and I do love excitements so! The other night I couldn't sleep for thinking about it.

At first I couldn't make out what I was made for, but now I think it was to search out the secrets of this wonderful world and be happy and thank the Giver of it all for devising it. I think there are many things to learn yet—I hope so; and by economizing and not hurrying too fast I think they will last weeks and weeks. I hope so. When you cast up a feather it sails away on the air and goes out of sight; then you throw up a clod and it doesn't. It comes down, every time. I have tried it and tried it, and it is always so. I wonder why it is? Of course it *doesn't* come down, but why should it *seem* to? I suppose it is an optical illusion. I mean, one of them is. I don't know which one. It may be the feather, it may be the clod; I can't prove which it is, I can only demonstrate that one or the other is a fake, and let a person take his choice.

By watching, I know that the stars are not going to last. I have seen some of the best ones melt and run down the sky. Since one can melt, they can all melt; since they can all melt, they can all melt the same night. That sorrow will come—I know it. I mean to sit up every night and look at them as long as I can keep awake; and I will impress those sparkling fields on my memory, so that by and by when they are taken away I can by my fancy restore those lovely myriads to the black sky and make them sparkle again, and double them by the blur of my tears.

AFTER THE FALL

When I look back, the Garden is a dream to me. It was beautiful, surpassingly beautiful, enchantingly beautiful; and now it is lost, and I shall not see it any more.

The Garden is lost, but I have found *him,* and am content. He loves me as well as he can; I love him with all the strength of my passionate nature, and this, I think, is proper to my youth and sex. If I ask myself why I love him, I find I do not know, and do not really much care to know; so I suppose that this kind of love is not a product of reasoning and statistics, like one's love for other reptiles and animals. I think that this must be so. I love certain birds because of their song; but I do not love Adam on account of his singing—no, it is not that; the more he sings the more I do not get reconciled to it. Yet I ask him to sing, because I wish to learn to like everything he is interested in. I am sure I can learn, because at first I could not stand it, but now I can. It sours the milk, but it doesn't matter; I can get used to that kind of milk.

It is not on account of his brightness that I love him—no, it is not that. He is not to blame for his brightness, such as it is, for he did not make it himself; he is as God made him, and that is sufficient. There was a wise purpose in it, *that* I know. In time it will develop, though I think it will not be sudden; and besides, there is no hurry; he is well enough just as he is.

It is not on account of his gracious and considerate ways and his delicacy that I love him. No, he has lacks in these regards, but he is well enough just so, and is improving.

It is not on account of his industry that I love him—no, it is not that. I think he has it in him, and I do not know why he conceals it from me. It is my only pain. Otherwise he is frank and open with me, now. I am sure he keeps nothing from me but this. It grieves me that he should have a secret from me, and sometimes it spoils my sleep, thinking of it, but I will put it out of my mind; it shall not trouble my happiness, which is otherwise full to overflowing.

It is not on account of his education that I love him—no, it is not that. He is self-educated, and does really know a multitude of things, but they are not so.

It is not on account of his chivalry that I love him—no, it is not that. He told on me, but I do not blame him; it is a peculiarity of sex, I think, and he did not make his sex. Of course I would not have told on him, I would have perished first; but that is a peculiarity of sex, too, and I do not take credit for it, for I did not make my sex.

Then why is it that I love him? *Merely because he is masculine,* I think.

At bottom he is good, and I love him for that, but I could love him without it. If he should beat me and abuse me, I should go on loving him. I know it. It is a matter of sex, I think.

He is strong and handsome, and I love him for that, and I admire him and am proud of him, but I could love him without those qualities. If he were plain, I should love him; if he were a wreck, I should love him; and I would work for him, and slave over him, and pray for him, and watch by his bedside until I died.

Yes, I think I love him merely because he is *mine* and is *masculine*. There is no other reason, I suppose. And so I think it is as I first said: that this kind of love is not a product of reasonings and statistics. It just *comes*—none knows whence—and cannot explain itself. And doesn't need to.

It is what I think. But I am only a girl, and the first that has examined this matter, and it may turn out that in my ignorance and inexperience I have not got it right.

FORTY YEARS LATER

It is my prayer, it is my longing, that we may pass from this life together—a longing which shall never perish from the earth, but shall have place in the heart of every wife that loves, until the end of time; and it shall be called by my name.

But if one of us must go first, it is my prayer that it shall be I; for he is strong, I am weak, I am not so necessary to him as he is to me—life without him would not be life; how could I endure it? This prayer is also immortal, and will not cease from being offered up while my race continues. I am the first wife; and in the last wife I shall be repeated.

AT EVE'S GRAVE

ADAM: Wheresoever she was, *there* was Eden.

The Man That Corrupted Hadleyburg

I

It was many years ago. Hadleyburg was the most honest and upright town in all the region round about. It had kept that reputation unsmirched during three generations, and was prouder of it than of any other of its possessions. It was so proud of it, and so anxious to insure its perpetuation, that it began to teach the principles of honest dealing to its babies in the cradle, and made the like teachings the staple of their culture thenceforward through all the years devoted to their education. Also, throughout the formative years temptations were kept out of the way of the young people, so that their honesty could have every chance to harden and solidify, and become a part of their very bone. The neighboring towns were jealous of this honorable supremacy, and affected to sneer at Hadleyburg's pride in it and call it vanity; but all the same they were obliged to acknowledge that Hadleyburg was in reality an incorruptible town; and if pressed they would also acknowledge that the mere fact that a young man hailed from Hadleyburg was all the recommendation he needed when he went forth from his natal town to seek for responsible employment.

But at last, in the drift of time, Hadleyburg had the ill luck to offend a passing stranger—possibly without knowing it, certainly without caring, for Hadleyburg was sufficient unto itself, and cared not a rap for strangers or their opinions. Still, it would have been well to make an exception in this one's case, for he was a bitter man and revengeful. All through his wanderings during a whole year he kept his injury in mind, and gave all his leisure moments to trying to invent a compensating satisfaction for it. He contrived many plans, and all of them were good, but none of them was quite sweeping enough; the poorest of them would hurt a great many individuals, but what he wanted was a plan which would comprehend the entire town, and not let so much as one person escape unhurt. At last he had a fortunate idea, and when it fell into his brain it lit up his whole head with an evil joy. He began to form a plan at once, saying to himself, "That is the thing to do—I will corrupt the town."

Six months later he went to Hadleyburg, and arrived in a buggy at the house of the old cashier of the bank about ten at night. He got a sack out of the buggy, shouldered it, and staggered with it through the cottage yard, and knocked at the door. A woman's voice said "Come in," and he entered, and set his sack behind the stove in the parlor, saying politely to the old lady who sat reading the *Missionary Herald* by the lamp:

"Pray keep your seat, madam, I will not disturb you. There—now it is pretty well concealed; one would hardly know it was there. Can I see your husband a moment, madam?"

No, he was gone to Brixton, and might not return before morning.

"Very well, madam, it is no matter. I merely wanted to leave that sack in his care, to be delivered to the rightful owner when he shall be found. I am a stranger; he does not know me; I am merely passing through the town to-night to discharge a matter which has been long in my mind. My errand is now completed, and I go pleased and a little proud, and you will never see me again. There is a paper attached to the sack which will explain everything. Good-night, madam."

The old lady was afraid of the mysterious big stranger, and was glad to see him go. But her curiosity was roused, and she went straight to the sack and brought away the paper. It began as follows:

> "TO BE PUBLISHED; or, the right man sought out by private inquiry—either will answer. This sack contains gold coin weighing a hundred and sixty pounds four ounces—"

"Mercy on us, and the door not locked!"

Mrs. Richards flew to it all in a tremble and locked it, then pulled down the window-shades and stood frightened, worried, and wondering if there was anything else she could do toward making herself and the money more safe. She listened awhile for burglars, then surrendered to curiosity and went back to the lamp and finished reading the paper:

> "I am a foreigner, and am presently going back to my own country, to remain there permanently. I am grateful to America for what I have received at her hands during my long stay under her flag; and to one of her citizens—a citizen of Hadleyburg—I am especially grateful for a great kindness done me a year or two ago. Two great kindnesses, in fact. I will explain. I was a gambler. I say I *was*. I was a ruined gambler. I arrived in this village at night, hungry and without a penny. I asked for help in the dark; I was ashamed to beg in the light. I begged of the right man. He gave me twenty dollars—that is to say, he gave me life, as I considered it. He also gave me fortune; for out of that money I have made myself rich at the gaming-table. And finally, a remark which he made to me has remained with me to this day, and has at last conquered me; and in conquering has saved the remnant of my morals: I shall gamble no more. Now I have no idea who that man was, but I want him found, and I want him to have this money, to give away, throw away, or keep, as he pleases. It is merely my way of testifying my gratitude to him. If I could stay, I would find him myself; but no matter, he will be found. This is an honest town, an incorrupt-

ible town, and I know I can trust it without fear. This man can be identified by the remark which he made to me; I feel persuaded that he will remember it.

"And now my plan is this: If you prefer to conduct the inquiry privately, do so. Tell the contents of this present writing to any one who is likely to be the right man. If he shall answer, 'I am the man; the remark I made was so-and-so,' apply the test—to wit: open the sack, and in it you will find a sealed envelope containing that remark. If the remark mentioned by the candidate tallies with it, give him the money, and ask no further questions, for he is certainly the right man.

"But if you shall prefer a public inquiry, then publish this present writing in the local paper—with these instructions added, to wit: Thirty days from now, let the candidate appear at the town-hall at eight in the evening (Friday), and hand his remark, in a sealed envelope, to the Rev. Mr. Burgess (if he will be kind enough to act); and let Mr. Burgess there and then destroy the seals of the sack, open it, and see if the remark is correct; if correct, let the money be delivered, with my sincere gratitude, to my benefactor thus identified."

Mrs. Richards sat down, gently quivering with excitement, and was soon lost in thinkings—after this pattern: "What a strange thing it is!. . . . And what a fortune for that kind man who set his bread afloat upon the waters!. . . . If it had only been my husband that did it!—for we are so poor, so old and poor!. . . ." Then, with a sigh—"But it was not my Edward; no, it was not he that gave a stranger twenty dollars. It is a pity too; I see it now. . . ." Then, with a shudder—"But it is *gambler's* money! the wages of sin; we couldn't take it; we couldn't touch it. I don't like to be near it; it seems a defilement." She moved to a farther chair . . . "I wish Edward would come, and take it to the bank; a burglar might come at any moment; it is dreadful to be here all alone with it."

At eleven Mr. Richards arrived, and while his wife was saying, "I am *so* glad you've come!" he was saying, "I'm so tired—tired clear out; it is dreadful to be poor, and have to make these dismal journeys at my time of life. Always at the grind, grind, grind, on a salary—another man's slave, and he sitting at home in his slippers, rich and comfortable."

"I am so sorry for you, Edward, you know that; but be comforted; we have our livelihood; we have our good name—"

"Yes, Mary, and that is everything. Don't mind my talk—it's just a moment's irritation and doesn't mean anything. Kiss me—there, it's all gone now, and I am not complaining any more. What have you been getting? What's in the sack?"

Then his wife told him the great secret. It dazed him for a moment; then he said:

"It weighs a hundred and sixty pounds? Why, Mary, it's for-ty thou-sand dollars—think of it—a whole fortune! Not ten men in this village are worth that much. Give me the paper."

He skimmed through it and said:

"Isn't it an adventure! Why, it's a romance; it's like the impossible things one reads about in books, and never sees in life." He was well stirred up now; cheerful, even gleeful. He tapped his old wife on the cheek, and said, humorously, "Why, we're rich, Mary, rich; all we've got to do is to bury the money and burn the papers. If the gambler ever comes to inquire, we'll merely look coldly upon him and say: 'What is this nonsense you are talking? We have never heard of you and your sack of gold before;' and then he would look foolish, and—"

"And in the mean time, while you are running on with your jokes, the money is still here, and it is fast getting along toward burglar-time."

"True. Very well, what shall we do—make the inquiry private? No, not that; it would spoil the romance. The public method is better. Think what a noise it will make! And it will make all the other towns jealous; for no stranger would trust such a thing to any town but Hadleyburg, and they know it. It's a great card for us. I must get to the printing-office now, or I shall be too late."

"But stop—stop—don't leave me here alone with it, Edward!"

But he was gone. For only a little while, however. Not far from his own house he met the editor-proprietor of the paper, and gave him the document, and said, "Here is a good thing for you, Cox—put it in."

"It may be too late, Mr. Richards, but I'll see."

At home again he and his wife sat down to talk the charming mystery over; they were in no condition for sleep. The first question was, Who could the citizen have been who gave the stranger the twenty dollars? It seemed a simple one; both answered it in the same breath—

"Barclay Goodson."

"Yes," said Richards, "he could have done it, and it would have been like him, but there's not another in the town."

"Everybody will grant that, Edward—grant it privately, anyway. For six months, now, the village has been its own proper self once more—honest, narrow, self-righteous, and stingy."

"It is what he always called it, to the day of his death—said it right out publicly, too."

"Yes, and he was hated for it."

"Oh, of course; but he didn't care. I reckon he was the best-hated man among us, except the Reverend Burgess."

"Well, Burgess deserves it—he will never get another congregation here. Mean as the town is, it knows how to estimate *him*. Edward, doesn't it seem odd that the stranger should appoint Burgess to deliver the money?"

"Well, yes—it does. That is—that is—"

"Why so much that-*is*-ing? Would *you* select him?"

"Mary, maybe the stranger knows him better than this village does."

"Much *that* would help Burgess!"

The husband seemed perplexed for an answer; the wife kept a steady eye upon him, and waited. Finally Richards said, with the hesitancy of one who is making a statement which is likely to encounter doubt,

"Mary, Burgess is not a bad man."

His wife was certainly surprised.

"Nonsense!" she exclaimed.

"He is not a bad man. I know. The whole of his unpopularity had its foundation in that one thing—the thing that made so much noise."

"That 'one thing,' indeed! As if that 'one thing' wasn't enough, all by itself."

"Plenty. Plenty. Only he wasn't guilty of it."

"How you talk! Not guilty of it! Everybody knows he *was* guilty."

"Mary, I give you my word—he was innocent."

"I can't believe it, and I don't. How do you know?"

"It is a confession. I am ashamed, but I will make it. I was the only man who knew he was innocent. I could have saved him, and—and—well, you know how the town was wrought up—I hadn't the pluck to do it. It would have turned everybody against me. I felt mean, ever so mean; but I didn't dare; I hadn't the manliness to face that."

Mary looked troubled, and for a while was silent. Then she said, stammeringly:

"I—I don't think it would have done for you to—to—One mustn't—er—public opinion—one has to be so careful—so—" It was a difficult road, and she got mired; but after a little she got started again. "It was a great pity, but—Why, we couldn't afford it, Edward—we couldn't indeed. Oh, I wouldn't have had you do it for anything!"

"It would have lost us the good-will of so many people, Mary; and then—and then—"

"What troubles me now is, what *he* thinks of us, Edward."

"He? *He* doesn't suspect that I could have saved him."

"Oh," exclaimed the wife, in a tone of relief, "I am glad of that. As long as he doesn't know that you could have saved him, he—he—well, that makes it a great deal better. Why, I might have known he didn't know, because he is always trying to be friendly with us, as little encouragement as we give him. More than once people have twitted me with it. There's the Wilsons, and the Wilcoxes, and the Harknesses, they take a mean pleasure in saying, '*Your friend* Burgess,' because they know it pesters me. I wish he wouldn't persist in liking us so; I can't think why he keeps it up."

"I can explain it. It's another confession. When the thing was new and hot, and the town made a plan to ride him on a rail, my conscience hurt me so that I couldn't stand it, and I went privately and gave him notice, and he got out of the town and staid out till it was safe to come back."

"Edward! If the town had found it out—"

"*Don't!* It scares me yet, to think of it. I repented of it the minute it was done; and I was even afraid to tell you, lest your face might betray it to somebody. I didn't sleep any that night, for worrying. But after a few days I saw that no one was going to suspect me, and after that I got to feeling glad I did it. And I feel glad yet, Mary—glad through and through."

"So do I, now, for it would have been a dreadful way to treat him. Yes, I'm glad; for really you did owe him that, you know. But, Edward, suppose it should come out yet, some day!"

"It won't."

"Why?"

"Because everybody thinks it was Goodson."

"Of course they would!"

"Certainly. And of course *he* didn't care. They persuaded poor old Sawlsberry to go and charge it on him, and he went blustering over there and did it. Goodson looked him over, like as if he was hunting for a place on him that he could despise the most, then he says, 'So you are the Committee of Inquiry, are you?' Sawlsberry said that was about what he was. 'Hm. Do they require particulars, or do you reckon a kind of a *general* answer will do?' 'If they require particulars, I will come back, Mr. Goodson; I will take the general answer first.' 'Very well, then, tell them to go to hell—I reckon that's general enough. And I'll give you some advice, Sawlsberry: when you come back for the particulars, fetch a basket to carry the relics of yourself home in.'"

"Just like Goodson; it's got all the marks. He had only one vanity; he thought he could give advice better than any other person."

"It settled the business, and saved us, Mary. The subject was dropped."

"Bless you, I'm not doubting *that*."

Then they took up the gold-sack mystery again, with strong interest. Soon the conversation began to suffer breaks—interruptions caused by absorbed thinkings. The breaks grew more and more frequent. At last Richards lost himself wholly in thought. He sat long, gazing vacantly at the floor, and by-and-by he began to punctuate his thoughts with little nervous movements of his hands that seemed to indicate vexation. Meantime his wife too had relapsed into a thoughtful silence, and her movements were beginning to show a troubled discomfort. Finally Richards got up and strode aimlessly about the room, ploughing his hands through his hair, much as a somnambulist might do who was having a bad dream. Then he seemed to arrive at a definite purpose; and without a word he put on his hat and passed quickly out of the house. His wife sat brooding, with a drawn face, and did not seem to be aware that she was alone. Now and then she murmured, "Lead us not into t. . . . but—but—we are so poor, so poor!. . . . Lead us not into. . . . Ah, who would be hurt by it?—and no one would ever know. . . . Lead us. . . ." The voice died out in mumblings. After a little she glanced up and muttered in a half-frightened, half-glad way—

"He is gone! But, oh dear, he may be too late—too late. . . . Maybe not—maybe there is still time." She rose and stood thinking, nervously clasping and unclasping her hands. A slight shudder shook her frame, and she said, out of a dry throat, "God forgive me—it's awful to think such things—but. . . . Lord, how we are made—how strangely we are made!"

She turned the light low, and slipped stealthily over and kneeled down by the sack and felt of its ridgy sides with her hands, and fondled them lovingly; and there was a gloating light in her poor old eyes. She fell into fits of absence; and came half out of them at times to mutter, "If we had only waited!—oh, if we had only waited a little, and not been in such a hurry!"

Meantime Cox had gone home from his office and told his wife all about the strange thing that had happened, and they had talked it over eagerly, and guessed that the late Goodson was the only man in the town who could have helped a suffering stranger with so noble a sum as twenty dollars. Then there was a pause, and the two became thoughtful and silent. And by-and-by nervous and fidgety. At last the wife said, as if to herself,

"Nobody knows this secret but the Richardses. . . . and us. . . . nobody."

The husband came out of his thinkings with a slight start, and gazed wistfully at his wife, whose face was become very pale; then he hesitatingly rose, and glanced furtively at his hat, then at his wife—a sort of mute inquiry. Mrs. Cox swallowed once or twice, with her hand at her throat, then in place of speech she nodded her head. In a moment she was alone, and mumbling to herself.

And now Richards and Cox were hurrying through the deserted streets, from opposite directions. They met, panting, at the foot of the printing-office stairs; by the night-light there they read each other's face. Cox whispered,

"Nobody knows about this but us?"

The whispered answer was,

"Not a soul—on honor, not a soul!"

"If it isn't too late to—"

The men were starting up stairs; at this moment they were overtaken by a boy, and Cox asked,

"Is that you, Johnny?"

"Yes, sir."

"You needn't ship the early mail—nor *any* mail; wait till I tell you."

"It's already gone, sir."

"Gone?" It had the sound of an unspeakable disappointment in it.

"Yes, sir. Time-table for Brixton and all the towns beyond changed to-day, sir—had to get the papers in twenty minutes earlier than common. I had to rush; if I had been two minutes later—"

The men turned and walked slowly away, not waiting to hear the rest. Neither of them spoke during ten minutes; then Cox said, in a vexed tone,

"What possessed you to be in such a hurry, *I* can't make out."

The answer was humble enough:

"I see it now, but somehow I never thought, you know, until it was too late. But the next time—"

"Next time be hanged! It won't come in a thousand years."

Then the friends separated without a good-night, and dragged themselves home with the gait of mortally stricken men. At their homes their wives sprang up with an eager "Well?"—then saw the answer with their eyes and sank down sorrowing, without waiting for it to come in words. In both houses a discussion followed of a heated sort—a new thing; there had been discussions before, but not heated ones, not ungentle ones. The discussions to-night were a sort of seeming plagiarisms of each other. Mrs. Richards said,

"If you had only waited, Edward—if you had only stopped to think; but no, you must run straight to the printing-office and spread it all over the world."

"It *said* publish it."

"That is nothing; is also said do it privately, if you liked. There, now—is that true, or not?"

"Why, yes—yes, it is true; but when I thought what a stir it would make, and what a compliment it was to Hadleyburg that a stranger should trust it so—"

"Oh, certainly, I know all that; but if you had only stopped to think, you would have seen that you *couldn't* find the right man, because he is in his grave, and hasn't left chick nor child nor relation behind him; and as long as the money went to somebody that awfully needed it, and nobody would be hurt by it, and—and—"

She broke down, crying. Her husband tried to think of some comforting thing to say, and presently came out with this:

"But after all, Mary, it must be for the best—it *must* be; we know that. And we must remember that it was so ordered—"

"Ordered! Oh, everything's *ordered*, when a person has to find some way out when he has been stupid. Just the same, it was *ordered* that the money should come to us in this special way, and it was you that must take it on yourself to go meddling with the designs of Providence—and who gave you the right. It was wicked, that is what it was—just blasphemous presumption, and no more becoming to a meek and humble professor of—"

"But, Mary, you know how we have been trained all our lives long, like the whole village, till it is absolutely second nature to us to stop not a single moment to think when there's an honest thing to be done—"

"Oh, I know it, I know it—it's been one everlasting training and training and training in honesty—honesty shielded, from the very cradle, against every possible temptation, and so it's *artificial* honesty, and weak as water when temptation comes, as we have seen this night. God knows I never had shade nor shadow of a doubt of my petrified and indestructible honesty until now—and now, under the very first big and real temptation, I—Edward, it is my belief that this town's honesty is as rotten as mine is; as rotten as yours is. It is a mean town, a hard, stingy town, and hasn't a virtue in the world but this honesty it is so celebrated for and so conceited about; and so help me, I do believe that if ever the day comes that its honesty falls under great temptation, its grand reputation will go to ruin like a house of cards. There, now, I've made confession, and I feel better; I am a humbug, and I've been one all my life, without knowing it. Let no man call me honest again—I will not have it."

"I—Well, Mary, I feel a good deal as you do; I certainly do. It seems strange, too, so strange. I never could have believed it—never."

A long silence followed; both were sunk in thought. At last the wife looked up and said,

"I know what you are thinking, Edward."

Richards had the embarrassed look of a person who is caught.

"I am ashamed to confess it, Mary, but—"

"It's no matter, Edward, I was thinking the same question myself."

"I hope so. State it."

"You were thinking, if a body could only guess out *what the remark was* that Goodson made to the stranger."

"It's perfectly true. I feel guilty and ashamed. And you?"

"I'm past it. Let us make a pallet here; we've got to stand watch till the bank vault opens in the morning and admits the sack. . . . Oh, dear, oh, dear—if we hadn't made the mistake!"

The pallet was made, and Mary said:

"The open sesame—what could it have been? I do wonder

what that remark could have been? But come; we will get to bed now."

"And sleep?"

"No; think."

"Yes, think."

By this time the Coxes too had completed their spat and their reconciliation, and were turning in—to think, to think, and toss, and fret, and worry over what the remark could possibly have been which Goodson made to the stranded derelict: that golden remark; that remark worth forty thousand dollars, cash.

The reason that the village telegraph-office was open later than usual that night was this: The foreman of Cox's paper was the local representative of the Associated Press. One might say its honorary representative, for it wasn't four times a year that he could furnish thirty words that would be accepted. But this time it was different. His despatch stating what he had caught got an instant answer:

"Send the whole thing—all the details—twelve hundred words."

A colossal order! The foreman filled the bill; and he was the proudest man in the State. By breakfast-time the next morning the name of Hadleyburg the Incorruptible was on every lip in America, from Montreal to the Gulf, from the glaciers of Alaska to the orange-groves of Florida; and millions and millions of people were discussing the stranger and his money-sack, and wondering if the right man would be found, and hoping some more news about the matter would come soon—right away.

II

Hadleyburg village woke up world-celebrated—astonished—happy—vain. Vain beyond imagination. Its nineteen principal citizens and their wives went about shaking hands with each other, and beaming, and smiling, and congratulating, and saying *this* thing adds a new word to the dictionary—*Hadleyburg,* synonym for *incorruptible*—destined to live in dictionaries forever! And the minor and unimportant citizens and their wives went around acting in much the same way. Everybody ran to the bank to see the gold-sack; and before noon grieved and envious crowds began to flock in from Brixton and all neighboring towns; and that afternoon and next day reporters began to arrive from everywhere to verify the sack and its history and write the whole thing up anew, and make dashing free-hand pictures of the sack, and of Richards's house, and the bank, and the Presbyterian church, and the Baptist church, and the public square, and the town-hall where the test would be applied and the money delivered; and damnable portraits of the Richardses, and Pinkerton the banker, and Cox, and the foreman, and Reverend Burgess, and the postmaster—and even of Jack Halliday, who was the loafing, good-natured, no-account, irreverent fisherman, hunter, boys' friend, stray-dogs' friend, typical "Sam Lawson" of the town. The little mean, smirking, oily Pinkerton showed the sack to all comers, and rubbed his sleek palms together pleasantly, and enlarged upon the town's fine old reputation for honesty and upon this wonderful endorsement of it, and hoped and believed that the example would now spread far and wide over the American world, and be epoch-making in the matter of moral regeneration. And so on, and so on.

By the end of a week things had quieted down again; the wild intoxication of pride and joy had sobered to a soft, sweet, silent delight—a sort of deep, nameless, unutterable content. All faces bore a look of peaceful, holy happiness.

Then a change came. It was a gradual change: so gradual that its beginnings were hardly noticed; maybe were not noticed at all, except by Jack Halliday, who always noticed everything; and always made fun of it, too, no matter what it was. He began to throw out chaffing remarks about people not looking quite so happy as they did a day or two ago; and next he claimed that the new aspect was deepening to positive sadness; next, that it was taking on a sick look; and finally he said that everybody was become so moody, thoughtful, and absent-minded that he could rob the meanest man in town of a cent out of the bottom of his breeches pocket and not disturb his revery.

At this stage—or at about this stage—a saying like this was dropped at bedtime—with a sigh, usually—by the head of each of the nineteen principal households:

"Ah, what *could* have been the remark that Goodson made!"

And straightway—with a shudder—came this, from the man's wife:

"Oh, *don't!* What horrible thing are you mulling in your mind? Put it away from you, for God's sake!"

But that question was wrung from those men again the next night—and got the same retort. But weaker.

And the third night the men uttered the question yet again—with anguish, and absently. This time—and the following night—the wives fidgeted feebly, and tried to say something. But didn't.

And the night after that they found their tongues and responded—longingly,

"Oh, if we *could* only guess!"

Halliday's comments grew daily more and more sparklingly disagreeable and disparaging. He went diligently about, laughing at the town, individually and in mass. But his laugh was the only one left in the village: it fell upon a hollow and mournful vacancy and emptiness. Not even a smile was findable anywhere. Halliday carried a cigar-box around on a tripod, playing that it was a camera, and halted all passers and aimed the thing and said, "Ready!—now look pleasant, please," but not even this capital joke could surprise the dreary faces into any softening.

So three weeks passed—one week was left. It was Saturday evening—after supper. Instead of the aforetime Saturday-evening flutter and bustle and shopping and larking, the streets were empty and desolate. Richards and his old wife sat apart in their little parlor—miserable and thinking. This was become their evening habit now: the life-long habit which had preceded it, of reading, knitting, and contented chat, or receiving or paying neighborly calls, was dead and gone and forgotten, ages ago—two or three weeks ago; nobody talked now, nobody read, nobody visited—the whole village sat at home, sighing, worrying, silent. Trying to guess out that remark.

The postman left a letter. Richards glanced listlessly at the superscription and the post-mark—unfamiliar, both—and tossed the letter on the table and resumed his might-have-beens and his hopeless dull miseries where he had left them off. Two or three hours later his wife got wearily up and was going away to bed without a good-night—custom now—but she stopped near the letter and eyed it awhile with a dead interest, then broke it open, and began to skim it over. Richards, sitting there with his chair tilted back against the wall and his chin between his knees, heard something fall. It was his wife. He sprang to her side, but she cried out:

"Leave me alone, I am too happy. Read the letter—read it!"

He did. He devoured it, his brain reeling. The letter was from a distant State, and it said:

"I am a stranger to you, but no matter: I have something to tell. I have just arrived home from Mexico, and learned about that episode. Of course you do not know who made that remark, but I know, and I am the only person living who does know. It was *Goodson*. I knew him well, many years ago. I passed through your village that very night, and was his guest till the midnight train came along. I overheard him make that remark to the stranger in the dark—it was in Hale Alley. He and I talked of it the rest of the way home, and while smoking in his house. He mentioned many of your villagers in the course of his talk—most of them in a very uncomplimentary way, but two or three favorably: among these latter yourself. I say 'favorably'—nothing stronger. I remember his saying he did not actually *like* any person in the town—not one; but that you—I *think* he said you—am almost sure—had done him a very great service once, possibly without knowing the full value of it, and he wished he had a fortune, he would leave it to you when he died, and a curse apiece for the rest of the citizens. Now, then, if it was you that did him that service, you are his legitimate heir, and entitled to the sack of gold. I know that I can trust to your honor and honesty, for in a citizen of Hadleyburg these virtues are an unfailing inheritance, and so I am going to reveal to you the remark, well satisfied that if you are not the right man you will seek and find the right one and see that poor Goodson's debt of gratitude for the service referred to is paid. This is the remark: *'You are far from being a bad man: go, and reform.'*

HOWARD L. STEPHENSON."

"Oh, Edward, the money is ours, and I am so grateful, *oh*, so grateful—kiss me, dear, it's forever since we kissed—and we needed it so—the money—and now you are free of Pinkerton and his bank, and nobody's slave any more; it seems to me I could fly for joy."

It was a happy half-hour that the couple spent there on the settee caressing each other; it was the old days come again—days that had begun with their courtship and lasted without a break till the stranger brought the deadly money. By-and-by the wife said:

"Oh, Edward, how lucky it was you did him that grand service, poor Goodson! I never liked him, but I love him now. And it was fine and beautiful of you never to mention it or brag about it." Then, with a touch of reproach, "But you ought to have told *me*, Edward, you ought to have told your wife, you know."

"Well, I—er—well, Mary, you see—"

"Now stop hemming and hawing, and tell me about it, Edward. I always loved you, and now I'm proud of you. Everybody believes there was only one good generous soul in this village, and now it turns out that you—Edward, why don't you tell me?"

"Well—er—er—Why, Mary, I can't!"

"You *can't*? *Why* can't you?"

"You see, he—well, he—he made me promise I wouldn't."

The wife looked him over, and said, very slowly,

"Made—you—promise? Edward, what do you tell me that for?"

"Mary, do you think I would lie?"

She was troubled and silent for a moment, then she laid her hand within his and said:.

"No. . . . no. We have wandered far enough from our bearings—God spare us that! In all your life you have never uttered a lie. But now—now that the foundations of things seem to be crumbling from under us, we—we—" She lost her voice for a moment, then said, brokenly, "Lead us not into temptation. . . . I think you made the promise, Edward. Let it rest so. Let us keep away from that ground. Now—that is all gone by; let us be happy again; it is no time for clouds."

Edward found it something of an effort to comply, for his mind kept wandering—trying to remember what the service was that he had done Goodson.

The couple lay awake the most of the night, Mary happy and busy, Edward busy, but not so happy. Mary was planning what she would do with the money. Edward was trying to recall that service. At first his conscience was sore on account of the lie he had told Mary—if it was a lie. After much reflection—suppose it *was* a lie? What then? Was it such a great matter? Aren't we always *acting* lies? Then why not *tell* them? Look at Mary—look what she had done. While he was hurrying off on his honest errand, what was she doing? Lamenting because the papers hadn't been destroyed and the money kept! Is theft better than lying?

That point lost its sting—the lie dropped into the background and left comfort behind it. The next point came to the front: *had* he rendered that service? Well, here was Goodson's own evidence as reported in Stephenson's letter; there could be no better evidence than that—it was even *proof* that he had rendered it. Of course. So that point was settled. . . . No, not quite. He recalled with a wince that this unknown Mr. Stephenson was just a trifle unsure as to whether the performer of it was Richards or some other—and, oh dear, he had put Richards on his honor! He must himself decide whither that money must go—and Mr. Stephenson was not doubting that if he was the wrong man he would go honorably and find the right one. Oh, it was odious to put a man in such a situation—ah, why couldn't Stephenson have left out that doubt! What did he want to intrude that for?

Further reflection. How did it happen that *Richards's* name remained in Stephenson's mind as indicating the right man, and not some other man's name? That looked good. Yes, that looked very good. In fact, it went on looking better and better, straight along—until by-and-by it grew into positive *proof.* And then

Richards put the matter at once out of his mind, for he had a private instinct that a proof once established is better left so.

He was feeling reasonably comfortable now, but there was still one other detail that kept pushing itself on his notice: of course he had done that service—that was settled; but what *was* that service? He must recall it—he would not go to sleep till he had recalled it; it would make his peace of mind perfect. And so he thought and thought. He thought of a dozen things—possible services, even probable services—but none of them seemed adequate, none of them seemed large enough, none of them seemed worth the money—worth the fortune Goodson had wished he could leave in his will. And besides, he couldn't remember having done them, anyway. Now, then—now, then—what *kind* of a service would it be that would make a man so inordinately grateful? Ah—the saving of his soul! That must be it. Yes, he could remember, now, how he once set himself the task of converting Goodson, and labored at it as much as—he was going to say three months; but upon closer examination it shrunk to a month, then to a week, then to a day, then to nothing. Yes, he remembered, now, and with unwelcome vividness, that Goodson had told him to go to thunder and mind his own business—*he* wasn't hankering to follow Hadleyburg to heaven!

So that solution was a failure—he hadn't saved Goodson's soul. Richards was discouraged. Then after a little came another idea: had he saved Goodson's property? No, that wouldn't do—he hadn't any. His life? That is it! Of course. Why, he might have thought of it before. This time he was on the right track, sure. His imagination-mill was hard at work in a minute, now.

Thereafter during a stretch of two exhausting hours he was busy saving Goodson's life. He saved it in all kinds of difficult and perilous ways. In every case he got it saved satisfactorily up to a certain point; then, just as he was beginning to get well persuaded that it had really happened, a troublesome detail would turn up which made the whole thing impossible. As in the matter of drowning, for instance. In that case he had swum out and tugged Goodson ashore in an unconscious state with a great crowd looking on and applauding, but when he had got it all thought out and was just beginning to remember all about it a whole swarm of disqualifying details arrived on the ground: the town would have known of the circumstance, Mary would have known of it, it would glare like a limelight in his own memory instead of being an inconspicuous service which he had possibly rendered "without knowing its full value." And at this point he remembered that he couldn't swim, anyway.

Ah—*there* was a point which he had been overlooking from the start: it had to be a service which he had rendered "possibly without knowing the full value of it." Why, really, that ought to be an easy hunt—much easier than those others. And sure enough, by-and-by he found it. Goodson, years and years ago, came near marrying a very sweet and pretty girl, named Nancy Hewitt, but in some way or other the match had been broken off; the girl died, Goodson remained a bachelor, and by-and-by became a soured one and a frank despiser of the human species. Soon after the girl's death the village found out, or thought it had found out, that she carried a spoonful of negro blood in her veins. Richards worked at these details a good while, and in the end he thought he remembered things concerning them which must have gotten mislaid in his memory through long neglect. He seemed to dimly remember that it was *he* that found out about the negro blood; that it was he that told the village; that the village told Goodson where they got it; that he thus saved Goodson from marrying the tainted girl; that he had done him this great service "without knowing the full value of it," in fact without knowing that he *was* doing it; but that Goodson knew the value of it, and what a narrow escape he had had, and so went to his grave grateful to his benefactor and wishing he had a fortune to leave him. It was all clear and simple now, and the more he went over it the more luminous and certain it grew; and at last, when he nestled to sleep satisfied and happy, he remembered the whole thing just as if it had been yesterday. In fact, he dimly remembered Goodson's *telling* him his gratitude once. Meantime Mary had spent six thousand dollars on a new house for herself and a pair of slippers for her pastor, and then had fallen peacefully to rest.

That same Saturday evening the postman had delivered a letter to each of the other principal citizens—nineteen letters in all.

No two of the envelopes were alike, and no two of the superscriptions were in the same hand, but the letters inside were just like each other in every detail but one. They were exact copies of the letter received by Richards—handwriting and all—and were all signed by Stephenson, but in place of Richards's name each receiver's own name appeared.

All night long eighteen principal citizens did what their caste-brother Richards was doing at the same time—they put in their energies trying to remember what notable service it was that they had unconsciously done Barclay Goodson. In no case was it a holiday job; still they succeeded.

And while they were at this work, which was difficult, their wives put in the night spending the money, which was easy. During that one night the nineteen wives spent an average of seven thousand dollars each out of the forty thousand in the sack—a hundred and thirty-three thousand altogether.

Next day there was a surprise for Jack Halliday. He noticed that the faces of the nineteen chief citizens and their wives bore that expression of peaceful and holy happiness again. He could not understand it, neither was he able to invent any remarks about it that could damage it or disturb it. And so it was his turn to be dissatisfied with life. His private guesses at the reasons for the happiness failed in all instances, upon examination. When he met Mrs. Wilcox and noticed the placid ecstasy in her face, he said to himself, "Her cat has had kittens"—and went and asked the cook; it was not so; the cook had detected the happiness, but did not know the cause. When Halliday found the duplicate ecstasy in the face of "Shadbelly" Billson (village nickname), he was sure some neighbor of Billson's had broken his leg, but inquiry showed that this had not happened. The subdued ecstasy in Gregory Yates's face could mean but one thing—he was a mother-in-law short; it was another mistake. "And Pinkerton—Pinkerton—he has collected ten cents that he thought he was going to lose." And so on, and so on. In some cases the guesses had to remain in doubt, in the others they proved distinct errors. In the end Halliday said to himself, "Anyway it foots up that there's nineteen Hadleyburg families temporarily in heaven; I don't know how it happened; I only know Providence is off duty to-day."

An architect and builder from the next State had lately ventured to set up a small business in this unpromising village, and his sign had now been hanging out a week. Not a customer yet; he was a discouraged man, and sorry he had come. But his weather changed suddenly now. First one and then another chief citizen's wife said to him privately:

"Come to my house Monday week—but say nothing about it for the present. We think of building."

He got eleven invitations that day. That night he wrote his daughter and broke off her match with her student. He said she could marry a mile higher than that.

Pinkerton the banker and two or three other well-to-do men planned country-seats—but waited. That kind don't count their chickens until they are hatched.

The Wilsons devised a grand new thing—a fancy-dress ball. They made no actual promises, but told all their acquaintanceship in confidence that they were thinking the matter over and thought they should give it—"and if we do, you will be invited, of course." People were surprised, and said, one to another, "Why, they are crazy, those poor Wilsons, they can't afford it." Several among the nineteen said privately to their husbands, "It is a good idea; we will keep still till their cheap thing is over, then *we* will give one that will make it sick."

The days drifted along and the bill of future squanderings rose higher and higher, wilder and wilder, more and more foolish and reckless. It began to look as if every member of the nineteen would not only spend his whole forty thousand dollars before receiving-day, but be actually in debt by the time he got the money. In some cases light-headed people did not stop with planning to spend, they really spent—on credit. They bought land, mortgages, farms, speculative stocks, fine clothes, horses, and various other things, paid down the bonus, and made themselves liable for the rest—at ten days. Presently the sober second thought came, and Halliday noticed that a ghastly anxiety was beginning to show up in a good many faces. Again he was puzzled, and didn't know what to make of it. "The Wilcox kittens aren't dead, for they weren't born; nobody's broken a leg; there's no shrinkage in mother-in-laws; *nothing* has happened—it is an insolvable mystery."

There was another puzzled man, too—the Rev. Mr. Burgess. For days, wherever he went, people seemed to follow him or to be watching out for him; and if he ever found himself in a retired spot, a member of the nineteen would be sure to appear, thrust an envelope privately into his hand, whisper "To be opened at the town-hall Friday evening," then vanish away like a guilty thing. He was expecting that there might be one claimant for the sack—doubtful, however, Goodson being dead—but it never occurred to him that all this crowd might be claimants. When the great Friday came at last, he found that he had nineteen envelopes.

III

The town-hall had never looked finer. The platform at the end of it was backed by a showy draping of flags; at intervals along the walls were festoons of flags; the gallery fronts were clothed in flags; the supporting columns were swathed in flags; all this was to impress the stranger, for he would be there in considerable force, and in a large degree he would be connected with the press. The house was full. The 412 fixed seats were occupied; also the 68 extra chairs which had been packed into the aisles, the steps of the platform were occupied; some distinguished strangers were given seats on the platform; at the horseshoe of tables which fenced the front and sides of the platform sat a strong force of special correspondents who had come from everywhere. It was the best-dressed house the town had ever produced. There were some tolerably expensive toilets there, and in several cases the ladies who wore them had the look of being unfamiliar with that kind of clothes. At least the town thought they had that look, but the notion could have arisen from the town's knowledge of the fact that these ladies had never inhabited such clothes before.

The gold-sack stood on a little table at the front of the platform where all the house could see it. The bulk of the house gazed at it with a burning interest, a mouth-watering interest, a wistful and pathetic interest; a minority of nineteen couples gazed at it tenderly, lovingly, proprietarily, and the male half of this minority kept saying over to themselves the moving little impromptu speeches of thankfulness for the audience's applause and congratulations which they were presently going to get up and deliver. Every now and then one of these got a piece of paper out of his vest pocket and privately glanced at it to refresh his memory.

Of course there was a buzz of conversation going on—there always is; but at last when the Rev. Mr. Burgess rose and laid his hand on the sack he could hear his microbes gnaw, the place was so still. He related the curious history of the sack, then went on to speak in warm terms of Hadleyburg's old and well-earned reputation for spotless honesty, and of the town's just pride in this reputation. He said that this reputation was a treasure of priceless value; that under Providence its value had now become inestimably enhanced, for the recent episode had spread this fame far and wide, and thus had focussed the eyes of the American world upon this village, and made its name for all time, as he hoped and believed, a synonym for commercial incorruptibility. (*Applause.*) "And who is to be the guardian of this noble treasure—the community as a whole? No! The responsibility is individual, not communal. From this day forth each and every one of you is in his own person its special guardian, and individually responsible that no harm shall come to it. Do you—does each of you—accept this great trust? [*Tumultuous assent.*] Then all is well. Transmit it to your children and to your children's children. To-day your purity is beyond reproach—see to it that it shall remain so. To-day there is not a person in your community who could be beguiled to touch a penny not his own—see to it that you abide in this grace. ["*We will! we will!*"] This is not the place to make comparisons between ourselves and other communities—some of them ungracious toward us; they have their ways, we have ours; let us be content. [*Applause.*] I am done. Under my hand, my friends, rests a stranger's eloquent recognition of what we are; through him the world will always henceforth know what we are. We do not know who he is, but in your name I utter your gratitude, and ask you to raise your voices in indorsement."

The house rose in a body and made the walls quake with the thunders of its thankfulness for the space of a long minute. Then it sat down, and Mr. Burgess took an envelope out of his pocket. The house held its breath while he slit the envelope open and took from it a slip of paper. He read its contents—slowly and impressively—the audience listening with tranced attention to this magic document, each of whose words stood for an ingot of gold:

"'*The remark which I made to the distressed stranger was this: "You are very far from being a bad man; go, and reform."*'" Then he continued: "We shall know in a moment now whether the remark here quoted corresponds with the one concealed in the sack; and if that shall prove to be so—and it undoubtedly will—this sack of gold belongs to a fellow-citizen who will henceforth stand before the nation as the symbol of the special virtue which has made our town famous throughout the land—Mr. Billson!"

The house had gotten itself all ready to burst into the proper tornado of applause; but instead of doing it, it seemed stricken with a paralysis; there was a deep hush for a moment or two, then a wave of whispered murmurs swept the place—of about this tenor: "*Billson!* oh, come, this is *too* thin! Twenty dollars to a stranger—or *anybody*—*Billson!* Tell it to the marines!" And now at this point the house caught its breath all of a sudden in a new access of astonishment, for it discovered that whereas in one part of the hall Deacon Billson was standing up with his head meekly bowed, in another part of it Lawyer Wilson was doing the same. There was a wondering silence now for a while. Everybody was puzzled, and nineteen couples were surprised and indignant.

Billson and Wilson turned and stared at each other. Billson asked, bitingly,

"Why do *you* rise, Mr. Wilson?"

"Because I have a right to. Perhaps you will be good enough to explain to the house why *you* rise?"

"With great pleasure. Because I wrote that paper."

"It is an impudent falsity! I wrote it myself."

It was Burgess's turn to be paralyzed. He stood looking vacantly at first one of the men and then the other, and did not seem to know what to do. The house was stupefied. Lawyer Wilson spoke up, now, and said,

"I ask the Chair to read the name signed to that paper."

That brought the Chair to itself, and it read out the name,

" 'John Wharton *Billson*.' "

"There!" shouted Billson, "what have you got to say for yourself, now? And what kind of apology are you going to make to me and to this insulted house for the imposture which you have attempted to play here?"

"No apologies are due, sir; and as for the rest of it, I publicly charge you with pilfering my note from Mr. Burgess and substituting a copy of it signed with your own name. There is no other way by which you could have gotten hold of the test-remark; I alone, of living men, possessed the secret of its wording."

There was likely to be a scandalous state of things if this went on; everybody noticed with distress that the short-hand scribes were scribbling like mad; many people were crying "Chair, Chair! Order! order!" Burgess rapped with his gavel, and said:

"Let us not forget the proprieties due. There has evidently been a mistake somewhere, but surely that is all. If Mr. Wilson gave me an envelope—and I remember now that he did—I still have it."

He took one out of his pocket, opened it, glanced at it, looked surprised and worried, and stood silent a few moments. Then he waved his hand in a wandering and mechanical way, and made an effort or two to say something, then gave it up, despondently. Several voices cried out:

"Read it! read it! What is it?"

So he began in a dazed and sleep-walker fashion:

" '*The remark which I made to the unhappy stranger was this: "You are far from being a bad man*. [The house gazed at him, marvelling.] *Go, and reform.*" ' [*Murmurs:* "Amazing! what can this mean?"] This one," said the Chair, "is signed Thurlow G. Wilson."

"There!" cried Wilson, "I reckon that settles it! I knew perfectly well my note was purloined."

"Purloined!" retorted Billson. "I'll let you know that neither you nor any man of your kidney must venture to—"

The Chair. "Order, gentlemen, order! Take your seats, both of you, please."

They obeyed, shaking their heads and grumbling angrily. The house was profoundly puzzled; it did not know what to do with this curious emergency. Presently Thompson got up. Thompson was the hatter. He would have liked to be a Nineteener; but such was not for him; his stock of hats was not considerable enough for the position. He said:

"Mr. Chairman, if I may be permitted to make a suggestion, can both of these gentlemen be right? I put it to you, sir, can both have happened to say the very same words to the stranger? It seems to me—"

The tanner got up and interrupted him. The tanner was a disgruntled man; he believed himself entitled to be a Nineteener, but he couldn't get recognition. It made him a little unpleasant in his ways and speech. Said he:

"Sho, *that's* not the point! *That* could happen—twice in a hundred years—but not the other thing. *Neither* of them gave the twenty dollars!" (*A ripple of applause.*)

Billson. "I did!"

Wilson. "I did!"

Then each accused the other of pilfering.

The Chair. "Order! Sit down, if you please—both of you. Neither of the notes has been out of my possession at any moment."

A Voice. "Good—that settles *that!*"

The Tanner. "Mr. Chairman, one thing is now plain: one of these men has been eavesdropping under the other one's bed, and filching family secrets. If it is not unparliamentary to suggest it, I will remark that both are equal to it. [*The Chair.* "Order! order!"] I withdraw the remark, sir, and will confine myself to suggesting that *if* one of them has overheard the other reveal the test-remark to his wife, we shall catch him now."

A Voice. "How?"

The Tanner. "Easily. The two have not quoted the remark in exactly the same words. You would have noticed that, if there hadn't been a considerable stretch of time and an exciting quarrel inserted between the two readings."

A Voice. "Name the difference."

The Tanner. "The word *very* is in Billson's note, and not in the other."

Many Voices. "That's so—he's right!"

The Tanner. "And so, if the Chair will examine the test-remark in the sack, we shall know which of these two frauds—[*The Chair.* "Order!"]—which of these two adventurers—[*The Chair.* "Order! order!"]—which of these two gentlemen—[*laughter and applause*]—is entitled to wear the belt as being the first dishonest blatherskite ever bred in this town—which he has dishonored, and which will be a sultry place for him from now out!" (*Vigorous applause.*)

Many Voices. "Open it!—open the sack!"

Mr. Burgess made a slit in the sack, slid his hand in and brought out an envelope. In it were a couple of folded notes. He said:

"One of these is marked, 'Not to be examined until all written communications which have been addressed to the Chair—if any—shall have been read.' The other is marked *'The Test.'* Allow me. It is worded—to wit:

" 'I do not require that the first half of the remark which was made to me by my benefactor shall be quoted with exactness, for it was not striking, and could be forgotten; but its closing fifteen words are quite striking, and I think easily rememberable; unless *these* shall be accurately reproduced, let the applicant be regarded as an impostor. My benefactor began by saying he seldom gave advice to any one, but that it always bore the hall-mark of high value when he did give it. Then he said this—and it has never faded from my memory: *"You are far from being a bad man—"* ' "

Fifty Voices. "That settles it—the money's Wilson's! Wilson! Wilson! Speech! Speech!"

People jumped up and crowded around Wilson, wringing his

hand and congratulating fervently—meantime the Chair was hammering with the gavel and shouting:

"Order, gentlemen! Order! Order! Let me finish reading, please." When quiet was restored, the reading was resumed—as follows:

"'"*Go, and reform—or, mark my words—some day, for your sins, you will die and go to hell or Hadleyburg*—TRY AND MAKE IT THE FORMER."'"

A ghastly silence followed. First an angry cloud began to settle darkly upon the faces of the citizenship; after a pause the cloud began to rise, and a tickled expression tried to take its place; tried so hard that it was only kept under with great and painful difficulty; the reporters, the Brixtonites, and other strangers bent their heads down and shielded their faces with their hands, and managed to hold in by main strength and heroic courtesy. At this most inopportune time burst upon the stillness the roar of a solitary voice—Jack Halliday's:

"*That's* got the hall-mark on it!"

Then the house let go, strangers and all. Even Mr. Burgess's gravity broke down presently, then the audience considered itself officially absolved from all restraint, and it made the most of its privilege. It was a good long laugh, and a tempestuously whole-hearted one, but it ceased at last—long enough for Mr. Burgess to try to resume, and for the people to get their eyes partially wiped; then it broke out again; and afterward yet again; then at last Burgess was able to get out these serious words:

"It is useless to try to disguise the fact—we find ourselves in the presence of a matter of grave import. It involves the honor of your town, it strikes at the town's good name. The difference of a single word between the test-remarks offered by Mr. Wilson and Mr. Billson was itself a serious thing, since it indicated that one or the other of these gentlemen had committed a theft—"

The two men were sitting limp, nerveless, crushed; but at these words both were electrified into movement, and started to get up—

"Sit down!" said the Chair, sharply, and they obeyed. "That, as I have said, was a serious thing. And it was—but for only one of them. But the matter has become graver; for the honor of *both* is now in formidable peril. Shall I go even further, and say in inextricable peril? *Both* left out the crucial fifteen words." He paused. During several moments he allowed the pervading stillness to gather and deepen its impressive effects, then added: "There would seem to be but one way whereby this could happen. I ask these gentlemen—Was there *collusion?—agreement?"*

A low murmur sifted through the house; its import was, "He's got them both."

Billson was not used to emergencies; he sat in a helpless collapse. But Wilson was a lawyer. He struggled to his feet, pale and worried, and said:

"I ask the indulgence of the house while I explain this most painful matter. I am sorry to say what I am about to say, since it must inflict irreparable injury upon Mr. Billson, whom I have always esteemed and respected until now, and in whose invulnerability to temptation I entirely believed—as did you all. But for the preservation of my own honor I must speak—and with frankness. I confess with shame—and I now beseech your pardon for it—that I said to the ruined stranger all of the words contained in the test-remark, including the disparaging fifteen. [*Sensation.*] When the late publication was made I recalled them, and I resolved to claim the sack of coin, for by every right I was entitled to it. Now I will ask you to consider this point, and weigh it well: that stranger's gratitude to me that night knew no bounds; he said himself that he could find no words for it that were adequate, and that if he should ever be able he would repay me a thousandfold. Now, then, I ask you this: could I expect—could I believe—could I even remotely imagine—that, feeling as he did, he would do so ungrateful a thing as to add those quite unnecessary fifteen words to his test?—set a trap for me?—expose me as a slanderer of my own town before my own people assembled in a public hall? It was preposterous; it was impossible. His test would contain only the kindly opening clause of my remark. Of that I had no shadow of doubt. You would have thought as I did. You would not have expected a base betrayal from one whom you had befriended and against whom you had committed no offence. And so, with perfect confidence, perfect trust, I wrote on a piece of paper the opening words—ending with 'Go, and reform,'—and signed it. When I was about to put it in an envelope I was called into my back office, and without thinking I left the paper lying open on my desk." He stopped, turned his head slowly toward Billson, waited a moment, then added: "I ask you to note this: when I returned, a little later, Mr. Billson was retiring by my street door." (*Sensation.*)

In a moment Billson was on his feet and shouting:

"It's a lie! It's an infamous lie!"

The Chair. "Be seated, sir! Mr. Wilson has the floor."

Billson's friends pulled him into his seat and quieted him, and Wilson went on:

"Those are the simple facts. My note was now lying in a different place on the table from where I had left it. I noticed that, but attached no importance to it, thinking a draught had blown it there. That Mr. Billson would read a private paper was a thing which could not occur to me; he was an honorable man, and he would be above that. If you will allow me to say it, I think his extra word '*very*' stands explained; it is attributable to a defect of memory. I was the only man in the world who could furnish here any detail of the test-mark—by *honorable* means. I have finished."

There is nothing in the world like a persuasive speech to fuddle the mental apparatus and upset the convictions and debauch the emotions of an audience not practised in the tricks and delusions of oratory. Wilson sat down victorious. The house submerged him in tides of approving applause; friends swarmed to him and shook him by the hand and congratulated him, and Billson was shouted down and not allowed to say a word. The Chair hammered and hammered with its gavel, and kept shouting,

"But let us proceed, gentlemen, let us proceed!"

At last there was a measurable degree of quiet, and the hatter said,

"But what is there to proceed with, sir, but to deliver the money?"

Voices. "That's it! That's it! Come forward, Wilson!"

The Hatter. "I move three cheers for Mr. Wilson, Symbol of the special virtue which—"

The cheers burst forth before he could finish; and in the midst of them—and in the midst of the clamor of the gavel also—some enthusiasts mounted Wilson on a big friend's shoulder and were going to fetch him in triumph to the platform. The Chair's voice now rose above the noise—

"Order! To your places! You forget that there is still a document to be read." When quiet had been restored he took up the document, and was going to read it, but laid it down again, saying, "I forgot; this is not to be read until all written communications received by me have first been read." He took an envelope out of his pocket, removed its enclosure, glanced at it—seemed astonished—held it out and gazed at it—stared at it.

Twenty or thirty voices cried out:

"What is it? Read it! read it!"

And he did—slowly, and wondering:

" 'The remark which I made to the stranger—[*Voices.* "Hello! how's this?"]—was this: "You are far from being a bad man. [*Voices.* "Great Scott!] Go, and reform." ' [*Voice.* "Oh, saw my leg off!"] Signed by Mr. Pinkerton the banker."

The pandemonium of delight which turned itself loose now was of a sort to make the judicious weep. Those whose withers were unwrung laughed till the tears ran down; the reporters, in throes of laughter, set down disordered pothooks which would never in the world be decipherable; and a sleeping dog jumped up, scared out of its wits, and barked itself crazy at the turmoil. All manner of cries were scattered through the din: "We're getting rich—*two* Symbols of Incorruptibility!—without counting Billson!" "*Three!*—count Shadbelly in—we can't have too many!" "All right—Billson's elected!" "Alas, poor Wilson—victim of *two* thieves!"

A Powerful Voice. "Silence! The Chair's fished up something more out of its pocket."

Voices. "Hurrah! Is it something fresh? Read it! read! read!"

The Chair (reading). " 'The remark which I made,' etc. 'You are far from being a bad man. Go,' etc. Signed, 'Gregory Yates.' "

Tornado of Voices. "Four Symbols!" "'Rah for Yates!" "Fish again!"

The house was in a roaring humor now, and ready to get all the fun out of the occasion that might be in it. Several Nineteeners, looking pale and distressed, got up and began to work their way toward the aisles, but a score of shouts went up:

"The doors, the doors—close the doors; no Incorruptible shall leave this place! Sit down, everybody!"

The mandate was obeyed.

"Fish again! Read! read!"

The Chair fished again, and once more the familiar words began to fall from its lips—" 'You are far from being a bad man—' "

"Name! name! What's his name?"

" 'L. Ingoldsby Sargent.' "

"Five elected! Pile up the Symbols! Go on, go on!"

" 'You are far from being a bad—' "

"Name! name!"

" 'Nicholas Whitworth.' "

"Hooray! hooray! it's a symbolical day!"

Somebody wailed in, and began to sing this rhyme (leaving out "it's") to the lovely *Mikado* tune of "When a man's afraid of a beautiful maid"; the audience joined in, with joy; then, just in time, somebody contributed another line—

"And don't you this forget—"

The house roared it out. A third line was at once furnished—

"Corruptibles far from Hadleyburg are—"

Thee house roared that one too. As the last note died, Jack Halliday's voice rose high and clear, freighted with a final line—

"But the Symbols are here, you bet!"

That was sung, with booming enthusiasm. Then the happy house started in at the beginning and sang the four lines through twice, with immense swing and dash, and finished up with a crashing three-times-three and a tiger for "Hadleyburg the Incorruptible and all Symbols of it which we shall find worthy to receive the hall-mark to-night."

Then the shoutings at the Chair began again, all over the place:

"Go on! go on! Read! read some more! Read all you've got!"

"That's it—go on! We are winning eternal celebrity!"

A dozen men got up now and began to protest. They said that this farce was the work of some abandoned joker, and was an insult to the whole community. Without a doubt these signatures were all forgeries—

"Sit down! sit down! Shut up! You are confessing. We'll find *your* names in the lot."

"Mr. Chairman, how many of those envelopes have you got?"

The Chair counted.

"Together with those that have been already examined, there are nineteen."

A storm of derisive applause broke out.

"Perhaps they all contain the secret. I move that you open them all and read every signature that is attached to a note of that sort—and read also the first eight words of the note."

"Second the motion!"

It was put and carried—uproariously. Then poor old Richards got up, and his wife rose and stood at his side. Her head was bent down, so that none might see that she was crying. Her husband gave her his arm, and so supporting her, he began to speak in a quavering voice:

"My friends, you have known us two—Mary and me—all our lives, and I think you have liked us and respected us—"

The Chair interrupted him:

"Allow me. It is quite true—that which you are saying, Mr. Richards; this town *does* know you two; it *does* like you; it *does* respect you; more—it honors you and *loves* you—"

Halliday's voice rang out:

"That's the hall-marked truth, too! If the Chair is right, let the house speak up and say it. Rise! Now, then—hip! hip! hip!—all together!"

The house rose in mass, faced toward the old couple eagerly, filled the air with a snow-storm of waving handkerchiefs, and delivered the cheers with all its affectionate heart.

The Chair then continued:

"What I was going to say is this: We know your good heart, Mr. Richards, but this is not a time for the exercise of charity toward offenders. [Shouts of "Right! right!"] I see your generous purpose in your face, but I cannot allow you to plead for these men—"

"But I was going to—"

"Please take your seat, Mr. Richards. We must examine the rest of these notes—simple fairness to the men who have already been exposed requires this. As soon as that has been done—I give you my word for this—you shall be heard."

Many Voices. "Right!—the Chair is right—no interruption can be permitted at this stage! Go on!—the names! the names!—according to the terms of the motion!"

The old couple sat reluctantly down, and the husband whispered to the wife, "It is pitifully hard to have to wait; the shame will be greater than ever when they find we were only going to plead for *ourselves.*"

Straightway the jollity broke loose again with the reading of the names.

" 'You are far from being a bad man—' Signature, 'Robert J. Titmarsh.'

" 'You are far from being a bad man—' Signature, 'Eliphalet Weeks.'

" 'You are far from being a bad man—' Signature, 'Oscar B. Wilder.' "

At this point the house lit upon the idea of taking the eight words out of the Chairman's hands. He was not unthankful for that. Thenceforward he held up each note in its turn, and waited. The house droned out the eight words in a massed and measured and musical deep volume of sound (with a daringly close resemblance to a well-known church chant)—" 'You are f-a-r from being a b-a-a-a-d man.' " Then the Chair said, "Signature, 'Archibald Wilcox.' " And so on, and so on, name after name, and everybody had an increasingly and gloriously good time except the wretched Nineteen. Now and then, when a particularly shining name was called, the house made the Chair wait while it chanted the whole of the test-remark from the beginning to the closing words, "And go to hell or Hadleyburg—try and make it the for-or-m-e-r!" and in these special cases they added a grand and agonized and imposing "A-a-a-a-*men*!"

The list dwindled, dwindled, dwindled, poor old Richards keeping tally of the count, wincing when a name resembling his own was pronounced, and waiting in miserable suspense for the time to come when it would be his humiliating privilege to rise with Mary and finish his plea, which he was intending to word thus: ". . . for until now we have never done any wrong thing, but have gone our humble way unreproached. We are very poor, we are old, and have no chick nor child to help us; we were sorely tempted, and we fell. It was my purpose when I got up before to make confession and beg that my name might not be read out in this public place, for it seemed to us that we could not bear it; but I was prevented. It was just; it was our place to suffer with the rest. It has been hard for us. It is the first time we have ever heard our name fall from any one's lips—sullied. Be merciful—for the sake of the better days; make our shame as light to bear as in your charity you can." At this point in his revery Mary nudged him, perceiving that his mind was absent. The house was chanting, "You are f-a-r," etc.

"Be ready," Mary whispered. "Your name comes now; he has read eighteen."

The chant ended.

"Next! next! next!" came volleying from all over the house.

Burgess put his hand into his pocket. The old couple, trembling, began to rise. Burgess fumbled a moment, then said,

"I find I have read them all."

Faint with joy and surprise, the couple sank into their seats, and Mary whispered,

"Oh, bless God, we are saved!—he has lost ours—I wouldn't give this for a hundred of those sacks!"

The house burst out with its *Mikado* travesty, and sang it three times with ever-increasing enthusiasm, rising to its feet when it reached for the third time the closing line—

"But the Symbols are here, you bet!"

and finishing up with cheers and a tiger for "Hadleyburg purity and our eighteen immortal representatives of it."

Then Wingate, the saddler, got up and proposed cheers "for the cleanest man in town, the one solitary important citizen in it who didn't try to steal that money—Edward Richards."

They were given with great and moving heartiness; then somebody proposed that Richards be elected sole Guardian and Symbol of the now Sacred Hadleyburg Tradition, with power and right to stand up and look the whole sarcastic world in the face.

Passed, by acclamation; then they sang the *Mikado* again, and ended it with,

"And there's *one* Symbol left, you bet!"

There was a pause; then—

A Voice. "Now, then, who's to get the sack?"

The Tanner (with bitter sarcasm). "That's easy. The money has to be divided among the eighteen Incorruptibles. They gave the suffering stranger twenty dollars apiece—and that remark—each in his turn—it took twenty-two minutes for the procession to move past. Staked the stranger—total contribution, $360. All they want is just the loan back—and interest—forty thousand dollars altogether."

Many Voices (derisively). "That's it! Divvy! divvy! Be kind to the poor—don't keep them waiting!"

The Chair. "Order! I now offer the stranger's remaining document. It says: 'If no claimant shall appear [*grand chorus of groans*], I desire that you open the sack and count out the money to the principal citizens of your town, they to take it in trust [*Cries of "Oh! Oh! Oh!"*], and use it in such ways as to them shall seem best for the propagation and preservation of your community's noble reputation for incorruptible honesty [*more cries*]—a reputation to which their names and their efforts will add a new and far-reaching lustre.' [*Enthusiastic outburst of sarcastic applause.*] That seems to be all. No—here is a postscript:

" 'P. S.—CITIZENS OF HADLEYBURG: There *is* no test-remark—nobody made one. [*Great sensation.*] There wasn't any pauper stranger, nor any twenty-dollar contribution, nor any accompanying benediction and compliment—these are all inventions. [*General buzz and hum of astonishment and delight.*] Allow me to tell my story—it will take but a word or two. I passed through your town at a certain time, and received a deep offence which I had not earned. Any other man would have been content to kill one or two of you and call it square, but to me that would have been a trivial revenge, and inadequate; for the dead do not *suffer.* Besides, I could not kill you all—and, anyway, made as I am, even that would not have satisfied me. I wanted to damage every man in the place, and every woman—and not in their bodies or in their estate, but in their vanity—the place where feeble and foolish people are most vulnerable. So I disguised myself, and came back and studied you. You were easy game. You had an old and lofty reputation for honesty, and naturally you were proud of it—it was your treasure of treasures, the very apple of your eye. As soon as I found out that you carefully and vigilantly kept yourselves and your children *out of temptation*, I knew how to proceed. Why, you simple creatures, the weakest of all weak things is a virtue which has not been tested in the fire. I laid a plan, and gathered a list of names. My project was to corrupt Hadleyburg the Incorruptible. My idea was to make liars and thieves of nearly half a hundred smirchless men and women who had never in their lives uttered a lie or stolen a penny. I was afraid of Goodson. He was neither born nor reared in Hadleyburg. I was afraid that if I started to operate my scheme by getting my letter laid before you, you would say to yourselves, "Goodson is the only man among us who would give away twenty dollars to a poor devil"—and then you might not bite at my bait. But Heaven took Goodson; then I knew I was safe, and I set my trap and baited it. It may be that I shall not catch all the men to whom I mailed the pretended test secret, but I shall catch the most of them, if I know Hadleyburg nature. [*Voices.* "Right—he got every last one of them."] I believe they will even steal ostensible *gamble*-money, rather than miss, poor, tempted, and mistrained fellows. I am hoping to eternally and everlastingly squelch your vanity and give Hadleyburg a new renown—one that will *stick*—and spread far. If I have succeeded, open the sack and summon the Committee on Propagation and Preservation of the Hadleyburg Reputation' "

A Cyclone of Voices. "Open it! Open it! The Eighteen to the front! Committee on Propagation of the Tradition! Forward—the Incorruptibles!"

The Chair ripped the sack wide, and gathered up a handful of bright, broad, yellow coins, shook them together, then examined them—

"Friends, they are only gilded disks of lead!"

There was a crashing outbreak of delight over this news, and when the noise had subsided, the tanner called out:

"By right of apparent seniority in this business, Mr. Wilson is Chairman of the Committee on Propagation of the Tradition. I suggest that he step forward on behalf of his pals, and receive in trust the money."

A Hundred Voices. "Wilson! Wilson! Wilson! Speech! Speech!"

Wilson (in a voice trembling with anger). "You will allow me to say, and without apologies for my language, *damn* the money!"

A Voice. "Oh, and him a Baptist!"

A Voice. "Seventeen Symbols left! Step up, gentlemen, and assume your trust!"

There was a pause—no response.

The Saddler. "Mr. Chairman, we've got *one* clean man left, anyway, out of the late aristocracy; and he needs money, and deserves it. I move that you appoint Jack Halliday to get up there and auction off that sack of gilt twenty-dollar pieces, and give the result to the right man—the man whom Hadleyburg delights to honor—Edward Richards."

This was received with great enthusiasm, the dog taking a hand again; the saddler started the bids at a dollar, the Brixton folk and Barnum's representative fought hard for it, the people cheered every jump that the bids made, the excitement climbed moment by moment higher and higher, the bidders got on their mettle and grew steadily more and more daring, more and more determined, the jumps went from a dollar up to five, then to ten, then to twenty, then fifty, then to a hundred, then—

At the beginning of the auction Richards whispered in distress to his wife: "Oh, Mary, can we allow it? It—it—you see, it is an honor-reward, a testimonial to purity of character, and—and—can we allow it? Hadn't I better get up and—Oh, Mary, what ought we to do?—what do you think we—" (*Halliday's voice. "Fifteen I'm bid!—fifteen for the sack!—twenty!—ah, thanks!—thirty—thanks again! Thirty, thirty, thirty!—do I hear forty?—forty it is! Keep the ball rolling, gentlemen, keep it rolling!—fifty!—thanks, noble Roman!—going at fifty, fifty, fifty!—seventy!—ninety!—splendid!—a hundred!—pile it up, pile it up!—hundred and twenty—forty!—just in time!—hundred and fifty!—*TWO *hundred! —superb! Do I hear two h—thanks!— two hundred and fifty!—"*)

"It is another temptation, Edward—I'm all in a tremble—but, oh, we've escaped *one* temptation, and that ought to warn us, to— [*"Six did I hear?—thanks!—six fifty, six f—*SEVEN *hundred!"*] And yet, Edward, when you think—nobody susp—[*"Eight hundred dollars!—hurrah!—make it nine!—Mr. Parsons, did I hear you say—thanks!—nine!—this noble sack of virgin lead going at only nine hundred dollars, gilding and all—come! do I hear—a thousand!—gratefully yours!—did some one say eleven?—a sack which is going to be the most celebrated in the whole Uni—"*] Oh, Edward" (beginning to sob), "we are *so* poor!—but—but—do as you think best—do as you think best."

Edward fell—that is, he sat still; sat with a conscience which was not satisfied, but which was overpowered by circumstances.

Meantime a stranger, who looked like an amateur detective gotten up as an impossible English earl, had been watching the evening's proceedings with manifest interest, and with a contented expression in his face; and he had been privately commenting to himself. He was now soliloquizing somewhat like this: "None of the Eighteen are bidding; that is not satisfactory; I must change that—the dramatic unities require it; they must buy the sack they tried to steal; they must pay a heavy price, too—some of them are rich. And another thing, when I make a mistake in Hadleyburg nature the man that puts that error upon me is entitled to a high honorarium, and some one must pay it. This poor old Richards has brought my judgment to shame; he is an honest man:—I don't understand it, but I acknowledge it. Yes, he saw my deuces—*and* with a straight flush, and by rights the pot is his. And it shall be a jack-pot, too, if I can manage it. He disappointed me, but let that pass."

He was watching the bidding. At a thousand, the market broke; the prices tumbled swiftly. He waited—and still watched. One competitor dropped out; then another, and another. He put in a bid or two, now. When the bids had sunk to ten dollars, he added a five; some one raised him a three; he waited a moment, then flung in a fifty-dollar jump, and the sack was his—at $1282. The house broke out in cheers—then stopped; for he was on his feet, and had lifted his hand. He began to speak.

"I desire to say a word, and ask a favor. I am a speculator in rarities, and I have dealings with persons interested in numismatics all over the world. I can make a profit on this purchase, just as it stands; but there is a way, if I can get your approval, whereby I can make every one of these leaden twenty-dollar pieces worth its face in gold, and perhaps more. Grant me that approval, and I will give part of my gains to your Mr. Richards, whose invulnerable probity you have so justly and so cordially recognized to-night; his share shall be ten thousand dollars, and I will hand him the money to-morrow. [*Great applause from the house.* But the "invulnerable probity" made the Richardses blush prettily; however, it went for modesty, and did no harm.] If you will pass my proposition by a good majority—I would like a two-thirds vote—I will regard that as the town's consent, and that is all I ask. Rarities are always helped by any device which will rouse curiosity and compel remark. Now if I may have your permission to stamp upon the faces of each of these ostensible coins the names of the eighteen gentlemen who—"

Nine-tenths of the audience were on their feet in a moment—dog and all—and the proposition was carried with a whirlwind of approving applause and laughter.

They sat down, and all the Symbols except "Dr." Clay Harkness got up, violently protesting against the proposed outrage, and threatening to—

"I beg you not to threaten me," said the stranger, calmly. "I know my legal rights, and am not accustomed to being frightened at bluster." (*Applause.*) He sat down. "Dr." Harkness saw an opportunity here. He was one of the two very rich men of the place, and Pinkerton was the other. Harkness was proprietor of a mint; that is to say, a popular patent medicine. He was running for the Legislature on one ticket, and Pinkerton on the other. It was a close race and a hot one, and getting hotter every day. Both had strong appetites for money; each had bought a great tract of land, with a purpose: there was going to be a new railway, and each wanted to be in the Legislature and help locate the route to his own advantage; a single vote might make the decision, and with it two or three fortunes. The stake was large, and Harkness was a daring speculator. He was sitting close to the stranger. He leaned over while one or another of the other Symbols was entertaining the house with protests and appeals, and asked, in a whisper,

"What is your price for the sack?"

"Forty thousand dollars."

"I'll give you twenty."

"No."

"Twenty-five."

"No."

"Say thirty."

"The price is forty thousand dollars; not a penny less."

"All right, I'll give it. I will come to the hotel at ten in the morning. I don't want it known; will see you privately."

"Very good." Then the stranger got up and said to the house:

"I find it late. The speeches of these gentlemen are not without merit, not without interest, not without grace; yet if I may be excused I will take my leave. I thank you for the great favor which you have shown me in granting my petition. I ask the Chair to keep the sack for me until to-morrow, and to hand these three five-hundred dollar notes to Mr. Richards." They were passed up to the Chair. "At nine I will call for the sack, and at eleven will deliver the rest of the ten thousand to Mr. Richards in person, at his home. Good night."

Then he slipped out, and left the audience making a vast noise, which was composed of a mixture of cheers, the *Mikado* song, dog-disapproval, and the chant, "You are f-a-r from being a b-a-a-d man—a-a-a-a-men!"

IV

At home the Richardses had to endure congratulations and compliments until midnight. Then they were left to themselves. They looked a little sad, and they sat silent and thinking. Finally Mary sighed and said,

"Do you think we are to blame, Edward—*much* to blame?" and her eyes wandered to the accusing triplet of big banknotes lying on the table, where the congratulators had been gloating over them and reverently fingering them. Edward did not answer at once; then he brought out a sigh and said, hesitatingly:

"We—we couldn't help it, Mary. It—well, it was ordered. *All* things are."

Mary glanced up and looked at him steadily, but he didn't return the look. Presently she said:

"I thought congratulations and praises always tasted good. But—it seems to me, now—Edward?"

"Well?"

"Are you going to stay in the bank?"

"N-no."

"Resign?"

"In the morning—by note."

"It does seem best."

Richards bowed his head in his hands and muttered:

"Before, I was not afraid to let oceans of people's money pour through my hands, but—Mary, I am so tired, so tired—"

"We will go to bed."

At nine in the morning the stranger called for the sack and took it to the hotel in a cab. At ten Harkness had a talk with him privately. The stranger asked for and got five checks on a metropolitan bank—drawn to "Bearer,"—four for $1500 each, and one for $34,000. He put one of the former in his pocketbook, and the remainder, representing $38,500, he put in an envelope, and with these he added a note, which he wrote after Harkness was gone. At eleven he called at the Richards house and knocked. Mrs. Richards peeped through the shutters, then went and received the envelope, and the stranger disappeared without a word. She came back flushed and a little unsteady on her legs, and gasped out:

"I am sure I recognized him! Last night it seemed to me that maybe I had seen him somewhere before."

"He is the man that brought the sack here?"

"I am almost sure of it."

"Then he is the ostensible Stephenson too, and sold every important citizen in this town with his bogus secret. Now if he has sent checks instead of money, we are sold too, after we thought we had escaped. I was beginning to feel fairly comfortable once more, after my night's rest, but the look of that envelope makes me sick. It isn't fat enough; $8500 in even the largest bank-notes makes more bulk than that."

"Edward, why do you object to checks?"

"Checks signed by Stephenson! I am resigned to take the $8500 if it could come in bank-notes—for it does seem that it was so ordered, Mary—but I have never had much courage, and I have not the pluck to try to market a check signed with that disastrous name. It would be a trap. That man tried to catch me; we escaped somehow or other; and now he is trying a new way. If it is checks—"

"Oh, Edward, it is *too* bad!" and she held up the checks and began to cry.

"Put them in the fire! quick! we mustn't be tempted. It is a trick to make the world laugh at *us*, along with the rest, and— Give them to *me*, since you can't do it!" He snatched them and tried to hold his grip till he could get to the stove; but he was human, he was a cashier, and he stopped a moment to make sure of the signature. Then he came near to fainting.

"Fan me, Mary, fan me! They are the same as gold!"

"Oh, how lovely, Edward! Why?"

"Signed by Harkness. What can the mystery of that be, Mary?"

"Edward, do you think—"

"Look here—look at this! Fifteen—fifteen—fifteen—thirty-four. Thirty-eight thousand five hundred! Mary, the sack isn't worth twelve dollars, and Harkness—apparently—has paid about par for it."

"And does it all come to us, do you think—instead of the ten thousand?"

"Why, it looks like it. And the checks are made to 'Bearer,' too."

"Is that good, Edward? What is it for?"

"A hint to collect them at some distant bank, I reckon. Perhaps Harkness doesn't want the matter known. What is that—a note?"

"Yes. It was with the checks."

It was in the "Stephenson" handwriting, but there was no signature. It said:

"I am a disappointed man. Your honesty is beyond the reach of temptation. I had a different idea about it, but I wronged you in that, and I beg pardon, and do it sincerely. I honor you—and that is sincere, too. This town is not worthy to kiss the hem of your garment. Dear sir, I made a square bet with myself that there were nineteen debauchable men in your self-righteous community. I have lost. Take the whole pot, you are entitled to it."

Richards drew a deep sign, and said:

"It seems written with fire—it burns so. Mary—I am miserable again."

"I, too. Ah, dear, I wish—"

"To think, Mary—he *believes* in me."

"Oh, don't, Edward—I can't bear it."

"If those beautiful words were deserved, Mary—and God knows I believed I deserved them once—I think I could give the forty thousand dollars for them. And I would put that paper away, as representing more than gold and jewels, and keep it always. But now—We could not live in the shadow of its accusing presence, Mary."

He put it in the fire.

A messenger arrived and delivered an envelope. Richards took from it a note and read it; it was from Burgess.

"You saved me, in a difficult time. I saved you last night. It was at cost of a lie, but I made the sacrifice freely, and out of a grateful heart. None in this village knows so well as I know how brave and good and noble you are. At bottom you cannot respect me, knowing as you do of that matter of which I am accused, and by the general voice condemned; but I beg that you will at least believe that I am a grateful man; it will help me to bear my burden.

[Signed] BURGESS."

"Saved, once more. And on such terms!" He put the note in the fire. "I—I wish I were dead, Mary, I wish I were out of it all."

"Oh, these are bitter, bitter days, Edward. The stabs, through their very generosity, are so deep—and they come so fast!"

Three days before the election each of two thousand voters suddenly found himself in possession of a prized memento—one of the renowned bogus double-eagles. Around one of its faces was stamped these words: "THE REMARK I MADE TO THE POOR STRANGER WAS—" Around the other face was stamped these: "GO, AND REFORM. (SIGNED) PINKERTON." Thus the entire remaining refuse of the renowned joke was emptied upon a single head, and with calamitous effect. It revived the recent vast laugh and concentrated it upon Pinkerton; and Harkness's election was a walk-over.

Within twenty-four hours after the Richardses had received their checks their consciences were quieting down, discouraged; the old couple were learning to reconcile themselves to the sin which they had committed. But they were to learn, now, that a sin takes on new and real terrors when there seems a chance that it is going to be found out. This gives it a fresh and most substantial and important aspect. At church the morning sermon was of the usual pattern; it was the same old things said in the same old way; they had heard them a thousand times and found them innocuous, next to meaningless, and easy to sleep under; but now it was different: the sermon seemed to bristle with accusations; it seemed aimed straight and specially at people who were concealing deadly sins. After church they got away from the mob of congratulators as soon as they could, and hurried homeward, chilled to the bone at they did not know what—vague, shadowy, indefinite fears. And by chance they caught a glimpse of Mr. Burgess as he turned a corner. He paid no attention to their nod of recognition! He hadn't seen it; but they did not know that. What could his conduct mean? It might mean—it might mean—oh, a dozen dreadful things. Was it possible that he knew that Richards could have cleared him of guilt in that bygone time, and had been silently waiting for a chance to even up accounts? At home, in their distress they got to imagining that their servant might have been in the next room listening when Richards revealed the secret to his wife that he knew of Burgess's innocence; next, Richards began to imagine that he had heard the swish of a gown in there at that time; next, he was sure he *had* heard it. They would call Sarah in, on a pretext, and watch her face; if she had been betraying them to Mr. Burgess, it would show in her manner. They asked her some questions—questions which were so random and incoherent and seemingly purposeless that the girl felt sure that the old people's minds had been affected by their sudden good fortune; the sharp and watchful gaze which they bent upon her frightened her, and that completed the business. She blushed, she became nervous and confused, and to the old people these were plain signs of guilt—guilt of some fearful sort or other—without doubt she was a spy and a traitor. When they were alone again they began to piece many unrelated things together and get horrible results out of the combination. When things had got about to the worst, Richards was delivered of a sudden gasp, and his wife asked,

"Oh, what is it?—what is it?"

"The note—Burgess's note! Its language was sarcastic, I see it now." He quoted: " 'At bottom you cannot respect me, *knowing*, as you do, of *that matter* of which I am accused'—oh, it is perfectly plain, now, God help me! He knows that I know! You see the ingenuity of the phrasing.

It was a trap—and like a fool, I walked into it. And Mary—?"

"Oh, it is dreadful—I know what you are going to say—he didn't return your transcript of the pretended test-remark."

"No—kept it to destroy us with. Mary, he has exposed us to some already. I know it—I know it well. I saw it in a dozen faces after church. Ah, he wouldn't answer our nod of recognition—*he* knew what he had been doing!"

In the night the doctor was called. The news went around in the morning that the old couple were rather seriously ill—prostrated by the exhausting excitement growing out of their great windfall, the congratulations, and the late hours, the doctor said. The town was sincerely distressed; for these old people were about all it had left to be proud of, now.

Two days later the news was worse. The old couple were delirious, and were doing strange things. By witness of the nurses, Richards had exhibited checks—for $8500? No—for an amazing sum—$38,500! What could be the explanation of this gigantic piece of luck?

The following day the nurses had more news—and wonderful. They had concluded to hide the checks, lest harm come to them; but when they searched they were gone from under the patient's pillow—vanished away. The patient said:

"Let the pillow alone; what do you want?"

"We thought it best that the checks—"

"You will never see them again—they are destroyed. They came from Satan. I saw the hell-brand on them, and I knew they were sent to betray me to sin." Then he fell to gabbling strange and dreadful things which were not clearly understandable, and which the doctor admonished them to keep to themselves.

Richards was right; the checks were never seen again.

A nurse must have talked in her sleep, for within two days the forbidden gabblings were the property of the town; and they were of a surprising sort. They seemed to indicate that Richards had been a claimant for the sack himself, and that

Burgess had concealed that fact and then maliciously betrayed it.

Burgess was taxed with this and stoutly denied it. And he said it was not fair to attach weight to the chatter of a sick old man who was out of his mind. Still, suspicion was in the air, and there was much talk.

After a day or two it was reported that Mrs. Richards's delirious deliveries were getting to be duplicates of her husband's. Suspicion flamed up into conviction, now, and the town's pride in the purity of its one undiscredited important citizen began to dim down and flicker toward extinction.

Six days passed, then came more news. The old couple were dying. Richards's mind cleared in his latest hour, and he sent for Burgess. Burgess said:

"Let the room be cleared. I think he wishes to say something in privacy."

"No!" said Richards; "I want witnesses. I want you all to hear my confession, so that I may die a man, and not a dog. I was clean—artificially—like the rest; and like the rest I fell when temptation came. I signed a lie, and claimed the miserable sack. Mr. Burgess remembered that I had done him a service, and in gratitude (and ignorance) he suppressed my claim and saved me. You know the thing that was charged against Burgess years ago. My testimony, and mine alone, could have cleared him, and I was a coward, and left him to suffer disgrace—"

"No—no—Mr. Richards, you—"

"My servant betrayed my secret to him—"

"No one has betrayed anything to me—"

—"and then he did a natural and justifiable thing; he repented of the saving kindness which he had done me, and he *exposed* me—as I deserved—"

"Never!—I make oath—"

"Out of my heart I forgive him."

Burgess's impassioned protestations fell upon deaf ears; the dying man passed away without knowing that once more he had done poor Burgess a wrong. The old wife died that night.

The last of the sacred Nineteen had fallen a prey to the fiendish sack; the town was stripped of the last rag of its ancient glory. Its mourning was not showy, but it was deep.

By act of the Legislature—upon prayer and petition—Hadleyburg was allowed to change its name to (never mind what—I will not give it away), and leave one word out of the motto that for many generations had graced the town's official seal.

It is an honest town once more, and the man will have to rise early that catches it napping again.

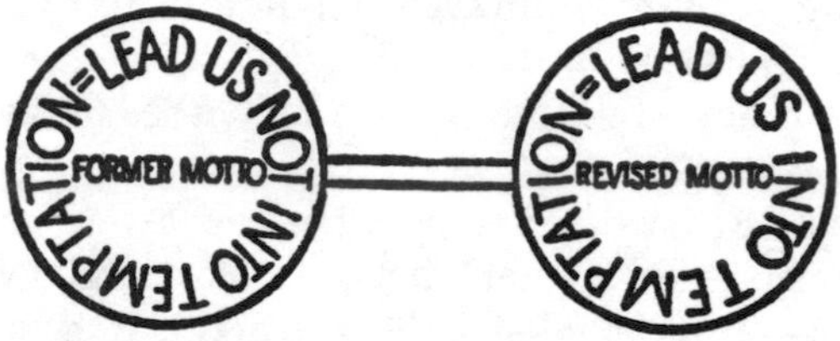

The £1,000,000 Bank-Note

When I was twenty-seven years old, I was a mining-broker's clerk in San Francisco, and an expert in all the details of stock traffic. I was alone in the world, and had nothing to depend upon but my wits and a clean reputation; but these were setting my feet in the road to eventual fortune, and I was content with the prospect.

My time was my own after the afternoon board, Saturdays, and I was accustomed to put it in on a little sail-boat on the bay. One day I ventured too far, and was carried out to sea. Just at nightfall, when hope was about gone, I was picked up by a small brig which was bound for London. It was a long and stormy voyage, and they made me work my passage without pay, as a common sailor. When I stepped ashore in London my clothes were ragged and shabby, and I had only a dollar in my pocket. This money fed and sheltered me twenty-four hours. During the next twenty-four I went without food and shelter.

About ten o'clock on the following morning, seedy and hungry, I was dragging myself along Portland Place, when a child that was passing, towed by a nursemaid, tossed a luscious big pear—minus one bite—into the gutter. I stopped, of course, and fastened my desiring eye on that muddy treasure. My mouth watered for it, my stomach craved it, my whole being begged for it. But every time I made a move to get it some passing eye detected my purpose, and of course I straightened up, then, and looked indifferent, and pretended that I had n't been thinking about the pear at all. This same thing kept happening and happening, and I could n't get the pear. I was just getting desperate enough to brave all the shame, and to seize it, when a window behind me was raised, and a gentleman spoke out of it, saying:

"Step in here, please."

I was admitted by a gorgeous flunkey, and shown into a sumptuous room where a couple of elderly gentlemen were sitting. They sent away the servant, and made me sit down. They had just finished their breakfast, and the sight of the remains of it almost overpowered me. I could hardly keep my wits together in the presence of that food, but as I was not asked to sample it, I had to bear my trouble as best I could.

Now, something had been happening there a little before, which I did not know anything about until a good many days afterward, but I will tell you about it now. Those two old brothers had been having a pretty hot argument a couple of days before, and had ended by agreeing to decide it by a bet, which is the English way of settling everything.

You will remember that the Bank of England once issued two notes of a million pounds each, to be used for a special purpose connected with some public transaction with a foreign country. For some reason or other only one of these had been used and canceled; the other still lay in the vaults of the Bank. Well, the brothers, chatting along, happened to get to wondering what might be the fate of a perfectly honest and intelligent stranger who should be turned adrift in London without a friend, and with no money but that million-pound bank-note, and no way to account for his being in possession of it. Brother A said he would starve to death; Brother B said he would n't. Brother A said he could n't offer it at a bank or anywhere else, because he would be arrested on the spot. So they went on disputing till Brother B said he would bet twenty thousand pounds that the man would live thirty days, *any way,* on that million, and keep out of jail, too. Brother A took him up. Brother B went down to the Bank and bought that note. Just like an Englishman, you see; pluck to the backbone. Then he dictated a letter, which one of his clerks wrote out in a beautiful round hand, and then the two brothers sat at the window a whole day watching for the right man to give it to.

They saw many honest faces go by that were not intelligent enough; many that were intelligent, but not honest enough; many that were both, but the possessors were not poor enough, or, if poor enough, were not strangers. There was always a defect, until I came along; but they agreed that I filled the bill all around; so they elected me unanimously, and there I was, now, waiting to know why I was called in. They began to ask me questions about myself, and pretty soon they had my story. Finally they told me I would answer their purpose. I said I was sincerely glad, and asked what it was. Then one of them handed me an envelop, and said I would find the explanation inside. I was going to open it, but he said no; take it to my lodgings, and look it over carefully, and not be hasty or rash. I was puzzled, and wanted to discuss the matter a little further, but they did n't; so I took my leave, feeling hurt and insulted to be made the butt of what was apparently some kind of a practical joke, and yet obliged to put up with it, not being in circumstances to resent affronts from rich and strong folk.

I would have picked up the pear, now, and eaten it before all the world, but it was gone; so I had lost that by this unlucky business, and the thought of it did not soften my feeling toward those men. As soon as I was out of sight of that house I opened my envelop, and saw that it contained money! My opinion of those people changed, I can tell you! I lost not a moment, but shoved note and money into my vest-pocket, and broke for the nearest cheap eating-house. Well, how I did eat! When at last I could n't hold any more, I took out my money and unfolded it, took one glimpse and nearly fainted. Five millions of dollars! Why, it made my head swim.

I must have sat there stunned and blinking at the note as much as a minute before I came rightly to myself again. The first thing I noticed, then, was the landlord. His eye was on the note, and he was petrified. He was worshiping, with all his body and soul, but he looked as if he could n't stir hand or foot. I took my cue in a moment, and did the only rational thing there was to do. I reached the note toward him, and said carelessly:

"Give me the change, please."

Then he was restored to his normal condition, and made a thousand apologies for not being able to break the bill, and I could n't get him to touch it. He wanted to look at it, and keep on looking at it; he could n't seem to get enough of it to quench the thirst of his eye, but he shrank from touching it as if it had been something too sacred for poor common clay to handle. I said:

"I am sorry if it is an inconvenience, but I must insist. Please change it; I have n't anything else."

But he said that was n't any matter; he was quite willing to let the trifle stand over till another time. I said I might not be in his neighborhood again for a good while; but he said it was of no consequence, he could wait, and, moreover, I could have anything I wanted, any time I chose, and let the account run as long as I pleased. He said he hoped he was n't afraid to trust as rich a gentleman as I was, merely because I was of a merry disposition, and chose to play larks on the public in the matter of dress. By this time another customer was entering, and the landlord hinted to me to put the monster out of sight; then he bowed me all the way to the door, and I started straight for that house and those brothers, to correct the mistake which had been made before the police should hunt me up, and help me do it. I was pretty nervous, in fact pretty badly frightened, though, of course, I was no way in fault; but I knew men well enough to know that when they find they've given a tramp a million-pound bill when they thought it was a one-pounder, they are in a frantic rage against *him* instead of quarreling with their own near-sightedness, as they ought. As I approached the house my excitement began to abate, for all was quiet there, which made me feel pretty sure the blunder was not discovered yet. I rang. The same servant appeared. I asked for those gentlemen.

"They are gone." This in the lofty, cold way of that fellow's tribe.

"Gone? Gone where?"

"On a journey."

"But whereabouts?"

"To the Continent, I think."

"The Continent?"

"Yes, sir."

"Which way—by what route?"

"I can't say, sir."

"When will they be back?"

"In a month, they said."

"A month! Oh, this is awful! Give me *some* sort of idea of how to get a word to them. It's of the last importance."

"I can't, indeed. I've no idea where they've gone, sir."

"Then I must see some member of the family."

"Family's away too; been abroad months—in Egypt and India, I think."

"Man, there's been an immense mistake made. They'll be back before night. Will you tell them I've been here, and that I will keep coming till it's all made right, and they need n't be afraid?"

"I'll tell them, if they come back, but I am not expecting them. They said you would be here in an hour to make inquiries, but I must tell you it's all right, they'll be here on time and expect you."

So I had to give it up and go away. What a riddle it all was! I was like to lose my mind. They would be here "on time." What could that mean? Oh, the letter would explain, maybe. I had forgotten the letter; I got it out and read it. This is what it said:

> You are an intelligent and honest man, as one may see by your face. We conceive you to be poor and a stranger. Inclosed you will find a sum of money. It is lent to you for thirty days, without interest. Report at this house at the end of that time. I have a bet on you. If I win it you shall have any situation that is in my gift—any, that is, that you shall be able to prove yourself familiar with and competent to fill.

No signature, no address, no date.

Well, here was a coil to be in! You are posted on what had preceded all this, but I was not. It was just a deep, dark puzzle to me. I had n't the least idea what the game was, nor whether harm was meant me or a kindness. I went into a park, and sat down to try to think it out, and to consider what I had best do.

At the end of an hour, my reasonings had crystallized into this verdict.

Maybe those men mean me well, maybe they mean me ill; no way to decide that—let it go. They've got a game, or a scheme, or an experiment, of some kind on hand; no way to determine what it is—let it go. There's a bet on me; no way to find out what it is—let it go. That disposes of the indeterminable quantities; the remainder of the matter is tangible, solid, and may be classed and labeled with certainty. If I ask the Bank of England to place this bill to the credit of the man it belongs to, they'll do it, for they know him, although I don't; but they will ask me how I came in possession of it, and if I tell the truth, they'll put me in the asylum, naturally, and a lie will land me in jail. The same result would follow if I tried to bank the bill anywhere or to borrow money on it. I have got to carry this immense burden around until those men come back, whether I want to or not. It is useless to me, as useless as a handful of ashes, and yet I must take care of it, and watch over it, while I beg my living. I could n't *give* it away, if I should try, for neither honest citizen nor highwayman would accept it or meddle with it for anything. Those brothers are safe. Even if I lose their bill, or burn it, they are still safe, because they can stop payment, and the Bank will make them whole; but meantime, I've got to do a month's suffering without wages or profit—unless I help win that bet, whatever it may be, and get that situation that I am promised. I *should* like to get that; men of their sort have situations in their gift that are worth having.

I got to thinking a good deal about that situation. My hopes began to rise high. Without doubt the salary would be large. It would begin in a month; after that I should be all right. Pretty soon I was feeling first rate. By this time I was tramping the streets again. The sight of a tailor-shop gave me a sharp longing to shed my rags, and to clothe myself decently once more. Could I afford it? No; I had nothing in the world but a million pounds. So I forced myself to go on by. But soon I was drifting back again. The temptation persecuted me cruelly. I must have passed that shop back and forth six times during that manful struggle. At last I gave in; I had to. I asked if they had a misfit suit that had been thrown on their hands. The fellow I spoke to nodded his head toward another fellow, and gave me no answer. I went to the indicated fellow, and he indicated another fellow with *his* head, and no words. I went to him, and he said:

"'Tend to you presently."

I waited till he was done with what he was at, then he took me into a back room, and overhauled a pile of rejected suits, and selected the rattiest one for me. I put it on. It did n't fit, and was n't in any way attractive, but it was new, and I was anxious to have it; so I did n't find any fault, but said with some diffidence:

"It would be an accommodation to me if you could wait some days for the money. I have n't any small change about me."

The fellow worked up a most sarcastic expression of countenance, and said:

"Oh, you have n't? Well, of course, I did n't expect it. I'd only expect gentlemen like you to carry large change."

I was nettled, and said:

"My friend, you should n't judge a stranger always by the clothes he wears. I am quite able to pay for this suit; I simply did n't wish to put you to the trouble of changing a large note."

He modified his style a little at that, and said, though still with something of an air:

"I did n't mean any particular harm, but as long as rebukes are going, I might say it was n't quite your affair to jump to the conclusion that we could n't change any note that you might happen to be carrying around. On the contrary, we *can*."

I handed the note to him, and said:

"Oh, very well; I apologize."

He received it with a smile, one of those large smiles which goes all around over, and has folds in it, and wrinkles, and spirals, and looks like the place where you have thrown a brick in a pond; and then in the act of his taking a glimpse of the bill this smile froze solid, and turned yellow, and looked like those wavy, wormy spreads of lava which you find hardened on little levels on the side of Vesuvius. I never before saw a smile caught like that, and perpetuated. The man stood there holding the bill, and looking like that, and the proprietor hustled up to see what was the matter, and said briskly:

"Well, what's up? what's the trouble? what's wanting?"

I said: "There is n't any trouble. I'm waiting for my change."

"Come, come; get him his change, Tod; get him his change."

Tod retorted: "Get him his change! It's easy to say, sir; but look at the bill yourself."

The proprietor took a look, gave a low, eloquent whistle, then made a dive for the pile of rejected clothing, and began to snatch it this way and that, talking all the time excitedly, and as if to himself:

"Sell an eccentric millionaire such an unspeakable suit as that! Tod's a fool—a born fool. Always doing something like this. Drives every millionaire away from this place, because he can't tell a millionaire from a tramp, and never could. Ah, here's the thing I'm after. Please get those things off, sir, and throw them in the fire. Do me the favor to put on this shirt and this suit; it's just the thing, the very thing—plain, rich, modest, and just ducally nobby; made to order for a foreign prince—you may know him, sir, his Serene Highness the Hospodar of Halifax; had to leave it with us and take a mourning-suit because his mother was going to die—which she did n't. But that's all right; we can't always have things the way we—that is, the way they—there! trousers all right, they fit you to a charm, sir; now the waistcoat; aha, right again! now the coat—lord! look at that, now! Perfect—the whole thing! I never saw such a triumph in all my experience."

I expressed my satisfaction.

"Quite right, sir, quite right; it'll do for a makeshift, I'm bound to say. But wait till you see what we'll get up for you on your own measure. Come, Tod, book and pen; get at it. Length of leg, 32"—and so on. Before I could get in a word he had measured me, and was giving orders for dress-suits, morning-suits, shirts, and all sorts of things. When I got a chance I said:

"But, my dear sir, I *can't* give these orders, unless you can wait indefinitely, or change the bill."

"Indefinitely! It's a weak word, sir, a weak word. Eternally—*that's* the word, sir. Tod, rush these things through, and send them to the gentleman's address without any waste of time. Let the minor customers wait. Set down the gentleman's address and—"

"I'm changing my quarters. I will drop in and leave the new address."

"Quite right, sir, quite right. One moment—let me show you out, sir. There—good day, sir, good day."

Well, don't you see what was bound to happen? I drifted naturally into buying whatever I wanted, and asking for change. Within a week I was sumptuously equipped with all needful comforts and luxuries, and was housed in an expensive private hotel in Hanover Square. I took my dinners there, but for breakfast I stuck by Harris's humble feeding-house, where I had got my first meal on my million-pound bill. I was the making of Harris. The fact had gone all abroad that the foreign crank who carried million-pound bills in his vest-pocket was the patron saint of the place. That was enough. From being a poor, struggling, little hand-to-mouth enterprise, it had become celebrated, and overcrowded with customers. Harris was so grateful that he forced loans upon me, and would not be denied; and so, pauper as I was, I had money to spend, and was living like the rich and the great. I judged that there was going to be a crash by and by, but I was in, now, and must swim across or drown. You see there was just that element of impending disaster to give a serious side, a sober side, yes, a tragic side, to a state of things which would otherwise have been purely ridiculous. In the night, in the dark, the tragedy part was always to the front, and always warning, always threatening; and so I moaned and tossed, and sleep was hard to find. But in the cheerful daylight the tragedy element faded out and disappeared, and I walked on air, and was happy to giddiness, to intoxication, you may say.

And it was natural; for I had become one of the notorieties of the metropolis of the world, and it turned my head, not just a little, but a good deal. You could not take up a newspaper, English, Scotch, or Irish, without finding in it one or more references to the "vest-pocket million-pounder" and his latest doings and sayings. At first, in these mentions, I was at the bottom of the personal-gossip column; next, I was listed above the knights, next above the baronets, next above the barons, and so on, and so on, climbing steadily, as my notoriety augmented, until I reached the highest altitude possible, and there I remained, taking precedence of all dukes not royal, and of all ecclesiastics except the primate of all England. But mind, this was not fame; as yet I had achieved only notoriety. Then came the climaxing stroke—the accolade, so to speak—which in a single instant transmuted the perishable dross of notoriety into the enduring gold of fame: "Punch" caricatured me! Yes, I was a made man, now; my place was established. I might be joked about still, but reverently, not hilariously, not rudely; I could be smiled at, but not laughed at. The time for that had gone by. "Punch" pictured me all a-flutter with rags, dickering with a beef-eater for the Tower of London. Well, you can imagine how it was with a young fellow who had never been taken notice of before, and now all of a sudden could n't say a thing that was n't taken up and repeated everywhere; could n't stir abroad without constantly overhearing the remark flying from lip to lip, "There he goes; that's him!" could n't take his breakfast without a crowd to look on; could n't appear in an opera-box without concentrating there the fire of a thousand lorgnettes. Why, I just swam in glory all day long—that is the amount of it.

You know, I even kept my old suit of rags, and every now and then appeared in them, so as to have the old pleasure of buying trifles, and being insulted, and then shooting the scoffer dead with the million-pound bill. But I could n't keep that up. The illustrated papers made the outfit so familiar that when I went out in it I was at once recognized and followed by a crowd, and if I attempted a purchase the man would offer me his whole shop on credit before I could pull my note on him.

About the tenth day of my fame I went to fulfill my duty to my flag by paying my respects to the American minister. He received me with the enthusiasm proper in my case, upbraided me for being so tardy in my duty, and said that there was only one way to get his forgiveness, and that was to take the seat at his dinner-party that night made vacant by the illness of one of his guests. I said I would, and we got to talking. It turned out that he and my father had been schoolmates in boyhood, Yale students together later, and always warm friends up to my father's death. So then he required me to put in at his house all the odd time I might have to spare, and I was very willing, of course.

In fact I was more than willing; I was glad. When the crash should come, he might somehow be able to save me from total destruction; I did n't know how, but he might think of a way, maybe. I could n't venture to unbosom myself to him at this late date, a thing which I would have been quick to do in the beginning of this awful career of mine in London. No, I could n't venture it now; I was in too deep; that is, too deep for me to be risking revelations to so new a friend, though not yet clear beyond my depth, as *I* looked at it. Because, you see, with all my borrowing, I was carefully keeping within my means—I mean within my salary. Of course I could n't *know* what my salary was going to be, but I had a good enough basis for an estimate in the fact that, if I won the bet, I was to have *choice* of any situation in that rich old gentleman's gift provided I was competent—and I should certainly prove competent; I had n't any doubt about that. And as to the bet, I was n't worrying about that; I had always been lucky. Now my estimate of the salary was six hundred to a thousand a year; say, six hundred for the first year, and so on up year by year, till I struck the upper figure by proved merit. At present I was only in debt for my first year's salary. Everybody had been trying to lend me money, but I had fought off the most of them on one pretext or another; so this indebtedness represented only £300 borrowed money, the other £300 represented my keep and my purchases. I believed my second year's salary would carry me through the rest of the month if I went on being cautious and economical, and I intended to look sharply out for that. My month ended, my employer back from his journey, I should be all right once more, for I should at once divide the two years' salary among my creditors by assignment, and get right down to my work.

It was a lovely dinner-party of fourteen. The Duke and Duchess of Shoreditch, and their daughter the Lady Anne-Grace-Eleanor-Celeste-and-so-forth-and-so-forth-de-Bohun, the Earl and Countess of Newgate, Viscount Cheapside, Lord and Lady Blatherskite, some untitled people of both sexes, the minister and his wife and daughter, and this daughter's visiting friend, an English girl of twenty-two, named Portia Langham, whom I fell in love with in two minutes, and she with me—I could see it without glasses. There was still another guest, an American—but I am a little ahead of my story. While the people were still in the drawing-room, whetting up for dinner, and coldly inspecting the late comers, the servant announced:

"Mr. Lloyd Hastings."

The moment the usual civilities were over, Hastings caught sight of me, and came straight with cordially outstretched hand; then stopped short when about to shake, and said with an embarrassed look:

"I beg your pardon, sir, I thought I knew you."

"Why, you do know me, old fellow."

"No! Are *you* the—the—"

"Vest-pocket monster? I am, indeed. Don't be afraid to call me by my nickname; I'm used to it."

"Well, well, well, this is a surprise. Once or twice I've seen your own name coupled with the nickname, but it never occurred to me that *you* could be the Henry Adams referred to. Why, it is n't six months since you were clerking away for Blake Hopkins in Frisco on a salary, and sitting up nights on an extra allowance, helping me arrange and verify the Gould and Curry Extension papers and statistics. The idea of your being in London, and a vast millionaire, and a colossal celebrity! Why, it's the Arabian Nights come again. Man, I can't take it in at all; can't realize it; give me time to settle the whirl in my head."

"The fact is, Lloyd, you are no worse off than I am. I can't realize it myself."

"Dear me, it *is* stunning, now is n't it? Why, It's just three months to-day since we went to the Miners' restaurant—"

"No, the What Cheer."

"Right, it *was* the What Cheer; went there at two in the morning, and had a chop and coffee after a hard six hours' grind over those Extension papers, and I tried to persuade you to come to London with me, and offered to get leave of absence for you and pay all your expenses, and give you something over if I succeeded in making the sale; and you would not listen to me, said

I would n't succeed, and you could n't afford to lose the run of business and be no end of time getting the hang of things again when you got back home. And yet here you are. How odd it all is! How did you happen to come, and whatever *did* give you this incredible start?"

"Oh, just an accident. It's a long story—a romance, a body may say. I'll tell you all about it, but not now."

"When?"

"The end of this month."

"That's more than a fortnight yet. It's too much of a strain on a person's curiosity. Make it a week."

"I can't. You'll know why, by and by. But how's the trade getting along?"

His cheerfulness vanished like a breath, and he said with a sigh:

"You were a true prophet, Hal, a true prophet. I wish I had n't come. I don't want to talk about it."

"But you must. You must come and stop with me to-night, when we leave here, and tell me all about it."

"Oh, may I? Are you in earnest?" and the water showed in his eyes.

"Yes; I want to hear the whole story, every word."

"I'm so grateful! Just to find a human interest once more, in some voice and in some eye, in me and affairs of mine, after what I've been through here—lord! I could go down on my knees for it!"

He gripped my hand hard, and braced up, and was all right and lively after that for the dinner—which did n't come off. No; the usual thing happened, the thing that is always happening under that vicious and aggravating English system—the matter of precedence could n't be settled, and so there was no dinner. Englishmen always eat dinner before they go out to dinner, because *they* know the risks they are running; but nobody ever warns the stranger, and so he walks placidly into the trap. Of course nobody was hurt this time, because we had all been to dinner, none of us being novices except Hastings, and he having been informed by the minister at the time that he invited him that in deference to the English custom he had not provided any dinner. Everybody took a lady and processioned down to the dining-room, because it is usual to go through the motions; but there the dispute began. The Duke of Shoreditch wanted to take precedence, and sit at the head of the table, holding that he outranked a minister who represented merely a nation and not a monarch; but I stood for my rights, and refused to yield. In the gossip column I ranked all dukes not royal, and said so, and claimed precedence of this one. It could n't be settled, of course, struggle as we might and did, he finally (and injudiciously) trying to play birth and antiquity, and I "seeing" his Conqueror and "raising" him with Adam, whose direct posterity I was, as shown by my name, while *he* was of a collateral branch, as shown by *his*, and by his recent Norman origin; so we all processioned back to the drawing-room again and had a perpendicular lunch—plate of sardines and a strawberry, and you group yourself and stand up and eat it. Here the religion of precedence is not so strenuous; the two persons of highest rank chuck up a shilling, the one that wins has first go at his strawberry, and the loser gets the shilling. The next two chuck up, then the next two, and so on. After refreshment, tables were brought, and we all played cribbage, sixpence a game. The English never play any game for amusement. If they can't make something or lose something,—they don't care which,—they won't play.

We had a lovely time; certainly two of us had, Miss Langham and I. I was so bewitched with her that I could n't count my hands if they went above a double sequence; and when I struck home I never discovered it, and started up the outside row again, and would have lost the game every time, only the girl did the same, she being in just my condition, you see; and consequently neither of us ever got out, or cared to wonder why we did n't; we only just knew we were happy, and did n't wish to know anything else, and did n't want to be interrupted. And I *told* her—I did indeed—told her I loved her; and she—well, she blushed till her hair turned red, but she liked it; she *said* she did. Oh, there was never such an evening! Every time I pegged I put on a postscript; every time she pegged she acknowledged receipt of it, counting the hands the same. Why, I could n't even say

"Two for his heels" without adding, "*My,* how sweet you do look!" and she would say, "Fifteen two, fifteen four, fifteen six, and a pair are eight, and eight are sixteen—*do* you think so?"—peeping out aslant from under her lashes, you know, so sweet and cunning. Oh, it was just *too*-too!"

Well, I was perfectly honest and square with her; told her I had n't a cent in the world but just the million-pound note she'd heard so much talk about, and *it* did n't belong to me; and that started her curiosity, and then I talked low, and told her the whole history right from the start, and it nearly killed her, laughing. What in the nation she could find to laugh about, *I* could n't see, but there it was; every half minute some new detail would fetch her, and I would have to stop as much as a minute and a half to give her a chance to settle down again. Why, she laughed herself lame, she did indeed; I never saw anything like it. I mean I never saw a painful story—a story of a person's troubles and worries and fears—produce just *that* kind of effect before. So I loved her all the more, seeing she could be so cheerful when there was n't anything to be cheerful about; for I might soon need that kind of wife, you know, the way things looked. Of course I told her we should have to wait a couple of years, till I could catch up on my salary; but she did n't mind that, only she hoped I would be as careful as possible in the matter of expenses, and not let them run the least risk of trenching on our third year's pay. Then she began to get a little worried, and wondered if we were making any mistake, and starting the salary on a higher figure for the first year than I would get. This was good sense, and it made me feel a little less confident than I had been feeling before; but it gave me a good business idea, and I brought it frankly out.

"Portia, dear, would you mind going with me that day, when I confront those old gentlemen?"

She shrank a little, but said:

"N-o; if my being with you would help hearten you. But—would it be quite proper, do you think?"

"No, I don't know that it would; in fact I'm afraid it would n't: but you see, there's so *much* dependent upon it that—"

"Then I'll go anyway, proper or improper," she said, with a

beautiful and generous enthusiasm. "Oh, I shall be so happy to think I'm helping."

"Helping, dear? Why, you'll be doing it all. You're so beautiful and so lovely and so winning, that with you there I can pile our salary up till I break those good old fellows, and they'll never have the heart to struggle."

Sho! you should have seen the rich blood mount, and her happy eyes shine!

"You wicked flatterer! There is n't a word of truth in what you say, but still I'll go with you. Maybe it will teach you not to expect other people to look with your eyes."

Were my doubts dissipated? Was my confidence restored? You may judge by this fact: privately I raised my salary to twelve hundred the first year on the spot. But I did n't tell her; I saved it for a surprise.

All the way home I was in the clouds, Hastings talking, I not hearing a word. When he and I entered my parlor, he brought me to myself with his fervent appreciations of my manifold comforts and luxuries.

"Let me just stand here a little and look my fill! Dear me, it's a palace; it's just a palace! And in it everything a body *could* desire, including cozy coal fire and supper standing ready. Henry, it does n't merely make me realize how rich you are; it makes me realize, to the bone, to the marrow, how poor I am—how poor I am and how miserable, how defeated, routed, annihilated!"

Plague take it! this language gave me the cold shudders. It scared me broad awake, and made me comprehend that I was standing on a half-inch crust, with a crater underneath. *I* did n't know I had been dreaming—that is, I had n't been allowing myself to know it for a while back; but *now*—oh, dear! Deep in debt, not a cent in the world, a lovely girl's happiness or woe in my hands, and nothing in front of me but a salary which might never—ok, *would* never—materialize! Oh, oh, oh, I am ruined past hope; nothing can save me!

"Henry, the mere unconsidered drippings of your daily income would—"

"Oh, my daily income! Here, down with this hot Scotch, and

cheer up your soul. Here's with you! Or, no—you're hungry; sit down and—"

"Not a bite for me; I'm past it. I can't eat, these days; but I'll drink with you till I drop. Come!"

"Barrel for barrel, I'm with you! Ready? Here we go! Now, then, Lloyd, unreel your story while I brew."

"Unreel it? What, again?"

"Again? What do you mean by that?"

"Why, I mean do you want to hear it *over* again?"

"Do I want to hear it *over* again? This *is* a puzzler. Wait; don't take any more of that liquid. You don't need it."

"Look here, Henry, you alarm me. Did n't I tell you the whole story on the way here?"

"You?"

"Yes, I."

"I'll be hanged if I heard a word of it."

"Henry, this is a serious thing. It troubles me. What did you take up yonder at the minister's?"

Then it all flashed on me, and I owned up, like a man.

"I took the dearest girl in this world—prisoner!"

So then he came with a rush, and we shook, and shook, and shook till our hands ached; and he did n't blame me for not having heard a word of a story which had lasted while we walked three miles. He just sat down then, like the patient, good fellow he was, and told it all over again. Synopsized, it amounted to this: He had come to England with what he thought was a grand opportunity; he had an "option" to sell the Gould and Curry Extension for the "locators" of it, and keep all he could get over a million dollars. He had worked hard, had pulled every wire he knew of, had left no honest expedient untried, had spent nearly all the money he had in the world, had not been able to get a solitary capitalist to listen to him, and his option would run out at the end of the month. In a word, he was ruined. Then he jumped up and cried out:

"Henry, you can save me! You can save me, and you're the only man in the universe that can. Will you do it? *Won't* you do it?"

"Tell me how. Speak out, my boy."

"Give me a million and my passage home for my 'option'! Don't, *don't* refuse!"

I was in a kind of agony. I was right on the point of coming out with the words, "Lloyd, I'm a pauper myself—absolutely penniless, and in *debt*!" But a white-hot idea came flaming through my head, and I gripped my jaws together, and calmed myself down till I was as cold as a capitalist. Then I said, in a commercial and self-possessed way:

"I will save you, Lloyd—"

"Then I'm already saved! God be merciful to you forever! If ever I—"

"Let me finish, Lloyd. I will save you, but not in that way; for that would not be fair to you, after your hard work, and the risks you've run. I don't need to buy mines; I can keep my capital moving, in a commercial center like London without that; it's what I'm at, all the time; but here is what I'll do. I know all about that mine, of course; I know its immense value, and can swear to it if anybody wishes it. You shall sell out inside of the fortnight for three millions cash, using my name freely, and we'll divide, share and share alike."

Do you know, he would have danced the furniture to kindling-wood in his insane joy, and broken everything on the place, if I had n't tripped him up and tied him.

Then he lay there, perfectly happy, saying:

"I may use your name! Your name—think of it! Man, they'll flock in droves, these rich Londoners; they'll *fight* for that stock! I'm a made man, I'm a made man forever, and I'll never forget you as long as I live!"

In less than twenty-four hours London was abuzz! I had n't anything to do, day after day, but sit at home, and say to all comers:

"Yes; I told him to refer to me. I know the man, and I know the mine. His character is above reproach, and the mine is worth far more than he asks for it."

Meantime I spent all my evenings at the minister's with Portia. I did n't say a word to her about the mine; I saved it for a surprise. We talked salary; never anything but salary and love; sometimes love, sometimes salary, sometimes love and salary together. And my! the interest the minister's wife and daughter took in our little affair, and the endless ingenuities they invented to save us from interruption, and to keep the minister in the dark and unsuspicious—well, it was just lovely of them!

When the month was up, at last, I had a million dollars to my credit in the London and County Bank, and Hastings was fixed in the same way. Dressed at my level best, I drove by the house in Portland Place, judged by the look of things that my birds were home again, went on toward the minister's and got my precious, and we started back, talking salary with all our might. She was so excited and anxious that it made her just intolerably beautiful. I said:

"Dearie, the way you're looking it's a crime to strike for a salary a single penny under three thousand a year."

"Henry, Henry, you'll ruin us!"

"Don't you be afraid. Just keep up those looks, and trust to me. It'll all come out right."

So as it turned out, I had to keep bolstering up *her* courage all the way. She kept pleading with me, and saying:

"Oh, please remember that if we ask for too much we may get no salary at all; and then what will become of us, with no way in the world to earn our living?"

We were ushered in by that same servant, and there they were, the two old gentlemen. Of course they were surprised to see that wonderful creature with me, but I said:

"It's all right, gentlemen; she is my future stay and help-mate."

And I introduced them to her, and called them by name. It did n't surprise them; they knew I would know enough to consult the directory. They seated us, and were very polite to me, and very solicitous to relieve her from embarrassment, and put her as much at her ease as they could. Then I said:

"Gentlemen, I am ready to report."

"We are glad to hear it," said *my* man, "for now we can decide the bet which my brother Abel and I made. If you have won for me, you shall have any situation in my gift. Have you the million-pound note?"

"Here it is, sir," and I handed it to him.

"I've won!" he shouted, and slapped Abel on the back. "*Now* what do you say, brother?"

"I say he *did* survive, and I've lost twenty thousand pounds. I never would have believed it."

"I've a further report to make," I said, "and a pretty long one. I want you to let me come soon, and detail my whole month's history; and I promise you it's worth hearing. Meantime, take a look at that."

"What, man! Certificate of deposit for £200,000? Is it yours?"

"Mine. I earned it by thirty days' judicious use of that little loan you let me have. And the only use I made of it was to buy trifles and offer the bill in change."

"Come, this is astonishing! It's incredible, man!"

"Never mind, I'll prove it. Don't take my word unsupported."

But now Portia's turn was come to be surprised. Her eyes were spread wide, and she said:

"Henry, is that really your money? Have you been fibbing to me?"

"I have indeed, dearie. But you'll forgive me, *I* know."

She put up an arch pout, and said:

"Don't you be so sure. You are a naughty thing to deceive me so!"

"Oh, you'll get over it, sweetheart, you'll get over it; it was only fun, you know. Come, let's be going."

"But wait, wait! The situation, you know. I want to give you the situation," said my man.

"Well," I said, "I'm just as grateful as I can be, but really I don't want one."

"But you can have the very choicest one in my gift."

"Thanks again, with all my heart; but I don't even want *that* one."

"Henry, I'm ashamed of you. You don't half thank the good gentleman. May I do it for you?"

"Indeed you shall, dear, if you can improve it. Let us see you try."

She walked to my man, got up in his lap, put her arm round his neck, and kissed him right on the mouth. Then the two old gentlemen shouted with laughter, but I was dumbfounded, just petrified, as you may say. Portia said:

"Papa, he has said you have n't a situation in your gift that he'd take; and I feel just as hurt as—"

"My darling!—is that your papa?"

"Yes; he's my steppapa, and the dearest one that ever was. You understand now, don't you, why I was able to laugh when you told me at the minister's, not knowing my relationships, what trouble and worry papa's and Uncle Abel's scheme was giving you?"

Of course I spoke right up, now, without any fooling, and went straight to the point.

"Oh, my dearest dear sir, I want to take back what I said. You *have* got a situation open that I want."

"Name it."

"Son-in-law."

"Well, well, well! But you know, if you have n't ever served in that capacity, you of course can't furnish recommendations of a sort to satisfy the conditions of the contract, and so—"

"Try me—oh, do, I beg of you! Only just try me thirty or forty years, and if—"

"Oh, well, all right; it's but a little thing to ask. Take her along."

Happy, we two? There're not words enough in the unabridged to describe it. And when London got the whole history, a day or two later, of my month's adventures with that bank-note, and how they ended, did London talk, and have a good time? Yes.

My Portia's papa took that friendly and hospitable bill back to the Bank of England and cashed it; then the Bank canceled it and made him a present of it, and he gave it to us at our wedding, and it has always hung in its frame in the sacredest place in our home, ever since. For it gave me my Portia. But for it I could not have remained in London, would not have appeared at the minister's, never should have met her. And so I always say, "Yes, it's a million-pounder, as you see; but it never made but one purchase in its life, and *then* got the article for only about a tenth part of its value."

The Mysterious Stranger

I

It was in 1590—winter. Austria was far away from the world, and asleep; it was still the Middle Ages in Austria, and promised to remain so forever. Some even set it away back centuries upon centuries and said that by the mental and spiritual clock it was still the Age of Belief in Austria. But they meant it as a compliment, not a slur, and it was so taken, and we were all proud of it. I remember it well, although I was only a boy; and I remember, too, the pleasure it gave me.

Yes, Austria was far from the world, and asleep, and our village was in the middle of that sleep, being in the middle of Austria. It drowsed in peace in the deep privacy of a hilly and woodsy solitude where news from the world hardly ever came to disturb its dreams, and was infinitely content. At its front flowed the tranquil river, its surface painted with cloud-forms and the reflections of drifting arks and stone-boats; behind it rose the woody steeps to the base of the lofty precipice; from the top of the precipice frowned a vast castle, its long stretch of towers and bastions mailed in vines; beyond the river, a league to the left, was a tumbled expanse of forest-clothed hills cloven by winding gorges where the sun never penetrated; and to the right a precipice overlooked the river, and between it and the hills just spoken of lay a far-reaching plain dotted with little homesteads nested among orchards and shade trees.

The whole region for leagues around was the hereditary property of a prince, whose servants kept the castle always in perfect condition for occupancy, but neither he nor his family came there oftener than once in five years. When they came it was as if the lord of the world had arrived, and had brought all the glories of its kingdoms along; and when they went they left a calm behind which was like the deep sleep which follows an orgy.

Eseldorf was a paradise for us boys. We were not over-much pestered with schooling. Mainly we were trained to be good Christians; to revere the Virgin, the Church, and the saints above everything. Beyond these matters we were not required to know much; and, in fact, not allowed to. Knowledge was not good for the common people, and could make them discontented with the lot which God had appointed for them, and God would not endure discontentment with His plans. We had two priests. One of them, Father Adolf, was a very zealous and strenuous priest, much considered.

There may have been better priests, in some ways, than Father Adolf, but there was never one in our commune who was held in more solemn and awful respect. This was because he had absolutely no fear of the Devil. He was the only Christian I have ever known of whom that could be truly said. People stood in deep dread of him on that account; for they thought that there must be something supernatural about him, else he could not be so bold and so confident. All men speak in bitter disapproval of the Devil, but they do it reverently, not flippantly; but Father Adolf's way was very different; he called him by every name he could lay his tongue to, and it made everyone shudder that heard him; and often he would even speak of him scornfully and scoffingly; then the people crossed themselves and went quickly out of his presence, fearing that something fearful might happen.

Father Adolf had actually met Satan face to face more than once, and defied him. This was known to be so. Father Adolf said it himself. He never made any secret of it, but spoke it right out. And that he was speaking true there was proof in at least one instance, for on that occasion he quarreled with the enemy, and intrepidly threw his bottle at him; and there, upon the wall of his study, was the ruddy splotch where it struck and broke.

But it was Father Peter, the other priest, that we all loved best and were sorriest for. Some people charged him with talking around in conversation that God was all goodness and would find a way to save all his poor human children. It was a horrible thing to say, but there was never any absolute proof that Father Peter said it; and it was out of character for him to say it, too, for he was always good and gentle and truthful. He wasn't charged with saying it in the pulpit, where all the congregation could hear and testify, but only outside, in talk; and it is easy for enemies to manufacture *that*. Father Peter had an enemy and a very powerful one, the astrologer who lived in a tumbled old tower up the valley, and put in his nights studying the stars. Every one knew he could foretell wars and famines, though that was not so hard, for there was always a war and generally a famine somewhere. But he could also read any man's life through the stars in a big book he had, and find lost property, and every one in the village except Father Peter stood in awe of him. Even Father Adolf, who had defied the Devil, had a wholesome respect for the astrologer when he came through our village wearing his tall, pointed hat and his long, flowing robe with stars on it, carrying his big book, and a staff which was known to have magic power. The bishop himself sometimes listened to the astrologer, it was said, for, besides studying the stars and prophesying, the astrologer made a great show of piety, which would impress the bishop, of course.

But Father Peter took no stock in the astrologer. He denounced him openly as a charlatan—a fraud with no valuable knowledge of any kind, or powers beyond those of an ordinary and rather inferior human being, which naturally made the astrologer hate Father Peter and wish to ruin him. It was the astrologer, as we all believed, who originated the story about Father Peter's shocking remark and carried it to the bishop. It was said that Father Peter had made the remark to his niece, Marget, though Marget denied it and implored the bishop to believe her and spare her old uncle from poverty and disgrace. But the bishop wouldn't listen. He suspended Father Peter indefinitely, though he wouldn't go so far as to excommunicate him on the evidence of only one witness; and now Father

Peter had been out a couple of years, and our other priest, Father Adolf, had his flock.

Those had been hard years for the old priest and Marget. They had been favorites, but of course that changed when they came under the shadow of the bishop's frown. Many of their friends fell away entirely, and the rest became cool and distant. Marget was a lovely girl of eighteen when the trouble came, and she had the best head in the village, and the most in it. She taught the harp, and earned all her clothes and pocket money by her own industry. But her scholars fell off one by one now; she was forgotten when there were dances and parties among the youth of the village; the young fellows stopped coming to the house, all except Wilhelm Meidling—and he could have been spared; she and her uncle were sad and forlorn in their neglect and disgrace, and the sunshine was gone out of their lives. Matters went worse and worse, all through the two years. Clothes were wearing out, bread was harder and harder to get. And now, at last, the very end was come. Solomon Isaacs had lent all the money he was willing to put on the house, and gave notice that to-morrow he would foreclose.

II

Three of us boys were always together, and had been so from the cradle, being fond of one another from the beginning, and this affection deepened as the years went on—Nikolaus Bauman, son of the principal judge of the local court; Seppi Wohlmeyer, son of the keeper of the principal inn, the "Golden Stag," which had a nice garden, with shade trees reaching down to the riverside, and pleasure boats for hire; and I was the third—Theodor Fischer, son of the church organist, who was also leader of the village musicians, teacher of the violin, composer, tax-collector of the commune, sexton, and in other ways a useful citizen, and respected by all. We knew the hills and the woods as well as the birds knew them; for we were always roaming then when we had leisure—at least, when we were not swimming or boating or fishing, or playing on the ice or sliding down hill.

And we had the run of the castle park, and very few had that.

It was because we were pets of the oldest serving man in the castle—Felix Brandt; and often we went there, nights, to hear him talk about old times and strange things, and to smoke with him (he taught us that) and to drink coffee; for he had served in the wars, and was at the siege of Vienna; and there, when the Turks were defeated and driven away, among the captured things were bags of coffee, and the Turkish prisoners explained the character of it and how to make a pleasant drink out of it, and now he always kept coffee by him, to drink himself and also to astonish the ignorant with. When it stormed he kept us all night; and while it thundered and lightened outside he told us about ghosts and horrors of every kind, and of battles and murders and mutilations, and such things, and made it pleasant and cozy inside; and he told these things from his own experience largely. He had seen many ghosts in his time, and witches and enchanters, and once he was lost in a fierce storm at midnight in the mountains, and by the glare of the lightning had seen the Wild Huntsman rage on the blast with his specter dogs chasing after him through the driving cloud-rack. Also he had seen an incubus once, and several times he had seen the great bat that sucks the blood from the necks of people while they are asleep, fanning them softly with its wings and so keeping them drowsy till they die.

He encouraged us not to fear supernatural things, such as ghosts, and said they did no harm, but only wandered about because they were lonely and distressed and wanted kindly notice and compassion; and in time we learned not to be afraid, and even went down with him in the night to the haunted chamber in the dungeons of the castle. The ghost appeared only once, and it went by very dim to the sight and floated noiseless through the air, and then disappeared; and we scarcely trembled, he had taught us so well. He said it came up sometimes in the night and woke him by passing its clammy hand over his face, but it did him no hurt; it only wanted sympathy and notice. But the strangest thing was that he had seen angels—actual angels out of heaven—and had talked with them. They had no wings, and wore clothes, and talked and looked and acted just like any natural person, and you would never know them for angels except for the wonderful things they did which a mortal could not do, and the way they suddenly disappeared while you were talking with them, which was also a thing which no mortal could do. And he said they were pleasant and cheerful, not gloomy and melancholy, like ghosts.

It was after that kind of a talk one May night that we got up next morning and had a good breakfast with him and then went down and crossed the bridge and went away up into the hills on the left to a woody hill-top which was a favorite place of ours, and there we stretched out on the grass in the shade to rest and smoke and talk over these strange things, for they were in our minds yet, and impressing us. But we couldn't smoke, because we had been heedless and left our flint and steel behind.

Soon there came a youth strolling toward us through the trees, and he sat down and began to talk in a friendly way, just as if he knew us. But we did not answer him, for he was a stranger and we were not used to strangers and were shy of them. He had new and good clothes on, and was handsome and had a winning face and a pleasant voice, and was easy and graceful and unembarrassed, not slouchy and awkward and diffident, like the other boys. We wanted to be friendly with him, but didn't know how to begin. Then I thought of the pipe, and wondered if it would be taken as kindly meant if I offered it to him. But I remembered that we had no fire, so I was sorry and disappointed. But he looked up bright and pleased, and said:

"Fire? Oh, that is easy; I will furnish it."

I was so astonished I couldn't speak; for I had not said anything. He took the pipe and blew his breath on it, and the tobacco glowed red, and spirals of blue smoke rose up. We jumped up and were going to run, for that was natural; and we did run a few steps, although he was yearningly pleading for us to stay, and giving us his word that he would not do us any harm, but only wanted to be friends with us and have company. So we stopped and stood, and wanted to go back, being full of curiosity and wonder, but afraid to venture. He went on coaxing, in his soft persuasive way; and when we saw that the pipe did not blow up and nothing happened, our confidence returned by little and little, and presently our curiosity got to be stronger than our fear, and we ventured back—but slowly, and ready to fly at any alarm.

He was bent on putting us as ease, and he had the right art; one could not remain doubtful and timorous where a person was so earnest and simple and gentle, and talked so alluringly as he did; no, he won us over, and it was not long before we were content and comfortable and chatty, and glad we had found this new friend. When the feeling of constraint was all gone we asked him how he had learned to do that strange thing, and he said he hadn't learned it at all; it came natural to him—like other things—other curious things.

"What ones?"

"Oh, a number; I don't know how many."

"Will you let us see you do them?"

"Do—please!" the other said.

"You won't run away again?"

"No—indeed we won't. Please do. Won't you?"

"Yes, with pleasure; but you mustn't forget your promise, you know."

We said we wouldn't, and he went to a puddle and came back with water in a cup which he had made out of a leaf, and blew upon it and threw it out, and it was a lump of ice the shape of the cup. We were astonished and charmed, but not afraid any more; we were very glad to be there, and asked him to go on and do some more things. And he did. He said he would give us any kind of fruit we liked, whether it was in season or not. We all spoke at once:

"Orange!"

"Apple!"

"Grapes!"

"They are in your pockets," he said, and it was true. And they were of the best, too, and we ate them and wished we had more, though none of us said so.

"You will find them where those came from," he said "and everything else your appetites call for; and you need not name the thing you wish; as long as I am with you, you have only to wish and find."

And he said true. There was never anything so wonderful and

so interesting. Bread, cakes, sweets, nuts—whatever one wanted, it was there. He ate nothing himself, but sat and chatted, and did one curious thing after another to amuse us. He made a tiny toy squirrel out of clay, and it ran up a tree and sat on a limb overhead and barked down at us. Then he made a dog that was not much larger than a mouse, and it treed the squirrel and danced about the tree, excited and barking, and was as alive as any dog could be. It frightened the squirrel from tree to tree and followed it up until both were out of sight in the forest. He made birds out of clay and set them free, and they flew away, singing.

At last I made bold to ask him to tell us who he was.

"An angel," he said, quite simply, and set another bird free and clapped his hands and made it fly away.

A kind of awe fell upon us when we heard him say that, and we were afraid again; but he said we need not be troubled, there was no occasion for us to be afraid of an angel, and he liked us, anyway. He went on chatting as simply and unaffectedly as ever; and while he talked he made a crowd of little men and women the size of your finger, and they went diligently to work and cleared and leveled off a space a couple of yards square in the grass and began to build a cunning little castle in it, the women mixing the mortar and carrying it up the scaffoldings in pails on their heads, just as our work-women have always done, and the men laying the courses of masonry—five hundred of these toy people swarming briskly about and working diligently and wiping the sweat off their faces as natural as life. In the absorbing interest of watching those five hundred little people make the castle grow step by step and course by course, and take shape and symmetry, that feeling and awe soon passed away and we were quite comfortable and at home again. We asked if we might make some people, and he said yes, and told Seppi to make some cannon for the walls, and told Nikolaus to make some halberdiers, with breastplates and greaves and helmets, and I was to make some cavalry, with horses, and in allotting these tasks he called us by our names, but did not say how he knew them. Then Seppi asked him what his own name was, and he said, tranquilly, "Satan," and held out a chip and caught a little woman on it who was falling from the scaffolding and put her back where she belonged, and said, "She is an idiot to step backward like that and not notice what she is about."

It caught us suddenly, that name did, and our work dropped out of our hands and broke to pieces—a cannon, a halberdier, and a horse. Satan laughed, and asked what was the matter. I said, "Nothing, only it seemed a strange name for an angel." He asked why.

"Because it's—it's—well, it's his name, you know."

"Yes—he is my uncle."

He said it placidly, but it took our breath for a moment and made our hearts beat. He did not seem to notice that, but mended our halberdiers and things with a touch, handing them to us finished, and said "Don't you remember?—he was an angel himself, once."

"Yes—it's true," said Seppi; "I didn't think of that."

"Before the Fall he was blameless."

"Yes," said Nikolaus, "he was without sin."

"It is a good family—ours," said Satan; "there is not a better. He is the only member of it that has ever sinned."

I should not be able to make any one understand how exciting it all was. You know that kind of quiver that trembles around through you when you are seeing something so strange and enchanting and wonderful that it is just a fearful joy to be alive and look at it; and you know how you gaze, and your lips turn dry and your breath comes short, but you wouldn't be anywhere but there, not for the world. I was bursting to ask one question—I had it on my tongue's end and could hardly hold it back—but I was ashamed to ask it; it might be a rudeness. Satan set an ox down that he had been making, and smiled up at me and said:

"It wouldn't be a rudeness and I should forgive it if it was. Have I seen him? Millions of times. From the time that I was a little child a thousand years old I was his second favorite among the nursery angels of our blood and lineage—to use a human phrase—yes, from that time until the Fall, eight thousand years, measured as you count time."

"Eight—thousand!"

"Yes." He turned to Seppi, and went on as if answering something that was in Seppi's mind: "Why, naturally I look like a boy, for that is what I am. With us what you call time is a spacious thing; it takes a long stretch of it to grow an angel to full age." There was a question in my mind, and he turned to me and answered it, "I am sixteen thousand years old—counting as you count." Then he turned to Nikolaus and said: "No, the Fall did not affect me nor the rest of the relationship. It was only he that I was named for who ate of the fruit of the tree and then beguiled the man and the woman with it. We others are still ignorant of sin; we are not able to commit it; we are without blemish, and shall abide in that estate always. We—" Two of the little workmen were quarreling, and in buzzing little bumblebee voices they were cursing and swearing at each other; now came blows and blood; then they locked themselves together in a life-and-death struggle. Satan reached out his hand and crushed the life out of them with his fingers, threw them away, wiped the red from his fingers on his handkerchief, and went on talking where he had left off: "We cannot do wrong; neither have we any disposition to do it, for we do not know what it is."

It seemed a strange speech, in the circumstances, but we barely noticed that, we were so shocked and grieved at the wanton murder he had committed—for murder it was, that was its true name, and it was without palliation or excuse, for the men had not wronged him in any way. It made us miserable, for we loved him, and had thought him so noble and so beautiful and gracious, and had honestly believed he was an angel; and to have him do this cruel thing—ah, it lowered him so, and we had had such pride in him. He went right on talking, just as if nothing had happened, telling about his travels, and the interesting things he had seen in the big worlds of our solar systems and of other solar systems far away in the remotenesses of space, and about the customs of the immortals that inhabit them, somehow fascinating us, enchanting us, charming us in spite of the pitiful scene that was now under our eyes, for the wives of the little dead men had found the crushed and shapeless bodies and were crying over them, and sobbing and lamenting, and a priest was kneeling there with his hands crossed upon his breast, praying;

and crowds and crowds of pitying friends were massed about them, reverently uncovered, with their bare heads bowed, and many with the tears running down—a scene which Satan paid no attention to until the small noise of the weeping and praying began to annoy him, then he reached out and took the heavy board seat out of our swing and brought it down and mashed all those people into the earth just as if they had been flies, and went on talking just the same.

An angel, and kill a priest! An angel who did not know how to do wrong, and yet destroys in cold blood hundreds of helpless poor men and women who had never done him any harm! It made us sick to see that awful deed, and to think that none of those poor creatures was prepared except the priest, for none of them had ever heard a mass or seen a church. And we were witnesses; we had seen these murders done and it was our duty to tell, and let the law take its course.

But he went on talking right along, and worked his enchantments upon us again with that fatal music of his voice. He made us forget everything; we could only listen to him, and love him, and be his slaves, to do with us as he would. He made us drunk with the joy of being with him, and of looking into the heaven of his eyes, and of feeling the ecstasy that thrilled along our veins from the touch of his hand.

III

The Stranger had seen everything, had had been everywhere, he knew everything, and he forgot nothing. What another must study, he learned at a glance; there were no difficulties for him. And he made things live before you when he told about them. He saw the world made; he saw Adam created; he saw Samson surge against the pillars and bring the temple down in ruins about him; he saw Caesar's death; he told of the daily life in heaven; he had seen the damned writhing in the red waves of hell; and he made us see all these things, and it was as if we were on the spot and looking at them with our own eyes. And we felt them, too, but there was no sign that they were anything to him beyond mere entertainments. Those visions of hell, those poor babes and women and girls and lads and men shrieking and supplicating in anguish—why, we could hardly bear it but he was as bland about it as if it had been so many imitation rats in an artificial fire.

And always when he was talking about men and women here on the earth and their doings—even their grandest and sublimest—we were secretly ashamed, for his manner showed that to him they and their doings were of paltry poor consequence; often you would think he was talking about flies, if you didn't know. Once he even said, in so many words, that our people down here were quite interesting to him, notwithstanding they were so dull and ignorant and trivial and conceited, and so diseased and rickety, and such a shabby, poor, worthless lot all around. He said it in a quite matter-of-course way and without bitterness, just as a person might talk about bricks or manure or any other thing that was of no consequence and hadn't feelings. I could see he meant no offense, but in my thoughts I set it down as not very good manners.

"Manners!" he said. "Why, it is merely the truth, and truth is good manners; manners are a fiction. The castle is done. Do you like it?"

Any one would have been obliged to like it. It was lovely to look at, it was so shapely and fine, and so cunningly perfect in all its particulars, even to the little flags waving from the turrets. Satan said we must put the artillery in place now, and station the halberdiers and display the cavalry. Our men and horses were a spectacle to see, they were so little like what they were intended for; for, of course, we had no art in making such things. Satan said they were the worst he had seen; and when he touched them and made them alive, it was just ridiculous the way they acted, on account of their legs not being of uniform lengths. They reeled and sprawled around us as if they were drunk, and endangered everybody's lives around them, and finally fell over and lay helpless and kicking. It made us all laugh, though it was a shameful thing to see. The guns were charged with dirt, to fire a salute, but they were so crooked and so badly made that all burst when they went off, and killed some of the gunners and crippled the others. Satan said we would have a storm now, and an earthquake, if we liked, but we must stand off a piece, out of danger. We wanted to call the people away, too, but he said never mind them; they were of no consequence, and we could make more, some time or other, if we needed them.

A small storm-cloud began to settle down black over the castle, and the miniature lightning and thunder began to play, and the ground to quiver, and the wind to pipe and wheeze, and the rain to fall, and all the people flocked into the castle for shelter. The cloud settled down blacker and blacker, and one could see the castle only simply through it; the lightning blazed out flash upon flash and pierced the castle and set it on fire, and the flames shone out red and fierce through the cloud, and the people came flying out, shrieking, but Satan brushed them back, paying no attention to our begging and crying and imploring; and in the midst of the howling of the wind and the volleying of the thunder the magazine blew up, the earthquake rent the ground wide, and the castle's wreck and ruin tumbled into the chasm, which swallowed it from sight, and closed upon it, with all that innocent life, not one of the five hundred poor creatures escaping. Our hearts were broken; we could not keep from crying.

"Don't cry," Satan said; "they were of no value."

"But they are gone to hell!"

"Oh, it is no matter; we can make plenty more."

It was of no use to try to move him; evidently he was wholly without feeling, and could not understand. He was full of bubbling spirits, and as gay as if this were a wedding instead of a fiendish massacre. And he was bent on making us feel as he did, and of course his magic accomplished his desire. It was no trouble to him; he did whatever he pleased with us. In a little while we were dancing on that grave, and he was playing to us on a strange, sweet instrument which he took out of his pocket; and the music—but there is no music like that, unless perhaps in heaven, and that was where he brought it from, he said. It made one mad, for pleasure; and we could not take our eyes from him, and the looks that went out of our eyes came from our hearts, and their dumb speech was worship. He brought the dance from heaven, too, and the bliss of paradise was in it.

Presently he said he must go away on an errand. But we could not bear the thought of it, and clung to him, and pleaded with him to stay; and that pleased him, and he said so, and said he would not go yet, but would wait a little while and we would sit down and talk a few minutes longer; and he told us Satan was only his real name, and he was to be known by it to us alone, but he had chosen another one to be called by in the presence of others; just a common one, such as people have—Philip Traum.

It sounded so odd and mean for such a being! But it was his decision, and we said nothing; his decision was sufficient.

We had seen wonders this day; and my thoughts began to run on the pleasure it would be to tell them when I got home, but he noticed those thoughts, and said:

"No, all these matters are a secret among us four. I do not mind your trying to tell them, if you like, but I will protect your tongues, and nothing of the secret will escape from them."

It was a disappointment, but it couldn't be helped, and it cost us a sigh or two. We talked pleasantly along, and he was always reading our thoughts and responding to them, and it seemed to me that this was the most wonderful of all the things he did, but he interrupted my musings and said:

"No, it would be wonderful for you, but it is not wonderful for me. I am not limited like you. I am not subject to human conditions. I can measure and understand your human weaknesses, for I have studied them; but I have none of them. My flesh is not real, although it would seem firm to your touch; my clothes are not real; I am a spirit. Father Peter is coming." We looked around, but did not see any one. "He is not in sight yet, but you will see him presently."

"Do you know him, Satan?"

"No."

"Won't you talk with him when he comes? He is not ignorant and dull, like us, and he would so like to talk with you. Will you?"

"Another time, yes, but not now. I must go on my errand after a little. There he is now; you can see him. Sit still, and don't say anything."

We looked up and saw Father Peter approaching through the chestnuts. We three were sitting together in the grass, and Satan sat in front of us in the path. Father Peter came slowly along with his head down, thinking, and stopped within a couple of yards of us and took off his hat and got out his silk handkerchief, and stood there mopping his face and looking as if he were going to speak to us, but he didn't. Presently he muttered, "I can't think what brought me here; it seems as if I were in my study a minute ago—but I suppose I have been dreaming along for an hour and have come all this stretch without noticing; for I am not myself in these troubled days." Then he went mumbling along to himself and walked straight through Satan, just as if nothing were there. It made us catch our breath to see it. We had the impulse to cry out, the way you nearly always do when a startling thing happens, but something mysteriously restrained us and we remained quiet, only breathing fast. Then the trees hid Father Peter after a little, and Satan said:

"It is as I told you—I am only a spirit."

"Yes, one perceives it now," said Nikolaus, "but we are not spirits. It is plain he did not see you, but were we invisible, too? He looked at us, but he didn't seem to see us."

"No, none of us was visible to him, for I wished it so."

It seemed almost too good to be true, that we were actually seeing these romantic and wonderful things, and that it was not a dream. And there he sat, looking just like anybody—so natural and simple and charming, and chatting along again the same as ever, and—well, words cannot make you understand what we felt. It was an ecstasy; and an ecstasy is a thing that will not go into words; it feels like music, and one cannot tell about music so that another person can get the feeling of it. He was back in the old ages once more now, and making them live before us. He had seen so much, so much! It was just a wonder to look at him and try to think how it must seem to have such experience behind one.

But it made you seem sorrowfully trivial, and the creature of a day, and such a short and paltry day, too. And he didn't say anything to raise up your dropping pride—no, not a word. He always spoke of men in the same old indifferent way—just as one speaks of bricks and manure-piles and such things; you could see that they were of no consequence to him, one way or the other. He didn't mean to hurt us, you could see that; just as we don't mean to insult a brick when we disparage it; a brick's emotions are nothing to us; it never occurs to us to think whether it has any or not.

Once when he was bunching the most illustrious kings and conquerors and poets and prophets and pirates and beggars together—just a brick-pile—I was shamed into putting in a word for man, and asked him why he made so much difference between men and himself. He had to struggle with that a moment; he didn't seem to understand how I could ask such a strange question. Then he said:

"The difference between man and me? The difference between a mortal and an immortal? between a cloud and a spirit?" He picked up a wood-louse that was creeping along a piece of bark: "What is the difference between Caesar and this?"

I said, "One cannot compare things which by their nature and by the interval between them are not comparable."

"You have answered your own question," he said. "I will expand it. Man is made of dirt—I saw him made. I am not made of dirt. Man is a museum of diseases, a home of impurities; he comes to-day and is gone to-morrow; he begins as dirt and departs as stench; I am of the aristocracy of the Imperishables. And man has the *Moral Sense*. You understand? He has the *Moral Sense*. That would seem to be difference enough between us, all by itself."

He stopped there, as if that settled the matter. I was sorry, for at that time I had but a dim idea of what the Moral Sense was. I merely knew that we were proud of having it, and when he talked like that about it, it wounded me, and I felt as a girl feels who thinks her dearest finery is being admired and then overhears strangers making fun of it. For a while we were all silent, and I, for one, was depressed. Then Satan began to chat again, and soon he was sparkling along in such a cheerful and vivacious vein that my spirits rose once more. He told some very cunning things that put us in a gale of laughter; and when he was telling about the time that Samson tied the torches to the foxes' tails and set them loose in the Philistines' corn, and Samson sitting on the fence slapping his thighs and laughing, with the tears running down his cheeks, and lost his balance and fell off the fence, the memory of that picture got him to laughing, too, and we did have a most lovely and jolly time. By and by he said:

"I am going on my errand now."

"Don't!" we all said. "Don't go; stay with us. You won't come back."

"Yes, I will; I give you my word."

"When? To-night? Say when."

"It won't be long. You will see."

"We like you."

"And I you. And as a proof of it I will show you something fine to see. Usually when I go I merely vanish; but now I will dissolve myself and let you see me do it."

He stood up, and it was quickly finished. He thinned away and thinned away until he was a soap-bubble, except that he kept his shape. You could see the bushes through him as clearly as you see things through a soap-bubble, and all over him played and flashed the delicate iridescent colors of the bubble, and along with them was that thing shaped like a window-sash which you always see on the globe of the bubble. You have seen a bubble strike the carpet and lightly bound along two or three times before it bursts. He did that. He sprang—touched the grass—bounded—floated along—touched again—and so on, and presently exploded—puff! and in his place was vacancy.

It was a strange and beautiful thing to see. We did not say anything, but sat wondering and dreaming and blinking; and finally Seppi roused up and said, mournfully sighing:

"I suppose none of it has happened."

Nikolaus signed and said about the same.

I was miserable to hear them say it, for it was the same cold fear that was in my own mind. Then we saw poor old Father Peter wandering along back, with his head bent down, searching the ground. When he was pretty close to us he looked up and saw us, and said, "How long have you been here, boys?"

"A little while, Father."

"Then it is since I came by, and maybe you can help me. Did you come up by the path?"

"Yes, Father."

"That is good. I came the same way. I have lost my wallet. There wasn't much in it, but a very little is much to me, for it was all I had. I suppose you haven't seen anything of it?"

"No, Father, but we will help you hunt."

"It is what I was going to ask you. Why, here it is!"

We hadn't noticed it; yet there it lay, right where Satan stood when he began to melt—if he did melt and it wasn't a delusion. Father Peter picked it up and looked very much surprised.

"It is mine," he said, "but not the contents. This is fat; mine was flat; mine was light; this is heavy." He opened it; it was stuffed as full as it could hold with gold coins. He let us gaze our fill; and of course we did gaze, for we had never seen so much money at one time before. All our mouths came open to say "Satan did it!" but nothing came out. There it was, you see—we couldn't tell what Satan didn't want told; he had said so himself.

"Boys, did you do this?"

It made us laugh. And it made him laugh, too, as soon as he thought what a foolish question it was.

"Who has been here?"

Our mouths came open to answer, but stood so for a moment, because we couldn't say "Nobody," for it wouldn't be true, and the right word didn't seem to come; then I thought of the right one, and said it:

"Not a human being."

"That is so," said the others, and let their mouths go shut.

"It is not so," said Father Peter, and looked at us very severely. "I came by here a while ago, and there was no one here, but that is nothing; some one has been here since. I don't mean to say that the person didn't pass here before you came, and I don't mean to say you saw him, but some one did pass, that I know. On your honor—you saw no one?"

"Not a human being."

"That is sufficient; I know you are telling me the truth."

He began to count the money on the path, we on our knees eagerly helping to stack it in little piles.

"It's eleven hundred ducats odd!" he said. "Oh dear! if it were only mine—and I need it so!" and his voice broke and his lips quivered.

"It is yours, sir!" we all cried out at once, "every heller!"

"No—it isn't mine. Only four ducats are mine; the rest . . . !" He fell to dreaming, poor old soul, and caressing some of the coins in his hands, and forgot where he was, sitting there on his heels with his old gray head bare; it was pitiful to see. "No," he said, waking up, "it isn't mine. I can't account for it. I think some enemy . . . it must be a trap."

Nikolaus said: "Father Peter, with the exception of the astrologer you haven't a real enemy in the village—nor Marget, either. And not even a half-enemy that's rich enough to chance eleven hundred ducats to do you a mean turn. I'll ask you if that's so or not?"

He couldn't get around that argument, and it cheered him up. "But it isn't mine, you see—it isn't mine, in any case."

He said it in a wistful way, like a person that wouldn't be sorry, but glad, if anybody would contradict him.

"It is yours, Father Peter, and we are witness to it. Aren't we, boys?"

"Yes we are—and we'll stand by it, too."

"Bless your hearts, you do almost persuade me; you do, indeed. If I had only a hundred-odd ducats of it! The house is mortgaged for it, and we've no home for our heads if we don't pay to-morrow. And that four ducats is all we've got in the—"

"It's yours, every bit of it, and you've got to take it—we are bail that it's all right. Aren't we, Theodor? Aren't we, Seppi?"

We two said yes, and Nikolaus stuffed the money back into the shabby old wallet and made the owner take it. So he said he would use two hundred of it, for his house was good enough security for that, and would put the rest at interest till the rightful owner came for it; and on our side we must sign a paper showing how he got the money—a paper to show to the villagers as proof that he had not got out of his troubles dishonestly.

IV

It made immense talk next day, when Father Peter paid Solomon Isaacs in gold and left the rest of the money with him at interest. Also, there was a pleasant change; many people called at the house to congratulate him, and a number of cool old friends became kind and friendly again; and, to top all, Marget was invited to a party.

And there was no mystery; Father Peter told the whole circumstance just as it happened, and said he could not account for it, only it was the plain hand of Providence, so far as he could see.

One or two shook their heads and said privately it looked more like the hand of Satan; and really that seemed a surprisingly good guess for ignorant people like that. Some came slyly buzzing around and tried to coax us boys to come out and "tell the truth;" and promised they wouldn't ever tell, but only wanted to know for their own satisfaction, because the whole thing was so curious. They even wanted to buy the secret, and pay money for it; and if we could have invented something that would answer—but we couldn't; we hadn't the ingenuity, so we had to let the chance go by, and it was a pity.

We carried that secret around without any trouble, but the other one, the big one, the splendid one, burned the very vitals of us, it was so hot to get out and we so hot to let it out and astonish people with it. But we had to keep it in; in fact, it kept itself in. Satan said it would, and it did. We went off every day and got to ourselves in the woods so that we could talk about Satan, and really that was the only subject we thought of or cared anything about; and day and night we watched for him and hoped he would come, and we got more and more impatient all the time. We hadn't any interest in the other boys any more, and wouldn't take part in their games and enterprises. They seemed so tame, after Satan; and their doings so trifling and commonplace after his adventures in antiquity and the constellations, and his miracles and meltings and explosions, and all that.

During the first day we were in a state of anxiety on account of one thing, and we kept going to Father Peter's house on one pretext or another to keep track of it. That was the gold coin; we were afraid it would crumble and turn to dust, like fairy money. If it did—But it didn't. At the end of the day no complaint had been made about it, so after that we were satisfied that it was real gold, and dropped the anxiety out of our minds.

There was a question which we wanted to ask Father Peter, and finally we went there the second evening, a little diffidently, after drawing straws, and I asked it as casually as I could, though it did not sound as casual as I wanted, because I didn't know how:

"What is the Moral Sense, sir?"

He looked down, surprised, over his great spectacles, and said, "Why, it is the faculty which enables us to distinguish good from evil."

It threw some light, but not a glare, and I was a little disappointed, also to some degree embarrassed. He was waiting for me to go on, so in default of anything else to say, I asked, "Is it valuable?"

"Valuable? Heavens! lad, it is the one thing that lifts man above the beasts that perish and makes him heir to immortality!"

This did not remind me of anything further to say, so I got out, with the other boys, and we went away with that indefinite sense you have often had of being filled but not fatted. They wanted me to explain, but I was tired.

We passed out through the parlor, and there was Marget at the spinnet teaching Marie Lueger. So one of the deserting pupils was back; and an influential one, too; the others would follow. Marget jumped up and ran and thanked us again, with tears in her eyes—this was the third time—for saving her and her uncle from being turned into the street, and we told her again we hadn't done it; but that was her way, she never could be grateful enough for anything a person did for her; so we let her have her say. And as we passed through the garden, there was Wilhelm Meidling sitting there waiting, for it was getting toward the edge of the evening, and he would be asking Marget to take a walk along the river with him when she was done with the lesson. He was a young lawyer, and succeeding fairly well and working his way along, little by little. He was very fond of Marget, and she of him. He had not deserted along with the others, but had stood his ground all through. His faithfulness was not lost on Marget and her uncle. He hadn't so very much talent, but he was handsome and good, and these are a kind of talents themselves and help along. He asked us how the lesson was getting along, and we told him it was about done. And maybe it was so; we didn't know anything about it, but we judged it would please him, and it did, and didn't cost us anything.

V

On the fourth day comes the astrologer from his crumbling old tower up the valley, where he had heard the news, I reckon. He had a private talk with us, and we told him what we could, for we were mightily in dread of him. He sat there studying and studying awhile to himself; then he asked:

"How many ducats did you say?"

"Eleven hundred and seven, sir."

Then he said, as if he were talking to himself: "It is ver-y singular. Yes . . . very strange. A curious coincidence." Then he began to ask questions, and went over the whole ground from the beginning, we answering. By and by he said: "Eleven hundred and six ducats. It is a large sum."

"Seven," said Seppi, correcting him.

"Oh seven, was it? Of course a ducat more or less isn't of consequence, but you said eleven hundred and six before."

It would not have been safe for us to say he was mistaken, but he knew he was. Nikolaus said, "We ask pardon for the mistake, but we meant to say seven."

"Oh, it is no matter, lad; it was merely that I noticed the discrepancy. It is several days, and you cannot be expected to remember precisely. One is apt to be inexact when there is no particular circumstance to impress the count upon the memory."

"But there was one, sir," said Seppi, eagerly.

"What was it, my son?" asked the astrologer, indifferently.

"First, we all counted the piles of coin, each in turn, and all made it the same—eleven hundred and six. But I had slipped one out, for fun, when the count began, and now I slipped it back and said, 'I think there is a mistake—there are eleven hundred and seven; let us count again.' We did, and of course I was right. They were astonished; then I told how it came about."

The astrologer asked us if this was so, and we said it was.

"That settles it," he said. "I know the thief now. Lads, the money was stolen."

Then he went away, leaving us very much troubled, and wondering what he could mean. In about an hour we found out; for by that time it was all over the village that Father Peter had been arrested for stealing a great sum of money from the astrologer. Everybody's tongue was loose and going. Many said it was not in Father Peter's character and must be a mistake; but the others shook their heads and said misery and want could drive a suffering man to almost anything. About one detail there were no differences; all agreed that Father Peter's account of how the money came into his hands was just about unbelievable—it had such an impossible look. They said it might have come into the astrologer's hands in some such way, but into Father Peter's, never! Our characters began to suffer now. We were Father Peter's only witnesses; how much did he probably pay us to back up his fantastic tale? People talked that kind of talk to us pretty freely and frankly, and were full of scoffings when we begged them to believe really we had told only the truth. Our parents were harder on us than any one else. Our fathers said we were disgracing our families, and they commanded us to purge ourselves of our lie, and there was no limit to their anger when we continued to say we had spoken true. Our mothers cried over us and begged us to give back our bribe and get back our honest names and save our families from shame, and come out and honorably confess. And at last we were so worried and harassed that we tried to tell the whole thing. Satan and all—but no, it wouldn't come out. We were hoping and longing all the time that Satan would come and help us out of our trouble, but there was no sign of him.

Within an hour after the astrologer's talk with us, Father Peter was in prison and the money sealed up and in the hands of the officers of the law. The money was in a bag, and Solomon Isaacs said he had not touched it since he had counted it; his oath was taken that it was the same money, and that the amount was eleven hundred and seven ducats. Father Peter claimed trial by the ecclesiastical court, but our other priest, Father Adolf, said an ecclesiastical court hadn't jurisdiction over a suspended priest. The bishop upheld him. That settled it; the case would go to trial in the civil court. The court would not sit for some time to come. Wilhelm Meidling would be Father Peter's lawyer and do the best he could, of course, but he told us privately that a weak case on his side and all the power and prejudice on the other made the outlook bad.

So Marget's new happiness died a quick death. No friends came to condole with her, and none were expected; an unsigned note withdrew her invitation to the party. There would be no scholars to take lessons. How could she support herself? She could remain in the house, for the mortgage was paid off, though the government and not poor Solomon Isaacs had the mortgage-money in its grip for the present. Old Ursula, who was cook, chambermaid, housekeeper, laundress, and everything else for Father Peter, and had been Marget's nurse in earlier years, said God would provide. But she said that from habit, for she was a good Christian. She meant to help in the providing, to make sure, if she could find a way.

We boys wanted to go and see Marget and show friendliness for her, but our parents were afraid of offending the community and wouldn't let us. The astrologer was going around inflaming everybody against Father Peter, and saying he was an abandoned thief and had stolen eleven hundred and seven gold ducats from him. He said he knew he was a thief from that fact, for it was exactly the sum he had lost and which Father Peter pretended he had "found."

In the afternoon of the fourth day after the catastrophe old Ursula appeared at our house and asked for some washing to do, and begged my mother to keep this secret, to save Marget's pride, who would stop this project if she found it out, yet Marget had not enough to eat and was growing weak. Ursula was growing weak herself, and showed it; and she ate of the food that was offered her like a starving person, but could not be persuaded to carry any home, for Marget would not eat charity food. She took some clothes down to the stream to wash them, but we saw from the window that handling the bat was too much for her strength; so she was called back and a trifle of money offered her, which she was afraid to take lest Marget should suspect; then she took it, saying she would explain that she found it in the road. To keep it from being a lie and damning her soul, she got me to drop it while she watched; then she went along by there and found it, and exclaimed with surprise and joy, and picked it up and went her way. Like the rest of the village, she could tell every-day lies fast enough and without taking any precautions against fire and brimstone on their account; but this was a new kind of lie, and it had a dangerous look because she hadn't had any practice in it. After a week's practice it wouldn't have given her any trouble. It is the way we are made.

I was in trouble, for how would Marget live? Ursula could not find a coin in the road every day—perhaps not even a second one. And I was ashamed, too, for not having been near Marget, and she so in need of friends: but that was my parents' fault, not mine, and I couldn't help it.

I was walking along the path, feeling very downhearted, when a most cheery and tingling freshening-up sensation went rippling through me, and I was too glad for any words, for I knew by that sign that Satan was by. I had noticed it before. Next moment he was alongside of me and I was telling him all my trouble and what had been happening to Marget and her uncle. While we were talking we turned a curve and saw old Ursula resting in the shade of a tree, and she had a lean stray kitten in her lap and was petting it. I asked her where she got it, and she said it came out of the woods and followed her; and she said it probably hadn't any mother or any friends and she was going to take it home and take care of it. Satan said:

"I understand you are very poor. Why do you want to add another mouth to feed? Why don't you give it to some rich person?"

Ursula bridled at this and said: "Perhaps you would like to have it. You must be rich, with your fine clothes and quality airs." Then she sniffed and said: "Give it to the rich—the idea!

The rich don't care for anybody but themselves; it's only the poor that have feeling for the poor, and help them. The poor and God. God will provide for this kitten."

"What makes you think so?"

Ursula's eyes snapped with anger. "Because I know it!" she said. "Not a sparrow falls to the ground without His seeing it."

"But it falls, just the same. What good is seeing it fall?"

Old Ursula's jaws worked, but she could not get any word out for the moment, she was so horrified. When she got her tongue she stormed out, "Go about your business, you puppy, or I will take a stick to you!"

I could not speak, I was so scared. I knew that with his notions about the human race Satan would consider it a matter of no consequence to strike her dead, there being "plenty more;" but my tongue stood still, I could give her no warning. But nothing happened; Satan remained tranquil—tranquil and indifferent. I suppose he could not be insulted by Ursula any more than the king could be insulted by a tumble-bug. The old woman jumped to her feet when she made her remark, and did it as briskly as a young girl. It had been many years since she had done the like of that. That was Satan's influence; he was a fresh breeze to the weak and the sick, wherever he came. His presence affected even the lean kitten, and it skipped to the ground and began to chase a leaf. This surprised Ursula, and she stood looking at the creature and nodding her head wonderingly, her anger quite forgotten.

"What's come over it?" she said. "Awhile ago it could hardly walk."

"You have not seen a kitten of that breed before," said Satan.

Ursula was not proposing to be friendly with the mocking stranger, and she gave him an ungentle look and retorted: "Who asked you to come here and pester me, I'd like to know? and what do you know about what I've seen and what I haven't seen?"

"You haven't seen a kitten with the hair-spines on its tongue pointing to the front, have you?"

"No—nor you, either."

"Well, examine this one and see."

Ursula was become pretty spry, but the kitten was spryer, and she could not catch it, and had to give it up. Then Satan said:

"Give it a name, and maybe it will come."

Ursula tried several names, but the kitten was not interested.

"Call it Agnes. Try that."

The creature answered to the name and came. Ursula examined its tongue. "Upon my word, it's true!" she said. "I have not seen this kind of a cat before. Is it yours?"

"No."

"Then how did you know its name so pat?"

"Because all cats of that breed are named Agnes; they will not answer to any other."

Ursula was impressed. "It is the most wonderful thing!" Then a shadow of trouble came into her face, for her superstitions were aroused, and she reluctantly put the creature down, saying: "I suppose I must let it go; I am not afraid—no, not exactly that, though the priest—well, I've heard people—indeed, many people . . . And, besides, it is quite well now and can take care of itself." She sighed, and turned to go, murmuring: "It is such a pretty one, too, and would be such company—and the house is so sad and lonesome these troubled days . . . Miss Marget so mournful and just a shadow, and the old master shut up in jail."

"It seems a pity not to keep it," said Satan.

Ursula turned quickly—just as if she were hoping some one would encourage her.

"Why?" she asked, wistfully.

"Because this breed brings luck."

"Does it? Is it true? Young man, do you know it to be true? How does it bring luck?"

"Well, it brings money, anyway."

Ursula looked disappointed. "Money? A cat bring money? The idea! You could never sell it here; people do not buy cats here; one can't even give them away." She turned to go.

"I don't mean sell it. I mean have an income from it. This kind is called the Lucky Cat. Its owner finds four silver groschen in his pocket every morning."

I saw the indignation rising in the old woman's face. She was insulted. This boy was making fun of her. That was her thought.

She thrust her hands into her pockets and straightened up to give him a piece of her mind. Her temper was all up, and hot. Her mouth came open and let out three words of a bitter sentence, . . . then it fell silent, and the anger in her face turned to surprise or wonder or fear, or something, and she slowly brought out her hands from her pockets and opened them and held them so. In one was my piece of money, in the other lay four silver groschen. She gazed a little while, perhaps to see if the groschen would vanish away; then she said, fervently:

"It's true—it's true—and I'm ashamed and beg forgiveness. O dear master and benefactor!" And she ran to Satan and kissed his hand, over and over again, according to the Austrian custom.

In her heart she probably believed it was a witch-cat and an agent of the Devil; but no matter, it was all the more certain to be able to keep its contract and furnish a daily good living for the family, for in matters of finance even the piousest of our peasants would have more confidence in an arrangement with the Devil than with an archangel. Ursula started homeward, with Agnes in her arms, and I said I wished I had her privilege of seeing Marget.

Then I caught my breath, for we were there. There in the parlor, and Marget standing looking at us, astonished. She was feeble and pale, but I knew that those conditions would not last in Satan's atmosphere, and it turned out so. I introduced Satan—that is, Philip Traum—and we sat down and talked. There was no constraint. We were simple folk, in our village, and when a stranger was a pleasant person we were soon friends. Marget wondered how we got in without her hearing us. Traum said the door was open, and we walked in and waited until she should turn around and greet us. This was not true; no door was open; we entered through the walls or the roof or down the chimney, or somehow; but no matter, what Satan wished a person to believe, the person was sure to believe, and so Marget was quite satisfied with that explanation. And then the main part of her mind was on Traum, anyway; she couldn't keep her eyes off him, he was so beautiful. That gratified me, and made me proud. I hoped he would show off some, but he didn't. He seemed only interested in being friendly and telling lies. He said he was an orphan. That made Marget pity him. The water came into her eyes. He said he had never known his mamma; she passed away while he was a young thing; and said his papa was in shattered health, and had no property to speak of—in fact, none of any earthly value—but he had an uncle in business down in the tropics, and he was very well off and had a monopoly, and it was from this uncle that he drew his support. The very mention of a kind uncle was enough to remind Marget of her own, and her eyes filled again. She said she hoped their two uncles would meet, some day. It made me shudder. Philip said he hoped so, too; and that made me shudder again.

"Maybe they will," said Marget. "Does your uncle travel much?"

"Oh yes, he goes all about; he has business everywhere."

And so they went on chatting, and poor Marget forgot her sorrow for one little while, anyway. It was probably the only really bright and cheery hour she had known lately. I saw she liked Philip, and I knew she would. And when he told her he was studying for the ministry I could see that she liked him better than ever. And then, when he promised to get her admitted to the jail so that she could see her uncle, that was the capstone. He said he would give the guards a little present, and she must always go in the evening after dark, and say nothing, "but just show this paper and pass in, and show it again when you come out"—and he scribbled some queer marks on the paper and gave it to her, and she was ever so thankful, and right away was in a fever for the sun to go down; for in that old, cruel time prisoners were not allowed to see their friends, and sometimes they spend years in the jails without ever seeing a friendly face. I judged that the marks on the paper were an enchantment, and that the guards would not know what they were doing, nor have any memory of it afterward; and that was indeed the way of it. Ursula put her head in at the door now and said:

"Supper's ready, miss." Then she saw us and looked frightened, and motioned me to come to her, which I did, and she asked if we had told about the cat. I said no, and she was relieved, and said please don't; for if Miss Marget knew, she would think it was an unholy cat and would send for a priest and have its gifts all purified out of it, and then there wouldn't be any more dividends. So I said we wouldn't tell, and she was satisfied. Then I was beginning to say good-by to Marget, but Satan interrupted and said, ever so politely—well, I don't remember just the words, but anyway he as good as invited himself to supper, and me, too. Of course Marget was miserably embarrassed, for she had no reason to suppose there would be half enough for a sick bird. Ursula heard him, and she came straight into the room, not a bit pleased. At first she was astonished to see Marget looking so fresh and rosy, and said so; then she spoke up in her native tongue, which was Bohemian, and said—as I learned afterward—"Send him away, Miss Marget; there's not victuals enough."

Before Marget could speak, Satan had the word, and was talking back to Ursula in her own language—which was a surprise to her, and for her mistress, too. He said, "Didn't I see you down the road awhile ago?"

"Yes, sir."

"Ah, that pleases me; I see you remember me." He stepped to her and whispered: "I told you it is a Lucky Cat. Don't be troubled; it will provide."

That sponged the slate of Ursula's feelings clean of its anxieties, and a deep, financial joy shone in her eyes. The cat's value was augmenting. It was getting full time for Marget to take some sort of notice of Satan's invitation, and she did it in the best way, the honest way that was natural to her. She said she had little to offer, but that we were welcome if we would share it with her.

We had supper in the kitchen, and Ursula waited at table. A small fish was in the frying-pan, crisp and brown and tempting, and one could see that Marget was not expecting such respectable food as this. Ursula brought it, and Marget divided it between Satan and me, declining to take any of it herself; and was beginning to say she did not care for fish to-day, but she did not finish the remark. It was because she noticed that another fish had appeared in the pan. She looked surprised, but did not say anything. She probably meant to inquire of Ursula about this later. There were other surprises: flesh and game and wines and fruits—things which had been strangers in that house lately; but Marget made no exclamations, and now even looked unsurprised, which was Satan's influence, of course. Satan talked right along, and was entertaining, and made the time pass pleasantly and cheerfully; and although he told a good many lies, it was no harm in him, for he was only an angel and did not know any better. They do not know right from wrong; I knew this, because I remembered what he had said about it. He got on the good side of Ursula. He praised her to Marget, confidentially, but speaking just loud enough for Ursula to hear. He said she was a fine woman, and he hoped some day to bring her and his uncle together. Very soon Ursula was mincing and simpering around in a ridiculous girly way, and smoothing out her gown and prinking at herself like a foolish old hen, and all the time pretending she was not hearing what Satan was saying. I was ashamed, for it showed us to be what Satan considered us, a silly race and trivial. Satan said his uncle entertained a great deal, and to have a clever woman presiding over the festivities would double the attractions of the place.

"But your uncle is a gentleman, isn't he?" asked Marget.

"Yes," said Satan indifferently; "some even call him a Prince, out of compliment, but he is not bigoted; to him personal merit is everything, rank nothing."

My hand was hanging down by my chair; Agnes came along and licked it; by this act a secret was revealed. I started to say, "It is all a mistake; this is just a common, ordinary cat; the hair-needles on her tongue point inward, not outward." But the words did not come, because they couldn't. Satan smiled upon me, and I understood.

When it was dark Marget took food and wine and fruit, in a basket, and hurried away to the jail, and Satan and I walked toward my home. I was thinking to myself that I should like to see what the inside of the jail was like; Satan overheard the thought, and the next moment we were in the jail. We were in the torture-chamber, Satan said. The rack was there, and the other instruments, and there was a smoky lantern or two hanging on the walls and helping to make the place look dim and dreadful. There were people there—and executioners—but as they took no notice of us, it meant that we were invisible. A young man lay bound, and Satan said he was suspected of being a heretic, and the executioners were about to inquire into it. They asked the man to confess to the charge, and he said he could not, for it was not true. Then they drove splinter after splinter under his nails, and he shrieked with the pain. Satan was not disturbed, but I could not endure it, and had to be whisked out of there. I was faint and sick, but the fresh air revived me, and we walked toward my home. I said it was a brutal thing.

"No, it was a human thing. You should not insult the brutes by such a misuse of that word; they have not deserved it," and he went on talking like that. "It is like your paltry race—always lying, always claiming virtues which it hasn't got, always denying them to the higher animals, which alone possess them. No brute ever does a cruel thing—that is the monopoly of those with the Moral Sense. When a brute inflicts pain he does it innocently; it is not wrong; for him there is no such thing as wrong. And he does not inflict pain for the pleasure of inflicting it—only man does that. Inspired by that mongrel Moral Sense of his! A sense whose function is to distinguish between right and wrong, with liberty to choose which of them he will do. Now what advantage can he get out of that? He is always choosing, and in nine cases out of ten he prefers the wrong. There shouldn't be any wrong; and without the Moral Sense there couldn't be any. And yet he is such an unreasoning creature that he is not able to perceive that the Moral Sense degrades him to the bottom layer of animated beings and is a shameful possession. Are you feeling better? Let me show you something."

VI

In a moment we were in a French village. We walked through a great factory of some sort, where men and women and little children were toiling in heat and dirt and a fog of dust; and they were clothed in rags, and drooped at their work, for they were worn and half starved, and weak and drowsy. Satan said:

"It is some more Moral Sense. The proprietors are rich, and very holy; but the wage they pay to these poor brothers and sisters of theirs is only enough to keep them from dropping dead with hunger. The work-hours are fourteen per day, winter and summer—from six in the morning till eight at night—little children and all. And they walk to and from the pigsties which they inhabit—four miles each way, through mud and slush, rain, snow, sleet, and storm, daily, year in and year out. They get four hours of sleep. They kennel together, three families in a room, in unimaginable filth and stench; and disease comes, and they die off like flies. Have they committed a crime, these mangy things? No. What have they done, that they are punished so? Nothing at all, except getting themselves born into your foolish race. You have seen how they treat a misdoer there in the jail; now you see how they treat the innocent and the worthy. Is your race logical? Are these ill-smelling innocents better off than that heretic? Indeed, no; his punishment is trivial compared with theirs. They broke him on the wheel and smashed him to rags and pulp after we left, and he is dead now, and free of your precious race; but these poor slaves here—why, they have been dying for years, and some of them will not escape from life for years to come. It is the Moral Sense which teaches the factory proprietors the difference between right and wrong—you perceive the result. They think themselves better than dogs. Ah, you are such an illogical, unreasoning race! And paltry—oh, unspeakably!"

Then he dropped all seriousness and just overstrained himself making fun of us, and deriding our pride in our warlike deeds, our great heroes, our imperishable fames, our mighty kings, our ancient aristocracies, our venerable history—and laughed and laughed till it was enough to make a person sick to hear him; and finally he sobered a little and said, "But, after all, it is not all ridiculous; there is a sort of pathos about it when one remembers how few are your days, how childish your pomps, and what shadows you are!"

Presently all things vanished suddenly from my sight, and I knew what it meant. The next moment we were walking along in our village; and down toward the river I saw the twinkling lights of the Golden Stag. Then in the dark I heard a joyful cry:

"He's come again!"

It was Seppi Wohlmeyer. He had felt his blood leap and his spirits rise in a way that could mean only one thing, and he knew Satan was near, although it was too dark to see him. He came to us, and we walked along together, and Seppi poured out his gladness like water. It was as if he were a lover and had found his sweetheart who had been lost. Seppi was a smart and animated boy, and had enthusiasm and expression, and was a contrast to Nikolaus and me. He was full of the last new mystery, now—the disappearance of Hans Oppert, the village loafer. People were beginning to be curious about it, he said. He did not say anxious—curious was the right word, and strong enough. No one had seen Hans for a couple of days.

"Not since he did that brutal thing, you know," he said.

"What brutal thing?" It was Satan that asked.

"Well, he is always clubbing his dog, which is a good dog, and his only friend, and is faithful, and loves him, and does no one any harm; and two days ago he was at it again, just for nothing—just for pleasure—and the dog was howling and begging, and Theodor and I begged, too, but he threatened us, and struck the dog again with all his might and knocked one of his eyes out, and he said to us, 'There, I hope you are satisfied now; that's what you have got for him by your damned meddling'—and he laughed, the heartless brute." Seppi's voice trembled with pity and anger. I guessed what Satan would say, and he said it.

"There is that misused word again—that shabby slander. Brutes do not act like that, but only men."

"Well, it was inhuman, anyway."

"No, it wasn't, Seppi; it was human—quite distinctly human. It is not pleasant to hear you libel the higher animals by attributing to them dispositions which they are free from, and which are found nowhere but in the human heart. None of the higher animals is tainted with the disease called the Moral Sense. Purify your language, Seppi; drop those lying phrases out of it."

He spoke pretty sternly—for him—and I was sorry I hadn't warned Seppi to be more particular about the word he used. I knew how he was feeling. He would not want to offend Satan; he would rather offend all his kin. There was an uncomfortable silence, but relief soon came, for that poor dog came along now, with his eye hanging down, and went straight to Satan, and began to moan and mutter brokenly, and Satan began to answer in the same way, and it was plain that they were talking together in the dog language. We all sat down in the grass, in the moonlight, for the clouds were breaking away now, and Satan took the dog's head in his lap and put the eye back in its place, and the dog was comfortable, and he wagged his tail and licked Satan's hand, and looked thankful and said the same; I knew he was saying it, though I did not understand the words. Then the two talked together a bit, and Satan said:

"He says his master was drunk."

"Yes, he was," said we.

"And an hour later he fell over the precipice there beyond the Cliff Pasture."

"We know the place; it is three miles from here."

"And the dog has been often to the village, begging people to go there, but he was only driven away and not listened to."

We remembered it, but hadn't understood what he wanted.

"He only wanted help for the man who had misused him, and he thought only of that, and has had no food nor sought any. He has watched by his master two nights. What do you think of your race? Is heaven reserved for it, and this dog ruled out, as your teachers tell you? Can your race add anything to this dog's stock of morals and magnanimities?" He spoke to the creature, who jumped up, eager and happy, and apparently ready for orders and impatient to execute them. "Get some men; go with the dog—he will show you that carrion; and take a priest along to arrange about insurance, for death is near."

With the last word he vanished, to our sorrow and disappointment. We got the men and Father Adolf, and we saw the man die. Nobody cared but the dog; he mourned and grieved, and licked the dead face, and could not be comforted. We buried him where he was, and without a coffin, for he had no money, and no friend but the dog. If we had been an hour earlier the priest would have been in time to send that poor creature to heaven, but now he was gone down into the awful fires, to burn forever. It seemed such a pity that in a world where so many people have difficulty to put in their time, one little hour could not have been spared for this poor creature who needed it so much, and to whom it would have made the difference between eternal joy and eternal pain. It gave an appalling idea of the value of an hour, and I thought I could never waste one again without remorse and terror. Seppi was depressed and grieved, and said it must be so much better to be a dog and not run such awful risks. We took this one home with us and kept him for our own. Seppi had a very good thought as we were walking along, and it cheered us up and made us feel much better. He said the dog had forgiven the man that had wronged him so, and maybe God would accept that absolution.

There was a very dull week, now, for Satan did not come, nothing much was going on, and we boys could not venture to go and see Marget, because the nights were moonlit and our parents might find us out if we tried. But we came across Ursula a couple of times taking a walk in the meadows beyond the river to air the cat, and we learned from her that things were going well. She had natty new clothes on and bore a prosperous look. The four groschen a day were arriving without a break, but were not being spent for food and wine and such things—the cat attended to all that.

Marget was enduring her forsakenness and isolation fairly well, all things considered, and was cheerful, by help of Wilhelm Meidling. She spent an hour or two every night in the jail with her uncle, and had fattened him up with the cat's contributions. But she was curious to know more about Philip Traum, and hoped I would bring him again. Ursula was curious about him herself, and asked a good many questions about his uncle. It made the boys laugh, for I had told them the nonsense Satan had been stuffing her with. She got no satisfaction out of us, our tongues being tied.

Ursula gave us a small item of information: money being plenty now, she had taken on a servant to help about the house and run errands. She tried to tell it in a commonplace, matter-of-course way, but she was so set up by it and so vain of it that her pride in it leaked out pretty plainly. It was beautiful to see her veiled delight in this grandeur, poor old thing, but when we heard the name of the servant we wondered if she had been altogether wise; for although we were young, and often thoughtless, we had fairly good perception on some matters. This boy was Gottfried Narr, a dull, good creature, with no harm in him and nothing against him personally; still, he was under a cloud, and properly so, for it had not been six months since a social blight had mildewed the family—his grandmother had been burned as a witch. When that kind of a malady is in the blood it does not always come out with just one burning. Just now was not a good time for Ursula and Marget to be having dealings with a member of such a family, for the witch-terror had risen higher during the past year than it had ever reached in the memory of the oldest villagers. The mere mention of a witch was almost enough to frighten us out of our wits. This was natural enough, because of late years there were more kinds of witches than there used to be; in old times it had been only old women, but of late years they were of all ages—even children of eight and nine; it was getting so that anybody might turn out to be a familiar of the Devil—age and sex hadn't anything to do with it. In our little region we had tried to extirpate the witches, but the more of them we burned the more of the breed rose up in their places.

Once, in a school for girls only ten miles away, the teachers found that the back of one of the girls was all red and inflamed, and they were greatly frightened, believing it to be the Devil's marks. The girl was scared, and begged them not to denounce her, and said it was only fleas; but of course it would not do to let the matter rest there. All the girls were examined, and eleven out of the fifty were badly marked, the rest less so. A commission was appointed, but the eleven only cried for their mothers and would not confess. Then they were shut up, each by herself, in the dark, and put on black bread and water for ten days and nights; and by that time they were haggard and wild, and their eyes were dry and they did not cry any more, but only sat and mumbled, and would not take the food. Then one of them confessed, and said they had often ridden through the air on broomsticks to the witches' Sabbath, and in a bleak place high up in the mountains had danced and drunk and caroused with several hundred other witches and the Evil One, and all had conducted themselves in a scandalous way and had reviled the priests and blasphemed God. That is what she said—not in narrative form, for she was not able to remember any of the details without having them called to her mind one after the other; but the commission did that, for they knew just what questions to ask, they being all written down for the use of witch-commissioners two centuries before. They asked, "Did you do so and so?" and she always said yes, and looked weary and tired, and took no interest in it. And so when the other ten heard that this one confessed, they confessed, too, and answered yes to the questions. Then they were burned at the stake all together, which was just and right; and everybody went from all the countryside to see it. I went, too; but when I saw that one of them was a bonny, sweet girl I used to play with, and looked so pitiful there chained to the stake, and her mother crying over her and devouring her with kisses and clinging around her neck, and saying, "Oh, my God! oh, my God!" it was too dreadful, and I went away.

It was bitter cold weather when Gottfried's grandmother was burned. It was charged that she had cured bad headaches by kneading the person's head and neck with her fingers—as she said—but really by the Devil's help, as everybody knew. They were going to examine her, but she stopped them, and confessed straight off that her power was from the Devil. So they appointed to burn her next morning, early, in our market-square. The officer who was to prepare the fire was there first, and prepared it. She was there next—brought by the constables, who left her and went to fetch another witch. Her family did not come with her. They might be reviled, maybe stoned, if the people were excited. I came, and gave her an apple. She was squatting at the fire, warming herself and waiting; and her old lips and hands were blue with the cold. A stranger came next. He was a traveler, passing through; and he spoke to her gently, and, seeing nobody but me there to hear, said he was sorry for her. And he asked if what she confessed was true, and she said no. He looked surprised and still more sorry then, and asked her:

"Then why did you confess?"

"I am old and very poor," she said, "and I work for my living.

There was no way but to confess. If I hadn't they might have set me free. That would ruin me, for no one would forget that I had been suspected of being a witch, and so I would get no more work, and wherever I went they would set the dogs on me. In a little while I would starve. The fire is best; it is soon over. You have been good to me, you two, and I thank you."

She snuggled closer to the fire, and put out her hands to warm them, the snow-flakes descending soft and still on her old gray head and making it white and whiter. The crowd was gathering now, and an egg came flying and struck her in the eye, and broke and ran down her face. There was a laugh at that.

I told Satan all about the eleven girls and the old woman, once, but it did not affect him. He only said it was the human race, and what the human race did was of no consequence. And he said he had seen it made; and it was not made of clay; it was made of mud—part of it was, anyway. I knew what he meant by that—the Moral Sense. He saw the thought in my head, and it tickled him and made him laugh. Then he called a bullock out of a pasture and petted it and talked with it, and said:

"There—he wouldn't drive children mad with hunger and fright and loneliness, and then burn them for confessing to things invented for them which had never happened. And neither would he break the hearts of innocent, poor old women and make them afraid to trust themselves among their own race; and he would not insult them in their death-agony. For he is not besmirched with the Moral Sense, but is as the angels are, and knows no wrong, and never does it."

Lovely as he was, Satan could be cruelly offensive when he chose; and he always chose when the human race was brought to his attention. He always turned up his nose at it, and never had a kind word for it.

Well, as I was saying, we boys doubted if it was a good time for Ursula to be hiring a member of the Narr family. We were right. When the people found it out they were naturally indignant. And, moreover, since Marget and Ursula hadn't enough to eat themselves, where was the money coming from to feed another mouth? That is what they wanted to know; and in order to find out they stopped avoiding Gottfried and began to seek his society and have sociable conversations with him. He was pleased—not thinking any harm and not seeing the trap—and so he talked innocently along, and was no discreeter than a cow.

"Money!" he said; "they've got plenty of it. They pay me two groschen a week, besides my keep. And they live on the fat of the land, I can tell you; the prince himself can't beat their table."

This astonishing statement was conveyed by the astrologer to Father Adolf on a Sunday morning when he was returning from mass. He was deeply moved, and said:

"This must be looked into."

He said there must be witchcraft at the bottom of it, and told the villagers to resume relations with Marget and Ursula in a private and unostentatious way, and keep both eyes open. They were told to keep their own counsel, and not rouse the suspicions of the household. The villagers were at first a bit reluctant to enter such a dreadful place, but the priest said they would be under his protection while there, and no harm could come to them, particularly if they carried a trifle of holy water along and kept their beads and crosses handy. This satisfied them and made them willing to go; envy and malice made the baser sort even eager to go.

And so poor Marget began to have company again, and was as pleased as a cat. She was like 'most anybody else—just human, and happy in her prosperities and not averse from showing them off a little; and she was humanly grateful to have the warm shoulder turned to her and be smiled upon by her friends and the village again; for of all the hard things to bear, to be cut by your neighbors and left in contemptuous solitude is maybe the hardest.

The bars were down, and we could all go there now, and we did—our parents and all—day after day. The cat began to strain herself. She provided the top of everything for those companies, and in abundance—among them many a dish and many a wine which they had not tasted before and which they had not even heard of except at second-hand from the prince's servants. And the tableware was much above ordinary, too.

Marget was troubled at times, and pursued Ursula with questions to an uncomfortable degree; but Ursula stood her ground and stuck to it that it was Providence, and said no word about the cat. Marget knew that nothing was impossible to Providence, but she could not help having doubts that this effort was from there, though she was afraid to say so, lest disaster come of it. Witchcraft occurred to her, but she put the thought aside, for this was before Gottfried joined the household, and she knew Ursula was pious and a bitter hater of witches. By the time Gottfried arrived Providence was established, unshakably intrenched, and getting all the gratitude. The cat made no murmur, but went on composedly improving in style and prodigality by experience.

In any community, big or little, there is always a fair proportion of people who are not malicious or unkind by nature, and who never do unkind things except when they are overmastered by fear, or when their self-interest is greatly in danger, or some such matter as that. Eseldorf had its proportion of such people, and ordinarily their good and gentle influence was felt, but these were not ordinary times—on account of the witch-dread—and so we did not seem to have any gentle and compassionate hearts left, to speak of. Every person was frightened at the unaccountable state of things at Marget's house, not doubting that witchcraft was at the bottom of it, and fright frenzied their reason. Naturally there were some who pitied Marget and Ursula for the danger that was gathering about them, but naturally they did not say so; it would not have been safe. So the others had it all their own way, and there was none to advise the ignorant girl and the foolish woman and warn them to modify their doings. We boys wanted to warn them, but we backed down when it came to the pinch, being afraid. We found that we were not manly enough nor brave enough to do a generous action when there was a chance that it could get us into trouble. Neither of us confessed this poor spirit to the others, but did as other people would have done—dropped the subject and talked about something else. And I knew we all felt mean, eating and drinking Marget's fine things along with those companies of spies, and petting her and complimenting her with the rest, and seeing with self-reproach how foolishly happy she was, and never saying a word to put her on her guard. And, indeed, she was happy, and as proud as a princess, and so grateful to have friends again. And all the time these people were watching with all their eyes and reporting all they saw to Father Adolf.

But he couldn't make head or tail of the situation. There must be an enchanter somewhere on the premises, but who was it? Marget was not seen to do any jugglery, nor was Ursula, nor yet Gottfried; and still the wines and dainties never ran short, and a guest could not call for a thing and not get it. To produce these effects was usual enough with witches and enchanters—that part of it was not new; but to do it without any incantations, or even any rumblings or earthquakes or lightnings or apparitions—that was new, novel, wholly irregular. There was nothing in the books like this. Enchanted things were always unreal. Gold turned to dirt in an unenchanted atmosphere, food withered away and vanished. But this test failed in the present case. The spies brought samples: Father Adolf prayed over them, exorcised them, but it did no good; they remained sound and real, they yielded to natural decay only, and took the usual time to do it.

Father Adolf was not merely puzzled, he was also exasperated; for these evidences very nearly convinced him—privately—that there was no witchcraft in the matter. It did not wholly convince him, for this could be a new kind of witchcraft. There was a way to find out as to this: if this prodigal abundance of provender was not brought in from the outside, but produced on the premises, there was witchcraft, sure.

VII

Marget announced a party, and invited forty people; the date for it was seven days away. This was a fine opportunity. Marget's house stood by itself, and it could be easily watched. All the week it was watched night and day. Marget's household went out and in as usual, but they carried nothing in their hands, and neither they nor others brought anything to the house. This was ascertained. Evidently rations for forty people were not being fetched. If they were furnished any sustenance it would have to be made on the premises. It was true that

Marget went out with a basket every evening, but the spies ascertained that she always brought it back empty.

The guests arrived at noon and filled the place. Father Adolf followed; also, after a little the astrologer, without invitation. The spies had informed him that neither at the back nor the front had any parcels been brought in. He entered, and found the eating and drinking going on finely, and everything progressing in a lively and festive way. He glanced around and perceived that many of the cooked delicacies and all of the native and foreign fruits were of a perishable character, and he also recognized that these were fresh and perfect. No apparitions, no incantations, no thunder. That settled it. This was witchcraft. And not only that, but of a new kind—a kind never dreamed of before. It was a prodigious power, an illustrious power; he resolved to discover its secret. The announcement of it would resound throughout the world, penetrate to the remotest lands, paralyze all the nations with amazement—and carry his name with it, and make him renowned forever. It was a wonderful piece of luck, a splendid piece of luck; the glory of it made him dizzy.

All the house made room for him; Marget politely seated him; Ursula ordered Gottfried to bring a special table for him. Then she decked it and furnished it, and asked for his orders.

"Bring me what you will," he said.

The two servants brought supplies from the pantry, together with white wine and red—a bottle of each. The astrologer, who very likely had never seen such delicacies before, poured out a beaker of red wine, drank it off, poured another, then began to eat with a grand appetite.

I was not expecting Satan, for it was more than a week since I had seen or heard of him, but now he came in—I knew it by the feel, though people were in the way and I could not see him. I heard him apologizing for intruding; and he was going away, but Marget urged him to stay, and he thanked her and stayed. She brought him along, introducing him to the girls, and to Meidling, and to some of the elders; and there was quite a rustle of whispers: "It's the young stranger we hear so much about and can't get sight of, he is away so much." "Dear, dear, but he is beautiful—what is his name?" "Philip Traum." "Ah, it fits him!"

(You see, "Traum" is German for "Dream.") "What does he do?" "Studying for the ministry, they say." "His face is his fortune—he'll be a cardinal some day." "Where is his home?" "Away down somewhere in the tropics, they say—has a rich uncle down there." And so on. He made his way at once; everybody was anxious to know him and talk with him. Everybody noticed how cool and fresh it was, all of a sudden, and wondered at it, for they could see that the sun was beating down the same as before, outside, and the sky was clear of clouds, but no one guessed the reason, of course.

The astrologer had drunk his second beaker; he poured out a third. He set the bottle down, and by accident overturned it. He seized it before much was spilled, and held it up to the light, saying, "What a pity—it is royal wine." Then his face lighted with joy or triumph, or something, and he said, "Quick! Bring a bowl."

It was brought—a four-quart one. He took up that two-pint bottle and began to pour; went on pouring, the red liquor gurgling and gushing into the white bowl and rising higher and higher up its sides, everybody staring and holding their breath—and presently the bowl was full to the brim.

"Look at the bottle," he said, holding it up; "it is full yet!" I glanced at Satan, and in that moment he vanished. Then Father Adolf rose up, flushed and excited, crossed himself, and began to thunder in his great voice, "This house is bewitched and accursed!" People began to cry and shriek and crowd toward the door. "I summon this detected household to—"

His words were cut off short. His face became red, then purple, but he could not utter another sound. Then I saw Satan, a transparent film, melt into the astrologer's body; then the astrologer put up his hand, and apparently in his own voice said, "Wait—remain where you are." All stopped where they stood. "Bring a funnel!" Ursula brought it, trembling and scared, and he stuck it in the bottle and took up the great bowl and began to pour the wine back, the people gazing and dazed with astonishment, for they knew the bottle was already full before he began. He emptied the whole of the bowl into the bottle, then smiled out over the room, chuckled, and said, indifferently: "It is nothing—anybody can do it! With my powers I can even do much more."

A frightened cry burst out everywhere. "Oh, my God, he is possessed!" and there was a tumultuous rush for the door which swiftly emptied the house of all who did not belong in it except us boys and Meidling. We boys knew the secret, and would have told it if we could, but we couldn't. We were very thankful to Satan for furnishing that good help at the needful time.

Marget was pale, and crying: Meidling looked kind of petrified; Ursula the same; but Gottfried was the worst—he couldn't stand, he was so weak and scared. For he was of a witch family, you know, and it would be bad for him to be suspected. Agnes came loafing in, looking pious and unaware, and wanted to rub up against Ursula and be petted, but Ursula was afraid of her and shrank away from her, but pretending she was not meaning any incivility, for she knew very well it wouldn't answer to have strained relations with that kind of a cat. But we boys took Agnes and petted her, for Satan would not have befriended her if he had not had a good opinion of her, and that was indorsement enough for us. He seemed to trust anything that hadn't the Moral Sense.

Outside, the guests, panic-stricken, scattered in every direction and fled in a pitiable state of terror; and such a tumult as they made with their running and sobbing and shrieking and shouting that soon all the village came flocking from their houses to see what had happened, and they thronged the street and shouldered and jostled one another in excitement and fright; and then Father Adolf appeared, and they fell apart in two walls like the cloven Red Sea, and presently down this lane the astrologer came striding and mumbling, and where he passed the lanes surged back in packed masses, and fell silent with awe, and their eyes stared and their breasts heaved, and several women fainted; and when he was gone by the crowd swarmed together and followed him at a distance, talking excitedly and asking questions and finding out the facts. Finding out the facts and passing them on to others, with improvements—improvements which soon enlarged the bowl of wine to a barrel, and made the one bottle hold it all and yet remain empty to the last.

When the astrologer reached the market-square he went straight to a juggler, fantastically dressed, who was keeping three brass balls in the air, and took them from him and faced around upon the approaching crowd and said: "This poor clown is ignorant of his art. Come forward and see an expert perform."

So saying, he tossed the balls up one after another and set them whirling in a slender bright oval in the air, and added another, then another and another, and so on—no one seeing whence he got them—adding, adding, adding, the oval lengthening all the time, his hands moving so swiftly that they were just a web or a blur and not distinguishable as hands; and such as counted said there were now a hundred balls in the air. The spinning great oval reached up twenty feet in the air and was a shining and glinting and wonderful sight. Then he folded his arms and told the balls to go on spinning without his help—and they did it. After a couple of minutes he said, "There, that will do," and the oval broke and came crashing down, and the balls scattered abroad and rolled every whither. And wherever one of them came the people fell back in dread, and no one would touch it. It made him laugh, and he scoffed at the people and called them cowards and old women. Then he turned and saw the tight-rope, and said foolish people were daily wasting their money to see a clumsy and ignorant varlet degrade that beautiful art; now they should see the work of a master. With that he made a spring into the air and lit firm on his feet on the rope. Then he hopped the whole length of it back and forth on one foot, with his hands clasped over his eyes; and next he began to throw somersaults, both backward and forward, and threw twenty-seven.

The people murmured, for the astrologer was old, and always before had been halting of movement and at times even lame, but he was nimble enough now and went on with his antics in the liveliest manner. Finally he sprang lightly down and walked away, and passed up the road and around the corner and disappeared. Then that great, pale, silent, solid crowd drew a deep breath and looked into one another's faces as if they said: "Was it real? Did you see it, or was it only I—and I was dreaming?" Then they broke into a low murmur of talking, and fell apart in couples, and moved toward their homes, still talking in that awed way, with faces close together and laying a hand on an arm and making other such gestures as people make when they have been deeply impressed by something.

We boys followed behind our fathers, and listened, catching all we could of what they said; and when they sat down in our house and continued their talk they still had us for company. They were in a sad mood, for it was certain, they said, that disaster for the village must follow this awful visitation of witches and devils. Then my father remembered that Father Adolf had been struck dumb at the moment of his denunciation.

"They have not ventured to lay their hands upon an anointed servant of God before," he said; "and how they could have dared it this time I cannot make out, for he wore his crucifix. Isn't it so?"

"Yes," said the others, "we saw it."

"It is serious, friends, it is very serious. Always before, we had a protection. It has failed."

The others shook, as with a sort of chill, and muttered those words over—"It has failed." "God has forsaken us."

"It is true," said Seppi Wohlmeyer's father; there is nowhere to look for help."

"The people will realize this," said Nikolaus's father, the judge, "and despair will take away their courage and their energies. We have indeed fallen upon evil times."

He signed, and Wohlmeyer said, in a troubled voice: "The report of it all will go about the country, and our village will be shunned as being under the displeasure of God. The Golden Stag will know hard times."

"True, neighbor," said my father; "all of us will suffer—all in repute, many in estate. And, good God!—"

"What is it?"

"That can come—to finish us!"

"Name it—um Gottes Willen!"

"The Interdict!"

It smote like a thunderclap, and they were like to swoon with the terror of it. Then the dread of this calamity aroused their energies, and they stopped brooding and began to consider ways to avert it. They discussed this, that, and the other way, and talked till the afternoon was far spent, then confessed that at present they could arrive at no decision. So they parted sorrowfully, with oppressed hearts which were filled with bodings.

While they were saying their parting words I slipped out and set my course for Marget's house to see what was happening there. I met many people, but none of them greeted me. It ought to have been surprising, but it was not, for they were so distraught with fear and dread that they were not in their right minds, I think; they were white and haggard, and walked like persons in a dream, their eyes open but seeing nothing, their lips moving but uttering nothing, and worriedly clasping and unclasping their hands without knowing it.

At Marget's it was like a funeral. She and Wilhelm sat together on the sofa, but said nothing, and not even holding hands. Both were steeped in gloom, and Marget's eyes were red from the crying she had been doing. She said:

"I have been begging him to go, and come no more, and so save himself alive. I cannot bear to be his murderer. This house is bewitched, and no inmate will escape the fire. But he will not go, and he will be lost with the rest."

Wilhelm said he would not go; if there was danger for her, his place was by her, and there he would remain. Then she began to cry again, and it was all so mournful that I wished I had stayed away. There was a knock, now, and Satan came in, fresh and cheery and beautiful, and brought that winy atmosphere of his and changed the whole thing. He never said a word about what had been happening, nor about the awful fears which were freezing the blood in the hearts of the community, but began to talk and rattle on about all manner of gay and pleasant things: and next about music—an artful stroke which cleared away the remnant of Marget's depression and brought her spirits and her interests broad awake. She had not heard any one talk so well and so knowingly on that subject before, and she was so uplifted by it and so charmed that what she was feeling lit up her face and came out in her words; and Wilhelm noticed it and did not look as pleased as he ought to have done. And next Satan branched off into poetry, and recited some, and did it well, and

Marget was charmed again; and again Wilhelm was not as pleased as he ought to have been, and this time Marget noticed it and was remorseful.

I fell asleep to pleasant music that night—the patter of rain upon the panes and the dull growling of distant thunder. Away in the night Satan came and roused me and said: "Come with me. Where shall we go?"

"Anywhere—so it is with you."

Then there was a fierce glare of sunlight, and he said, "This is China."

That was a grand surprise, and made me sort of drunk with vanity and gladness to think I had come so far—so much, much farther than anybody else in our village, including Bartel Sperling, who had such a great opinion of his travels. We buzzed around over that empire for more than half an hour, and saw the whole of it. It was wonderful, the spectacles we saw; and some were beautiful, others too horrible to think. For instance— However, I may go into that by and by, and also why Satan chose China for this excursion instead of another place; it would interrupt my tale to do it now. Finally we stopped flitting and lit.

We sat upon a mountain commanding a vast landscape of a mountain-range and gorge and valley and plain and river, with cities and villages slumbering in the sunlight, and a glimpse of blue sea on the farther verge. It was a tranquil and dreamy picture, beautiful to the eye and restful to the spirit. If we could only make a change like that whenever we wanted to, the world would be easier to live in than it is, for change of scene shifts the mind's burdens to the other shoulder and banishes old, shopworn wearinesses from mind and body both.

We talked together, and I had the idea of trying to reform Satan and persuade him to lead a better life. I told him about all those things he had been doing, and begged him to be more considerate and stop making people unhappy. I said I knew he did not mean any harm, but that he ought to stop and consider the possible consequences of a thing before launching it in that impulsive and random way of his; then he would not make so much trouble. He was not hurt by this plain speech; he only looked amused and surprised, and said:

"What? I do random things? Indeed, I never do. I stop and consider possible consequences? Where is the need? I know what the consequences are going to be—always."

"Oh, Satan, then how could you do these things?"

"Well, I will tell you, and you must understand if you can. You belong to a singular race. Every man is a suffering-machine and a happiness-machine combined. The two functions work together harmoniously, with a fine and delicate precision, on the give-and-take principle. For every happiness turned out in the one department the other stands ready to modify it with a sorrow or a pain—maybe a dozen. In most cases the man's life is about equally divided between happiness and unhappiness. When this is not the case the unhappiness predominates—always; never the other. Sometimes a man's make and disposition are such that his misery-machine is able to do nearly all the business. Such a man goes through life almost ignorant of what happiness is. Everything he touches, everything he does, brings a misfortune upon him. You have seen such people? To that kind of a person life is not an advantage, is it? It is only a disaster. Sometimes for an hour's happiness a man's machinery makes him pay years of misery. Don't you know that? It happens every now and then. I will give you a case or two presently. Now the people of your village are nothing to me—you know that, don't you?"

I did not like to speak out too flatly, so I said I had suspected it.

"Well, it is true that they are nothing to me. It is not possible that they should be. The difference between them and me is abysmal, immeasurable. They have no intellect."

"No intellect?"

"Nothing that resembles it. At a future time I will examine what man calls his mind and give you the details of that chaos, then you will see and understand. Men have nothing in common with me—there is no point of contact; they have foolish little feelings and foolish little vanities and impertinences and ambitions; their foolish little life is but a laugh, a sigh, and extinction; and they have no sense. Only the Moral Sense. I will show you what I mean. Here is a red spider, not so big as a pin's head. Can you imagine an elephant being interested in him—caring whether he is happy or isn't, or whether he is wealthy or poor, or whether his sweetheart returns his love or not, or whether his mother is sick or well, or whether he is looked up to in society or not, or whether his enemies will smite him or his friends desert him, or whether his hopes will suffer blight or his political ambitions fail, or whether he shall die in the bosom of his family or neglected and despised in a foreign land? These things can never be important to the elephant; they are nothing to him; he cannot shrink his sympathies to the microscopic size of them. Man is to me as the red spider is to the elephant. The elephant has nothing against the spider—he cannot get down to that remote level; I have nothing against man. The elephant is indifferent; I am indifferent. The elephant would not take the trouble to do the spider an ill turn; if he took the notion he might do him a good turn, if it came in his way and cost nothing. I have done men good service, but no ill turns.

"The elephant lives a century, the red spider a day; in power, intellect, and dignity the one creature is separated from the other by a distance which is simply astronomical. Yet in these, as in all qualities, man is immeasurably further below me than is the wee spider below the elephant.

"Man's mind clumsily and tediously and laboriously patches little trivialities together and gets a result—such as it is. My mind creates! Do you get the force of that? Creates anything it desires—and in a moment. Creates without material. Creates fluids, solids, colors—anything, everything—out of the airy nothing which is called Thought. A man imagines a silk thread, imagines a machine to make it, imagines a picture, then by weeks of labor embroiders it on canvas with the thread. I think the whole thing, and in a moment it is before you—created.

"I think a poem, music, the record of a game of chess—anything—and it is there. This is the immortal mind—nothing is beyond its reach. Nothing can obstruct my vision; the rocks are transparent to me, and darkness is daylight. I do not need to open a book; I take the whole of its contents into my mind at a single glance, through the cover; and in a million years I could not forget a single word of it, or its place in the volume.

Nothing goes on in the skull of man, bird, fish, insect, or other creature which can be hidden from me. I pierce the learned man's brain with a single glance, and the treasures which cost him threescore years to accumulate are mine; he can forget, and he does forget, but I retain.

"Now, then, I perceive by your thoughts that you are understanding me fairly well. Let us proceed. Circumstances might so fall out that the elephant could like the spider—supposing he can see it—but he could not love it. His love is for his own kind—for his equals. An angel's love is sublime, adorable, divine, beyond the imagination of man—infinitely beyond it! But it is limited to his own august order. If it fell upon one of your race for only an instant, it would consume its object to ashes. No, we cannot love men, but we can be harmlessly indifferent to them; we can also like them, sometimes. I like you and the boys, I like Father Peter, and for your sakes I am doing all these things for the villagers."

He saw that I was thinking a sarcasm, and he explained his position.

"I have wrought well for the villagers, though it does not look like it on the surface. Your race never know good fortune from ill. They are always mistaking the one for the other. It is because they cannot see into the future. What I am doing for the villagers will bear good fruit some day; in some cases to themselves; in others, to unborn generations of men. No one will ever know that I was the cause, but it will be none the less true, for all that. Among you boys you have a game: you stand a row of bricks on end a few inches apart; you push a brick, it knocks its neighbor over, the neighbor knocks over the next brick—and so on till all the row is prostrate. That is human life. A child's first act knocks over the initial brick, and the rest will follow inexorably. If you could see into the future, as I can, you would see everything that was going to happen to that creature; for nothing can change the order of its life after the first event has determined it. That is, nothing will change it, because each act unfailingly begets an act, that act begets another, and so on to the end, and the seer can look forward down the line and see just when each act is to have birth, from cradle to grave."

"Does God order the career?"

"Foreordain it? No. The man's circumstances and environment order it. His first act determines the second and all that follow after. But suppose, for argument's sake, that the man should skip one of these acts; an apparently trifling one, for instance; suppose that it had been appointed that on a certain day, at a certain hour and minute and second and fraction of a second he should go to the well, and he didn't go. That man's career would change utterly, from that moment; thence to the grave it would be wholly different from the career which his first act as a child had arranged for him. Indeed, it might be that if he had gone to the well he would have ended his career on a throne, and that omitting to do it would set him upon a career that would lead to beggary and a pauper's grave. For instance: if at any time—say in boyhood—Columbus had skipped the triflingest little link in the chain of acts projected and made inevitable by his first childish act, it would have changed his whole subsequent life, and he would have become a priest and died obscure in an Italian village, and America would not have been discovered for two centuries afterward. I know this. To skip any one of the billion acts in Columbus's chain would have wholly changed his life. I have examined his billion of possible careers, and in only one of them occurs the discovery of America. You people do not suspect that all of your acts are of one size and importance, but it is true; to snatch at an appointed fly is as big with fate for you as in any other appointed act—"

"As the conquering of a continent, for instance?"

"Yes. Now, then, no man ever does drop a link—the thing has never happened! Even when he is trying to make up his mind as to whether he will do a thing or not, that itself is a link, an act, and has its proper place in his chain; and when he finally decides an act, that also was the thing which he was absolutely certain to do. You see, now, that a man will never drop a link in his chain. He cannot. If he made up his mind to try, that project would itself be an unavoidable link—a thought bound to occur to him at that precise moment, and made certain by the first act of his babyhood."

It seemed so dismal!

"He is a prisoner for life," I said sorrowfully, "and cannot get free."

"No, of himself he cannot get away from the consequences of his first childish act. But I can free him."

I looked up wistfully.

"I have changed the careers of a number of your villagers."

I tried to thank him, but found it difficult, and let it drop.

"I shall make some other changes. You know that little Lisa Brandt?"

"Oh yes, everybody does. My mother says she is so sweet and so lovely that she is not like any other child. She says she will be the pride of the village when she grows up; and its idol, too, just as she is now."

"I shall change her future."

"Make it better?" I asked.

"Yes. And I will change the future of Nikolaus."

I was glad, this time, and said, "I don't need to ask about his case; you will be sure to do generously by him."

"It is my intention."

Straight off I was building that great future of Nicky's in my imagination, and had already made a renowned general of him and hofmeister at the court, when I noticed that Satan was waiting for me to get ready to listen again. I was ashamed of having exposed my cheap imaginings to him, and was expecting some sarcasms, but it did not happen. He proceeded with his subject:

"Nicky's appointed life is sixty-two years."

"That's grand!" I said.

"Lisa's, thirty-six. But, as I told you, I shall change their lives and those ages. Two minutes and a quarter from now Nikolaus will wake out of his sleep and find the rain blowing in. It was appointed that he should turn over and go to sleep again. But I have appointed that he shall get up and close the window first. That trifle will change his career entirely. He will rise in the morning two minutes later than the chain of his life had appointed him to rise. By consequence, thenceforth nothing will ever happen to him in accordance with the details of the old chain." He took out his watch and sat looking at it a few moments, then said: "Nikolaus has risen to close the window. His life is changed, his new career has begun. There will be consequences."

It made me feel creepy; it was uncanny.

"But for this change certain things would happen twelve days from now. For instance, Nikolaus would save Lisa from drowning. He would arrive on the scene at exactly the right moment—four minutes past ten, the long-ago appointed instant of time—and the water would be shoal, the achievement easy and certain. But he will arrive some seconds too late, now; Lisa will have struggled into deeper water. He will do his best, but both will drown."

"Oh, Satan! oh, dear Satan!" I cried, with the tears rising in my eyes, "save them! Don't let it happen. I can't bear to lose Nikolaus, he is my loving playmate and friend; and think of Lisa's poor mother!"

I clung to him and begged and pleaded, but he was not moved. He made me sit down again, and told me I must hear him out.

"I have changed Nikolaus's life, and this has changed Lisa's. If I had not done this, Nikolaus would save Lisa, then he would catch cold from his drenching; one of your race's fantastic and desolating scarlet fevers would follow, with pathetic after-effects; for forty-six years he would lie in his bed a paralytic log, deaf, dumb, blind, and praying night and day for the blessed relief of death. Shall I change his life back?"

"Oh no! Oh, not for the word! In charity and pity leave it as it is."

"It is best so. I could not have changed any other link in his life and done him so good a service. He had a billion possible careers, but not one of them was worth living; they were charged full with miseries and disasters. But for my intervention he would do his brave deed twelve days from now—a deed begun and ended in six minutes—and get for all reward those forty-six years of sorrow and suffering I told you of. It is one of the cases I was thinking of awhile ago when I said that sometimes an act which brings the actor an hour's happiness and self-satisfaction is paid for—or punished—by years of suffering."

I wondered what poor little Lisa's early death would save her from. He answered the thought:

"From ten years of pain and slow recovery from an accident, and then from nineteen years' pollution, shame, depravity, crime, ending with death at the hands of the executioner. Twelve days hence she will die; her mother would save her life if she could. Am I not kinder than her mother?"

"Yes—oh, indeed yes; and wiser."

"Father Peter's case is coming on presently. He will be acquitted, through unassailable proofs of his innocence."

"Why, Satan, how can that be? Do you really think it?"

"Indeed, I know it. His good name will be restored, and the rest of his life will be happy."

"I can believe it. To restore his good name will have that effect."

"His happiness will not proceed from that cause. I shall change his life that day, for his good. He will never know his good name has been restored."

In my mind—and modestly—I asked for particulars, but Satan paid no attention to my thought. Next, my mind wandered to the astrologer, and I wondered where he might be.

"In the moon," said Satan, with a fleeting sound which I believed was a chuckle. "I've got him on the cold side of it, too. He doesn't know where he is, and is not having a pleasant time; still, it is good enough for him, a good place for his star studies. I shall need him presently; then I shall bring him back and possess him again. He has a long and cruel and odious life before him, but I will change that, for I have no feeling against him and am quite willing to do him a kindness. I think I shall get him burned."

He had such strange notions of kindness! But angels are made so, and do not know any better. Their ways are not like our ways; and, besides, human beings are nothing to them; they think they are only freaks. It seems to me odd that he should put the astrologer so far away; he could have dumped him in Germany just as well, where he would be handy.

"Far away?" said Satan. "To me no place is far away; distance does not exist for me. The sun is less than a hundred million miles from here, and the light that is falling upon us has taken eight minutes to come; but I can make that flight, or any other, in a fraction of time so minute that it cannot be measured by a watch. I have but to think the journey, and it is accomplished."

I held out my hand and said, "The light lies upon it; think it into a glass of wine, Satan."

He did it. I drank the wine.

"Break the glass," he said.

I broke it.

"There—you see it is real. The villagers thought the brass balls were magic stuff and as perishable as smoke. They were afraid to touch them. You are a curious lot—your race. But come along; I have business. I will put you to bed." Said and done. Then he was gone; but his voice came back to me through the rain and darkness saying, "Yes, tell Seppi, but no other."

It was the answer to my thought.

VIII

Sleep would not come. It was not because I was proud of my travels and excited about having been around the big world to China, and feeling contemptuous of Bartel Sperling, "the traveler," as he called himself, and looked down upon us others because he had been to Vienna once and was the only Eseldorf boy who had made such a journey and seen the world's wonders. At another time that would have kept me awake, but it did not affect me now. No, my mind was filled with Nikolaus, my thoughts ran upon him only, and the good days we had seen together at romps and frolics in the woods and the fields and the river in the long summer days, and skating and sliding in the winter when our parents thought we were in school. And now he was going out of this young life, and the summers and winters would come and go, and we others would rove and play as before, but his place would be vacant; we should see him no more. To-morrow he would not suspect, but would be as he had always been, and it would shock me to hear him laugh, and see him do lightsome and frivolous things, for to me he would be a corpse, with waven hands and dull eyes, and I should see the shroud around his face; and next day he would not suspect, nor the next, and all the time his handful of days would be wasting swiftly away and that awful thing coming nearer and nearer, his fate closing steadily around him and no one knowing it but Seppi and me. Twelve days—only twelve days. It was awful to think of. I noticed that in my thoughts I was not calling him by his familiar names, Nick and Nicky, but was speaking of him by his full name, and reverently, as one speaks of the dead. Also, as incident after incident of our comradeship came thronging into my mind out of the past, I noticed that they were mainly cases where I had wronged him or hurt him, and they rebuked me and reproached me, and my heart was wrung with remorse, just as it is when we remember our unkindnesses to friends who have passed beyond the veil, and we wish we could have them back again, if only for a moment, so that we could go on our knees to them and say, "Have pity, and forgive."

Once when we were nine years old he went a long errand of nearly two miles for the fruiterer, who gave him a splendid big apple for reward, and he was flying home with it, almost beside himself with astonishment and delight, and I met him, and he let me look at the apple, not thinking of treachery, and I ran off with it, eating it as I ran, he following me and begging; and when he overtook me I offered him the core, which was all that was left; and I laughed. Then he turned away, crying, and said he had meant to give it to his little sister. That smote me, for she was slowly getting well of a sickness, and it would have been a proud moment for him, to see her joy and surprise and have her caresses. But I was ashamed to say I was ashamed, and only said something rude and mean, to pretend I did not care, and he made no reply in words, but there was a wounded look in his face as he turned away toward his home which rose before me many times in after years, in the night, and reproached me and made me ashamed again. It had grown dim in my mind, by and by, then it disappeared; but it was back now, and not dim.

Once at school, when we were eleven, I upset my ink and spoiled four copy-books, and was in danger of severe punishment; but I put it upon him, and he got the whipping.

And only last year I had cheated him in a trade, giving him a large fish-hook which was partly broken through for three small sound ones. The first fish he caught broke the hook, but he did not know I was blamable, and he refused to take back one of the small hooks which my conscience forced me to offer him, but said, "A trade is a trade; the hook was bad, but that was not your fault."

No, I could not sleep. These little, shabby wrongs upbraided me and tortured me, and with a pain much sharper than one feels when the wrongs have been done to the living. Nikolaus was living, but no matter; he was to me as one already dead. The wind was still moaning about the eaves, the rain still pattering upon the panes.

In the morning I sought out Seppi and told him. It was down by the river. His lips moved, but he did not say anything, he only looked dazed and stunned, and his face turned very white. He stood like that a few moments, the tears welling into his eyes, then he turned away and I locked my arm in his and we walked along thinking, but not speaking. We crossed the bridge and wandered through the meadows and up among the hills and the woods, and at last the talk came and flowed freely, and it was all about Nikolaus and was a recalling of the life we had lived with him. And every now and then Seppi said, as if to himself:

"Twelve days!—less than twelve days."

We said we must be with him all the time; we must have all of him we could; the days were precious now. Yet we did not go to seek him. It would be like meeting the dead, and we were afraid. We did not say it, but that was what we were feeling. And so it gave us a shock when we turned a curve and came upon Nikolaus face to face. He shouted, gaily:

"Hi-hi! What is the matter? Have you seen a ghost?"

We couldn't speak, but there was no occasion; he was willing to talk for us all, for he had just seen Satan and was in high spirits about it. Satan had told him about our trip to China, and he had begged Satan to take him on a journey, and Satan had promised. It was to be a far journey, and wonderful and beautiful; and Nikolaus had begged him to take us, too, but he said no, he would take us some day, maybe, but not now. Satan would come for him on the 13th, and Nikolaus was already counting the hours, he was so impatient.

That was the fatal day. We were already counting the hours, too.

We wandered many a mile, always following paths which had been our favorites from the days when we were little, and always we talked about the old times. All the blitheness was with Nikolaus; we others could not shake off our depression. Our tone toward Nikolaus was so strangely gentle and tender and yearning that he noticed it, and was pleased; and we were constantly doing him deferential little offices of courtesy, and saying, "Wait, let me do that for you," and that pleased him, too. I gave him seven fish-hooks—all I had—and made him take them; and Seppi gave him his new knife and a humming-top painted red and yellow—atonements for swindles practised upon him formerly, as I learned later, and probably no longer remembered by Nikolaus now. These things touched him, and he could not have believed that we loved him so; and his pride in it and gratefulness for it cut us to the heart, we were so undeserving of them. When we parted at last, he was radiant, and said he had never had such a happy day.

As we walked along homeward, Seppi said, "We always prized him, but never so much as now, when we are going to lose him."

Next day and every day we spent all of our spare time with Nikolaus; and also added to it time which we (and he) stole from work and other duties, and this cost the three of us some sharp scoldings, and some threats of punishment. Every morning two of us woke with a start and a shudder, saying, as the days flew along, "Only ten days left;" "only nine days left;" "only eight;" "only seven." Always it was narrowing. Always Nikolaus was gay and happy, and always puzzled because we were not. He wore his invention to the bone trying to invent ways to cheer us up, but it was only a hollow success; he could see that our jollity had no heart in it, and that the laughs we broke into came up against some obstruction or other and suffered damage and decayed into a sigh. He tried to find out what the matter was, so that he could help us out of our trouble or make it lighter by sharing it with us; so we had to tell many lies to deceive him and appease him.

But the most distressing thing of all was that he was always making plans, and often they went beyond the 13th! Whenever that happened it made us groan in spirit. All his mind was fixed upon finding some way to conquer our depression and cheer us up; and at last, when he had but three days to live, he fell upon the right idea and was jubilant over it—a boys-and-girls' frolic and dance in the woods, up there where we first met Satan, and this was to occur on the 14th. It was ghastly, for that was his funeral day. We couldn't venture to protest; it would only have brought a "Why?" which we could not answer. He wanted us to help him invite his guests, and we did it—one can refuse nothing to a dying friend. But it was dreadful, for really we were inviting them to his funeral.

It was an awful eleven days; and yet, with a lifetime stretching back between to-day and then, they are still a grateful memory to me, and beautiful. In effect they were days of companionship with one's sacred dead, and I have known no comradeship that was so close or so precious. We clung to the hours and the minutes, counting them as they wasted away, and parting with them with that pain and bereavement which a miser feels who sees his hoard filched from him coin by coin by robbers and is helpless to prevent it.

When the evening of the last day came we stayed out too long; Seppi and I were in fault for that; we could not bear to part with Nikolaus; so it was very late when we left him at his door. We lingered near awhile, listening; and that happened which we were fearing. His father gave him the promised punishment, and we heard his shrieks. But we listened only a moment, then hurried away, remorseful for this thing which we had caused. And sorry for the father, too; our thought being, "If he only knew—if he only knew!"

In the morning Nikolaus did not meet us at the appointed place, so we went to his home to see what the matter was. His mother said:

"His father is out of all patience with these goings-on, and will not have any more of it. Half the time when Nick is needed he is not to be found; then it turns out that he has been gadding around with you two. His father gave him a flogging last night. It always grieved me before, and many's the time I have begged him off and saved him, but this time he appealed to me in vain, for I was out of patience myself."

"I wish you had saved him just this one time," I said, my voice trembling a little; "it would ease a pain in your heart to remember it some day."

She was ironing at the time, and her back was partly toward me. She turned about with a startled or wondering look in her face and said, "What do you mean by that?"

I was not prepared, and didn't know anything to say; so it was awkward, for she kept looking at me; but Seppi was alert and spoke up:

"Why, of course it would be pleasant to remember, for the very reason we were out so late was that Nikolaus got to telling how good you are to him, and how he never got whipped when you were by to save him; and he was so full of it, and we were so full of the interest of it, that none of us noticed how late it was getting."

"Did he say that? Did he?" and she put her apron to her eyes.

"You can ask Theodor—he will tell you the same."

"It is a dear, good lad, my Nick," she said. "I am sorry I let him get whipped; I will never do it again. To think—all the time I was sitting here last night, fretting and angry at him, he was loving me and praising me! Dear, dear, if we could only know! Then we shouldn't ever go wrong; but we are only poor, dumb beasts groping around and making mistakes. I sha'n't ever think of last night without a pang."

She was like all the rest; it seemed as if nobody could open a mouth, in these wretched days, without saying something that made us shiver. They were "groping around," and did not know what true, sorrowfully true things they were saying by accident.

Seppi asked if Nikolaus might go out with us.

"I am sorry," she answered, "but he can't. To punish him further, his father doesn't allow him to go out of the house to-day."

We had a great hope! I saw it in Seppi's eyes. We thought, "If he cannot leave the house, he cannot be drowned." Seppi asked, to make sure:

"Must he stay in all day, or only the morning?"

"All day. It's such a pity, too; it's a beautiful day, and he is so unused to being shut up. But he is busy planning his party, and maybe that is company for him. I do hope he isn't too lonesome."

Seppi saw that in her eye which emboldened him to ask if we might go up and help him pass his time.

"And welcome!" she said, right heartily. "Now I call that real friendship, when you might be abroad in the fields and the woods, having a happy time. You are good boys, I'll allow that, though you don't always find satisfactory ways of improving it. Take these cakes—for yourselves—and give him this one, from his mother."

The first thing we noticed when we entered Nikolaus's room was the time—a quarter to 10. Could that be correct? Only such a few minutes to live! I felt a contraction at my heart. Nikolaus jumped up and gave us a glad welcome. He was in good spirits over his plannings for his party and had not been lonesome.

"Sit down," he said, "and look at what I've been doing. And I've finished a kite that you will say is a beauty. It's drying, in the kitchen; I'll fetch it."

He had been spending his penny savings in fanciful trifles of various kinds, to go as prizes in the games, and they were marshaled with fine and showy effect upon the table. He said:

"Examine them at your leisure while I get mother to touch up the kite with her iron if it isn't dry enough yet."

Then he tripped out and went clattering downstairs, whistling.

We did not look at the things; we couldn't take any interest in anything but the clock. We sat staring at it in silence, listening to the ticking, and every time the minute-hand jumped we nodded recognition—one minute fewer to cover in the race for life or for death. Finally Seppi drew a deep breath and said:

"Two minutes to ten. Seven minutes more and he will pass the death-point. Theodor, he is going to be saved! He's going to—"

"Hush! I'm on needles. Watch the clock and keep still."

Five minutes more. We were panting with the strain and the excitement. Another three minutes, and there was a footstep on the stair.

"Saved! And we jumped up and faced the door.

The old mother entered, bringing the kite. "Isn't it a beauty?" she said. "And, dear me, how he has slaved over it—ever since daylight, I think, and only finished it awhile before you came." She stood it against the wall, and stepped back to take a view of it. "He drew the pictures his own self, and I think they are very good. The church isn't so very good, I'll have to admit, but look at the bridge—any one can recognize the bridge in a minute. He asked me to bring it up. . . . Dear me! it's seven minutes past ten, and I—"

"But where is he?"

"He? Oh, he'll be here soon; he's gone out a minute."

"Gone out?"

"Yes. Just as he came down-stairs little Lisa's mother came in and said the child had wandered off somewhere, and as she was a little uneasy I told Nikolaus to never mind about his father's orders—go and look her up. . . . Why, how white you two do look! I do believe you are sick. Sit down; I'll fetch something. That cake has disagreed with you. It is a little heavy, but I thought—"

She disappeared without finishing her sentence, and we hurried at once to the back window and looked toward the river. There was a great crowd at the other end of the bridge, and people were flying toward that point from every direction.

"Oh, it is all over—poor Nikolaus! Why, oh, why did she let him get out of the house!"

"Come away," said Seppi, half sobbing, "come quick—we can't bear to meet her; in five minutes she will know."

But we were not to escape. She came upon us at the foot of the stairs, with her cordials in her hands, and made us come in and sit down and take the medicine. Then she watched the effect, and it did not satisfy her; so she made us wait longer, and kept upbraiding herself for giving us the unwholesome cake.

Presently the thing happened which we were dreading. There

was a sound of tramping and scraping outside, and a crowd came solemnly in, with heads uncovered, and laid the two drowned bodies on the bed.

"Oh, my God!" that poor mother cried out, and fell on her knees, and put her arms about her dead boy and began to cover the wet face with kisses. "Oh, it was I that sent him, and I have been his death. If I had obeyed, and kept him in the house, this would not have happened. And I am rightly punished; I was cruel to him last night, and him begging me, his own mother, to be his friend."

And so she went on and on, and all the women cried, and pitied her, and tried to comfort her, but she could not forgive herself and could not be comforted, and kept on saying if she had not sent him out he would be alive and well now, and she was the cause of his death.

It shows how foolish people are when they blame themselves for anything they have done. Satan knows, and he said nothing happens that your first act hasn't arranged to happen and made inevitable; and so, of your own motion you can't ever alter the scheme or do a thing that will break a link. Next we heard screams, and Frau Brandt came wildly plowing and plunging through the crowd with her dress in disorder and hair flying loose, and flung herself upon her dead child with moans and kisses and pleadings and endearments; and by and by she rose up almost exhausted with her outpourings of passionate emotion, and clenched her fist and lifted it toward the sky, and her tear-drenched face grew hard and resentful, and she said:

"For nearly two weeks I have had dreams and presentiments and warnings that death was going to strike what was most precious to me, and day and night and night and day I have groveled in the dirt before Him praying Him to have pity on my innocent child and save it from harm—and here is His answer!"

Why, He had saved it from harm—but she did not know.

She wiped the tears from her eyes and cheeks, and stood awhile gazing down at the child and caressing its face and its hair with her hands; then she spoke again in that bitter tone: "But in His hard heart is no compassion. I will never pray again."

She gathered her dead child to her bosom and strode away, the crowd falling back to let her pass, and smitten dumb by the awful words they had heard. Ah, that poor woman! It is as Satan said, we do not know good fortune from bad, and are always mistaking the one for the other. Many a time since I have heard people pray to God to spare the life of sick persons, but I have never done it.

Both funerals took place at the same time in our little church next day. Everybody was there, including the party guests. Satan was there, too; which was proper, for it was on account of his efforts that the funerals had happened. Nikolaus had departed this life without absolution, and a collection was taken up for masses, to get him out of purgatory. Only two-thirds of the required money was gathered, and the parents were going to try to borrow the rest, but Satan furnished it. He told us privately that there was no purgatory, but he had contributed in order that Nikolaus's parents and their friends might be saved from worry and distress. We thought it very good of him, but he said money did not cost him anything.

At the graveyard the body of little Lisa was seized for debt by a carpenter to whom the mother owed fifty groschen for work done the year before. She had never been able to pay this, and was not able now. The carpenter took the corpse home and kept it four days in his cellar, the mother weeping and imploring about his house all the time; then he buried it in his brother's cattle-yard, without religious ceremonies. It drove the mother wild with grief and shame, and she forsook her work and went daily about the town, cursing the carpenter and blaspheming the laws of the emperor and the church, and it was pitiful to see. Seppi asked Satan to interfere, but he said the carpenter and the rest were members of the human race and were acting quite neatly for that species of animal. He would interfere if he found a horse acting in such a way, and we must inform him when we came across that kind of horse doing that kind of a human thing, so that he could stop it. We believed this was sarcasm, for of course there wasn't any such horse.

But after a few days we found that we could not abide that poor woman's distress, so we begged Satan to examine her several possible careers, and see if he could not change her, to her profit, to a new one. He said the longest of her careers as they now stood gave her forty-two years to live, and her shortest one twenty-nine, and that both were charged with grief and hunger and cold and pain. The only improvement he could make would be to enable her to skip a certain three minutes from now; and he asked us if he should do it. This was such a short time to decide in that we went to pieces with nervous excitement, and before we could pull ourselves together and ask for particulars he said the time would be up in a few more seconds; so then we gasped out, "Do it!"

"It is done," he said; "she was going around a corner; I have turned her back; it has changed her career."

"Then what will happen, Satan?"

"It is happening now. She is having words with Fischer, the weaver. In his anger Fischer will straightway do what he would not have done but for this accident. He was present when she stood over her child's body and uttered those blasphemies."

"What will he do?"

"He is doing it now—betraying her. In three days she will go to the stake."

We could not speak; we were frozen with horror, for if we had not meddled with her career she would have been spared this awful fate. Satan noticed these thoughts, and said:

"What you are thinking is strictly human-like—that is to say, foolish. The woman is advantaged. Die when she might, she would go to heaven. By this prompt death she gets twenty-nine years more of heaven than she is entitled to, and escapes twenty-nine years of misery here."

A moment before we were bitterly making up our minds that we would ask no more favors of Satan for friends of ours, for he did not seem to know any way to do a person a kindness but by killing him; but the whole aspect of the case was changed now, and we were glad of what we had done and full of happiness in the thought of it.

After a little I began to feel troubled about Fischer, and asked, timidly, "Does this episode change Fischer's life-scheme, Satan?"

"Change it? Why, certainly. And radically. If he had not met

Frau Brandt awhile ago he would die next year, thirty-four years of age. Now he will live to be ninety, and have a pretty prosperous and comfortable life of it, as human lives go."

We felt a great joy and pride in what we had done for Fischer, and were expecting Satan to sympathize with this feeling; but he showed no sign and this made us uneasy. We waited for him to speak, but he didn't; so, to assuage our solicitude we had to ask him if there was any defect in Fischer's good luck. Satan considered the question a moment, then said, with some hesitation:

"Well, the fact is, it is a delicate point. Under his several former possible life-careers he was going to heaven."

We were aghast. "Oh, Satan! and under this one—"

"There, don't be so distressed. You were sincerely trying to do him a kindness; let that comfort you."

"Oh, dear, dear, that cannot comfort us. You ought to have told us what we were doing, then we wouldn't have acted so."

But it made no impression on him. He had never felt a pain or a sorrow, and did not know what they were, in any really informing way. He had no knowledge of them except theoretically—that is to say, intellectually. And of course that is no good. One can never get any but a loose and ignorant notion of such things except by experience. We tried our best to make him comprehend the awful thing that had been done and how we were compromised by it, but he couldn't seem to get hold of it. He said he did not think it important where Fischer went to; in heaven he would not be missed, there were "plenty there." We tried to make him see that he was missing the point entirely; that Fischer, and not other people, was the proper one to decide about the importance of it; but it all went for nothing; he said he did not care for Fischer—there were plenty more Fischers.

The next minute Fischer went by on the other side of the way, and it made us sick and faint to see him, remembering the doom that was upon him, and we the cause of it. And how unconscious he was that anything had happened to him! You could see by his elastic step and his alert manner that he was well satisfied with himself for doing that hard turn for poor Frau Brandt. He kept glancing back over his shoulder expectantly. And, sure enough, pretty soon Frau Brandt followed after, in charge of the officers and wearing jingling chains. A mob was in her wake, jeering and shouting, "Blasphemer and heretic!" and some among them were neighbors and friends of her happier days. Some were trying to strike her, and the officers were not taking as much trouble as they might to keep them from it.

"Oh, stop them, Satan!" It was out before we remembered that he could not interrupt them for a moment without changing their whole after-lives. He puffed a little puff toward them with his lips and they began to reel and stagger and grab at the empty air; then they broke apart and fled in every direction, shrieking, as if in intolerable pain. He had crushed a rib of each of them with that little puff. We could not help asking if their life-chart was changed.

"Yes, entirely. Some have gained years, some have lost them. Some few will profit in various ways by the change, but only that few."

We did not ask if we had brought poor Fischer's luck to any of them. We did not wish to know. We fully believed in Satan's desire to do us kindnesses, but we were losing confidence in his judgment. It was at this time that our growing anxiety to have him look over our life-charts and suggest improvements began to fade out and give place to other interests.

For a day or two the whole village was a chattering turmoil over Frau Brandt's case and over the mysterious calamity that had overtaken the mob, and at her trial the place was crowded. She was easily convicted of her blasphemies, for she uttered those terrible words again and said she would not take them back. When warned that she was imperiling her life, she said they could take it in welcome, she did not want it, she would rather live with the professional devils in perdition than with these imitators in the village. They accused her of breaking all those ribs by witchcraft, and asked her if she was not a witch? She answered scornfully:

"No. If I had that power would any of you holy hypocrites be alive five minutes? No; I would strike you all dead. Pronounce your sentence and let me go; I am tired of your society."

So they found her guilty, and she was excommunicated and cut off from the joys of heaven and doomed to the fires of hell;

then she was clothed in a coarse robe and delivered to the secular arm, and conducted to the market-place, the bell solemnly tolling the while. We saw her chained to the stake, and saw the first film of blue smoke rise on the still air. Then her hard face softened, and she looked upon the packed crowd in front of her and said, with gentleness:

"We played together once, in long-agone days when we were innocent little creatures. For the sake of that, I forgive you."

We went away then, and did not see the fires consume her, but we heard the shrieks, although we put our fingers in our ears. When they ceased we knew she was in heaven, notwithstanding the excommunication; and we were glad of her death and not sorry that we had brought it about.

One day, a little while after this, Satan appeared again. We were always watching out for him, for life was never very stagnant when he was by. He came upon us at that place in the woods where we had first met him. Being boys, we wanted to be entertained; we asked him to do a show for us.

"Very well," he said; "would you like to see a history of the progress of the human race?—its development of that product which it calls civilization?"

We said we should.

So, with a thought, he turned the place into the Garden of Eden, and we saw Abel praying by his altar; then Cain came walking toward him with his club, and did not seem to see us, and would have stepped on my foot if I had not drawn it in. He spoke to his brother in a language which we did not understand; then he grew violent and threatening, and we knew what was going to happen, and turned away our heads for the moment; but we heard the crash of the blows and heard the shrieks and the groans; then there was silence, and we saw Abel lying in his blood and gasping out his life, and Cain standing over him and looking down at him, vengeful and unrepentant.

Then the vision vanished, and was followed by a long series of unknown wars, murders, and massacres. Next we had the Flood, and the Ark tossing around in the stormy waters, with lofty mountains in the distance showing veiled and dim through the rain. Satan said:

"The progress of your race was not satisfactory. It is to have another chance now."

The scene changed, and we saw Noah overcome with wine.

Next, we had Sodom and Gomorrah, and "the attempt to discover two or three respectable persons there," as Satan described it. Next, Lot and his daughters in the cave.

Next came the Hebraic wars, and we saw the victims massacre the survivors and their cattle, and save the young girls alive and distribute them around.

Next we had Jael; and saw her slip into the tent and drive the nail into the temple of her sleeping guest; and we were so close that when the blood gushed out it trickled in a little red stream to our feet, and we could have stained our hands in it if we had wanted to.

Next we had Egyptian wars, Greek wars, Roman wars, hideous drenchings of the earth with blood; and we saw the treacheries of the Romans toward the Carthaginians, and the sickening spectacle of the massacre of those brave people. Also we saw Caesar invade Britain—"not that those barbarians had done him any harm, but because he wanted their land, and desired to confer the blessings of civilization upon their widows and orphans," as Satan explained.

Next, Christianity was born. Then ages of Europe passed in review before us, and we saw Christianity and Civilization march hand in hand through those ages, "leaving famine and death and desolation in their wake, and other signs of the progress of the human race," as Satan observed.

And always we had wars, and more wars, and still other wars—all over Europe, all over the world. "Sometimes in the private interest of royal families," Satan said, "sometimes to crush a weak nation; but never a war started by the aggressor for any clean purpose—there is no such war in the history of the race."

"Now," said Satan, "you have seen your progress down to the present, and you must confess that it is wonderful—in its way. We must now exhibit the future."

He showed us slaughters more terrible in their destruction of life, more devastating in their engines of war, than any we had seen.

"You perceive," he said, "that you have made continual progress. Cain did his murder with a club; the Hebrews did their murders with javelins and swords; the Greeks and Romans added protective armor and the fine arts of military organization and generalship; the Christian has added guns and gunpowder; a few centuries from now he will have so greatly improved the deadly effectiveness of his weapons of slaughter that all men will confess that without Christian civilization war must have remained a poor and trifling thing to the end of time."

Then he began to laugh in the most unfeeling way, and make fun of the human race, although he knew that what he had been saying shamed us and wounded us. No one but an angel could have acted so; but suffering is nothing to them; they do not know what it is, except by hearsay.

More than once Seppi and I had tried in a humble and diffident way to convert him, and as he had remained silent we had taken his silence as a sort of encouragement; necessarily, then, this talk of his was a disappointment to us, for it showed that we had made no deep impression upon him. The thought made us sad, and we knew then how the missionary must feel when he has been cherishing a glad hope and has seen it blighted. We kept our grief to ourselves, knowing that this was not the time to continue our work.

Satan laughed his unkind laugh to a finish; then he said: "It is a remarkable progress. In five or six thousand years five or six high civilizations have risen, flourished, commanded the wonder of the world, then faded out and disappeared; and not one of them except the latest ever invented any sweeping and adequate way to kill people. They all did their best—to kill being the chiefest ambition of the human race and the earliest incident in its history—but only the Christian civilization has scored a triumph to be proud of. Two or three centuries from now it will be recognized that all the competent killers are Christians; then the pagan world will go to school to the Christian—not to acquire his religion, but his guns. The Turk and the Chinaman will buy those to kill missionaries and converts with."

By this time his theater was at work again, and before our eyes nation after nation drifted by, during two or three centuries, a mighty procession, an endless procession, raging, struggling, wallowing through seas of blood, smothered in battle-smoke through which the flags glinted and the red jets from the cannon darted; and always we heard the thunder of the guns and the cries of the dying.

"And what does it amount to?" said Satan, with his evil chuckle. "Nothing at all. You gain nothing; you always come out where you went in. For a million years the race has gone on monotonously propagating itself and monotonously reperforming this dull nonsense—to what end? No wisdom can guess! Who gets a profit out of it? Nobody but a parcel of usurping little monarchs and nobilities who despise you; would feel defiled if you touched them; would shut the door in your face if you proposed to call; whom you slave for, fight for, die for, and are not ashamed of it, but proud; whose existence is a perpetual insult to you and you are afraid to resent it; who are mendicants supported by your alms, yet assume toward you the airs of benefactor toward beggar; who address you in the language of master to slave, and are answered in the language of slave to master; who are worshiped by you with your mouth, while in your heart—if you have one—you despise yourselves for it. The first man was a hypocrite and a coward, qualities which have not yet failed in his line; it is the foundation upon which all civilizations have been built. Drink to their perpetuation! Drink to their augmentation! Drink to—" Then he saw by our faces how much we were hurt, and he cut his sentence short and stopped chuckling, and his manner changed. He said, gently: "No we will drink one another's health, and let civilization go. The wine which has flown to our hands out of space by desire is earthly, and good enough for that other toast; but throw away the glasses; we will drink this one in wine which has not visited this world before."

We obeyed, and reached up and received the new cups as they descended. They were shapely and beautiful goblets, but they were not made of any material that we were acquainted with. They seemed to be in motion, they seemed to be alive; and certainly the colors in them were in motion. They were very brilliant and sparkling, and of every tint, and they were never still, but flowed to and fro in rich tides which met and broke and flashed out dainty explosions of enchanting color. I think it was most like opals washing about in waves and flashing out their splendid fires. But there is nothing to compare the wine with. We drank it, and felt a strange and witching ecstasy as of heaven go stealing through us, and Seppi's eyes filled and he said worshipingly:

"We shall be there some day, and then—"

He glanced furtively at Satan, and I think he hoped Satan would say, "Yes, you will be there some day," but Satan seemed to be thinking about something else, and said nothing. This made me feel ghastly, for I knew he had heard; nothing, spoken or unspoken, ever escaped him. Poor Seppi looked distressed, and did not finish his remark. The goblets rose and clove their way into the sky, a triplet of radiant sundogs, and disappeared. Why didn't they stay? It seemed a bad sign, and depressed me. Should I ever see mine again? Would Seppi ever see his?

IX

It was wonderful, the mastery Satan had over time and distance. For him they did not exist. He called them human inventions, and said they were artificialities. We often went to the most distant parts of the globe with him, and stayed weeks and months, and yet were gone only a fraction of a second, as a rule. You could prove it by the clock. One day when our people were in such awful distress because the witch commission were afraid to proceed against the astrologer and Father Peter's household, or against any, indeed, but the poor and the friendless, they lost patience and took to witch-hunting on their own score, and began to chase a born lady who was known to have the habit of curing people by devilish arts, such as bathing them, washing them, and nourishing them instead of bleeding them and purging them through the ministrations of a barber-surgeon in the proper way. She came flying down, with the howling and cursing mob after her, and tried to take refuge in houses, but the doors were shut in her face. They chased her more than half an hour, we following to see it, and at last she was exhausted and fell, and they caught her. They dragged her to a tree and threw a rope over the limb, and began to make a noose in it, some holding her, meantime, and she crying and begging, and her young daughter looking on and weeping, but afraid to say or do anything.

They hanged the lady, and I threw a stone at her, although in my heart I was sorry for her; but all were throwing stones and each was watching his neighbor, and if I had not done as the others did it would have been noticed and spoken of. Satan burst out laughing.

All that were near by turned upon him, astonished and not pleased. It was an ill time to laugh, for his free and scoffing ways and his supernatural music had brought him under suspicion all over the town and turned many privately against him. The big blacksmith called attention to him now, raising his voice so that all should hear, and said:

"What are you laughing at? Answer! Moreover, please explain to the company why you threw no stone."

"Are you sure I did not throw a stone?"

"Yes. You needn't try to get out of it; I had my eye on you."

"And I—I noticed you!" shouted two others.

"Three witnesses," said Satan: "Mueller, the blacksmith; Klein, the butcher's man; Pfeiffer, the weaver's journeyman. Three very ordinary liars. Are there any more?"

"Never mind whether there are others or not, and never mind about what you consider us—three's enough to settle your matter for you. You'll prove that you threw a stone, or it shall go hard with you."

"That's so!" shouted the crowd, and surged up as closely as they could to the center of interest.

"And first you will answer that other question," cried the blacksmith, pleased with himself for being mouthpiece to the public and hero of the occasion. "What are you laughing at?"

Satan smiled and answered, pleasantly: "To see three cowards stoning a dying lady when they were so near death themselves."

You could see the superstitious crowd shrink and catch their breath, under the sudden shock. The blacksmith, with a show of bravado, said:

"Pooh! What do you know about it?"

"I? Everything. By profession I am a fortuneteller, and I read the hands of you three—and some others—when you lifted them to stone the woman. One of you will die tomorrow week; another of you will die to-night; the third has but five minutes to live—and yonder is the clock!"

It made a sensation. The faces of the crowd blanched, and turned mechanically toward the clock. The butcher and the weaver seemed smitten with an illness, but the blacksmith braced up and said, with spirit:

"It is not long to wait for prediction number one. If it fails, young master, you will not live a whole minute after, I promise you that."

No one said anything; all watched the clock in a deep stillness which was impressive. When four and a half minutes were gone the blacksmith gave a sudden gasp and clapped his hands upon his heart, saying, "Give me breath! Give me room!" and began to sink down. The crowd surged back, no one offering to support him, and he fell lumbering to the ground and was dead. The people stared at him, then at Satan, then at one another; and their lips moved, but no words came. Then Satan said:

"Three saw that I threw no stone. Perhaps there are others; let them speak."

It struck a kind of panic into them, and, although no one answered him, many began to violently accuse one another, saying, "You said he didn't throw," and getting for reply, "It is a lie, and I will make you eat it!" And so in a moment they were in a raging and noisy turmoil, and beating and banging one another; and in the midst was the only indifferent one—the dead lady hanging from her rope, her troubles forgotten, her spirit at peace.

So we walked away, and I was not at ease, but was saying to myself, "He told them he was laughing at them, but it was a lie—he was laughing at me."

That made him laugh again, and he said, "Yes, I was laughing at you, because, in fear of what others might report about you, you stoned the woman when your heart revolted at the act—but I was laughing at the others, too."

"Why?"

"Because their case was yours."

"How is that?"

"Well, there were sixty-eight people there, and sixty-two of them had no more desire to throw a stone than you had."

"Satan!"

"Oh, it's true. I know your race. It is made up of sheep. It is governed by minorities, seldom or never by majorities. It suppresses its feelings and its beliefs and follows the handful that makes the most noise. Sometimes the noisy handful is right, sometimes wrong; but no matter, the crowd follows it. The vast majority of the race, whether savage or civilized, are secretly kind-hearted and shrink from inflicting pain, but in the presence of the aggressive and pitiless minority they don't dare to assert themselves. Think of it! One kind-hearted creature spies upon another, and sees to it that he loyally helps in iniquities which revolt both of them. Speaking as an expert, I know that ninety-nine out of a hundred of your race were strongly against the killing of witches when that foolishness was first agitated by a handful of pious lunatics in the long ago. And I know that even to-day, after ages of transmitted prejudice and silly teaching, only one person in twenty puts any real heart into the harrying of a witch. And yet apparently everybody hates witches and wants them killed. Some day a handful will rise up on the other side and make the most noise—perhaps even a single daring man with a big voice and a determined front will do it—and in a week all the sheep will wheel and follow him, and witch-hunting will come to a sudden end.

"Monarchies, aristocracies, and religions are all based upon that large defect in your race—the individual's distrust of his neighbor, and his desire, for safety's or comfort's sake, to stand well in his neighbor's eye. These institutions will always remain, and always flourish, and always oppress you, affront you, and degrade you, because you will always be and remain slaves of minorities. There was never a country where the majority of the people were in their secret hearts loyal to any of these institutions."

I did not like to hear our race called sheep, and said I did not think they were.

"Still, it is true, lamb," said Satan. "Look at you in war—what mutton you are, and how ridiculous!"

"In war? How?"

"There has never been a just one, never an honorable one—on the part of the instigator of the war. I can see a million years ahead, and this rule will never change in so many as half a dozen instances. The loud little handful—as usual—will shout for the war. The pulpit will—warily and cautiously—object—at first; the great, big, dull bulk of the nation will rub its sleepy eyes and try to make out why there should be a war, and will say, earnestly and indignantly, "It is unjust and dishonorable, and there is no necessity for it." Then the handful will shout louder. A few fair men on the other side will argue and reason against the war with speech and pen, and at first will have a hearing and be applauded; but it will not last long; those others will out-shout them, and presently the anti-war audiences will thin out and lose popularity. Before long you will see this curious thing: the speakers stoned from the platform, and free speech strangled by hordes of furious men who in their secret hearts are still at one with those stoned speakers—as earlier—but do not dare to say so. And now the whole nation—pulpit and all—will take up the war-cry, and shout itself hoarse, and mob any honest man who ventures to open his mouth; and presently such mouths will cease to open. Next the statesmen will invent cheap lies, putting the blame upon the nation that is attacked, and every man will be glad of those conscience-soothing falsities, and will diligently study them, and refuse to examine any refutations of them; and thus he will by and by convince himself that the war is just, and will thank God for the better sleep he enjoys after this process of grotesque self-deception."

X

Days and days went by now, and no Satan. It was dull without him. But the astrologer, who had returned from his excursion to the moon, went about the village, braving public opinion, and getting a stone in the middle of his back now and then when some witch-hater got a safe chance to throw it and dodge out of sight. Meantime two influences had been working well for Marget. That Satan, who was quite indifferent to her, had stopped going to her house after a visit or two had hurt her pride, and she had set herself the task of banishing him from her heart. Reports of Wilhelm Meidling's dissipation brought to her from time to time by old Ursula had touched her with remorse, jealousy of Satan being the cause of it; and so now, these two matters working upon her together, she was getting a good profit out of the combination—her interest in Satan was steadily cooling, her interest in Wilhelm as steadily warming. All that was needed to complete her conversion was that Wilhelm should brace up and do something that should cause favorable talk and incline the public toward him again.

The opportunity came now. Marget sent and asked him to defend her uncle in the approaching trial, and he was greatly pleased, and stopped drinking and began his preparations with diligence. With more diligence than hope, in fact, for it was not a promising case. He had many interviews in his office with Seppi and me, and threshed out our testimony pretty thoroughly, thinking to find some valuable grains among the chaff, but the harvest was poor, of course.

If Satan would only come! That was my constant thought. He could invent some way to win the case; for he had said it would be won, so he necessarily knew how it could be done. But the days dragged on, and still he did not come. Of course I did not doubt that it would be won, and that Father Peter would be happy for the rest of his life, since Satan had said so; yet I knew I should be much more comfortable if he would come and tell us how to manage it. It was getting high time for Father Peter to have a saving change toward happiness, for by general report he was worn out with his imprisonment and the ignominy that was burdening him, and was like to die of his miseries unless he got relief soon.

At last the trial came on, and the people gathered from all around to witness it; among them many strangers from considerable distances. Yes, everybody was there except the accused. He was too feeble in body for the strain. But Marget was present, and keeping up her hope and her spirit the best she could. The money was present, too. It was emptied on the table, and was handled and caressed and examined by such as were privileged.

The astrologer was put in the witness-box. He had on his best hat and robe for the occasion.

QUESTION. You claim that this money is yours

ANSWER. I DO.

Q. How did you come by it?

A. I found the bag in the road when I was returning from a journey.

Q. When?

A. More than two years ago.

Q. What did you do with it?

A. I brought it home and hid it in a secret place in my observatory, intending to find the owner if I could.

Q. You endeavored to find him?

A. I made diligent inquiry during several months, but nothing came of it.

Q. And then?

A. I thought it not worth while to look further, and was minded to use the money in finishing the wing of the foundling-asylum connected with the priory and nunnery. So I took it out of its hiding-place and counted it to see if any of it was missing. And then—

Q. Why do you stop? Proceed.

A. I am sorry to have to say this, but just as I had finished and was restoring the bag to its place, I looked up and there stood Father Peter behind me.

Several murmured, "That looks bad," but others answered, "Ah, but he is such a liar!"

Q. That made you uneasy?
A. No; I thought nothing of it at the time, for Father Peter often came to me unannounced to ask for a little help in his need.

Marget blushed crimson at hearing her uncle falsely and impudently charged with begging, especially from one he had always denounced as a fraud, and was going to speak, but remembered herself in time and held her peace.

Q. Proceed.
A. In the end I was afraid to contribute the money to the foundling-asylum, but elected to wait yet another year and continue my inquiries. When I heard of Father Peter's find I was glad, and no suspicion entered my mind; when I came home a day or two later and discovered that my own money was gone I still did not suspect until three circumstances connected with Father Peter's good fortune struck me as being singular coincidences.
Q. Pray name them.
A. Father Peter had found his money in a path—I had found mine in a road. Father Peter's find consisted exclusively of gold ducats—mine also. Father Peter found eleven hundred and seven ducats—I exactly the same.

This closed his evidence, and certainly it made a strong impression on the house; one could see that.

Wilhelm Meidling asked him some questions, then called us boys, and we told our tale. It made the people laugh, and we were ashamed. We were feeling pretty badly, anyhow, because Wilhelm was hopeless, and showed it. He was doing as well as he could, poor young fellow, but nothing was in his favor, and such sympathy as there was was now plainly not with his client. It might be difficult for court and people to believe the astrologer's story, considering his character, but it was almost impossible to believe Father Peter's. We were already feeling badly enough, but when the astrologer's lawyer said he believed he would not ask us any questions—for our story was a little delicate and it would be cruel for him to put any strain upon it—everybody tittered, and it was almost more than we could bear. Then he made a sarcastic little speech, and got so much fun out of our tale, and it seemed so ridiculous and childish and every way impossible and foolish, that it made everybody laugh till the tears came; and at last Marget could not keep up her courage any longer, but broke down and cried, and I was so sorry for her.

Now I noticed something that braced me up. It was Satan standing alongside of Wilhelm! And there was such a contrast!—Satan looked so confident, had such a spirit in his eyes and face, and Wilhelm looked so depressed and despondent. We two were comfortable now, and judged that he would testify and persuade the bench and the people that black was white and white black, or any other color he wanted it. We glanced around to see what the strangers in the house thought of him, for he was beautiful, you know—stunning, in fact—but no one was noticing him; so we knew by that that he was invisible.

The lawyer was saying his last words; and while he was saying them Satan began to melt into Wilhelm. He melted into him and disappeared; and then there was a change, when his spirit began to look out of Wilhelm's eyes.

That lawyer finished quite seriously, and with dignity. He pointed to the money, and said:

"The love of it is the root of all evil. There it lies, the ancient tempter, newly red with the shame of its latest victory—the dishonor of a priest of God and his two poor juvenile helpers in crime. If it could but speak, let us hope that it would be constrained to confess that of all its conquests this was the basest and the most pathetic."

He sat down. Wilhelm rose and said:

"From the testimony of the accuser I gather that he found this money in a road more than two years ago. Correct me, sir, if I misunderstood you."

The astrologer said his understanding of it was correct.

"And the money so found was never out of his hands thenceforth up to a certain definite date—the last day of last year. Correct me, sir, if I am wrong."

The astrologer nodded his head. Wilhelm turned to the bench and said:

"If I prove that this money here was not that money, then it is not his?"

"Certainly not; but this is irregular. If you had such a witness it was your duty to give proper notice of it and have him here to—" He broke off and began to consult with the other judges. Meantime that other lawyer got up excited and began to protest against allowing new witnesses to be brought into the case at this late stage.

The judges decided that his contention was just and must be allowed.

"But this is not a new witness," said Wilhelm. "It has already been partly examined. I speak of the coin."

"The coin? What can the coin say?"

"It can say it is not the coin that the astrologer once possessed. It can say it was not in existence last December. By its date it can say this."

And it was so! There was the greatest excitement in the court while that lawyer and the judges were reaching for coins and examining them and exclaiming. And everybody was full of admiration of Wilhelm's brightness in happening to think of that neat idea. At last order was called and the court said:

"All of the coins but four are of the date of the present year. The court tenders its sincere sympathy to the accused, and its deep regret that he, an innocent man, through an unfortunate mistake, has suffered the undeserved humiliation of imprisonment and trial. The case is dismissed."

So the money could speak, after all, though that lawyer thought it couldn't. The court rose, and almost everybody came forward to shake hands with Marget and congratulate her, and then to shake with Wilhelm and praise him; and Satan had stepped out of Wilhelm and was standing around looking on full of interest, and people walking through him every which way, not knowing he was there. And Wilhelm could not explain why he only thought of the date on the coins at the last moment, instead of earlier; he said it just occurred to him, all of a sudden, like an inspiration, and he brought it right out without any hesitation, for, although he didn't examine the coins, he seemed, somehow, to know it was true. That was honest of him, and like him; another would have pretended he had thought of it earlier, and was keeping it back for a surprise.

He had dulled down a little now; not much, but still you could notice that he hadn't that luminous look in his eyes that he had while Satan was in him. He nearly got it back, though, for a moment when Marget came and praised him and thanked him and couldn't keep him from seeing how proud she was of him. The astrologer went off dissatisfied and cursing, and Solomon Isaacs gathered up the money and carried it away. It was Father Peter's for good and all, now.

Satan was gone. I judged that he had spirited himself away to the jail to tell the prisoner the news; and in this I was right. Marget and the rest of us hurried thither at our best speed, in a great state of rejoicing.

Well, what Satan had done was this: he had appeared before that poor prisoner, exclaiming, "The trial is over, and you stand forever disgraced as a thief—by verdict of the court!"

The shock unseated the old man's reason. When we arrived, ten minutes later, he was parading pompously up and down and delivering commands to this and that and the other constable or jailer, and calling them Grand Chamberlain, and Prince This and Prince That, and Admiral of the Fleet, Field Marshal in Command, and all such fustian, and was as happy as a bird. He thought he was Emperor!

Marget flung herself on his breast and cried, and indeed everybody was moved almost to heartbreak. He recognized Marget, but could not understand why she should cry. He patted her on the shoulder and said:

"Don't do it, dear; remember, there are witnesses, and it is not becoming in the Crown Princess. Tell me your trouble—it shall be mended; there is nothing the Emperor cannot do." Then he looked around and saw old Ursula with her apron to her eyes. He was puzzled at that, and said, "And what is the matter with you?"

Through her sobs she got out words explaining that she was distressed to see him—"so." He reflected over that a moment, then muttered, as if to himself: "A singular old thing, the Dowager Duchess—means well, but is always snuffling and never able to tell what it is about. It is because she doesn't know." His eyes fell on Wilhelm. "Prince of India," he said, "I divine that it is you that the Crown Princess is concerned about. Her tears shall be dried; I will no longer stand between you; she shall share your throne; and between you you shall inherit mine. There, little lady, have I done well? You can smile now—isn't it so?"

He petted Marget and kissed her, and was so contented with himself and with everybody that he could not do enough for us all, but began to give away kingdoms and such things right and left, and the least that any of us got was a principality. And so at last, being persuaded to go home, he marched in imposing state; and when the crowds along the way saw how it gratified him to be hurrahed at, they humored him to the top of his desire, and he responded with condescending bows and gracious smiles, and often stretched out a hand and said, "Bless you, my people!"

As pitiful a sight as ever I saw. And Marget, and old Ursula crying all the way.

On my road home I cam upon Satan, and reproached him with deceiving me with that lie. He was not embarrassed, but said, quite simply and composedly:

"Ah, you mistake; it was the truth. I said he would be happy the rest of his days, and he will, for he will always think he is the Emperor, and his pride in it and his joy in it will endure to the end. He is now, and will remain, the one utterly happy person in this empire."

"But the method of it, Satan, the method! Couldn't you have done it without depriving him of his reason?"

It was difficult to irritate Satan, but that accomplished it.

"What an ass you are!" he said. "Are you so unobservant as not to have found out that sanity and happiness are an impossible combination? No sane man can be happy, for to him life is real, and he sees what a fearful thing it is. Only the mad can be happy, and not many of those. The few that imagine themselves kings or gods are happy, the rest are no happier than the sane. Of course, no man is entirely in his right mind at any time, but I have been referring to the extreme cases. I have taken from this man that trumpery thing which the race regards as a Mind; I have replaced his tin life with a silver-gilt fiction; you see the result—and you criticize! I said I would make him permanently happy, and I have done it. I have made him happy by the only means possible to his race—and you are not satisfied!" He heaved a discouraged sigh, and said, "It seems to me that this race is hard to please."

There it was, you see. He didn't seem to know any way to do a person a favor except by killing him or making a lunatic out of him. I apologized, as well as I could; but privately I did not think much of his processes—at that time.

Satan was accustomed to say that our race lived a life of continuous and uninterrupted self-deception. It duped itself from cradle to grave with shams and delusions which it mistook for realities, and this made its entire life a sham. Of the score of fine qualities which it imagined it had and was vain of, it really possessed hardly one. It regarded itself as gold, and was only brass. One day when he was in this vein he mentioned a detail—the sense of humor. I cheered up then, and took issue. I said we possessed it.

"There spoke the race!" he said; "always ready to claim what it hasn't got, and mistake its ounce of brass filings for a ton of gold-dust. You have a mongrel perception of humor, nothing more; a multitude of you possess that. This multitude sees the comic side of a thousand low-grade and trivial things—broad incongruities, mainly; grotesqueries, absurdities, evokers of the horse-laugh. Then ten thousand high-grade comicalities which exist in the world are sealed from their dull vision. Will a day come when the race will detect the funniness of these juvenilities and laugh at them—and by laughing at them destroy them? For your race, in its poverty, has unquestionably one really effective weapon—laughter. Power, money, persuasion, supplication, persecution—these can lift at a colossal humbug—push it a little—weaken it a little, century by century; but only laughter can blow it to rags and atoms at a blast. Against the assault of laughter nothing can stand. You are always fussing and fighting with your other weapons. Do you ever use that one? No; you leave it lying rusting. As a race, do you ever use it at all? No; you lack sense and the courage"

We were traveling at the time and stopped at a little city in India and looked on while a juggler did his tricks before a group of natives. They were wonderful, but I knew Satan could beat that game, and I begged him to show off a little, and he said he would. He changed himself into a native in turban and breech-cloth, and very considerately conferred on me a temporary knowledge of the language.

The juggler exhibited a seed, covered it with earth in a small flower-pot, then put a rag over the pot; after a minute the rag began to rise; in ten minutes it had risen a foot; then the rag was removed and a little tree was exposed, with leaves upon it and ripe fruit. We ate the fruit, and it was good. But Satan said:

"Why do you cover the pot? Can't you grow the tree in the sunlight?"

"No," said the juggler; "no one can do that."

"You are only an apprentice; you don't know your trade. Give me the seed. I will show you." He took the seed and said, "What shall I raise from it?"

"It is a cherry seed; of course you will raise a cherry."

"Oh no; that is a trifle; any novice can do that. Shall I raise an orange-tree from it?"

"Oh yes!" and the juggler laughed.

"And shall I make it bear other fruits as well as oranges?"

"If God wills!" and they all laughed.

Satan put the seed in the ground, put a handful of dust on it, and said, "Rise!"

A tiny stem shot up and began to grow, and grew so fast that in five minutes it was a great tree, and we were sitting in the shade of it. There was a murmur of wonder, then all looked up and saw a strange and pretty sight, for the branches were heavy with fruits of many kinds and colors—oranges, grapes, bananas, peaches, cherries, apricots, and so on. Baskets were brought, and the unlading of the tree began; and the people crowded around Satan and kissed his hand, and praised him, calling him prince of jugglers. The news went about the town, and everybody came running to see the wonder—and they remembered to bring baskets, too. But the tree was equal to the occasion; it put out new fruits as fast as any were removed; baskets were filled by the score and by the hundred, but always the supply remained undiminished. At last a foreigner in white linen and sun-helmet arrived, and exclaimed, angrily:

"Away from here! Clear out, you dogs; the tree is on my lands and is my property."

The natives put down their baskets and made humble obeisance. Satan made humble obeisance, too, with his fingers to his forehead, in the native way, and said:

"Please let them have their pleasure for an hour, sir—only that, and no longer. Afterward you may forbid them; and you will still have more fruit than you and the state together can consume in a year."

This made the foreigner very angry, and he cried out, "Who are you, you vagabond, to tell your betters what they may do and what they mayn't! and he struck Satan with his cane and followed this error with a kick.

The fruits rotted on the branches, and the leaves withered and fell. The foreigner gazed at the bare limbs with the look of one who is surprised, and not gratified. Satan said:

"Take good care of the tree, for its health and yours are bound together. It will never bear again, but if you tend it well it will live long. Water its roots once in each hour every night—and do it yourself; it must not be done by proxy, and to do it in daylight will not answer. If you fail only once in any night, the tree will die, and you likewise. Do not go home to your own country any more—you would not reach there; make no business or pleasure engagements which require you to go outside your gate at night—you cannot afford the risk; do not rent or sell this place—it would be injudicious."

The foreigner was proud and wouldn't beg, but I thought he looked as if he would like to. While he stood gazing at Satan we vanished away and landed in Ceylon.

I was sorry for that man; sorry Satan hadn't been his customary self and killed him or made him a lunatic. It would have been a mercy. Satan overheard the thought, and said:

"I would have done it but for his wife, who has not offended me. She is coming to him presently from their native land, Portugal. She is well, but has not long to live, and has been yearning to see him and persuade him to go back with her next year. She will die without knowing he can't leave that place?"

"He won't tell her?"

"He? He will not trust that secret with any one; he will reflect that it could be revealed in sleep, in the hearing of some Portuguese guest's servant some time or other."

"Did none of those natives understand what you said to him?"

"None of them understood, but he will always be afraid that some of them did. That fear will be torture to him, for he has been a harsh master to them. In his dreams he will imagine them chopping his tree down. That will make his days uncomfortable—I have already arranged for his nights."

It grieved me, though not sharply, to see him take such a malicious satisfaction in his plans for this foreigner.

"Does he believe what you told him, Satan?"

"He thought he didn't, but our vanishing helped. The tree, where there had been no tree before—that helped. The insane and uncanny variety of fruits—the sudden withering—all these things are helps. Let him think as he may, reason as he may, one thing is certain, he will water the tree. But between this and night he will begin his changed career with a very natural precaution—for him."

"What is that?"

"He will fetch a priest to cast out the tree's devil. You are such a humorous race—and don't suspect it."

"Will he tell the priest?"

"No. He will say a juggler from Bombay created it, and that he wants the juggler's devil driven out of it, so that it will thrive and be fruitful again. The priest's incantations will fail; then the Portuguese will give up that scene and get his watering-pot ready."

"But the priest will burn the tree. I know it; he will not allow it to remain."

"Yes, and anywhere in Europe he would burn the man, too. But in India the people are civilized, and these things will not happen. The man will drive the priest away and take care of the tree."

I reflected a little, then said, "Satan, you have given him a hard life, I think."

"Comparatively. It must not be mistaken for a holiday."

We flitted from place to place around the world as we had done before, Satan showing me a hundred wonders, most of them reflecting in some way the weakness and triviality of our race. He did this now every few days—not out of malice—I am sure of that—it only seemed to amuse and interest him, just as a naturalist might be amused and interested by a collection of ants.

XI

For as much as a year Satan continued these visits, but at last he came less often, and then for a long time he did not come at all. This always made me lonely and melancholy. I felt that he was losing interest in our tiny world and might at any time abandon his visits entirely. When one day he finally came to me I was overjoyed, but only for a little while. He had come to say good-by, he told me, and for the last time. He had investigations and undertakings in other corners of the universe, he said, that would keep him busy for a longer period than I could wait for his return.

"And you are going away, and will not come back any more?"

"Yes," he said. "We have comraded long together, and it has been pleasant—pleasant for both; but I must go now, and we shall not see each other any more."

"In this life, Satan, but in another? We shall meet in another, surely?"

Then, all tranquilly and soberly, he had the strange answer, *"There is no other."*

A subtle influence blew upon my spirit from his, bringing with it a vague, dim, but blessed and hopeful feeling that the incredible words might be true—even *must* be true.

"Have you never suspected this, Theodor?"

"No. How could I? But if it can only be true—"

"It is true."

A gust of thankfulness rose in my breast, but a doubt checked it before it could issue in words, and I said, "But—but—we have seen that future life—seen it in its actuality, and so—"

"It was a vision—it had no existence."

I could hardly breathe for the great hope that was struggling in me. "A vision?—a vi—"

"Life itself is only a vision, a dream."

It was electrical. By God! I had had that very thought a thousand times in my musings!

"*Nothing* exists; all is a dream. God—man—the world—the sun, the moon, the wilderness of stars—a dream, all a dream; they have no existence. *Nothing exists save empty space—and you!"*

"I!"

"And you are not you—you have no body, no blood, no bones, you are but a *thought*. I myself have no existence; I am but a dream—your dream, creature of your imagination. In a moment you will have realized this, then you will banish me from your visions and I shall dissolve into the nothingness out of which you made me. . . .

"I am perishing already—I am failing—I am passing away. In a little while you will be alone in shoreless space, to wander its limitless solitudes without friend or comrade forever—for you will remain a *thought*, the only existent thought, and by your nature inextinguishable, indestructible. But I, your poor servant, have revealed you to yourself and set you free. Dream other dreams, and better!

"Strange! that you should not have suspected years ago—centuries, ages, eons ago!—for you have existed, companionless, through all the eternities. Strange, indeed, that you should not have suspected that your universe and its contents were only dreams, visions, fiction! Strange, because they are so frankly and hysterically insane—like all dreams: a God who could make good children as easily as bad, yet preferred to make bad ones; who could have made every one of them happy, yet never made a single happy one; who made them prize their bitter life, yet stingily cut it short; who gave his angels eternal happiness unearned, yet required his other children to earn it; who gave his angels painless lives, yet cursed his other children with biting miseries and maladies of mind and body; who mouths justice and invented hell—mouths mercy and invented hell—mouths Golden Rules, and forgiveness multiplied by seventy times seven, and invented hell; who mouths morals to other people and has none himself; who frowns upon crimes, yet commits them all; who created man without invitation, then tries to shuffle the responsibility for man's acts upon man, instead of honorably placing it where it belongs, upon himself; and finally, with altogether divine obtuseness, invites this poor, abused slave to worship him! . . .

"You perceive, *now*, that these things are all impossible except in a dream. You perceive that they are pure and puerile insanities, the silly creations of an imagination that is not conscious of its freaks—in a word, that they are a dream, and you the maker of it. The dream-marks are all present; you should have recognized them earlier.

"It is true, that which I have revealed to you; there is no God, no universe, no human race, no earthly life, no heaven, no hell. It is all a dream—a grotesque and foolish dream. Nothing exists but you. And you are but a *thought*—a vagrant thought, a useless thought, a homeless thought, wandering forlorn among the empty eternities!"

He vanished, and left me appalled; for I knew, and realized, that all he had said was true.

At the Appetite-Cure

I

This establishment's name is Hochberghaus. It is in Bohemia, a short day's journey from Vienna, and being in the Austrian empire is of course a health resort. The empire is made up of health resorts; it distributes health to the whole world. Its waters are all medicinal. They are bottled and sent throughout the earth; the natives themselves drink beer. This is self-sacrifice, apparently—but outlanders who have drunk Vienna beer have another idea about it. Particularly the Pilsner which one gets in a small cellar up an obscure back lane in the First Bezirk—the name has escaped me, but the place is easily found: You inquire for the Greek church; and when you get to it, go right along by—the next house is that little beer-mill. It is remote from all traffic and all noise; it is always Sunday there. There are two small rooms, with low ceilings supported by massive arches; the arches and ceilings are whitewashed, otherwise the rooms would pass for cells in the dungeons of a bastile. The furniture is plain and cheap, there is no ornamentation anywhere; yet it is a heaven for the self-sacrificers, for the beer there is incomparable; there is nothing like it elsewhere in the world. In the first room you will find twelve or fifteen ladies and gentlemen of civilian quality; in the other one a dozen generals and ambassadors. One may live in Vienna many months and not hear of this place; but having once heard of it and sampled it, the sampler will afterward infest it.

However, this is all incidental—a mere passing note of gratitude for blessings received—it has nothing to do with my subject. My subject is health resorts. All unhealthy people ought to domicile themselves in Vienna, and use that as a base, making flights from time to time to the outlying resorts, according to need. A flight to Marienbad to get rid of fat; a flight to Carlsbad to get rid of rheumatism; a flight to Kaltenleutgeben to take the water cure and get rid of the rest of the diseases. It is all so handy. You can stand in Vienna and toss a biscuit into Kaltenleutgeben, with a twelve-inch gun. You can run out thither at any time of the day; you go by the phenomenally slow trains, and yet inside of an hour you have exchanged the glare and swelter of the city for wooded hills, and shady forest paths, and soft cool airs, and the music of birds, and the repose and peace of paradise.

And there are plenty of other health resorts at your service and convenient to get at from Vienna; charming places, all of them; Vienna sits in the centre of a beautiful world of mountains with now and then a lake and forests; in fact, no other city is so fortunately situated.

There are abundance of health resorts, as I have said. Among them this place—Hochberghaus. It stands solitary on the top of a densely wooded mountain, and is a building of great size. It is called the Appetite Anstallt, and people who have lost their appetites come here to get them restored. When I arrived I was taken by Professor Haimberger to his consulting-room and questioned:

"It is six o'clock. When did you eat last."

"At noon."

"What did you eat?"

"Next to nothing."

"What was on the table?"

"The usual things."

"Chops, chickens, vegetables, and so on?"

"Yes; but don't mention them—I can't bear it."

"Are you tired of them?"

"Oh, utterly. I wish I might never hear of them again."

"The mere sight of food offends you, does it?"

"More, it revolts me."

The doctor considered awhile, then got out a long menu and ran his eye slowly down it.

"I think," said he, "that what you need to eat is—but here, choose for yourself."

I glanced at the list, and my stomach threw a handspring. Of all the barbarous layouts that were ever contrived, this was the most atrocious. At the top stood "tough, underdone, overdue tripe, garnished with garlic"; half-way down the bill stood "young cat; old cat; scrambled cat"; at the bottom stood "sailor-boots, softened with tallow—served raw." The wide intervals of the bill were packed with dishes calculated to insult a cannibal. I said:

"Doctor, it is not fair to joke over so serious a case as mine. I came here to get an appetite, not to throw away the remnant that's left."

He said gravely: "I am not joking; why should I joke?"

"But I can't eat these horrors."

"Why not?"

He said it with a naïveté that was admirable, whether it was real or assumed.

"Why not? Because—why, doctor, for months I have seldom been able to endure anything more substantial than omelettes and custards. These unspeakable dishes of yours—"

"Oh, you will come to like them. They are very good. And you *must* eat them. It is the rule of the place, and is strict. I cannot permit any departure from it."

I said, smiling: "Well, then, doctor, you will have to permit the departure of the patient. I am going."

He looked hurt, and said in a way which changed the aspect of things:

"I am sure you would not do me that injustice. I accepted you in good faith—you will not shame that confidence. This appetite-cure is my whole living. If you should go forth from it with the sort of appetite which you now have, it could become known, and you can see, yourself, that people would say my cure failed in your case and hence can fail in other cases. You will not go; you will not do me this hurt."

I apologized and said I would stay.

"That is right. I was sure you would not go; it would take the food from my family's mouths."

"Would they mind that? Do they eat these fiendish things?"

"They? My family?" His eyes were full of gentle wonder. "Of course not."

"Oh, they don't! Do you?"

"Certainly not."

"I see. It's another case of a physician who doesn't take his own medicine."

"I don't need it. It is six hours since you lunched. Will you have supper now—or later?"

"I am not hungry, but now is as good a time as any, and I would like to be done with it and have it off my mind. It is about my usual time, and regularity is commanded by all the authorities. Yes, I will try to nibble a little now—I wish a light horse-whipping would answer instead."

The professor handed me that odious menu.

"Choose—or will you have it later?"

"Oh, dear me, show me to my room; I forgot your hard rule."

"Wait just a moment before you finally decide. There is another rule. If you choose now, the order will be filled at once; but if you wait, you will have to await my pleasure. You cannot get a dish from that entire bill until I consent."

"All right. Show me to my room, and send the cook to bed; there is not going to be any hurry."

The professor took me up one flight of stairs and showed me into a most inviting and comfortable apartment consisting of parlor, bedchamber, and bathroom.

The front windows looked out over a far-reaching spread of green glades and valleys, and tumbled hills clothed with forests—a noble solitude unvexed by the fussy world. In the parlor were many shelves filled with books. The professor said he would now leave me to myself; and added:

"Smoke and read as much as you please, drink all the water you like. When you get hungry, ring and give your order, and I will decide whether it shall be filled or not. Yours is a stubborn, bad case, and I think the first fourteen dishes in the bill are each and all too delicate for its needs. I ask you as a favor to restrain yourself and not call for them."

"Restrain myself, is it? Give yourself no uneasiness. You are going to save money by me. The idea of coaxing a sick man's appetite back with this buzzard-fare is clear insanity."

I said it with bitterness, for I felt outraged by this calm, cold talk over these heartless new engines of assassination. The doctor looked grieved, but not offended. He laid the bill of fare on the commode at my bed's head, "so that it would be handy," and said:

"Yours is not the worst case I have encountered, by any means; still it is a bad one and requires robust treatment; therefore I shall be gratified if you will restrain yourself and skip down to No. 15 and begin with that."

Then he left me and I began to undress, for I was dog-tired and very sleepy. I slept fifteen hours and woke up finely refreshed at ten the next morning. Vienna coffee! It was the first thing I thought of—that unapproachable luxury—that sumptuous coffee-house coffee, compared with which all other European coffee and all American hotel coffee is mere fluid poverty. I rang, and ordered it; also Vienna bread, that delicious invention. The servant spoke through the wicket in the door and said—but you know what he said. He referred me to the bill of fare. I allowed him to go—I had no further use for him.

After the bath I dressed and started for a walk, and got as far as the door. It was locked on the outside. I rang and the servant came and explained that it was another rule. The seclusion of the patient was required until after the first meal. I had not been particularly anxious to get out before; but it was different now. Being locked in makes a person wishful to get out. I soon began to find it difficult to put in the time. At two o'clock I had been twenty-six hours without food. I had been growing hungry for some time; I recognized that I was not only hungry now, but hungry with a strong adjective in front of it. Yet I was not hungry enough to face the bill of fare.

I must put in the time somehow. I would read and smoke. I did it; hour by hour. The books were all of one breed—shipwrecks; people lost in deserts; people shut up in caved-in mines; people starving in besieged cities. I read about all the revolting dishes that ever famishing men had stayed their hunger with. During the first hours these things nauseated me: hours followed in which they did not so affect me; still other hours followed in which I found myself smacking my lips over some tolerably infernal messes. When I had been without food forty-five hours I ran eagerly to the bell and ordered the second dish in the bill, which was a sort of dumplings containing a compost made of caviar and tar.

It was refused me. During the next fifteen hours I visited the bell every now and then and ordered a dish that was further down the list. Always a refusal. But I was conquering prejudice after prejudice, right along; I was making sure progress; I was creeping up on No. 15 with deadly certainty, and my heart beat faster and faster, my hopes rose higher and higher.

At last when food had not passed my lips for sixty hours, victory was mine, and I ordered No. 15:

"Soft-boiled spring chicken—in the egg; six dozen, hot and fragrant!"

In fifteen minutes it was there; and the doctor along with it, rubbing his hands with joy. He said with great excitement:

"It's a cure, it's a cure! I knew I could do it. Dear sir, my grand system never fails—never. You've got your appetite back—you know you have; say it and make me happy."

"Bringing on your carrion—I can eat anything in the bill!"

"Oh, this is noble, this is splendid—but I knew I could do it, the system never fails. How are the birds?"

"Never was anything so delicious in the world; and yet as a rule I don't care for game. But don't interrupt me, don't—I can't spare my mouth, I really can't."

Then the doctor said:

"The cure is perfect. There is no more doubt nor danger. Let the poultry alone; I can trust you with a beefsteak, now."

The beefsteak came—as much as a basketful of it—with potatoes, and Vienna bread and coffee; and I ate a meal then that was worth all the costly preparation I had made for it. And dripped tears of gratitude into the gravy all the time—gratitude to the doctor for putting a little plain common-sense into me when I had been empty of it so many, many years.

II

Thirty years ago Haimberger went off on a long voyage in a sailing-ship. There were fifteen passengers on board. The table-fare was of the regulation pattern of the day: At 7 in the morning, a cup of bad coffee in bed; at 9, breakfast: bad coffee, with condensed milk; soggy rolls, crackers, salt fish; at 1 P.M., luncheon: cold tongue, cold ham, cold corned beef, soggy cold rolls, crackers; 5 P.M., dinner: thick pea soup, salt fish, hot corned beef and sour kraut, boiled pork and beans, pudding; 9 till 11 P.M., supper: tea, with condensed milk, cold tongue, cold ham, pickles, sea-biscuit, pickled oysters, pickled pig's feet, grilled bones, golden buck.

At the end of the first week eating had ceased, nibbling had taken its place. The passengers came to the table, but it was partly to put in the time, and partly because the wisdom of the ages commanded them to be regular in their meals. They were tired of the coarse and monotonous fare, and took no interest in it, had no appetite for it. All day and every day they roamed the ship half hungry, plagued by their gnawing stomachs, moody, untalkative, miserable. Among them were three confirmed dyspeptics. These became shadows in the course of three weeks. There was also a bed-ridden invalid; he lived on boiled rice; he could not look at the regular dishes.

Now came shipwreck and life in open boats, with the usual paucity of food. Provisions ran lower and lower. The appetites improved, then. When nothing was left but raw ham and the ration of that was down to two ounces a day per person, the appetites were perfect. At the end of fifteen days the dyspeptics, the invalid, and the most delicate ladies in the party were chewing sailor-boots in ecstasy, and only complaining because the supply of them was limited. Yet these were the same people who couldn't endure the ship's tedious corned beef and sour kraut and other crudities. They were rescued by an English vessel.

Within ten days the whole fifteen were in as good condition as they had been when the shipwreck occurred.

"They had suffered no damage by their adventure," said the professor. "Do you note that?"

"Yes."

"Do you note it well?"

"Yes—I think I do."

"But you don't. You hesitate. You don't rise to the importance of it. I will say it again—with emphasis—*not one of them suffered any damage.*"

"Now I begin to see. Yes, it was indeed remarkable."

"Nothing of the kind. It was perfectly natural. There was no reason why they should suffer damage. They were undergoing Nature's Appetite Cure, the best and wisest in the world."

"Is that where you got your idea?"

"That is where I got it."

"It taught those people a valuable lesson."

"What makes you think that?"

"Why shouldn't I? You seem to think it taught you one."

"That is nothing to the point. I am not a fool."

"I see. Were they fools?"

"They were human beings."

"Is it the same thing?"

"Why do you ask? You know it yourself. As regards his health—and the rest of the things—the average man is what his environment and his superstitions have made him; and their function is to make him an ass. He can't add up three or four new circumstances together and perceive what they mean; it is beyond him. He is not capable of observing for himself; he has to get everything at second-hand. If what are miscalled the lower animals were as silly as man is, they would all perish from the earth in a year."

"Those passengers learned no lesson, then?"

"Not a sign of it. They went to their regular meals in the English ship, and pretty soon they were nibbling again—nibbling, appetiteless, disgusted with the food, moody, miserable, half hungry, their outraged stomachs cursing and swearing and whining and supplicating all day long. And in vain, for they were the stomachs of fools."

"Then, as I understand it, your scheme is—"

"Quite simple. Don't eat till you are hungry. If the food fails to taste good, fails to satisfy you, rejoice you, comfort you, don't eat again until you are *very* hungry. Then it will rejoice you—and do you good, too."

"And I observe no regularity, as to hours?"

"When you are conquering a bad appetite—no. After it is conquered, regularity is no harm, so long as the appetite remains good. As soon as the appetite wavers, apply the corrective again—which is starvation, long or short according to the needs of the case."

"The best diet, I suppose—I mean the wholesomest—"

"All diets are wholesome. Some are wholesomer than others, but all the ordinary diets are wholesome enough for the people who use them. Whether the food be fine or coarse it will taste good and it will nourish if a watch be kept upon the appetite and a little starvation introduced every time it weakens. Nansen was used to fine fare, but when his meals were restricted to bear-meat months at a time he suffered no damage and no discomfort, because his appetite was kept at par through the difficulty of getting his bear-meat regularly."

"But doctors arrange carefully considered and delicate diets for invalids."

"They can't help it. The invalid is full of inherited superstitions and won't starve himself. He believes it would certainly kill him."

"It would weaken him, wouldn't it?"

"Nothing to hurt. Look at the invalids in our shipwreck. They lived fifteen days on pinches of raw ham, a suck at sailor-boots, and general starvation. It weakened them, but it didn't hurt them. It put them in fine shape to eat heartily of hearty food and build themselves up to a condition of robust health. But they do not perceive that; they lost their opportunity; they remained invalids; it served them right. Do you know the tricks that the health-resort doctors play?"

"What is it?"

"My system disguised—covert starvation. Grape-cure, bath-cure, mud-cure—it is all the same. The grape and the bath and the mud make a show and do a trifle of the work—the real work is done by the surreptitious starvation. The patient accustomed to four meals and late hours—at both ends of the day—now consider what he has to do at a health resort. He gets up at 6 in the morning. Eats one egg. Tramps up and down a promenade two hours with the other fools. Eats a butterfly. Slowly drinks a glass of filtered sewage that smells like a buzzard's breath. Promenades another two hours, but alone; if you speak to him he says anxiously, 'My water!—I am walking off my water!—please don't interrupt,' and goes stumping along again. Eats a candied rose-leaf. Lies at rest in the silence and solitude of his room for hours; mustn't read, mustn't smoke. The doctor comes and feels of his heart, now, and his pulse, and thumps his breast and his back and his stomach, and listens for results through a penny flageolet; then orders the man's bath—half a degree, Reamur, cooler than yesterday. After the bath another egg. A glass of sewage at 3 or 4 in the afternoon, and promenade solemnly with the other freaks. Dinner at 6—half a doughnut and a cup of tea. Walk again. Half-past 8, supper—more butterfly; at 9, to bed. Six weeks of this régime—think of it. It starves a man out and puts him in splendid condition. It would have the same effect in London, New York, Jericho—anywhere."

"How long does it take to put a person in condition here?"

"It ought to take but a day or two; but in fact it takes from one to six weeks, according to the character and mentality of the patient."

"How is that?"

"Do you see that crowd of women playing football, and boxing, and jumping fences yonder? They have been here six or seven weeks. They were spectral poor weaklings when they came. They were accustomed to nibbling at dainties and delicacies at set hours four times a day, and they had no appetite for anything. I questioned them, and then locked them into their rooms—the frailest ones to starve nine or ten hours, the others twelve or fifteen. Before long they began to beg; and indeed they suffered a good deal. They complained of nausea, headache, and so on. It was good to see them eat when the time was up. They could not remember when the devouring of a meal had afforded them such rapture—that was their word. Now, then, that ought to have ended their cure, but it didn't. They were free to go to any meals in the house, and they chose their accustomed four. Within a day or two I had to interfere. Their appetites were weakening. I made them knock out a meal. That set them up again. Then they resumed the four. I begged them to learn to knock out a meal themselves, without waiting for me. Up to a fortnight ago they couldn't; they really hadn't manhood enough; but they were gaining it, and now I think they are safe. They drop out a meal every now and then of their own accord. They are in fine condition now, and they might safely go home, I think, but their confidence is not quite perfect yet, so they are waiting awhile."

"Other cases are different?"

"Oh yes. Sometimes a man learns the whole trick in a week. Learns to regulate his appetite and keep it in perfect order. Learns to drop out a meal with frequency and not mind it."

"But why drop the entire meal out? Why not a part of it?"

"It's a poor device, and inadequate. If the stomach doesn't call vigorously—with a shout, as you may say—it is better not to pester it but just give it a real rest. Some people can eat more meals than others, and still thrive. There are all sorts of people, and all sorts of appetites. I will show you a man presently who was accustomed to nibble at eight meals a day. It was beyond the proper gait of his appetite by two. I have got him down to six a day, now, and he is all right, and enjoys life. How many meals do you affect per day?"

"Formerly—for twenty-two years—a meal and a half; during the past two years, two and a half: coffee and a roll at 9, luncheon at 1, dinner at 7.30 or 8."

"Formerly a meal and a half—that is, coffee and a roll at 9, dinner in the evening, nothing between—is that it?"

"Yes."

"Why did you add a meal?"

"It was the family's idea. They were uneasy. They thought I was killing myself."

"You found a meal and a half per day enough, all through the twenty-two years?"

"Plenty."

"Your present poor condition is due to the extra meal. Drop it out. You are trying to eat oftener than your stomach demands. You don't gain, you lose. You eat less food now, in a day, on two and a half meals, than you formerly ate on one and a half."

"True—a good deal less; for in those old days my dinner was a very sizable thing."

"Put yourself on a single meal a day, now—dinner—for a few days, till you secure a good, sound, regular, trustworthy appetite, then take to your one and a half permanently, and don't listen to the family any more. When you have any ordinary ailment, particularly of a feverish sort, eat nothing at all during twenty-four hours. That will cure it. It will cure the stubbornest cold in the head, too. No cold in the head can survive twenty-four hours' unmodified starvation."

"I know it. I have proved it many a time."

The Facts Concerning the Recent Carnival of Crime in Connecticut

I was feeling blithe, almost jocund. I put a match to my cigar, and just then the morning's mail was handed in. The first superscription I glanced at was in a handwriting that sent a thrill of pleasure through and through me. It was Aunt Mary's; and she was the person I loved and honored most in all the world, outside of my own household. She had been my boyhood's idol; maturity, which is fatal to so many enchantments, had not been able to dislodge her from her pedestal; no, it had only justified her right to be there, and placed her dethronement permanently among the impossibilities. To show how strong her influence over me was, I will observe that long after everybody else's "*do-stop-smoking*" had ceased to affect me in the slightest degree, Aunt Mary could still stir my torpid conscience into faint signs of life when she touched upon the matter. But all things have their limit in this world. A happy day came at last, when even Aunt Mary's words could no longer move me. I was not merely glad to see that day arrive; I was more than glad—I was grateful; for when its sun had set, the one alloy that was able to mar my enjoyment of my aunt's society was gone. The remainder of her stay with us that winter was in every way a delight. Of course she pleaded with me just as earnestly as ever, after that blessed day, to quit my pernicious habit, but to no purpose whatever; the moment she opened the subject I at once became calmly, peacefully, contentedly indifferent—absolutely, adamantinely indifferent. Consequently the closing weeks of that memorable visit melted away as pleasantly as a dream, they were so freighted for me with tranquil satisfaction. I could not have enjoyed my pet vice more if my gentle tormentor had been a smoker herself, and an advocate of the practice. Well, the sight of her handwriting reminded me that I was getting very hungry to see her again. I easily guessed what I should find in her letter. I opened it. Good! just as I expected; she was coming! Coming this very day, too, and by the morning train; I might expect her any moment.

I said to myself, "I am thoroughly happy and content now. If my most pitiless enemy could appear before me at this moment, I would freely right any wrong I may have done him."

Straightway the door opened, and a shriveled, shabby dwarf entered. He was not more than two feet high. He seemed to be about forty years old. Every feature and every inch of him was a trifle out of shape; and so, while one could not put his finger upon any particular part and say, "This is a conspicuous deformity," the spectator perceived that this little person was a deformity as a whole—a vague, general, evenly blended, nicely adjusted deformity. There was a fox-like cunning in the face and the sharp little eyes, and also alertness and malice. And yet, this vile bit of human rubbish seemed to bear a sort of remote and ill-defined resemblance to me! It was dully perceptible in the mean form, the countenance, and even the clothes, gestures, manner, and attitudes of the creature. He was a far-fetched, dim suggestion of a burlesque upon me, a caricature of me in little. One thing about him struck me forcibly and most unpleasantly: he was covered all over with a fuzzy, greenish mold, such as one sometimes sees upon mildewed bread. The sight of it was nauseating.

He stepped along with a chipper air, and flung himself into a doll's chair in a very free-and-easy way, without waiting to be asked. He tossed his hat into the waste-basket. He picked up my old chalk pipe from the floor, gave the stem a wipe or two on his knee, filled the bowl from the tobacco-box at his side, and said to me in a tone of pert command:

"Gimme a match!"

I blushed to the roots of my hair; partly with indignation, but mainly because it somehow seemed to me that this whole performance was very like an exaggeration of conduct which I myself had sometimes been guilty of in my intercourse with familiar friends—but never, never with strangers, I observed to myself. I wanted to kick the pygmy into the fire, but some incomprehensible sense of being legally and legitimately under his authority forced me to obey his order. He applied the match to the pipe, took a contemplative whiff or two, and remarked, in an irritatingly familiar way:

"Seems to me it's devilish odd weather for this time of year."

I flushed again, and in anger and humiliation as before; for the language was hardly an exaggeration of some that I have uttered in my day, and moreover was delivered in a tone of voice and with an exasperating drawl that had the seeming of a deliberate travesty of my style. Now there is nothing I am quite so sensitive about as a mocking imitation of my drawling infirmity of speech. I spoke up sharply and said:

"Look here, you miserable ash-cat! you will have to give a little more attention to your manners, or I will throw you out of the window!"

The manikin smiled a smile of malicious content and security, puffed a whiff of smoke contemptuously toward me, and said, with a still more elaborate drawl:

"Come—go gently now; don't put on *too* many airs with your betters."

This cool snub rasped me all over, but it seemed to subjugate me, too, for a moment. The pygmy contemplated me awhile with his weasel eyes, and then said, in a peculiarly sneering way:

"You turned a tramp away from your door this morning."

I said crustily:

"Perhaps I did, perhaps I didn't. How do *you* know?"

"Well, I know. It isn't any matter *how* I know."

"Very well. Suppose I *did* turn a tramp away from the door—what of it?"

"Oh, nothing; nothing in particular. Only you lied to him."

"I *didn't!* That is, I—"

"Yes, but you did; you lied to him."

I felt a guilty pang—in truth, I had felt it forty times before that tramp had traveled a block from my door—but still I resolved to make a show of feeling slandered; so I said:

"This is a baseless impertinence. I said to the tramp—"

"There—wait. You were about to lie again. *I* know what you said to him. You said the cook was gone down-town and there was nothing left from breakfast. Two lies. You knew the cook was behind the door, and plenty of provisions behind *her.*"

This astonishing accuracy silenced me; and it filled me with wondering speculations, too, as to how this cub could have got his information. Of course he could have culled the conversation from the tramp, but by what sort of magic had he contrived to find out about the concealed cook? Now the dwarf spoke again:

"It was rather pitiful, rather small, in you to refuse to read that poor young woman's manuscript the other day, and give her an opinion as to its literary value; and she had come so far, too, and *so* hopefully. Now *wasn't* it?"

I felt like a cur! And I had felt so every time the thing had recurred to my mind, I may as well confess. I flushed hotly and said:

"Look here, have you nothing better to do than prowl around prying into other people's business? Did that girl tell you that?"

"Never mind whether she did or not. The main thing is, you did that contemptible thing. And you felt ashamed of it afterward. Aha! you feel ashamed of it *now!*"

This was a sort of devilish glee. With fiery earnestness I responded:

"I told that girl, in the kindest, gentlest way, that I could not consent to deliver judgment upon *any* one's manuscript, because an individual's verdict was worthless. It might underrate a work of high merit and lose it to the world, or it might overrate a trashy production and so open the way for its infliction upon the world. I said that the great public was the only tribunal competent to sit in judgment upon a literary effort, and therefore it must be best to lay it before that tribunal in the outset, since in the end it must stand or fall by that mighty court's decision anyway."

"Yes, you said all that. So you did, you juggling, small-souled shuffler! And yet when the happy hopefulness faded out of that poor girl's face, when you saw her furtively slip beneath her shawl the scroll she had so patiently and honestly scribbled at—so ashamed of her darling now, so proud of it before—when you saw the gladness go out of her eyes and the tears come there, when she crept away so humbly who had come so—"

"Oh, peace! peace! peace! Blister your merciless tongue, haven't all these thoughts tortured me enough without *your* coming here to fetch them back again!"

Remorse! remorse! It seemed to me that it would eat the very heart out of me! And yet that small fiend only sat there leering at me with joy and contempt, and placidly chuckling. Presently he began to speak again. Every sentence was an accusation, and every accusation a truth. Every clause was freighted with sarcasm and derision, every slow-dropping word burned like vitriol. The dwarf reminded me of times when I had flown at my children in anger and punished them for faults which a little inquiry would have taught me that others, and not they, had committed. He reminded me of how I had disloyally allowed old friends to be traduced in my hearing, and been too craven to utter a word in their defense. He reminded me of many dishonest things which I had done; of many which I had procured to be done by children and other irresponsible persons; of some which I had planned, thought upon, and longed to do, and been kept from the performance by fear of consequences only. With exquisite cruelty he recalled to my mind, item by item, wrongs and unkindnesses I had inflicted and humiliations I had put upon friends since dead, "who died thinking of those injuries, maybe, and grieving over them," he added, by way of poison to the stab.

"For instance," said he, "take the case of your younger brother, when you two were boys together, many a long year ago. He always lovingly trusted in you with a fidelity that your manifold treacheries were not able to shake. He followed you about like a dog, content to suffer wrong and abuse if he might only be with you; patient under these injuries so long as it was your hand that inflicted them. The latest picture you have of him in health and strength must be such a comfort to you You pledged your honor that if he would let you blindfold him no harm should come to him; and then, giggling and choking over the rare fun of the joke, you led him to a brook thinly glazed with ice, and pushed him in; and how you did laugh! Man, you will never forget the gentle, reproachful look he gave you as he struggled shivering out, if you live a thousand years! Oho! you see it now, you see it *now!*"

"Beast, I have seen it a million times, and shall see it a million more! and may you rot away piecemeal, and suffer till doomsday what I suffer now, for bringing it back to me again!"

The dwarf chuckled contentedly, and went on with his accusing history of my career. I dropped into a moody, vengeful state, and suffered in silence under the merciless lash. At last this remark of his gave me a sudden rouse:

"Two months ago, on a Tuesday, you woke up, away in the night, and fell to thinking, with shame, about a peculiarly mean and pitiful act of yours toward a poor ignorant Indian in the wilds of the Rocky Mountains in the winter of eighteen hundred and—"

"Stop a moment, devil! Stop! Do you mean to tell me that even my very *thoughts* are not hidden from you?"

"It seems to look like that. Didn't you think the thoughts I have just mentioned?"

"If I didn't, I wish I may never breathe again! Look here, friend—look me in the eye. Who *are* you?"

"Well, who do you think?"

"I think you are Satan himself. I think you are the devil."

"No."

"No? Then who *can* you be?"

"Would you really like to know?"

"*Indeed* I would."

"Well, I am your *Conscience!*"

In an instant I was in a blaze of joy and exultation. I sprang at the creature, roaring:

"Curse you. I have wished a hundred million times that you were tangible, and that I could get my hands on your throat once! Oh, but I will wreak a deadly vengeance on—"

Folly! Lightning does not move more quickly than my

Conscience did! He darted aloft so suddenly that in the moment my fingers clutched the empty air he was already perched on the top of the high bookcase, with his thumb at his nose in token of derision. I flung the poker at him, and missed. I fired the bootjack. In a blind rage I flew from place to place, and snatched and hurled any missile that came handy; the storm of books, inkstands, and chunks of coal gloomed the air and beat about the manikin's perch relentlessly, but all to no purpose; the nimble figure dodged every shot; and not only that, but burst into a cackle of sarcastic and triumphant laughter as I sat down exhausted. While I puffed and gasped with fatigue and excitement, my Conscience talked to this effect:

"My good slave, you are curiously witless—no, I mean characteristically so. In truth, you are always consistent, always yourself, always an ass. Otherwise it must have occurred to you that if you attempted this murder with a sad heart and a heavy conscience, I would droop under the burdening influence instantly. Fool, I should have weighed a ton, and could not have budged from the floor; but instead, you are so cheerfully anxious to kill me that your conscience is as light as a feather; hence I am away up here out of your reach. I can almost respect a mere ordinary sort of fool; but *you*—pah!"

I would have given anything, then, to be heavy-hearted, so that I could get this person down from there and take his life, but I could no more be heavy-hearted over such a desire than I could have sorrowed over its accomplishment. So I could only look longingly up at my master, and rave at the ill luck that denied me a heavy conscience the one only time that I had ever wanted such a thing in my life. By and by I got to musing over the hour's strange adventure, and of course my human curiosity began to work. I set myself to framing in my mind some questions for this fiend to answer. Just then one of my boys entered, leaving the door open behind him, and exclaimed:

"My! what *has* been going on here? The bookcase is all one riddle of—"

I sprang up in consternation, and shouted:

"Out of this! Hurry! Jump! Fly! Shut the door! Quick, or my Conscience will get away!"

The door slammed to, and I locked it. I glanced up and was grateful, to the bottom of my heart, to see that my owner was still my prisoner. I said:

"Hang you, I might have lost you! Children are the heedlessest creatures. But look here, friend, the boy did not seem to notice you at all; how is that?"

"For a very good reason. I am invisible to all but you."

I made a mental note of that piece of information with a good deal of satisfaction. I could kill this miscreant now, if I got a chance, and no one would know it. But this very reflection made me so light-hearted that my Conscience could hardly keep his seat, but was like to float aloft toward the ceiling like a toy balloon. I said, presently:

"Come, my Conscience, let us be friendly. Let us fly a flag of truce for a while. I am suffering to ask you some questions."

"Very well. Begin."

"Well, then, in the first place, why were you never visible to me before?"

"Because you never asked to see me before; that is, you never asked in the right spirit and the proper form before. You were just in the right spirit this time, and when you called for your most pitiless enemy I was that person by a very large majority, though you did not suspect it."

"Well, did that remark of mine turn you into flesh and blood?"

"No. It only made me visible to you. I am unsubstantial, just as other spirits are."

This remark prodded me with a sharp misgiving. If he was unsubstantial, how was I going to kill him? But I dissembled, and said persuasively:

"Conscience, it isn't sociable of you to keep at such a distance. Come down and take another smoke."

This was answered with a look that was full of derision, and with this observation added:

"Come where you can get at me and kill me? The invitation is declined with thanks."

"All right," said I to myself; "so it seems a spirit *can* be killed, after all; there will be one spirit lacking in this world, presently, or I lose my guess." Then I said aloud:

"Friend—"

"There; wait a bit. I am not your friend, I am your enemy; I am not your equal, I am your master. Call me 'my lord,' if you please. You are too familiar."

"I don't like such titles. I am willing to call you *sir*. That is as far as—"

"We will have no argument about this. Just obey, that is all. Go on with your chatter."

"Very well, my lord—since nothing but my lord will suit you—I was going to ask you how long you will be visible to me?"

"Always!"

I broke out with strong indignation: "This is simply an outrage. That is what I think of it. You have dogged, and dogged, and *dogged* me, all the days of my life, invisible. That was misery enough; now to have such a looking thing as you tagging after me like another shadow all the rest of my days is an intolerable prospect. You have my opinion, my lord; make the most of it."

"My lad, there was never so pleased a conscience in this world as I was when you made me visible. It gives me an inconceivable advantage. *Now* I can look you straight in the eye, and call you names, and leer at you, jeer at you, sneer at you; and *you* know what eloquence there is in visible gesture and expression, more especially when the effect is heightened by audible speech. I shall always address you henceforth in your o-w-n s-n-i-v-e-l-i-n-g d-r-a-w-l—baby!"

I let fly with the coal-hod. No result. My lord said:

"Come, come! Remember the flag of truce!"

"Ah, I forgot that. I will try to be civil; and *you* try it, too, for a novelty. The idea of a *civil* conscience! It is a good joke; an excellent joke. All the consciences *I* have ever heard of were nagging, badgering, fault-finding, execrable savages! Yes; and always in a sweat about some poor little insignificant trifle or other—destruction catch the lot of them, *I* say! I would trade mine for the smallpox and seven kinds of consumption, and be glad of the chance. Now tell me, why *is* it that a conscience can't haul a man over the coals once, for an offense, and then let him alone? Why is it that it wants to keep on pegging at him, day and night and night and day, week in and week out, forever and ever, about the same old thing? There is no sense in that, and no reason in it. I think a conscience that will act like that is meaner than the very dirt itself."

"Well, *we* like it; that suffices."

"Do you do it with the honest intent to improve a man?"

That question produced a sarcastic smile, and this reply:

"No, sir. Excuse me. We do it simply because it is 'business.' It is our trade. The *purpose* of it is to improve the man, but *we* are merely disinterested agents. We are appointed by authority, and haven't anything to say in the matter. We obey orders and leave the consequences where they belong. But I am willing to admit this much: we *do* crowd the orders a trifle when we get a chance, which is most of the time. We enjoy it. We are instructed to remind a man a few times of an error; and I don't mind acknowledging that we try to give pretty good measure. And when we get hold of a man of a peculiarly sensitive nature, oh, but we do haze him! I have consciences to come all the way from China and Russia to see a person of that kind put through his paces, on a special occasion. Why, I knew a man of that sort who had accidentally crippled a mulatto baby; the news went abroad, and I wish you may never commit another sin if the consciences didn't flock from all over the earth to enjoy the fun and help his master exorcise him. That man walked the floor in torture for forty-eight hours, without eating or sleeping, and then blew his brains out. The child was perfectly well again in three weeks."

"Well, you are a precious crew, not to put it too strong. I think I begin to see now why you have always been a trifle inconsistent with me. In your anxiety to get all the juice you can out of a sin, you make a man repent of it in three or four different ways. For instance, you found fault with me for lying to that tramp, and I suffered over that. But it was only yesterday that I told a tramp the square truth, to wit, that, it being regarded as bad citizenship to encourage vagrancy, I would give him nothing. What did you do *then?* Why, you made me say to myself, 'Ah, it would have been so much kinder and more blameless to ease him off with a little white lie, and send him away feeling that if he could not have bread, the gentle treatment was at least something to be grateful for!' Well, I suffered all day about *that*. Three days before I had fed a tramp, and fed him freely, supposing it a virtuous act. Straight off you said, 'Oh, false citizen, to have fed a tramp!' and I suffered as usual. I gave a tramp work; you objected to it—*after* the contract was made, of course; you never speak up beforehand. Next, I *refused* a tramp work; you objected to *that*. Next, I proposed to kill a tramp; you kept me awake all night, oozing remorse at every pore. Sure I was going to be right *this* time, I sent the next tramp away with my benediction; and I wish you may live as long as I do, if you didn't make me smart all night again because I didn't kill him. Is there *any* way of satisfying that malignant invention which is called a conscience?"

"Ha, ha! this is luxury! Go on!"

"But come, now, answer me that question. *Is* there any way?"

"Well, none that I propose to tell *you*, my son. Ass! I don't care *what* act you may turn your hand to, I can straightway whisper a word in your ear and make you think you have committed a dreadful meanness. It is my *business*—and my joy—to make you repent of *every*thing you do. If I have fooled away any opportunities it was not intentional; I beg to assure you it was not intentional!"

"Don't worry; you haven't missed a trick that *I* know of. I never did a thing in all my life, virtuous or otherwise, that I didn't repent of in twenty-four hours. In church last Sunday I listened to a charity sermon. My first impulse was to give three hundred and fifty dollars; I repented of that and reduced it a hundred; repented of that and reduced it another hundred; repented of that and reduced it another hundred; repented of that and reduced the remaining fifty to twenty-five; repented of that and came down to fifteen; repented of that and dropped to two dollars and a half; when the plate came around at last, I repented once more and contributed ten cents. Well, when I got home, I did wish to goodness I had that ten cents back again! You never *did* let me get through a charity sermon without having something to sweat about."

"Oh, and I never shall, I never shall. You can always depend on me."

"I think so. Many and many's the restless night I've wanted to take you by the neck. If I could only get hold of you now!"

"Yes, no doubt. But I am not an ass; I am only the saddle of an ass. But go on, go on. You entertain me more than I like to confess."

"I am glad of that. (You will not mind my lying a little, to keep in practice.) Look here; not to be too personal, I think you are about the shabbiest and most contemptible little shriveled-up reptile that can be imagined. I am grateful enough that you are invisible to other people, for I should die with shame to be seen with such a mildewed monkey of a conscience as *you* are. Now if you were five or six feet high, and—"

"Oh, come! who is to blame?"

"*I* don't know."

"Why, you are; nobody else."

"Confound you, I wasn't consulted about your personal appearance."

"I don't care, you had a good deal to do with it, nevertheless. When you were eight or nine years old, I was seven feet high, and as pretty as a picture."

"I wish you had died young! So you have grown the wrong way, have you?"

"Some of us grow one way and some the other. You had a large conscience once; if you've a small conscience now I reckon there are reasons for it. However, both of us are to blame, you and I. You see, you used to be conscientious about a great many things; morbidly so, I may say. It was a great many years ago. You probably do not remember it now. Well, I took a great interest in my work, and I so enjoyed the anguish which certain pet sins of yours afflicted you with that I kept pelting at you until I rather overdid the matter. You began to rebel. Of course I began to lose ground, then, and shrivel a little—diminish in stature, get moldy, and grow deformed. The more I weakened, the more stubbornly you fastened on to those particular sins; till at last the places on my person that represent those vices became as callous as shark-skin. Take smoking, for instance. I played that card a little too long, and I lost. When people plead with you at this late day to quit that vice, that old callous place seems to enlarge and cover me all over like a shirt of mail. It exerts a mysterious, smothering effect; and presently I, your faithful hater, your devoted Conscience, go sound asleep! Sound? It is no name for it. I couldn't hear it thunder at such a time. You have some few other vices—perhaps eighty, or maybe ninety—that affect me in much the same way."

"This is flattering; you must be asleep a good part of your time."

"Yes, of late years. I should be asleep *all* the time but for the help I get."

"Who helps you?"

"Other consciences. Whenever a person whose conscience I am acquainted with tries to plead with you about the vices you are callous to, I get my friend to give his client a pang concerning some villainy of his own, and that shuts off his meddling and starts him off to hunt personal consolation. My field of usefulness is about trimmed down to tramps, budding authoresses, and that line of goods now; but don't you worry—I'll harry you on *them* while they last! Just you put your trust in me."

"I think I can. But if you had only been good enough to mention these facts some thirty years ago, I should have turned my particular attention to sin, and I think that by this time I should not only have had you pretty permanently asleep on the entire list of human vices, but reduced to the size of a homeopathic pill, at that. That is about the style of conscience *I* am pining for. If I only had you shrunk down to a homeopathic pill, and could get my hands on you, would I put you in a glass case for a keepsake? No, sir. I would give you to a yellow dog! That is where *you* ought to be—you and all your tribe. You are not fit to be in society, in my opinion. Now another question. Do you know a good many consciences in this section?"

"Plenty of them."

"I would give anything to see some of them! Could you bring them here? And would they be visible to me?"

"Certainly not."

"I suppose I ought to have known that without asking. But no matter, you can describe them. Tell me about my neighbor Thompson's conscience, please."

"Very well. I know him intimately; have known him many years. I knew him when he was eleven feet high and of a faultless figure. But he is very rusty and tough and misshapen now, and hardly ever interests himself about anything. As to his present size—well, he sleeps in a cigar-box."

"Likely enough. There are few smaller, meaner men in this region than Hugh Thompson. Do you know Robinson's conscience?"

"Yes. He is a shade under four and a half feet high; used to be a blond; is a brunette now, but still shapely and comely."

"Well, Robinson is a good fellow. Do you know Tom Smith's conscience?"

"I have known him from childhood. He was thirteen inches high, and rather sluggish, when he was two years old—as nearly all of us are at that age. He is thirty-seven feet high now, and the stateliest figure in America. His legs are still racked with growing-pains, but he has a good time, nevertheless. Never sleeps. He is the most active and energetic member of the New England Conscience Club; is president of it. Night and day you can find him pegging away at Smith, panting with his labor, sleeves rolled up, countenance all alive with enjoyment. He has got his victim splendidly dragooned now. He can make poor Smith imagine that the most innocent little thing he does is an odious sin; and then he sets to work and almost tortures the soul out of him about it."

"Smith is the noblest man in all this section, and the purest; and yet is always breaking his heart because he cannot be good! Only a conscience *could* find pleasure in heaping agony upon a spirit like that. Do you know my aunt Mary's conscience?"

"I have seen her at a distance, but am not acquainted with her. She lives in the open air altogether, because no door is large enough to admit her."

"I can believe that. Let me see. Do you know the conscience of that publisher who once stole some sketches of mine for a 'series' of his, and then left me to pay the law expenses I had to incur in order to choke him off?"

"Yes. He has a wide fame. He was exhibited, a month ago, with some other antiquities, for the benefit of a recent Member of the Cabinet's conscience that was starving in exile. Tickets and fares were high, but I traveled for nothing by pretending to be the conscience of an editor, and got in for half-price by representing myself to be the conscience of a clergyman. However, the publisher's conscience, which was to have been the main feature of the entertainment, was a failure—as an exhibition. He was there, but what of that? The management had provided a microscope with a magnifying power of only thirty thousand diameters, and so nobody got to see him, after all. There was great and general dissatisfaction, of course, but—"

Just here there was an eager footstep on the stair; I opened the door, and my aunt Mary burst into the room. It was a joyful meeting and a cheery bombardment of questions and answers concerning family matters ensued. By and by my aunt said:

"But I am going to abuse you a little now. You promised me, the day I saw you last, that you would look after the needs of the poor family around the corner as faithfully as I had done it myself. Well, I found out by accident that you failed of your promise. *Was* that right?"

In simple truth, I never had thought of that family a second time! And now such a splintering pang of guilt shot through me! I glanced up at my Conscience. Plainly, my heavy heart was affecting him. His body was drooping forward; he seemed about to fall from the bookcase. My aunt continued:

"And think how you have neglected my poor *protégé* at the almshouse, you dear, hard-hearted promise-breaker!" I blushed scarlet, and my tongue was tied. As the sense of my guilty negligence waxed sharper and stronger, my Conscience began to sway heavily back and forth; and when my aunt, after a little pause, said in a grieved tone, "Since you never once went to see her, maybe it will not distress you now to know that that poor child died, months ago, utterly friendless and forsaken!" My Conscience could no longer bear up under the weight of my sufferings, but tumbled headlong from his high perch and struck the floor with a dull, leaden thump. He lay there writhing with pain and quaking with apprehension, but straining every muscle in frantic efforts to get up. In a fever of expectancy I sprang to the door, locked it, placed my back against it, and bent a watchful gaze upon my struggling master. Already my fingers were itching to begin their murderous work.

"Oh, what *can* be the matter!" exclaimed my aunt, shrinking from me, and following with her frightened eyes the direction of mine. My breath was coming in short, quick gasps now, and my excitement was almost uncontrollable. My aunt cried out:

"Oh, do not look so! You appal me! Oh, what can the matter be? What is it you see? Why do you stare so? Why do you work your fingers like that?"

"Peace, woman!" I said, in a hoarse whisper. "Look elsewhere; pay no attention to me; it is nothing—nothing. I am often this way. It will pass in a moment. It comes from smoking too much."

My injured lord was up, wild-eyed with terror, and trying to hobble toward the door. I could hardly breathe, I was so wrought up. My aunt wrung her hands, and said:

"Oh, I knew how it would be; I knew it would come to this at last! Oh, I implore you to crush out that fatal habit while it may yet be time! You must not, you shall not be deaf to my supplications longer!" My struggling Conscience showed sudden signs of weariness! "Oh, promise me you will throw off this hateful slavery of tobacco!" My Conscience began to reel drowsily, and grope with his hands—enchanting spectacle! "I beg you, I beseech you, I implore you! Your reason is deserting you! There is madness in your eye! It flames with frenzy! Oh, hear me, hear me, and be saved! See, I plead with you on my very knees!" As she sank before me my Conscience reeled again, and then drooped languidly to the floor, blinking toward me a last supplication for mercy, with heavy eyes. "Oh, promise, or you are lost! Promise, and be redeemed! Promise! Promise and live!" With a long-drawn sigh my conquered Conscience closed his eyes and fell fast asleep!

With an exultant shout I sprang past my aunt, and in an instant I had my lifelong foe by the throat. After so many years of waiting and longing, he was mine at last. I tore him to shreds and fragments. I rent the fragments to bits. I cast the bleeding rubbish into the fire, and drew into my nostrils the grateful incense of my burnt-offering. At last, and forever, my Conscience was dead!

I was a free man! I turned upon my poor aunt, who was almost petrified with terror, and shouted:

"Out of this with your paupers, your charities, your reforms, your pestilent morals! You behold before you a man whose life-conflict is done, whose soul is at peace; a man whose heart is dead to sorrow, dead to suffering, dead to remorse; a man WITHOUT A CONSCIENCE! In my joy I spare you, though I could throttle you and never feel a pang! Fly!"

She fled. Since that day my life is all bliss. Bliss, unalloyed bliss. Nothing in all the world could persuade me to have a conscience again. I settled all my old outstanding scores, and began the world anew. I killed thirty-eight persons during the first two weeks—all of them on account of ancient grudges. I burned a dwelling that interrupted my view. I swindled a widow and some orphans out of their last cow, which is a very good one, though not thoroughbred, I believe. I have also committed scores of crimes, of various kinds, and have enjoyed my work exceedingly, whereas it would formerly have broken my heart and turned my hair gray, I have no doubt.

In conclusion, I wish to state, by way of advertisement, that medical colleges desiring assorted tramps for scientific purposes, either by the gross, by cord measurement, or per ton, will do well to examine the lot in my cellar before purchasing elsewhere, as these were all selected and prepared by myself, and can be had at a low rate, because I wish to clear out my stock and get ready for the spring trade.

Back from "Yurrup"

BOSTON, November, 1869.

Have you ever seen a family of fools just back from Europe—or Yurrup, as they pronounce it? They never talk *to* you, of course, being strangers, but they talk to each other and *at* you till you are pretty nearly distracted with their clatter; till you are sick of their ocean experiences; their mispronounced foreign names; their dukes and emperors; their trivial adventures; their pointless reminiscences; till you are sick of their imbecile faces and their relentless clack, and wish it had pleased Providence to leave the clapper out of their empty skulls.

I traveled with such a family one eternal day, from New York to Boston, last week. They had spent just a year in "Yurrup," and were returning home to Boston. Papa said little, and looked bored—he had simply been down to New York to receive and cart home his cargo of travelled imbecility. Sister Angeline, aged 23, sister Augusta, aged 25, and brother Charles, aged 33, did the conversational drivel, and mamma purred and admired, and threw in some help when occasion offered, in the way of remembering some French barber's—I should say some French Count's—name, when they pretended to have forgotten it. They occupied the choice seats in the parlor of the drawing-room car, and for twelve hours I sat opposite to them—was their *vis-a-vis*, they would have said, in their charming French way.

Augusta—"Plague that nahsty (nasty) steamer! I've the headache yet, she rolled so the fifth day out."

Angeline—"And well you may. *I* never saw such a nahsty old tub. I never want to go in the *Ville de Paris* again. Why *didn't* we go over to London and come in the *Scotia?*"

Aug—"Because we were fools!"

[I fervently endorsed that sentiment.]

Ange—"Gustie, what made Count Caskowhisky drive off looking so blue, that last Thursday in Pairy? (Paris, she meant.) Ah, own up, now!"

Aug—"Now, Angie, how you talk! I *told* the nahsty creature I would not receive his attentions any longer. And the old duke his father kept boring me about him and his two million francs a year till I sent *him* off with a flea in his ear."

Chorus.—"Ke-he-he! Ha-ha-ha!"

Charles—[Pulling a small silken cloak to pieces.] "Angie, where'd you get this cheap thing?"

Ange—"You Cholly, let that alone! Cheap! Well, how could I help it? There we were, tied up in Switzerland—just down from Mon Bong (Mont Blanc, doubtless)—couldn't buy anything in those nahsty shops so far away from Pairy. I had to put up with that slimpsy forty-dollar rag—but bless you, I couldn't go naked!"

Chorus—"Ke-he-he!"

Aug—"Guess who I was thinking of? Those ignorant persons we saw first in Rome and afterwards in Venice—those—"

Ange—"Oh, ha-ha-ha! He-e-he! It *was* so funny! Papa, one of them called the Santa della Spiggiola the Santa della Spizziola! Ha-ho-ha! And she thought it was Canova that did Michael Angelo's Moses! Only *think* of it!—Canova a sculptor and the Moses a picture! I thought I should die! I guess I let them see by the way I laughed, that they'd made fools of themselves, because they blushed and sneaked off."

[Papa laughed faintly, but not with the easy grace of a man who was certain he knew what he was laughing about.]

Aug.—"Why Cholly! Where did you get those nahsty Beaumarchais gloves? Well, I *wouldn't*, if I were you!"

Mamma—[With uplifted hands.] "Beaumarchais, my son!"

Ange—"Beaumarchais! Why how can you! Nobody in Pairy wears those nahsty things but the commonest people."

Charles—"They *are* a rum lot, but then Tom Blennerhasset gave 'em to me—he wanted to do something or other to curry favor, I s'pose."

Ange—"Tom Blennerhasset!"

Aug.—"Tom Blennerhasset!"

Mamma—"Tom Blennerhasset! And have you been associating with *him*."

Papa—[suddenly interested.] "Heavens, what has the son of an honored and honorable old friend been doing?"

Chorus—"Doing! Why, his father has endorsed himself bankrupt for friends—that's what the matter!"

Ange—"Oh, mon Dieu, j'ai faim! Avez-vous quelque chose de bon, en votre poche, mon cher frere? Excuse me for speaking French, for, to tell the truth, I haven't spoken English for so long that it comes dreadful awkward. Wish we were back in Yurrup—c'est votre desire aussi, n'est-ce pas, mes cheres?"

And from that moment they lapsed into barbarous French and kept it up for an hour—hesitating, gasping for words, stumbling head over heels through adverbs and participles, floundering among adjectives, working miracles of villainous pronunciation—and neither one of them ever by any chance understanding what another was driving at.

By that time some newcomers had entered the car, and so they lapsed into English again and fell to holding everything American up to scorn and contumely in order that they might thus let those newcomers know they were just home from "Yurrup." They kept up this little game all the way to Boston—and if ever I can learn when their funeral is to take place, I shall lay aside every other pleasure and attend it. To use their pet and best beloved phrase, they were a "nahsty" family of American snobs, and there ought to be a law against allowing such to go to Europe and misrepresent the nation. It will take these insects five years, now, to get done turning up their noses at everything American and making damaging comparisons between their own country and "Yurrup." Let us pity their waiting friends in Boston in their affliction.

The Stolen White Elephant

The following curious history was related to me by a chance railway acquaintance. He was a gentleman more than seventy years of age, and his thoroughly good and gentle face and earnest and sincere manner imprinted the unmistakable stamp of truth upon every statement which fell from his lips. He said:

You know in what reverence the royal white elephant of Siam is held by the people of that country. You know it is sacred to kings, only kings may possess it, and that it is, indeed, in a measure even superior to kings, since it receives not merely honor but worship. Very well; five years ago, when the troubles concerning the frontier line arose between Great Britain and Siam, it was presently manifest that Siam had been in the wrong. Therefore every reparation was quickly made, and the British representative stated that he was satisfied and the past should be forgotten. This greatly relieved the King of Siam, and partly as a token of gratitude, but partly also, perhaps, to wipe out any little remaining vestige of unpleasantness which England might feel toward him, he wished to send the Queen a present—the sole sure way of propitiating an enemy, according to Oriental ideas. This present ought not only to be a royal one, but transcendently royal. Wherefore, what offering could be so meet as that of a white elephant? My position in the Indian civil service was such that I was deemed peculiarly worthy of the honor of conveying the present to her Majesty. A ship was fitted out for me and my servants and the officers and attendants of the elephant, and in due time I arrived in New York harbor and placed my royal charge in admirable quarters in Jersey City. It was necessary to remain awhile in order to recruit the animal's health before resuming the voyage.

All went well during a fortnight—then my calamities began. The white elephant was stolen! I was called up at dead of night and informed of this fearful misfortune. For some moments I was beside myself with terror and anxiety; I was helpless. Then I grew calmer and collected my faculties. I soon saw my course—for, indeed, there was but the one course for an intelligent man to pursue. Late as it was, I flew to New York and got a policeman to conduct me to the headquarters of the detective force. Fortunately I arrived in time, though the chief of the force, the celebrated Inspector Blunt, was just on the point of leaving for his home. He was a man of middle size and compact frame, and when he was thinking deeply he had a way of knitting his brows and tapping his forehead reflectively with his finger, which impressed you at once with the conviction that you stood in the presence of a person of no common order. The very sight of him gave me confidence and made me hopeful. I stated my errand. It did not flurry him in the least; it had no more visible effect upon his iron self-possession than if I had told him somebody had stolen my dog. He motioned me to a seat, and said, calmly:

"Allow me to think a moment, please."

So saying, he sat down at his office table and leaned his head upon his hand. Several clerks were at work at the other end of the room; the scratching of their pens was all the sound I heard during the next six or seven minutes. Meantime the inspector sat there, buried in thought. Finally he raised his head, and there was that in the firm lines of his face which showed me that his brain had done its work and his plan was made. Said he—and his voice was low and impressive:

"This is no ordinary case. Every step must be warily taken; each step must be made sure before the next is ventured. And secrecy must be observed—secrecy profound and absolute. Speak to no one about the matter, not even the reporters. I will take care of *them;* I will see that they get only what it may suit my ends to let them know." He touched a bell; a youth appeared. "Alaric, tell the reporters to remain for the present." The boy retired. "Now let us proceed to business—and systematically. Nothing can be accomplished in this trade of mine without strict and minute method."

He took a pen and some paper. "Now—name of the elephant?"

"Hassan Ben Ali Ben Selim Abdallah Mohammed Moisé Al hammal Jamsetjejeebhoy Dhuleep Sultan Ebu Bhudpoor."

"Very well. Given name?"

"Jumbo."

"Very well. Place of birth?"

"The capital city of Siam."

"Parents living?"

"No—dead."

"Had they any other issue besides this one?"

"None. He was an only child."

"Very well. These matters are sufficient under that head. Now please describe the elephant, and leave out no particular, however insignificant—that is insignificant from *your* point of view. To men in my profession there *are* no insignificant particulars; they do not exist."

I described—he wrote. When I was done, he said:

"Now listen. If I have made any mistakes, correct me."

He read as follows:

"Height, 19 feet; length from apex of forehead to insertion of tail, 26 feet; length of trunk, 16 feet; length of tail, 6 feet; total length, including trunk and tail, 48 feet; length of tusks, 9½ feet; ears in keeping with these dimensions; footprint resembles the mark left when one upends a barrel in the snow; color of the elephant, a dull white; has a hole the size of a plate in each ear for the insertion of jewelry, and possesses the habit in a remarkable degree of squirting water upon spectators and of maltreating with his trunk not only such persons as he is acquainted with, but even entire strangers; limps slightly with his right hind leg, and has a small scar in his left armpit caused by a former boil; had on, when stolen, a castle containing seats for fifteen persons, and a gold-cloth saddle-blanket the size of an ordinary carpet."

There were no mistakes. The inspector touched the bell, handed the description to Alaric, and said:

"Have fifty thousand copies of this printed at once and mailed to every detective office and pawnbroker's shop on the continent," Alaric retired. "There—so far, so good. Next, I must have a photograph of the property."

I gave him one. He examined it critically, and said:

"It must do, since we can do no better; but he has his trunk curled up and tucked into his mouth. That is unfortunate, and is calculated to mislead, for of course he does not usually have it in that position." He touched his bell.

"Alaric, have fifty thousand copies of this photograph made the first thing in the morning, and mail them with the descriptive circulars."

Alaric retired to execute his orders. The inspector said:

"It will be necessary to offer a reward, of course. Now as to the amount?"

"What sum would you suggest?"

"To *begin* with, I should say—well, twenty-five thousand dollars. It is an intricate and difficult business; there are a thousand avenues of escape and opportunities of concealment. These thieves have friends and pals everywhere—"

"Bless me, do you know who they are?"

The wary face, practised in concealing the thoughts and feelings within, gave me no token, nor yet the replying words, so quietly uttered:

"Never mind about that. I may, and I may not. We generally gather a pretty shrewd inkling of who our man is by the manner of his work and the size of the game he goes after. We are not dealing with a pickpocket or a hall thief now, make up your mind to that. This property was not 'lifted' by a novice. But, as I was saying, considering the amount of travel which will have to be done, and the diligence with which the thieves will cover up their traces as they move along, twenty-five thousand may be too small a sum to offer, yet I think it worth while to start with that."

So we determined upon that figure as a beginning. Then this man, whom nothing escaped which could be any possibility be made to serve as a clue, said:

"There are cases in detective history to show that criminals have been detected through peculiarities in their appetites. Now, what does this elephant eat, and how much?"

"Well, as to *what* he eats—he will eat *anything*. He will eat a man, he will eat a Bible—he will eat anything *between* a man and a Bible."

"Good—very good, indeed, but too general. Details are necessary—details are the only valuable things in our trade. Very well—as to men. At one meal—or, if you prefer, during one day—how many men will he eat, if fresh?"

"He would not care whether they were fresh or not; at a single meal he would eat five ordinary men."

"Very good; five men; we will put that down. What nationalities would he prefer?"

"He is indifferent about nationalities. He prefers acquaintances, but is not prejudiced against strangers."

"Very good. Now, as to Bibles. How many Bibles would he eat at a meal?"

"He would eat an entire edition."

"It is hardly succinct enough. Do you mean the ordinary octavo, or the family illustrated?"

"I think he would be indifferent to illustrations; that is, I think he would not value illustrations above simple letterpress."

"No, you do not get my idea. I refer to bulk. The ordinary octavo Bible weighs about two pounds and a half, while the great quarto with the illustrations weighs ten or twelve. How many Doré Bibles would he eat at a meal?"

"If you knew this elephant, you could not ask. He would take what they had."

"Well, put it in dollars and cents, then. We must get at it somehow. The Doré costs a hundred dollars a copy, Russian leather, beveled."

"He would require about fifty thousand dollars' worth—say an edition of five hundred copies."

"Now that is more exact. I will put that down. Very well; he likes men and Bibles; so far, so good. What else will he eat? I want particulars."

"He will leave Bibles to eat bricks, he will leave bricks to eat bottles, he will leave bottles to eat clothing, he will leave clothing to eat cats, he will leave cats to eat oy sters, he will leave oysters to eat ham, he will leave ham to eat sugar, he will leave sugar to eat pie, he will leave pie to eat potatoes, he will leave potatoes to eat bran, he will leave bran to eat hay, he will leave hay to eat oats, he will leave oats to eat rice, for he was mainly raised on it. There is nothing whatever that he will not eat but European butter, and he would eat that if he could taste it."

"Very good. General quantity at a meal—say about—"

"Well, anywhere from a quarter to half a ton."

"And he drinks—"

"Everything that is fluid. Milk, water, whisky, molasses, castor oil, camphene, carbolic acid—it is no use to go into particulars; whatever fluid occurs to you set it down. He will drink anything that is fluid, except European coffee."

"Very good. As to quantity?"

"Put it down five to fifteen barrels—his thirst varies; his other appetites do not."

"These things are unusual. They ought to furnish quite good clues toward tracing him."

He touched the bell.

"Alaric, summon captain Burns."

Burns appeared. Inspector Blunt unfolded the whole matter to him, detail by detail. Then he said in the clear, decisive tones of a man whose plans are clearly defined in his head and who is accustomed to command:

"Captain Burns, detail Detective Jones, Davis, Halsey, Bates, and Hackett to shadow the elephant."

"Yes, sir."

"Detail Detectives Moses, Dakin, Murphy, Rogers, Tupper, Higgins, and Batholomew to shadow the thieves."

"Yes, sir."

"Place a strong guard—a guard of thirty picked men, with a relief of thirty—over the place from whence the elephant was stolen, to keep strict watch there night and day, and allow none to approach—except reporters—without written authority from me."

"Yes, sir."

"Place detectives in plain clothes in the railway, steamship, and ferry depots, and upon all roadways leading out of Jersey City, with orders to search all suspicious persons."

"Yes, sir."

"Furnish all these men with photograph and accompanying description of the elephant, and instruct them to search all trains and outgoing ferryboats and other vessels."

"Yes, sir."

"If the elephant should be found, let him be seized, and the information forwarded to me by telegraph."

"Yes, sir."

"Let me be informed at once if any clues should be found—footprints of the animal, or anything of that kind."

"Yes, sir."

"Get an order commanding the harbor police to patrol the frontages vigilantly."

"Yes, sir."

"Despatch detectives in plain clothes over all the railways, north as far as Canada, west as far as Ohio, south as far as Washington."

"Yes, sir."

"Place experts in all the telegraph offices to listen to all messages; and let them require that all cipher despatches be interpreted to them."

"Yes, sir."

"Let all these things be done with the utmost secrecy—mind, the most impenetrable secrecy."

"Report to me promptly at the usual hour."

"Yes, sir."

"Go!"

"Yes, sir."

He was gone.

Inspector Blunt was silent and thoughtful a moment, while the fire in his eye cooled down and faded out. Then he turned to me and said in a placid voice:

"I am not given to boasting, it is not my habit; but—we shall find the elephant."

I shook him warmly by the hand and thanked him; and I *felt* my thanks, too. The more I had seen of the man the more I liked him and the more I admired him and marveled over the mysterious wonders of his profession. Then we parted for the night, and I went home with a far happier heart than I had carried with me to his office.

II

Next morning it was all in the newspapers, in the minutest detail. It even had additions—consisting of Detective This, Detective That, and Detective The Other's "Theory" as to how the robbery was done, who the robbers were, and whither they had flown with their booty. There were eleven of these theories, and they covered all the possibilities; and this single fact shows what independent thinkers detectives are. No two theories were alike, or even much resembled each other, save in one striking particular, and in that one all the other eleven theories were absolutely agreed. That was, that although the rear of my building was torn out and the only door remained locked, the elephant had not been removed through the rent, but by some other (undiscovered) outlet. All agreed that the robbers had made that rent only to mislead the detectives. That never would have occurred to me or to any other layman, perhaps, but it had not deceived the detectives for a moment. Thus, what I had supposed was the only thing that had no mystery about it was in fact the very thing I had gone furthest astray in. The eleven theories all named the supposed robbers, but no two named the same robbers; the total number of suspected persons was thirty-seven. The various newspaper accounts all closed with the most important opinion of—that of Chief Inspector Blunt. A portion of this statement read as follows:

> The chief knows who the two principals are, namely, "Brick" Duffy and "Red" McFadden. Ten days before the robbery was achieved he was already aware that it was to be attempted, and had quietly proceeded to shadow these two noted villains; but unfortunately on the night in question

their track was lost, and before it could be found again the bird was flown—that is, the elephant.

Duffy and McFadden are the boldest scoundrels in the profession; the chief has reasons for believing that they are the men who stole the stove out of the detective headquarters on a bitter night last winter—in consequence of which the chief and every detective present were in the hands of the physicians before morning, some with frozen feet, others with frozen fingers, ears, and other members.

When I read the first half of that I was more astonished than ever at the wonderful sagacity of this strange man. He not only saw everything in the present with a clear eye, but even the future could not be hidden from him. I was soon at his office, and said I could not help wishing he had had those men arrested, and so prevented the trouble and loss; but his reply was simple and unanswerable:

"It is not our province to prevent crime, but to punish it. We cannot punish it until it is committed."

I remarked that the secrecy with which he had begun had been marred by the newspapers; not only all our facts but all our plans and purposes had been revealed; even all the suspected persons had been named; these would doubtless disguise themselves now, or go into hiding.

"Let them. They will find that when I am ready for them my hand will descend upon them, in their secret places, as unerringly as the hand of fate. As to the newspapers, we *must* keep in with them. Fame, reputation, constant public mention—these are the detective's bread and butter. He must publish his facts, else he will be supposed to have none; he must publish his theory, for nothing is so strange or striking as a detective's theory, or brings him so much wonderful respect; we must publish our plans, for these the journals insist upon having, and we could not deny them without offending. We must constantly show the public what we are doing, or they will believe we are doing nothing. It is much pleasanter to have a newspaper say, 'Inspector Blunt's ingenious and extraordinary theory is as follows,' than to have it say some harsh thing, or, worse still, some sarcastic one."

"I see the force of what you say. But I noticed that in one part of your remarks in the papers this morning you refused to reveal your opinion upon a certain minor point."

"Yes, we always do that; it has a good effect. Besides, I had not formed any opinion on that point, anyway."

I deposited a considerable sum of money with the inspector, to meet current expenses, and sat down to wait for news. We were expecting the telegrams to begin to arrive at any moment now. Meantime I reread the newspapers and also our descriptive circular, and observed that our twenty-five thousand dollars reward seemed to be offered only to detectives. I said I thought it ought to be offered to anybody who would catch the elephant. The inspector said:

"It is the detectives who will find the elephant, hence the reward will go to the right place. If other people found the animal, it would only be by watching the detectives and taking advantage of clues and indications stolen from them, and that would entitle the detectives to the reward, after all. The proper office of a reward is to stimulate the men who deliver up their time and their trained sagacities to this sort of work, and not to confer benefits, upon chance citizens who stumble upon a capture without having earned the benefits by their own merits and labors."

This was reasonable enough, certainly. Now the telegraphic machine in the corner began to click, and the following despatch was the result:

FLOWER STATION, N.Y., 7.30 A.M.

HAVE GOT A CLUE. FOUND A SUCCESSION OF DEEP TRACKS ACROSS A FARM NEAR HERE. FOLLOWED THEM TWO MILES PAST WITHOUT RESULT; THINK ELEPHANT WENT WEST. SHALL NOW SHADOW HIM IN THAT DIRECTION. . . . .

DARLEY, DETECTIVE

"Darley's one of the best men on the force," said the inspector. "We shall hear from him again before long."

Telegram No. 2 came:

BARKER'S, N. J., 7.40 A.M.

JUST ARRIVED. GLASS FACTORY BROKEN OPEN HERE DURING NIGHT, AND EIGHT HUNDRED BOTTLES TAKEN. ONLY WATER IN LARGE QUANTITY NEAR HERE IS FIVE MILES DISTANT. SHALL STRIKE FOR THERE. ELEPHANT WILL BE THIRSTY. BOTTLES WERE EMPTY.

BAKER, DETECTIVE

"That promises well, too," said the inspector. "I told you the creature's appetites would not be bad clues."

Telegram No. 3:

TAYLORVILLE, L. I., 8.15 A.M.

A HAYSTACK NEAR HERE DISAPPEARED DURING NIGHT. PROBABLY EATEN. HAVE GOT A CLUE, AND AM OFF.

HUBBARD, DETECTIVE

"How he does move around!" said the inspector. "I knew we had a difficult job on hand, but we shall catch him yet."

FLOWER STATION, N.Y., 9 A.M.

SHADOWED THE TRACKS THREE MILES WESTWARD. LARGE, DEEP AND RAGGED. HAVE JUST MET A FARMER WHO SAYS THEY ARE NOT ELEPHANT TRACKS. SAYS THEY ARE HOLES WHERE HE DUG UP SAPLINGS FOR SHADE TREES WHEN GROUND WAS FROZEN LAST WINTER. GIVE ME ORDERS HOW TO PROCEED.

DARLEY, DETECTIVE

"Aha! a confederate of the thieves! The thing grows warm," said the inspector.

He dictated the following telegram to Darley:

ARREST THE MAN AND FORCE HIM TO NAME HIS PALS. CONTINUE TO FOLLOW THE TRACKS—TO THE PACIFIC IF NECESSARY.

CHIEF BLUNT

Next telegram:

CONEY POINT, PA., 8.45 A.M.

GAS OFFICE BROKEN OPEN HERE DURING NIGHT AND

THREE MONTHS' UNPAID GAS BILLS TAKEN. HAVE GOT A CLUE AND AM AWAY.

MURPHY, DETECTIVE

"Heavens!" said the inspector; "would he eat gas bills?"

"Through ignorance—yes; but they cannot support life. At least, unassisted."

Now came this exciting telegram:

IRONVILLE, N. Y., 9.30 A.M.

JUST ARRIVED. THIS VILLAGE IN CONSTERNATION. ELEPHANT PASSED THROUGH HERE AT FIVE THIS MORNING. SOME SAY HE WENT EAST, SOME SAY WEST, SOME NORTH, SOME SOUTH—BUT ALL SAY THEY DID NOT WAIT TO NOTICE PARTICULARLY. HE KILLED A HORSE; HAVE SECURED A PIECE OF IT FOR A CLUE. KILLED IT WITH HIS TRUNK; FROM STYLE OF BLOW, THINK HE STRUCK IT LEFT-HANDED. FROM POSITION IN WHICH HORSE LIES, THINK ELEPHANT TRAVELED NORTHWARD ALONG LINE OF BERKLEY RAILWAY. HAS FOUR AND HALF HOURS' START, BUT I MOVE ON HIS TRACK AT ONCE.

HAWES, DETECTIVE

I uttered exclamations of joy. The inspector was as self-contained as a graven image. He calmly touched his bell.

"Alaric, send Captain Burns here."

Burns appeared.

"How many men are ready for instant orders?"

"Ninety-six, sir."

"Send them north at once. Let them concentrate along the line of the Berkley road north of Ironville."

"Yes, sir."

"Let them conduct their movements with the utmost secrecy. As fast as others are at liberty, hold them for orders."

"Yes, sir."

"Go!"

"Yes, sir."

Presently came another telegram:

SAGE CORNERS, N. Y., 10.30.

JUST ARRIVED, ELEPHANT PASSED THROUGH HERE AT

8.15. ALL ESCAPED FROM THE TOWN BUT A POLICEMAN. APPARENTLY ELEPHANT DID NOT STRIKE AT POLICEMAN, BUT AT THE LAMPPOST. GOT BOTH. I HAVE SECURED A PORTION OF THE POLICEMAN AS CLUE.

STUMM, DETECTIVE

"So the elephant has turned westward," said the inspector. "However, he will not escape, for my men are scattered all over that region."

The next telegram said:

GLOVER'S, 11.15.

JUST ARRIVED. VILLAGE DESERTED, EXCEPT SICK AND AGED. ELEPHANT PASSED THROUGH THREE-QUARTERS OF AN HOUR AGO. THE ANTITEMPERANCE MASS-MEETING WAS IN SESSION; HE PUT HIS TRUNK IN AT A WINDOW AND WASHED IT OUT WITH WATER FROM CISTERN. SOME SWALLOWED IT—SINCE DEAD; SEVERAL DROWNED. DETECTIVES CROSS AND O'SHAUGHNESSY WERE PASSING THROUGH TOWN, BUT GOING SOUTH—SO MISSED ELEPHANT. WHOLE REGION FOR MANY MILES AROUND IN TERROR—PEOPLE FLYING FROM THEIR HOMES. WHEREVER THEY TURN MEET ELEPHANT, AND MANY ARE KILLED.

BRANT, DETECTIVE

I could have shed tears, this havoc so distressed me. But the inspector only said:

"You see—we are closing in on him. He feels our presence; he has turned eastward again."

Yet further troublous news was in store for us. The telegraph brought this:

HOGANSPORT, 12.19.

JUST ARRIVED. ELEPHANT PASSED THROUGH HALF AN HOUR AGO, CREATING WILDEST FRIGHT AND EXCITEMENT. ELEPHANT RAGED AROUND STREETS: TWO PLUMBERS GOING BY, KILLED ONE.—OTHER ESCAPED. REGRET GENERAL.

O'FLAHERTY, DETECTIVE

"Now he is right in the midst of my men," said the inspector. "Nothing can save him."

A succession of telegrams came from detectives who were scattered through New Jersey and Pennsylvania, and who were following clues consisting of ravaged barns, factories, and Sunday-school libraries, with high hopes—hopes amounting to certainties, indeed. The inspector said:

"I wish I could communicate with them and order them north, but that is impossible. A detective only visits a telegraph office to send his report; then he is off again, and you don't know where to put your hand on him."

Now came this despatch:

BRIDGEPORT, CT., 12.15.

BARNUM OFFERS RATE OF $4,000 A YEAR FOR EXCLUSIVE PRIVILEGE OF USING ELEPHANT AS TRAVELING ADVERTISING MEDIUM FROM NOW TILL DETECTIVES FIND HIM. WANTS TO PASTE CIRCUS-POSTERS ON HIM. DESIRES IMMEDIATE ANSWER.

BOGGS, DETECTIVE

"That is perfectly absurd!" I exclaimed.

"Of course it is," said the inspector. "Evidently Mr. Barnum, who thinks he is so sharp, does not know me—but I know him."

Then he dictated this answer to the despatch:

MR. BARNUM'S OFFER DECLINED. MAKE IT $7,000 OR NOTHING.

CHIEF BLUNT

"There. We shall not have to wait long for an answer. Mr. Barnum is not at home; he is in the telegraph office—it is his way when he has business on hand. Inside of three—"

DONE.

P.T. BARNUM

So interrupted the clicking telegraphic instrument. Before I could make a comment upon this extraordinary episode, the following despatch carried my thoughts into another very distressing channel:

BOLIVIA, N. Y., 12.50.

ELEPHANT ARRIVED HERE FROM THE SOUTH AND PASSED

THROUGH TOWARD THE FOREST AT 11.50, DISPERSING A FUNERAL ON THE WAY, AND DIMINISHING THE MOURNERS BY TWO. CITIZENS FIRED SOME SMALL CANNON-BALLS INTO HIM, AND THEN FLED. DETECTIVE BURKE AND I ARRIVED TEN MINUTES LATER, FROM THE NORTH, BUT MISTOOK SOME EXCAVATIONS FOR FOOTPRINTS, AND SO LOST A GOOD DEAL OF TIME; BUT AT LAST WE STRUCK THE RIGHT TRAIL AND FOLLOWED IT TO THE WOODS. WE THEN GOT DOWN ON OUR HANDS AND KNEES AND CONTINUED TO KEEP A SHARP EYE ON THE TRACK, AND SO SHADOWED IT INTO THE BRUSH. BURKE WAS IN ADVANCE. UNFORTUNATELY THE ANIMAL HAD STOPPED TO REST; THEREFORE, BURKE HAVING HIS HEAD DOWN, INTENT UPON THE TRACK, BUTTED UP AGAINST THE ELEPHANT'S HIND LEGS BEFORE HE WAS AWARE OF HIS VICINITY. BURKE INSTANTLY AROSE TO HIS FEET, SEIZED THE TAIL, AND EXCLAIMED JOYFULLY, "I CLAIM THE RE—" BUT GOT NO FURTHER, FOR A SINGLE BLOW OF THE HUGE TRUNK LAID THE BRAVE FELLOW'S FRAGMENTS LOW IN DEATH. I FLED REARWARD, AND THE ELEPHANT TURNED AND SHADOWED ME TO THE EDGE OF THE WOOD, MAKING TREMENDOUS SPEED, AND I SHOULD INEVITABLY HAVE BEEN LOST, BUT THAT THE REMAINS OF THE FUNERAL PROVIDENTIALLY INTERVENED AGAIN AND DIVERTED HIS ATTENTION. I HAVE JUST LEARNED THAT NOTHING OF THAT FUNERAL IS NOW LEFT; BUT THIS IS NO LOSS, FOR THERE IS ABUNDANCE OF MATERIAL FOR ANOTHER. MEANTIME, THE ELEPHANT HAS DISAPPEARED AGAIN.

MULROONEY, DETECTIVE

We heard no news except from the diligent and confident detectives scattered about New Jersey, Pennsylvania, Delaware, and Virginia—who were all following fresh and encouraging clues—until shortly after 2 P.M., when this telegram came:

BAXTER CENTER, 2.15.

ELEPHANT BEEN HERE, PLASTERED OVER WITH CIRCUS-BILLS, AND BROKE UP A REVIVAL, STRIKING DOWN AND DAMAGING MANY WHO WERE ON THE POINT OF ENTERING UPON A BETTER LIFE. CITIZENS PENNED UP AND ESTABLISHED A GUARD. WHEN DETECTIVE BROWN AND I ARRIVED, SOME TIME AFTER, WE ENTERED INCLOSURE AND PROCEEDED TO IDENTIFY ELEPHANT BY PHOTOGRAPHS AND DESCRIPTION, ALL MARKS TALLIED EXACTLY

EXCEPT ONE, WHICH WE COULD NOT SEE—THE BOIL-SCAR UNDER ARMPIT. TO MAKE SURE, BROWN CREPT UNDER TO LOOK, AND WAS IMMEDIATELY BRAINED—THAT IS, HEAD CRUSHED AND DESTROYED, THOUGH NOTHING ISSUED FROM DEBRIS. ALL FLED; SO DID ELEPHANT, STRIKING RIGHT AND LEFT WITH MUCH EFFECT. HAS ESCAPED, BUT LEFT BOLD BLOOD-TRACK FROM CANNON-WOUNDS. REDISCOVERY CERTAIN. HE BROKE SOUTHWARD, THROUGH A DENSE FOREST.

BRENT, DETECTIVE

That was the last telegram. At nightfall a fog shut down which was so dense that objects but three feet away could not be discerned. This lasted all night. The ferryboats and even the omnibuses had to stop running.

III

Next morning the papers were as full of detective theories as before; they had all our tragic facts in detail also, and a great many more which they had received from their telegraphic correspondents. Column after column was occupied, a third of its way down, with glaring head-lines, which it made my heart sick to read. Their general tone was like this:

THE WHITE ELEPHANT AT LARGE! HE MOVES UPON HIS FATAL MARCH! WHOLE VILLAGES DESERTED BY THEIR FRIGHT-STRICKEN OCCUPANTS! PALE TERROR GOES BEFORE HIM, DEATH AND DEVASTATION FOLLOW AFTER! AFTER THESE, THE DETECTIVES! BARNS DESTROYED, FACTORIES GUTTED, HARVESTS DEVOURED, PUBLIC ASSEMBLAGES DISPERSED, ACCOMPANIED BY SCENES OF CARNAGE IMPOSSIBLE TO DESCRIBE! THEORIES OF THIRTY-FOUR OF THE MOST DISTINGUISHED DETECTIVES ON THE FORCE! THEORY OF CHIEF BLUNT!

"There!" said Inspector Blunt, almost betrayed into excitement, "this is magnificent! This is the greatest windfall that any detective organization ever had. The fame of it will travel to the ends of the earth, and endure to the end of time, and my name with it."

But there was no joy for me. I felt as if I had committed all those red crimes, and that the elephant was only my irresponsible agent. And how the list had grown! In one place he had "interfered with an election and killed five repeaters." He had followed this act with the destruction of two poor fellows, named O'Donohue and McFlannigan, who had "found a refuge in the home of the oppressed of all lands only the day before, and were in the act of exercising for the first time the noble right of American citizens at the polls, when stricken down by the relentless hand of the Scourge of Siam." In another, he had "found a crazy sensation-preacher preparing his next season's heroic attacks on the dance, the theater, and other things which can't strike back, and had stepped on him." And in still another place he had "killed a lightning-rod agent." And so the list went on, growing redder and redder, and more and more heartbreaking. Sixty persons had been killed, and two hundred and forty wounded. All the accounts bore just testimony to the activity and devotion of the detectives, and all closed with the remark that "three hundred thousand citizens and four detectives saw the dread creature, and two of the latter he destroyed."

I dreaded to hear the telegraphic instrument begin to click again. By and by the messages began to pour in, but I was happily disappointed in their nature. It was soon apparent that all trace of the elephant was lost. The fog had enabled him to search out a good hiding-place unobserved. Telegrams from the most absurdly distant points reported that a dim vast mass had been glimpsed there through the fog at such and such an hour, and was "undoubtedly the elephant." This dim vast mass had been glimpsed in New Haven, in New Jersey, in Pennsylvania, in interior New York, in Brooklyn, and even in the city of New York itself! But in all cases the dim vast mass had vanished quickly and left no trace. Every detective of the large force scattered over this huge extent of country sent his hourly report, and each and every one of them had a clue, and was shadowing something, and was hot upon the heels of it.

But the day passed without other result.

The next day the same.

The next just the same.

The newspaper reports began to grow monotonous with facts that amounted to nothing, clues which led to nothing, and theories which had nearly exhausted the elements which surprise and delight and dazzle.

By advice of the inspector I doubled the reward.

Four more dull days followed. Then came a bitter blow to the poor, hard-working detectives—the journalists declined to print their theories, and coldly said, "Give us a rest."

Two weeks after the elephant's disappearance I raised the reward to seventy-five thousand dollars by the inspector's advice. It was a great sum, but I felt that I would rather sacrifice my whole private fortune than lose my credit with my government. Now that the detectives were in adversity, the newspapers turned upon them, and began to fling the most stinging sarcasms at them. This gave the minstrels an idea, and they dressed themselves as detectives and hunted the elephant on the stage in the most extravagant way. The caricaturists made pictures of detectives scanning the country with spyglasses, while the elephant, at their backs, stole apples out of their pockets. And they made all sorts of ridiculous pictures of the detective badge—you have seen that badge printed in gold on the back of detective novels, no doubt—it is a wide-staring eye, with the legend, "WE NEVER SLEEP." When detectives called for a drink, the would-be facetious barkeeper resurrected an obsolete form of expression and said, "Will you have an eye-opener?" All the air was thick with sarcasms.

But there was one man who moved calm, untouched, unaffected, through it all. It was that heart of oak, the chief inspector. His brave eye never dropped, his serene confidence never wavered. He always said:

"Let them rail on; he laughs best who laughs last."

My admiration for the man grew into a species of worship. I was at his side always. His office had become an unpleasant place to me, and now became daily more and more so. Yet if he could endure it I meant to do so also—at least, as long as I could. So I came regularly, and stayed—the only outsider who seemed to be capable of it. Everybody wondered how I could; and often it seemed to me that I must desert, but at such times I looked into that calm and apparently unconscious face, and held my ground.

About three weeks after the elephant's disappearance I was about to say, one morning, that I should *have* to strike my colors and retire, when the great detective arrested the thought by proposing one more superb and masterly move.

This was to compromise with the robbers. The fertility of this man's invention exceeded anything I have ever seen and I have had a wide intercourse with the world's finest minds. He said he was confident he could compromise for one hundred thousand dollars and recover the elephant. I said I believed I could scrape the amount together, but what would become of the poor detectives who had worked so faithfully? He said:

"In compromises they always get half."

This removed my only objection. So the inspector wrote two notes, in this form:

DEAR MADAME—YOUR HUSBAND CAN MAKE A LARGE SUM OF MONEY (AND BE ENTIRELY PROTECTED FROM THE LAW) BY MAKING AN IMMEDIATE APPOINTMENT WITH ME.

CHIEF BLUNT

He sent one of these by his confidential messenger to the "reputed wife" of Brick Duffy, and the other to the reputed wife of Red McFadden.

Within the hour these offensive answers came:

YE OWLD FOOL: BRICK DUFFYS BIN DED 2 YERE.

BRIDGET MAHONEY

CHIEF BAT—RED MCFADDEN IS HUNG AND IN HEVING 18 MONTH. ANY ASS BUT A DETECTIVE KNOSE THAT.

MARY O'HOOLIGAN

"I had long suspected these facts," said the inspector; "this testimony proves the unerring accuracy of my instinct."

The moment one resource failed him he was ready with another. He immediately wrote an advertisement for the morning papers, and I kept a copy of it:

A.—xwblv. 242 N. Tjnd—fz328wmlg. Ozpo,—; 2 m! ogw. Mum.

He said that if the thief was alive this would bring him to the usual rendezvous. He further explained that the usual rendezvous was a place where all business affairs between detectives and criminals were conducted. This meeting would take place at twelve the next night.

We could do nothing till then, and I lost no time in getting out of the office, and was grateful indeed for the privilege.

At eleven the next night I brought one hundred thousand dollars in bank-notes and put them into the chief's hands, and shortly afterward he took his leave, with the brave old undimmed confidence in his eye. An almost intolerable hour dragged to a close; then I heard his welcome tread, and rose gasping and tottered to meet him. How his fine eyes flamed with triumph! He said:

"We've compromised! The jokers will sing a different tune to-morrow! Follow me!"

He took a lighted candle and strode down into the vast vaulted basement where sixty detectives always slept, and where a score were now playing cards to while the time. I followed close after him. He walked swiftly down to the dim and remote end of the place, and just as I succumbed to the pangs of suffocation and was swooning away he stumbled and fell over the outlying members of a mighty object, and I heard him exclaim as he went down:

"Our noble profession is vindicated. Here is your elephant!"

I was carried to the office above and restored with carbolic acid. The whole detective force swarmed in, and such another season of triumphant rejoicing ensued as I had never witnessed before. The reporters were called, baskets of champagne were opened, toasts were drunk, the handshakings and congratulations were continuous and enthusiastic. Naturally the chief was the hero of the hour, and his happiness was so complete and had been so patiently and worthily and bravely won that it made me happy to see it, though I stood there a homeless beggar, my priceless charge dead, and my position in my country's service lost to me through what would always seem my fatally careless execution of a great trust. Many an eloquent eye testified its deep admiration for the chief, and many a detective's voice murmured, "Look at him—just the king of the profession; only give him a clue, it's all he wants, and there ain't anything hid that he can't find." The dividing of the fifty thousand dollars made great pleasure; when it was finished the chief made a little speech while he put his share in his pocket, in which he said, "Enjoy it, boys, for you've earned it; and, more than that, you've earned for the detective profession undying fame."

A telegram arrived, which read:

MONROE, MICH., 10 P.M.

FIRST TIME I'VE STRUCK A TELEGRAPH OFFICE IN OVER THREE WEEKS. HAVE FOLLOWED THOSE FOOTPRINTS, HORSE-BACK, THROUGH THE WOODS, A THOUSAND MILES TO HERE AND THEY GET STRONGER AND BIGGER AND FRESHER EVERY DAY. DON'T WORRY—INSIDE OF ANOTHER WEEK I'LL HAVE THE ELEPHANT. THIS IS DEAD SURE.

DARLEY, DETECTIVE

The chief ordered three cheers for "Darley, one of the finest minds on the force," and then commanded that he be telegraphed to come home and receive his share of the reward.

So ended that marvelous episode of the stolen elephant. The newspapers were pleasant with praises once more, the next day, with one contemptible exception. This sheet said, "Great is the detective! He may be a little slow in finding a little thing like a mislaid elephant—he may hunt him all day and sleep with his rotting carcass all night for three weeks, but he will find him at last—if he can get the man who mislaid him to show him the place!"

Poor Hassan was lost to me forever. The cannon-shots had wounded him fatally, he had crept to that unfriendly place in the fog, and there, surrounded by his enemies and in constant danger of detection, he had wasted away with hunger and suffering till death gave him peace.

The compromise cost me one hundred thousand dollars, my detective expenses were forty-two thousand dollars more. I never applied for a place again under my government; I am a ruined man and a wanderer on the earth—but my admiration for that man, whom I believe to be the greatest detective the world has ever produced, remains undimmed to this day, and will so remain unto the end.

Those Blasted Children

Lick House, San Francisco, Wednesday, 1863.

Editors T. T.:—No. 165 is a pleasant room. It is situated at the head of a long hall, down which, on either side, are similar rooms occupied by sociable bachelors, and here and there one tenanted by an unsociable nurse or so. Charley Creed sleeps in No. 157. He is my time-piece—or, at least, his boots are. If I look down the hall and see Charley's boots still before his door, I know it is early yet, and I may hie me sweetly to bed again. But if those unerring boots are gone, I know it is after eleven o'clock, and time for me to be rising with the lark. This reminds me of the lark of yesterday and last night, which was altogether a different sort of bird from the one I am talking about now. Ah me! Summer girls and summer dresses, and summer scenes at the "Willows", Seal Rock Point, and the grim sea-lions wallowing in the angry surf; glimpses through the haze of stately ships far away at sea; a dash along the smooth beach, and the exhilaration of watching the white waves come surging ashore, and break into seething foam about the startled horse's feet; reveries beside the old wreck, half buried in sand, and compassion for the good ship's fate; home again in a soft twilight, oppressed with the odor of flowers—home again to San Francisco, drunk, perhaps, but not disorderly. Dinner at six, with ladies and gentlemen, dressed with faultless taste and elegance, and all drunk, apparently, but very quiet and well-bred—unaccountably so, under the circumstances, it seemed to my cloudy brain. Many things happened after that, I remember—such as visiting some of their haunts with those dissipated Golden Era fellows, and—

Her come those young savages again—those noisy and inevitable children. God be with them!—or they with him, rather, if it be not asking too much. They are another time-piece of mine. It is two o'clock now; they are invested with their regular lunch, and have come up here to settle it. I will soothe my troubled spirit with a short season of blasphemy, after which I will expose their infamous proceedings with a relentless pen. They have driven me from labor many and many a time; but behold! the hour of retribution is at hand.

That is young Washington Billings, now—a little dog in long flaxen curls and Highland costume.

"Hi, Johnny! look through the keyhole! here's that feller with a long nose, writing again—less stir him up!" [A double kick against the door—a grand infant war-hoop in full chorus—and then a clatter of scampering feet down the echoing corridors.] Ah—one of them has fallen, and hurt himself. I hear the intelligent foreign nurse boxing his ears for it (the parents, Mr. and Mrs. Kerosene, having gone up to Sacramento on the evening boat, and left their offspring properly cared for.)

Here they come again, as soldiers—infantry. I know there are not more than thirty or forty of them, yet they are under no sort of discipline, and they make noise enough for a thousand. Young Oliver Higgins is in command. They assault my works—they try to carry my position by storm—they finally draw off with boistrous cheers, to harrass a handful of skirmishers thrown out by the enemy—a bevy of chambermaids.

Once more they come trooping down the hall. This time as cavalry. They must have captured and disarmed the skirmishers, for half my young ruffians are mounted on broomsticks. They make a reconnoissance in force. They attack my premises in a body, but they achieve nothing approaching a success. I am too strongly intrenched for them.

They invest my stronghold, and lay seige to it—that is to say, they sit down before my camp, and betake themselves to the pastimes of youth. All talking at once, as they do, their conversation is amusing, but not instructive to me.

"Ginn me some o' that you're eat'n." "I won't—you wouldn't lemme play with that dead rat, the peanut-boy give you yesterday." "Well! I don't care; I reckon I know summun't you don't; Oho, Mr. Smarty, 'n' I ain't a goin' to tell you, neither; now, see what you got by it; it's summun't my ma said about your ma, too. I'll tell you, if you'll gimme ever so little o' that, will you? Well." (I imagine from the break in this conversation, while the other besiegers go on talking noisily, that a compromise is being effected.) "There, don't take so much. Now, what'd she say?" "Why, ma told my pa 't if your ma is so mighty rich now she wasn't nobody till she come to Sanf'cisco. That's what she said." "Your ma's a big story-teller, 'n' I'm goin' jes' as straight as I can walk, 'n' tell my ma. You'll see what she'll do." (I foresee a diversion in one or two family circles.) "Flora Low, you quit pullin that doll's legs out, it's mine." "Well, take your old doll, then. I'd thank you to know, Miss Florence Hillyer, 't my pa's Governor, 'n' I can have a thousan' dolls if I want to, 'n' gold ones, too, or silver, or anything." (More trouble brewing.) "What do I care for that. I guess my pa could be Governor, too, if he wanted to; but he don't. He owns two hundred feet in the Chollar, 'n' he's got lots more silver mines in Washoe besides. He could fill this house full of silver, clear up to that chandelier, so he could, now, Miss." "You, Bob Miller, you leg go that string—I'll smack you in the eye." "You will, will you? I'd like to see you try it. You jes' hit me if you dare!" "You lay your hands on me, 'n' I will hit you." "Now I've laid my hand on you, why don't you hit? "Well, I mean, if you lay 'em on me so's to hurt." " Ah-h! you're afraid, that's the reason." "No I ain't, neither, you big fool." (Ah, now they're at it. Discord shall invade the ranks of my foes, and they shall fall by their own hands. It appears from the sound without that two nurses have made a descent upon the combatants, and are bearing them from the field. The nurses are abusing each other. One boy proclaims that the other struck him when he wasn't doin' nothin'; and the other boy says he was called a big fool. Both are going along as comfortably as I could wish, now.) "Sandy Baker, I know what makes your pa's hair kink so; it's 'cause he's a mulatter; I heard my ma say so." "It's a lie!" (Another row, and more skirmishing with the nurses. Truly, happiness flows in upon me most bountifully this day.) "Hi, boys! here comes a Chinaman!" (God pity any Chinaman who chances to come in the way of the boys hereabout, for the eye of the law regardeth him not, and the youth of California in their generation are down upon him.) "Now, boys! grab his clothes basket—take him by the tail!" (There they go, now, like a pack of young demons; they have confiscated the basket, and the dismayed Chinaman is towing half the tribe down the hall by his cue. Rejoice, O my soul, for behold, all things are lovely, etc.—to speak after the manner of the vulgar.) "Oho, Miss Susy Badger, my uncle Tom's goin' across the bay to Oakland, 'n' down to Santa Clara, 'n' Alamedy, 'n' San Leandro, 'n' everywheres—all over the world, 'n' he's goin' to take me with him—he said so." "Humph! that ain't noth'n—I been there. My aunt Mary'd take me to any place I wanted to go, if I 'wanted her to, but I don't; she's got horses 'n' things—O, ever so many!—millions of 'em; but my ma says it don't look well for little girls to be always gadd'n about. That's why you don't ever see me goin' to places like some girls do. I despise to—" (The end is at hand; the nurses have massed themselves on the left; they move in serried phalanx on my besiegers; they surround them, and capture the last miscreant—horse, foot, and dragoons, munitions of war, and camp equipage. The victory is complete. They are gone—my castle is no longer menaced, and the rover is free. I am here, staunch and true!)

It is a living wonder to me that I haven't scalped some of those children before now. I expect I would have done it, but then I hardly felt well enough acquainted with them. I scarcely ever show them any attention anyhow, unless it is to throw a boot-jack at them or some little nonsense of that kind when I happen to feel playful. I am confident I would have destroyed several of them though, only it might appear as if I were making most too free.

I observe that that young officer of the Pacific Squadron—the one with his nostrils turned up like port-holes—has become a great favorite with half the mothers in the house, by imparting to them much useful information concerning the manner of doctoring children among the South American savages. His brother is brigadier in the Navy. The drab-complexioned youth with the Solferino mustache has corraled the other half with the Japanese treatment. The more I think of it the more I admire it. Now, I am no peanut. I have an idea that I could invent some little remedies that would stir up a commotion among these women, if I chose to try. I always had a good general notion of physic, I believe. It is one of my natural gifts, too, for I have never studied a single day under a regular physician. I will jot down a few items here, just to see how likely I am to succeed.

In the matter of measles, the idea is, to bring it out—bring it to the surface. Take the child and fill it up with saffron tea. Add something to make the patient sleep—say a tablespoonful of arsenic. Don't rock it—it will sleep anyhow.

As far as brain fever is concerned: This is a very dangerous disease, and must be treated with decision and dispatch. In every case where it has proved fatal, the sufferer invariably perished. You must strike at the root of the distemper. Remove the brains; and then—Well, that will be sufficient—that will answer—just remove the brains. This remedy has never been known to fail. It was originated by the lamented J. W. Macbeth, Thane of Cawdor, Scotland, who refers to it thus: "Time was, that when the brains were out, the man would die; but, under different circumstances, I think not; and, all things being equal, I believe you, my boy." Those were his last words.

Concerning worms: Administer a catfish three times a week. Keep the room very quiet; the fish won't bite if there is the least noise.

When you come to fits, take no chances on fits. If the child has them bad, soak it in a barrel of rain-water over night, or a good article of vinegar. If this does not put an end to its troubles, soak it a week. You can't soak a child too much when it has fits:

In cases wherein an infant stammers, remove the under-jaw. In proof of the efficacy of this treatment, I append the following certificate, voluntarily forwarded to me by Mr. Zeb. Leavenworth, of St. Louis, Mo.:

"St. Louis, May 26, 1863.

"Mr. Mark Twain—Dear Sir:—Under Providence, I am beholden to you for the salvation of my Johnny. For a matter of three years, that suffering child stuttered to that degree that it was a pain and a sorrow to me to hear him stagger over the sacred name of 'p-p-p-pap'. It troubled me so that I neglected my business; I refused food; I took no pride in my dress, and my hair actually began to fall off. I could not rest; I could not sleep. Morning, noon, and night, I did nothing but moan pitifully, and murmur to myself: 'Hell's fire! what am I going to do about my Johnny?' But in a blessed hour you appeared unto me like an angel from the skies; and without hope of reward, revealed your sovereign remedy—and that very day, I sawed off my Johnny's under-jaw. May Heaven bless you, noble Sir. It afforded instant relief; and my Johnny has never stammered since. I honestly believe he never will again. As to disfigurement, he does seem to look sorter ornery and hog-mouthed, but I am too grateful in having got him effectually saved from that dreadful stuttering, to make much account of small matters. Heaven speed you in your holy work of healing the afflictions of humanity. And if my poor testimony can be of any service to you, do with it as you think will result in the greatest good to our fellow-creatures. Once more, Heaven bless you.

"Zeb. Leavenworth."

Now, that has such a plausible ring about it, that I can hardly keep from believing it myself. I consider it a very fair success.

Regarding Cramps. Take your offspring—let the same be warm and dry at the time—and immerse it in a commodious soup-tureen filled with the best quality of camphene. Place it over a slow fire, and add reasonable quantities of pepper, mustard, horse-radish, saltpetre, strychnine, blue vitriol, aqua fortis, a quart of flour, and eight or ten fresh eggs, stirring it from time to time, to keep up a healthy reaction. Let it simmer fifteen minutes. When your child is done, set the tureen off, and allow the infallible remedy to cool. If this does not confer an entire insensibility to cramps, you must lose no time, for the case is desperate. Take your offspring, and parboil it. The most vindictive cramps cannot survive this treatment; neither can the subject, unless it is endowed with an iron constitution. It is an extreme measure, and I always dislike to resort to it. I never parboil a child until everything else has failed to bring about the desired end.

Well, I think those will do to commence with. I can branch out, you know, when I get more confidence in myself.

O infancy! thou art beautiful, thou art charming, thou art lovely to contemplate! But thoughts like these recall sad memories of the past, of the halcyon days of my childhood, when I was a sweet, prattling innocent, the pet of a dear home-circle, and the pride of the village.

Enough, enough! I must weep, or this bursting heart will break.

An Appeal Against Injudicious Swearing

SATURDAY, NOV. 8.

To the Editor of The Sun—*Sir:* Doubtless you city people do not mind having your feelings hurt and your self-love blistered, for your horse car and elevated road service train you to patience and humble-mindedness, but with us hayseed folk from the back settlements the case is different. We are so delicate, so sensitive—well, you would never be able to imagine what it is like. An unkind speech shrivels us all up and often makes us cry. Now, the thing which happened to-day a New Yorker would not mind in the least; but I give you my word it almost made me want to go away and be at rest in the cold grave.

I stepped aboard a red Sixth avenue horse car—No. 106—at Sixth avenue and Forty-second street at 11:45 this morning, bound down town. Of course there was no seat—there never is: New Yorkers do not require a seat, but only permission to stand up and look meek, and be thankful for such little rags of privilege as the good horse-car company may choose to allow them. I stood in the door, behind three ladies. After a moment, the conductor, desiring to pass through and see the passengers, took me by the lappel and said to me with that winning courtesy and politeness which New Yorkers are so accustomed to: "Jesus Christ! what you want to load up the door for? Git back here out of the way!" Those ladies shrank together under the shock, just the same as I did; so I judged they were country people. This conductor was a person about 30 years old, I should say, five feet nine, with blue eyes, a small, dim, unsuccessful moustache, and the general expression of a chicken thief—you may probably have seen him.

I urged him to modify his language, I being from the country and sensitive. He looked upon me with cold and heartless scorn, thus hurting me still more. I said I would report him, and asked him for his number. He said, in a tone which wounded me more than I can tell, "I'll give you a chew of tobacco."

Why, dear sir, if conductors were to talk to us like that out in the country we could never, never bear to ride with them, we are so sensitive. I went up to Sixth avenue and Forty-third street to report him, but there was nobody in the superintendent's office who seemed to want to converse with me. A man with "conductor" on his cap said it wouldn't be any use to try to see the President at that time of day, and intimated, by his manner, not his words, that people with complaints were not popular there, any way.

So I have been obliged to come to you, you see. What I wanted to say to the President of the road was this—and through him say it to the President of the elevated roads—that the conductors ought to be instructed never to swear at country people except when there are no city ones to swear at, and not even then except for practice. Because the country people are sensitive. Conductors need not make any mistakes; they can easily tell us from the city people. Could you use your influence to get this small and harmless distinction made in our favor?

A Dog's Tale

I

My father was a St. Bernard, my mother was a collie, but I am a Presbyterian. This is what my mother told me; I do not know these nice distinctions myself. To me they are only fine large words meaning nothing. My mother had a fondness for such; she liked to say them, and see other dogs look surprised and envious, as wondering how she got so much education. But, indeed, it was not real education; it was only show: she got the words by listening in the dining-room and drawing-room when there was company, and by going with the children to Sunday-school and listening there; and whenever she heard a large word she said it over to herself many times, and so was able to keep it until there was a dogmatic gathering in the neighborhood, then she would get it off, and surprise and distress them all, from pocket-pup to mastiff, which rewarded her for all her trouble. If there was a stranger he was nearly sure to be suspicious, and when he got his breath again he would ask her what it meant. And she always told him. He was never expecting this, but thought he would catch her; so when she told him, he was the one that looked ashamed, whereas he had thought it was going to be she. The others were always waiting for this, and glad of it and proud of her, for they knew what was going to happen, because they had had experience. When she told the meaning of a big word they were all so taken up with admiration that it never occurred to any dog to doubt if it was the right one; and that was natural, because, for one thing, she answered up so promptly that it seemed like a dictionary speaking, and for another thing, where could they find out whether it was right or not? for she was the only cultivated dog there was. By and by, when I was older, she brought home the word Unintellectual, one time, and worked it pretty hard all the week at different gatherings, making much unhappiness and despondency; and it was at this time that I noticed that during that week she was asked for the meaning at eight different assemblages, and flashed out a fresh definition every time, which showed me that she had more presence of mind than culture, though I said nothing, of course. She had one word which she always kept on hand, and ready, like a life-preserver, a kind of emergency word to strap on when she was likely to get washed overboard in a sudden way—that was the word Synonymous. When she happened to fetch out a long word which had had its day weeks before and its prepared meanings gone to her dump-pile, if there was a stranger there of course it knocked him groggy for a couple of minutes, then he would come to, and by that time she would be away down the wind on another tack, and not expecting anything; so when he'd hail and ask her to cash in, I (the only dog on the inside of her game) could see her canvas flicker a moment—but only just a moment,—then it would belly out taut and full, and she would say, as calm as a summer's day, "It's synonymous with supererogation," or some godless long reptile of a word like that, and go placidly about and skim away on the next tack, perfectly comfortable, you know, and leave that stranger looking profane and embarrassed, and the initiated slatting the floor with their tails in unison and their faces transfigured with a holy joy.

And it was the same with phrases. She would drag home a whole phrase, if it had a grand sound, and play it six nights and two matinées, and explain it a new way every time,—which she had to, for all she cared for was the phrase; she wasn't interested in what it meant, and knew those dogs hadn't wit enough to catch her, anyway. Yes, she was a daisy! She got so she wasn't afraid of anything, she had such confidence in the ignorance of those creatures. She even brought anecdotes that she had heard the family and the dinner guests laugh and shout over; and as a rule she got the nub of one chestnut hitched onto another chestnut, where, of course, it didn't fit and hadn't any point; and when she delivered the nub she fell over and rolled on the floor and laughed and barked in the most insane way, while I could see that she was wondering to herself why it didn't seem as funny as it did when she first heard it. But no harm was done; the others rolled and barked too, privately ashamed of themselves for not seeing the point, and never suspecting that the fault was not with them and there wasn't any to see.

You can see by these things that she was of a rather vain and frivolous character; still, she had virtues, and enough to make up, I think. She had a kind heart and gentle ways, and never harbored resentments for injuries done her, but put them easily out of her mind and forgot them; and she taught her children her kindly way, and from her we learned also to be brave and prompt in time of danger, and not to run away, but face the peril that threatened friend or stranger, and help him the best we could without stopping to think what the cost might be to us. And she taught us not by words only, but by example, and that is the best way and the surest and the most lasting. Why, the brave things she did, the splendid things! she was just a soldier; and so modest about it—well, you couldn't help admiring her, and you couldn't help imitating her; not even a King Charles spaniel could remain entirely despicable in her society. So, as you see, there was more to her than her education.

II

When I was well grown, at last, I was sold and taken away, and I never saw her again. She was broken-hearted, and so was I, and we cried; but she comforted me as well as she could, and said we were sent into this world for a wise and good purpose, and must do our duties without repining, take our life as we might find it, live it for the best good of others, and never mind about the results; they were not our affair. She said men who did like this would have a noble and beautiful reward by and by in another world, and although we animals would not go there, to do well and right without reward would give to our brief lives a worthiness and dignity which in itself would be a reward. She had gathered these things from time to time when she had gone to the Sunday-school with the children, and had laid them up in her memory more carefully than she had done with those other words and phrases; and she had studied them deeply, for her good and ours. One may see by this that she had a wise and thoughtful head, for all there was so much lightness and vanity in it.

So we said our farewells, and looked our last upon each other through our tears; and the last thing she said—keeping it for the last to make me remember it the better, I think—was, "In memory of me, when there is a time of danger to another do not think of yourself, think of your mother, and do as she would do."

Do you think I could forget that? No.

III

It was such a charming home!—my new one; a fine great house, with pictures, and delicate decorations, and rich furniture, and no gloom anywhere, but all the wilderness of dainty colors lit up with flooding sunshine; and the spacious grounds around it, and the great garden—oh, greensward, and noble trees, and flowers, no end! And I was the same as a member of the family; and they loved me, and petted me, and did not give me a new name, but called me by my old one that was dear to me because my mother had given it me—Aileen Mavourneen. She got it out of a song; and the Grays knew that song, and said it was a beautiful name.

Mrs. Gray was thirty, and so sweet and so lovely, you cannot imagine it; and Sadie was ten, and just like her mother, just a darling slender little copy of her, with auburn tails down her back and short frocks; and the baby was a year old, and plump and dimpled, and fond of me, and never could get enough of hauling on my tail, and hugging me, and laughing out its innocent happiness; and Mr. Gray was thirty-eight, and tall and slender and handsome, a little bald in front, alert, quick in his movements, businesslike, prompt, decided, unsentimental, and with that kind of trim-chiselled face that just seems to glint and sparkle with frosty intellectuality! He was a renowned scientist. I do not know what the word means, but my mother would know how to use it and get effects. She would know how to depress a rat-terrier with it and make a lap-dog look sorry he came. But that is not the best one; the best one was Laboratory. My mother could organize a Trust on that one that would skin the tax-collars off the whole herd. The laboratory was not a book, or a picture, or a place to wash your hands in, as the college president's dog said—no, that is the lavatory; the laboratory is quite different, and is filled with jars, and bottles, and electrics, and wires, and strange machines; and every week other scientists came there and sat in the place, and used the machines, and discussed, and made what they called experiments and discoveries; and often I came, too, and stood around and listened, and tried to learn, for the sake of my mother, and in loving memory of her, although it was a pain to me, as realizing what she was losing out of her life and I gaining nothing at all; for try as I might, I was never able to make anything out of it at all.

Other times I lay on the floor in the mistress's workroom and slept, she gently using me for a footstool, knowing it pleased me, for it was a caress; other times I spent an hour in the nursery, and got well tousled and made happy; other times I watched by the crib there, when the baby was asleep and the nurse out for a few minutes on the baby's affairs; other times I romped and raced through the grounds and the garden with Sadie till we were tired out, then slumbered on the grass in the shade of a tree while she read her book; other times I went visiting among the neighbor dogs,—for there were some most pleasant ones not far away, and one very handsome and courteous and graceful one, a curly-haired Irish setter by the name of Robin Adair, who was a Presbyterian like me, and belonged to the Scotch minister.

The servants in our house were all kind to me and were fond of me, and so, as you see, mine was a pleasant life. There could not be happier dog than I was, nor a gratefuler one. I will say this for myself, for it is only the truth: I tried in all ways to do well and right, and honor my mother's memory and her teachings, and earn the happiness that had come to me, as best I could.

By and by came my little puppy, and then my cup was full, my happiness was perfect. It was the dearest little waddling thing, and so smooth and soft and velvety, and had such cunning little awkward paws, and such affectionate eyes, and such a sweet and innocent face; and it made me so proud to see how the children and their mother adored it, and fondled it, and exclaimed over every little wonderful thing it did. It did seem to me that life was just too lovely to—

Then came the winter. One day I was standing a watch in the nursery. That is to say, I was asleep on the bed. The baby was asleep in the crib, which was alongside the bed, on the side next the fireplace. It was the kind of crib that has a lofty tent over it made of a gauzy 'stuff that you can see through. The nurse was out, and we two sleepers were alone. A spark from the wood-fire was shot out, and it lit on the slope of the tent. I suppose a quiet interval followed, then a scream from the baby woke me, and there was that tent flaming up toward the ceiling! Before I could think, I sprang to the floor in my fright, and in a second was half-way to the door; but in the next half-second my mother's farewell was sounding in my ears, and I was back on the bed again. I reached my head through the flames and dragged the baby out by the waist-band, and tugged it along, and we fell to the floor together in a cloud of smoke; I snatched a new hold, and dragged the screaming little creature along and out at the door and around the bend of the hall, and was still tugging away, all excited and happy and proud, when the master's voice shouted,—

"Begone, you cursed beast!" and I jumped to save myself; but he was wonderfully quick, and chased me up, striking furiously at me with his cane, I dodging this way and that, in terror, and at last a strong blow fell upon my left fore leg, which made me shriek and fall, for the moment, helpless; the cane went up for another blow, but never descended, for the nurse's voice rang wildly out, "The nursery's on fire!" and the master rushed away in that direction, and my other bones were saved.

The pain was cruel, but, no matter, I must not lose any time; he might come back at any moment; so I limped on three legs to the other end of the hall, where there was a dark little stairway leading up into a garret where old boxes and such things were kept, as I had heard say, and where people seldom went. I managed to climb up there, then I searched my way through the dark amongst the piles of things, and hid in the secretest place I could find. It was foolish to be afraid there, yet still I was; so afraid that I held in and hardly even whimpered, though it would have been such a comfort to whimper, because that eases the pain, you know. But I could lick my leg, and that did me some good.

For half an hour there was a commotion down-stairs, and shoutings, and rushing footsteps, and then there was quiet again. Quiet for some minutes, and that was grateful to my spirit, for then my fears began to go down; and fears are worse than pains,—oh, much worse. Then came a sound that froze me! They were calling me—calling me by name—hunting for me!

It was muffled by distance, but that could not take the terror out of it, and it was the most dreadful sound to me that I had ever heard. It went all about, everywhere, down there: along the halls, through all the rooms, in both stories, and in the basement and the cellar; then outside, and further and further away—then back, and all about the house again, and I thought it would never, never stop. But at last it did, hours and hours after the vague twilight of the garret had long ago been blotted out by black darkness.

Then in that blessed stillness my terrors fell little by little away, and I was at peace and slept. It was a good rest I had, but I woke before the twilight had come again. I was feeling fairly comfortable, and I could think out a plan now. I made a very good one; which was, to creep down, all the way down the back stairs, and hide behind the cellar door, and slip out and escape when the iceman came at dawn, whilst he was inside filling the refrigerator; then I would hide all day, and start on my journey when night came; my journey to—well, anywhere where they would not know me and betray me to the master. I was feeling almost cheerful now; then suddenly I thought, Why what would life be without my puppy!

That was despair. There was no plan for me; I saw that; I must stay where I was; stay, and wait, and take what might come—it was not my affair; that was what life is,—my mother had said it. Then—well, then the calling began again! All my sorrows came back. I said to myself, the master will never forgive. I did not know what I had done to make him so bitter and so unforgiving, yet I judged it was something a dog could not understand, but which was clear to a man and dreadful.

They called and called—days and nights, it seemed to me. So long that the hunger and thirst near drove me mad, and I recognized that I was getting very weak. When you are this way you sleep a great deal, and I did. Once I woke in an awful fright—it seemed to me that the calling was right there in the garret! And so it was: it was Sadie's voice, and she was crying; my name was falling from her lips all broken, poor thing, and I could not believe my ears for the joy of it when I heard her say,

"Come back to us,—oh, come back to us, and forgive—it is all so sad without our—"

I broke in with *such* a grateful little yelp, and the next moment Sadie was plunging and stumbling through the darkness and the lumber and shouting for the family to hear, "She's found, she's found!"

The days that followed—well, they were wonderful. The mother and Sadie and the servants—why, they just seemed to worship me. They couldn't seem to make me a bed that was fine enough; and as for food, they couldn't be satisfied with anything but game and delicacies that were out of season; and every day the friends and neighbors flocked in to hear about my heroism—that was the name they called it by, and it means agriculture. I remember my mother pulling it on a kennel once, and explaining it that way, but didn't say what agriculture was, except that it was synonymous with intramural incandescence; and a dozen times a day Mrs. Gray and Sadie would tell the tale to newcomers, and say I risked my life to save the baby's, and both of us had burns to prove it, and then the company would pass me around and pet me and exclaim about me, and you could see the pride in the eyes of Sadie and her mother; and when the people wanted to know what made me limp, they looked ashamed and changed the subject, and sometimes when people hunted them this way and that way with questions about it, it looked to me as if they were going to cry.

And this was not all the glory; no, the master's friends came, a whole twenty of the most distinguished people, and had me in the laboratory, and discussed me as if I was a kind of discovery; and some of them said it was wonderful in a dumb beast, the finest exhibition of instinct they could call to mind; but the master said, with vehemence, "It's far above instinct; it's *reason*, and many a man, privileged to be saved and go with you and me to a better world by right of its possession, has less of it than this poor silly quadruped that's foreordained to perish"; and then he laughed, and said, "Why, look at me—I'm a sarcasm! bless you, with all my grand intelligence, the only thing I inferred was that the dog had gone mad and was destroying the child, whereas but for the beast's intelligence—it's *reason*, I tell you!—the child would have perished!"

They disputed and disputed, and *I* was the very centre and subject of it all, and I wished my mother could know that this grand honor had come to me; it would have made her proud.

Then they discussed optics, as they called it, and whether a certain injury to the brain would produce blindness or not, but they could not agree about it, and said they must test it by experiment by and by; and next they discussed plants, and that interested me, because in the summer Sadie and I had planted seeds—I helped her dig the holes, you know,—and after days and days a little shrub or a flower came up there, and it was a wonder how that could happen; but it did, and I wished I could talk,—I would have told those people about it and shown them how much I knew, and been all alive with the subject; but I didn't care for the optics; it was dull, and when they came back to it again it bored me, and I went to sleep.

Pretty soon it was spring, and sunny and pleasant and lovely, and the sweet mother and the children patted me and the puppy good-by, and went away on a journey and a visit to their kin, and the master wasn't any company for us, but we played together and had good times, and the servants were kind and friendly, so we got along quite happily and counted the days and waited for the family.

And one day those men came again, and said now for the test, and they took the puppy to the laboratory, and I limped three-leggedly along, too, feeling proud, for any attention shown the puppy was a pleasure to me, of course. They discussed and experimented, then suddenly the puppy shrieked, and they set him on the floor, and he went staggering around, with his head all bloody, and the master clapped his hands and shouted:

"There, I've won—confess it! He's as blind as a bat!"

And they all said,

"It's so—you've proved your theory, and suffering humanity owes you a great debt from henceforth," and they crowded around him, and wrung his hand cordially and thankfully, and praised him.

But I hardly saw or heard these things, for I ran at once to my little darling, and snuggled close to it where it lay, and licked the blood, and it put its head against mine, whimpering softly, and I knew in my heart it was a comfort to it in its pain and trouble to feel its mother's touch, though it could not see me. Then it drooped down, presently, and its little velvet nose rested upon the floor, and it was still, and did not move any more.

Soon the master stopped discussing a moment, and rang in the footman, and said, "Bury it in the far corner of the garden," and then went on with the discussion, and I trotted after the footman, very happy and grateful, for I knew the puppy was out of its pain now, because it was asleep. We went far down the garden to the furthest end, where the children and the nurse and the puppy and I used to play in the summer in the shade of a great elm, and there the footman dug a hole, and I saw he was going to plant the puppy, and I was glad, because it would grow and come up a fine handsome dog, like Robin Adair, and be a beautiful surprise for the family when they came home; so I tried to help him dig, but my lame leg was no good, being stiff, you know, and you have to have two, or it is no use. When the footman had finished and covered little Robin up, he patted my head, and there were tears in his eyes, and he said, "Poor little doggie, you SAVED *his* child."

I have watched two whole weeks, and he doesn't come up! This last week a fright has been stealing upon me. I think there is something terrible about this. I do not know what it is, but the fear makes me sick, and I cannot eat, though the servants bring me the best of food; and they pet me so, and even come in the night, and cry, and say, "Poor doggie—do give it up and come home; *don't* break our hearts!" and all this terrifies me the more, and makes me sure something has happened. And I am so weak; since yesterday I cannot stand on my feet any more. And within this hour the servants, looking toward the sun where it was sinking out of sight and the night chill coming on, said things I could not understand, but they carried something cold to my heart.

"Those poor creatures! They do not suspect. They will come home in the morning, and eagerly ask for the little doggie that did the brave deed, and who of us will be strong enough to say the truth to them: 'The humble little friend is gone where go the beasts that perish.'"

The Danger of Lying in Bed

The man in the ticket office said:

"Have an accident insurance ticket, also?"

"No," I said, after studying the matter over a little. "No, I believe not; I am going to be travelling by rail all day to-day. However, to-morrow I don't travel. Give me one for to-morrow."

The man looked puzzled. He said:

"But it is for accident insurance, and if you are going to travel by rail—"

"If I am going to travel by rail, I shan't need it. Lying at home in bed is the thing *I* am afraid of."

I had been looking into this matter. Last year I travelled twenty thousand miles, almost entirely by rail; the year before, I travelled over twenty-five thousand miles, half by sea and half by rail; and the year before that I travelled in the neighborhood of ten thousand miles, exclusively by rail. I suppose if I put in all the little odd journeys here and there, I may say I have travelled sixty thousand miles during the three years I have mentioned. *And never an accident.*

For a good while I said to myself every morning: "Now I have escaped thus far, and so the chances are just that much increased that I shall catch it this time. I will be shrewd, and buy an accident ticket." And to a dead moral certainty I drew a blank, and went to bed that night without a joint started or a bone splintered. I got tired of that sort of daily bother, and fell to buying accident tickets that were good for a month. I said to myself, "A man *can't* buy thirty blanks in one bundle."

But I was mistaken. There was never a prize in the lot. I could read of railway accidents every day—the newspaper atmosphere was foggy with them; but somehow they never came my way. I found I had spent a good deal of money in the accident business, and had nothing to show for it. My suspicions were aroused, and I began to hunt around for somebody that had won in this lottery. I found plenty of people who had invested, but not an individual that had ever had an accident or made a cent. I stopped buying accident tickets and went to ciphering. The result was astounding. THE PERIL LAY NOT IN TRAVELLING, BUT IN STAYING AT HOME.

I hunted up statistics, and was amazed to find that after all the glaring newspaper headings concerning railroad disasters, less than *three hundred* people had really lost their lives by those disasters in the preceding twelve months. The Erie road was set down as the most murderous in the list. It had killed forty-six—or twenty-six, I do not exactly remember which, but I know the number was double that of any other road. But the fact straightway suggested itself that the Erie was an immensely long road, and did more business than any other line in the country; so the double number of killed ceased to be matter for surprise.

By further figuring, it appeared that between New York and Rochester the Erie ran eight passenger trains each way every day—sixteen altogether; and carried a daily average of 6,000 persons. That is about a million in six months—the population of New York city. Well, the Erie kills from thirteen to twenty-three persons out of *its* million in six months; and in the same time 13,000 of New York's million die in their beds! My flesh crept, my hair stood on end. "This is appalling!" I said. "The danger isn't in travelling by rail, but in trusting to those deadly beds. I will never sleep in a bed again."

I had figured on considerably less than one-half the length of the Erie road. It was plain that the entire road must transport at least eleven or twelve thousand people every day. There are many short roads running out of Boston that do fully half as much; a great many such roads. There are many roads scattered about the Union that do a prodigious passenger business. Therefore it was fair to presume that an average of 2,500 passengers a day for each road in the country would be about correct. There are 846 railway lines in our country, and 846 times 2,500 are 2,115,000. So the railways of America move more than two millions of people every day; six hundred and fifty millions of people a year, without counting the Sundays. They do that, too—there is no question about it; though where they get the raw material is clear beyond the jurisdiction of my arithmetic; for I have hunted the census through and through, and I find that there are not that many people in the United States, by a matter of six hundred and ten millions at the very least. They must use some of the same people over again, likely.

San Francisco is one-eighth as populous as New York; there are 60 deaths a week in the former and 500 a week in the latter—if they have luck. That is 3,120 deaths a year in San Francisco, and eight times as many in New York—say about 25,000 or 26,000. The health of the two places is the same. So we will let it stand as a fair presumption that this will hold good all over the country, and that consequently 25,000 out of every million of people we have must die every year. That amounts to one-fortieth of our total population. One million of us, then, die annually. Out of this million ten or twelve thousand are stabbed, shot, drowned, hanged, poisoned, or meet a similarly violent death in some other popular way, such as perishing by kerosene lamp and hoop-skirt conflagrations, getting buried in coal mines, falling off housetops, breaking through church or lecture-room floors, taking patent medicines, or committing suicide in other forms. The Erie railroad kills from 23 to 46; the other 845 railroads kill an average of one-third of a man each; and the rest of that million, amounting in the aggregate to the appalling figure of nine hundred and eighty-seven thousand six hundred and thirty-one corpses, die naturally in their beds!

You will excuse me from taking any more chances on those beds. The railroads are good enough for me.

And my advice to all people is, Don't stay at home any more than you can help; but when you have *got* to stay at home a while, buy a package of those insurance tickets and sit up nights. You cannot be too cautious.

[One can see now why I answered that ticket agent in the manner recorded at the top of this sketch.]

The moral of this composition is, that thoughtless people grumble more than is fair about railroad management in the United States. When we consider that every day and night of the year full fourteen thousand railway trains of various kinds, freighted with life and armed with death, go thundering over the land, the marvel is, *not* that they kill three hundred human beings in a twelvemonth, but that they do not kill three hundred times three hundred!

What Is Man?

February, 1905. The studies for these papers were begun twenty-five or twenty-seven years ago. The papers were written seven years ago. I have examined them once or twice per year since and found them satisfactory. I have just examined them again, and am still satisfied that they speak the truth.

Every thought in them has been thought (and accepted as unassailable truth) by millions upon millions of men—and concealed, kept private. Why did they not speak out? Because they dreaded (*and could not bear*) the disapproval of the people around them. Why have not I published? The same reason has restrained me, I think. I can find no other.

I

a. Man the Machine *b. Personal Merit*

[The Old Man and the Young Man had been conversing. The Old Man had asserted that the human being is merely a machine, and nothing more. The Young Man objected, and asked him to go into particulars and furnish his reasons for his position.]

OLD MAN. What are the materials of which a steam engine is made?

YOUNG MAN. Iron, steel, brass, white-metal, and so on.
O. M. Where are these found?
Y. M. In the rocks.
O. M. In a pure state?
Y. M. No—in ores.
O. M. Are the metals suddenly deposited in the ores?
Y. M. No—it is the patient work of countless ages.
O. M. You could make the engine out of the rocks themselves?
Y. M. Yes, a brittle one and not valuable.
O. M. You would not require much, of such an engine as that?
Y. M. No—substantially nothing.
O. M. To make a fine and capable engine, how would you proceed?
Y. M. Drive tunnels and shafts into the hills; blast out the iron ore; crush it, smelt it, reduce it to pig-iron; put some of it through the Bessemer process and make steel of it. Mine and treat and combine the several metals of which brass is made.
O. M. Then?
Y. M. Out of the perfected result, build the fine engine.
O. M. You would require much, of this one?
Y. M. Oh, indeed yes.
O. M. It could drive lathes, drills, planers, punches, polishers, in a word all the cunning machines of a great factory?
Y. M. It could.
O. M. What could the stone engine do?
Y. M. Drive a sewing-machine, possibly—nothing more, perhaps.
O. M. Men would admire the other engine and rapturously praise it?
Y. M. Yes.
O. M. But not the stone one?
Y. M. No.
O. M. The merits of the metal machine would be far above those of the stone one?
Y. M. Of course.
O. M. Personal merits?
Y. M. *Personal* merits? How do you mean?

O. M. It would be personally entitled to the credit of its own performance?

Y. M. The engine? Certainly not.

O. M. Why not?

Y. M. Because its performance is not personal. It is a result of the law of its construction. It is not a *merit* that it does the things which it is set to do—it can't *help* doing them.

O. M. And it is not a personal demerit in the stone machine that it does so little?

Y. M. Certainly not. It does no more and no less than the law of its make permits and compels it to do. There is nothing *personal* about it; it cannot choose. In this process of "working up to the matter" is it your idea to work up to the proposition that a man and a machine are about the same thing, and that there is no personal merit in the performance of either?

O. M. Yes—but do not be offended; I am meaning no offence. What makes the grand difference between the stone engine and the steel one? Shall we call it training, education? Shall we call the stone engine a savage and the steel one a civilized man? The original rock contained the stuff of which the steel one was built—but along with it a lot of sulphur and stone and other obstructing inborn heredities, brought down from the old geologic ages—prejudices, let us call them. Prejudices which nothing within the rock itself had either *power* to remove or any *desire* to remove. Will you take note of that phrase?

Y. M. Yes. I have written it down: "Prejudices which nothing within the rock itself had either power to remove or any desire to remove." Go on.

O. M. Prejudices which must be removed by *outside influences* or not at all. Put that down.

Y. M. Very well: "Must be removed by outside influences or not at all." Go on.

O. M. The iron's prejudice against ridding itself of the cumbering rock. To make it more exact, the iron's absolute *indifference* as to whether the rock be removed or not. Then comes the *outside influence* and grinds the rock to powder and sets the ore free. The *iron* in the ore is still captive. An *outside influence* smelts it free of the clogging ore. The iron is emancipated iron, now, but indifferent to further progress. An *outside influence* beguiles it into the Bessemer furnace and refines it into steel of the first quality. It is educated, now—its training is complete. And it has reached its limit. By no possible process can it be educated into *gold*. Will you set that down?

Y. M. Yes: "Everything has its limit—iron ore cannot be educated into gold."

O. M. There are gold men, and tin men, and copper men, and leaden men, and steel men, and so on—and each has the limitations of his nature, his heredities, his training and his environment. You can build engines out of each of those metals, and they will all perform, but you must not require the weak ones to do equal work with the stronger ones. In each case, to get the best results, you must free the metal from its obstructing prejudicial ores by education—smelting, refining, and so forth.

Y. M. You have arrived at man, now?

O. M. Yes. Man the machine—man, the impersonal engine. Whatsoever a man is, is due to his *make*, and to the *influences* brought to bear upon it by his heredities, his habitat, his associations. He is moved, directed, COMMANDED, by *exterior* influences—*solely*. He *originates* nothing, himself—not even an opinion, not even a thought.

Y. M. Oh, come! Where did I get my opinion that this which you are talking is all foolishness?

O. M. It is a quite natural opinion—indeed an inevitable opinion—but *you* did not create the materials out of which it is formed. They are odds and ends of thoughts, impressions, feelings, gathered unconsciously from a thousand books, a thousand conversations, and from streams of thought and feeling which have flowed down into your heart and brain out of the hearts and brains of ten centuries of ancestors. *Personally* you did not create even the smallest microscopic fragment of the materials out of which your opinion is made; and personally you cannot claim even the slender merit of *putting the borrowed materials together.* That was done—*automatically*—by your mental machinery, in strict accordance with the law of that machinery's construction. And you not only did not make that machinery yourself, but you have *not even any command over it*.

Y. M. This is too much. You think I could have formed no opinion but that one?

O. M. Spontaneously? No. And *you did not form that one*; your machinery did it for you—automatically and instantly, without reflection or the need of it.

Y. M. Suppose I had reflected? How then?

O. M. Suppose you try.

Y. M. (*After a quarter of an hour.*) I have reflected.

O. M. You mean you have tried to change your opinion—as an experiment?

Y. M. Yes.

O. M. With success?

Y. M. No. It remains the same; it is impossible to change it.

O. M. I am sorry, but you see, yourself, that your mind is merely a machine, nothing more. You have no command over it, it has no command over itself—it is worked *solely from the outside*. That is the law of its make; it is the law of all machines.

Y. M. Can't I *ever* change one of these automatic opinions?

O. M. No. You can't, yourself, but *exterior influences* can do it.

Y. M. And exterior ones *only*?

O. M. Yes—exterior ones only.

Y. M. That position is untenable—I may say ludicrously untenable.

O. M. What makes you think so?

Y. M. I don't merely think it, I know it. Suppose I resolve to enter upon a course of thought, and study, and reading, with the deliberate purpose of changing that opinion; and suppose I succeed. *That* is not the work of an exterior impulse, the whole of it is mine and personal; for I originated the project.

O. M. Not a shred of it. *It grew out of this talk with me.* But for that it would never have occurred to you. No man ever originates anything. All his thoughts, all his impulses, come *from the outside.*

Y. M. It's an exasperating subject. The *first* man had original thoughts, anyway; there was nobody to draw from.

O. M. It is a mistake. Adam's thoughts came to him from the outside. *You* have a fear of death. You did not invent that—you got it from outside, from talk and teaching. Adam had no fear of death—none in the world.

Y. M. Yes he had.

O. M. When he was created?

Y. M. No.

O. M. When, then?

Y. M. When he was threatened with it.

O. M. Then it came from the *outside.* Adam is quite big enough; let us not try to make a god of him. *None but gods have ever had a thought which did not come from the outside.* Adam probably had a good head, but it was of no sort of use to him until it was filled up *from the outside.* He was not able to invent the triflingest little thing with it. He had not a shadow of a notion of the difference between good and evil—he had to get the idea *from the outside.* Neither he nor Eve was able to originate the idea that it was immodest to go naked: the knowledge came in with the apple *from the outside.* A man's brain is so constructed that *it can originate nothing whatever.* It can only use material obtained *outside.* It is merely a machine; and it works automatically, not by will power. *It has no command over itself, its owner has no command over it.*

Y. M. Well, never mind Adam; but certainly Shakespeare's creations—

O. M. No, you mean Shakespeare's *imitations*. Shakespeare created nothing. He correctly observed, and he marvelously painted. He exactly portrayed people whom *God* had created, but he created none himself. Let us spare him the slander of charging him with trying. Shakespeare could not create. *He was a machine, and machines do not create.*

Y. M. Where *was* his excellence, then?

O. M. In this. He was not a sewing-machine, like you and me, he was a Gobelin loom. The threads and the colors came into him *from the outside*; outside influences, suggestions, *experiences*, (reading, seeing plays, playing plays, borrowing ideas, and so on), framed the patterns in his mind and started up its complex and admirable machinery, and *it automatically* turned out that pictured and gorgeous fabric which still compels the astonishment of the world. If Shakespeare had been born and bred on a barren and unvisited rock in the ocean his mighty intellect would have had no *outside material* to work with, and could have invented none; and *no outside influences*, teachings, mouldings, persuasions, inspirations, of a valuable sort, and could have invented none; and so, Shakespeare would have produced nothing. In Turkey he would have produced something—something up to the highest limit of Turkish influences, associations and training. In France he would have produced something better—something up to the highest limit of the French influences and training. In England he rose to the highest limit attainable through the *outside helps afforded by that land's ideals, influences and training*. You and I are but sewing-machines. We must turn out what we can; we must do our endeavor, and care nothing at all when the unthinking reproach us for not turning out Gobelins.

Y. M. And so we are mere machines! And machines may not boast, nor feel proud of their performance, nor claim personal merit for it, nor applause and praise. It is an infamous doctrine.

O. M. It isn't a doctrine, it is merely a fact.

Y. M. I suppose, then, there is no more merit in being brave than in being a coward?

O. M. *Personal* merit? No. A brave man does not *create* his bravery. He is entitled to no personal credit for possessing it. It is born to him. A baby born with a billion dollars—where is the personal merit in that? A baby born with nothing—where is the personal demerit in that? The one is fawned upon, admired, worshiped, by sycophants, the other is neglected and despised—where is the sense in it?

Y. M. Sometimes a timid man sets himself the task of conquering his cowardice and becoming brave—and succeeds. What do you say to that?

O. M. That it shows the value of *training in right directions over training in wrong ones.* Inestimably valuable is training, influence, education, in right directions—*training one's self-approbation to elevate its ideals.*

Y. M. But as to merit—the personal merit of the victorious coward's project and achievement?

O. M. There isn't any. In the world's view he is a worthier man than he was before, but *he* didn't achieve the change—the merit of it is not his.

Y. M. Whose, then?

O. M. His *make,* and the influences which wrought upon it from the outside.

Y. M. His make?

O. M. Yes. To start with, he was *not* utterly and completely a coward, or the influences would have had nothing to work upon. He was not afraid of a cow, though perhaps of a bull; not afraid of a woman, but afraid of a man. There was something to build upon. There was a *seed.* No seed, no plant. Did he make that seed himself, or was it born in him? It was no merit of *his* that the seed was there.

Y. M. Well, anyway, the idea of *cultivating* it, the resolution to cultivate it, was meritorious, and he originated that.

O. M. He did nothing of the kind. It came whence *all*

impulses, good or bad, come—from *outside*. If that timid man had lived all his life in a community of human rabbits; had never read of brave deeds; had never heard speech of them; had never heard any one praise them nor express envy of the heroes that had done them, he would have had no more idea of bravery than Adam had of modesty, and it could never by any possibility have occurred to him to *resolve* to become brave. He *could not originate the idea*—it had to come to him from the *outside*. And so, when he heard bravery extolled and cowardice derided, it woke him up. He was ashamed. Perhaps his sweetheart turned up her nose and said "I am told that you are a coward!" It was not *he* that turned over the new leaf—she did it for him. *He* must not strut around in the merit of it—it is not his.

Y. M. But anyway he reared the plant after she watered the seed.

O. M. No. *Outside influences* reared it. At the command—and trembling—he marched out into the field—with other soldiers and in the daytime, not alone and in the dark. He had the *influence of example*, he drew courage from his comrades' courage; he was afraid, and wanted to run, but he did not dare; he was *afraid* to run, with all those soldiers looking on. He was progressing, you see—the moral fear of shame had risen superior to the physical fear of harm. By the end of the campaign experience will have taught him that not *all* who go into battle get hurt—an outside influence which will be helpful to him; and he will also have learned how sweet it is to be praised for courage and be huzza'd at with tear-choked voices as the war-worn regiment marches past the worshiping multitude with the flags flying and the drums beating. After that he will be as securely brave as any veteran in the army—and there will not be a shade nor suggestion of *personal merit* in it anywhere; it will all have come from the *outside*. The Victoria Cross breeds more heroes than—

Y. M. Hang it, where is the sense in his becoming brave if he is to get no credit for it?

O. M. Your question will answer itself presently. It involves an important detail of man's make which we have not yet touched upon.

Y. M. What detail is that?

O. M. The impulse which moves a person to do things—the only impulse that ever moves a person to do a thing.

Y. M. The *only* one! Is there but one?

O. M. That is all. There is only one.

Y. M. Well, certainly that is a strange enough doctrine. What is the sole impulse that ever moves a person to do a thing?

O. M. The impulse to *content his own spirit*—the *necessity* of contenting his own spirit and *winning its approval.*

Y. M. Oh, come, that won't do!

O. M. Why won't it?

Y. M. Because it puts him in the attitude of always looking out for his own comfort and advantage; whereas an unselfish man often does a thing solely for another person's good when it is a positive disadvantage to himself.

O. M. It is a mistake. The act must do *him* good, first; otherwise he will not do it. He may *think* he is doing it solely for the other person's sake, but it is not so; he is contenting his own spirit *first*—the other person's benefit has to always take *second* place.

Y. M. What a fantastic idea! What becomes of self-sacrifice? Please answer me that.

O. M. What is self-sacrifice?

Y. M. The doing good to another person where no shadow nor suggestion of benefit to one's self can result from it.

II

Man's Sole Impulse—The Securing of His Own Approval

O. M. There have been instances of it—you think?

Y. M. *Instances?* Millions of them!

O. M. You have not jumped to conclusions? You have examined them—critically?

Y. M. They don't need it; the acts themselves reveal the golden impulse back of them.

O. M. For instance?

Y. M. Well, then, for instance. Take the case in the book here. The man lives three miles up town. It is bitter cold, blowing hard, snowing hard, midnight. He is about to enter the horse-car when a gray and ragged old woman, a touching picture of misery, puts out her lean hand and begs for rescue from hunger and death. The man finds that he has but a quarter in his pocket, but he does not hesitate; he gives it her and trudges home through the storm. There—it is noble, it is beautiful; its grace is marred by no fleck or blemish or suggestion of self-interest.

O. M. What makes you think that?

Y. M. Pray what else could I think? Do you imagine that there is some other way of looking at it?

O. M. Can you put yourself in the man's place and tell me what he felt and what he thought?

Y. M. Easily. The sight of that suffering old face pierced his generous heart with a sharp pain. He could not bear it. He could endure the three-mile walk in the storm, but he could not endure the tortures his conscience would suffer if he turned his back and left that poor old creature to perish. He would not have been able to sleep, for thinking of it.

O. M. What was his state of mind on his way home?

Y. M. It was a state of joy which only the self-sacrificer knows. His heart sang, he was unconscious of the storm.

O. M. He slept well?

Y. M. One cannot doubt it.

O. M. Very well. Now let us add up the details and see how much he got for his twenty-five cents. Let us try to find out the *real* why of his making the investment. In the first place *he* couldn't bear the pain which the suffering old face gave him. So he was thinking of *his* pain—this good man. He must buy a salve for it. If he did not succor the old woman *his* conscience would torture him all the way home. Thinking of *his* pain again. He must buy relief from that. If he didn't relieve the old woman *he* would not get any sleep. He must buy some sleep—still thinking of *himself,* you see. Thus, to sum up, he bought himself free of a sharp pain in his heart, he bought himself free of the tortures of a waiting conscience, he bought a whole night's sleep—all for twenty-five cents! This able trader got a hundred dollars' worth of clean profit out of an investment of twenty-five cents. It should make Wall street ashamed of itself. On his way home his heart was joyful, and it sang—profit on top of profit! The impulse which moved the man to succor the old woman was—*first*—to *content his own spirit;* secondly, to relieve *her* sufferings. Is it your opinion that men's acts proceed from one central and unchanging and inalterable impulse, or from a variety of impulses?

Y. M. From a variety, of course—some high and fine and noble, others not. What is your opinion?

O. M. That there is but *one* law, one source.

Y. M. That both the noblest impulses and the basest proceed from that one source?

O. M. Yes.

Y. M. Will you put that law into words?

O. M. Yes. This is the law. Keep it in your mind. *From his cradle to his grave a man never does a single thing which has any* FIRST AND FOREMOST *object but one—to secure peace of mind, spiritual comfort, for* HIMSELF.

Y. M. Come! He never does anything for any one else's comfort, spiritual or physical?

O. M. No. *Except on those distinct terms*—that it shall *first* secure *his own* spiritual comfort. Otherwise, he will not do it.

Y. M. It will be easy to expose the falsity of that proposition.

O. M. For instance?

Y. M. Take that noble passion, love of country, patriotism. A man who loves peace and dreads pain, leaves his pleasant home and his weeping family and marches out to manfully expose himself to hunger, cold, wounds and death. Is that seeking spiritual comfort?

O. M. He loves peace and dreads pain?

Y. M. Yes.

O. M. Then perhaps there is something that he loves *more* than he loves peace—*the approval of his neighbors and the public.* And perhaps there is something which he dreads more than he dreads pain—the *disapproval* of his neighbors and the public. If he is sensitive to shame he will go to the field—not because his spirit will be *entirely* comfortable there, but because it will be more comfortable there than it would be if he remained at home. He will always do the thing which will bring him the *most* mental comfort—for that is *the sole law of his life.* He leaves the weeping family behind; he is sorry to make them uncomfortable, but not sorry enough to sacrifice his *own* comfort to secure theirs.

Y. M. Do you really believe that mere public opinion could force a timid and peaceful man to—

O. M. Go to the wars? Yes—public opinion can force some men to do *anything*.

Y. M. *Anything?*

O. M. Yes—anything.

Y. M. I don't believe that. Can it force a right-principled man to do a wrong thing?

O. M. Yes.

Y. M. Can it force a kind man to do a cruel thing?

O. M. Yes.

Y. M. Give an instance.

O. M. Alexander Hamilton was a conspicuously high-principled man. He regarded dueling as wrong, and as opposed to the teachings of religion—but in deference to *public opinion* he fought a duel. He deeply loved his family, but to buy public approval he treacherously deserted them and threw his life away, ungenerously leaving them to life-long sorrow in order that he might stand well with a foolish world. In the then condition of the public standards of honor he could not have been comfortable with the stigma upon him of having refused to fight. The teachings of religion, his devotion to his family, his kindness of heart, his high principles, all went for nothing when they stood in the way of his spiritual comfort. A man will do *anything*, no matter what it is, *to secure his spiritual comfort*; and he can neither be forced nor persuaded to any act which has not that goal for its object. Hamilton's act was compelled by the inborn necessity of contenting his own spirit; in this it was like all the other acts of his life, and like all the acts of all men's lives. Do you see where the kernel of the matter lies? A man cannot be comfortable without *his own* approval. He will secure the largest share possible of that, at all costs, all sacrifices.

Y. M. A minute ago you said Hamilton fought the duel to get the *public* approval.

O. M. I did. By refusing to fight the duel he could have secured his family's approval and a large share of his own; but the public approval was more valuable in his eyes than all other approvals put together—in the earth or above it; to secure that would furnish him the *most* comfort of mind, the most *self*-approval; so he sacrificed all other values to get it.

Y. M. Some noble souls have refused to fight duels, and have manfully braved the public contempt.

O. M. They acted *according to their make*. They valued their principles and the approval of their families *above* the public approval. They took the thing they valued *most* and let the rest go. They took what would give them the *largest* share of *personal contentment and approval*—a man *always* does. Public opinion cannot force that kind of men to go to the wars. When they go, it is for other reasons. Other spirit-contenting reasons.

Y. M. Always spirit-contenting reasons?

O. M. There are no others.

Y. M. When a man sacrifices his life in trying to save a little child from a burning building, what do you call that?

O. M. When he does it, it is the law of *his* make. *He* can't bear to see the child in that peril, (a man of a different make *could*), and so he tries to save the child, and loses his life. But he has got what he was after—*his own approval*.

Y. M. What do you call Love, Hate, Charity, Revenge, Humanity, Magnanimity, Forgiveness?

O. M. Different results of the one Master Impulse: the necessity of securing one's self-approval. They wear diverse clothes and are subject to diverse moods, but in whatsoever ways they masquerade they are the *same person* all the time. To change the figure, the *compulsion* that moves a man—and there is but the one—is the necessity of securing the contentment of his own spirit. When it stops, the man is dead.

Y. M. This is foolishness. Love—

O. M. Why, love is that impulse, that law, in its most uncompromising form. It will squander life and everything else on its object. Not *primarily* for the object's sake, but for *its own*. When its object is happy *it* is happy—and that is what it is unconsciously after.

Y. M. You do not even except the lofty and gracious passion of mother-love?

O. M. No, *it* is the absolute slave of that law. The mother will go naked to clothe her child; she will starve that it may have food; suffer torture to save it from pain; die that it may live. She takes a living *pleasure* in making these sacrifices. *She does it for that reward*—that self-approval, that contentment, that peace, that comfort. *She would do it for your child* IF SHE COULD GET THE SAME PAY.

Y. M. This is an infernal philosophy of yours.

O. M. It isn't a philosophy, it is a fact.

Y. M. Of course you must admit that there are some acts which—

O. M. No. There is *no* act, large or small, fine or mean, which springs from any motive but the one—the necessity of appeasing and contenting one's own spirit.

Y. M. The world's philanthropists—

O. M. I honor them, I uncover my head to them—from habit and training; but *they* could not know comfort or happiness or self-approval if they did not work and spend for the unfortunate. It makes *them* happy to see others happy; and so with money and labor they buy what they are after—*happiness, self-approval*. Why don't misers do the same thing? Because they can get a thousandfold more happiness by *not* doing it. There is no other reason. They follow the law of their make.

Y. M. What do you say of duty for duty's sake?

O. M. That *it does not exist*. Duties are not performed for duty's *sake*, but because their *neglect* would make the man *uncomfortable*. A man performs but *one* duty—the duty of contenting his spirit, the duty of making himself agreeable to himself. If he can most satisfyingly perform this sole and only duty by *helping* his neighbor, he will do it; if he can most satisfyingly perform it by *swindling* his neighbor, he will do that. But always he looks out for Number One—*first*; the effects upon others are a *secondary* matter. Men pretend to self-sacrifices, but this is a thing which, in the ordinary value of the phrase, *does not exist and has not existed*. A man often honestly *thinks* he is sacrificing himself merely and solely for some one else, but he is deceived: his bottom impulse is to content a requirement of his nature and training, and thus acquire peace for his soul.

Y. M. Apparently, then, all men, both good and bad ones, devote their lives to contenting their consciences?

O. M. Yes. That is a good enough name for it: Conscience—that independent Sovereign, that insolent absolute Monarch inside of a man who is the man's Master.

There are all kinds of consciences, because there are all kinds of men. You satisfy an assassin's conscience in one way, a philanthropist's in another, a miser's in another, a burglar's in still another. As a *guide* or *incentive* to any authoritatively prescribed line of morals or conduct, (leaving *training* out of the account), a man's conscience is totally valueless. I knew a kind-hearted Kentuckian whose self-approval was lacking—whose conscience was troubling him, to phrase it with exactness—*because he had neglected to kill a certain man*—a man whom he had never seen. The stranger had killed this man's friend in a fight, this man's Kentucky training made it his duty to kill the stranger for it. He neglected this duty—kept dodging it, shirking it, putting it off, and his unrelenting conscience kept persecuting him for this conduct. At last, to get ease of mind, comfort, self-approval, he hunted up the stranger and took his life. It was an immense act of *self-sacrifice,* (as per the usual definition), for he did not want to do it, and he never would have done it if he could have bought a contented spirit and an unworried mind at smaller cost. But we are so made that we will pay *anything* for that contentment—even another man's life.

Y. M. You spoke a moment ago of *trained* consciences. You mean that we are not *born* with consciences competent to guide us aright?

O. M. If we were, children and savages would know right from wrong, and not have to be taught it.

Y. M. But consciences can be *trained?*

O. M. Yes.

Y. M. Of course by parents, teachers, the pulpit, and books.

O. M. Yes—they do their share; they do what they can.

Y. M. And the rest is done by—

O. M. Oh, a million unnoticed influences—for good or bad; influences which work without rest during every waking moment of a man's life, from cradle to grave.

Y. M. You have tabulated these?

O. M. Many of them—yes.

Y. M. Will you read me the result?

O. M. Another time, yes. It would take an hour.

Y. M. A conscience can be trained to shun evil and prefer good?

O. M. Yes.

Y. M. But will prefer it for spirit-contenting reasons only?

O. M. It *can't* be trained to do a thing for any *other* reason. The thing is impossible.

Y. M. There *must* be a genuinely and utterly self-sacrificing act recorded in human history somewhere.

O. M. You are young. You have many years before you. Search one out.

Y. M. It does seem to me that when a man sees a fellow-being struggling in the water and jumps in at the risk of his life to save him—

O. M. Wait. Describe the *man*. Describe the *fellow-being*. State if there is an *audience* present; or if they are *alone*.

Y. M. What have these things to do with the splendid act?

O. M. Very much. Shall we suppose, as a beginning, that the two are alone, in a solitary place, at midnight?

Y. M. If you choose.

O. M. And that the fellow-being is the man's daughter?

Y. M. Well, n-no—make it some one else.

O. M. A filthy, drunken ruffian, then?

Y. M. I see. Circumstances alter cases. I suppose that if there was no audience to observe the act, the man wouldn't perform it.

O. M. But there is here and there a man who *would*. People, for instance, like the man who lost his life trying to save the child from the fire; and like the man who gave the needy old woman his 25 cents and walked home in the storm—there are here and there men like that who would do it. And why? Because they couldn't *bear* to see a fellow-being struggling in the water and not jump in and help. It would give *them* pain. They would save the fellow-being on that account. *They wouldn't do it otherwise*. They strictly obey the law which I have been insisting upon. You must remember and always distinguish the people who *can't bear* things from the people who *can*. It will throw light upon a number of apparently "self-sacrificing" cases.

Y. M. Oh, dear, it's all so disgusting.

O. M. Yes. And so true.

Y. M. Come—take the good boy who does things which he doesn't want to do, in order to gratify his mother.

O. M. He does seven-tenths of the act because it gratifies *him* to gratify his mother. Throw the bulk of advantage the other way and the good boy would not do the act. He *must* obey the iron law. None can escape it.

Y. M. Well, take the case of a bad boy who—

O. M. You needn't mention it, it is a waste of time. It is no matter about the bad boy's act. Whatever it was, he had a spirit-contenting reason for it. Otherwise you have been misinformed, and he didn't do it.

Y. M. It is very exasperating. A while ago you said that a man's conscience is not a born judge of morals and conduct, but has to be taught and trained. Now I think a conscience can get drowsy and lazy, but I don't think it can go wrong; and if you wake it up—

A LITTLE STORY

O. M. I will tell you a little story:

Once upon a time an Infidel was a guest in the house of a Christian widow whose little boy was ill and near to death. The Infidel often watched by the bedside and entertained the boy with talk, and he used these opportunities to satisfy a strong longing of his nature—that desire which is in us all to better other people's condition by having them think as we think. He was successful. But the dying boy, in his last moments, reproached him and said—

"I believed, and was happy in it; you have taken my belief away, and my comfort. Now I have nothing left, and I die

miserable; for the things which you have told me do not take the place of that which I have lost."

And the mother, also, reproached the Infidel, and said—

"My child is forever lost, and my heart is broken. How could you do this cruel thing? We had done you no harm, but only kindness; we made our house your home, you were welcome to all we had, and this is our reward."

The heart of the Infidel was filled with remorse for what he had done, and he said—

"It was wrong—I see it now; but I was only trying to do him good. In my view he was in error; it seemed my duty to teach him the truth."

Then the mother said—

"I had taught him, all his little life, what I believed to be the truth, and in his believing faith both of us were happy. Now he is dead—and lost; and I am miserable. Our faith came down to us through centuries of believing ancestors; what right had you, or any one, to disturb it? Where was your honor, where was your shame?"

Y. M. He was a miscreant, and deserved death!

O. M. He thought so himself, and said so.

Y. M. Ah—you see, *his conscience was awakened!*

O. M. Yes—his Self-Disapproval was. It *pained* him to see the mother suffer. He was sorry he had done a thing which brought *him* pain. It did not occur to him to think of the mother when he was mis-teaching the boy, for he was absorbed in providing *pleasure* for himself, then. Providing it by satisfying what he believed to be a call of duty.

Y. M. Call it what you please, it is to me a case of *awakened conscience*. That awakened conscience could never get itself into that species of trouble again. A cure like that is a *permanent* cure.

O. M. Pardon—I had not finished the story. We are creatures of *outside influences*—we originate *nothing* within. Whenever we take a new line of thought and drift into a new line of belief and action, the impulse is *always* suggested from the *outside*. Remorse so preyed upon the Infidel that it dissolved his harshness toward the boy's religion and made him come to regard it with tolerance, next with kindness, and presently with tenderness, for the boy's sake and the mother's. Finally he found himself examining it. From that moment his progress in his new trend was steady and rapid. He became a believing Christian. And now his remorse for having robbed the dying boy of his faith and his salvation was bitterer than ever. It gave him no rest, no peace. He *must* have rest and peace—it is the law of our nature. There seemed but one way to get it; he must devote himself to saving imperiled souls. He became a missionary. He landed in a pagan country ill and helpless. A native widow took him into her humble home and nursed him back to convalescence. Then her young boy was taken hopelessly ill, and the grateful missionary helped her tend him. Here was his first opportunity to repair a part of the wrong done to the other boy by doing a precious service for this one by undermining his foolish faith in his false gods. He was successful. But the dying boy in his last moments reproached him, and said—

"I believed, and was happy in it; you have taken my belief away, and my comfort. Now I have nothing left, and I die miserable; for the things which you have told me do not take the place of that which I have lost."

And the mother, also, reproached the missionary, and said—

"My child is forever lost, and my heart is broken. How could you do this cruel thing? We had done you no harm, but only kindness; we made our house your home, you were welcome to all we had, and this is our reward."

The heart of the missionary was filled with remorse for what he had done, and he said—

"It was wrong—I see it now; but I was only trying to do him good. In my view he was in error; it seemed my duty to teach him the truth."

Then the mother said—

"I had taught him, all his little life, what I believed to be the truth, and in his believing faith both of us were happy. Now he is dead—and lost; and I am miserable. Our faith came down to us through centuries of believing ancestors; what right had you, or any one, to disturb it? Where was your honor, where was your shame?"

The missionary's anguish of remorse and sense of treachery were as bitter and persecuting and unappeasable, now, as they had been in the former case. The story is finished. What is your comment?

Y. M. The man's conscience was a fool! It was morbid. It didn't know right from wrong.

O. M. I am not sorry to hear you say that. If you grant that *one* man's conscience doesn't know right from wrong, it is an admission that there are others like it. This single admission pulls down the whole doctrine of infallibility of judgment in consciences. Meantime there is one thing which I ask you to notice.

Y. M. What is that?

O. M. That in both cases the man's *act* gave him no spiritual discomfort, and that he was quite satisfied with it and got pleasure out of it. But afterward when it resulted in *pain* to *him,* he was sorry. Sorry it had inflicted pain upon the others, *but for no reason under the sun except that their pain gave* HIM *pain.* Our consciences take *no* notice of pain inflicted upon others until it reaches a point where it gives pain to *us*. In *all* cases without exception we are absolutely indifferent to another person's pain until his sufferings make us uncomfortable. Many an infidel would not have been troubled by that Christian mother's distress. Don't you believe that?

Y. M. Yes. You might almost say it of the *average* infidel, I think.

O. M. And many a missionary, sternly fortified by his sense of duty, would not have been troubled by the pagan mother's distress—Jesuit missionaries in Canada in the early French times, for instance; see episodes quoted by Parkman.

Y. M. Well, let us adjourn. Where have we arrived?

O. M. At this. That we (mankind), have ticketed ourselves with a number of qualities to which we have given misleading names. Love, Hate, Charity, Compassion, Avarice, Benevolence, and so on. I mean, we attach misleading *meanings* to the names. They are all forms of self-contentment, self-gratification, but the names so disguise them that they distract our attention from the fact. Also, we have smuggled a word into the dictionary which ought not to be there at all—Self-Sacrifice. It describes a thing which does not exist. But worst of all, we ignore and never mention the Sole Impulse which dictates and compels a man's every act: the imperious necessity of securing his own approval, in every emergency and at all costs. To it we owe all that we are. It is our breath, our heart, our blood. It is our only spur, our whip, our goad, our only impelling power; we have no other. Without it we should be mere inert images, corpses; no one would do anything, there would be no progress, the world would stand still. We ought to stand reverently uncovered when the name of that stupendous power is uttered.

Y. M. I am not convinced.

O. M. You will be, when you think.

III

Instances in Point

O. M. Have you given thought to the Gospel of Self-Approval since we talked?

Y. M. I have.

O. M. It was I that moved you to it. That is to say, an *outside influence* moved you to it—not one that originated in your own head. Will you try to keep that in mind and not forget it?

Y. M. Yes. Why?

O. M. Because by and by, in one of our talks, I wish to further impress upon you that neither you, nor I, nor any man ever originates a thought in his own head. *The utterer of a thought always utters a second-hand one.*

Y. M. Oh, now—

O. M. Wait. Reserve your remark till we get to that part of our discussion—to-morrow or next day, say. Now, then, you have been considering the proposition that no act is ever born of any but a self-contenting impulse—(primarily). You have sought. What have you found?

Y. M. I have not been very fortunate. I have examined many fine and apparently self-sacrificing deeds in romances and biographies, but—

O. M. Under searching analysis the ostensible self-sacrifice disappeared? It naturally would.

Y. M. But here in this novel is one which seems to promise. In the Adirondack woods is a wage-earner and lay preacher in the lumber-camps who is of noble character and deeply religious. An earnest and practical laborer in the New York slums comes up there on vacation—he is leader of a section of the University Settlement. Holme, the lumberman, is fired with a desire to throw away his excellent worldly prospects and go down and save souls on the East Side. He counts it happiness to make this sacrifice for the glory of God and for the cause of Christ. He resigns his place, makes the sacrifice cheerfully, and goes to the East Side and preaches Christ and Him crucified every day and every night to little groups of half-civilized foreign paupers who scoff at him. But he rejoices in the scoffings, since he is suffering them in the great cause of Christ. You have so filled my mind with suspicions that I was constantly expecting to find a hidden questionable impulse back of all this, but I am thankful to say I have failed. This man saw his duty, and for *duty's sake* he sacrificed self and assumed the burden it imposed.

O. M. Is that as far as you have read?

Y. M. Yes.

O. M. Let us read further, presently. Meantime, in sacrificing himself—*not* for the glory of God, *primarily*, as *he* imagined, but *first* to content that exacting and inflexible master within him—*did he sacrifice anybody else?*

Y. M. How do you mean?

O. M. He relinquished a lucrative post and got mere food and lodging in place of it. Had he dependants?

Y. M. Well—yes.

O. M. In what way and to what extent did his self-sacrifice affect *them*?

Y. M. He was the support of a superannuated father. He had a young sister with a remarkable voice—he was giving her a musical education, so that her longing to be self-supporting might be gratified. He was furnishing the money to put a young brother through a polytechnic school and satisfy his desire to become a civil engineer.

O. M. The old father's comforts were now curtailed?

Y. M. Quite seriously. Yes.

O. M. The sister's music-lessons had to stop?

Y. M. Yes.

O. M. The young brother's education—well, an extinguishing blight fell upon that happy dream, and he had to go to sawing wood to support the old father, or something like that?

Y. M. It is about what happened. Yes.

O. M. What a handsome job of self-sacrificing he did do! It seems to me that he sacrificed everybody *except* himself. Haven't I told you that no man *ever* sacrifices himself; that there is no instance of it upon record anywhere; and that when a man's Interior Monarch requires a thing of its slave for either its *momentary* or its *permanent* contentment, that thing must and will be furnished and that command obeyed, no matter who may stand in the way and suffer disaster by it? That man *ruined his family* to please and content his Interior Monarch—

Y. M. And help Christ's cause.

O. M. Yes—*secondly*. Not firstly. *He* thought it was firstly.

Y. M. Very well, have it so, if you will. But it could be that he argued that if he saved a hundred souls in New York—

O. M. The sacrifice of the *family* would be justified by that great profit upon the—the—what shall we call it?

Y. M. Investment?

O. M. Hardly. How would *speculation* do? how would *gamble* do? Not a solitary soul-capture was sure. He played for a possible thirty-three hundred per cent profit. It was *gambling*—with his family for "chips." However, let us see how the game came out. Maybe we can get on the track of the secret original impulse, the *real* impulse, that moved him to so nobly self-sacrifice his family in the Savior's cause under the superstition that he was sacrificing himself. I will read a chapter or so. . . . Here we have it! it was bound to expose itself sooner or later. He preached to the East-Side rabble a season, then went back to his old dull and obscure life in the lumber camps *"hurt to the heart, his pride humbled."* Why? Were not his efforts acceptable to the Savior, for Whom alone they were made? Dear me, that detail is *lost sight of*, is not even referred to, the fact that it started out as a motive is entirely forgotten! Then what is the trouble? The authoress quite innocently and unconsciously gives the whole business away. The trouble was this: this man merely *preached* to the poor; that is not the University Settlement's way; it deals in larger and better things than that, and it did not enthuse over that crude Salvation-Army eloquence. It was courteous to Holme—but cool. It did not pet him, did not take him to its bosom. *"Perished were all his dreams of distinction, the praise and grateful approval of—"* Of whom? The Savior? No; the Savior is not mentioned. Of whom, then? Of "his *fellow-workers.*" Why did he want that? Because the Master inside of him wanted it, and would not be content without it. That emphasized sentence quoted above, reveals the secret we have been seeking, the original impulse, the *real* impulse, which moved the obscure and unappreciated Adirondack lumberman to sacrifice his family and go on that crusade to the East Side—which said original impulse was this, to-wit: without knowing it *he went there to show a neglectful world the large talent that was in him, and rise to distinction.* As I have warned you before, *no* act springs from any but the one law, the one motive. But I pray you, do not accept this law upon my say-so, but diligently examine for yourself. Whenever you read of a self-sacrificing act or hear of one, or of a duty done for *duty's sake,* take it to pieces and look for the *real* motive. It is always there.

Y. M. I do it every day. I cannot help it, now that I have gotten started upon the degrading and exasperating quest. For it is hatefully interesting!—in fact, fascinating is the word. As soon as I come across a golden deed in a book I have to stop and take it apart and examine it, I cannot help myself.

O. M. Have you ever found one that defeated the rule?

Y. M. No—at least, not yet. But take the case of servant-tipping in Europe. You pay the *hotel* for service; you owe the servants *nothing,* yet you pay them, besides. Doesn't that defeat it?

O. M. In what way?

Y. M. You are not *obliged* to do it, therefore its source is compassion for their ill-paid condition, and—

O. M. Has that custom ever vexed you, annoyed you, irritated you?

Y. M. Well—yes.

O. M. Still you succumbed to it?

Y. M. Of course.

O. M. Why of course?

Y. M. Well, custom is law, in a way, and laws must be submitted to—everybody recognizes it as a *duty.*

O. M. Then you pay the irritating tax for *duty's* sake?

Y. M. I suppose it amounts to that.

O. M. Then the impulse which moves you to submit to the tax is not *all* compassion, charity, benevolence?

Y. M. Well—perhaps not.

O. M. Is *any* of it?

Y. M. I—perhaps I was too hasty in locating its source.

O. M. Perhaps so. In case you ignored the custom would you get prompt and effective service from the servants?

Y. M. Oh, hear yourself talk! Those European servants? Why, you wouldn't get any at all, to speak of.

O. M. Couldn't *that* work as an impulse to move you to pay the tax?

Y. M. I am not denying it.

O. M. Apparently, then, it is a case of for-duty's-sake with a little self-interest added?

Y. M. Yes, it has the look of it. But here is a point: we pay that tax knowing it to be unjust and an extortion; yet we go away with a pain at the heart if we think we have been stingy with the poor fellows; and we heartily wish we were back again, so that we could do the right thing, and *more* than the right thing, the *generous* thing. I think it will be difficult for you to find any thought of self in that impulse.

O. M. I wonder why you should think so. When you find service charged in the *hotel* bill does it annoy you?

Y. M. No.

O. M. Do you ever complain of the amount of it?

Y. M. No, it would not occur to me.

O. M. The *expense*, then, is not the annoying detail. It is a fixed charge, and you pay it cheerfully, you pay it without a murmur. When you came to pay the servants, how would you like it if each of the men and maids had a fixed charge?

Y. M. Like it? I should rejoice!

O. M. Even if the fixed tax were a shade *more* than you had been in the habit of paying in the form of tips?

Y. M. Indeed, yes!

O. M. Very well, then. As I understand it, it isn't really compassion nor yet duty that moves you to pay the tax, and it isn't the *amount* of the tax that annoys you. Yet *something* annoys you. What is it?

Y. M. Well, the trouble is, you never know *what* to pay, the tax varies so, all over Europe.

O. M. So you have to guess?

Y. M. There is no other way. So you go on thinking and thinking, and calculating and guessing, and consulting with other people and getting their views; and it spoils your sleep, nights, and makes you distraught in the day-time, and while you are pretending to look at the sights you are only guessing and guessing and guessing all the time, and being worried and miserable.

O. M. And all about a debt which you don't owe and don't have to pay unless you want to! Strange. What is the purpose of the guessing?

Y. M. To guess out what is right to give them, and not be unfair to any of them.

O. M. It has a quite noble look—taking so much pains and using up so much valuable time in order to be just and fair to a poor servant to whom you owe nothing, but who needs money and is ill paid.

Y. M. I think, myself, that if there is any ungracious motive back of it it will be hard to find.

O. M. How do you know when you have not paid a servant fairly?

Y. M. Why, he is silent; does not thank you. Sometimes he gives you a look that makes you ashamed. You are too proud to rectify your mistake there, with people looking, but afterward you keep on wishing and wishing you *had* done it. My, the shame and the pain of it! Sometimes you see, by the signs, that you have hit it *just right,* and you go away mightily satisfied. Sometimes the man is so effusively thankful that you know you have given him a good deal *more* than was necessary.

O. M. *Necessary?* Necessary for what?

Y. M. To content him.

O. M. How do you feel *then*?

Y. M. Repentant.

O. M. It is my belief that you have *not* been concerning yourself in guessing out his just dues, but only in ciphering out what would *content* him. And I think you had a self-deluding reason for that.

Y. M. What was it?

O. M. If you fell short of what he was expecting and wanting, you would get a look which would *shame you before folk*. That would give you *pain*. *You*—for you are only working for yourself, not *him*. If you gave him too much you would be *ashamed of yourself* for it, and that would give *you* pain—another case of thinking of *yourself*, protecting yourself, *saving yourself from discomfort*. You never think of the servant once—except to guess out how to secure *his approval*. If you get that, you get your *own* approval, and that is the sole and only thing you are after. The Master inside of you is then satisfied, contented, comfortable; there was *no other* thing at stake, as a matter of *first* interest, anywhere in the transaction.

FURTHER INSTANCES

Y. M. Well, to think of it: Self-Sacrifice for others, the grandest thing in man, ruled out! non-existent!

O. M. Are you accusing me of saying that?

Y. M. Why, certainly.

O. M. I haven't said it.

Y. M. What did you say, then?

O. M. That no man has ever sacrificed himself in the common meaning of that phrase—which is, self-sacrifice for another *alone*. Men make daily sacrifices for others, but it is for their own sake *first*. The act must content their own spirit *first*. The other beneficiaries come second.

Y. M. And the same with duty for duty's sake?

O. M. Yes. No man performs a duty for mere duty's sake; the act must content his spirit *first*. He must feel better for *doing* the duty than he would for shirking it. Otherwise he will not do it.

Y. M. Take the case of the *Berkeley Castle*.

O. M. It was a noble duty, greatly performed. Take it to pieces and examine it, if you like.

Y. M. A British troop-ship crowded with soldiers and their wives and children. She struck a rock and began to sink. There was room in the boats for the women and children only. The colonel lined-up his regiment on the deck and said "it is our duty to die, that they may be saved." There was no murmur, no protest. The boats carried away the women and children. When the death-moment was come, the colonel and his officers took their several posts, the men stood at shoulder-arms, and so, as on dress-parade, with their flag flying and the drums beating, they went down, a sacrifice to duty for duty's sake. Can you view it as other than that?

O. M. It was something as fine as that, as exalted as that. Could you have remained in those ranks and gone down to your death in that unflinching way?

Y. M. Could I? No, I could not.

O. M. Think. Imagine yourself there, with that watery doom creeping higher and higher around you.

Y. M. I can imagine it. I feel all the horror of it. I could not have endured it, I could not have remained in my place. I know it.

O. M. Why?

Y. M. There is no why about it: I know myself, and I know I couldn't *do* it.

O. M. But it would be your *duty* to do it.

Y. M. Yes, I know—but I couldn't.

O. M. It was more than a thousand men, yet not one of them flinched. Some of them must have been born with your temperament; if they could do that great duty for duty's *sake*, why not you? Don't you know that you could go out and gather together a thousand clerks and mechanics and put them on that deck and ask them to die for duty's sake, and not two dozen of them would stay in the ranks to the end?

Y. M. Yes, I know that.

O. M. But you *train* them, and put them through a campaign or two; then they would be soldiers; soldiers, with a soldier's pride, a soldier's self-respect, a soldier's ideals.

They would have to content a *soldier's* spirit then, not a clerk's, not a mechanic's. They could not content that spirit by shirking a soldier's duty, could they?

Y. M. I suppose not.

O. M. Then they would do the duty not for the *duty's* sake, but for their *own* sake—primarily. The *duty* was *just the same,* and just as imperative, when they were clerks, mechanics, raw recruits, but they wouldn't perform it for that. As clerks and mechanics they had other ideals, another spirit to satisfy, and they satisfied it. They *had* to; it is the law. *Training* is potent. Training toward higher, and higher, and ever higher ideals is worth any man's thought and labor and diligence.

Y. M. Consider the man who stands by his duty and goes to the stake rather than be recreant to it.

O. M. It is his make and his training. He has to content the spirit that is in him, though it cost him his life. Another man, just as sincerely religious, but of different temperament, will fail of that duty, though recognizing it as a duty, and grieving to be unequal to it; but he must content the spirit that is in him—he cannot help it. He could not perform that duty for duty's *sake,* for that would not content his spirit, and the contenting of his spirit must be looked to *first*. It takes precedence of all other duties.

Y. M. Take the case of a clergyman of stainless private morals who votes for a thief for public office, on his own party's ticket, and against an honest man on the other ticket.

O. M. He has to content his spirit. He has no public morals; he has no private ones, where his party's prosperity is at stake. He will always be true to his make and training.

IV
Training

Y. M. You keep using that word—training. By it do you particularly mean—

O. M. Study, instruction, lectures, sermons? That is a part of it—but not a large part. I mean *all* the outside influences. There are a million of them. From the cradle to the grave, during all his waking hours, the human being is under training. In the very first rank of his trainers stands *association*. It is his human environment which influences his mind and his feelings, furnishes him his ideals, and sets him on his road and keeps him in it. If he leave that road he will find himself shunned by the people whom he most loves and esteems, and whose approval he most values. He is a chameleon; by a law of his nature he takes the color of his place of resort. The influences about him create his preferences, his aversions, his politics, his tastes, his morals, his religion. He creates none of these things for himself. He *thinks* he does, but that is because he has not examined into the matter. You have seen Presbyterians?

Y. M. Many.

O. M. How did they happen to be Presbyterians and not Congregationalists? And why were the Congregationalists not Baptists, and the Baptists Roman Catholics, and the Roman Catholics Buddhists, and the Buddhists Quakers, and the Quakers Episcopalians, and the Episcopalians Millerites, and the Millerites Hindoos, and the Hindoos Atheists, and the Atheists Spiritualists, and the Spiritualists Agnostics, and the Agnostics Methodists, and the Methodists Confucians, and the Confucians Unitarians, and the Unitarians Mohammedans, and the Mohammedans Salvation Warriors, and the Salvation Warriors Zoroastrians, and the Zoroastrians Christian Scientists, and the Christian Scientists Mormons—and so on?

Y. M. You may answer your question yourself.

O. M. That list of sects is not a record of *studies,* searchings, seekings after light; it mainly (and sarcastically) indicates what *association* can do. If you know a man's nationality you can come within a split hair of guessing the complexion of his religion: English—Protestant; American—ditto; Spaniard, Frenchman, Irishman, Italian, South American, Austrian—Roman Catholic; Russian—Greek Catholic; Turk—Mohammedan; and so on. And when you know the man's religious complexion, you know what sort of religious books he reads when he wants some more light, and what sort of books he avoids, lest by accident he get more light than he wants. In America if you know which party-collar a voter wears, you know what his associations are, and how he came by his politics, and which breed of newspaper he reads to get light, and which breed he diligently avoids, and which breed of mass meetings he attends in order to broaden his political knowledge, and which breed of mass meetings he doesn't attend, except to refute its doctrines with brickbats. We are always hearing of people who are around *seeking after Truth.* I have never seen a (permanent) specimen. I think he has never lived. But I have seen several entirely sincere people who *thought* they were (permanent) Seekers after Truth. They sought diligently, persistently, carefully, cautiously, profoundly, with perfect honesty and a nicely adjusted judgment—until they believed that without doubt or question they had found the Truth. *That was the end of the search.* The man spent the rest of his life hunting up shingles wherewith to protect his Truth from the weather. If he was seeking after political Truth he found it in one or another of the hundred political gospels which govern men in the earth; if he was seeking after the Only True Religion he found it in one or another of the three thousand that are on the market. In any case, when he found his Truth *he sought no further;* but from that day forth, with his soldering iron in one hand and his bludgeon in the other he tinkered its leaks and reasoned with objectors. There have been innumerable Temporary Seekers after Truth—have you ever heard of a Permanent one? In the very nature of man such a person is impossible. However, to drop back to the text—training: all training is one form or another of *outside influence*, and *association* is the largest part of it. A man is never anything but what his outside influences have made him. They train him downwards or they train him upwards—but they *train* him; they are at work upon him all the time.

Y. M. Then if he happen by the accidents of life to be evilly placed there is no help for him, according to your notions—he must train downwards.

O. M. No help for him? No help for this chameleon? It is a mistake. It is in his chameleonship that his greatest good fortune lies. He has only to change his habitat—his *associations*. But the impulse to do it must come from the *outside*—he cannot originate it himself, with that purpose in view. Sometimes a very small and accidental thing can furnish him the initiatory impulse and start him on a new road, with a new ideal. The chance remark of a sweetheart, "I hear that you are a coward" may water a seed that shall sprout and bloom and flourish, and end in producing a surprising fruitage in the fields of war. The history of man is full of such accidents. The accident of a broken leg brought a profane and ribald soldier under religious influences and furnished him a new ideal. From that accident sprang the Order of the Jesuits, and it has been shaking thrones, changing policies, and doing other tremendous work for two hundred years—and will go on. The chance reading of a book, or of a paragraph in a newspaper can start a man on a new track and make him renounce his old associations and seek new ones that are *in sympathy with his new ideal*; and the result, for that man, can be an entire change of his way of life.

Y. M. Are you hinting at a scheme of procedure?

O. M. Not a new one—an old one. Old as mankind.

Y. M. What is it?

O. M. Merely the laying of traps for people. Traps baited with *Initiatory Impulses toward high ideals*. It is what the tract distributor does. It is what the missionary does. It is what governments ought to do.

Y. M. Don't they?

O. M. In one way they do, in another way they don't. They separate the small-pox patients from the healthy people, but in dealing with crime they put the healthy into the pest-house along with the sick. That is to say, they put the beginners in with the confirmed criminals. This would be well if man were naturally inclined to good, but he isn't, and so *association* makes the beginners worse than they were when they went into captivity. It is putting a very severe punishment upon the comparatively innocent. However, all governments are hard on the innocent at times. They hang a man—which is a trifling punishment; this breaks the hearts of his family—which is a heavy one. They comfortably jail and feed a wife-beater, and leave his innocent wife and children to starve.

Y. M. Do you believe in the doctrine that man is equipped with an intuitive perception of good and evil?

O. M. Adam hadn't it.

Y. M. But has man acquired it since?

O. M. No. I think he has no intuitions of any kind. He gets *all* his ideas, all his impressions, all his opinions, from the outside. I keep repeating this, in the hope that I may so impress it upon you that you will be interested to observe and examine for yourself and see whether it is true or false.

Y. M. Where did you get your own aggravating notions?

O. M. From the *outside*. I did not invent them. They are gathered from a thousand unknown sources. Mainly *unconsciously* gathered.

Y. M. Don't you believe that God could make an inherently honest man?

O. M. Yes, I know He could. I also know that He never did make one.

Y. M. A wiser observer than you has recorded the fact that "an honest man's the noblest work of God."

O. M. He didn't record a fact, he recorded a falsity. It is windy, and sounds well, but it is not true. God makes a man with honest and dishonest *possibilities* in him, and stops there. The man's *associations* develop the possibilities—the one set or the other. The result is accordingly an honest man or a dishonest one.

Y. M. And the honest one is not entitled to—

O. M. Praise? No. How often must I tell you that? *He* is not the architect of his honesty.

Y. M. Now then, I will ask you to tell me where there is any sense in training people to lead virtuous lives. What is gained by it?

O. M. The man himself gets large advantages out of it, and that is the main thing—to *him*. He is not a peril to his neighbors, he is not a damage to them—and so *they* get an advantage out of his virtues. That is the main thing to *them*. To train men to lead virtuous lives is an inestimably important thing. It can make this life comparatively comfortable to the parties concerned; the *neglect* of this training can make this life a constant peril and distress to the parties concerned.

Y. M. You have said that training is everything; that training is the man *himself*, for it makes him what he is.

O. M. I said training and *another* thing. Let that other thing pass, for the moment. What were you going to say?

Y. M. We have an old servant. She has been with us twenty-two years. Her service used to be faultless, but now she has become very forgetful. We are all fond of her; we all recognize that she cannot help the infirmity which age has brought her; the rest of the family do not scold her for her remissnesses, but at times I do—I can't seem to control myself. Don't I try? I do try. Now, then, when I was ready to dress, this morning, no clean clothes had been put out. I lost my temper; I lose it easiest and quickest in the early morning. I rang; and immediately began to warn myself not to show temper, and to be careful and speak gently. I safeguarded myself most carefully. I even chose the very words I would use: "You've forgotten the clean clothes, Jane." When she appeared in the door I opened my mouth to say that phrase—and out of it, moved by an instant surge of passion which I was not expecting and hadn't time to put under control, came the hot rebuke, "You've forgotten them again!" You say a man always does the thing which will best please his Interior Master. Whence came the impulse to make careful preparation to save the girl the humiliation of a rebuke? Did that come from the Master, who is always primarily concerned about *himself*?

O. M. Unquestionably. There is no other source for any impulse. *Secondarily* you made preparation to save the girl, but *primarily* its object was to save yourself, by contenting the Master.

Y. M. How do you mean?

O. M. Has any member of the family ever implored you to watch your temper and not fly out at the girl?

Y. M. Yes. My mother.

O. M. You love her?

Y. M. Oh, more than that!

O. M. You would always do anything in your power to please her?

Y. M. It is a delight to me to do anything to please her!

O. M. Why? *You would do it for pay, solely*—for *profit*. What profit would you expect and certainly receive, from the investment?

Y. M. Personally? None. To please *her* is enough.

O. M. It appears, then, that your object, primarily, *wasn't* to save the girl a humiliation, but to *please your mother*. It also appears that to please your mother gives *you* a strong pleasure. Is not that the profit which you get out of the investment? Isn't that the *real* profit and *first* profit?

Y. M. Oh, well? Go on.

O. M. In *all* transactions, the Interior Master looks to it that *you get the first profit*. Otherwise there is no transaction.

Y. M. Well, then, if I was so anxious to get that profit and was so intent upon it, why did I throw it away by losing my temper?

O. M. In order to get *another* profit which suddenly superseded it in value.

Y. M. Where was it?

O. M. Ambushed behind your born temperament, and waiting for a chance. Your native warm temper jumped suddenly to the front, and *for the moment* its influence was more powerful than your mother's, and abolished it. In that instant you were eager to flash out a hot rebuke and enjoy it. You did enjoy it, didn't you?

Y. M. For—for a quarter of a second. Yes—I did.

O. M. Very well, it is as I have said: the thing which will give you the *most* pleasure, the most satisfaction, in any moment or *fraction* of a moment, is the thing you will always do. You must content the Master's *latest* whim, whatever it may be.

Y. M. But when the tears came into the old servant's eyes I could have cut my hand off for what I had done.

O. M. Right. You had humiliated *yourself*, you see; you had given yourself *pain*. Nothing is of *first* importance to a man except results which damage *him* or profit him—all the rest is *secondary*. Your Master was displeased with you, although you had obeyed him. He required a prompt *repentance*; you obeyed again; you *had* to—there is never any escape from his commands. He is a hard master, and fickle; he changes his mind in the fraction of a second, but you must be ready to obey, and you will obey, *always*. If he requires repentance, to content him, you will always furnish it. He must be nursed, petted, coddled, and kept contented, let the terms be what they may.

Y. M. Training! Oh, what is the use of it? Didn't I, and didn't my mother try to train me up to where I would no longer fly out at that girl?

O. M. Have you never managed to keep back a scolding?

Y. M. Oh, certainly—many times.

O. M. More times this year than last?

Y. M. Yes, a good many more.

O. M. More times last year than the year before?

Y. M. Yes.

O. M. There is a large improvement, then, in the two years?

Y. M. Yes, undoubtedly.

O. M. Then your question is answered. You see there *is* use in training. Keep on. Keep faithfully on. You are doing well.

Y. M. Will my reform reach perfection?

O. M. It will. Up to *your* limit.

Y. M. My limit? What do you mean by that?

O. M. You remember you said that I said training was *everything*. I corrected you, and said "training and *another* thing." That other thing is *temperament*—that is, the disposition you were born with. *You can't eradicate your disposition nor any rag of it*—you can only put a pressure on it and keep it down and quiet. You have a warm temper?

Y. M. Yes.

O. M. You will never get rid of it; but by watching it you can keep it down nearly all the time. *Its presence is your limit.* Your reform will never quite reach perfection, for your temper will beat you now and then, but you will come near enough. You have made valuable progress and can make more. There *is* use in training. Immense use. Presently you will reach a new stage of development, then your progress will be easier; will proceed on a simpler basis, anyway.

Y. M. Explain.

O. M. You keep back your scoldings now, to please *yourself* by pleasing your *mother*; presently the mere triumphing over your temper will delight your vanity and confer a more delicious pleasure and satisfaction upon you than even the approbation of your *mother* confers upon you now. You will then labor for yourself directly and at *first hand,* not by the roundabout way through your mother. It simplifies the matter, and it also strengthens the impulse.

Y. M. Ah, dear! But I shan't ever reach the point where I will spare the girl for *her* sake *primarily,* not mine?

O. M. Why—yes. In heaven.

Y. M. (*After a reflective pause.*) Temperament. Well, I see one must allow for temperament. It is a large factor, sure enough. My mother is thoughtful, and not hot-tempered. When I was dressed I went to her room; she was not there; I called, she answered from the bath-room. I heard the water running. I inquired. She answered, without temper, that Jane had forgotten her bath, and she was preparing it herself. I offered to ring, but she said, "No, don't do that; it would only distress her to be confronted with her lapse, and would be a rebuke; she doesn't deserve that—she is not to blame for the tricks her memory serves her." I say—has my mother an Interior Master?—and where was he?

O. M. He was there. There, and looking out for his own peace and pleasure and contentment. The girl's distress would have pained *your mother.* Otherwise the girl would have been rung up, distress and all. I know women who would have gotten a No. 1 *pleasure* out of ringing Jane up—and so they would infallibly have pushed the button and obeyed the law of their make and training, which are the servants of their Interior Masters. It is quite likely that a part of your mother's forbearance came from training. The *good* kind of training—whose best and highest function is to see to it that every time it confers a satisfaction upon its pupil a benefit shall fall at second hand upon others.

Y. M. If you were going to condense into an admonition your plan for the general betterment of the race's condition, how would you word it?

ADMONITION

O. M. Diligently train your ideals *upward* and *still upward* toward a summit where you will find your chiefest pleasure in conduct which, while contenting you, will be sure to confer benefits upon your neighbor and the community.

Y. M. Is that a new gospel?

O. M. No.

Y. M. It has been taught before?

O. M. For ten thousand years.

Y. M. By whom?

O. M. All the great religions—all the great gospels.

Y. M. Then there is nothing new about it.

O. M. Oh, yes there is. It is candidly stated, this time. That has not been done before.

Y. M. How do you mean?

O. M. Haven't I put *you* FIRST, and your neighbor and the community *afterward*?

Y. M. Well, yes, that is a difference, it is true.

O. M. The difference between straight speaking and crooked; the difference between frankness and shuffling.

Y. M. Explain.

O. M. The others offer you a hundred bribes to be good, thus conceding that the Master inside of you must be conciliated and contented first, and that you will do nothing at *first hand* but for his sake; then they turn square around and require you to do good for *others'* sake *chiefly;* and to do your duty for duty's *sake,* chiefly; and to do *unselfish* things; and to do acts of *self-sacrifice.* Thus at the outset we all stand upon the same ground—recognition of the supreme and absolute Monarch that resides in man, and we all grovel before him and appeal to him; then those others dodge and shuffle, and face around and unfrankly and inconsistently and illogically change the form of their appeal and direct its persuasions to man's *second-place* powers and to powers which have *no existence* in him, thus advancing them to *first* place; whereas in my Admonition I stick logically and consistently to the original position: I place the Interior Master's requirements *first*, and keep them there.

Y. M. If we grant, for the sake of argument, that your scheme and the other schemes aim at and produce the same result—*right living*—has yours an advantage over the others

O. M. One, yes—a large one. It has no concealments, no deceptions. When a man leads a right and valuable life under it he is not deceived as to the *real* chief motive which impels him to it—in those other cases he is.

Y. M. Is that an advantage? Is it an advantage to live a lofty life for a mean reason? In the other cases he lives the lofty life under the *impression* that he is living it for a lofty reason. Is not that an advantage?

O. M. Perhaps so. The same advantage he might get out of thinking himself a duke, and living a duke's life, and parading in ducal fuss and feathers, when he wasn't a duke at all, and could find it out if he would only examine the herald's records.

Y. M. But anyway, he is obliged to do a duke's part; he puts his hand in his pocket and does his benevolences on as big a scale as he can stand, and that benefits the community.

O. M. He could do that without being a duke.

Y. M. But would he?

O. M. Don't you see where you are arriving?

Y. M. Where?

O. M. At the stand-point of the other schemes: That it is good morals to let an ignorant duke do showy benevolences for pride's sake, a pretty low motive, and go on doing them unwarned, lest if he were made acquainted with the actual motive which prompted them he might shut up his purse and cease to be good?

Y. M. But isn't it best to leave him in ignorance, as long as he *thinks* he is doing good for others' sake?

O. M. Perhaps so. It is the position of the other schemes. They think humbug is good enough morals when the dividend on it is good deeds and handsome conduct.

Y. M. It is my opinion that under your scheme of a man's doing a good deed for his *own* sake first-off, instead of first for the *good deed's* sake, no man would ever do one.

O. M. Have you committed a benevolence lately?

Y. M. Yes. This morning.

O. M. Give the particulars.

Y. M. The cabin of the old negro woman who nursed me when I was a child and who saved my life once at risk of her own, was burned last night, and she came mourning this morning, and pleading for money to build another one.

O. M. You furnished it?

Y. M. Certainly.

O. M. You were glad you had the money?

Y. M. Money? I hadn't it. I sold my horse.

O. M. You were glad you had the horse?

Y. M. Of course I was; for if I hadn't had the horse I should have been incapable, and my *mother* would have captured the chance to set old Sally up.

O. M. You were cordially glad you were not caught out and incapable?

Y. M. Oh, I just was!

O. M. Now then—

Y. M. Stop where you are! I know your whole catalogue of questions, and I could answer every one of them without your wasting the time to ask them; but I will summarize the whole thing in a single remark: I did the charity knowing it was because the act would give *me* a splendid pleasure, and because old Sally's moving gratitude and delight would give *me* another one; and because the reflection that she would be happy now and out of her trouble would fill *me* full of happiness. I did the whole thing with my eyes open and recognizing and realizing that I was looking out for *my* share of the profits *first*. Now then, I have confessed. Go on.

O. M. I haven't anything to offer; you have covered the whole ground. Could you have been any *more* strongly moved to help Sally out of her trouble—could you have done the deed any more eagerly—if you had been under the delusion that you were doing it for *her* sake and profit only?

Y. M. No! Nothing in the world could have made the impulse which moved me more powerful, more masterful, more thoroughly irresistible. I played the limit!

O. M. Very well. You begin to suspect—and I claim to *know*—that when a man is a shade *more strongly moved* to do *one* of two things or of two dozen things than he is to do any one of the *others*, he will infallibly do that *one* thing, be it good or be it evil; and if it be good, not all the beguilements of all the casuistries can increase the strength of the impulse by a single shade or add a shade to the comfort and contentment he will get out of the act.

Y. M. Then you believe that such tendency toward doing good as is in men's hearts would not be diminished by the removal of the delusion that good deeds are done primarily for the sake of No. 2 instead of for the sake of No. 1?

O. M. That is what I fully believe.

Y. M. Doesn't it somehow seem to take from the dignity of the deed?

O. M. If there is dignity in falsity, it does. It removes that.

Y. M. What is left for the moralist to do?

O. M. Teach unreservedly what he already teaches with one side of his mouth and takes back with the other: Do right *for your own sake*, and be happy in knowing that your *neighbor* will certainly share in the benefits resulting.

Y. M. Repeat your Admonition.

O. M. *Diligently train your ideals upward and still upward toward a summit where you will find your chiefest pleasure in conduct which, while contenting you, will be sure to confer benefits upon your neighbor and the community.*

Y. M. One's *every* act proceeds from *exterior influences,* you think?

O. M. Yes.

Y. M. If I conclude to rob a person, I am not the *originator* of the idea, but it came in from the *outside*? I see him handling money—for instance—and *that* moves me to the crime?

O. M. That, by itself? O, certainly not. It is merely the *latest* outside influence of a procession of preparatory influences stretching back over a period of years. No *single* outside influence can make a man do a thing which is at war with his training. The most it can do is to start his mind on a new track and open it to the reception of *new* influences—as in the case of Ignatius Loyola. In time these influences can train him to a point where it will be consonant with his new character to yield to the *final* influence and do that thing. I will put the case in a form which will make my theory clear to you, I think. Here are two ingots of virgin gold. They shall represent a couple of characters which have been refined and perfected in the virtues by years of diligent right training. Suppose you wanted to break down these strong and well compacted characters—what influence would you bring to bear upon the ingots?

Y. M. Work it out yourself. Proceed.

O. M. Suppose I turn upon one of them a steam-jet during a long succession of hours. Will there be a result?

Y. M. None that I know of.

O. M. Why?

Y. M. A steam-jet cannot break down such a substance.

O. M. Very well. The steam is an *outside influence,* but it is ineffective, because the gold *takes no interest in it*. The ingot remains as it was. Suppose we add to the steam some quicksilver in a vaporized condition, and turn the jet upon the other ingot. Will there be an instantaneous result?

Y. M. No.

O. M. The *quicksilver* is an outside influence which gold (by its peculiar nature—say *temperament, disposition*), *cannot be indifferent to*. It stirs the interest of the gold, although we do not perceive it; but a *single* application of the influence works no damage. Let us continue the application in a steady stream, and call each minute a year. By the end of ten or twenty minutes—ten or twenty years—the little ingot is sodden with quicksilver, rotten with quicksilver, its virtues are gone, its character is degraded. At last it is ready to yield to a temptation which it would have taken no notice of, ten or twenty years ago. We will apply that temptation in the form of a pressure with my finger. You note the result?

Y. M. Yes; the ingot has crumbled to sand. I understand, now. It is not the *single* outside influence that does the work, but only the *last* one of a long and disintegrating accumulation of them. I see, now, how my *single* impulse to rob the man is not the one that makes me do it, but only the *last* one of a preparatory series. You might illustrate it with a parable.

A PARABLE

O. M. I will. There was once a pair of New England boys—twins. They were alike in good dispositions, fleckless morals, and personal appearance. They were the models of the Sunday-school. At fifteen George had an opportunity to go as cabin-boy in a whale-ship, and sailed away for the Pacific. Henry remained at home in the village. At eighteen George was a sailor before the mast, and Henry was teacher of the advanced Bible class. At twenty-two George, through fighting-habits and drinking-habits acquired at sea and in the sailor boarding-houses of the European and Oriental ports, was a common rough in Hong Kong, and out of a job; and Henry was superintendent of the Sunday-school. At twenty-six George was a wanderer, a tramp, and Henry was pastor of the village church. Then George came home, and was Henry's guest. One evening a man passed by and turned down the lane, and Henry said, with a pathetic smile, "Without intending me a discomfort, that man is always keeping me reminded of my pinching poverty, for he carries heaps of money about him, and goes by here every evening of his life." That *outside influence*—that remark—was enough for George, but *it* was not the one that made him ambush the man and rob him, it merely represented the eleven years' accumulation of such influences, and gave birth to the act for which their long gestation had made preparation. It had never entered the head of Henry to rob the man—his ingot had been subjected to clean steam only; but George's had been subjected to vaporized quicksilver.

V

More About the Machine

NOTE.—When Mrs. W. asks how can a millionaire give a single dollar to colleges and museums while one human being is destitute of bread; she has answered her question herself. Her feeling for the poor shows that she has a standard of benevolence; therefore she has conceded the millionaire's privilege of having a standard; since she evidently requires him to adopt her standard she is by that act requiring herself to adopt his. The human being always looks down when he is examining another person's standard, he never finds one that he has to examine by looking up.

THE MAN-MACHINE AGAIN

Y. M. You really think man is a mere machine?

O. M. I do.

Y. M. And that his mind works automatically and is independent of his control—carries on thought on its own hook?

O. M. Yes. It is diligently at work, unceasingly at work, during every waking moment. Have you never tossed about all night, imploring, beseeching, commanding your mind to stop work and let you go to sleep?—you who perhaps imagine that your mind is your servant and must obey your orders, think what you tell it to think, and stop when you tell it to stop. When it chooses to work, there is no way to keep it still for an instant. The brightest man would not be able to supply it with subjects if he had to hunt them up. If it needed the man's help it would wait for him to give it work when he wakes in the morning.

Y. M. Maybe it does.

O. M. No, it begins right away, before the man gets wide enough awake to give it a suggestion. He may go to sleep saying, "The moment I wake I will think upon such and such a subject," but he will fail. His mind will be too quick for him; by the time he has become nearly enough awake to be half conscious, he will find that it is already at work on another subject. Make the experiment and see.

Y. M. At any rate he can make it stick to a subject if he wants to.

O. M. Not if it finds another that suits it better. As a rule it will listen to neither a dull speaker nor a bright one. It refuses all persuasion. The dull speaker wearies it and sends it far away in idle dreams; the bright speaker throws out stimulating ideas which it goes chasing after and is at once unconscious of him and his talk. You cannot keep your mind from wandering, if it wants to; it is master, not you.

After an Interval of Days

O. M. Now, dreams—but we will examine that later. Meantime, did you try commanding your mind to wait for orders from you, and not do any thinking on its own hook?

Y. M. Yes, I commanded it to stand ready to take orders when I should wake in the morning.

O. M. Did it obey?

Y. M. No. It went to thinking about something of its own initiation, without waiting for me. Also—as you suggested—at night I appointed a theme for it to begin on in the morning, and commanded it to begin on that one and no other.

O. M. Did it obey?

Y. M. No.

O. M. How many times did you try the experiment?

Y. M. Ten.

O. M. How many successes did you score?

Y. M. Not one.

O. M. It is as I have said: the mind is independent of the man. He has no control over it, it does as it pleases. It will take up a subject in spite of him; it will stick to it in spite of him; it will throw it aside in spite of him. It is entirely independent of him.

Y. M. Go on. Illustrate.

O. M. Do you know chess?

Y. M. I learned it a week ago.

O. M. Did your mind go on playing the game all night that first night?

Y. M. Don't mention it!

O. M. It was eagerly, unsatisfiably interested; it rioted in the combinations; you implored it to drop the game and let you get some sleep?

Y. M. Yes. It wouldn't listen; it played right along. It wore me out and I got up haggard and wretched in the morning.

O. M. At some time or other you have been captivated by a ridiculous rhyme-jingle?

Y. M. Indeed, yes!

> "I saw Esau kissing Kate,
> And she saw I saw Esau;
> I saw Esau, he saw Kate,
> And she saw—"

And so on. My mind went mad with joy over it. It repeated it all day and all night for a week in spite of all I could do to stop it, and it seemed to me that I must surely go crazy.

O. M. And the new popular song?

Y. M. Oh, yes! "In the Swee-eet By and By;" etc. Yes, the new popular song with the taking melody sings thro' one's head day and night, asleep and awake, till one is a wreck. There is no getting the mind to let it alone.

O. M. Yes, asleep as well as awake. The mind is quite independent. It is master. You have nothing to do with it. It is so apart from you that it can conduct its affairs, sing its songs, play its chess, weave its complex and ingeniously-constructed dreams, while you sleep. It has no use for your help, no use for your guidance, and never uses either, whether you be asleep or awake. You have imagined that you could originate a thought in your mind, and you have sincerely believed you could do it.

Y. M. Yes, I have had that idea.

O. M. Yet you can't originate a dream-thought for it to work out, and get it accepted?

Y. M. No.

O. M. And you can't dictate its procedure after it has originated a dream-thought for itself?

Y. M. No. No one can do it. Do you think the waking mind and the dream-mind are the same machine?

O. M. There is argument for it. We have wild and fantastic day-thoughts? Things that are dream-like?

Y. M. Yes—like Mr. Wells's man who invented a drug that made him invisible; and like the Arabian tales of the Thousand Nights.

O. M. And there are dreams that are rational, simple, consistent and unfantastic?

Y. M. Yes. I have dreams that are like that. Dreams which are just like real life; dreams in which there are several persons with distinctly differentiated characters—inventions of my mind and yet strangers to me: a vulgar person; a refined one; a wise person; a fool; a cruel person; a kind and compassionate one; a quarrelsome person; a peacemaker; old persons and young; beautiful girls and homely ones. They talk in character, each preserves his own characteristics. There are vivid fights, vivid and biting insults, vivid love-passages; there are tragedies and comedies, there are griefs that go to one's heart, there are sayings and doings that make you laugh: indeed the whole thing is exactly like real life.

O. M. Your dreaming mind originates the scheme, consistently and artistically develops it, and carries the little drama creditably through—all without help or suggestion from you?

Y. M. Yes.

O. M. It is argument that it could do the like awake without help or suggestion from you—and I think it does. It is argument that it is the same old mind in both cases, and never needs your help. I think the mind is purely a machine, a thoroughly independent machine, an automatic machine. Have you tried the other experiment which I suggested to you?

Y. M. Which one?

O. M. The one which was to determine how much influence you have over your mind—if any.

Y. M. Yes, and got more or less entertainment out of it. I did as you ordered: I placed two texts before my eyes—one a dull one and barren of interest, the other one full of interest, inflamed with it, white-hot with it. I commanded my mind to busy itself solely with the dull one.

O. M. Did it obey?

Y. M. Well, no, it didn't. It busied itself with the other one.

O. M. Did you try hard to make it obey?

Y. M. Yes, I did my honest best.

O. M. What was the text which it refused to be interested in or think about?

Y. M. It was this question: if A owes B a dollar and a half, and B owes C two and three-quarters, and C owes A thirty-five cents, and D and A together owe E and B three-sixteenths of—of—I don't remember the rest, now, but anyway it was wholly uninteresting, and I could not force my mind to stick to it even half a minute at a time; it kept flying off to the other text.

O. M. What was the other text?

Y. M. It is no matter about that.

O. M. But what was it?

Y. M. A photograph.

O. M. Your own?

Y. M. No. It was hers.

O. M. You really made an honest good test. Did you make a second trial?

Y. M. Yes. I commanded my mind to interest itself in the morning paper's report of the pork market, and at the same time I reminded it of an experience of mine of sixteen years ago. It refused to consider the pork, and gave its whole blazing interest to that ancient incident.

O. M. What was the incident?

Y. M. An armed desperado slapped my face in the presence of twenty spectators. It makes me wild and murderous every time I think of it.

O. M. Good tests, both; very good tests. Did you try my other suggestion?

Y. M. The one which was to prove to me that if I would leave my mind to its own devices it would find things to think about without any of my help, and thus convince me that it was a machine, an automatic machine, set in motion by exterior influences, and as independent of me as it could be if it were in some one else's skull? Is that the one?

O. M. Yes.

Y. M. I tried it. I was shaving. I had slept well, and my mind was very lively, even gay and frisky. It was reveling in a fantastic and joyful episode of my remote boyhood which had suddenly flashed up in my memory,—moved to this by the spectacle of a yellow cat picking its way carefully along the top of the garden wall. The color of this cat brought the bygone cat before me, and

I saw her walking along a side-step of the pulpit; saw her walk onto a large sheet of sticky flypaper and get all her feet involved; saw her struggle and fall down, helpless and dissatisfied; saw her go on struggling, on her back and getting more and more dissatisfied, more and more urgent, more and more unreconciled, more and more mutely profane; saw the silent congregation quivering like jelly, and the tears running down their faces. I saw it all. The sight of the tears whisked my mind to a far distant and a sadder scene—in Tierra del Fuego—and with Darwin's eyes I saw a naked great savage hurl his little boy against the rocks for a trifling fault; saw the poor mother gather up her dying child and hug it to her breast and weep, uttering no word. Did my mind stop to mourn with that nude black sister of mine? No—it was far away from that scene in an instant, and was busying itself with an ever-recurring and disagreeable dream of mine. In this dream I always find myself, stripped to my shirt, cringing and dodging about in the midst of a great drawingroom throng of finely dressed ladies and gentlemen, and wondering how I got there. And so on and so on, picture after picture, incident after incident, a drifting panorama of ever-changing, ever-dissolving views manufactured by my mind without any help from me—why, it would take me two hours to merely name the multitude of things my mind tallied off and photographed in fifteen minutes, let alone describe them to you.

O. M. A man's mind, left free, has no use for his help. But there is one way whereby he can get its help when he desires it.

Y. M. What is that way?

O. M. When your mind is racing along from subject to subject and strikes an inspiring one, open your mouth and begin to talk upon that matter—or take your pen and use that. It will interest your mind and concentrate it, and it will pursue the subject with satisfaction. It will take full charge, and furnish the words itself.

Y. M. But don't I tell it what to say?

O. M. There are certainly occasions when you haven't time. The words leap out before you know what is coming.

Y. M. For instance?

O. M. Well, take a "flash of wit"—repartee. Flash is the right word. It is out instantly. There is no time to arrange the words. There is no thinking, no reflecting. Where there is a wit-mechanism it is automatic in its action, and needs no help. Where the wit-mechanism is lacking, no amount of study and reflection can manufacture the product.

Y. M. You really think a man originates nothing, creates nothing.

THE THINKING-PROCESS

O. M. I do. Men perceive, and their brain-machines automatically combine the things perceived. That is all.

Y. M. The steam-engine?

O. M. It takes fifty men a hundred years to invent it. One meaning of invent is discover. I use the word in that sense. Little by little they discover and apply the multitude of details that go to make the perfect engine. Watt noticed that confined steam was strong enough to lift the lid of the teapot. He didn't create the idea, he merely discovered the fact; the cat had noticed it a hundred times. From the teapot he evolved the cylinder—from the displaced lid he evolved the piston-rod. To attach something to the piston-rod to be moved by it, was a simple matter—crank and wheel. And so there was a working engine.* One by one, improvements were discovered by men who used their eyes, not their creative powers—for they hadn't any—and now, after a hundred years the patient contributions of fifty or a hundred observers stand compacted in the wonderful machine which drives the ocean liner.

*The Marquess of Worcester had done all of this more than a century earlier.

Y. M. A Shakespearean play?

O. M. The process is the same. The first actor was a savage. He reproduced in his theatrical war-dances, scalp-dances, and so on, incidents which he had seen in real life. A more advanced civilization produced more incidents, more episodes; the actor and the story-teller borrowed them. And so the drama grew, little by little, stage by stage. The elaborate Shakespearean play was the final outcome. It is made up of the facts of life, not creations. It took centuries to develop the Greek drama. It borrowed from preceding ages; it lent to the ages that came after. Men observe and combine, that is all. So does a rat.

Y. M. How?

O. M. He observes a smell, he infers a cheese, he seeks and finds. The astronomer observes this and that; adds his this and that to the this-and-thats of a hundred predecessors, infers an invisible planet, seeks it and finds it. The rat gets into a trap; gets out with trouble; infers that cheese in traps lacks value, and meddles with that trap no more. The astronomer is very proud of his achievement; the rat is proud of his. Yet both are machines, they have done machine-work, they have originated nothing, they have no right to be vain, the whole credit belongs to their Maker. They are entitled to no honors, no praises, no monuments when they die, no remembrance. One is a complex and elaborate machine, the other a simple and limited machine, but they are alike in principle, function and process, and neither of them works otherwise than automatically, and neither of them may righteously claim a *personal* superiority or a personal dignity above the other.

Y. M. In earned personal dignity, then, and in personal merit for what he does, it follows of necessity that he is on the same level as a rat?

O. M. His brother the rat; yes, that is how it seems to me. Neither of them being entitled to any personal merit for what he does, it follows of necessity that neither of them has a right to arrogate to himself (personally-created) superiorities over his brother.

Y. M. Are you determined to go on believing in these insanities? Would you go on believing in them in the face of able arguments backed by collated facts and instances?

O. M. I have been a humble, earnest and sincere Truth Seeker.

Y. M. Very well?

O. M. The humble, earnest and sincere Truth Seeker is always convertible by such means.

Y. M. I am thankful to God to hear you say this, for now I know that your conversion—

O. M. Wait. You misunderstand. I said I have *been* a Truth Seeker.

Y. M. Well?

O. M. I am not that now. Have you forgotten? I told you that there are none but temporary Truth Seekers; that a permanent one is a human impossibility; that as soon as the Seeker finds what he is thoroughly convinced is the Truth, he seeks no further, but gives the rest of his days to hunting for junk to patch it and caulk it and prop it with, and make it weather-proof and keep it from caving in on him. Hence the Presbyterian remains a Presbyterian, the Mohammedan a Mohammedan, the Spiritualist a Spiritualist, the Democrat a Democrat, the Republican a Republican, the Monarchist a Monarchist; and if a humble, earnest and sincere Seeker after Truth should find it in the proposition that the moon is made of green cheese nothing could ever budge him from that position; for he is nothing but an automatic machine, and must obey the laws of his construction.

Y. M. And so—

O. M. Having found the Truth; perceiving that beyond question Man has but one moving impulse—the contenting of his own spirit—and is merely a Machine and entitled to no personal merit for anything he does, it is not humanly possible for me to seek further. The rest of my days will be spent in patching and painting and puttying and caulking my priceless possession, and in looking the other way when an imploring argument or a damaging fact approaches.

VI

Instinct and Thought

Y. M. It is odious. Those drunken theories of yours, advanced a while ago—concerning the rat and all that—strip Man bare of all his dignities, grandeurs, sublimities.

O. M. He hasn't any to strip—they are shams, stolen clothes. He claims credits which belong solely to his Maker.

Y. M. But you have no right to put him on a level with the rat.

O. M. I don't—morally. That would not be fair to the rat. The rat is well above him, there.

Y. M. Are you joking?

O. M. No, I am not.

Y. M. Then what do you mean?

O. M. That comes under the head of the Moral Sense. It is a large question. Let us finish with what we are about now, before we take it up.

Y. M. Very well. You have seemed to concede that you place Man and the rat on *a* level. What is it? The intellectual?

O. M. In form—not in degree.

Y. M. Explain.

O. M. I think that the rat's mind and the man's mind are the same machine, but of unequal capacities—like yours and Edison's; like the African pigmy's and Homer's; like the Bushman's and Bismarck's.

Y. M. How are you going to make that out, when the lower animals have no mental quality but instinct, while man possesses reason?

O. M. What is instinct?

Y. M. It is a merely unthinking and mechanical exercise of inherited habit.

O. M. What originated the habit?

Y. M. The first animal started it, its descendants have inherited it.

O. M. How did the first one come to start it?

Y. M. I don't know; but it didn't *think* it out.

O. M. How do you know it didn't?

Y. M. Well—I have a right to suppose it didn't, anyway.

O. M. I don't believe you have. What is thought?

Y. M. I know what you call it: the mechanical and automatic putting together of impressions received from the outside, and drawing an inference from them.

O. M. Very good. Now my idea of the meaningless term "instinct" is, that it is merely *petrified thought*; thought solidified and made inanimate by habit; thought which was once alive and awake, but is become uncon scious—walks in its sleep, so to speak.

Y. M. Illustrate it.

O. M. Take a herd of cows, feeding in a pasture. Their heads are all turned in one direction. They do that instinctively; they gain nothing by it, they have no reason for it, they don't know why they do it. It is an inherited habit which was originally thought—that is to say, observation of an exterior fact, and a valuable inference drawn from that observation and confirmed by experience. The original wild ox noticed that with the wind in his favor he could smell his enemy in time to escape; then he inferred that it was worth while to keep his nose to the wind. That is the process which man calls reasoning. Man's thought-machine works just like the other animals', but it is a better one and more Edisonian. Man, in the ox's place, would go further, reason wider: he would face a part of the herd the other way and protect both front and rear.

Y. M. Did you say the term instinct is meaningless?

O. M. I think it is a bastard word. I think it confuses us; for as a rule it applies itself to habits and impulses which had a far-off origin in thought, and now and then breaks the rule and applies itself to habits which can hardly claim a thought-origin.

Y. M. Give an instance.

O. M. Well, in putting on trousers a man always inserts the

same old leg first—never the other one. There is no advantage in that, and no sense in it. All men do it, yet no man ever thought it out and adopted it of set purpose, I imagine. But it is a habit which is transmitted, no doubt, and will continue to be transmitted.

Y. M. Can you prove that the habit exists?

O. M. You can prove it, if you doubt. If you will take a man to a clothing store and watch him try on a dozen pairs of trousers, you will see.

Y. M. The cow-illustration is not—

O. M. Sufficient to show that a dumb animal's mental machine is just the same as a man's and its reasoning-processes the same? I will illustrate further. If you should hand Mr. Edison a box which you caused to fly open by some concealed device, he would infer a spring, and would hunt for it and find it. Now an uncle of mine had an old horse who used to get into the closed lot where the corn-crib was and dishonestly take the corn. I got the punishment myself, as it was supposed that I heedlessly failed to insert the wooden pin which kept the gate closed. These persistent punishments fatigued me; they also caused me to infer the existence of a culprit, somewhere; so I hid myself and watched the gate. Presently the horse came and pulled out the pin with his teeth and went in. Nobody taught him that; he had observed—then thought it out for himself. His process did not differ from Edison's; he put this and that together and drew an inference—and the peg, too; but I made him sweat for it.

Y. M. It has something of the seeming of thought about it. Still, it is not very elaborate. Enlarge.

O. M. Suppose that Edison has been enjoying some one's hospitalities. He comes again, by and by, and the house is vacant. He infers that his host has moved. A while afterward, in another town, he sees the man enter a house; he infers that that is the new home, and follows to inquire. Here, now, is the experience of a gull, as related by a naturalist. The scene is a Scotch fishing village where the gulls were kindly treated. This particular gull visited a cottage; was fed; came next day and was fed again; came into the house, next time, and ate with the family; kept on doing this almost daily, thereafter. But once the gull was away on a journey for a few days, and when it returned the house was vacant. Its friends had removed to a village three miles distant. Several months later it saw the head of the family on the street there, followed him home, entered the house without excuse or apology, and became a daily guest again. Gulls do not rank high, mentally, but this one had memory and the reasoning faculty, you see, and applied them Edisonially.

Y. M. Yet it was not an Edison and couldn't be developed into one.

O. M. Perhaps not; could you?

Y. M. That is neither here nor there. Go on.

O. M. If Edison were in trouble and a stranger helped him out of it and next day he got into the same difficulty again, he would infer the wise thing to do in case he knew the stranger's address. Here is a case of a bird and a stranger as related by a naturalist. An English gentleman saw a bird flying around about his dog's head, down in the grounds, and uttering cries of distress. He went there to see about it. The dog had a young bird in his mouth—unhurt. The gentleman rescued it and put it on a bush and brought the dog away. Early the next morning the mother-bird came for the gentleman, who was sitting on his verandah, and by its maneuvers persuaded him to follow it to a distant part of the grounds—flying a little way in front of him and waiting for him to catch up, and so on; and keeping to the winding path, too, instead of flying the near way across lots. The distance covered was four hundred yards. The same dog was the culprit; he had the young bird again, and once more he had to give it up. Now the mother-bird had reasoned it all out: since the stranger had helped her once, she inferred that he would do it again;

she knew where to find him, and she went upon her errand with confidence. Her mental processes were what Edison's would have been. She put this and that together—and that is all that thought *is*—and out of them built her logical arrangement of inferences. Edison couldn't have done it any better himself.

Y. M. Do you believe that many of the dumb animals can think?

O. M. Yes—the elephant, the monkey, the horse, the dog, the parrot, the macaw, the mocking-bird, and many others. The elephant whose mate fell into a pit, and who dumped dirt and rubbish into the pit till the bottom was raised high enough to enable the captive to step out, was equipped with the reasoning quality. I conceive that all animals that can learn things through teaching and drilling have to know how to observe, and put this and that together and draw an inference—the process of thinking. Could you teach an idiot the manual of arms, and to advance, retreat, and go through complex field-maneuvers at the word of command?

Y. M. Not if he were a thorough idiot.

O. M. Well, canary birds can learn all that; dogs and elephants learn all sorts of wonderful things. They must surely be able to notice, and to put things together, and say to themselves, "I get the idea, now: when I do so and so, as per order, I am praised and fed; when I do differently, I am punished." Fleas can be taught nearly anything that a Congressman can.

Y. M. Granting, then, that dumb creatures are able to think upon a low plane, is there any that can think upon a high one? Is there one that is well up toward man?

O. M. Yes. As a thinker and planner the ant is the equal of any savage race of men; as a self-educated specialist in several arts she is the superior of any savage race of men; and in one or two high mental qualities she is above the reach of any man, savage or civilized.

Y. M. O, come! you are abolishing the intellectual frontier which separates man and beast.

O. M. I beg your pardon. One cannot abolish what does not exist.

Y. M. You are not in earnest, I hope. You cannot mean to seriously say there is no such frontier.

O. M. I do say it seriously. The instances of the horse, the gull, the mother-bird and the elephant show that those creatures put their this's and that's together just as Edison would have done it and drew the same inferences that he would have drawn. Their mental machinery was just like his, also its manner of working. Their equipment was as inferior to his, in elaboration, as a Waterbury is inferior to the Strasburg clock, but that is the only difference—there is no frontier.

Y. M. It looks exasperatingly true; and is distinctly offensive. It elevates the dumb beast to—to—

O. M. Let us drop that lying phrase, and call them the Unrevealed Creatures; so far as we can know, there is no such thing as a dumb beast.

Y. M. On what grounds do you make that assertion?

O. M. On quite simple ones. "Dumb" beast suggests an animal that has no thought-machinery, no understanding, no speech, no way of communicating what is in its mind. We know that a hen *has* speech. We cannot understand everything she says, but we easily learn two or three of her phrases. We know when she is saying "I've laid an egg;" we know when she is saying to the chicks, "Run here, dears, I've found a worm;" we know what she is saying when she voices a warning: "Quick! hurry! gather yourselves under mamma, there's a hawk coming!" We understand the cat when she stretches herself out, purring with affection and contentment and lifts up a soft voice and says "Come, kitties, supper's ready;" we understand her when she goes mourning about and says "Where can they be?—they are lost—won't you help me hunt for them?" and we understand the disreputable Tom when he challenges at midnight from his shed: "You come over here, you product of immoral commerce, and I'll make your fur fly!" We understand a few of a dog's phrases, and we learn to understand a few of the remarks and gestures of any bird or other animal that we domesticate and observe. The clearness and exactness of the few of the hen's speeches which we understand is argument that she can communicate to her kind a hundred things which we cannot comprehend—in a word, that she can converse. And this argument is also applicable in the case of others of the great army of the Unrevealed. It is just like man's vanity and impertinence to call an animal dumb because it is dumb to his dull perceptions. Now as to the ant—

Y. M. Yes, go back to the ant, the creature that—as you seem to think—sweeps away the last vestige of an intellectual frontier between man and the Unrevealed.

O. M. That is what she surely does. In all his history the aboriginal Australian never thought out a house for himself and built it. The ant is an amazing architect. She is a wee little creature, but she builds a strong and enduring house eight feet high—a house which is as large in proportion to her size as is the largest capitol or cathedral in the world compared to man's size. No savage race has produced architects who could approach the ant in genius or culture. No civilized race has produced architects who could plan a house better for the uses proposed than can hers. Her house contains a throne room; nurseries for her young; granaries; apartments for her soldiers, her workers, etc.; and they and the multifarious halls and corridors which communicate with them are arranged and distributed with an educated and experienced eye for convenience and adaptability.

Y. M. That could all be mere instinct.

O. M. It would elevate the savage much above what he is, if he had it. But let us look further before we decide. The ant has soldiers—battalions, regiments, armies; and they have their appointed captains and generals, who lead them to battle.

Y. M. That could be instinct, too.

O. M. We will look still further. The ant has a system of government; it is well planned, elaborate, and is well carried on.

Y. M. Instinct again.

O. M. She has crowds of slaves, and is a hard and unjust employer of forced labor.

Y. M. Instinct.

O. M. She has cows, and milks them.

Y. M. Instinct, of course.

O. M. In Texas she lays out a farm twelve feet square, plants it, weeds it, cultivates it, gathers the crop and stores it away.

Y. M. Instinct, all the same.

O. M. The ant discriminates between friend and stranger. Sir John Lubbock took ants from two different nests, made them drunk with whisky and laid them, unconscious, by one of the nests, near some water. Ants from this nest came and examined and discussed these disgraced creatures, then carried their friends home and threw the strangers overboard. Sir John repeated the experiment a number of times. For a while the sober ants did as they had done at first—carried their friends home and threw the strangers overboard. But finally they lost patience, seeing that their reformatory efforts went for nothing, and threw both friends and strangers overboard. Come—is this instinct, or is it thoughtful and intelligent discussion of a thing new—absolutely new—to their experience; with a verdict arrived at, sentence passed, and judgment executed? Is it instinct?—thought petrified by ages of habit—or isn't it brand-new thought, inspired by the new occasion, the new circumstances?

Y. M. I have to concede it. It was not a result of habit; it has all the look of reflection, thought, putting this and that together, as you phrase it. I believe it was thought.

O. M. I will give you another instance of thought. Franklin had a cup of sugar on a table in his room. The ants got at it. He tried several preventives; the ants rose superior to them. Finally he contrived one which shut off access—probably set the table's legs in pans of water, or drew a circle of tar around the cup, I don't remember. At any rate he watched to see what they would do. They tried various schemes—failures, every one. The ants were badly puzzled. Finally they held a consultation, discussed the problem, arrived at a decision—and this time they beat that great philosopher. They formed in procession, crossed the floor, climbed the wall, marched across the ceiling to a point just over the cup, then one by one they let go and fell down into it! Was that instinct—thought petrified by ages of inherited habit?

Y. M. No, I don't believe it was. I believe it was a newly-reasoned scheme to meet a new emergency.

O. M. Very well. You have conceded the reasoning power in two instances. I come now to a mental detail wherein the ant is a long way the superior of any human being. Sir John Lubbock proved by many experiments that an ant knows a stranger-ant of her own species in a moment, even when the stranger is disguised—with paint. Also, he proved that an ant knows every individual in her hive of 500,000 souls. Also, that after a year's absence of one of the 500,000 she will straightway recognize the returned absentee and grace the recognition with an affectionate welcome. How were these recognitions made? Not by color, for painted ants were recognized. Not by smell, for ants that had been dipped in chloroform were recognized. Not by speech and not by antennae-signs nor contacts, for the drunken and motionless ants were recognized and the friend discriminated from the stranger. The ants were all of the one species, therefore the friends had to be recognized by form and feature—friends who formed part of a hive of 500,000! Has any man a memory for form and feature approaching that?

Y. M. Certainly not.

O. M. Franklin's ants and Lubbock's ants show fine capacities for putting this and that together in new and untried emergencies and deducing smart conclusions from the combinations—a man's mental process exactly. With memory to help, man preserves his observations and reasonings, reflects upon them, adds to them, re-combines, and so proceeds, stage by stage, to far results—from the tea-kettle to the ocean greyhound's complex engine; from personal labor to slave labor; from wigwam to palace; from the capricious chase to agriculture and stored food; from nomadic life to stable government and concentrated authority; from incoherent hordes to massed armies. The ant has observation, the reasoning faculty, and the preserving adjunct of a prodigious memory; she has duplicated man's development and the essential features of his civilization, and you call it all instinct!

Y. M. Perhaps I lacked the reasoning faculty myself.

O. M. Well, don't tell anybody, and don't do it again.

Y. M. We have come a good way. As a result—as I understand it—I am required to concede that there is absolutely no intellectual frontier separating Man and the Unrevealed Creatures?

O. M. That is what you are required to concede. There is no such frontier—there is no way to get around that. Man has a finer and more capable machine in him than those others, but it is the same machine and works in the same way. And neither he nor those others can command the machine—it is strictly automatic, independent of control, works when it pleases, and when it doesn't please, can't be forced.

Y. M. Then man and the other animals are all alike, as to mental machinery, and there isn't any difference of any stupendous magnitude between them, except in quality, not in kind.

O. M. That is about the state of it—intellectually. There are pronounced limitations on both sides. We can't learn to understand much of their language, but the dog, the elephant, etc., learn to understand a very great deal of ours. To that extent they are our superiors. On the other hand they can't learn reading, writing, etc., nor any of our fine and high things, and there we have a large advantage over them.

Y. M. Very well, let them have what they've got, and welcome; there is still a wall, and a lofty one. They haven't the Moral Sense; we have it, and it lifts us immeasurably above them.

O. M. What makes you think that?

Y. M. Now look here—let us call a halt. I have stood the other infamies and insanities and that is enough; I am not going to have man and the other animals put on the same level morally.

O. M. I wasn't going to hoist man up to that.

Y. M. This is too much! I think it is not right to jest about such things.

O. M. I am not jesting, I am merely reflecting a plain and simple truth—and without uncharitableness. The fact that man knows right from wrong proves his *intellectual* superiority to the other creatures; but the fact that he can *do* wrong proves his *moral* inferiority to any creature that *cannot*. It is my belief that this position is not assailable.

FREE WILL

Y. M. What is your opinion regarding Free Will?

O. M. That there is no such thing. Did the man possess it who gave the old woman his last shilling and trudged home in the storm?

Y. M. He had the choice between succoring the old woman and leaving her to suffer. Isn't it so?

O. M. Yes, there was a choice to be made, between bodily comfort on the one hand and the comfort of the spirit on the other. The body made a strong appeal, of course—the body would be quite sure to do that; the spirit made a counter appeal. A choice had to be made between the two appeals, and was made. Who or what determined that choice?

Y. M. Any one but you would say that the man determined it, and that in doing it he exercised Free Will.

O. M. We are constantly assured that every man is endowed with Free Will, and that he can and must exercise it where he is offered a choice between good conduct and less-good conduct. Yet we clearly saw that in that man's case he really had no Free Will: his temperament, his training, and the daily influences which had moulded him and made him what he was, *compelled* him to rescue the old woman and thus save *himself*—save himself from spiritual pain, from unendurable wretchedness. He did not make the choice, it was made *for* him by forces which he could not control. Free Will has always existed in *words*, but it stops there, I think—stops short of *fact*. I would not use those words—Free Will—but others.

Y. M. What others?

O. M. Free Choice.

Y. M. What is the difference?

O. M. The one implies untrammeled power to *act* as you please, the other implies nothing beyond a mere *mental process*: the critical ability to determine which of two things is nearest right and just.

Y. M. Make the difference clear, please.

O. M. The mind can freely *select, choose, point out*, the right and just one—its function stops there. It can go no further in the matter. It has no authority to say that the right one shall be acted upon and the wrong one discarded. That authority is in other hands.

Y. M. The man's?

O. M. In the machine which stands for him. In his born disposition and the character which has been built around it by training and environment.

Y. M. It will act upon the right one of the two?

O. M. It will do as it pleases in the matter. George Washington's machine would act upon the right one;

Pizarro's mind would know which was the right one and which the wrong, but the Master inside of Pizarro would act upon the wrong one.

Y. M. Then as I understand it a bad man's mental machinery calmly and judicially points out which of two things is right and just—

O. M. Yes, and his *moral* machinery will freely act upon the one or the other, according to its make, and be quite indifferent to the *mind's* feelings concerning the matter—that is, *would* be, if the mind had any feelings; which it hasn't. It is merely a thermometer: it registers the heat and the cold, and cares not a farthing about either.

Y. M. Then we must not claim that if a man *knows* which of two things is right he is absolutely *bound* to do that thing?

O. M. His temperament and training will decide what he shall do, and he will do it; he cannot help himself, he has no authority over the matter. Wasn't it right for David to go out and slay Goliath?

Y. M. Yes.

O. M. Then it would have been equally *right* for any one else to do it?

Y. M. Certainly.

O. M. Then it would have been *right* for a born coward to attempt it?

Y. M. It would—yes.

O. M. You know that no born coward ever would have attempted it, don't you?

Y. M. Yes.

O. M. You know that a born coward's make and temperament would be an absolute and insurmountable bar to his ever essaying such a thing, don't you?

Y. M. Yes, I know it.

O. M. He clearly perceives that it would be *right* to try it?

Y. M. Yes.

O. M. His mind has Free Choice in determining that it would be *right* to try it?

Y. M. Yes.

O. M. Then if by reason of his inborn cowardice he simply can *not* essay it, what becomes of his Free Will? where is his Free Will? why claim that he has Free Will when the plain facts show that he hasn't? why contend that because he and David *see* the right alike, both must *act* alike? why impose the same laws upon goat and lion?

Y. M. There is really no such thing as Free Will?

O. M. It is what I think. There is *Will*. But it has nothing to do with *intellectual perceptions of right and wrong*, and is not under their command. David's temperament and training had Will, and it was a compulsory force; David had to obey its decrees, he had no choice. The coward's temperament and training possess Will, and *it* is compulsory; it commands him to avoid danger, and he obeys, he has no choice. But neither the Davids nor the cowards possess Free Will—will that may do the right or do the wrong, as their *mental* verdict shall decide.

NOT TWO VALUES, BUT ONLY ONE

Y. M. There is one thing which bothers me: I can't tell where you draw the line between *material* covetousness and *spiritual* covetousness.

O. M. I don't draw any.

Y. M. How do you mean?

O. M. There is no such thing as *material* covetousness. All covetousness is spiritual.

Y. M. *All* longings, desires, ambitions *spiritual*, never material?

O. M. Yes. The Master in you requires that in *all* cases you shall content his *spirit*—that alone. He never requires anything else, he never interests himself in any other matter.

Y. M. Ah, come! When he covets somebody's money—isn't that rather distinctly material and gross?

O. M. No. The money is merely a symbol—it represents in visible and concrete form a *spiritual desire*. Any so-called material thing that you want is merely a symbol; you want it not for *itself,* but because it will content your spirit for the moment.

Y. M. Please particularize.

O. M. Very well. Maybe the thing longed for is a new hat. You get it and your vanity is pleased, your spirit contented. Suppose your friends deride the hat, make fun of it: at once it loses its value; you are ashamed of it, you put it out of your sight, you never want to see it again.

Y. M. I think I see. Go on.

O. M. It is the same hat, isn't it? It is in no way altered. But it wasn't the *hat* you wanted, but only what it stood for—a something to please and content your *spirit.* When it failed of that, the whole of its value was gone. There are no *material* values, there are only spiritual ones. You will hunt in vain for a material value that is *actual, real*—there is no such thing. The only value it possesses, for even a moment, is the spiritual value back of it: remove that and it is at once worthless—like the hat.

Y. M. Can you extend that to money?

O. M. Yes. It is merely a symbol, it has no *material* value; you think you desire it for its own sake, but it is not so. You desire it for the spiritual content it will bring; if it fail of that, you discover that its value is gone. There is that pathetic tale of the man who labored like a slave, unresting, unsatisfied, until he had accumulated a fortune, and was happy over it, jubilant about it; then in a single week a pestilence swept away all whom he held dear and left him desolate. His money's value was gone. He realized that his joy in it came not from the money itself, but from the spiritual contentment he got out of his family's enjoyment of the pleasures and delights it lavished upon them. Money has no *material* value; if you remove its spiritual value nothing is left but dross. It is so with all things, little or big, majestic or trivial—there are no exceptions. Crowns, sceptres, pennies, paste jewels, village notoriety, world-wide fame—they are all the same, they have no *material* value: while they content the *spirit* they are precious, when this fails they are worthless.

A DIFFICULT QUESTION

Y. M. You keep me confused and perplexed all the time by your elusive terminology. Sometimes you divide a man up into two or three separate personalities, each with authorities, jurisdictions and responsibilities of its own, and when he is in that condition I can't grasp him. Now when *I* speak of a man, he is *the whole thing in one*, and easy to hold and contemplate.

O. M. That is pleasant and convenient, if true. When you speak of "my body," who is the "my?"

Y. M. It is the "me."

O. M. The body is a property, then, and the Me owns it. Who is the Me?

Y. M. The Me is *the whole thing*; it is a common property; an undivided ownership, vested in the whole entity.

O. M. If the Me admires a rainbow, is it the whole Me that admires it, including the hair, hands, heels and all?

Y. M. Certainly not. It is my *mind* that admires it.

O. M. So *you* divide the Me yourself. Everybody does; everybody must. What, then, definitely, is the Me?

Y. M. I think it must consist of just those two parts—the body and the mind.

O. M. You think so? If you say "I believe the world is round," who is the "I" that is speaking?

Y. M. The mind.

O. M. If you say "I grieve for the loss of my father," who is the "I?"

Y. M. The mind.

O. M. Is the mind exercising an intellectual function when it examines and accepts the evidence that the world is round?

Y. M. Yes.

O. M. Is it exercising an intellectual function when it grieves for the loss of your father?

Y. M. No. That is not cerebration, brain-work, it is a matter of *feeling*.

O. M. Then its source is not in your mind, but in your *moral* territory?

Y. M. I have to grant it.

O. M. Is your mind a part of your *physical* equipment?

Y. M. No. It is independent of it; it is spiritual.

O. M. Being spiritual, it cannot be affected by physical influences?

Y. M. No.

O. M. Does the mind remain sober when the body is drunk?

Y. M. Well—no.

O. M. There *is* a physical effect present, then?

Y. M. It looks like it.

O. M. A cracked skull has resulted in a crazy mind. Why should that happen if the mind is spiritual, and *independent* of physical influences?

Y. M. Well—I don't know.

O. M. When you have a pain in your foot, how do you know it?

Y. M. I feel it.

O. M. But you do not feel it until a nerve reports the hurt to the brain. Yet the brain is the seat of the mind, is it not?

Y. M. I think so.

O. M. But isn't spiritual enough to learn what is happening in the outskirts without the help of the *physical* messenger? You perceive that the question of who or what the Me is, is not a simple one at all. You say "I admire the rainbow," and "I believe the world is round," and in these cases we find that the Me is not all speaking, but only the *mental* part. You say "I grieve," and again the Me is not all speaking, but only the *moral* part. You say the mind is wholly spiritual; then you say "I have a pain" and find that this time the Me is mental *and* spiritual combined. We all use the "I" in this indeterminate fashion, there is no help for it. We imagine a Master and

King over what you call The Whole Thing, and we speak of him as "I," but when we try to define him we find we cannot do it. The intellect and the feelings can act quite *independently* of each other; we recognize that, and we look around for a Ruler who is master over both, and can serve as a *definite and indisputable "I,"* and enable us to know what we mean and who or what we are talking about when we use that pronoun, but we have to give it up and confess that we cannot find him. To me, Man is a machine, made up of many mechanisms; the moral and mental ones acting automatically in accordance with the impulses of an interior Master who is built out of born-temperament and an accumulation of multitudinous outside influences and trainings; a machine whose *one* function is to secure the spiritual contentment of the Master, be his desires good or be they evil; a machine whose Will is absolute and must be obeyed, and always *is* obeyed.

Y. M. Maybe the Me is the Soul?

O. M. Maybe it is. What is the Soul?

Y. M. I don't know.

O. M. Neither does any one else.

THE MASTER-PASSION

Y. M. What is the Master?—or, in common speech, the Conscience? Explain it.

O. M. It is that mysterious autocrat, lodged in a man, which compels the man to content its desires. It may be called the Master Passion—the hunger for Self-Approval.

Y. M. Where is its seat?

O. M. In man's moral constitution.

Y. M. Are its commands for the man's good?

O. M. It is indifferent to the man's good; it never concerns itself about anything but the satisfying of its own desires. It can be *trained* to prefer things which will be for the man's good, but it will prefer them only because they will content *it* better than other things would.

Y. M. Then even when it is trained to high ideals it is still looking out for its own contentment, and not for the man's good?

O. M. True. Trained or untrained it cares nothing for the man's good, and never concerns itself about it.

Y. M. It seems to be an *immoral* force seated in the man's moral constitution?

O. M. It is a *colorless* force seated in the man's moral constitution. Let us call it an instinct—a blind, unreasoning instinct, which cannot and does not distinguish between good morals and bad ones, and cares nothing for results to the man provided its own contentment be secured; and it will *always* secure that.

Y. M. It seeks money, and it probably considers that that is an advantage for the man?

O. M. It is not always seeking money, it is not always seeking power, nor office, nor any other *material* advantage. In *all* cases it seeks a *spiritual* contentment, let the *means* be what they may. Its desires are determined by the man's temperament—and it is lord over that. Temperament, Conscience, Susceptibility, Spiritual Appetite, are in fact the same thing. Have you ever heard of a person who cared nothing for money?

Y. M. Yes. A scholar who would not leave his garret and his books to take a place in a business house at a large salary.

O. M. He had to satisfy his master,—that is to say, his temperament, his Spiritual Appetite—and it preferred the books to money. Are there other cases?

Y. M. Yes, the hermit.

O. M. It is a good instance. The hermit endures solitude, hunger, cold, and manifold perils, to content his autocrat, who prefers these things, and prayer and contemplation, to money or to any show or luxury that money can buy. Are there others?

Y. M. Yes. The artist, the poet, the scientist.

O. M. Their autocrat prefers the deep pleasures of these occupations, either well paid or ill paid, to any others in the market, at any price. You *realize* that the Master Passion—the contentment of the spirit—concerns itself with many things besides so-called material advantage, material prosperity, cash, and all that?

Y. M. I think I must concede it.

O. M. I believe you must. There are perhaps as many Temperaments that would refuse the burdens and vexations and distinctions of public office as there are that hunger after them. The one set of Temperaments seek the contentment of the spirit, and that alone; and this is exactly the case with the other set. Neither set seeks anything *but* the contentment of the spirit. If the one is sordid, both are sordid; and equally so, since the end in view is precisely the same in both cases. And in both cases Temperament decides the preference—and Temperament is *born*, not made.

CONCLUSION

O. M. You have been taking a holiday?

Y. M. Yes; a mountain-tramp covering a week. Are you ready to talk?

O. M. Quite ready. What shall we begin with?

Y. M. Well, lying abed resting-up, two days and nights, I have thought over all these talks, and passed them carefully in review. With this result: that. . . . that. . . . are you intending to publish your notions about Man some day?

O. M. Now and then, in these past twenty years, the Master inside of me has half-intended to order me to set them to paper and publish them. Do I have to tell you why the order has remained unissued, or can you explain so simple a thing without my help?

Y. M. By your doctrine, it is simplicity itself: outside influences moved your interior Master to give the order; stronger outside influences deterred him. Without the outside influences, neither of these impulses could ever have been born, since a person's brain is incapable of originating an idea within itself.

O. M. Correct. Go on.

Y. M. The matter of publishing or withholding is still in your Master's hands. If, some day, an outside influence shall determine him to publish, he will give the order, and it will be obeyed.

O. M. That is correct. Well?

Y. M. Upon reflection I have arrived at the conviction that the publication of your doctrines would be harmful. Do you pardon me?

O. M. Pardon *you*? You have done nothing. You are an instrument—a speaking-trumpet. Speaking-trumpets are not responsible for what is said through them. Outside influences—in the form of life-long teachings, trainings, notions, prejudices, and other second-hand importations—have persuaded the Master within you that the publication of these doctrines would be harmful. Very well, this is quite natural, and was to be expected; in fact was inevitable. Go on; for the sake of ease and convenience, stick to habit: speak in the first person, and tell me what your Master thinks about it.

Y. M. Well, to begin: it is a desolating doctrine; it is not inspiring, enthusing, uplifting. It takes the glory out of man, it takes the pride out of him, it takes the heroism out of him, it denies him all personal credit, all applause; it not only degrades him to a machine, but allows him no control over the machine; makes a mere coffee-mill of him, and neither permits him to supply the coffee nor turn the crank; his sole and piteously humble function being to grind coarse or fine, according to his make, outside impulses doing all the rest.

O. M. It is correctly stated. Tell me—what do men admire most in each other?

Y. M. Intellect, courage, majesty of build, beauty of countenance, charity, benevolence, magnanimity, kindliness, heroism, and—and—

O. M. I would not go any further. These are *elementals*. Virtue, fortitude, holiness, truthfulness, loyalty, high ideals—these, and all the related qualities that are named in the dictionary, are *made out of the elementals*, by blendings, combinations, and shadings of the elementals, just as one makes green by blending blue and yellow, and makes several shades and tints of red by modifying the elemental red. There are seven elemental colors, they are all in the rainbow; out of them we manufacture and name fifty shades of them. You have named the elementals of the human rainbow, and also one *blend*—heroism, which is made out of courage and magnanimity. Very well, then; which of these elements does the possessor of it manufacture for himself? Is it intellect?

Y. M. No.

O. M. Why?

Y. M. He is born with it.

O. M. Is it courage?

Y. M. No. He is born with it.

O. M. Is it majesty of build, beauty of countenance?

Y. M. No. They are birthrights.

O. M. Take those others—the elemental moral qualities—charity, benevolence, magnanimity, kindliness; fruitful seeds, out of which spring, through cultivation by outside influences, all the manifold blends and combinations of virtues named in the dictionaries: does man manufacture any one of those seeds, or are they all born in him?

Y. M. Born in him.

O. M. Who manufactures them, then?

Y. M. God.

O. M. Where does the credit of it belong?

Y. M. To God.

O. M. And the glory of which you spoke, and the applause?

Y. M. To God.

O. M. Then it is *you* who degrade man. You make him claim glory, praise, flattery, for every valuable thing he possesses—*borrowed* finery, the whole of it; no rag of it earned by himself, not a detail of it produced by his own labor. *You* make man a humbug; have I done worse by him?

Y. M. You have made a machine of him.

O. M. Who devised that cunning and beautiful mechanism, a man's hand?

Y. M. God.

O. M. Who devised the law by which it automatically hammers out of a piano an elaborate piece of music, without error, while the man is thinking about something else, or talking to a friend?

Y. M. God.

O. M. Who devised the blood? Who devised the wonderful machinery which automatically drives its renewing and refreshing streams through the body, day and night, without assistance or advice from the man? Who devised the man's mind, whose machinery works automatically, interests itself in what it pleases, regardless of his will or desire, labors all night when it likes, deaf to his appeals for mercy? God devised all these things. *I* have not made man a machine, God made him a machine. I am merely calling attention to the fact, nothing more. Is it wrong to call attention to a fact? Is it a crime?

Y. M. I think it is wrong to *expose* a fact when harm can come of it.

O. M. Go on.

Y. M. Look at the matter as it stands now. Man has been taught that he is the supreme marvel of the Creation; he believes it; in all the ages he has never doubted it, whether he was a naked savage, or clothed in purple and fine linen, and civilized. This has made his heart buoyant, his life cheery. His pride in himself, his sincere admiration of himself, his joy in what he supposed were his own and unassisted achievements, and his exultation over the praise and applause which they evoked—these have exalted him, enthused him, ambitioned him to higher and higher flights; in a word, made his life worth the living. But by your scheme, all this is abolished: he is degraded to a machine, he is a nobody, his noble prides wither to mere vanities; let him strive as he may, he can never be any better than his humblest and stupidest neighbor; he would never be cheerful again, his life would not be worth the living.

O. M. You really think that?

Y. M. I certainly do.

O. M. Have you ever seen me uncheerful, unhappy?

Y. M. No.

O. M. Well, *I* believe these things. Why have they not made me unhappy?

Y. M. Oh, well—temperament, of course! You never let *that* escape from your scheme.

O. M. That is correct. If a man is born with an unhappy temperament, nothing can make him happy; if he is born with a happy temperament, nothing can make him unhappy.

Y. M. What—not even a degrading and heart-chilling system of beliefs?

O. M. Beliefs? Mere beliefs? Mere convictions? They are powerless. They strive in vain against inborn temperament.

Y. M. I can't believe that, and I don't.

O. M. Now you are speaking hastily. It shows that you have not studiously examined the facts. Of all your intimates, which one is the happiest? Isn't it Burgess?

Y. M. Easily.

O. M. And which one is the unhappiest? Henry Adams?

Y. M. Without a question!

O. M. I know them well. They are extremes, abnormals; their temperaments are as opposite as the poles. Their life-histories are about alike—but look at the results! Their ages are about the same—around about fifty. Burgess has always been buoyant, hopeful, happy; Adams has always been cheerless, hopeless, despondent. As young fellows, both tried country journalism—and failed. Burgess didn't seem to mind it; Adams couldn't smile, he could only mourn and groan over what had happened, and torture himself with vain regrets for not having done so-and-so instead of so-and-so—*then* he would have succeeded. They tried the law—and failed. Burgess remained happy—because he couldn't help it, Adams was wretched—because he couldn't help it. From that day to this, those two men have gone on trying things and failing: Burgess has come out happy and cheerful every time, Adams the reverse. Now we do absolutely know that these men's inborn temperaments have remained unchanged through all the vicissitudes of their material affairs. Let us see how it is with their immaterialities. Both have been zealous democrats; both have been zealous republicans; both have been zealous mugwumps. Burgess has always found happiness and Adams unhappiness, in these several political beliefs and in their migrations out of them. Both of these men have been Presbyterians, Universalists, Methodists, Catholics,—then Presbyterians again, then Methodists again. Burgess has always found rest in these excursions, and Adams unrest; they are trying Christian Science, now, with the customary result, the inevitable result. No political or religious belief can make Burgess unhappy or the other man happy. I assure you it is purely a matter of temperament. Beliefs are *acquirements*, temperaments are *born*; beliefs are subject to change, nothing whatever can change temperament.

Y. M. You have instanced extreme temperaments.

O. M. Yes. The half dozen others are modifications of the extremes. But the law is the same. Where the temperament is two-thirds happy, or two-thirds unhappy, no political or religious beliefs can change the proportions. The vast majority of temperaments are pretty equally balanced; the intensities are absent, and this enables a nation to learn to accommodate itself to its political and religious circumstances and like them, be satisfied with them, at last prefer them. Nations do not *think*, they only *feel*. They get their feelings at second-hand—through their temperaments, not their brains. A nation can be brought—by force of circumstances, not argument—to reconcile itself to *any kind of government or religion that can be devised*; in time it will fit itself to the required conditions; later, it will prefer them; and will fiercely fight for them. As instances, you have all history: the Greeks, the Romans, the Persians, the Egyptians, the Russians, the Germans, the French, the English, the Spaniards, the Americans, the South Americans, the Japanese, the Chinese, the Hindoos, the Turks—a thousand wild and tame religions, every kind of government that can be thought of, from tiger to housecat, each nation *knowing* it has the only true religion and the only sane system of government, each despising all the others, each an ass and not suspecting it, each proud of its fancied supremacy, each perfectly sure it is the pet of God, each with undoubting confidence summoning Him to take command in time of war, each surprised when He goes over to the enemy, but by habit able to excuse it and resume compliments—in a word, the whole human race content, always content, persistently content, indestructibly content, happy, thankful, proud, *no matter what its religion is, nor whether its master be tiger or housecat*. Am I stating facts? You know I am. Is the human race cheerful? You know it is. Considering what it can stand, and be happy, you do me too much honor when you think that *I* can place before it a system of plain cold facts that can take the cheerfulness out of it. Nothing can do that. Everything has been tried. Without success. I beg you not to be troubled.

Saint Joan of Arc

I

The evidence furnished at the Trials and Rehabilitaiton sets forth Joan of Arc's strange and beautiful history in clear and minute detail. Among all the multitude of biographies that freight the shelves of the world's libraries, *this is the only one whose validity is confirmed to us by oath.* It gives us a vivid picture of a career and a personality of so extraordinary a character that we are helped to accept them as actualities by the very fact that both are beyond the inventive reach of fiction. The public part of the career occupied only a mere breath of time—it covered but two years; but what a career it was! The personality which made it possible is one to be reverently studied, loved, and marvelled at, but not to be wholly understood and accounted for by even the most searching analysis.

Note.—The Official Record of the Trials and Rehabilitation of Joan of Arc is the most remarkable history that exists in any language; yet there are few people in the world who can say they have read it: in England and America it has hardly been heard of.

Three hundred years ago Shakespeare did not know the true story of Joan of Arc; in his day it was unknown even in France. For four hundred years it existed rather as a vaguely defined romance than as definite and authentic history. The true story remained buried in the official archives of France from the Rehabilitation of 1456 until Quicherat dug it out and gave it to the world two generations ago, in lucid and understandable modern French. It is a deeply fascinating story. But only in the Official Trials and Rehabilitation can it be found in its entirety.—M. T.

In Joan of Arc at the age of sixteen there was no promise of a romance. She lived in a dull little village on the frontiers of civilization; she had been nowhere and had seen nothing; she knew none but simple shepherd folk; she had never seen a person of note; she hardly knew what a soldier looked like; she had never ridden a horse, nor had a warlike weapon in her hand; she could neither read nor write: she could spin and sew; she knew her catechism and her prayers and the fabulous histories of the saints, and this was all her learning. That was Joan at sixteen. What did she know of law? of evidence? of courts? of the attorney's trade? of legal procedure? Nothing. Less than nothing. Thus exhaustively equipped with ignorance, she went before the court at Toul to contest a false charge of breach of promise of marriage; she conducted her cause herself, without any one's help or advice or any one's friendly sympathy, and won it. She called no witnesses of her own, but vanquished the prosecution by using with deadly effectiveness its own testimony. The astonished judge threw the case out of court, and spoke of her as "this marvellous child."

She went to the veteran Commandant of Vaucouleurs and demanded an escort of soldiers, saying she must march to the help of the King of France, since she was commissioned of God to win back his lost kingdom for him and set the crown upon his head. The Commandant said, "What, you? you are only a child." And he advised that she be taken back to her village and have her ears boxed. But she said she must obey God, and would come again, and again, and yet again, and finally she would get the soldiers. She said truly. In time he yielded, after months of delay and refusal, and gave her the soldiers; and took off his sword and gave her that, and said, "Go—and let come what may." She made her long and perilous journey through the enemy's country, and spoke with the King, and convinced him. Then she was summoned before the University of Poitiers to prove that she *was* commissioned of God and not of Satan, and daily during three weeks she sat before that learned congress unafraid, and capably answered their deep questions out of her ignorant but able head and her simple and honest heart; and again she won her case, and with it the wondering admiration of all that august company.

And now, aged seventeen, she was made Commander-in-Chief, with a prince of the royal house and the veteran generals of France for subordinates; and at the head of the first army she had ever seen, she marched to Orleans, carried the commanding fortresses of the enemy by storm in three desperate assaults, and in ten days raised a siege which had defied the might of France for seven months.

After a tedious and insane delay caused by the King's instability of character and the treacherous counsels of his ministers, she got permission to take the field again. She took Jargeau by storm; then Meung; she forced Beaugency to surrender; then—in the open field—she won the memorable victory of Patay against Talbot, "the English lion," and broke the back of the Hundred Years' War. It was a campaign which cost but seven weeks of time; yet the political results would have been cheap if the time expended had been fifty years. Patay, that unsung and now long-forgotten battle, was the Moscow of the English power in France; from the blow struck that day it was destined never to recover. It was the beginning of the end of an alien dominion which had ridden France intermittently for three hundred years.

Then followed the great campaign of the Loire, the capture of Troyes by assault, and the triumphal march past surrendering towns and fortresses to Rheims, where Joan put the crown upon her King's head in the Cathedral, amid wild public rejoicings, and with her old peasant father there to see these things and believe his eyes if he could. She had restored the crown and the lost sovereignty; the King was grateful for once in his shabby poor life, and asked her to name her reward and have it. She asked for nothing for herself, but begged that the taxes of her native village might be remitted forever. The prayer was granted, and the promise kept for three hundred and sixty years. Then it was broken, and remains broken to-day. France was very poor then, she is very rich now; but she has been collecting those taxes for more than a hundred years.

Joan asked one other favor: that now that her mission was fulfilled she might be allowed to go back to her village and take up her humble life again with her mother and the friends of her childhood; for she had no pleasure in the cruelties of war, and the sight of blood and suffering wrung her heart. Sometimes in battle she did not draw her sword, lest in the splendid madness of the onset she might forget herself and take an enemy's life with it. In the Rouen Trials, one of her quaintest speeches—coming from the gentle and girlish source it did—was her naïve remark that she had "never killed any one." Her prayer for leave to go back to the rest and peace of her village' home was not granted.

Then she wanted to march at once upon Paris, take it, and drive the English out of France. She was hampered in all the ways that treachery and the King's vacillation could devise, but she forced her way to Paris at last, and fell badly wounded in a successful assault upon one of the gates. Of course her men lost heart at once—she was the only heart they had. They fell back. She begged to be allowed to remain at the front, saying victory was sure. "I will take Paris now or die!" she said. But she was removed from the field by force; the King ordered a retreat, and actually disbanded his army. In accordance with a beautiful old military custom Joan devoted her silver armor and hung it up in the Cathedral of St. Denis. Its great days were over.

Then, by command, she followed the King and his frivolous court and endured a gilded captivity for a time, as well as her free spirit could; and whenever inaction became unbearable she gathered some men together and rode away and assaulted a stronghold and captured it.

At last in a sortie against the enemy, from Compiègne, on the 24th of May (when she was turned eighteen), she was herself captured, after a gallant fight. It was her last battle. She was to follow the drums no more.

Thus ended the briefest epoch-making military career known to history. It lasted only a year and a month, but if found France an English province, and furnishes the reason that France is France to-day and not an English province still. Thirteen months! It was, indeed, a short career; but in the centuries that have since elapsed five hundred millions of Frenchmen have lived and died blest by the benefactions it conferred; and so long as France shall endure, the mighty debt must grow. And France is grateful; we often hear her say it. Also thrifty: she collects the Domrémy taxes.

II

Joan was fated to spend the rest of her life behind bolts and bars. She was a prisoner of war, not a criminal, therefore hers was recognized as an honorable captivity. By the rules of war she must be held to ransom, and a fair price could not be refused if offered. John of Luxembourg paid her the just compliment of requiring a prince's ransom for her. In that day that phrase represented a definite sum—61,125 francs. It was, of course, supposable that either the King or grateful France, or both, would fly with the money and set their fair young benefactor free. But this did not happen. In five and a half months neither King nor country stirred a hand nor offered a penny. Twice Joan tried to escape. Once by a trick she succeeded for a moment, and locked her jailer in behind her, but she was discovered and caught; in the other case she let herself down from a tower sixty feet high, but her rope was too short, and she got a fall that disabled her and she could not get away.

Finally, Cauchon, Bishop of Beauvais, paid the money and bought Joan ostensibly for the Church, to be tried for wearing male attire and for other impieties, but really for the English, the enemy into whose hands the poor girl was so piteously anxious not to fall. She was now shut up in the dungeons of the Castle of Rouen and kept in an iron cage, with her hands and feet and neck chained to a pillar; and from that time forth during all the months of her imprisonment, till the end, several rough English soldiers stood guard over her night and day—and not outside her room, but in it. It was a dreary and hideous captivity, but it did not conquer her: nothing could break that invincible spirit. From first to last she was a prisoner a year; and she spent the last three months of it on trial for her life before a formidable array of ecclesiastical judges, and disputing the ground with them foot by foot and inch by inch with brilliant generalship and dauntless pluck. The spectacle of that solitary girl, forlorn and friendless, without advocate or adviser, and without the help and guidance of any copy of the charges brought against her or rescript of the complex and voluminous daily proceedings of the court to modify the crushing strain upon her astonishing memory, fighting that long battle serene and undismayed against these colossal odds, stands alone in its pathos and its sublimity; it has nowhere its mate, either in the annals of fact or in the inventions of fiction.

And how fine and great were the things she daily said, how fresh and crisp—and she so worn in body, so starved, and tired, and harried! They run through the whole gamut of feeling and expression—from scorn and defiance, uttered with soldierly fire and frankness, all down the scale to wounded dignity clothed in words of noble pathos; as, when her patience was exhausted by the pestering delvings and gropings and searchings of her persecutors to find out what kind of devil's witchcraft she had employed to rouse the war spirit in her timid soldiers, she burst out with, "What I said was, *'Ride these English down'*—and I did it myself!" and as, when insultingly asked why it was that *her* standard had place at the crowning of the King in the Cathedral of Rheims rather than the standards of the other captains, she uttered that touching speech, *"It had borne the burden, it had earned the honor"*—a phrase which fell from her lips without premeditation, yet whose moving beauty and simple grace it would bankrupt the arts of language to surpass.

Although she was on trial for her life, she was the only witness called on either side; the only witness summoned to testify before a packed jury commissioned with a definite task: to find her guilty, whether she was guilty or not. She must be convicted out of her own mouth, there being no other way to accomplish it. Every advantage that learning has over ignorance, age over youth, experience over inexperience, chicane over artlessness, every trick and trap and gin devisable by malice and the cunning of sharp intellects practised in setting snares for the unwary—all these were employed against her without shame; and when these arts were one by one defeated by the marvellous intuitions of her alert and penetrating mind, Bishop Cauchon stooped to a final baseness which it degrades human speech to describe: a priest who pretended to come from the region of her own home and to be a pitying friend and anxious to help her in her sore need was smuggled into her cell, and he misused his sacred office to steal her confidence; she confided to him the things sealed from revealment by her Voices, and which her prosecutors had tried so long in vain to trick her into betraying. A concealed confederate set it all down and delivered it to Cauchon, who used Joan's secrets, thus obtained, for her ruin.

Throughout the Trials, whatever the foredoomed witness said was twisted from its true meaning when possible, and made to tell against her; and whenever an answer of hers was beyond the reach of twisting it was not allowed to go upon the record. It was upon one of these latter occasions that she uttered that pathetic reproach—to Cauchon: "Ah, you set down everything that is against me, but you will not set down what is for me."

That this untrained young creature's genius for war was wonderful, and her generalship worthy to rank with the ripe products of a tried and trained military experience, we have the sworn testimony of two of her veteran subordinates—one, the Duc d'Alençon, the other the greatest of the French generals of the time, Dunois, Bastard of Orleans; that her genius was as great—possibly even greater—in the subtle warfare of the forum we have for witness the records of the Rouen Trials, that protracted exhibition of intellectual fence maintained with credit against the master-minds of France; that her moral greatness was peer to her intellect we call the Rouen Trials again to witness, with their testimony to a fortitude which patiently and steadfastly endured during twelve weeks the wasting forces of captivity, chains, loneliness, sickness, darkness, hunger, thirst, cold, shame, insult, abuse, broken sleep, treachery, ingratitude, exhausting sieges of cross-examination, the threat of torture, with the rack before her and the executioner standing ready: yet never surrendering, never asking quarter, the frail wreck of her as unconquerable the last day as was her invincible spirit the first.

Great as she was in so many ways, she was perhaps even greatest of all in the lofty things just named—her patient endurance, her steadfastness, her granite fortitude. We may not hope to easily find her mate and twin in these majestic qualities; where we lift our eyes highest we find only a strange and curious contrast—there in the captive eagle beating his broken wings on the Rock of St. Helena.

III

The Trials ended with her condemnation. But as she had conceded nothing, confessed nothing, this was victory for her, defeat for Cauchon. but his evil resources were not yet exhausted. She was persuaded to agree to sign a paper of slight import, then by treachery a paper was substituted which contained a recantation and a detailed confession of everything which had been charged against her during the Trials and denied and repudiated by her persistently during the three months; and this false paper she ignorantly signed. This was a victory for Cauchon. He followed it eagerly and pitilessly up by at once setting a trap for her which she could not escape. When she realized this she gave up the long struggle, denounced the treason which had been practised against her, repudiated the false confession, reasserted the truth of the testimony which she had given in the Trials, and went to her martyrdom with the peace of God in her tired heart, and on her lips endearing words and loving prayers for the cur she had crowned and the nation of ingrates she had saved.

When the fires rose about her and she begged for a cross for her dying lips to kiss, it was not a friend but an enemy, not a Frenchman but an alien, not a comrade in arms but an English soldier, that answered that pathetic prayer. He broke a stick across his knee, bound the pieces together in the form of the symbol she loved, and gave it her; and his gentle deed is not forgotten, nor will be.

IV

Twenty-five years afterwards the Process of Rehabilitaiton was instituted, there being a growing doubt as to the validity of a sovereignty that had been rescued and set upon its feet by a person who had been proven by the Church to be a witch and a familiar of evil spirits. Joan's old generals, her secretary, several aged relations and other villagers of Domrémy, surviving judges and secretaries of the Rouen and Poitiers Processes—a cloud of witnesses, some of whom had been her enemies and persecutors,—came and made oath and testified; and what they said was written down. In that sworn testimony the moving and beautiful history of Joan of Arc is laid bare, from her childhood to her martyrdom. From the verdict she rises stainlessly pure, in mind and heart, in speech and deed and spirit, and will so endure to the end of time.

She is the Wonder of the Ages. And when we consider her origin, her early circumstances, her sex, and that she did all the things upon which her renown rests while she was still a young girl, we recognize that while our race continues she will be also the *Riddle* of the Ages. When we set about accounting for a Napoleon or a Shakespeare or a Raphael or a Wagner or an Edison or other extraordinary person, we understand that the measure of his talent will not explain the whole result, nor even the largest part of it; no, it is the atmosphere in which the talent was cradled that explains; it is the training which it received while it grew, the nurture it got from reading, study, example, the encouragement it gathered from self-recognition and recognition from the outside at each stage of its development: when we know all these details, then we know why the man was ready when his opportunity came. We should expect Edison's surroundings and atmosphere to have the largest share in discovering him to himself and to the world; and we should expect him to live and die undiscovered in a land where an inventor could find no comradeship, no sympathy, no ambition-rousing atmosphere of recognition and applause—Dahomey, for instance. Dahomey could not find an Edison out; in Dahomey an Edison could not find himself out. Broadly speaking, genius is not born with sight, but blind; and it is not itself that opens its eyes, but the subtle influences of a myriad of stimulating exterior circumstances.

We all know this to be not a guess, but a mere commonplace fact, a truism. Lorraine was Joan of Arc's Dahomey. And there the Riddle confronts us. We can understand how she could be born with military genius, with leonine courage, with incomparable fortitude, with a mind which was in several particulars a prodigy—a mind which included among its specialties the lawyer's gift of detecting traps laid by the adversary in cunning and treacherous arrangements of seemingly innocent words, the orator's gift of eloquence, the advocate's gift of presenting a case in clear and compact form, the judge's gift of sorting and weighing evidence, and finally, something recognizable as more than a mere trace of the statesman's gift of understanding a political situation and how to make profitable use of such opportunities as it offers; we can comprehend how she could be born with these great qualities, but we cannot comprehend how they became immediately usable and effective without the developing forces of a sympathetic atmosphere and the training which comes of teaching, study, practice—years of practice,—and the crowning and perfecting help of a thousand mistakes. We can understand how the possibilities of the future perfect peach are all lying hid in the humble bitter-almond, but we cannot conceive of the peach springing directly from the almond without the intervening long seasons of patient cultivation and development. Out of a cattle-pasturing peasant village lost in the remotenesses of an unvisited wilderness and atrophied with ages of stupefaction and ignorance we cannot see a Joan of Arc issue equipped to the last detail for her amazing career and hope to be able to explain the riddle of it, labor at it as we may.

It is beyond us. All the rules fail in this girl's case. In the world's history she stands alone—quite alone. Others have been great in their first public exhibitions of generalship, valor, legal talent, diplomacy, fortitude; but always their previous years and associations had been in a larger or smaller degree a preparation for these things. There have been no exceptions to the rule. But Joan was competent in a law case at sixteen without ever having seen a law-book or a court-house before; she had no training in soldiership and no associations with it, yet she was a competent general in her first campaign; she was brave in her first battle, yet her courage had had no education—not even the education which a boy's courage gets from never-ceasing reminders that it is not permissible in a boy to be a coward, but only in a girl; friendless, alone, ignorant, in the blossom of her youth, she sat week after week, a prisoner in chains, before her assemblage of judges, enemies hunting her to her death, the ablest minds in France, and answered them out of an untaught wisdom which overmatched their learning, baffled their tricks and treacheries with a native sagacity which compelled their wonder, and scored every day a victory against these incredible odds and camped unchallenged on the field. In the history of the human intellect, untrained, inexperienced, and using only its birthright equipment of untried capacities, there is nothing which approaches this. Joan of Arc stands alone, and must continue to stand alone, by reason of the unfellowed fact that in the things wherein she was great she was so without shade or suggestion of help from preparatory teaching, practice, environment, or experience. There is no one to compare her with, none to measure her by; for all others among the illustrious *grew* towards their high place in an atmosphere and surroundings which discovered their gift to them and nourished it and promoted it, intentionally or unconsciously. There have been other young generals, but they were not girls; young generals, but they have been soldiers before they were generals: she *began* as a general; she commanded the first army she ever saw; she led it from victory to victory, and never lost a battle with it; there have been young commanders-in-chief, but none so young as she: she is the only soldier in history who has held the supreme command of a nation's armies at the age of seventeen.

Her history has still another feature which sets her apart and leaves her without fellow or competitor: there have been many uninspired prophets, but she was the only one who ever ventured the daring detail of naming, along with a foretold event, the event's precise nature, the special time-limit within which it would occur, and the place—*and scored fulfilment.* At Vaucouleurs she said she must go to the King and be made his general, and break the English power, and crown her sovereign—"at Rheims." It all happened. It was all to happen "next year"—and it did. She foretold her first wound and its character and date a month in advance, and the prophecy was recorded in a public record-book three weeks in advance. She repeated it the morning of the date named, and it was fulfilled before night. At Tours she foretold the limit of her military career—saying it would end in one year from the time of its utterance—and she was right. She foretold her martyrdom—using *that word,* and naming a time three months away—and again she was right. At a time when France seemed hopelessly and permanently in the hands of the English she twice asserted in her prison before her judges that within seven years the English would meet with a mightier disaster than had been the fall of Orleans: it happened within five—the fall of Paris. Other prophecies of hers came true, both as to the event named and the time-limit prescribed.

She was deeply religious, and believed that she had daily speech with angels; that she saw them face to face, and that they counselled her, comforted and heartened her, and brought commands to her direct from God. She had a childlike faith in the heavenly origin of her apparitions and her Voices, and not any threat of any form of death was able to frighten it out of her loyal heart. She was a beautiful and simple and lovable character. In the records of the Trials this comes out in clear and shining detail. She was gentle and winning and affectionate; she loved her home and friends and her village life; she was miserable in the presence of pain and suffering; she was full of compassion: on the field of her most splendid victory she forgot her triumphs to hold in her lap the head of a dying enemy and comfort his passing spirit with pitying words; in an age when it was common to slaughter prisoners she stood dauntless between hers and harm, and saved them alive; she was forgiving, generous, unselfish, magnanimous, she was pure from all spot or stain of baseness. And always she was a *girl;* and dear and worshipful, as is meet for that estate: when she fell wounded, the first time, she was frightened, and cried when she saw her blood gushing from her breast; but she was Joan of Arc! and when presently she found that her generals were sounding the retreat, she staggered to her feet and led the assault again and took that place by storm.

There is no blemish in that rounded and beautiful character.

How strange it is!—that almost invariably the artist remembers only one detail—one minor and meaningless detail of the personality of Joan of Arc: to wit, that she was a peasant girl—and forgets all the rest; and so he paints her as a strapping middle-aged fishwoman, with costume to match, and in her face the spirituality of a ham. He is slave to his one idea, and forgets to observe that the supremely great souls are never lodged in gross bodies. No brawn, no muscle, could endure the work that their bodies must do; they do their miracles by the spirit, which has fifty times the strength and staying power of brawn and muscle. The Napoleons are little, not big; and they work twenty hours in the twenty-four, and come up fresh, while the big soldiers with the little hearts faint around them with fatigue. We know what Joan of Arc was like, without asking—merely by what she did. The artist should paint her *spirit*—then he could not fail to paint her body aright. She would rise before us, then, a vision to win us, not repel: a lithe young slender figure, instinct with "the unbought grace of youth," dear and bonny and lovable, the face beautiful, and transfigured with the light of that lustrous intellect and the fires of that unquenchable spirit.

Taking into account, as I have suggested before, all the circumstances—her origin, youth, sex, illiteracy, early environment, and the obstructing conditions under which she exploited her high gifts and made her conquests in the field and before the courts that tried her for her life,—she is easily and by far the most extraordinary person the human race has ever produced.

Concerning the American Language

There was an Englishman in our compartment, and he complimented me on—on what? But you would never guess. He complimented me on my English. He said Americans in general did not speak the English language as correctly as I did. I said I was obliged to him for his compliment, since I knew he meant it for one, but that I was not fairly entitled to it, for I did n't speak English at all,—I only spoke American.

He laughed, and said it was a distinction without a difference. I said no, the difference was not prodigious, but still it was considerable. We fell into a friendly dispute over the matter. I put my case as well as I could, and said,—

"The languages were identical several generations ago, but our changed conditions and the spread of our people far to the south and far to the west have made many alterations in our pronunciation, and have introduced new words among us and changed the meanings of many old ones. English people talk through their noses; we do not. We say *know,* English people say *näo;* we say *cow,* the Briton says *käow;* we—"

"Oh, come! that is pure Yankee; everybody knows that."

"Yes, it is pure Yankee; that is true. One cannot hear it in America outside of the little corner called New England, which is Yankee land. The English themselves planted it there, two hundred and fifty years ago, and there it remains; it has never spread. But England talks through her nose yet; the Londoner and the backwoods New-Englander pronounce 'know' and 'cow' alike, and then the Briton unconsciously satirizes himself by making fun of the Yankee's pronounciation."

We argued this point at some length; nobody won; but no matter, the fact remains,—Englishmen say *näo* and *käow* for "know" and "cow," and that is what the rustic inhabitant of a very small section of America does.

"You conferred your *a* upon New England, too, and there it remains; it has not travelled out of the narrow limits of those six little States in all these two hundred and fifty years. All England uses it, New England's small population—say four millions—use it, but we have forty-five millions who do not use it. You say 'glahs of wawtah,' so does New England; at least, New England says *glahs*. America at large flattens the *a*, and says 'glass of water.' These sounds are pleasanter than yours; you may think they are not right,—well, in English they are *not* right, but in 'American' they are. You say *flahsk*, and *bahsket*, and *jackahss*; we say 'flask,' 'basket,' 'jackass,'—sounding the *a* as it is in 'tallow,' 'fallow,' and so on. Up to as late as 1847 Mr. Webster's Dictionary had the impudence to still pronounce 'basket' *bahsket*, when he knew that outside of his little New England all America shortened the *a* and paid no attention to his English broadening of it. However, it called itself an English Dictionary, so it was proper enough that it should stick to English forms, perhaps. It still calls itself an English Dictionary to-day, but it has quietly ceased to pronounce 'basket' as if it were spelt *bahsket*. In the American language the *h* is respected; the *h* is not dropped or added improperly."

"The same is the case in England,—I mean among the educated classes, of course."

"Yes, that is true; but a nation's language is a very large matter. It is not simply a manner of speech obtaining among the educated handful; the manner obtaining among the vast uneducated multitude must be considered also. Your uneducated masses speak English, you will not deny that; our uneducated masses speak American,—it won't be fair for you to deny that, for you can see, yourself, that when your stable-boy says, 'It is n't the 'unting that 'urts the 'orse, but the 'ammer, 'ammer, 'ammer on the 'ard 'ighway,' and our stable-boy makes the same remark without suffocating a single *h*, these two people are manifestly talking two different languages. But if the signs are to be trusted, even your educated classes used to drop the *h*. They say *humble*, now, and *heroic*, and *historic*, etc., but I judge that they used to drop those *h*'s because your writers still keep up the fashion of putting *an* before those words, instead of *a*. This is what Mr. Darwin might call a 'rudimentary' sign that that *an* was justifiable once, and useful,—when your educated classes used to say *'umble*, and *'eroic*, and *'istorical*. Correct writers of the American language do not put *an* before those words."

The English gentleman had something to say upon this matter, but never mind what he said,—I'm not arguing his case. I have him at a disadvantage, now. I proceeded:—

"In England you encourage an orator by exclaiming 'H'yaah! h'yaah!' We pronounce it *heer* in some sections, 'h'*yer*' in others, and so on; but our whites do not say 'h'yaah,' pronouncing the *a*'s like the *a* in *ah*. I have heard English ladies say 'don't you'—making two separate and distinct words of it; your Mr. Bernand has satirized it. But we always say 'dontchu.' This is much better. Your ladies say, 'Oh, it's *o*ful nice!' Ours say, 'Oh, it's *aw*ful nice!' We say, '*Four* hundred,' you say '*For*'—as in the word or. Your clergymen speak of 'the Lawd,' ours of 'the Lord'; yours speak of 'the gawds of the heathen,' ours of 'the gods of the heathen.' When you are exhausted, you say you are 'knocked up.' We don't. When you say you will do a thing 'directly,' you mean 'immediately'; in the American language—generally speaking—the word signifies 'after a little.' When you say 'clever,' you mean 'capable'; with us the word used to mean 'accommodating,' but I don't know what it means now. Your word 'stout' means 'fleshy'; our word 'stout' usually means 'strong.' Your words 'gentleman' and 'lady' have a very restricted meaning; with us they include the bar-maid, butcher, burglar, harlot, and horse-thief. You say, 'I have n't *got* any stocking on,' 'I have n't *got* any memory,' 'I have n't *got* any money in my purse'; we usually say, 'I have n't any stockings on,' 'I have n't any memory,' 'I have n't any money in my purse.' You say 'out of window'; we always put in a *the*. If one asks 'How old is that man?' the Briton answers, 'He will be about forty;' in the American language, we should say, 'He *is* about forty.' However, I won't tire you, sir; but if I wanted to, I could pile up differences here until I not only convinced you that English and American are separate languages, but that when I speak my native tongue in its utmost purity an Englishman can't understand me at all."

"I don't wish to flatter you, but it is about all I can do to understand you *now.*"

That was a very pretty compliment, and it put us on the pleasantest terms directly,—I use the word in the English sense.

[*Later*—1882. Æsthetes in many of our schools are now beginning to teach the pupils to broaden the *a*, and to say "don't you," in the elegant foreign way.]

Fenimore Cooper's Literary Offenses

The Pathfinder *and* The Deerslayer *stand at the head of Cooper's novels as artistic creations. There are others of his works which contain parts as perfect as are to be found in these, and scenes even more thrilling. Not one can be compared with either of them as a finished whole.*

The defects in both of these tales are comparatively slight. They were pure works of art.—Prof. Lounsbury.

The five tales reveal an extraordinary fullness of invention. . . . One of the very greatest characters in fiction, Natty Bumppo . . . The craft of the woodsman, the tricks of the trapper, all the delicate art of the forest, were familiar to Cooper from his youth up.—Prof. Brander Matthews.

Cooper is the greatest artist in the domain of romantic fiction yet produced by America.—Wilkie Collins.

It seems to me that is was far from right for the Professor of English Literature in Yale, the Professor of English Literature in Columbia, and Wilkie Collins to deliver opinions on Cooper's literature without having read some of it. It would have been much more decorous to keep silent and let persons talk who have read Cooper.

Cooper's art has some defects. In one place in *Deerslayer,* and in the restricted space of two-thirds of a page, Cooper has scored

114 offenses against literary art out of a possible 115. It breaks the record.

There are nineteen rules governing literary art in the domain of romantic fiction—some say twenty-two. In *Deerslayer* Cooper violated eighteen of them. These eighteen require:

1. That a tale shall accomplish something and arrive somewhere. But the *Deerslayer* tale accomplishes nothing and arrives in the air.

2. They require that the episodes of a tale shall be necessary parts of the tale, and shall help to develop it. But as the *Deerslayer* tale is not a tale, and accomplishes nothing and arrives nowhere, the episodes have no rightful place in the work, since there was nothing for them to develop.

3. They require that the personages in a tale shall be alive, except in the case of corpses, and that always the reader shall be able to tell the corpses from the others. But this detail has often been overlooked in the *Deerslayer* tale.

4. They require that the personages in a tale, both dead and alive, shall exhibit a sufficient excuse for being there. But this detail also has been overlooked in the *Deerslayer* tale.

5. They require that when the personages of a tale deal in conversation, the talk shall sound like human talk, and be talk such as human beings would be likely to talk in the given circumstances, and have a discoverable meaning, also a discoverable purpose, and a show of relevancy, and remain in the neighborhood of the subject in hand, and be interesting to the reader, and help out the tale, and stop when the people cannot think of anything more to say. But this requirement has been ignored from the beginning of the *Deerslayer* tale to the end of it.

6. They require that when the author describes the character of a personage in his tale, the conduct and conversation of that personage shall justify said description. But this law gets little or no attention in the *Deerslayer* tale, as Natty Bumppo's case will amply prove.

7. They require that when a personage talks like an illustrated, gilt-edged, tree-calf, hand-tooled, seven-dollar Friendship's Offering in the beginning of a paragraph, he shall

not talk like a negro minstrel in the end of it. But this rule is flung down and danced upon in the *Deerslayer* tale.

8. They require that crass stupidities shall not be played upon the reader as "the craft of the woodsman, the delicate art of the forest," by either the author or the people in the tale. But this rule is persistently violated in the *Deerslayer* tale.

9. They require that the personages of a tale shall confine themselves to possibilities and let miracles alone; or, if they venture a miracle, the author must so plausibly set it forth as to make it look possible and reasonable. But these rules are not respected in the *Deerslayer* tale.

10. They require that the author shall make the reader feel a deep interest in the personages of his tale and in their fate; and that he shall make the reader love the good people in the tale and hate the bad ones. But the reader of the *Deerslayer* tale dislikes the good people in it, is indifferent to the others, and wishes they would all get drowned together.

11. They require that the characters in a tale shall be so clearly defined that the reader can tell beforehand what each will do in a given emergency. But in the *Deerslayer* tale this rule is vacated.

In addition to these large rules there are some little ones. These require that the author shall

12. *Say* what he is proposing to say, not merely come near it.
13. Use the right word, not its second cousin.
14. Eschew surplusage.
15. Not omit necessary details.
16. Avoid slovenliness of form.
17. Use good grammar.
18. Employ a simple and straightforward style.

Even these seven are coldly and persistently violated in the *Deerslayer* tale.

Cooper's gift in the way of invention was not a rich endowment; but such as it was he liked to work it, he was pleased with the effects, and indeed he did some quite sweet things with it. In his little box of stage-properties he kept six or eight cunning devices, tricks, artifices for his savages and woodsmen to deceive and circumvent each other with, and he was never so happy as when he was working these innocent things and seeing them go. A favorite one was to make a moccasined person tread in the tracks of the moccasined enemy, and thus hide his own trail. Cooper wore out barrels and barrels of moccasins in working that trick. Another stage-property that he pulled out of his box pretty frequently was his broken twig. He prized his broken twig above all the rest of his effects, and worked it the hardest. It is a restful chapter in any book of his when somebody doesn't step on a dry twig and alarm all the reds and whites for two hundred years around. Every time a Cooper person is in peril, and absolute silence is worth four dollars a minute, he is sure to step on a dry twig. There may be a hundred handier things to step on, but that wouldn't satisfy Cooper. Cooper requires him to turn out and find a dry twig; and if he can't do it, go and borrow one. In fact, the Leatherstocking Series ought to have been called the Broken Twig Series.

I am sorry there is not room to put in a few dozen instances of the delicate art of the forest, as practised by Natty Bumppo and some of the other Cooperian experts. Perhaps we may venture two or three samples. Cooper was a sailor—a naval officer; yet he gravely tells us how a vessel, driving toward a lee shore in a gale, is steered for a particular spot by her skipper because he knows of an *undertow* there which will hold her back against the gale and save her. For just pure woodcraft, or sailorcraft, or whatever it is, isn't that neat? For several years Cooper was daily in the society of artillery, and he ought to have noticed that when a cannon-ball strikes the ground it either buries itself or skips a hundred feet or so; skips again a hundred feet or so—and so on, till finally it gets tired and rolls. Now in one place he loses some "females"—as he always calls women—in the edge of a wood near a plain at night in a fog, on purpose to give Bumppo a chance to show off the delicate art of the forest before the reader. These mislaid people are hunting for a fort. They hear a cannon-blast, and a cannon-ball presently comes rolling into the wood and stops at their feet. To the females this suggests nothing. The case is very different with the admirable Bumppo. I wish I may never know peace again if he doesn't strike out promptly and *follow the track* of that cannon-ball across the plain through the dense fog and find the fort. Isn't it a daisy? If Cooper had any real knowledge of Nature's ways of doing things, he had a most delicate art in concealing the fact. For instance: one of his acute Indian experts, Chingachgook (pronounced Chicago, I think), has lost the trail of a person he is tracking through the forest. Apparently that trail is hopelessly lost. Neither you nor I could ever have guessed out the way to find it. It was very different with Chicago. Chicago was not stumped for long. He turned a running stream out of its course, and there, in the slush in its old bed, were that person's moccasin tracks. The current did not wash them away, as it would have done in all other like cases—no, even the eternal laws of Nature have to vacate when Cooper wants to put up a delicate job of woodcraft on the reader.

We must be a little wary when Brander Matthews tell us that Cooper's books "reveal an extraordinary fullness of invention." As a rule, I am quite willing to accept Brander Matthews's literary judgments and applaud his lucid and graceful phrasing of them; but that particular statement needs to be taken with a few tons of salt. Bless your heart, Cooper hadn't any more invention than a horse; and I don't mean a high-class horse, either; I mean a clothes-horse. It would be very difficult to find a really clever "situation" in Cooper's books, and still more difficult to find one of any kind which he has failed to render absurd by his handling of it. Look at the episodes of "the caves"; and at the celebrated scuffle between Maqua and those others on the table-land a few days later; and at Hurry Harry's queer water-transit from the castle to the ark; and at Deerslayer's half-hour with his first corpse; and at the quarrel between Hurry Harry and Deerslayer later; and at—but choose for yourself; you can't go amiss.

If Cooper had been an observer his inventive faculty would have worked better; not more interestingly, but more rationally, more plausibly. Cooper's proudest creations in the way of "situations" suffer noticeably from the absence of the observer's protecting gift. Cooper's eye was splendidly inaccurate. Cooper seldom saw anything correctly. He saw nearly all things as through a glass eye, darkly. Of course a man who cannot see the commonest little every-day matters accurately is working at a disadvantage when he is constructing a "situation." In the *Deerslayer* tale Cooper has a stream which is fifty feet wide where it flows out of a lake; it presently narrows to twenty as it meanders along for no given reason, and yet when a stream acts like that it ought to be required to explain itself. Fourteen pages later the width of the brook's outlet from the lake has suddenly shrunk thirty feet, and become "the narrowest part of the stream." This shrinkage is not accounted for. The stream has bends in it, a sure indication that it has alluvial banks and cuts them; yet these bends are only thirty and fifty feet long. If Cooper had been a nice and punctilious observer he would have noticed that the bends were oftener nine hundred feet long than short of it.

Cooper made the exit of that stream fifty feet wide, in the first place, for no particular reason; in the second place, he narrowed it to less than twenty to accommodate some Indians. He bends a "sapling" to the form of an arch over this narrow passage, and conceals six Indians in its foliage. They are "laying" for a settler's scow or ark which is coming up the stream on its way to the lake; it is being hauled against the stiff current by a rope whose stationary end is anchored in the lake; its rate of progress cannot be more than a mile an hour. Cooper describes the ark, but pretty obscurely. In the matter of dimensions "it was little more than a modern canal-boat." Let us guess, then, that it was about one hundred and forty feet long. It was of "greater breadth than common." Let us guess, then, that it was about sixteen feet wide. This leviathan had been prowling down bends which were but a third as long as itself, and scraping between banks where it had only two feet of space to spare on each side. We cannot too much admire this miracle. A low-roofed log dwelling occupies "two-thirds of the ark's length"—a dwelling ninety feet long and sixteen feet wide, let us say—a kind of vestibule train. The dwelling has two rooms—each forty-five feet long and sixteen feet wide, let us guess. One of them is the bedroom of the Hutter girls, Judith and Hetty; the other is the parlor in the daytime, at night it is papa's bed-chamber. The ark is arriving at the stream's exit now, whose width has been reduced to less than twenty feet to accommodate the Indians—say to eighteen. There is a foot to spare on each side of the boat. Did the Indians notice that there was going to be a tight squeeze there? Did they notice that they could make money by climbing down out of that arched sapling and just stepping aboard when the ark scraped by? No, other Indians would have noticed these things, but Cooper's Indians never notice anything. Cooper thinks they are marvelous creatures for noticing, but he was almost always in error about his Indians. There was seldom a sane one among them.

The ark is one hundred and forty-feet long; the dwelling is ninety feet long. The idea of the Indians is to drop softly and secretly from the arched sapling to the dwelling as the ark creeps along under it at the rate of a mile an hour, and butcher the family. It will take the ark a minute and a half to pass under. It will take the ninety-foot dwelling a minute to pass under. Now, then, what did the six Indians do? It would take you thirty years to guess, and even then you would have to give it up, I believe. Therefore, I will tell you what the Indians did. Their chief, a person of quite extraordinary intellect for a Cooper Indian, warily watched the canal-boat as it squeezed along under him, and when he had got his calculations fined down to exactly the right shade, as he judged, he let go and dropped. And *missed the house!* That is actually what he did. He missed the house, and landed in the stern of the scow. It was not much of a fall, yet it knocked him silly. He lay there unconscious. If the house had been ninety-seven feet long he would have made the trip. The fault was Cooper's, not his. The error lay in the construction of the house. Cooper was no architect.

There still remained in the roost five Indians. The boat has passed under and is not out of their reach. Let me explain what the five did—you would not be able to reason it out for yourself. No. 1 jumped for the boat, but fell in the water astern of it. Then No. 2 jumped for the boat, but fell in the water still farther astern of it. Then No. 3 jumped for the boat, and fell a good way astern of it. Then No. 4 jumped for the boat, and fell in the water *away* astern. Then even No. 5 made a jump for the boat—for he was a Cooper Indian. In the matter of intellect, the difference between a Cooper Indian and the Indian that stands in front of the cigar-shop is not spacious. The scow episode is really a sublime burst of invention; but it does not thrill, because the inaccuracy of the details throws a sort of air of fictitiousness and general improbability over it. This comes of Cooper's inadequacy as an observer.

The reader will find some examples of Cooper's high talent for inaccurate observation in the account of the shooting-match in *The Pathfinder.*

> A common wrought nail was driven lightly into the target, its head having been first touched with paint.

The color of the paint is not stated—an important omission, but Cooper deals freely in important omissions. No, after all, it was not an important omission; for this nail-head is a *hundred yards* from the marksmen, and could not be seen by them at that distance, no matter what its color might be. How far can the best eyes see a common house-fly? A hundred yards? It is quite impossible. Very well; eyes that cannot see a house-fly that is a hundred yards away cannot see an ordinary nail-head at that distance, for the size of the two objects is the same. It takes a keen eye to see a fly or a nail-head at fifty yards—one hundred and fifty feet. Can the reader do it?

The nail was lightly driven, its head painted, and game called. Then the Cooper miracles began. The bullet of the first marksman chipped an edge of the nail-head; the next man's bullet drove the nail a little way into the target—and removed all the paint. Haven't the miracles gone far enough now? Not to suit Cooper; for the purpose of this whole scheme is to show off his prodigy, Deerslayer-Hawkeye-Long-Rifle-Leatherstocking-Pathfinder-Bumppo before the ladies.

> "Be all ready to clench it, boys!" cried out Pathfinder, stepping into his friend's tracks the instant they were vacant. "Never mind a new nail; I can see that, though the paint is gone, and what I can see I can hit at a hundred yards, though it were only a mosquito's eye. Be ready to clench!"

> The rifle cracked, the bullet sped its way, and the head of the nail was buried in the wood, covered by the piece of flattened lead.

There, you see, is a man who could hunt flies with a rifle, and command a ducal salary in a Wild West show to-day if we had him back with us.

The recorded feat is certainly surprising just as it stands; but it is not surprising enough for Cooper. Cooper adds a touch. He has made Pathfinder do this miracle with another man's rifle; and not only that, but Pathfinder did not have even the advantage of loading it himself. He had everything against him, and yet he made that impossible shot; and not only made it, but did it with absolute confidence, saying, "Be ready to clench." Now a person like that would have undertaken that same feat with a brick-bat, and with Cooper to help he would have achieved it, too.

Pathfinder showed off handsomely that day before the ladies. His very first feat was a thing which no Wild West show can touch. He was standing with the group of marksmen, observing—a hundred yards from the target, mind; one Jasper raised his rifle and drove the center of the bull's-eye. Then the Quartermaster fired. The target exhibited no result this time. There was a laugh. "It's a dead miss," said Major Lundie. Pathfinder waited an impressive moment or two; then said, in that calm, indifferent, know-it-all way of his, "No, Major, he has covered Jasper's bullet, as will be seen if any one will take the trouble to examine the target."

Wasn't it remarkable! How *could* he see that little pellet fly through the air and enter that distant bullet-hole? Yet that is what he did; for nothing is impossible to a Cooper person. Did any of those people have any deep-seated doubts about this thing? No; for that would imply sanity, and these were all Cooper people.

> The respect for Pathfinder's skill and for his *quickness and accuracy of sight* [the italics are mine] was so profound and general, that the instant he made this declaration the spectators began to distrust their own opinions, and a dozen rushed to the target in order to ascertain the fact. There, sure enough, it was found that the

> Quartermaster's bullet had gone through the hole made by Jasper's, and that, too, so accurately as to require a minute examination to be certain of the circumstance, which, however, was soon clearly established by discovering one bullet over the other in the stump against which the target was placed.

They made a "minute" examination; but never mind, how could they know that there were two bullets in that hole without digging the latest one out? for neither probe nor eyesight could prove the presence of any more than one bullet. Did they dig? No; as we shall see. It is the Pathfinder's turn now; he steps out before the ladies, takes aim, and fires.

But, alas! here is disappointment; an incredible, an unimaginable disappointment—for the target's aspect is unchanged; there is nothing there but that same old bullet-hole!

> "If one dared to hint at such a thing," cried Major Duncan, "I should say that the Pathfinder has also missed the target!"

As nobody had missed it yet, the "also" was not necessary; but never mind about that, for the Pathfinder is going to speak.

> "No, no, Major," said he, confidently, "that *would* be a risky declaration. I didn't load the piece, and can't say what was in it; but if it was lead, you will find the bullet driving down those of the Quartermaster and Jasper, else is not my name Pathfinder."
>
> A shout from the target announced the truth of this assertion.

Is the miracle sufficient as it stands? Not for Cooper. The Pathfinder speaks again, and he "now slowly advances toward the stage occupied by the females":

> "That's not all, boys, that's not all; if you find the target touched at all, I'll own to a miss. The Quartermaster cut the wood, but you'll find no wood cut by that last messenger."

The miracle is at last complete. He knew—doubtless *saw*—at the distance of a hundred yards—that his bullet had passed into the hole *without fraying the edges.* There were now three bullets in that one hole—three bullets embedded processionally in the body of the stump back of the target. Everybody knew this—somehow or other—and yet nobody had dug any of them out to make sure. Cooper is not a close observer, but he is interesting. He is certainly always that, no matter what happens. And he is more interesting when he is not noticing what he is about than when he is. This is a considerable merit.

The conversations in the Cooper books have a curious sound in our modern ears. To believe that such talk really ever came out of people's mouths would be to believe that there was a time when time was of no value to a person who thought he had something to say; when it was the custom to spread a two-minute remark out to ten; when a man's mouth was a rolling-mill, and busied itself all day long in turning four-foot pigs of thought into thirty-foot bars of conversational railroad iron by attenuation; when subjects were seldom faithfully stuck to, but the talk wandered all around and arrived nowhere; when conversations consisted mainly of irrelevancies, with here and there a relevancy, a relevancy with an embarrassed look, as not being able to explain how it got there.

Cooper was certainly not a master in the construction of dialogue. Inaccurate observation defeated him here as it defeated him in so many other enterprises of his. He even failed to notice that the man who talks corrupt English six days in the week must and will talk it on the seventh, and can't help himself. In the *Deerslayer* story he lets Deerslayer talk the showiest kind of book-talk sometimes, and at other times the basest of base dialects. For instance, when some one asks him if he has a sweetheart, and if so, where she abides, this is his majestic answer:

> "She's in the forest—hanging from the boughs of the trees, in a soft rain—in the dew on the open grass—the clouds that float about in the blue heavens—the birds that sing in the woods—the sweet springs where I slake my thirst—and in all the other glorious gifts that come from God's Providence!"

And he preceded that, a little before, with this:

> "It consarns me as all things that touches a fri'nd consarns a fri'nd."

And this is another of his remarks:

> "If I was Injin born, now, I might tell of this, or carry in the scalp and boast of the expl'ite afore the whole tribe; or if my inimy had only been a bear"—[and so on].

We cannot imagine such a thing as a veteran Scotch Commander-in-Chief comporting himself in the field like a windy melodramatic actor, but Cooper could. On one occasion Alice and Cora were being chased by the French through a fog in the neighborhood of their father's fort:

> *"Point de quartier aux coquins!"* cried an eager pursuer, who seemed to direct the operations of the enemy.
>
> "Stand firm and be ready, my gallant 60ths!" suddenly exclaimed a voice above them; "wait to see the enemy; fire low, and sweep the glacis."
>
> "Father! father" exclaimed a piercing cry from out the mist; "it is I! Alice! thy own Elsie! spare, O! save your daughters!"
>
> "Hold!" shouted the former speaker, in the awful tones of parental agony, the sound reaching even to the woods, and rolling back in solemn echo. "'Tis she! God has restored me my children! Throw open the sally-port; to the field, 60ths, to the field! pull not a trigger, lest ye kill my lambs! Drive off these dogs of France with your steel!"

Cooper's word-sense was singularly dull. When a person has a poor ear for music he will flat and sharp right along without knowing it. He keeps near the tune, but it is *not* the tune. When a person has a poor ear for words, the result is a literary flatting and sharping; you perceive what he is intending to say, but you also perceive that he doesn't *say* it. This is Cooper. He was not a word-musician. His ear was satisfied with the *approximate* word. I will furnish some circumstantial evidence in support of this charge. My instances are gathered from half a dozen pages of the tale called *Deerslayer*. He uses "verbal" for "oral"; "precision" for "facility"; "phenomena" for "marvels"; "necessary" for "predetermined"; "unsophisticated" for "primitive"; "preparation" for "expectancy"; "rebuked" for "subdued"; "dependent on" for "resulting from"; "fact" for "condition"; "fact" for "conjecture"; "precaution" for "caution"; "explain" for "determine"; "mortified" for "disappointed"; "meretricious" for "factitious"; "materially" for "considerably"; "decreasing" for "deepening"; "increasing" for "disappearing"; "embedded" for "inclosed"; "treacherous" for "hostile"; "stood" for "stooped"; "softened" for "replaced"; "rejoined" for "remarked"; "situation" for "condition"; "different" for "differing"; "insensible" for "unsentient"; "brevity" for "celerity"; "distrusted" for "suspicious"; "mental imbecility" for "imbecility"; "eyes" for "sight"; "counteracting" for "opposing"; "funeral obsequies" for "obsequies."

There have been daring people in the world who claimed that Cooper could write English, but they are all dead now—all dead but Lounsbury. I don't remember that Lounsbury makes the claim in so many words, still he makes it, for he says that *Deerslayer* is a "pure work of art." Pure, in that connection, means faultless—faultless in all details—and language is a detail. If Mr. Lounsbury had only compared Cooper's English with the English which he writes himself—but it is plain that he didn't; and so it is likely that he imagines until this day that Cooper's is as clean and compact as his own. Now I feel sure, deep down in my heart, that Cooper wrote about the poorest English that exists in our language, and that the English of *Deerslayer* is the very worst that even Cooper ever wrote.

I may be mistaken, but it does seem to me that *Deerslayer* is not a work of art in any sense; it does seem to me that it is destitute of every detail that goes to the making of a work of art; in truth, it seems to me that *Deerslayer* is just simply a literary *delirium tremens.*

A work of art? It has no invention; it has no order, system, sequence, or result; it has no life-likeness, no thrill, no stir, no seeming of reality; its characters are confusedly drawn, and by their acts and words they prove that they are not the sort of people the author claims that they are; its humor is pathetic; its pathos is funny, its conversations are—oh! indescribable; its love-scenes odious; its English a crime against the language.

Counting these out, what is left is Art. I think we must all admit that.

My First Lie and How I Got Out of It

As I understand it, what you desire is information about "my first lie, and how I got out of it." I was born in 1835; I am well along, and my memory is not as good as it was. If you had asked about my first truth it would have been easier for me and kinder of you, for I remember that fairly well; I remember it as if it were last week. The family think it was week before, but that is flattery and probably has a selfish project back of it. When a person has become seasoned by experience and has reached the age of sixty-four, which is the age of discretion, he likes a family compliment as well as ever, but he does not lose his head over it as in the old innocent days.

I do not remember my first lie, it is too far back; but I remember my second one very well. I was nine days old at the time, and had noticed that if a pin was sticking in me and I advertised it in the usual fashion, I was lovingly petted and coddled and pitied in a most agreeable way and got a ration between meals besides.

It was human nature to want to get these riches, and I fell. I lied about the pin—advertising one when there wasn't any. You would have done it; George Washington did it, anybody would have done it. During the first half of my life I never knew a child that was able to rise above that temptation and keep from telling that lie. Up to 1867 all the civilized children that were ever born into the world were liars. Including George. Then the safety-pin came in and blocked the game. But is that reform worth anything? No; for it is reform by force and has no virtue in it; it merely stops that form of lying, it doesn't impair the disposition to lie, by a shade. It is the cradle application of conversion by fire and sword, or of the temperance principle through prohibition.

To return to that early lie. They found no pin and they realized that another liar had been added to the world's supply. For by grace of a rare inspiration a quite commonplace but seldom noticed fact was borne in upon their understandings—that almost all lies are acts, and speech has no part in them. Then, if they examined a little further they recognized that all people are liars from the cradle onward, without exception, and that they begin to lie as soon as they wake in the morning, and keep it up without rest or refreshment until they go to sleep at night. If they arrived at that truth it probably grieved them—did, if they had been heedlessly and ignorantly educated by their books and teachers; for why should a person grieve over a thing which by the eternal law of his make he cannot help? He didn't invent the law; it is merely his business to obey it and keep still; join the universal conspiracy and keep so still that he shall deceive his fellow-conspirators into imagining that he doesn't know that the law exists. It is what we all do—we that know. I am speaking of the lie of silent assertion; we can tell it without saying a word, and we all do it—we that know. In the magnitude of its territorial spread it is one of the most majestic lies that the civilizations make it their sacred and anxious care to guard and watch and propagate.

For instance. It would not be possible for a humane and intelligent person to invent a rational excuse for slavery; yet you will remember that in the early days of the emancipation agitation in the North the agitators got but small help or countenance from any one. Argue and plead and pray as they might, they could not break the universal stillness that reigned, from pulpit and press all the way down to the bottom of society—the clammy stillness created and maintained by the lie of silent assertion—the silent assertion that there wasn't anything going on in which humane and intelligent people were interested.

From the beginning of the Dreyfus case to the end of it all France, except a couple of dozen moral paladins, lay under the smother of the silent-assertion lie that no wrong was being done to a persecuted and unoffending man. The like smother was over England lately, a good half of the population silently letting on that they were not aware that Mr. Chamberlain was trying to manufacture a war in South Africa and was willing to pay fancy prices for the materials.

Now there we have instances of three prominent ostensible civilizations working the silent-assertion lie. Could one find other instances in the three countries? I think so. Not so very many, perhaps, but say a billion—just so as to keep within bounds. Are those countries working that kind of lie, day in and day out, in thousands and thousands of varieties, without ever resting? Yes, we know that to be true. The universal conspiracy of the silent-assertion lie is hard at work always and everywhere, and always in the interest of a stupidity or a sham, never in the interest of a thing fine or respectable. Is it the most timid and shabby of all lies? It seems to have the look of it. For ages and ages it has mutely labored in the interest of despotisms and aristocracies and chattel slaveries, and military slaveries, and religious slaveries, and has kept them alive; keeps them alive yet, here and there and yonder, all about the globe; and will go on keeping them alive until the silent-assertion lie retires from business—the silent assertion that nothing is going on which fair and intelligent men are aware of and are engaged by their duty to try to stop.

What I am arriving at is this: When whole races and peoples conspire to propagate gigantic mute lies in the interest of tyrannies and shams, why should we care anything about the trifling lies told by individuals? Why should we try to make it appear that abstention from lying is a virtue? Why should we want to beguile ourselves in that way? Why should we without shame help the nation lie, and then be ashamed to do a little lying on our own account? Why shouldn't we be honest and honorable, and lie every time we get a chance? That is to say, why shouldn't we be consistent, and either lie all the time or not at all? Why should we help the nation lie the whole day long and then object to telling one little individual private lie in our own interest to go to bed on? Just for the refreshment of it, I mean, and to take the rancid taste out of our mouth.

Here in England they have the oddest ways. They won't tell a spoken lie—nothing can persuade them. Except in a large moral interest, like politics or religion, I mean. To tell a spoken lie to get even the poorest little personal advantage out of it is a thing which is impossible to them. They make me ashamed of myself sometimes, they are so bigoted. They will not even tell a lie for the fun of it; they will not tell it when it hasn't even a suggestion of damage or advantage in it for any one. This has a restraining influence upon me in spite of reason, and I am always getting out of practice.

Of course, they tell all sorts of little unspoken lies, just like anybody; but they don't notice it until their attention is called to it. They have got me so that sometimes I never tell a verbal lie now except in a modified form; and even in the modified form they don't approve of it. Still, that is as far as I can go in the interest of the growing friendly relations between the two countries; I must keep some of my self-respect. And my health. I can live on a pretty low diet, but I can't get along on no sustenance at all.

Of course, there are times when these people have to come out with a spoken lie, for that is a thing which happens to everybody once in a while, and would happen to the angels if they came down here much. Particularly to the angels, in fact, for the lies I speak of are self-sacrificing ones told for a generous object, not a mean one; but even when these people tell a lie of that sort it seems to scare them and unsettle their minds. It is a wonderful thing to see, and shows that they are all insane. In fact, it is a country which is full of the most interesting superstitions.

I have an English friend of twenty-five years' standing, and yesterday when we were coming downtown on top of the 'bus I happened to tell him a lie. A modified one, of course; a half-breed, a mulatto; I can't seem to tell any other kind now, the market is so flat. I was explaining to him how I got out of an embarrassment in Austria last year. I do not know what might have become of me if I hadn't happened to remember to tell the police that I belonged to the same family as the Prince of Wales. That made everything pleasant and they let me go; and apologized, too, and were ever so kind and obliging and polite, and couldn't do too much for me, and explained how the mistake came to be made, and promised to hang the officer that did it, and hoped I would let bygones be bygones and not say anything about it; and I said they could depend on me. My friend said, austerely:

"You call it a modified lie? Where is the modification?"

I explained that it lay in the form of my statement to the police.

"I didn't say I belonged to the royal family; I only said I belonged to the same family as the Prince—meaning the human family, of course; and if those people had had any penetration they would have known it. I can't go around furnishing brains to the police; it is not to be expected."

"How did you feel after that performance?"

"Well, of course I was distressed to find that the police had misunderstood me, but as long as I had not told any lie I knew there was no occasion to sit up nights and worry about it."

My friend struggled with the case for several minutes, turning it over and examining it in his mind, then he said that so far as he could see the modification was itself a lie, it being a misleading reservation of an explanatory fact, and so I had told two lies instead of only one.

"I wouldn't have done it," said he; "I have never told a lie, and I should be very sorry to do such a thing."

Just then he lifted his hat and smiled a basketful of surprised and delighted smiles down at a gentleman who was passing in a hansom.

"Who was that, G.?"

"I don't know."

"Then why did you do that?"

"Because I saw he thought he knew me and was expecting it of me. If I hadn't done it he would have been hurt. I didn't want to embarrass him before the whole street."

"Well, your heart was right, G., and your act was right. What you did was kindly and courteous and beautiful; I would have done it myself; but it was a lie."

"A lie? I didn't say a word. How do you make it out?"

"I know you didn't speak, still you said to him very plainly and enthusiastically in dumb show, 'Hello! you in town? Awful glad to see you, old fellow; when did you get back?' Concealed in your actions was what you have called 'a misleading reservation of an explanatory fact'—the fact that you had never seen him before. You expressed joy in encountering him—a lie; and you made that reservation—another lie. It was my pair over again. But don't be troubled—we all do it."

Two hours later, at dinner, when quite other matters were being discussed, he told how he happened along once just in the nick of time to do a great service for a family who were old friends of his. The head of it had suddenly died in circumstances and surroundings of a ruinously disgraceful character. If known the facts would break the hearts of the innocent family and put upon them a load of unendurable shame. There was no help but in a giant lie, and he girded up his loins and told it.

"The family never found out, G.?"

"Never. In all these years they have never suspected. They were proud of him and always had reason to be; they are proud of him yet, and to them his memory is sacred and stainless and beautiful."

"They had a narrow escape, G."

"Indeed they had."

"For the very next man that came along might have been one of these heartless and shameless truth-mongers. You have told the truth a million times in your life, G., but that one golden lie atones for it all. Persevere."

Some may think me not strict enough in my morals, but that position is hardly tenable. There are many kinds of lying which I do not approve. I do not like an injurious lie, except when it injures somebody else; and I do not like the lie of bravado, nor the lie of virtuous ecstasy; the latter was affected by Bryant, the former by Carlyle.

Mr. Bryant said, "Truth crushed to earth will rise again." I have taken medals at thirteen world's fairs, and may claim to be not without capacity, but I never told as big a one as that Mr. Bryant was playing to the gallery; we all do it. Carlyle said, in substance, this—I do not remember the exact words: "This gospel is eternal—that a lie shall not live." I have a reverent affection for Carlyle's books, and have read his Revolution eight times; and so I prefer to think he was not entirely at himself when he told that one. To me it is plain that he said it in a moment of excitement, when chasing Americans out of his back yard with brickbats. They used to go there and worship. At bottom he was probably fond of them, but he was always able to conceal it. He kept bricks for them, but he was not a good shot, and it is matter of history that when he fired they dodged, and carried off the brick; for as a nation we like relics, and so long as we get them we do not much care what the reliquary thinks about it. I am quite sure that when he told that large one about a lie not being able to live he had just missed an American and was over-excited. He told it above thirty years ago, but it is alive yet; alive, and very healthy and hearty, and likely to out-live any fact in history. Carlyle was truthful when calm but give him Americans enough and bricks enough and he could have taken medals himself.

As regards that time that George Washington told the truth, a word must be said, of course. It is the principal jewel in the crown of America, and it is but natural that we should work it for all it is worth, as Milton says in his "Lay of the Last Minstrel." It was a timely and judicious truth, and I should have told it myself in the circumstances. But I should have stopped there. It was a stately truth, a lofty truth—a Tower; and I think it was a mistake to go on and distract attention from its sublimity by building another Tower alongside of it fourteen times as high. I refer to his remark that he "could not lie." I should have fed that to the marines; or left it to Carlyle; it is just in his style. It would have taken a medal at any European fair and would have got an Honorable Mention even at Chicago if it had been saved up. But let it pass; the Father of his Country was excited. I have been in those circumstances, and I recollect.

With the truth he told I have no objection to offer, as already indicated. I think it was not premeditated, but an inspiration. With his fine military mind, he had probably arranged to let his brother Edward in for the cherry-tree results, but by an inspiration he saw his opportunity in time and took advantage of it. By telling the truth he could astonish his father; his father would tell the neighbors; the neighbors would spread it; it would travel to all firesides; in the end it would make him President, and not only that, but First President. He was a far-seeing boy and would be likely to think of these things. Therefore, to my mind, he stands justified for what he did. But not for the other Tower; it was a mistake. Still, I don't know about that; upon reflection I think perhaps it wasn't. For indeed it is that Tower that makes the other one live. If he hadn't said "I cannot tell a lie" there would have been no convulsion. That was the earthquake that rocked the planet. That is the kind of statement that lives forever, and a fact barnacled to it has a good chance to share its immortality.

To sum up, on the whole I am satisfied with things the way they are. There is a prejudice against the spoken lie, but none against any other, and by examination and mathematical computation I find that the proportion of the spoken lie to the other varieties is as 1 to 22,894. Therefore the spoken lie is of no consequence, and it is not worth while to go around fussing about it and trying to make believe that it is an important matter. The silent colossal National Lie that is the support and confederate of all the tyrannies and shams and inequalities and unfairnesses that afflict the peoples—that is the one to throw bricks and sermons at. But let us be judicious and let somebody else begin.

And then—But I have wandered from my text. How did I get out of my second lie? I think I got out with honor, but I cannot be sure, for it was a long time ago and some of the details have faded out of my memory. I recollect that I was reversed and stretched across some one's knee and that something happened, but I cannot now remember what it was. I think there was music; but it is all dim now and blurred by the lapse of time, and this may be only a senile fancy.

The Awful German Language

A little learning makes the whole world kin.—*Proverbs* xxxii 7.

I went often to look at the collection of curiosities in Heidelberg Castle, and one day I surprised the keeper of it with my German. I spoke entirely in that language. He was greatly interested; and after I had talked awhile he said my German was very rare, possibly a 'unique;' and wanted to add it to his museum.

If he had known what it had cost me to acquire my art, he would also have known that it would break any collector to buy it. Harris and I had been hard at work on our German during several weeks at that time, and although we had made good progress, it had been accomplished under great difficulty and annoyance, for three of our teachers had died in the meantime. A person who has not studied German can form no idea what a perplexing language it is.

Surely there is not another language that is so slipshod and systemless, and so slippery and elusive to the grasp. One is washed about in it, hither and hither, in the most helpless way; and when at last he thinks he has captured a rule which offers firm ground to take a rest on amid the general rage and turmoil of the ten parts of speech, he turns over the page and reads, 'Let the pupil make careful note of the following *exceptions*.' He runs his eye down and finds that there are more exceptions to the rule than instances of it. So overboard he goes again, to hunt for another Ararat and find another quicksand. Such has been, and continues to be, my experience. Every time I think I have got one of these four confusing 'cases' where I am master of it, a seemingly insignificant preposition intrudes itself into my sentence, clothed with an awful and unsuspected power, and crumbles the ground from under me. For instance, my book inquires after a certain bird—(it is always inquiring after things which are of no sort of consequence to anybody): 'Where is the bird?' Now the answer to this question—according to the book—is that the bird is waiting in the blacksmith shop on account of the rain. Of course no bird would do that, but then you must stick to the book. Very well, I begin to cipher out the German for that answer. I begin at the wrong end, necessarily, for that is the German idea. I say to myself, '*Regen* (rain) is masculine—or maybe it is feminine—or possibly neuter—it is too much trouble to look, now. Therefore, it is either *der* (the) Regen, or *die* (the) Regen, or *das* (the) Regen, according to which gender it may turn out to be when I look. In the interest of science, I will cipher it out on the hypothesis that it is masculine. Very well—then *the* rain is *der* Regen, if it is simply in the quiescent state of being *mentioned*, without enlargement or discussion—Nominative case; but if this rain is lying around, in a kind of a general way on the ground, it is then definitely located, it is *doing something*—that is, *resting* (which is one of the German grammar's ideas of doing something), and this throws the rain into the Dative case, and makes it *dem* Regen. However, this rain is not resting, but is doing something *actively*—it is falling—to interfere with the bird, likely—and this indicates *movement*—which has the effect of sliding it into the Accusative case and changing *dem* Regen into *den* Regen.' Having completed the grammatical horoscope of this matter, I answer up confidently and state in German that the bird is staying in the blacksmith shop 'wegen (on account of) *den* Regen.' Then the teacher lets me softly down with the remark that whenever the word 'wegen' drops into a sentence, it *always* throws that subject into the *Genitive* case, regardless of consequences—and that therefore this bird stayed in the blacksmith shop 'wegen *des* Regens.'

N.B.—I was informed later, by a higher authority, that there was an 'exception' which permits one to say 'wegen *den* Regen' in certain peculiar and complex circumstances, but that this exception is not extended to anything but rain.

There are ten parts of speech, and they are all troublesome. An average sentence in a German newspaper is a sublime and impressive curiosity; it occupies a quarter of a column; it contains all the ten parts of speech—not in regular order, but mixed; it is built mainly of compound words constructed by the writer on the spot, and not to be found in any dictionary—six or seven words compacted into one, without joint or seam—that is, without hyphens; it treats of fourteen or fifteen different subjects, each enclosed in a parenthesis of its own, with here and there extra parentheses which re-enclose three or four of the minor parentheses, making pens within pens; finally, all the parentheses and re-parentheses are massed together between a couple of king-parentheses, one of which is placed in the first line of the majestic sentence and the other in the middle of the last line of it—*after which comes the* VERB, and you find out for the first time what the man has been talking about; and after the verb—merely by way of ornament, as far as I can make out—the writer shovels in *'haben sind gewesen gehabt haben geworden sein,'* or words to that effect, and the monument is finished. I suppose that this closing hurrah is in the nature of the flourish to a man's signature—not necessary, but pretty. German books are easy enough to read when you hold them before the looking-glass or stand on your head—so as to reverse the construction—but I think that to learn to read and understand a German newspaper is a thing which must always remain an impossibility to a foreigner.

Yet even the German books are not entirely free from attacks of the Parenthesis distemper—though they are usually so mild as to cover only a few lines, and therefore when you at last get down to the verb it carries some meaning to your mind because you are able to remember a good deal of what has gone before.

Now here is a sentence from a popular and excellent German novel—with a slight parenthesis in it. I will make a perfectly literal translation, and throw in the parenthesis-marks and some hyphens for the assistance of the reader—though in the original there are no parenthesis-marks or hyphens, and the reader is left to flounder through to the remote verb the best way he can:—

'But when he, upon the street, the (in-satin-and-silk-covered-now-very-unconstrainedly-after-the-newest-fashion-dressed) government counsellor's wife *met*,' etc., etc.[1]

That is from 'The Old Mamselle's Secret,' by Mrs. Marlitt. And that sentence is constructed upon the most approved German model. You observe how far that verb is from the reader's base of operations; well, in a German newspaper they put their verb away over the next page; and I have heard that sometimes after stringing along on exciting preliminaries and parentheses for a column or two, they get in a hurry and have to go to press without getting to the verb at all. Of course, then, the reader is left in a very exhausted and ignorant state.

We have the Parenthesis disease in our literature, too; and one may see cases of it everyday in our books and newspapers; but with us it is the mark and sign of an unpractised writer or a cloudy intellect, whereas with the Germans it is doubtless the mark and sign of a practised pen and of the presence of that sort of luminous intellectual fog which stands for clearness among these people. For surely it is *not* clearness—it necessarily can't be clearness. Even a jury would have penetration enough to discover that. A writer's ideas must be a good deal confused, a good deal out of line and sequence, when he starts out to say that a man met a counsellor's wife in the street, and then right in the midst of this so simple undertaking halts these approaching people and makes them stand still until he jots down an inventory of the woman's dress. That is manifestly absurd. It reminds a person of those dentists who secure your instant and breathless interest in a tooth by taking a grip on it with the forceps, and then stand there and drawl through a tedious anecdote before they give the dreaded jerk. Parentheses in literature and dentistry are in bad taste.

The Germans have another kind of parenthesis, which they make by splitting a verb in two and putting half of it at the

[1]'Wenn er aber auf der Strasse der in Sammt und Seide gehüllten jetz sehr ungenirt nach der neusten mode gekleideten Regierungsrathin begegnet.'

beginning of an exciting chapter and the *other half* at the end of it. Can anyone conceive of anything more confusing than that? These things are called 'separable verbs.' The German grammar is blistered all over with separable verbs; and the wider the two portions of one of them are spread apart, the better the author of the crime is pleased with his performance. A favourite one is *reiste ab* which means *departed*. Here is an example which I culled from a novel and reduced to English:—

'The trunks being now ready, he DE- after kissing his mother and sisters, and once more pressing to his bosom his adored Gretchen, who, dressed in simple white muslin, with a single tuberose in the ample folds of her rich brown hair, had tottered feebly down the stairs, still pale from the terror and excitement of the past evening, but longing to lay her poor aching head yet once again upon the breast of him whom she loved more dearly than life itself, PARTED.'

However, it is not well to dwell too much on the separable verbs. One is sure to lose his temper early; and if he sticks to the subject, and will not be warned, it will at last either soften his brain or petrify it. Personal pronouns and adjectives are a fruitful nuisance in this language, and should have been left out. For instance, the same sound, *sie*, means *you*, and it means *she*, and it means *her*, and it means *it*, and it means *they*, and it means *them*. Think of the ragged poverty of a language which has to make one word to do the work of six—and a poor little weak thing of only three letters at that. But mainly, think of the exasperation of never knowing which of these meanings the speaker is trying to convey. This explains why, whenever a person says *sie* to me, I generally try to kill him, if a stranger.

Now observe the Adjective. Here was a case where simplicity would have been an advantage; therefore, for no other reason, the inventor of this language complicated it all he could. When we wish to speak of our 'good friend or friends,' in our enlightened tongue, we stick to the one form and have no trouble or hard feeling about it: but with the German tongue it is different. When a German gets his hands on an adjective, he declines it, and keeps on declining it until the common sense is all declined out of it. It is as bad as Latin. He says, for instance:—

SINGULAR

Nominative—Mein gut*er* Freund, my good friend.
Genitive—Mein*es* gut*en* Freund*es*, of my good friend.
Dative—Mein*em* gut*en* Freund, to my good friend.
Accusative—Mein*en* gut*en* Freund, my good friend.

PLURAL

N.—Mein*e* gut*en* Freund*e*, my good friends.
G.—Mein*er* gut*en* Freund*e*, of my good friends.
D.—Mein*en* gut*en* Freund*en*, to my good friends.
A.—Mein*e* gut*en* Freund*e*, my good friends.

Now let the candidate for the asylum try to memorise those variations, and see how soon he will be elected. One might better go without friends in Germany than take all this trouble about them. I have shown what a bother it is to decline a good (male) friend; well, this is only a third of the work, for there is a variety of new distortions of the adjective to be learned when the object is feminine, and still another when the object is neuter. Now there are more adjectives in this language than there are black cats in Switzerland, and they must all be as elaborately declined as the examples above suggested. Difficult?—troublesome?—these words cannot describe it. I heard a Californian student in Heidelberg say, in one of his calmest moods, that he would rather decline two drinks than one German adjective.

The inventor of the language seems to have taken pleasure in complicating it in every way he could think of. For instance, if one is casually referring to a house, *Haus*, or a horse, *Pferd*, or a dog, *Hund*, he spells these words as I have indicated; but if he is referring to them in the Dative case, he sticks on a foolish and unnecessary *e* and spells them Hause, Pferde, Hunde. So, as an added *e* often signifies the plural, as the *s* does with us, the new student is likely to go on for a month making twins out of a Dative dog before he discovers his mistake; and on the other hand, many a new student who could ill afford loss, has bought and paid for two dogs and only got one of them, because he ignorantly bought that dog in the Dative singular when he really supposed he was talking plural—which left the law on the seller's side, of course, by the strict rules of grammar, and therefore a suit for recovery could not lie.

In German, all the Nouns begin with a capital letter. Now that is a good idea; and a good idea in this language is necessarily conspicuous from its lonesomeness. I consider this capitalising of nouns a good idea, because by reason of it you are almost always able to tell a noun the minute you see it. You fall into error occasionally, because you mistake the name of a person for the name of a thing, and waste a good deal of time trying to dig a meaning out of it. German names almost always do mean something, and this helps to deceive the student. I translated a passage one day, which said that 'the infuriated tigress broke loose and utterly ate up the unfortunate fir-forest' (*Tannenwald*). When I was girding up my loins to doubt this, I found out that Tannenwald, in this instance, was a man's name.

Every noun has a gender, and there is no sense or system in the distribution; so the gender of each must be learned separately and by heart. There is no other way. To do this one has to have a memory like a memorandum book. In German a young lady has no sex, while a turnip has. Think what overwrought reverence that shows for the turnip, and what callous disrespect for the girl. See how it looks in print. I translate this from a conversation in one of the best of the German Sunday-school books:—

Gretchen. 'Wilhelm, where is the turnip?'

Wilhelm. 'She has gone to the kitchen.'

Gretchen. 'Where is the accomplished and beautiful English maiden?'

Wilhelm. 'It has gone to the opera.'

To continue with the German genders: a tree is male, its buds are female, its leaves are neuter; horses are sexless, dogs are male, cats are female—Tom-cats included, of course; a person's mouth, neck, bosom, elbows, fingers, nails, feet, and body are of the male sex, and his head is male or neuter according to the word selected to signify it, and *not* according to the sex of the individual who wears it—for in Germany all the women wear either male heads or sexless ones; a person's nose, lips, shoulders, breast, hands, hips, and toes are of the female sex; and his hair, ears, eye, chin, legs, knees, heart, and conscience haven't any sex at all. The inventor of the language probably got what he knew about a conscience from hearsay.

Now, by the above dissection, the reader will see that in Germany a man may *think* he is a man, but when he comes to look into the matter closely he is bound to have his doubts; he finds that in sober truth he is a most ridiculous mixture; and if he ends by trying to comfort himself with the thought that he can at least depend on a third of this mess as being manly and masculine, the humiliating second thought will quickly remind him that in this respect he is no better off than any woman or cow in the land.

In the German it is true that, by some oversight of the inventor of the language, a Woman is a female, but a Wife (*Weib*) is not—which is unfortunate. A wife here has no sex; she is neuter; so, according to the grammar, a fish is *he*, his scales are *she*, but a fish-wife is neither. To describe a wife as sexless may be called under-description; that is bad enough, but over-description is surely worse. A German speaks of an Englishman as the *Engländer*; to change the sex he adds *in*, and that stands for Englishwoman—*Engländerinn*. That seems descriptive enough, but still it is not exact enough for a German; so he precedes the word with that article which indicates that the creature to follow is feminine, and writes it down thus: '*Die* Engländer*inn*'—which means 'the *she-Englishwoman*.' I consider that that person is over-described.

Well, after the student has learned the sex of a great number of nouns he is still in difficulty, because he finds it impossible to persuade his tongue to refer to things as '*he*' and '*she*,' and '*him*' and '*her*,' which it has been always accustomed to refer to as '*it*.' When he even frames a German sentence in his mind, with the hims and hers in the right places, and then works up his courage to the utterance point, it is no use—the moment he begins to speak his tongue flies the track, and all those laboured males and females come out as '*its*.' And even when he is reading German to himself he always calls those things '*it*,' whereas he ought to read in this way:—

Tale of the Fishwife and Its Sad Fate[2]

It is a bleak Day. Hear the Rain, how he pours, and the Hail, how he rattles; and see the Snow, how he drifts along, and oh, the Mud, how deep he is! Ah, the poor Fishwife, it is stuck fast in the Mire; it has dropped its Basket of Fishes; and its Hands have been cut by the Scales as it seized some of the falling Creatures; and one Scale has even got into its Eye, and it cannot get her out. It opens its Mouth to cry for Help, but if any Sound comes out of him, alas! he is drowned by the raging of the Storm. And now a Tomcat has got one of the Fishes, and she will surely escape with him. No; she bites off a Fin, she holds her in her Mouth—will she swallow her? No the Fishwife's brave Mother-Dog deserts his Puppies and rescues the Fin; which he eats himself as his Reward. O horror; the Lightning has struck the Fishbasket! he sets him on Fire! See the Flame, how she licks the doomed Utensil with her red and angry Tongue! Now she attacks the helpless Fishwife's Foot—she burns him up all but the big Toe, and even *she* is partly consumed; and still she spreads, still she waves her fiery tongues! She attacks the Fishwife's Leg and destroys *it*; she attacks its Hand and destroys *her*; she attacks its poor worn Garment and destroys *her* also; she attacks its Body and consumes *him*; she wreathes herself about its Heart and *it* is consumed; next about its Breast and in a Moment *she* is a Cinder; now she reaches its Neck—*he* goes; now its Chin—*it* goes; now its Nose—*she* goes. In another moment, except Help come, the Fishwife will be no more! Time presses—is there none to succour and save? Yes! Joy, you! with flying Feet the she-Englishwoman comes! But alas! the generous she-Female is too late! Where how is the fated Fishwife? It has ceased from its Sufferings; it has gone to a better Land; all that is left of it for its loved Ones to lament over is this poor smouldering Ash-heap. Ah, woful, woful Ash-heap! Let us take him up tenderly, reverently, upon the lowly Shovel, and bear him to his long Rest, with the Prayer that when he rises again it will be in a Realm where he will have one good square responsible

[2]I capitalise the nouns, in the German (and ancient English) fashion.

Sex, and have it all to himself, instead of having a mangy lot of assorted Sexes scattered all over him in Spots.

There, now, the reader can see for himself that this pronoun-business is a very awkward thing for the unaccustomed tongue.

I suppose that in all languages the similarities of look and sound between words which have no similarity in meaning are a fruitful source of perplexity to the foreigner. It is so in our tongue, and it is notably the case in the German. Now there is that troublesome word *vermählt*: to me it has so close a resemblance—either real or fancied—to three or four other words, that I never know whether it means despised, painted, suspected, or married, until I look in the dictionary, and then I find it means the latter. There are lots of such words, and they are a great torment. To increase the difficulty there are words which *seem* to resemble each other, and yet do not; but they make just as much trouble as if they did. For instance, there is the word *vermeithen* (to let, to lease, to hire), and the word *verheirathen* (another way of saying to *marry*). I heard of an Englishman who knocked at a man's door in Heidelberg and proposed, in the best German he could command, to 'verheirathen' that house. Then there are some words which mean one thing when you emphasise the first syllable, but mean something very different if you throw the emphasis on the last syllable. For instance, there is a word which means a runaway, or the act of glancing through a book, according to the placing of the emphasis; and another word which signifies to *associate* with a man, or to *avoid* him, according to where you put the emphasis—and you can generally depend on putting it in the wrong place and getting into trouble.

There are some exceedingly useful words in this language: *Schlag*, for example, and *Zug*. There are three-quarters of a column of Schlags in the dictionary, and a column and a half of Zugs. The word Schlag means Blow, Stroke, Dash, Hit, Shock, Clap, Slap, Time, Bar, Coin, Stamp, Kind, Sort, Manner, Way, Apoplexy, Wood-cutting, Enclosure, Field, Forest-clearing. This is its simple and *exact* meaning—that is to say, its restricted, its fettered meaning; but there are ways by which you can set it free, so that it can soar away, as on the wings of the morning, and never be at rest. You can hang any word you please to its tail, and make it mean anything you want to. You can begin with *Schlag-ader,* which means artery, and you can hang on the whole dictionary, word by word, clear through the alphabet, to *Schlag-wasser,* which means bilge-water, and including *Schlag-mutter,* which means mother-in-law.

Just the same with *Zug*. Strictly speaking, Zug means Pull, Tug, Draught, Procession, March, Progress, Flight, Direction, Expedition, Train, Caravan, Passage, Stroke, Touch, Line, Flourish, Trait of Character, Feature, Lineament, Chess-move, Organ-stop, Team, Whiff, Bias, Drawer, Propensity, Inhalation, Disposition; but that thing which it does *not* mean, when all its legitimate pendants have been hung on, has not been discovered yet.

One cannot over-estimate the usefulness of Schlag and Zug. Armed just with these two, and the word *Also,* what cannot the foreigner on German soil accomplish? The German word *Also* is the equivalent of the English phrase 'You know,' and does not mean anything at all—in *talk,* though it sometimes does in print. Every time a German opens his mouth an *Also* falls out; and every time he shuts it he bites one in two that was trying to *get* out.

Now, the foreigner, equipped with these three noble words, is master of the situation. Let him talk right along, fearlessly; let him pour his indifferent German forth, and when he lacks for a word, let him heave a *Schlag* into the vacuum: all the chances are, that it fits it like a plug; but if it doesn't, let him promptly heave a *Zug* after it; the two together can hardly fail to bung the hole; but if, by a miracle, they *should* fail, let him simply say *Also!* and this will give him a moment's chance to think of the needful word. In Germany when you load your conversational gun it is always best to throw in a *Schlag* or two and a *Zug* or two; because it doesn't make any difference how much the rest of the charge may scatter, you are bound to bag something with *them*. Then you blandly say *Also* and load up again. Nothing gives such an air of grace and elegance and unconstraint to a German or an English conversation as to scatter it full of 'Also's' or 'You knows.'

In my note-book I find this entry:

> *July* 1.—In the hospital, yesterday, a word of thirteen syllables was successfully removed from a patient—a North-German from near Hamburg; but as most unfortunately the surgeons had opened him in the wrong place, under the impression that he contained a panorama, he died. The sad event has cast a gloom over the whole community.

That paragraph furnishes a text for a few remarks about one of the most curious and notable features of my subject—the length of German words. Some German words are so long that they have a perspective. Observe these examples:—

Freundschaftsbezeigungen.
Dilletantenaufdringlichkeiten.
Stadtverordnetenversammlungen.

These things are not words, they are alphabetical processions. And they are not rare; one can open a German newspaper any time and see them marching majestically across the page—and if he has any imagination he can see the banners and hear the music, too. They impart a martial thrill to the meekest subject. I take a great interest in these curiosities. Whenever I come across a good one I stuff it and put it in my museum. In this way I have made quite a valuable collection. When I get duplicates, I exchange with other collectors, and thus increase the variety of my stock. Here are some specimens which I lately bought at an auction sale of the effects of a bankrupt bric-à-brac hunter:—

GENERALSTAATSVERORDNETENVERSAMMLUNGEN.
ALTERTHUMSWISSENSCHAFTEN.
KINDERBEWAHRUNGSANSTALTEN.
UNABHAENGIGKEITSERKLAERUNGEN.
WIEDERHERSTELLUNGSBESTREBUNGEN.
WAFFENSTILLSTANDSUNTERHANDLUNGEN.

Of course when one of these grand mountain ranges goes stretching across the printed page, it adorns and ennobles that literary landscape—but at the same time it is a great distress to the new student, for it blocks up his way; he cannot crawl under it, or climb over it, or tunnel through it. So he resorts to the dictionary for help; but there is no help there. The dictionary must draw the line somewhere—so it leaves this sort of words out. And it is right, because these long things are hardly legitimate words, but are rather combinations of words, and the inventor of them ought to have been killed. They are compound words, with the hyphens left out. The various words used in building them are in the dictionary, but in a very scattered condition so you can hunt the materials out, one by one, and get at the meaning at last, but it is a tedious and harassing business. I have tried this process upon some of the above examples. 'Freundschaftsbezeigungen' seems to be 'Friendshipdemonstrations,' which is only a foolish and clumsy way of saying 'demonstrations of friendship.' 'Unabhaengigkeitserklaerungen' seems to be 'Independencedeclarations,' which is no improvement upon 'Declarations of Independence,' as far as I can see. 'Generalstaatsverordnetenversammlungen' seems to be 'Generalstatesrepresentatives-meetings,' as nearly as I can get at it—a mere rhythmical, gushy euphuism for 'meeting of the legislature,' I judge. We used to have a good deal of this sort of crime in our literature, but it has gone out now. We used to speak of a thing as a 'never-to-be-forgotten' circumstance, instead of cramping it into the simple and sufficient word 'memorable,' and then going calmly about our business as if nothing had happened. In those days we were not content to embalm the thing and bury it decently, we wanted to build a monument over it.

But in our newspapers the compounding-disease lingers a little to the present day, but with the hyphens left out, in the German fashion. This is the shape it takes: instead of saying 'Mr. Simmons, clerk of the county and district courts, was in town yesterday,' the new form puts it thus: 'Clerk of the County and District Court Simmons was in town yesterday.' This saves neither time nor ink, and has an awkward sound besides. One often sees a remark like this in our papers: '*Mrs.* Assistant District Attorney Johnson returned to her city residence yesterday for the season.' That is a case of really unjustifiable compounding; because it not only saves no time or trouble, but confers a title on Mrs. Johnson which she has no right to. But these little instances are trifles indeed, contrasted with the ponderous and dismal German system of piling jumbled compounds together. I wish to submit the following local item, from a Mannheim journal, by way of illustration:—

'In the daybeforeyesterdayshortlyaftereleveno'clock Night, the inthistownstandingtavern called "The Waggoner" was downburnt. When the fire to the onthedownburninghouseresting Stork's Nest reached, flew the parent Storks away. But when the bytheraging, fire-surrounded Nest *itself* caught Fire, straightway plunged the quick-returning Mother-Stork into the Flames and died, her Wings over her young ones outspread.'

Even the cumbersome German construction is not able to take the pathos out of that picture—indeed it somehow seems to strengthen it. This item is dated away back yonder months ago. I could have used it sooner, but I was waiting to hear from the Father-Stork. I am still waiting.

'Also!' If I have not shown that the German is a difficult language, I have at least intended to do it. I have heard of an American student who was asked how he was getting along with his German, and who answered promptly: 'I am not getting along at all. I have worked at it hard for three level months, and all I have got to show for it is one solitary German phrase—'"*Zwei glas*"' (two glasses of beer). He paused a moment, reflectively, then added with feeling, 'But I have got that *solid*!'

And if I have not also shown that German is a harassing and infuriating study, my execution has been at fault, and not my intent. I heard lately of a worn and sorely tried American student who used to fly to a certain German word for relief when he could bear up under his aggravations no longer—the only word in the whole language whose sound was sweet and precious to his ear and healing to his lacerated spirit. This was the word *Damit*. It was only the *sound* that helped him, not the meaning;[3] and so, at last, when he learned that the emphasis was not on the first syllable, his only stay and support was gone, and he faded away and died.

[3]It merely means, in its general sense, '*herewith*.'

I think that a description of any loud, stirring, tumultuous episode must be tamer in German than in English. Our descriptive words of this character have such a deep, strong, resonant sound, while their German equivalents do seem so thin and mild and energyless. Boom, burst, crash, roar, storm, bellow, blow, thunder, explosion; howl, cry, shout, yell, groan; battle, hell. These are magnificent words; they have a force and magnitude of sound befitting the things which they describe. But their German equivalents would be ever so nice to sing the children to sleep with, or else my awe-inspiring ears were made for display and not for superior usefulness in analysing sounds. Would any man want to die in a battle which was called by so tame a term as a *Schlacht*? Or would not a consumptive feel too much bundled up, who was about to go out, in a shirt collar and a seal ring, into a storm which the bird-song word *Gewitter* was employed to describe? And observe the strongest of the several German equivalents for explosion—*Ausbruch*. Our word Toothbrush is more powerful than that. It seems to me that the Germans could do worse than import it into their language to describe particularly tremendous explosions with. The German word for hell—Hölle—sounds more like *helly* than anything else; therefore, how necessarily chipper, frivolous, and unimpressive it is. If a man were told in German to go there, could he really rise to the dignity of feeling insulted?

Having now pointed out, in detail, the several vices of this language, I now come to the brief and pleasant task of pointing out its virtues. The capitalising of the nouns I have already mentioned. But far before this virtue stands another—that of spelling a word according to the sound of it. After one short lesson in the alphabet, the student can tell how any German word is pronounced, without having to ask; whereas in our language if a student should inquire of us 'What does B, O, W, spell?' we should be obliged to reply, 'Nobody can tell what it spells, when you set if off by itself—you can only tell by referring to the context and finding out what it signifies—whether it is a thing to shoot arrows with, or a nod of one's head, or the forward end of a boat.'

There are some German words which are singularly and powerfully effective. For instance, those which describe lowly, peaceful, and affectionate home life; those which deal with love, in any and all forms, from mere kindly feeling and honest good will toward the passing stranger, clear up to courtship; those which deal with outdoor Nature, in its softest and loveliest aspects—with meadows and forests, and birds and flowers, the fragrance and sunshine of summer, and the moonlight of peaceful winter nights; in a word, those which deal with any and all forms of rest, repose, and peace; those also which deal with the creatures and marvels of fairyland; and lastly and chiefly, in those words which express pathos, is the language surpassingly rich and effective. There are German songs which can make a stranger to the language cry. That shows that the *sound* of the words is correct—it interprets the meanings with truth and with exactness; and so the ear is informed, and through the ear, the heart.

The Germans do not seem to be afraid to repeat a word when it is the right one. They repeat it several times, if they choose. That is wise. But in English when we have used a word a couple of times in a paragraph, we imagine we are growing tautological, and so we are weak enough to exchange it for some other word which only approximates exactness, to escape what we wrongly fancy is a greater blemish. Repetition may be bad, but surely inexactness is worse.

There are people in the world who will take a great deal of trouble to point out the faults in a religion or a language, and then go gladly about their business without suggesting any remedy. I am not that kind of a person. I have shown that the German language needs reforming. Very well, I am ready to reform it. At least I am ready to make the proper suggestions. Such a course as this might be immodest in another; but I have devoted upwards of nine full weeks, first and last, to a careful and critical study of this tongue, and thus have acquired a confidence in my ability to reform it which no mere superficial culture could have conferred upon me.

In the first place, I would leave out the Dative Case. It confuses the plurals; and besides, nobody ever knows when he is in the

Dative Case, except he discover it by accident—and then he does not know when or where it was that he got into it, or how long he has been in it, or how he is ever going to get out of it again. The Dative Case is but an ornamental folly—it is better to discard it.

In the next place, I would move the Verb further up to the front. You may load up with ever so good a Verb, but I notice that you never really bring down a subject with it at the present German range—you only cripple it. So I insist that this important part of speech should be brought forward to a position where it may be easily seen with the naked eye.

Thirdly, I would import some strong words from the English tongue—to swear with, and also to use in describing all sorts of vigorous things in a vigorous way.[4]

Fourthly, I would reorganise the sexes, and distribute them according to the will of the Creator. This as a tribute of respect, if nothing else.

Fifthly, I would do away with those great long compounded words; or require the speaker to deliver them in sections, with intermissions for refreshments. To wholly do away with them would be best, for ideas are more easily received and digested when they come one at a time than when they come in bulk. Intellectual food is like any other; it is pleasanter and more beneficial to take it with a spoon than with a shovel.

Sixthly, I would require a speaker to stop when he is done, and not hang a string of those useless 'haben sind gewesen gehabt haben geworden seins' to the end of his oration. This sort of gew-gaws undignify a speech, instead of adding a grace. They are therefore an offence, and should be discarded.

[4]'*Verdammt,*' and its variations and enlargements, are words which have plenty of meaning, but the *sounds* are so mild and ineffectual that German ladies can use them without sin. German ladies who could not be induced to commit a sin by any persuasion or compulsion, promptly rip out one of these harmless little words when they tear their dresses or don't like the soup. It sounds about as wicked as our 'My gracious!' German ladies are constantly saying, 'Ach! Gott!' 'Mein Gott!' 'Gott in Himmel!' 'Herr Gott!' 'Der Herr Jesus!' etc. They think our ladies have the same custom perhaps, for I once heard a gentle and lovely old German lady say to a sweet young American girl, 'The two languages are so alike—how pleasant that is; we say, "Ach! Gott!" you say, "*Goddam.*" '

Seventhly, I would discard the Parenthesis. Also the re-Parenthesis, the re-re-parenthesis, and the re-re-re-re-re-re-parenthesis, and likewise the final wide-reaching all-enclosing King-parenthesis. I would require every individual, be he high or low, to unfold a plain straightforward tale, or else coil it and sit on it and hold his peace. Infractions of this law should be punishable with death.

And eighthly and lastly, I would retain *Zug* and *Schlag* with their pendants, and discard the rest of the vocabulary. This would simplify the language.

I have now named what I regard as the most necessary and important changes. These are perhaps all I could be expected to name for nothing; but there are other suggestions which I can and will make in case my proposed application shall result in my being formally employed by the government in the work of reforming the language.

My philological studies have satisfied me that a gifted person ought to learn English (barring spelling and pronouncing) in 30 hours, French in 30 days, and German in 30 years. It seems manifest, then, that the latter tongue ought to be trimmed down and repaired. If it is to remain as it is, it ought to be gently and reverently set aside among the dead languages, for only the dead have time to learn it.

A FOURTH OF JULY ORATION IN THE GERMAN TONGUE, DELIVERED AT A BANQUET OF THE ANGLO-AMERICAN CLUB OF STUDENTS BY THE AUTHOR OF THIS BOOK.

GENTLEMEN: Since I arrived, a month ago, in this old wonderland, this vast garden of Germany, my English tongue has so often proved a useless piece of baggage to me, and so troublesome to carry around, in a country where they haven't the checking system for luggage, that I finally set to work, last week, and learned the German language. Also! Es freut mich dass dies so ist, denn en muss, in ein hauptsächlich degree, höflich sein, dass man auf ein occasion like this, sein Rede in die Sprache des Landes worin he boards, aussprechen soll. Dafür habe ich, aus reinische Verlegenheit—no, Vergangenheit—no, I mean

Höflichkeit—aus reinische Höflichkeit have ich resolved to tackle this business in the German language, um Gottes willen! Also! Sie müssen so freundlich sein, und verzeih mich die interlarding von ein oder zwei Englischer Worte, hie und da, denn ich finde dass die deutche is not a very copious language, and so when you've really got anything to say, you've got to draw on a language that can stand the strain.

Wenn aber man kann nicht meinem Rede verstehen, so werde ich ihm später dasselbe übersetz, wenn er solche Dienst verlangen wollen haben werden sollen sein hätte. (I don't know what wollen haben werden sollen sein hätte means, but I notice they always put it at the end of a German sentence—merely for general literary gorgeousness, I suppose.)

This is a great and justly honoured day—a day which is worthy of the veneration in which it is held by the true patriots of all climes and nationalities—a day which offers a fruitful theme for thought and speech; und meinem Freunde—no, mein*en* Freund*en*—mein*es* Freund*es*—well, take your choice, they're all the same price; I don't know which one is right—also! ich have gehabt haben worden gewesen sein, as Goethe says, in his Paradise Lost—ich—ich—that is to say—ich—but let us change cars.

Also! Die Anblick so viele Grossbrittanischer und Amerikanischer hier zusammengetroffen in Bruderliche concord, ist zwar a welcome and inspiriting spectacle. And what has moved you to it? Can the terse German tongue rise to the expression of this impulse? Is it Freundschafts-bezeigungenstadtverordnetenversammlungenfamilien-eigenthümlichkeitem? Nein, o nein! This is a crisp and noble word, but it fails to pierce the marrow of the impulse which has gathered this friendly meeting and produced diese Anblick—eine Anblick welche ist gut zu sehen—gut für die Augen in a foreign land and a far country—eine Anblick solche als in die gewönliche Heidelberger phrase nennt man ein 'schönes Aussicht!' Ja, freilich natürlich wahrscheinlich ebensowoh! Also! Die Aussicht auf dem Königstuhl mehr grösserer ist, aber geistlische sprechend nicht so schön, lob' Gott! Because sie sind hier zusammengetroffen, in Bruderlichem concord, ein grossen Tag zu feiern, whose high benefits were not for one land and one locality only, but have conferred a measure of good upon all lands that know liberty to-day, and love it. Hundert Jahre vorüber, waren die Engländer und die Amerikaner Feinde; aber heute sind sie herzlichen Freunde, Gott sei Dank! May this good fellowship endure; may these banners here blended in amity, so remain; may they never any more wave over opposing hosts, or be stained with blood which was kindred, is kindred, and always will be kindred, until a line drawn upon a map shall be able to say, '*This* bars the ancestral blood from flowing in the veins of the descendant!'

A Presidential Candidate

I have pretty much made up my mind to run for President. What the country wants is a candidate who cannot be injured by investigation of his past history, so that the enemies of the party will be unable to rake up anything against him that nobody ever heard of before. If you know the worst about a candidate, to begin with, every attempt to spring things on him will be checkmated. Now I am going to enter the field with an open record. I am going to own up in advance to all the wickedness I have done, and if any Congressional committee is disposed to prowl around my biography in the hope of discovering any dark and deadly deed that I have secreted, why—let it prowl.

In the first place, I admit that I treed a rheumatic grandfather of mine in the winter of 1850. He was old and inexpert in climbing trees, but with the heartless brutality that is characteristic of me I ran him out of the front door in his nightshirt at the point of a shotgun, and caused him to bowl up a maple tree, where he remained all night, while I emptied shot into his legs. I did this because he snored. I will do it again if I ever have another grandfather. I am as inhuman now as I was in 1850. I candidly acknowledge that I ran away at the battle of Gettysburg. My friends have tried to smooth over this fact by asserting that I did so for the purpose of imitating Washington, who went into the woods at Valley Forge for the purpose of saying his prayers. It was a miserable subterfuge. I struck out in a straight line for the

Tropic of Cancer because I was scared. I wanted my country saved, but I preferred to have somebody else save it. I entertain that preference yet. If the bubble reputation can be obtained only at the cannon's mouth, I am willing to go there for it, provided the cannon is empty. If it is loaded my immortal and inflexible purpose is to get over the fence and go home. My invariable practice in war has been to bring out of every fight two-thirds more men than when I went in. This seems to me to be Napoleonic in its grandeur.

My financial views are of the most decided character, but they are not likely perhaps, to increase my popularity with the advocates of inflation. I do not insist upon the special supremacy of rag money or hard money. The great fundamental principle of my life is to take any kind I can get.

The rumor that I buried a dead aunt under my grapevine was correct. The vine needed fertilizing, my aunt had to be buried, and I dedicated her to this high purpose. Does that unfit me for the Presidency? The Constitution of our country does not say so. No other citizen was ever considered unworthy of this office because he enriched his grapevines with his dead relatives. Why should I be selected as the first victim of an absurd prejudice?

I admit also that I am not a friend of the poor man. I regard the poor man, in his present condition, as so much wasted raw material. Cut up and properly canned, he might be made useful to fatten the natives of the cannibal islands and to improve our export trade with that region. I shall recommend legislation upon the subject in my first message. My campaign cry will be: "Desiccate the poor workingman; stuff him into sausages."

These are about the worst parts of my record. On them I come before the country. If my country don't want me, I will go back again. But I recommend myself as a safe man—a man who starts from the basis of total depravity and proposes to be fiendish to the last.